CHEERS FOR ELIZABETH GAGE'S
TABOO

"Gage's latest opus starts out like gangbusters and doesn't let up for a single chapter. In the grand tradition of Krantz and Collins, Gage has written a thoroughly racy yet romantic novel, full of sordid pasts, intrigues and Hollywood egos. . . . *TABOO* is steamy, romantic fiction at its absolute finest. Juicy romance just doesn't get any better than this."
—*West Coast Review of Books*

"*TABOO* is a great tale of revenge and of those who pay the price for their own sins. . . . The glory of the tale comes in the heartrending manner in which Gage presents her characters. No one can create sorrow better. No one can spin a tale tighter. . . . For those who love weeping buckets of tears, Elizabeth Gage's new novel is perfect." —*Ocala Star Banner*

"**Completely absorbing** . . . Elizabeth Gage has worked her magic again. . . . [A] must-read novel."
—*Affaire de Coeur*

"**Compelling** . . . packed with double crosses and delicious revenge . . . the kind of page-turner that immediately transforms readers into casting directors . . ."
—*Detroit Free Press*

"Excellent portrayal of Hollywood and the movie industry in its heyday in the late '30s and '40s. [Gage's] unique writing style makes this shocking, engrossing, sexually explicit story incredible reading." —*Rendezvous*

A Literary Guild Featured Alternate
A Doubleday Book Club Featured Alternate

AND PRAISE FOR . . .

THE MASTER STROKE

"A delicious tale of injustice and revenge . . . utterly captivating."
—*Kirkus Reviews*

"*The Master Stroke* will surely enhance Elizabeth Gage's reputation as the thinking woman's Danielle Steel. On her third outing, Gage turns her shrewd attention to the ruthless world of international business. . . . Once again, Gage proves herself to be a master—or would that be mistress?—of the sex scene. Her writing is erotic. . . ."
—*Houston Post*

"Gage writes with amazing intensity. . . ."
—*San Jose Mercury News*

PANDORA'S BOX

"Rife with plot twists, comeuppances and bed-hopping . . . Gage proves herself a shrewd chronicler of the rich and rotten."
—*New York Daily News*

"Exuberantly racy romance . . . Engrossing, *Pandora's Box* glows with perceptive characterization."
—*Publishers Weekly*

"The author's theme is as timeless and intriguing as the myth from which she takes her title."
—*Chicago Tribune*

A GLIMPSE OF STOCKING

"A blockbuster . . . in the grand Krantz/Collins tradition . . ."
—*Kirkus Reviews*

"One of [the season's] steamiest books . . . *A Glimpse of Stocking*'s pleasures emerge from Gage's sincerity. The heroine [Annie] is an obvious labor of love. The scenes of Christine bringing men to their financial and physical knees add a certain *je ne sais quoi*. . . ."
—*USA Today*

"Has blockbuster written all over it. Writing in the tradition of Judith Krantz . . . Gage stirs up a . . . stew of greed, eroticism, and violence. . . . *A Glimpse of Stocking* builds to an appalling series of climaxes. . . ."
—*Chicago Sun-Times*

"The ultimate page-turner of the year; shocking and sensational . . . Unlike most of the high-powered glitz novels on the shelves, *A Glimpse of Stocking* is an unusually well-plotted story with three-dimensional, intense characters, fascinating and unique, who leap off the page to entertain. . . . A riveting story, chilling violence, searing passion, boundless ambition and its bloody price . . . a must read."
—*Rave Reviews*

"Revenge may be sweet, but it's also over the top of the sexual Richter scale; the earth moves in pretty astounding ways in *A Glimpse of Stocking*."
—*Los Angeles Times*

Books by Elizabeth Gage

A Glimpse of Stocking
Pandora's Box
The Master Stroke
Taboo

Published by POCKET BOOKS

Taboo

a novel by

Elizabeth Gage

POCKET STAR BOOKS

New York   London   Toronto   Sydney   Tokyo   Singapore

This book is a work of fiction. Names, characters, places and
incidents are either products of the author's imagination or are
used fictitiously. Any resemblance to actual events or locales or
persons, living or dead, is entirely coincidental.

 A Pocket Star Book published by
POCKET BOOKS, a division of Simon & Schuster Inc.
1230 Avenue of the Americas, New York, NY 10020

Copyright © 1992 by Gage Productions, Ltd.

All rights reserved, including the right to reproduce
this book or portions thereof in any form whatsoever.
For information address Pocket Books, 1230 Avenue
of the Americas, New York, NY 10020

ISBN: 0-671-78644-X

First Pocket Books paperback printing December 1993

10 9 8 7 6 5 4 3 2 1

POCKET STAR BOOKS and colophon are registered
trademarks of Simon & Schuster Inc.

Cover photo by Jim Galante

Printed in the U.S.A.

To Sidney J. Ritchie
and to Andi
with love

ACKNOWLEDGMENTS

The author wishes to thank the following for their cooperation and advice in the preparation of this novel:

Twentieth Century-Fox Film Corporation
The Hollywood Chamber of Commerce
The Beverly Hills Visitors' Bureau
Columbia Pictures
Metro-Goldwyn-Mayer/United Artists Entertainment Company
The California Historical Society
The American Film Institute
The Academy of Motion Picture Arts and Sciences
The National Film Archive
Ernst H. Huneck, M.D.

Special thanks to Jim Ghent for his patient instruction in the technical arcana of filmmaking, and to Sally Dubose for her encyclopedic knowledge of the unwritten side of Hollywood history.

Finally, I would like to thank those individuals who generously shared with me their recollections about the studio era, its great achievements as well as its dark side, without wishing to be named here. Ironically, the history of an institution such as Hollywood is often rooted in events which, by their very nature, were not intended to see the light of day and can be documented only by the private testimony of individuals who do not feel safe in making these statements public, even sixty years after the fact. This is a characteristic of Hollywood itself, and a part of its mystery. It might well be observed that many other institutions share the same mystery.

My heartfelt appreciation goes to Ms. Tina Gerrard and Mr. Jon Kirsh for their tireless and thorough assistance in my research. And sincere thanks as always to Jay Garon, for his support and encouragement.

Elizabeth Gage

CONTENTS

CONTENTS

As I felt my way forward, at each step I ventured, I seemed to hear something within me cry out: No farther! Not a step farther! And yet I could not stop. I had to venture the least little bit farther. Only one hair's-breadth more. And then one more, and always one more . . . And then it happened.

That is the way such things come about.

—Ibsen
Rosmersholm

PROLOGUE

PROLOGUE

April 22, 1947

DARKNESS FILLED THE ROOM, JOINING ALL THOSE PRESENT in watchful silence.

Before them, magnified to a hundred times human size, was the face of a woman.

She stood with a man in a place of parting, a station of some sort. Behind them one had the feeling of other people, many people, gathered here to say goodbye to each other.

But the woman's face dominated everything. The man was reflected in her eyes, which grew more beautiful as despair swept over them.

"Must you go?" she asked. "Does it have to happen?" She had a smooth, husky voice. On the surface it was sweet and natural, like the voice of a young girl. But underneath it seemed ageless and full of secrets.

The golden eyes were larger now, anguish shading their glow like clouds passing across the moon.

"Yes," he said. "I've got to go. I'd give anything to change that. But there's no way."

She sighed, as though he were enunciating a terrible law, cruel and inflexible as life itself.

"Somehow I feel my heart is losing you," she said.

3

"That I've committed a sin without realizing it, and that's why you're leaving me."

The man shook his head.

"You've committed no sin," he said. "Unless love is a crime."

He held her close. Her hand fluttered at his shoulder, afraid to pull him to her since he was about to take his leave.

"Promise me you'll make the best of things," he said, "and try to be happy."

"Happy," she murmured with a tense little smile, as though he had told a silly joke. Then her face darkened, and she buried her head against his chest so that he would not see the depth of her grief.

"It's so strange," she said, more to herself than to him. "When love comes, you plunge without thinking. You see that your life was an empty shell before love came, so you turn your back on the past without a second thought."

She closed her eyes, her hands touching his strong back.

"And then," she said, "when the world comes back to claim its own, there's no way to fight it, because you have no heart to endure loneliness any more. You've thrown it away, like a child throwing away a paper toy. There's no turning back the clock, no way to go back and be more careful, to look ahead and see the danger."

Now she looked into his face.

"That's the crime, you see," she said. "That's what has to be paid for."

The man said nothing. He could see her heart opening before him, and was silenced by the pain he saw there.

She hugged him hard. "Love is so much more important than life," she said. "But life is the stronger. It's not fair . . ."

He put his hands on her cheeks.

"I'll come back," he said.

"Will you?" The look in her eyes did not express belief. Instead she seemed to take comfort from his desire to return to her, as though that alone must suffice now. "Will you?"

"Yes. I will come back." Still he tried to reassure her.

4

And yet it was clear that she knew something he didn't, that she was facing it already, though he couldn't, because his own love blinded him.

She hugged him, kissed him. Her touch was full of renunciation.

"Goodbye," she said. "You have to go. There's no more time."

He embraced her, murmured his last farewell, and was gone. Her face, alone at last, was more beautiful than ever in its desolation.

"The whole of life gone by," came a voice inside her. "And nothing left but goodbye . . ."

She watched him recede. She raised a hand to signal her love.

"Was that the word I heard that first day?" came the inner voice. "When the past was obliterated by your face, and suddenly the future stretched before me like heaven? Was that what I heard? *Goodbye* . . ."

"Goodbye . . ." The word was not spoken, but only formed on her lips. The camera moved closer to her. Each shade and contour of her face, famous the world over for its beauty, was transfigured by grief. Every woman's dream, every woman's loss, were united in her eyes.

Sobs were heard in the audience. People hugged each other, unable to take their eyes from the screen even as their tears colored the image before them.

The face of the young woman began to fade away. Yet the eyes disappeared more slowly than the rest, so that as the film ended the look in them was still visible, like a shadow that cannot be entirely dimmed even by time.

Then the last words appeared on the screen.

THE END

No one moved. A sort of awe had overtaken the spectators. They knew they were witnessing something more final than the end of a film.

Kate Hamilton, the star who shone so powerfully before them, would never be seen on the screen again. This farewell to love was also the end of her career, the shortest and most extraordinary in the history of the screen.

And Joseph Knight, the man who was behind the camera recording that image, the man who had made Kate a star with his love as well as his great talent, would never make another film.

The words the heroine had spoken on the screen hung like a knell over movie history. With Kate Hamilton the Hollywood film had aspired to a depth of emotion it had never expressed before. Thanks to Joseph Knight, who had captured Kate for all time at the height of her genius.

But now it was finished. Just as the film told of beginnings and inevitable endings, it seemed to foretell the future for those who had given themselves to its creation. In so many ways, with this film, life had imitated art . . .

The credits moved slowly up the screen.

Anne .... Kate Hamilton
Susan .... Eve Sinclair
Sam .... Samuel Raines

The audience sat transfixed. No one got up to leave. Sobs continued to be heard. Men comforted their women, and tried to hide their own emotion.

At the back of the theater, unobserved, sat a young woman who watched the names pass before her eyes with particular interest.

Kate Hamilton . . .

Eve Sinclair . . .

She stared straight in front of her. She could still see the projected face, and the fateful words, THE END.

"Goodbye," she murmured soundlessly.

Yes, this was the end. For the talent that had made Joseph Knight a prodigy among filmmakers, and for the bigger-than-life image of Kate Hamilton on the screen. They would be seen no more by an admiring public.

The end of hope? Perhaps. Not the end of love, though . . .

Gradually the theater began to empty. People walked

slowly, in silence, so profound was the spell the film had cast on them. But the young woman did not move.

To the audience filing quietly from the theater, the film just seen was a work of art. A great one, to be sure. Already it had drawn more people into theaters than any film in memory. No one could stay away from it. Back and back they came, as though, despite the searing of their hearts by this tragic story, they were drawn to it like moths to a flame. It seemed to contain a truth that nourished their sense of who they were, more than ever at this moment of their nation's history.

To the young woman seated in the shadows, it was more than a film. It was her own goodbye—and her last.

She did not cry. There were no tears left for her to shed.

She could still hear the words that had come from the screen only moments ago. Words that seemed to tell the whole story far better than her own memory could tell it.

I feel as though I've committed a sin without realizing it, and that's why I'm losing you now . . .

That's the crime that has to be paid for . . .

The screen was blank now. She was alone in the theater, gazing at the enormous curtains that reared before her like a shroud. No one had thought to look at her as they filed from the theater. Their hearts were still too full of the images they had just seen. Had they noticed her, they might not have recognized her, so profound is the difference between those bigger-than-life images and a mere human being.

But they were distracted. And that was what the movies were all about. To distract the eye from something real, something close at hand, and to open it to something unreal, to an illusion. She knew only too well that illusion can be the door to emptiness and evil. But only now did she realize that it can also be the only door to the heart's deepest truth. Joseph Knight had taught her that.

Perhaps, she mused, there was another reason why no one would recognize her today. For she was not the same any more, and never would be. Time and fate had changed her, uprooting her from the past she once took for granted, and then annihilating the future she had looked forward to like a beautiful dream.

A fitting ending, she thought. A curtain drawn.

And behind the curtain, the eyes still gazing out at her, with their eternal hurt and their bottomless, infinite love. Eyes looking not at her, not at this room or this day, but at Joseph Knight. The eyes that would not fade, the love that would not die.

Was that the word I was hearing that first day? When the past was obliterated by your face, and suddenly the future stretched before me like heaven? Was that what I heard? Goodbye . . .

Let that be her epitaph, then. The heroine on the screen, an illusion made real only by the impression film can make upon the heart, had said it better than she ever could. At the dawn of love lurks the ending that sunders, the final separation, shedding its wondrous light upon all human joy and hiding from us, until it is too late, what must come after.

Goodbye . . .

BOOK
ONE

BOOK

ONE

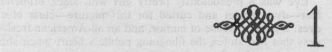

1

Seventeen Years Earlier

September 12, 1930

KATE HAMILTON WAS ELEVEN YEARS OLD.

She sat in the darkened movie theater, her eyes riveted to the screen.

Her own existence was forgotten. So was the small California town outside this theater, and the house she lived in with her mother and stepfather. So were Kate's schoolmates, her memories, her worries and disappointments.

The movie theater was like an exotic womb to her, a warm and wonderful place where dreams came true. Every aspect of the experience was touched by a special charm— the smell of candy, the distant aroma of smoke from the smokers' section in the rear, the broken seat springs, the occasional sound of a child's voice asking its mother for a drink of water or a trip to the bathroom. The torpor of the spectators, their own languid absorption in the film, and above all the secret darkness of the theater were pure magic for Kate.

And it was at the core of this private womb that she gazed rapt at the figure on the screen.

It was a young girl. Her name was Eve Sinclair. She was one of the biggest child stars in Hollywood. The movie being shown today was her latest feature role, an antebel-

11

lum costume drama in which Eve played an adorable daughter who saved her parents' plantation and their marriage to boot.

Kate was not paying attention to the story. She had seen the film seven times, and knew nearly all the dialogue, as well as the tired, sentimental plot by heart. She had eyes only for Eve.

Eve was a precociously pretty girl with sleek brunette hair—dyed russet and curled for this picture—clear blue eyes, a puckish sense of humor, and an all-American freshness that had stolen the filmgoing public's heart when she was eight and had kept her star rising ever since.

Kate sat entranced. Eve Sinclair was her heroine and her ideal.

According to the fan magazines Eve lived with her parents in Pasadena. She had a dog named Muffy who slept in her room every night. Her favorite hobbies were ice-skating, reading (Kate had saved long and hard to buy copies of the books that were said to be Eve's favorites—*Little Women, Great Expectations, Rebecca of Sunnybrook Farm*), and playing the flute. Her favorite performer was Clark Gable, on whom she claimed to have a hopeless crush, and with whom she dreamed of making a film one day. Her cherished hope was to travel to Egypt, see the Pyramids, and ride an elephant.

All these things Kate knew as a zealot knows the Gospel. She lived, breathed, and dreamed Eve Sinclair. In her room at home, carefully hidden from the prying eye of her mother, was a private folder containing hundreds of photos of Eve and fan articles about her, as well as ads for all her movies. Kate knew Eve's entire filmography, from her earliest comedy short to her contract with Worldwide Pictures, the studio that had made her a star.

In her early roles Eve had been typecast as a plucky little girl who charmed adults and twisted them around her little finger. As she grew older, and her limbs got longer, she developed a special prettiness, clean and sparkling and intelligent. New roles were created for her in which she displayed a precocious seriousness of character to go along with her adorable looks. She used her sharp wits and her sure sense of right and wrong to settle disputes between the adults around her, and to make appropriate marital matches where the Hollywood screenwriters deemed it necessary.

In this era of "hard times," which would soon come to be called the Depression, Eve had come to represent pre-adolescent courage and resourcefulness, but also a deeper moral quality, a sure instinct for the right and honest thing, which ran through all the characters she played and made her a household name. Filmgoers identified her with sincerity and uprightness as well as beauty. This was easy to do, for the combination of her clear eyes with their candid, honest smile, her pearly skin, and her fresh young body seemed to incarnate everything a mother wishes for in a daughter.

As Kate sat watching the film wind down to its stereotyped conclusion, she felt a familiar pang of inadequacy. Eve was everything Kate was not and wished she could be. Eve had no rough edges. She never had a hair out of place, or a spill or stain to mar her lovely clothes, or a moment of clumsiness that might bring reproach from the adults around her. Her body was slim, lithe, without any of the lumpy contours that made normal girls curse themselves.

Compared to Eve, Kate thought herself a poor excuse for a human being. She was messy, sloppy, and ordinary. In the mirror she looked at her sandy hair, her undistinguished nose, her faraway eyes, and decided that she was a crude and misshapen thing, in every way the opposite of sweet, pert, ideal Eve Sinclair.

Her first five minutes in the theater were always marred by this painful comparison. But then she forgot herself and plunged into the spell of Eve's beauty and charm, only coming to herself again two hours later. For those precious two hours, she dared to identify with the perfection of Eve's bright smile, her lilting voice, her impish humor, and—perhaps most important of all—the happy ending that Eve brought about for herself, her fictional family, and all those around her in the magical world on the screen.

* * *

The film was over. It was time to go home.

Kate emerged blinking into the harsh sunlight of afternoon. The main street of Plainfield, California lay before her, sleepy, drab, and demoralized, like every other small town in America these days.

It was a hot little town exiled in the fruit-growing fields of the San Joaquin Valley. Though in Kate's mind it seemed worlds away from the glamour of Hollywood, in reality it was only separated from the film capital by about a hundred and fifty miles. Such was the difference between geography and dreams.

In the center of town there were a handful of shoppers pausing before the dusty display windows of the stores and a few cars going up and down the street. But most people were at home on this hot Saturday, too poor to go out and buy anything and too tired to go out for fun.

Kate walked the eight blocks to the poor neighborhood in which she lived with her mother. She watched the little bungalows and ramshackle houses grow dingier, grayer, as she neared home. A scattering of young children played desultorily in the heat or wandered here and there. Few of them could afford bicycles, so almost all were on foot. Their clothes were threadbare. The hard times had hit everywhere, but most of all here, in the poorer neighborhoods of the small towns, where people had difficulty getting work even in good times. The atmosphere was one of peevish fatigue and boredom.

The spell of Eve Sinclair and her fictional world began to fade as the drabness of town settled into Kate's senses. This gradual process of erosion was the last and saddest part of Kate's Eve Sinclair experiences. It made her so sick of her own life that she quickly began looking forward to a way to get hold of another quarter so she could go back to the theater to see the picture again.

At last Kate reached home. It was a tiny two-story stucco house with warped shutters, faded curtains, and an air of seediness that Kate had never noticed in her early years but had become acutely aware of as she grew older.

She entered through the front door and passed into the kitchen. Her mother was talking on the phone to one of her friends and at the same time carefully applying polish to her toenails. She did not look up to greet Kate.

Kate opened the refrigerator and poured herself a glass of milk. Then she turned to go upstairs.

She had to pass through the living room, with its shabby overstuffed furniture, its cheap throw pillows with silk screens of Niagara Falls and Yosemite, its unwashed windows and huge console radio, to get to the staircase. The radio was on. A ball game was in progress. In one of the old easy chairs sat her stepfather, whom she thought of only as Ray. Like her mother, he did not look up to notice her arrival. He held a bottle of beer in his hand and was smoking a cigarette. He was dressed, as always, in dirty slacks and an undershirt.

He was not really her stepfather. That was a euphemism used by Kate's mother to hide the fact that Ray had simply moved in, not long after the death of Kate's father, a mild-mannered bank clerk who had succumbed to a heart attack five years ago, when he was not yet fifty.

Ray was a young man, ten years younger at least than Kate's real father, and was what some women would call good-looking. He had a strong body, olive skin, and shiny black hair. When he dressed up to go out with Mother, he looked very fancy. But the suits he wore, the colorful ties, the wing-tip shoes and the hats with their loud hatbands, were in poor taste and branded him as the lowlife he was. Though Kate did not admire him and spoke to him as little as possible, she felt a glimmer of understanding of why her mother had chosen him. He had a tacky sort of virility which he showed off with his loud clothes.

With a silence bordering on stealth Kate hurried up the stairs and went into her room, closing the door behind her.

The walls were bare, except for one poster for an Eve Sinclair movie that Kate had managed to talk the theater owner out of a year ago. Kate quickly opened her desk drawer and took out her folder of Eve Sinclair memorabilia. She drank her milk as she looked through the fan magazines for the hundredth time, noticing the little details about Eve's private and public life that she already knew by heart.

At last the real world beckoned, and she could hold it back no longer. She got out her books and began to do her homework. There was an arithmetic exam tomorrow, and she had to write an essay about what she had done over the summer.

The latter filled her with disgust. For one thing, Kate hated to write. She had no talent with words. They came out of her pen like clumsy little inked animals, foreign and meaningless. She could no more put her feelings into words than she could put the man in the moon into a lunch box. Words were irrelevant to her existence. She lived for images, for impressions. Even with her best friends she spent much of her time in silence.

At home she rarely spoke at all.

Her mother had no use for her and had made that clear years ago. Irma Hamilton thought only about herself. Her daughter was at best an encumbrance, at worst an enemy. As for Ray, he had been polite to Kate when he first started romancing Irma immediately after her husband's death, as suitors of women are always polite to their children. But he had never been interested in Kate as a person. After he had moved in he ceased even speaking to her.

Kate had encouraged this silence, for she hated Ray. He was greasy and oily and he smelled of beer and sweat and tobacco. And he was lazy.

He never seemed to work. He was always around the house, sitting with his can of beer and doing nothing. A couple of days a week he put on a suit and went into town, on "business," as Mother said. But something about the languor of his demeanor made it obvious he was not really working. Mother suspected he was seeing other women, and often made scenes about this.

The two of them also fought about money. Every so often they would get into a savage fray, usually made worse by alcohol—Mother drank gin when she could afford it, and beer the rest of the time—and she would scream at him, calling him a "no-good bum" and a "cheap heel." Sometimes these fights came to blows, and Kate, upstairs, put her pillow over her head or her hands over her ears.

But eventually, in their rather sour and unsmiling way,

they made up. Kate would hear them go upstairs to the bedroom, where they closed the door. A long silence followed, and then the uncanny noises of sighing bedsprings and woman's moans that made Kate want to escape at all costs, to go anywhere to get away from them.

Whenever she wanted to forget them, Kate thought of her father.

Kate kept a photo of him on her dresser. Sometimes she would look at the picture for long minutes at a time, studying the gentle bespectacled face with its mild features, and struggling to remember what it had looked like in life.

Though the face was dim now, Kate remembered her father as a quiet presence, comforting and warm. She could still recall sitting on his lap as he read his evening paper. He had been a trifle plump around the middle, and she had felt his stomach against her tiny back as his arms encircled her. He had murmured the words of the newspaper aloud as he ran his finger along the lines, and occasionally she would learn to make out a word as he spoke it.

Words like "assembly" and "commission" and "ordinance" had become familiar to her in those days, like foreign toys for adults that had peeked into her world. She enjoyed seeing them wend their way down the columns of the newspaper.

It had been so much fun for her, and made her feel so close to Father, that after he died she could not bring herself to look at a newspaper again. In fact, perhaps it was Father's brief introduction of her to the world of words that made them seem so foreign and inhospitable since his death. She had taken leave of that world after he went.

She could remember him bathing her when she was a little girl, and helping her on with her clothes and listening to her say her prayers at night. It was as though he was the one who had the physical closeness of a mother with her, soothing her tears and cleaning her little cuts and bruises—while, at that period, her mother was a distant presence, hardly real.

Kate still had an unnaturally clear memory of having run into the living room naked from the bathroom one night when she was no more than three or four. Her mother had scolded her, but her father had gathered her in his arms and said, "Now, now, Katie. There's plenty of time to become a pin-up girl in the future. Let's get your pajamas on."

No one had called her "Katie" since Father died. Her mother rarely called her by name at all, and treated her with a distant irritability in which there was no love. Mother was absorbed in herself, always putting makeup on or taking it off, always fixing her hair, always talking on the phone or on her way out somewhere. She never had time for Kate.

Kate sensed that Mother's marriage to Father had not been perfect. Indeed, the suddenness with which Ray came to take Father's place had suggested that the previous world had never been as happy or secure as it seemed.

In retrospect Kate decided that her mother had only been acting the whole time she was married to her father. A side of her mother she had never suspected suddenly overwhelmed her mother's whole personality as soon as Daddy was in the ground. Thus Kate lost both her parents instead of just one when her father died.

Nowadays when Kate studied the photo of her father, watching it grow more foreign as time pulled her away from him and made memory fade, it was as though she was looking into the mirror of her own mystery. For her own self became more of a dark crystal each day. As she grew older she seemed to understand herself less rather than more.

And this was where Eve Sinclair came in. Where Kate herself was muddled, unformed, Eve was perfect and beautiful. How much easier it was to disappear into that dark movie theater and spend two precious hours identifying with Eve than to wander confusedly through the outer world in search of one's own self!

At five o'clock there was a brief, curt knock, and Kate's door was unceremoniously opened.

Irma Hamilton looked in without warmth.

"Your father and I are going out for dinner," she said. *He's not my father.*

"I've left a plate for you in the refrigerator," Mother added. "Put it in the oven whenever you want."

Kate looked at her mother. Her eyes were gray-green, her hair a dyed auburn. She was somewhat overweight from the beer she drank and the candy she liked to eat, but there was a voluptuousness about her that was accentuated by the flashy, colorful dresses she wore, dresses that hugged her breasts and hips. There was a sort of permanent curl to her lip that expressed her aggravation at the world and her absorption in her own empty pleasures. Kate had heard Ray call her a "bitch" a thousand times, and she had to admit that the word seemed to suit her.

Kate said nothing. She knew that Mother and Ray were going out to a local grill where they ate their dinner at least twice a week. Children were not allowed in the place. They would have drinks with their meal, too many drinks. They would return late, at nine-thirty or later, and have more drinks at home. Perhaps they would fight. Kate was delighted not to have to be with them. She wished they would go out every night.

Mother glanced around the room with a look of bored speculation in her eyes.

"And clean up this place," she said. "It looks like a goddamned hurricane hit it."

Without another word she closed the door and was gone.

Kate spent the evening trying without much success to concentrate on her homework and poring occasionally over her folder of Eve Sinclair memorabilia. By the time the downstairs door opened and shut at ten o'clock she was in her pajamas, having bathed, washed her hair, and accepted the unwelcome fact that she still had not memorized the math and had left the English essay only half written.

No one said goodnight to her. She could tell by the sound of the conversation downstairs that the adults had drunk more than usual. There was a crackle of menace in Mother's strident bantering and Ray's brooding responses.

Kate got into bed. She tried to shut out the sound of their talk, and of the ice clinking in their glasses, with her memory of the movie she had seen today. She saw Eve cross the parlor to run to her father's arms, saw Eve running gaily across the lawn of the plantation, saw Eve's sparkling smile fill the screen. And her own world receded in proportion as Eve filled her fantasies.

She was just drifting off to welcome sleep when the remote sound of the adults mounting the stairs reached her ears. Then the door of the other bedroom opened and closed. And, as dreams struggled against reality in her sleepy mind, the muted gasps and squeaking bedsprings of their lovemaking reached her ears. It was a foreign sound, loathsome and lewdly comical. It was the hoarse mutter of a world in which she could not imagine herself living, a desert that could not support life.

For a moment Kate frowned. Then, with an effort of will, she plunged deeper into her dreams of the happy plantation house, the beautiful little girl in her white dress, the loving parents, the spreading lawn, and the whispering wind in the trees. For this one precious moment, Kate actually was Eve Sinclair, was inside her skin and inside the character she played, and lived in another and better world.

Kate fell asleep.

Hollywood, California
September 12, 1930

EVE SINCLAIR WAS HUNGRY.

In fact, she was starving. Her young body, craving quick energy, cried out for something sweet and good-tasting.

More than anything in the world she wanted a big dish of chocolate-swirl ice cream with whipped cream and a cherry on top.

No, she mused: make that three cherries.

Eve was tired and irritable after an exhausting morning on the set of her latest picture, *Mischief and Miracles*. She had had to squeeze in her history and English lessons with her studio tutor on the set this morning, between learning new lines for her latest scene and rehearsing a difficult dance number with the choreographer.

At eleven-thirty, after five straight hours of work, her mind had begun to wander under the hot lights, and the tutor had scolded her. Then the director had reprimanded her, more gently, for her repeated failure to get one of the lines right. Finally her exhaustion had begun to show to the cameras, and shooting was halted while she took a thirty-minute rest.

Now she was between scenes, and her mother was touching up her makeup. It was a job that Mother reserved jealously for herself. She considered Eve's appearance her personal responsibility, not only during shooting but during publicity work as well. She was not about to let her beautiful daughter's image and career be ruined by a sloppy studio makeup artist who was not paying proper attention to his work.

Mother sat beside Eve, carefully applying a touch of color to her cheeks to hide their pallor.

"You rebounded well, dear," she was saying. "You had a tough morning, but you came back. You're a damned good actress, and you showed them who was the star."

There was a curiously impersonal firmness in her voice. Eve listened without comment. Her own mind was still on her painful hunger.

"Mother, can I have some ice cream?" The girl asked the question without real hope.

Mother laughed. "Ice cream!" she exclaimed. "At this hour? Why, you know ice cream ruins your voice, honey. No ice cream, certainly not. You can have some soup after the next scene."

Eve said nothing. She accepted her mother's rules without question, as always. It was only thanks to Mother's tireless work on her behalf that she was where she was today. It was Mother who had started her in singing and dancing lessons when she was scarcely out of diapers and had got her into the profitable vaudeville career that netted her a screen test in Hollywood at age eight.

The test had been successful, for Eve had possessed a precocious acting talent to go along with her adorable looks and her ability to sing and dance. She had become a contract player at Worldwide Pictures, earning fifty dollars a week and performing in small roles in innumerable "B" pictures and comedy trailers before she got her first big chance at age nine in a feature film called *Prairie Girl*.

Thanks to her long preparation before the cameras and the arduous training she had undergone in the interim, Eve had been ready when the call came. In *Prairie Girl* she played the perky, adorable daughter of a young farmer who must fight to save his land from unscrupulous bankers, and she had made the most of the part. Her extraordinary poise and naturalness before the cameras impressed everyone. The picture was an unexpected hit, and Eve began a new round of roles, this time featured ones with good billing. Her mother and her agent, Irving Fine, negotiated a new and far more lucrative contract for her, and the routine of shooting and behind-the-scenes training in singing, dancing, and acting accelerated.

Being young and strong, Eve stood up under the pressure. By age eleven she was one of the best-known child actresses in Hollywood. Her reputation for professionalism and dependability made her a sought-after loan-out as well as one of Worldwide's most pampered stars.

For all this Eve had to thank Mother. It was Mother who had pushed her to prepare herself before she got her chance and pushed her to make the most of it when it came. And it was Mother, even today, who kept after her to hone her talent ever sharper and make it shine, so that she would be ready when her next big opportunity came.

Mother had sacrificed a lot of herself to get Eve where she was today. Eve was her only child. After she discovered Eve's precocious talent, she had refused to have more children, preferring to devote herself entirely to Eve's career.

Eve's father, a modest pharmacist in the small Illinois town of Eve's birth, had wanted a normal life for his daughter, and more children. But his wife had overruled him, insisting on pushing Eve into show business, and a divorce followed soon afterward. Mother and Eve had moved to Hollywood, leaving Father behind forever.

Eve missed her father's quiet, reassuring personality. She often longed for him when the pace of show business got too hectic. She sensed on some ever-receding level of her consciousness that life with him would have been peaceful and happy in a way she could not clearly conceive nowadays.

But he was in her past now. Mother was Eve's only real companion, her only friend, and her stern taskmaster. Eve lived to please Mother, and to prevent the dark look of anger and disapproval that came into Mother's eyes whenever it seemed that Eve was not giving "one hundred and fifty percent," as Mother put it, to her work.

So Eve said nothing more about her hunger for ice cream now. She was a "trouper," and everyone admired her for that. Unlike other child stars, Eve never burst into tears when a scene went wrong, never became peevish or ill-behaved when the long, boring hours on the set got on her nerves, never threw temper tantrums when the pressure of work got to be simply too much. She was so uncannily poised, so quiet and professional, that her directors held her up as a model even to the adult performers who worked with her.

Eve was a marvel. She was the creation of eight straight years of unrelenting work in the toughest business in the world. Her talent, very considerable from the outset, had been combined with a personality trained almost from the cradle to handle the rigors of Hollywood. She needed no praise, no cajoling, to do her best. She was a star to the marrow of her bones.

The fact that somewhere behind the armor of her talent and experience there lurked an unformed young girl, innocent of the real world outside Hollywood, bereft of friends her own age or any experience at the activities of ordinary children—this fact did not interest those who lived off her talent, first among them her mother. Their only concern was to sharpen that talent, get her more opportunities to use it, and push her as far as she could go in her career. After all, there was so much money involved, for themselves as well as for little Evie . . .

Hollywood had no time for childhood. The only playing Eve had ever done with children her own age had been for the publicity cameras. And those children had been extras hired by the casting department for the occasion.

Surprisingly enough, Eve herself was not really aware of the secret chasm of loneliness inside her. For as long as she could remember she had done what adults expected of her and lived off the approval she got from them. She knew nothing else. She could not consciously miss a normal childhood, because she had no idea of what it was. She knew only work, and more work, and Mother to help her get work and push her to do her best.

Somewhere along the line, as Eve's ability as an actress had developed, her untapped talent at being a person had been sacrificed. What she was today was an accomplished star, a brilliant performer, and the dead, empty embryo of a human being who had never had her chance to grow and be normal, to be loved for who she was instead of what she could do.

And perhaps it was the very fact that Eve floated atop her own emptiness without feeling the vertigo of that emptiness that made her so brilliant and poised a performer. There was nothing behind the mask she put on before the cameras—nothing personal to trouble the perfect surface of her performance. She could laugh or cry on cue, without ever looking self-conscious, and stop on a dime the instant she heard the word "Cut!" Nothing stood in the way of the perfect illusion she showed the cameras. For she was a creature made of illusion itself.

So today Eve Sinclair stood at the threshold of a long and successful career, a career earned by a lot of talent and even more hard work. But it was a delicate moment for her. She was growing out of childhood roles, and it was time for the transition to adolescent parts. This was a transition that few child actors survived. Though Eve herself had given no thought to this dilemma, her mother had been thinking about it very seriously for a long time.

And today she had important news to tell her daughter.

"Listen, honey," Mother said as she finished touching up Eve's makeup. "I have something to tell you. I didn't want to tell you before, because I knew it would make you nervous and spoil your scene. Sit up straight, dear—that's right."

Stifling a yawn, Eve sat up straight. In the mirror she saw her mother's eyes fixed on her.

"As of last month," Mother said, "you were number-eighteen box-office in the nation. You're the fourth most important star the studio has. Your pictures have been grossing millions. Your talent has never been better. But you're getting older now. The time has come to make a transition to a higher level. This will mean more money for you, and more responsibility."

She paused to replace an errant lock of her daughter's beautiful sable hair.

"Irving and I have negotiated a very important deal for you," she went on. "The studio is going to loan you out to Olympic Pictures to make a comedy with Tommy Valentine."

Eve's ears perked up at the mention of the name. Tommy Valentine was a highly visible and famous child actor, two years older than Eve. He had scored tremendous successes on Broadway and in films, playing a variety of roles with great versatility. He had an all-American look of bright humor and boyish sensitivity that endeared him to the public. He was well above Eve in the box-office rankings and was the hottest adolescent star in Hollywood.

"Now," Mother said, "this will not be just any old comedy. It's a romantic story in which you and Tommy will fall in love. Mr. Donath and the head men at Olympic are very high on the property. They think that with a little bit of luck the picture could produce sequels. That would be tremendous, Eve, the best possible thing for your career. The publicity blitz will be all-out for this picture."

Eve said nothing. She was listening carefully. She knew that Tommy Valentine was a far bigger star than herself. Performing opposite him would be the biggest step she had yet taken in her career.

"Well?" her mother asked, a trace of impatience in her voice. "Aren't you pleased?"

Eve smiled. "Of course I'm pleased, Mother," she said. The mother smiled, mollified.

"Now, I shouldn't have told you this, because it's supposed to be a surprise," she said. "Mr. Donath is going to tell you himself this afternoon after shooting. But I wanted you to know about it, and to know how important it is, so you'll make the right impression when you go in to see him. Do you understand?"

"Yes, Mother."

Mother smiled.

"That's my girl," she said. "You've worked hard for this studio, and you deserve only the best. These people know when they've got a good thing."

The daughter looked into her mother's eyes in the mirror.

"What will my salary be?" she asked quietly.

The mother frowned at the question.

"You let me and Irving worry about that," she said. "It's not a child's business to be thinking about money."

The young girl nodded obediently. In previous years she had never thought about money. But recently she had become curious about it, and always took note when Mother and Irving let slip contract talk about dollars in her hearing.

"Now," Mother said. "All the groundwork has been done. The official signing will take place next week. As soon as you're finished shooting today you'll have a private meeting with Mr. Donath. It is essential that you impress him with your enthusiasm for the project and your ability to handle it. He likes you already, but he has to be convinced that you're ready, willing, and able to throw *one hundred and fifty percent* effort into this. Do you understand?"

"Yes, Mother."

Carl Donath was the head of the studio. Under his stern aegis Worldwide Pictures produced high-gloss, quality films, with an emphasis on musicals and family pictures. He kept an eye on every detail of production, and was a valuable friend to any performer to whom he took a liking. He had long been impressed by Eve's astonishing professionalism, like everyone else at Worldwide.

But he could hardly be unaware that her age was now working against her. He was giving her a crucial chance to turn the corner into romantic teenage parts, and he must be treated well.

"Good," said Mother. "Now let's get back to work. After this scene you can have something to eat."

With a last look at her face in the mirror, Eve got up to leave the dressing room. She was already beginning to file away her mother's news as she concentrated on the scene she had to do.

She only hoped that the hunger pangs that were making her knees weak would not cause her stomach to rumble during the scene.

The director would never forgive her if her restless tummy forced him into re-takes.

At six o'clock that evening shooting was over.

Eve was whisked from the set to her dressing room, where her mother hurriedly took off her makeup and helped her on with a pretty dress that showed off her shapely young legs and her slim shoulders. In the blue garment she looked like a prim schoolgirl, her clear complexion glowing around her intelligent eyes.

Eve was exhausted and hungry. The bowl of soup she had been promised at eleven-thirty had finally materialized at one. But she had never had a proper lunch. The ice-cream sundae she had fantasized about was not even a memory now. She felt weak and found it hard to concentrate. She had just done the work of an adult Hollywood professional, from six in the morning until six at night, and she was drained.

But the four difficult scenes that had been on the schedule for today were completed and printed, thanks to Eve's brilliant performance. The director was pleased, the producer was relieved, and Mother was proud.

Now it was time to see Mr. Donath. When that meeting was over, Eve would at last be taken home to dinner.

As they left the dressing room Eve yawned.

Her mother stopped her in her tracks with hands on both her shoulders. "No yawning," she said. "Mr. Donath demands complete loyalty from his stars. You must be at your absolute best today. Do you understand, Eve?"

The girl nodded, stifling the second yawn that stirred in her throat.

Ethel Sonnenbaum—that was Mother's married name, and Eve's real last name—walked her daughter through the studio streets, filled with false building fronts, false telephone booths and fire hydrants and manholes, even false mountains, while dozens of actors, from extras to stars, passed on either side of them, some greeting them with friendly hellos.

They left the lot behind and arrived at the executive office building. Mother held Eve's hand tightly as they entered the elevator.

The top floor was reserved for Mr. Donath's office. There were three outer secretaries' offices to get through. Each secretary greeted Eve and her mother warmly. They were expected.

As they approached the innermost office the mother caught her daughter's arm and pulled her aside.

"Remember what I told you," she said. "Be at your best. You are not a little girl any more. You are a star. You are a professional. You can be depended on. It took me and Irving a long time to convince Mr. Donath to give you this chance. Now he needs to be sure that you are ready to do anything necessary to help this studio. Do you understand?"

Eve nodded, hiding her exhaustion behind wide, attentive eyes.

"Be nice, be pretty," the mother said. "And do *whatever he asks*. Is that clear?"

Eve nodded, her expression unreadable.

At the last office the inner door was open. Carl Donath

was standing in the doorway. He was a tall man in his fifties, with thinning gray hair and a distinguished air.

"Evie," he smiled, holding out his arms to Eve. "My brightest little star. Come in, dear. I've been waiting for you."

Eve's mother bent to straighten her daughter's dress. As she did so she whispered in Eve's ear, "Don't forget: *it's your career.*"

With a smile she sent her daughter forward and stepped back as the door was closed.

This was to be a private meeting.

Inside the office Mr. Donath held out his arms.

"Eve," he said. "How delightfully pretty you look today. Come right here and sit beside me on the couch."

Eve did as she was told. She smelled his expensive cologne and the aroma of cigars as she sat beside him. She felt the aura of his considerable charm. He affected a paternal air toward all his stars, and particularly toward the children, since the studio made a lot of its money off child stars, who were a staple of entertainment nowadays. Hard times had made the public sentimental, and it liked as much fantasy as possible in the films it went out to see with its hard-earned money. Children filled the bill perfectly.

"And how are you, my darling?" he asked. "Work going well?"

"Yes, Mr. Donath," she replied, putting on a grateful smile.

"They're not tiring you out too much, I hope?" he asked. "Studies going all right?"

"Yes, sir."

"Ah, that's wonderful. You know, Evie, you're my brightest star. The brightest star in my firmament." He patted her thigh, which seemed tiny under his large hand. "If you don't feel well treated, you must always come straight to me. Straight to Papa. You know that, don't you?"

She nodded.

"I have a very pleasant surprise for you," he said. "The studio has some exciting new plans for your career. Plans

29

that will make that rising star of yours shoot upward all the faster. I hope no one has spilled the beans. I wanted to tell you myself."

Now both his hands were on her thighs, patting and soothing.

Don't feel anything. Behind her sunny, childish smile Eve was preparing herself for what must come. No performance she had put on for the cameras today matched the challenge before her now. But she was equal to it. Her mother's words still echoed in her ears: *It's your career.* This was the single most important of all Mother's maxims, the essence of all her teaching. One could not shrink from any sacrifice where Career was concerned.

"You know that all I want is your happiness, don't you?" the studio head murmured. "All the pictures in the world, and all the millions at the box office, don't mean anything if my little darling isn't happy. You know that, don't you?"

"Yes, sir."

"Ah, that's good. That's right."

Now the hands were pulling up her skirt, inch by inch. The large fingers were slipping up her thighs toward the center of her. She heard heavy breathing in her ear, and felt his smile close to her hair.

Don't feel anything. You're not here. You're somewhere else.

And she was. As the hands found their way under her skirt to her waist, Eve withdrew far behind her skin to a place where no feeling existed, no emotion, no dread, no pain. It was a place she had learned to visit during a thousand sessions before the camera or before the publicity people, when her fatigue, her hunger, or her need to go to the bathroom were so unbearable that she could not stand it a second longer. This refuge had stood her in good stead through her years as a Hollywood actress, years in which her youthful identity had been sacrificed to her career. It would stand her in good stead now.

"That's my girl," murmured Carl Donath, nuzzling her little ear with his thick lips. A groan stirred in his throat as he pulled her closer to him. "That's Daddy's girl."

 3

September 12, 1930

FOURTEEN HUNDRED MILES FROM THE HOLLYWOOD STUDIO where Eve Sinclair was hard at work improving her career, a half dozen men sweated under the hot Oklahoma sun, their combined strength barely a match for the enormous weight of the drill assembly they were lifting.

They were oil workers, and they were replacing a drill bit that had been dulled and deformed by its work deep under the ground, pulverizing rock at the bottom of the well. It was attached to the heavy tools that followed it down the shaft, tools whose weight would add to the tremendous force of each blow of the new bit.

Grunting under the effort, the men pushed it this way and that, some of them cursing as the bit assembly swayed and banged at the hole, until at last it found its fit and slid into place.

Watching them from his privileged position as lookout, Julian Flagg took off his cap and wiped his brow. Unlike the roughnecks, he wore his shirt despite the heat. He was skinny and pale, and did not like to expose his skin to the merciless Oklahoma sun. He hated sun almost as much as he hated work.

Julian Flagg had wangled himself the job of lookout today, thanks to the foreman, who deemed him his special pet thanks to a lot of small favors and obsequious behavior

31

over four years on the job. Julian looked at the men, satisfied not to be among them. Most of them were complaining mightily, for they hated the danger of dealing with the heavy equipment. More than one man had been seriously injured in the past by drill parts.

They were aware that they were lucky to have jobs at all. Because of the hard times, thousands of oil men had been laid off throughout the West. Though the wells were still making money, the owners felt they were doing men a favor by hiring them, and offered them low salaries and no benefits. The men had to face backbreaking work, long hours, and poor working conditions for rock-bottom wages. As a result many of them did as little work as possible, and shirked danger whenever they could. But a job like today's could not be avoided, and forced them into both risk and hard physical effort. So they complained.

But one of them did not make a sound. And it was this man that Julian Flagg was looking at.

His name was Joseph Knight. He had come to the field six months ago, a young man of nineteen who looked, somehow, much older. Perhaps it was because of his thick muscles and his ruddy skin—which were visible now as he worked shirtless with the others. His hard pectorals, powerful back and shoulders, and strong arms made him look at least twenty-five. And there was an air of purpose in his square jaw and his calm dark eyes that belied his youth.

His physical superiority over the other men was obvious. Not only did he not make a sound as he strained, his heavy muscles standing out in the sun under the coating of dirt that covered all the men's skin. There was a quality of silent leadership even in his exertion. He was stronger than the others, and he was intentionally taking on a greater portion of the weight in order to spare them. They saw this sacrifice on his part, and were encouraged to give their best.

Knight was a natural leader. This was one reason—though far from the only reason—why Julian Flagg hated him.

Knight had been hired routinely as a roughneck. He had no experience and nothing to recommend him except his strong arms. In the last six months he had shown not only his willingness to work hard and to learn, but also his striking leadership. His crews always seemed to do the job faster and better than anyone else's. Though he was a quiet young man who did not take a conscious leadership role, something serious in him struck a chord in the other men, and they worked harder when they were beside him.

This quality of Knight's was appreciated by the foreman. These were not union men. There was no union in the fields. As a matter of fact, the company had fought the union organizers so savagely over the last five years that it seemed there would never be a union here. The men had reasons to be disgruntled. They knew the company was making millions while they themselves made almost nothing, because the company used the excuse of the hard times to pay as little as possible. All the more reason why they needed a man like Knight to set an example of dedication to the work.

This alone had attracted the attention of the foreman within the first few weeks after Knight's arrival. But there was more. After his first month on the job, Knight had made a suggestion as to how better to organize the drilling schedule and to manage the site. The foreman, impressed, took the idea to the owner, Mr. Lowry. The next week it was implemented.

As of today Joseph Knight was well on his way to being named head of the field team. In another six months he might even become a foreman himself.

In his four years here, Julian Flagg, a cunning and dishonest worker, had managed to avoid most of the hardest work while endearing himself to the foreman through a variety of small favors. He had informed on the men who were slacking (though he was a master slacker himself) and had reported to the foreman every rumor he heard about the union and its activities. More than once a disgruntled worker who dared to speak to the union people found himself beaten up and fired because of a secret denunciation at the hands of Julian Flagg.

The other men were not stupid, and had come to distrust Flagg and keep their distance from him. But he was very thick with the foreman, who in turn passed along a good word about him to the owner every once in a while.

Thus it was with frustration and simmering rage that Flagg, a natural jackal, saw youthful Joseph Knight, with his quiet competence and his great strength, upstaging him. Flagg himself would have liked to be promoted to gang leader one of these days. Now it looked as though Knight would steal that honor from him.

Like all jackals, Flagg hated a man who was his moral superior. Thus he hated Joseph Knight. He hated that upright manhood in Knight that impressed the men and made them do their best. It was a quality that made Flagg look pathetic and contemptible by comparison. It made Flagg fume with jealous resentment.

And there was a final reason why Flagg hated Knight.

Joseph Knight, with his precociously manly looks, was irresistible to women. Every weekend, when the men went into town to spend their week's wages on liquor and women, Knight found himself surrounded by the most desirable girls of the town, who vied for the opportunity to spend the night with him. As for Julian Flagg, he had to content himself with paying one of the sleazy whores for an hour in bed, for he was a pimply, unattractive young man whose dishonesty shone in his pasty face.

What bothered him the most was that it was not just Joseph Knight's brawny torso or handsome, ruddy face that attracted the women. It was that same mysterious air of masculine strength and integrity. Women could not keep their hands off him. His very silence, his aloofness, seemed to drive them crazy with desire.

For this reason, along with everything else, Julian Flagg hated Joseph Knight.

And soon, if things went on the way they were going, Knight would be Julian Flagg's boss. This would be intolerable.

But today, as he watched the men work, Julian Flagg had an idea of how to get this menace, this Joseph Knight, out of his hair.

And he was going to act on it.

*　　*　　*

That night Denning Lowry, the owner of the company that ran the oil field and two others in the same county, sat having dinner in the big house with his daughter, Beth, who was home for the summer from her boarding school in Massachusetts.

Beth was his only child and his pet. Since his wife's death six years ago Beth had been the light of his life. At seventeen she was polished and refined by finishing-school life, but she still had the pert, vixenish ways that had always endeared her to him and allowed her to twist him around her little finger.

Now that she was a "real young lady," as the county folks liked to call her, she was bored to tears around the big house, with its crude Oklahoma decor and its silent servants. She spent most of her time shopping or driving to visit friends, the daughters of other oil men or big ranchers, and going to parties. But she always had dinner with her father, for she knew how he doted on her. She listened to his news of the day and told him of her doings. This was part of the strategy that allowed her to get a new dress or new horse out of him whenever she wanted. Or a promise for a tour of Europe, which she was now working to cajole from him.

Denning Lowry was glad to see his daughter gadding about the county and flirting with her many beaux. He intended to marry her into one of the best families in the state. It was for this that he had worked all these years. Though his late wife had come from a good family, Lowry himself was the son of poor farm people in Texas and had come up the hard way.

It had not been easy for him to amass enough property and money to match himself up with the big oil families in the county. He had had to play the game rough. He had forced more than one competitor out of business, and acquired more than one parcel of land through intimidation and questionable business tactics.

For the last seventeen years—the length of young Beth's life—he had worked to consolidate his position in the county's economy and political life by doing a thousand favors for everybody who was anybody. He had enough influential politicians in his pocket to get any ordinance passed that would be beneficial to himself and the other oil men. And he worked with all his strength to keep the unions out.

Over the years the oil men had come to respect him as a crude but effective ally. Though they looked down on him socially, laughed at his vulgar ways, and made a show of disapproving of his business tactics, they knew his shenanigans served their own interests as well as his. He did the dirty work they needed done but did not want to soil their hands with.

In a strongbox under the floor of his bedroom, Denning Lowry kept a secret cash fund, which was used for political payoffs, bribes, and the hiring of outsiders to break the unions. This fund presently contained forty thousand dollars, culled from his own illegal profits and from a secret organization of oil men who used Denning Lowry as their bag man. Thanks to Lowry, several union organizers had disappeared in the last two years, and several more had been beaten so badly that they ran for their lives.

Denning Lowry hated the union above all things on earth. It was a gang of troublemakers who intended to restrain free trade and throttle the booming oil business before it could reach its potential. One had to fight the evil of union organization with every weapon possible.

This was truer than ever nowadays, for the union was aggressively trying to turn Lowry's own men against him. There were constant rumors of secret meetings, and the murmur of discontent among the men was unmistakable.

Lowry had taken a good many steps to keep a lid on things. In the first place, he kept his men as happy as such men had a right to be. He gave them decent bunkhouses to sleep in, three square meals a day prepared by a skilled cook, and regular bonuses for their visits to the whores in town. In the second place, he had an intricate network of paid informers who kept him abreast of what the men were thinking, what they were saying in the privacy of their bunkhouses and in their bars. Even some of the whores were on Denning Lowry's payroll. He got invaluable information from them, for a working man far from home and family, like most of the roughnecks, has no one to unburden himself to except his favorite whore.

Thanks to Lowry's vigilance, the union had been held at bay in Will County, though it had made disturbing inroads among workers in other parts of the state. Lowry was proud that his county was non-union, and was determined that it would remain that way as long as he had anything to say about it. His peers among the oil men respected his vigilance and his ruthlessness in this regard.

So Denning Lowry had become an accepted member of the oil-rich community. And soon, thanks to his years of toil, he would marry Beth into one of the best oil families in the county. Beth's children would enjoy all the advantages he had never had, and she would grow up to become one of the great ladies of the state. Perhaps Denning Lowry's grandchildren would include a governor, a senator, a congressman.

The seeds were sown. It fell to pretty, coquettish young Beth to make them grow into a great future.

Tonight Denning Lowry was quieter than usual as he sat at the dinner table with his daughter.

"Penny for your thoughts, Daddy," Beth said, wrinkling her pretty nose.

He smiled, admiring her fresh young face. The auburn curls and milky complexion always charmed him, as did the vixenish look in her eyes.

"Oh, nothing that would interest you, darlin'," he said. "Just business."

He did not want to burden her with what was on his mind, though it was sorely preoccupying him.

He had heard through his grapevine that one of the promising young field men he had hired in the last few months was a secret union sympathizer.

The fellow's name was Joseph Knight. He had shown himself a strong and willing worker and a natural leader. He had impressed the foreman with a clever idea or two about the field organization, and Lowry, always on top of things, had heard about this. He liked the young man and was keeping him in mind for a future promotion.

Knight was a good-looking young fellow, with dark hair, intense black eyes, and a thickly muscled body that made him an ideal worker. He said little, but his reticence only made his few words carry more weight. He did not attract attention to himself but got the work done quickly and well. This was an unusual quality in a profession in which laziness was the hallmark of almost all the men. Denning Lowry considered Knight one of the best men he had hired in twenty years.

Now, however, there was bad news about Knight.

The informer, a reliable man named Flagg, was categorical. Knight was not to be trusted. He had been seen in the company of some union men in the town and had been overheard encouraging discontent among the men of his crew.

This came as a disappointment to Lowry. He had hoped to make Knight a team leader by the end of the year and perhaps foreman by next summer. Knight would make an ideal foreman, with his quiet intelligence, his seriousness, and the way he commanded respect from the men.

But unfortunately, as Lowry had learned in two decades in the business, it was just this seriousness, this inner integrity, that was a danger. For such men too often turned to the union to fight for better working conditions. Despite their superiority as workers, they often had to be torn out of the organization the way a weed is torn out of a garden. For they sowed discord and potential rebellion. A boss like Lowry had to know how to find men who worked hard without having too much integrity, men who took the job seriously, but not seriously enough to want to unionize. This was a delicate balance.

Evidently Knight had slipped over the line to the wrong side.

Beth had said something, but her father, lost in his worry, had not heard her.

"What, honey?" he said.

She laughed. "You're a million miles away," she said. "The problem can't be *that* bad, can it?"

He sighed and patted her hand.

"One of my men is turning out to be a troublemaker,"

he said. "Too bad. He was a good man. At least I thought he was."

"What's his name?" Beth asked.

"Knight," he said. "Fellow by the name of Joe Knight."

Beth's lips curled in a look of distaste.

"I could have told you that about him," she said.

Her father looked at her in surprise.

"What?" he asked. "How do you know Joe Knight?" It amazed him that his daughter could know any of the roughnecks by name.

"Well, I don't *know* him," she corrected. "But I've seen him. He's stuck-up."

The father looked at his daughter incredulously.

"Has he insulted you?" he asked, bristling.

She laughed.

"Oh, no, Daddy," she said. "I've never even talked to him. It's just that he's—well, he thinks he's God's gift to women, or something. I'm not surprised he's a troublemaker. Anyone can see he thinks he's the be-all and end-all . . ."

Denning Lowry was perplexed and disturbed. Apparently Knight had made no improper advances toward his cherished daughter. But her words sufficed to alarm him. He knew how popular Knight was with the girls in town. And he had seen with his own eyes how handsome the young man was.

Thus Beth's words, combined with what he had heard from his informer, made up his mind.

He had to get rid of Joseph Knight.

That night Denning Lowry had a long talk with his foreman. He told him to pick four of the strongest men in the field, men who had been used before to deal with troublemakers, men who knew how to beat a man within an inch of his life without leaving too many marks for the police to investigate.

"Give him something to remember us by," he told the foreman. "I don't want him ever to be in shape to work on an oil rig again. Dump him over the county line. And make sure he understands that if he ever shows his face in these parts while I'm alive, he's a dead man. Got it?"

The foreman grinned. "Got it, boss," he said. "You can count on me. He'll never forget us."

Satisfied, Denning Lowry went to bed early that night and fell into a deep sleep.

At three o'clock that morning Denning Lowry was awakened from troubled dreams by a cold touch underneath his chin and a hand that closed over his mouth, keeping him from crying out.

He realized there was a knife at his throat. The feel of the cold steel was unmistakable.

A quiet voice spoke in his ear.

"Get up," it said.

Clumsily, trembling as the blade pressed angrily at his throat, Denning Lowry sat up in the bed. He could feel the breath of the intruder against his ear.

For an instant Denning Lowry wondered how the intruder had got past the guard dogs and groundskeeper. This house was kept under tight security.

But that did not matter now. The man was here, and there was no stopping him.

"Don't cry out. If you do, I'll kill you. Get up," said the voice. Denning Lowry was pulled roughly to his feet and placed in the chair beside the window. He shivered in his pajamas, despite the heat of the Oklahoma night.

Then the light on the bureau was turned on.

Lowry caught his breath. It was the young man, Joseph Knight. He was covered with bruises and caked dirt. It was obvious he had been in a fight. But he looked calm and strong. It was clear he had been the winner. The powerful muscles of his neck and shoulders, close up, were frightening to look at.

"Four weren't enough," Knight said. "Next time send more."

Lowry gulped uncomfortably. "I don't know what you're talking about . . ." he began. "I assure you, I had nothing to do . . ."

Then he fell silent as he saw the knife in the young man's

hand. It was a long, sharp stiletto, the kind of knife that professional killers use. The sight of the erect, shiny blade made him feel sick to his stomach.

Slowly, silently, so as not to awaken the house, the young man pulled the bed aside from its position on the floor. Underneath it was a small braided rug.

He kicked aside the rug. The panel of flooring above the secret strongbox was revealed.

"Open it," the young man said. "Get me the money."

"Money?" Lowry said, trembling. "There isn't any money. You're crazy. This is private property, young man. I'd advise you to . . ."

He was thinking fast. How had the fellow found out about the money box, and its hiding place? No one knew about it. Not even the servants. There were over forty thousand dollars in that box, in cash and negotiable securities. Denning Lowry had to try to protect his money.

"There is no money," he insisted.

The young man seized Lowry roughly by the neck with one hand. With the other he shoved the blade of the knife against the oil man's upper lip, the edge grazing his nose.

"Don't bother to lie," he said. "Do as I say."

Denning Lowry got down on his knees and pulled up the floorboards beneath which the strongbox was located. He reached down. His hand found the gun that was kept on top of the strongbox, and began to emerge from the hole.

He heard a low laugh. Before he could raise the gun to shoot, a powerful arm curled around his neck and squeezed. Almost at once a red wave rose up before his eyes, blinding him as the air to his lungs was cut off.

Then a finger grasped his ear. A sudden, horrific stab of pain shot through him, a pain that would have made him shriek in agony had not the strong arm remained around his throat, choking off his voice.

In the light of the lamp he saw gouts of his own blood spattering over the floor. Amid them was a small piece of flesh that a moment ago had been Denning Lowry's earlobe.

The young man had taken the gun and thrown it on the bed. The stiletto was at Lowry's neck again.

"Open the box," Joseph Knight said. "Or I'll kill you and do it myself."

Bleeding like a stuck pig, Denning Lowry pulled out the strongbox with trembling hands, produced a key from the pocket of his pajamas, and opened the box.

"On the bed," came Joseph Knight's voice, calm and businesslike. "Lie down."

Denning Lowry lay curled up like a child, clutching his bleeding ear. The ringing of his panic in his ears made it almost impossible to hear the sounds of Joseph Knight taking his money.

At last the voice returned.

"Get up," it said.

Still holding his ear, Lowry staggered to his feet.

"That's not your money," he dared to say. Even at this desperate moment he had enough courage to protest the theft of his ill-gotten gain.

Joseph Knight smiled. It was the coldest smile Denning Lowry had ever seen. Looking at it he easily understood how four strong men had been no match for this fellow. He seemed inhuman, heavy and powerful as an anvil. There was nothing young about him, despite his chronological age. He had obviously been through things that had tempered his intelligence and courage while hardening his heart. The glare in his black eyes was ageless, terrifying. Denning Lowry realized the money was no longer the issue. He must get out of this night alive.

The young man had stuffed the cash and securities inside his shirt. He put the gun in his pocket. Then he picked up the knife and took a step toward his victim.

"Beg for your life," Joseph Knight said quietly.

Lowry struggled for words. No man had dared humble him in over twenty years. He could not beg.

Seeing him hesitate, Knight attacked quickly. In one fluid motion he forced him to his knees and grasped him about the neck. The needle-shaped blade was sticking straight into Denning Lowry's ear, a half inch from his brain.

"You have three seconds," Knight said. "No one will hear you die."

Lowry felt the point of the blade stir against his flesh.

"I . . . please don't kill me," Lowry stammered. "I've given you what you wanted. Just leave. Please . . . please don't kill me. I have a daughter. She needs a father."

Knight looked at him appraisingly. He saw a middle-aged man in his nightshirt, covered with blood, his trembling hand at his ear.

Knight seemed satisfied.

"I'm going to let you live," he said. "If you decide to send anyone after me, they'd better be good. Because next time it won't be your earlobe I take off."

"I . . ."

"Lie down on your bed." The authority in the voice silenced Lowry. He got into his bed. He lay holding his ear, shuddering as the blood continued to flow over his hand.

He did not hear Joseph Knight leave. Whether this was because of the tumult of his own fear and pain, or because of some inhuman subtlety of movement on Knight's part, he did not know. He was afraid to move or cry out, for Knight might still be within striking distance.

So Denning Lowry lay listening to the silence of the house, pressing the pillow against his ear to slow the bleeding, until he could stand it no longer.

At last, afraid he would bleed to death, he rang for the servants. A few moments later his manservant, James, came to the door in his own nightshirt. Blinking from his sleep, he asked what was the matter.

Lowry looked past him down the hall. He could not help wondering if Knight was still here, watching him.

"Call Dr. Martin," he said. "I've—I've cut myself. Hurry!"

The manservant's eyes opened wide at the sight of the blood all over his master.

"Yes, sir," he cried. "Right away, sir."

Denning Lowry watched the servant rush away down the hall. Then he returned to the bedroom, sat down on the bed, and wept.

Part of him had already decided he would pay any price to have Joseph Knight hunted down and killed.

Another part, more wise, was recalling that the young

man had entered this house despite the burglar alarms, the guard dogs, and the servants. He also recalled that the young man had known where the strongbox was. Clearly Joseph Knight had an intelligence and foresight to match his heartless will.

If Lowry were to send someone after him, and the someone did not succeed—the thought was too terrifying to bear. He could still hear Knight's warning words—*Next time it won't be your earlobe I take off*. The defenseless genitals between his legs tingled, making him shudder in fear.

Better not to throw good money after bad, he decided at last. What was gone was gone. He could not call the police, for the money stolen had been obtained through illegal means. None of it had been declared for tax purposes. He would face charges of bribery, conspiracy, illegal payoffs, and tax evasion if the authorities found out about the fund. And, of course, he would lose the confidence of the oil men whose favor he had spent so many years currying.

Joseph Knight had no doubt known all this. In taking the money he was stealing something whose owner could never come after it.

Better, then, to be thankful for his life, Denning Lowry decided. As things stood he would have a lost earlobe to remember Knight by, but his future was safe.

And his empire was secure.

Yes, Denning Lowry thought. He was alive. That was what counted.

• • •

Denning Lowry never saw Joseph Knight again.

He could not know what happened to his money.

Thirty thousand dollars of it went into a canny investment in an oil field in Texas, nine hundred miles away from the Lowry spread. Joseph Knight had made good use of the technical education he had got in the oil fields. The two wells he invested in came in six months later. The thirty thousand dollars he had taken from Denning Lowry had

44

him well on his way to being a millionaire before he was twenty-one.

The other ten thousand dollars never left the county. It was donated quietly and anonymously to the leaders of the union movement.

The four men who had attempted to beat up Joseph Knight spent a combined total of thirteen months in the hospital, their dislocated jaws, broken ribs, cracked spines, and crushed hands giving thousands of dollars of expense to Denning Lowry.

The foreman, one Delmer Goss, had to give up his job, because he could no longer ambulate around the field sites. His back had been broken, and he was confined to a wheelchair for the rest of his life. Unluckily for him, Denning Lowry held him personally responsible for the lack of success his strong-arm men had had in disciplining Joseph Knight. Lowry never contributed a penny to Goss's medical expenses.

As for Julian Flagg, the field worker who had denounced Knight to the foreman as a union man, he was never again to tell tales on his fellow workers.

His tongue had been cut out in the early morning hours not long after Joseph Knight's visit to Denning Lowry's bedroom. When asked to write down the name of the person who had done this to him, Julian Flagg refused. His whole body trembled as he shook his head.

As for Beth Lowry, she was never told the truth about what had happened that fateful night in the silence of her house.

When her father refused to explain the bandage on his ear the next morning, Beth said nothing. And when he insisted on sending her back East to her finishing school immediately instead of waiting for the fall semester, she agreed obediently.

After all, she had no reason to be here any longer, now that Joseph Knight was gone.

Never again would she feel his caresses on her naked body, or know the delight of being possessed by him.

Though only seventeen, Beth Lowry knew something

about men. She knew she would never see Joseph Knight again.

But she knew he would remember her.

For it was thanks to Beth, who knew her father like the back of her hand, and who had overheard many a whispered conversation in her time, that Joseph Knight had known in advance about the four men coming to beat him up.

And it was thanks to her also that he had known where the strongbox was located.

4

October 15, 1935

AT AGE SIXTEEN KATE HAMILTON WAS, IF ANYTHING, EVEN more removed from the world around her than she had been as a little girl.

Her teachers at school were mystified by her. She never raised her hand in the classroom, and nearly always answered their questions incorrectly. Her grades were mediocre, and she was criticized for being "a million miles away" in class, though more than once the complex, kaleidoscopic expression in her golden eyes made teachers suspect that she was far above her peers in intelligence.

Kate had blossomed into a nubile and very beautiful teenager, with rich sandy hair and a lush figure. But she was not popular in school, because she came from the wrong side of town, was poor, and had a mother with a somewhat tainted reputation.

The most sympathetic of her teachers understood that a combination of adolescent self-consciousness and alienation from the mainstream of popular students kept Kate from reaching her academic potential. But not even these well-meaning outsiders could see how cut off Kate was from the everyday reality they took for granted.

When Kate seemed "a million miles away" in class, she was also light-years away from herself. She did not know where her mind was or who she was. Behind her golden eyes there were no girlish dreams, no obsessions, no crushes on boys, no romantic aspirations for the future. Inside her there was only a spreading emptiness that walled her off from the world and from herself.

Sometimes she felt as though, under different circumstances, this unseen force that dragged her away from her life might have led her toward something meaningful, perhaps something wonderful. She felt momentary flashes of hope and even excitement about her life, as though a thrilling future were winking coyly at her from behind the drab curtain of today.

But these flashes quickly gave way to darkness, as an image in a crystal ball fades, and Kate continued to sleepwalk through her days and weeks and months, floating outside herself as though in a void.

One day when she arrived home from high school her mother was not there.

Ray was alone in the living room, reading the paper and listening to the radio.

Surprisingly, he got up to greet her.

"Your mother had to go to your grandmother's," he said. "Grandma's pretty sick. Irma's going to spend the night."

Listlessly Kate nodded. Then she turned to go up the stairs to her room.

"Kate," he called after her. "I thought you and I might go downtown for supper if you've a mind to."

She paused. He was standing with the paper in his hand, looking up at her. The look in his eyes was more friendly than she was used to.

He was older now, and heavier around the middle. But he still had that overpolished, oily air she had known since he moved in with her mother, that look of a slick, cologned man-about-town caught in his undershirt without having shaven. It made her faintly ill, as always.

"I have a lot of homework," she said. "You go ahead."

He looked at her for a moment, and then turned away.

She went into her room and closed the door. She could still see the look of unaccustomed interest in his eyes. He had seemed glad that Irma was out.

The last few years had brought disturbing changes to the family. As Kate had flowered into a creature of striking charms, her ungainly early adolescence eclipsed by a ripe beauty that made men turn to stare at her in the street, Mother had gotten older, fatter, more lined and sallow from liquor and lack of exercise.

And Mother's fights with Ray had become more frequent. She was more jealous. Sometimes he was out until late at night. When he returned they fought.

There was a continual quiet discord between them. The old days of their shared torpor in the living room, the occasional rollicking laughter after a few drinks, were gone. Their quarrels were many now, their reconciliations fewer. Kate had the impression that Ray was just waiting for Grandmother to die in order to find out whether there was any money in her will for Irma.

As for Mother, she paid less and less attention to Kate. She was too wrapped up in her own problems to care about those of her teenage daughter. When she did notice Kate, she treated her with suspicion and resentment, as though Kate had committed some sort of crime by merely being alive.

Kate dumped her books on her bed, selected the history textbook, and sat down to study. She had an exam in history on Friday and a paper to write for her English teacher on *King Lear*.

She knew it was all hopeless. She would get a C or C-minus on the history exam, and perhaps a C-plus on the English paper. In both courses her work would reflect the distraction that owned her soul. The teachers would upbraid her, try to reason with her, and tell her she was not making full use of her innate talent. She would make a show of listening, then try to forget them and hope they would leave her alone.

After an hour, bored to distraction by her studies, Kate stood up and stretched her young body. She felt tired enough to go to sleep right now, though it was only five-thirty.

She opened her closet door, looked on the shelf and saw her old folder of Eve Sinclair material. She opened it and saw a movie fan magazine with a publicity photo of Eve on the cover.

Her adoration of Eve had waned during the last few years. Eve had gone on to more successes in films, moving from her Adorable Child roles to a series of adolescent comedies with a young actor named Tommy Valentine. The series was successful, especially with young people. Eve was quite beautiful now, though lacking in the sultry looks that made today's sex symbols of the screen. There was a cleanness, a straightness and honesty about her that made her a popular star.

But Kate seldom went to the movies nowadays. She had no girlfriend to go with her, and when she went alone she always found a male sitting next to her with puffing breath and wandering hands.

So she stayed home in her room when her parents were out and left the house when they were home. She wandered the town window-shopping or just walking. People saw this, and it increased her reputation as a loose or fast girl. Nothing could have been further from the truth. Sex was utterly foreign to her. It was just something that interested other people, like all the pastimes and preoccupations of the outer world that Kate never touched.

At length she closed the folder of Eve Sinclair materials and looked back at her history book. The little concentration she had begun with was ebbing fast. She realized she needed something to eat.

She went downstairs silently to make herself dinner of a sandwich and a glass of milk, and then stole back upstairs.

In the living room Ray was still listening to the radio. She did not speak to him.

Upstairs she studied for another two hours, and then her eyes got heavy. It was time for bed. She had to get up early for school tomorrow, and she knew Mother would not bother to call from Grandma's tonight. She brushed her teeth, took off her clothes, and turned off the light at nine o'clock. She plummeted quickly into dreamless sleep.

Sometime later she was awakened by a touch at her shoulder.

"Mother . . ." she murmured as she came awake. She assumed it was Irma, home early with some news about the old lady's illness.

But it was Ray. He was kneeling by the side of her bed. She smelled liquor on his breath, a lot of liquor. She sat up on one elbow. She could feel an odd tension in him.

"What . . . What's the matter?" she asked.

"Nothing. Nothing's the matter," he said. His voice was thick with alcohol. "Take it easy, will you?"

"What are you doing here?" She was beginning to worry. She had only her nightgown on under the sheets. "Where's Mother?"

"She's at your grandmother's, like I told you," he said. "What's the matter, anyway?"

"I . . . What do you want?" Kate asked.

Ray was smiling in the darkness.

"She won't be home until morning," he said. "It's just you and me, kid."

She shrank back into the sheets.

"Leave me alone," she said. "Go away. Just go to bed."

He shook his head.

"Not so fast," he said.

Slowly he touched at the sheets covering her. She tried to hold them back, but he pulled them away. He could see the outline of her young breasts under the nightgown, and the slim waist leading to rounded hips and long beautiful thighs.

"You're a gorgeous girl, princess," he said. "You've avoided me long enough."

Her eyes opened wide. She could not believe this was

happening. For years Ray had been nothing but an unpleasant fixture in her life, a formless male presence on the sofa downstairs, and the uglier half of her mother's indifference.

Only now did she clearly recall the way he had been looking at her for the past few months, the liquid gleam in his eyes. And only now did she understand the secret reason for the new savagery that had come over her mother's quarrels with him. Her intuition told her that this night, having silently approached over several years, was upon her at last with absolute inevitability.

A long arm had settled over her chest. She felt her breasts pushed down as Ray inched his weight over her. She tried to turn away from him, but his arm held her fast.

"Don't fight me," he said. "This is the natural way. I know you want it."

Suddenly he was atop her. His sour-smelling breath came close to her face as he gripped her. She could feel the hardness between his legs pressed to her loins. She had never felt so trapped before, so violated.

Rage overtook her suddenly. She would not allow this boozehound to have his way with her.

She lunged this way and that, but he had her pinned to the bed. For some reason she did not cry out. She did not want to attract the neighbors and have them know about her shame. She had to fight Ray off by herself somehow.

She managed to get her hands poised against his chest and gave a mighty push. But he held firm. He was too strong for her.

"Come on, princess. Where do you get off being so high and mighty?" he mumbled thickly.

She held one hand against his chest and slapped him with the other.

He slapped her back, hard. Then, with a quick lunge, he tore her nightgown down the front. Clearly he was very drunk and would stop at nothing.

The creamy girlish breasts were bared to him. A long sigh escaped his lips. Pinning both her hands with his, he bent to nuzzle at the nipples.

A huge spasm of terror shot through her at the touch of his tongue.

"Get off me," she hissed. "Get off me or I'll kill you."

He did not answer. His lips and tongue were all over her breasts now, licking and sucking. Her body trembled madly under his weight. She felt him begin to move atop her, his pelvis grinding into her.

"You'll see," he murmured. "I know how to show a girl a good time."

He ground faster. He tried to kiss her, but she turned her face away. Madly she squirmed under him, on the verge of screaming.

A voice from the doorway came to her rescue.

"You little tramp."

She looked up to see her mother glaring down at her.

"Mother, make him stop!" Kate cried.

Ray paused. She felt his body go tense.

The mother leapt forward and struck Ray a hard blow to the temple with her open hand.

"Get off her," she hissed. "Get the hell out of here."

Somehow, in the next instant, Ray disappeared. Now it was her mother astride Kate, hitting her face with both hands.

"You goddamned little tramp," she hissed. "I might have known. I might have known. You scheming little bitch . . . It's a lucky thing I came home. I suspected something like this. I know men . . ."

Kate was thunderstruck. She could not understand why her mother was hitting her. She was, after all, the victim.

"How long has this been going on between you two?" the mother hissed. "When did you cook this up? My God, I'll kill you for this. I should have known sooner. You little whore . . ."

She kept striking Kate hard, her hands moving with an almost mechanical ferocity.

"Stinking little tramp," she hissed. "I should have known. God, what a fool I've been . . ."

Over and over again she struck her daughter. At length Kate stopped struggling. She kept her hands joined in front of her face and felt the blows fall, violent and imprecise, on her arms, her breasts, her ears. She felt nothing now, neither pain nor anger nor disbelief. Everything was dissolving into a bottomless resignation, an infinite shame.

At last, exhausted by her own effort, the mother backed away.

"Get out," she said. "Get out of this house. I don't want to see you here in the morning."

She stormed out, slamming the door behind her. Kate lay where she was.

In the other bedroom she could hear Mother slapping Ray and upbraiding him in savage terms. There were confused sounds of drawers being opened and shut.

Then, after an interval, quick steps were heard on the stairs, and the downstairs door opened and closed.

They had both left. Kate was alone in the house.

She lay for a long time in her bed. Then she got up, stripped off the torn nightgown, and took a long hot shower, scrubbing her lips and breasts hard where Ray had kissed them.

When she came out of the shower she got the old suitcase out of her closet and started to pack enough things to leave with. She found a few dresses, some slacks and blouses, underwear. She picked up the framed picture of her father from her desk and placed it carefully among her soft underthings, where it would not get broken.

In the closet Kate noticed her old folders of Eve Sinclair material. She smiled wanly at this evidence of her youthful heart's yearnings for something fine, something immaculate, a place to belong and be happy.

Despite the pain she felt at this terrible moment, there was also a cold sense of relief, and of liberation. This house had been a prison ever since her father died. Her departure from Irma Hamilton's life was long overdue. It had only taken Ray's pickled lust to break down the last barrier and open the door for her escape.

She went downstairs, got her raincoat out of the closet, and stood with her suitcase in her hand, taking a last look around. For a long time she had already been without a home. Now she was at last to face her future in the real world.

Without a goodbye or a backward look, Kate turned and left the house.

5

KATE WALKED SLOWLY TOWARD THE CENTER OF TOWN.

She was still a child as far as practical knowledge of the world went, and did not know the county geographically, not to mention the state. She had no idea where to go. It was late, and the darkness of the streets made her nervous. She had to make a decision.

She went to the bus station. She would catch the first bus out of town, she decided, regardless of its destination.

She had taken her small nest egg of money before leaving the house. It totaled eighteen dollars. It came from Christmas presents and occasional baby-sitting jobs.

The first bus out of town was headed for Stockton. Kate bought a ticket and sat down in the waiting room. She had to wait only fifteen minutes for the bus to leave. Somehow she knew she did not have to fear that her mother or Ray would come after her.

When the call came she got on the bus, gave the driver her ticket, and sat in a window seat toward the back. The bus was half filled with sleepy-eyed travelers who stared blankly out the windows. Kate noticed two servicemen sitting together, a lonely salesman, and a couple of poor families who looked like they were bound somewhere in search of work. They had their few possessions in large paper bags and beat-up cardboard suitcases. Their children looked hungry.

The bus left the station. Soon the town was far behind. Kate gazed through tired eyes at the strange nocturnal landscape of her home state. She had never come this way before. Her mother's relatives were in Mendota, in the other direction from home. So now the orange groves and wide rolling fields passing by her window looked entirely foreign. She seemed to be literally in the middle of nowhere. Her lack of a real destination made the land itself seem alien, without compass or meaning.

All at once Kate felt more alone than she could bear. She took her picture of her father out of her suitcase and sat looking at it. The eyes were the same, mild and dreamy, the old suit and waistcoat testifying to Father's poverty as well as his quiet gentility. She noticed the shape of his face and forehead and reflected for the first time that she really looked like him. This comforted her.

But it also made her realize she was alone in the world. Father was gone forever, and Mother was behind her. She would be on her own from now on. There was no home for her to go back to.

With this impression in her mind and her hand clutched around the picture of her father, Kate fell asleep.

Two hours later she was awakened by the lurch of the bus stopping at the Stockton station.

She got off the bus, carried her suitcase out of the station, and moved a few uncertain steps along the sidewalk. It was still dark outside. The station was located in the business district, a much bigger downtown area than Kate was used to. Afraid to wander about in the nocturnal city, Kate went back into the station and sat in the waiting room until dawn broke. Then she struck out on foot, carrying her suitcase. Trucks rumbled down the streets, and city buses, and cars. Kate was awed by the number of large office buildings and factories and warehouses. The small town of her girlhood had not prepared her for a city this size.

But it was still too early for any of the businesses to be open. Kate passed the time by continuing her solitary walk. She felt tired, and the suitcase seemed heavier, but she did not want to slow down. She was afraid that if she sat down to rest the last of her courage would leave her.

Soon the air got warm. It would be a hot day. There was a fetid smell of garbage, gasoline, and greasy restaurant cooking in the air. It made Kate both hungry and nauseated.

She passed clothing stores where cloth coats could be bought for $6.95, leather shoes for $1.75, raincoats for $2.69. A barber shop advertised a haircut and shave for 30 cents. In an appliance store window an electric washing machine was advertised at $47.50, and a gas stove at $23.95. She passed a restaurant where a meal of pork chops or ham cost 25 cents, and a plate of stew or goulash cost 15 cents.

She realized she had had nothing to eat since her sandwich last night, and almost entered the restaurant. But the smells around her had taken away her appetite. Besides, she wanted to save money. She bought an apple for a penny from an impoverished apple seller and carried it along with her.

She stopped in her tracks as she passed an alley. In it was a woman, dressed thickly in layer upon layer of threadbare clothing, with two tiny children by her side and two huge shopping bags. The woman was bent over a garbage can, reaching inside. Kate could see flies buzzing in dive-bomb patterns above the foul-smelling garbage.

As she watched, the woman lifted up a rotten piece of food—perhaps a potato—and, shaking the flies off it, handed it to one of the children, a little boy. He began to bring it to his lips, an empty look in his little eyes.

Kate turned away and walked on, faster.

She continued her peregrination around the downtown area. She felt completely at sea. No destination beckoned to her, no purpose gave her a bearing.

Then she saw a billboard on the side of an office building. JOBS FOR HIGH SCHOOL GRADUATES, the sign read. GOOD

PAY FOR REGULAR HOURS. APPLY AT RBI STENOGRAPHIC INC., 223 CENTER STREET.

Kate looked long and hard at the sign. She could, she mused, lie about her education. Why not? It was easy enough. And she had studied typing in high school. She was not a very good typist, but perhaps she could get by.

Now she had a place to go. With renewed energy she walked a couple of blocks in what she thought was the right direction, saw a traffic cop, and asked him how to get to Center Street.

"Go back the way you came," he said tiredly. "Three blocks west, then turn left. That's Center."

"Thank you."

She retraced her steps, noticing the same landmarks she had passed on her way here. When she found Center Street she turned into it quickly. Her feet were tired now, but she walked with a sense of purpose.

The numbers inched up slowly on the doorways of apartments and small businesses and office buildings. From 37 to 78 took three whole blocks.

By the time Kate reached the two hundreds she had walked seven blocks and was very tired.

She stopped in her tracks when she looked at the building that bore the number 223.

It was deserted, the windows boarded up.

She stood gazing at the hollow shell, unable to make up her mind whether to go on or turn back.

A voice sounded in her ear.

"Looking for something, young lady?"

Startled, she turned to see another policeman, this one much older. He was looking at her suspiciously.

"I—yes," she said. "I'm looking for a place called RBI Stenographic. I thought this was the address."

He smiled sourly.

"They went under about a year ago," he said. "No sense in looking them up."

"Oh. Thank you."

He turned away and continued on his beat, tapping his billy club against his thigh.

Suddenly Kate felt deeply tired. She wanted to sit down,

but there were no benches in sight. She walked slowly back the way she had come.

She felt weaker and very hungry, and began to raise the apple she had bought to her lips. But the memory of the woman with the two children in the alley by the garbage cans made her ill, and she put the apple in her bag and forgot it.

At last she found a bench at a bus stop and sat down.

She allowed her eyes to close for a moment. She saw her bedroom at home. She saw her closet, her scrapbook of Eve Sinclair memorabilia, her few books, her stuffed animals and school notebooks. Somehow the item she missed the most was her own pillow. She knew she would not sleep in a warm, familiar bed for a long time.

It all seemed as far away as the moon now. And the void of that parting spread through Kate like a dark potion, draining her of everything she had ever felt, thought, and hoped for, until there was nothing left of her but the anticipation of something faceless and cold that approached from the future.

She was floating in that empty reverie when the lurch of large tires and the muffled ding of a stop wire brought her awake.

It was the bus. An old city bus, with the legend CENTRAL ST.–CITY LIMITS above the driver's window.

On an impulse Kate got on the bus. She had had enough of the city. She just wanted to get away from here, no matter what the destination. She paid the fare from the coins in the bottom of her purse and sat down.

Very tired now, almost dozing, she watched the city pass her by. The strange streets, the sad faces of people she did not know and would never know, the complaining car horns, the smoke-filled air, turned a cold shoulder to her, and she was glad to leave them behind her.

She actually slept for a while. When she woke up she saw that the streets the bus was passing were less busy. The stores and businesses had given way to cheap little homes, and then there were vacant lots and even a farm field or pasture.

At last the bus, empty now save Kate and one other passenger, reached the city limits.

"End of the line," said the driver, coming to a stop.

The other passenger, a man in work clothes with a black metal lunchbox, got out of the bus. Kate remained in her seat, undecided.

The driver peered at her through his oversized rearview mirror.

"End of the line, miss," he repeated.

Reluctantly Kate got up from her seat, picked up her suitcase, and got off the bus. The old vehicle drove away with a whine and a belch of oily smoke, and she stood at a crossroads surrounded by fields and orchards.

The other passenger stood looking at her for a moment. Then an aged pickup truck appeared from nowhere and stopped by his side. He got in. Behind the wheel was a woman wearing work clothes. The truck disappeared down one of the country roads.

Kate looked around her. There were route signs at the crossroads.

SACRAMENTO 40, said one arrow. MODESTO 22, said another.

Kate felt confused and irritated with herself. She wondered why she had not simply ridden the bus back into Stockton. Surely there was nothing out in this godforsaken country for her. It was nearly noon now. The day was wending its way toward a nightfall which meant home and security for other people, people like that worker who had been picked up by his wife just now, but meant only wandering and loneliness to Kate.

Impelled by the vague idea of reaching a small town and finding a rooming house, she walked along the side of the road.

A mile went by, then another. The day was blazing hot. Kate's feet were tired and sore. She did not seem to be getting any nearer to a town. She was walking further and further into the country. Orange groves and fields of sugar beets flanked the baking road. She passed an occasional farmhouse, but saw no indication of a town.

At last, unsure whether she was making the right decision

or not, she turned and began to retrace her steps. She would catch the bus back into Stockton and try to find a cheap rooming house.

The overheated countryside seemed to blur before her tired eyes. She hoped she had not lost her way in her fatigue and confusion. The monotonous look of the landscape made things worse. She was no longer entirely sure of her direction.

She was beginning to feel panicky when a car came roaring along the country road at high speed and pulled up beside her with a screech. There were three young men in it.

"Need a lift?" asked the driver. "Where you headed?"

Kate looked in the window. The driver was a young man in jeans and a T-shirt, apparently a working man. He looked serious and rather impatient.

"The bus stop back into town," she said.

"Have you there in two minutes," he smiled. "Jump in."

She got into the car.

There was silence for a moment as they drove.

The driver looked at her seriously and asked, "You from around here?"

She shook her head.

"Where you from?" he asked.

She sought for a lie, and settled for the first one that came to mind. "Sacramento," she said.

A laugh broke out from the back seat.

Kate did not turn around. She kept her eyes on the road ahead.

"What you doing in these parts?" the driver asked, still wearing his serious look of inquiry.

"Oh . . . Just visiting," Kate said.

Again the laugh broke out in the back, lower and more meaningful now.

"Visiting," repeated the driver. Now he smiled, an unpleasant smile.

Kate stole a glance into the back seat. There were two young men, both smoking cigarettes and holding bottles of beer between their knees. One of them leered at her, seeing her look at him.

They had gained speed. The car must be doing fifty or sixty at least. It leapt along the country roads as the orchards and irrigation ditches careened by.

Then they shot very quickly across a road that looked familiar. In that split second Kate recognized the road she had come from town on, and even saw the bus stop.

"That was my stop," she said.

"No, it wasn't," said the driver, with his serious look.

Suddenly she realized that that strange, intent expression on his face came not from impatience or unfriendliness, but from drunkenness. The leer in his eyes was unmistakable. She cursed herself for not having seen it when he first stopped to pick her up.

The car was going faster now. The driver was pushing the accelerator with deliberate violence.

"Can I get out, please?" Kate asked.

The driver looked at her in feigned surprise. He raised an ironic eyebrow. "Be my guest," he said.

But the car did not slow down.

"Are you going to slow down?" she asked.

Suddenly he slammed on the brakes and swerved into a dirt road that went straight as an arrow between endless rows of orange trees. Picking up speed again, they raced between the trees. Low-hanging branches snapped and clawed at the sides of the car.

Kate was frightened now.

"Slow down," she said. "Let me out."

Suddenly an arm curled round her neck from behind. She smelled a beery mouth close to her ear.

"What's the matter, honey? Don't you feel sociable?"

The arm closed tighter around her neck. She began to struggle. She heard drunken laughter from the back seat. The hand slid lower to touch her breast.

All at once Kate could feel Ray's face pressed close to her own last night, and his body pushing hers to the bed, his alcohol-scented breath foul in her nostrils.

Something snapped as the memory came back. She

turned and bit the arm around her neck as hard as she could, just below the elbow.

She heard a hoarse cry from the back seat.

"Goddamn bitch! Jesus Christ!"

Then a hand grabbed her hair. She felt panicked. The car was still going very fast. They were going deeper into nowhere.

Her scalp hurt. She struggled, squirming this way and that.

"Stop!" she cried. "Let me out!"

The hand in her hair clenched harder. Thrashing in her pain, she kicked the driver in his side. He let out an oath.

"God damn her," a voice said.

The car screeched to a halt, clouds of dust billowing around it from the dirt road.

The angry hand was still in Kate's hair. The driver got out and crossed to her side. She felt herself dragged from the car. She was pulled along the ground between two orange trees. Now she could see the young men's faces. They were insignificant country boys, ignorant beer drinkers on the prowl. She knew the type from back home, though she had never been at close quarters with any of them before.

But these young men were very drunk and were enraged by her struggles in the car. The driver especially, for she had endangered them all by kicking him when he was behind the wheel. The two from the back seat had grabbed her arms and were preparing to hold her down. The driver was approaching. She realized he was the leader. He was wearing a twisted smile and fiddling with his belt.

"You ought to be more polite," he said. "Now I'm going to have to teach you a lesson. Hold her legs, Earl . . ."

Kate felt male arms pushing her back onto the ground. One of the boys fumbled to spread her legs. The driver, a look of contempt in his face, was taking off his jeans.

Kate suddenly saw red. She thought of Ray and her mother, and the life they had led all these years since her father's death. She heard Ray's quarrels with Irma and the hideous squeak of the bedsprings during their couplings, and she thought of the oily male body that had so often possessed her mother, trying only last night to enjoy Kate herself.

And now these ignorant, foul-mouthed country punks wanted the same thing. Well, she was not going to let them have it.

She squirmed madly in the arms of the two young men holding her. They tried to hold her down, but their drunkenness made them weak, and her rage made her strong. She managed to free her legs, and when the driver approached, she kicked him in his groin with all her strength.

Then she turned on the other two. They were still holding onto her, but she fought with a rage so unexpected that before long she had freed herself and was battling them as an equal.

It was all over in a few moments. Kate had a vague impression of them punching and kicking at her in unison, their ugly faces distorted by drunken anger. She fought back with spasmodic lunges, kicking and scratching and punching. She tasted her own blood as the blows rained on her. Her skirt was ripped, as was her blouse. A strange force, greater than her hunger or her fatigue, kept her fighting until they gave up on her and fled.

She heard cursing, then laughter, then the car's engine. There was an angry roar and a cloud of dust. She was alone. They had pushed her to the ground and driven off. She could still hear their laughter and their oaths.

She lay on the ground for a long time. She smelled the odd mixture of orange blossoms along with that of her own blood and the beery saliva still on her skin. She knew she had got off lucky. They could have had their way with her had they not been confused by drink.

Then it occurred to her that they might come back.

She struck out through the orange grove, at right angles to where they had dropped her. She came to a road. She started walking. She did not know where she was going. She only knew she must hurry.

An occasional car or truck passed her. No one slowed down. For this she was grateful.

She tasted blood inside her mouth. She realized she had been hit harder than she thought.

Only now did she realize that her suitcase and purse were gone. They were still in the young men's car. She was penniless, without clothes, staggering along this country road in her torn skirt and blouse.

Somehow this extremity did not hurt as much as the fact that her photo of her father, the only thing in the world that meant anything to her, was gone forever. A stifled sob sounded in her throat as she thought of her loss.

She kept walking without noticing where she was going. How long she walked she did not know. The torrid sun began to sag toward the horizon. Soon it would be dusk.

Kate passed a picnic ground by the side of the road. There was a drinking fountain. She used the tepid water to wash the blood from her face. She took a long drink and felt better.

Then her hunger smote her with sudden violence. She realized that she had eaten nothing since last night's sandwich. The apple she had bought this morning was still in her bag, long gone now.

She walked on weak legs around the little parking area. There was a picnic table with a few crumbs of potato chips and bread scattered on the ground beneath it.

There was also an uncovered garbage can for picnic refuse. On a whim Kate peered into it.

She saw what looked like a bag of potato chips with a few pieces left in the bottom. Tentatively she reached for it.

She heard a sudden scuffling noise and realized there was an animal in the can. Too late she dropped the bag and straightened up. A large gray rat was looking fearfully out at her from inside the can.

In that instant Kate saw the impoverished mother back in Stockton, feeding a rotten potato to her son from the garbage can in the alley. A wave of nausea overtook her as the image blended with those of the three young men in the car, the liquid eyes of Ray in her bedroom, and her mother's snarling face as she banished her from home.

Kate fell to her knees in the dust and threw up.

She stayed where she was for what seemed a long time, afraid another wave of retching would attack if she stood up. But it was getting darker. She knew she had to get moving.

Unfortunately there was no restroom at the parking area, so she could not look in a mirror to fix her face. She adjusted her torn blouse and skirt as best she could and struck out along the road again.

She walked for what seemed hours. In the darkness of evening the valley heat quickly dissipated, and she felt cold. Her entire body ached from her struggle with the young men in the car.

After a while she noticed that her neck hurt from her erect posture. Then twinges of pain began to start from her neck down her back each time she took a step. The kicks and punches of her attackers must have hurt her more than she had noticed at first.

She realized she could not go much farther. Walking was an agony. Her condition was worse for the fact that she had slept little in the last twenty-four hours.

But she went on. A brute instinct for survival drove her, along with the conviction that she could not turn back, would never turn back. No matter what ordeals lay in wait for her, she would leave her past life further and further behind her. For as long as she could remember she had been spiritually adrift. Now she at least knew what she was running away from.

But soon even these thoughts abandoned her, and she put one foot in front of the other mechanically, hopeless and empty, contemplating the hostile world through dulled, indifferent eyes, like the homeless children she had seen in Stockton.

Hours later, alone in the night, she noticed a gas station–restaurant at a country crossroads. LAST GAS FOR FORTY MILES, read a sign in front of the place.

Kate came closer, looking for signs of life. She was beyond embarrassment or modesty now. She would ask for help if she could find anyone on the place.

ALWAYS OPEN, said a sign before the darkened windows of the diner.

There was not a light on in the place. A smaller sign in the window of the front door read CLOSED.

Kate was too exhausted to smile at the irony of the two contradictory messages.

She noticed a large house behind the diner, about fifty yards up a low hill. A light seemed to be burning somewhere inside it.

She knew she could go no farther on her own. She dragged herself up the hill, climbed the rickety old steps, and rang the doorbell.

There was a long silence. She rang again. Her hands were trembling. The breath in her throat was shallow and raspy.

Finally a light went on inside the house. Then she heard steps. Someone was approaching the door.

The light over the door went on, blinding Kate. The door opened to reveal an old man in a worn flannel bathrobe. He peered at her through the screen door.

"What's the matter?" he asked.

"My neck," she said dazedly. "I've been . . ."

Before she could go on she fell in a heap at his feet.

 6

WHEN KATE AWOKE SHE WAS IN A BED UNDER A WARM comforter.

Blinking, she looked around her. The walls bore photographs, a couple of pennants, and a diploma whose text she could not read. There was the bed she was in, an old easy chair, and a cheap writing desk.

The lamp by the bed was not lit. She saw a light coming from the hall. She heard steps.

There was a timid knock at the door.

"Are you awake, young lady?"

The old man she had seen at the front door of the house entered with a tray.

"I brought you some soup and a glass of milk," he said. "It's not the Ritz, but it will help perk you up. You looked awfully weak."

Kate stared at him without speaking. She was dazed and frightened.

He came to her side.

"I sponged the blood off you," he said. "I left your clothes on, though. Didn't want you to feel embarrassed. You can take a shower when you're up to it. I have some clothes you can put on afterward."

He placed the tray on her lap and adjusted the pillows behind her head.

"You took quite a beating," he said. "But I think you'll be all right."

He smiled. His eyes were tired behind his wire-rimmed glasses. His face was gentle and a bit apologetic.

She was gazing at him in silence, her eyes like those of a wild animal that has blundered into captivity. Perhaps because of this he asked her no questions about what had happened to her.

He gestured to the diploma and the pennants.

"This is my daughter's room," he said. "Well, not exactly. She's only been in it twice. When we moved from Missouri she was already away at school. But I kind of missed her, so I put some of her stuff in here. Frances—that's my wife—didn't like it. Wanted it to be a guest room. But I was sentimental."

He gestured to the diploma.

"Cassie was a fine student," he said. "She was seventh in her high-school class back home. Of course, there were only eighty students in the class—it was a small high school—but she was smart as a whip anyway, I'll tell you. I never could beat her in an argument. I guess she took after her mother. They were both smart women."

He sighed.

"Frances died three and a half years ago. TB. Too bad for me, I'll tell you. She was the one who did all the work on this place. We retired out here, you see, after I got my pension back in Joplin. Frances bought this land, built the station and the diner, hired the help, and even baked all the pies and doughnuts herself. She was quite a dynamo. I pumped the gas, but she handled the accounts. What a whiz that girl was. She henpecked me, but I figure I deserved it. I'm not the kind of fellow who will get the lead out without a kick in the pants."

Kate listened in silence. She felt less frightened now. Despite the strangeness of her surroundings and the struggles she had been through since she left home, she could see that this old man was harmless and lonely.

He looked around the room. "Since Frances went, things have gone downhill," he said. "Cassie got married back in Pennsylvania, to a fellow she met at school. They have their own kids now. I don't see them; this country of ours is too big for folks to travel such distances. But she writes now and then, and sends pictures of the little ones. I can't complain. Young people have to live their own lives. As for me, I keep working, but business isn't what it once was. I have trouble keeping help in the diner. And I'm not as ambitious as I should be. A fellow wanted to sell me some billboard space back on the highway, but I kind of shrank from it. I suppose I should have taken the plunge."

Kate managed a weak smile. She sensed that the old man was as much at sea in his own life as she was in hers. He was so desperate for someone to talk to that he was pouring out his life's history to a total stranger. This made her feel less alone somehow.

He looked down at Kate, who was quietly sipping her soup. He laughed.

"But listen to me," he said. "I'm boring you with my life's story, and I don't even know your name."

"Kate," she said. "Katherine, actually."

"That's a nice name," he said. "Same as Cassie's. Strange, isn't it?"

"Mr.—" Kate said.

"Stimson," he said. "Ewell Stimson. Pleased to meet you, Kate. How's that soup?"

"Fine," she replied. "Thank you."

"It came out of a can," he said. "But I eat it myself for dinner half the time. To tell you the truth, I'm not much of a cook. That's quite a disadvantage when you run a diner, isn't it? But that's the way it is."

"Don't you employ a cook in the diner?" Kate asked.

"My last full-time man ran off with one of the customers, three months ago," he smiled. "Too bad. That feller could whip up burgers with the best of 'em. Made a darned good meat loaf, too. Business was just beginning to pick up when he lit out."

He looked at Kate. "How about a nice piece of chocolate cake to help that soup down?" he asked. "Don't worry, I didn't bake it. Came from the bakery in town. They put out good cakes and pies there."

"Town?" Kate asked. "Are we near a town?"

"Town of Tracy," he said. "Ten miles that way." He gestured to the window. "On the way to Modesto."

She said nothing. She remembered the road sign pointing to Modesto this noon, when she had got off the bus from Stockton. It seemed a lifetime ago. A brief image of the three young men who had beaten her up flashed before her mind's eye. It made her feel weak and nauseated. She forced it out of her mind.

The man named Ewell Stimson was looking down at her with a smile. There was inquiry in his eyes, but he still asked her no questions.

"Well, now," he said. "Some of the color is coming back into your cheeks, young lady. I'm glad to see that. Reminds me of the time Cassie sprained her ankle, when she was in the eighth grade. Lordy, how I worried. But young people bounce back quick."

There was a silence as he looked away from her, his eyes scanning the room.

"Too bad she couldn't have spent some time out here with us before she got married," he said. "I really liked that girl. Got along almost better with her than with Frances. But young people have their own lives to live."

He looked back down at Kate. "How about that cake?" he asked.

She smiled.

"That would be nice. Thank you."

With a spring in his step that belied his tired exterior, he went to get it.

Kate breathed a sigh of relief. The man was so lonely that all he wanted was to talk about himself, his past, and his family. He was not about to interrogate her about what had happened to her. He had not even asked her what her last name was.

Kate began to relax.

An hour later Ewell Stimson had gone to bed after showing Kate where the shower was and giving her fresh towels and a bathrobe and pajamas that belonged to his daughter.

"I'm up by five, generally," he said. "Have to be ready to serve these truckers. But you sleep in. Get your strength back. I've left some of Cassie's clothes in the closet for you, and a few things that belonged to Frances. I hope you can find something that will fit. Now, you be sure to let me know if you think you need a doctor. You look all right to me, but I'm no judge. Sleep well, now."

After he left she got up to take her shower.

She took off her clothes and folded them on the chair by the door. As she did so she noticed aches in most of her joints, and sharp pains in her breasts and thighs where she had been struck by the young men in the car.

Wearing her borrowed nightgown, she stole down the hall to the bathroom. The light was out in the old man's bedroom. She heard his breathing as he slept.

She went in and took off her nightgown. She looked at herself in the mirror. There were black and blue marks all over her face and neck, as well as her arms and legs. Her lower lip was swollen. A large scratch on her cheek had been cleansed by Ewell Stimson.

Her body was dirty from her struggles in the dust with the three young men. She had not noticed until now how sweaty she was. She needed a shower badly.

Her eyes seemed strange in the mirror. The golden irises

had dulled to an odd, murky color. Perhaps this was because of the unfamiliar light in the bathroom. And their expression seemed alien, inscrutable. It was as though she had already been changed by her uprooting from home in a way she could not yet fully appreciate. She was both fascinated and scared by this. She wondered if she would ever again look the same as she had looked only a day and a half ago.

She turned on the shower and got in. At first the water was icy cold. The shower head didn't work well. The water came out in noisy splats. She guessed that Ewell Stimson took baths.

She found a bar of soap and began to soap herself. She saw dirt from the bottoms of her feet swirling down the drain.

She ran the soap along her stomach and over her breasts. Despite the aches in her body the warm slippery soap felt good. Her nipples tingled and stood up at the touch of her fingers. The excitement starting in her breasts spread deep inside her.

She sighed. The bar of soap slipped from her hand, but she caught it in mid-air before it could clatter to the bottom of the tub. Her quick reflexes did not surprise her. Ever since she was a little girl she had been a fine athlete, often better than the boys her age.

She soaped her stomach, then her thighs—they were longer now, for she had grown in the last year—and then the place between her legs. She felt a sharp tingle, almost painful, as she touched herself. She realized that she was a woman now. The changes she had seen in the girls at school in the last couple of years—the sudden obsessive interest in boys, the narcissistic concern about their appearance—were taking place in her, too.

The feeling hovered on the edge of pleasure for an instant, and then lurched into discomfort as she recalled Ray assaulting her in her bed and the country boys in the car pawing at her body.

Then she put these thoughts away from her. She was starting a new life. The girls at school would never see her again. There would be no boys for her to fantasize about, no dances for her to be invited to. All that was behind her now.

Her destiny was a different one. And perhaps it had always been so. She resolved not to look back. If she was adrift and homeless, she was also free. With this in mind, the hunger in her body took on a different meaning. It was part of the great change that was turning her life in a new direction.

So she let her fingers linger for a split-second on the slippery flesh of her sex, pondering the fact that, as she grew into her womanhood, this place might become crucially important to her.

But not more important than her brain. Not more important than her freedom.

With this thought Kate finished soaping between her legs and turned to run the water over her body.

It never occurred to her that every move she made was being watched.

7

November 18, 1935

THE SOUND STAGE WAS SILENT.

Stagehands, sound men, makeup people, assistant directors, and grips stood watching as the camera moved in close on the two young people seated on a park bench before a dark backdrop.

The park to be shown behind them was nowhere to be

seen. It would be created later by the set designer and his staff as a painted matte background. Today's job was to shoot the scene. By the time the backdrop was painted and the superimposition achieved by the special effects department, the two young actors would be at work on another film.

But for today they were totally concentrated on the job at hand. The director, behind the camera, was giving them their last-minute instructions. He was one of the best in the business, and had worked on several films with these stars before. The atmosphere on the set was one of cool, disciplined professionalism, without a moment wasted.

At the back of the sound stage, where no one noticed him, stood the producer of the film. His name was Justin Garza, and he was one of the most influential producers at Olympic Pictures. He had made his name in silent comedies, working with some of the best talent in the business, and had made the transition to sound film as a producer of family dramas and romantic comedies.

The two young people on the sound stage were the key to the current wave of success he was riding. Their names were Tommy Valentine and Eve Sinclair. Together they had made seven films in the series that had come to be known as "Jill and Johnny." Their collaboration had made them household names, and their stories of wholesome small-town romance had captured the imagination of the nation.

The producer watched with a half smile as Tommy delivered his line and Eve responded. These two performers worked together with a special symbiosis, playing off each other brilliantly thanks to long familiarity. Tommy played a confused but spunky young man with a touching delicacy. Eve, with consummate skill and conviction, played her patented role as the tomboyish girl-next-door who blossoms into adolescent beauty through her dawning love for Tommy.

They were a perfect couple, and their films had paid huge dividends. At present Eve Sinclair was number nine box-office among actresses, and Tommy Valentine number six among men. The "Jill and Johnny" films were money in the bank, and the studio got enormous publicity mileage

out of sparking constant speculation about an offscreen romance between the two stars that might one day blossom
into marriage.

On the surface these facts indicated a formula for success
that could be counted on to continue in the future. But
Justin Garza saw the danger signs behind the statistics. For
example, this was the first time Tommy Valentine had
fallen out of the top five since the "Jill and Johnny" series
took off, four years ago. As for Eve, she had climbed into
the top ten among women only this year. And she showed
every sign of being poised to climb higher, while Tommy,
though still a big star, was visibly on the decline.

Justin Garza had studied the rushes of this picture carefully, and the camera did not lie. Tommy Valentine was
losing his wholesome, freckled looks. He was older now,
and looked tired and flaccid on screen. He was no more
than a film or two away from the end of his days as a
screen adolescent. He would soon have to take the plunge
into adult roles and sink or swim. Given the nature of his
talent and today's competition, it was unlikely he would
survive.

As for Eve, her situation was the opposite of Tommy's.
Four years ago she had been an adorable little teenager,
fresh from a career in a long series of child roles similar to
those of Shirley Temple. As a nubile young romantic lead
she had been a perfect foil for Tommy, playing her innocent
freshness off against his somewhat more mature characterization of Johnny Hogan, the all-American boy. Eve had
brilliantly hidden her blossoming adolescent attractiveness
under her tomboy mannerisms, and unveiled herself at the
end of each film as a truly desirable young girl just in time
for Tommy to declare his love for her.

But now Eve was eighteen years old, going on nineteen
(though the publicity propaganda had her at seventeen).
Her face had matured, and so had her body. She was slim
and smooth, with raven hair and limpid blue eyes in which
a great intelligence mingled with a complex, chameleonlike
personality. Though she was hardly a sex symbol on the
order of a Harlow or a Marlene Dietrich, she was very
beautiful, and ready to take her shot at romantic female

leads. Nowadays she was obviously holding herself back in order to communicate the innocence of young Jill Garnett. Her range was widening beyond her character.

The handwriting was on the wall, thought Justin Garza. The "Jill and Johnny" series was on the way out. And when it went, Garza would lose his main meal ticket at Olympic Pictures.

It would soon be time for him to think about picking up the pieces and starting something new. But it would not be easy to confect something that would bring in the box-office dollars of "Jill and Johnny." Hit films that engendered successful series were rare.

Justin Garza had a lot of thinking to do. His own position as one of the hottest producers in Hollywood was at stake. He would have to find something to follow the "Jill and Johnny" series, and soon.

As he left the sound stage to return to his office, Garza made a classic Hollywood business decision. He would delay the inevitable as long as possible. Perhaps he could milk three more "Jill and Johnny" films out of Tommy Valentine, instead of two or only one. After all, a good makeup man can work wonders. Then he would deal with the future when the future came.

Lovely Eve Sinclair, he knew, would have no trouble landing on her feet when "Jill and Johnny" was behind her. She would go on to do whatever she liked and would be brilliant as always.

As for Tommy Valentine, he would soon be adrift in the shark-infested waters of the cruelest business on earth. One could only hope that Tommy had saved some of the money he had earned during his starring years. He would probably need it.

With that depressing thought Justin Garza put both young performers out of his mind. Thanking his lucky stars that producers did not age as fast as actors, he went off to his lunch date with the head of the studio.

A half hour later Tommy Valentine sat in his dressing room, taking off the last of his makeup while Eve Sinclair lolled on the couch watching him.

The two were good friends. Though they had known each other only casually as child stars working for different studios, their seven films together had made them very close. Eve felt she owed Tommy a great deal, since it was "Jill and Johnny," launched with the help of his powerful box-office appeal, that had allowed her to make the transition from child roles to adolescent stardom. She often listened to his complaints about the studio, his agent, or their producer, and had done him more than one favor in the last five years.

Of course, there was no truth to the rumors about their off-screen love affair. But they both recognized the necessity of such stories, and their agents, along with the studio's publicity department, had been hard at work on the campaign for four years.

After seven films together they were almost like brother and sister. They knew each other better than anyone else, and could help each other out in difficult moments before the camera without anyone else even noticing. Their uncanny intimacy on screen was a key to the success of the series.

"How about dinner tonight?" Tommy was saying. "I'll take you to Perino's. Maybe we could meet Terri and Ralph and go to Cloudy's."

Cloudy's was a gambling casino tucked away behind a security fence high in the Hollywood hills. It was tolerated by the Beverly Hills police because most of its clients were stars and studio bigwigs, and it was a sort of tourist attraction for wealthy show-business people from all over the world. Tommy loved to gamble, and had often drawn attention to himself by risking huge sums at the roulette tables. He enjoyed living dangerously; besides, he could afford the financial losses he incurred.

Eve smiled. "I'll have dinner with you," she said. "But you'll have to gamble on your own. I'm going home to bed."

Tommy laughed. "Spoilsport," he said. "You sure know how to kill an evening."

Eve hated gambling. Money meant a great deal to her, and she could not imagine risking it on the antics of a little steel ball dancing on a roulette wheel. Acting was a business with her, and she had perfected her performing technique in a lot of subtle ways in order to achieve stardom. Though she was acknowledged as one of the finest actresses in Hollywood despite her tender age—the only reason she had not won awards for her acting was the commercial nature of the films she had been given to do—she did not think of herself as an artist. She was a professional in a highly competitive field. And she was a success. She never lost sight of the job at hand—namely, to reach the top at whatever cost, and then to stay there.

She was smiling at Tommy's reflected face in the mirror when a knock at the door interrupted them.

It was a young stagehand with a note for Tommy. Tommy took it eagerly and reached into his pocket. He handed the stagehand a five-dollar tip. The stagehand let himself out, giving Tommy an odd, knowing look as he did so.

Tommy opened the note quickly and read it without sitting down.

Then he turned to Eve.

"Listen, Evie," he said a trifle embarrassedly. "Could I take a rain check on that dinner? Something has come up."

Eve smiled. "Sure," she said. "I'm not the one to cramp your style. You know that. Just be careful, okay?"

Tommy threw the note on his dressing table and looked down at her, a pained expression on his face.

"I don't know what I'd do without you," he said. "I never thought I'd make a friend in this business. What makes you so nice?"

"Probably the fact that it takes one pain in the neck to appreciate another one," she joked, smiling up at him from the couch.

There was a silence. Each knew approximately what the other was thinking.

Eve had known for a long time that Tommy was a homosexual. It was an open secret throughout Hollywood but jealously guarded from the outside world, which saw Tommy as an all-American boy whose offscreen romance with his beautiful co-star might one day lead to marriage.

Tommy had told Eve the truth about his sex life soon after they began working together. Since then she had often had occasion to cover for him when one of his amorous adventures made him late for shooting or caused enough emotional distress to hurt his concentration.

Tonight, as so often in the past, Eve respected Tommy's right to his private pleasures, but warned him to be careful.

She noticed the look of sadness in his eyes as he glanced at his own face in the dressing-room mirror. She could read his thoughts. No one could be more painfully conscious of the effects of aging than he was. For Tommy, this sad reality concerned his love life as well as his career.

"Come here," she said. "Sit by me."

He came to the couch and lay down with his head in her lap. Suddenly he seemed like a little boy clinging to his mother.

"Oh, Evie . . ." he murmured.

Neither of them said anything for a time. Eve stroked his hair with a gentle finger, and he closed his eyes.

"Tell me something," she said at length.

"Anything, pal," he smiled.

"What's it like?"

There was a silence.

"You mean . . . ?" he asked.

"With boys, I mean," she said.

There was a long pause. She could feel him collecting his thoughts. As he did so, he seemed to become softer and more feminine in her arms.

"They tell you all through your youth that you're supposed to be tough," he said. "Just like Douglas Fairbanks. Running around beating people up, and showing off, and sweeping the heroine away on a white horse. But one day— I can't say exactly when, but it's when you're very young— you realize you don't want to do the fighting, Evie. You want to be held. You want someone else to be strong, and to take care of you. That's what it's all about."

Eve stroked his hair. "I think I understand," she said.

"Do you?" Tommy laughed. "Girls aren't supposed to understand a thing like that."

"I do, though," Eve insisted. "You want the same thing

from a boy that I do. To be taken care of. To be protected. It's very natural. You're just more girl than boy inside. There's no crime in that."

He laughed. "Tell that to the Legion of Decency," he said.

She patted his shoulder. "I'm here to make sure they don't find out," she said.

He sat up and grinned at her. "You know," he said, "you're a pretty nice girl. Have I told you that lately?"

She smiled, touching his cheek with her palm. Then she grew serious.

"Do you still like me?" she asked. "I mean . . . You know what I mean. I need to be liked, too, you know."

He kissed her softly on her cheek. "I'll always love you, kid," he said. "You're the one who knew me when."

He looked at his watch.

"God damn it," he said. "I've got to call my agent. He's been waiting all day. I'll be right back, honey."

He leapt up and hurried out of the dressing room, bound for the phone down the corridor.

Eve sat alone for a moment, as though lost in thought.

Then she got up and moved to Tommy's dressing table. She looked at her own face in his mirror. She could see she was growing more beautiful every day. She noted the fact with detached satisfaction, much as a sprinter measures his latest time or a weight lifter notes a slight increase in his strength. Beauty was important to her career now. It was a key element in her plans.

She looked at the glossies of Tommy on the walls around the mirror. They showed a young man who was fast losing his looks. Only the expert efforts of the studio photographers and cameramen could hide the loss of his boyish glow, and the onset of a distinctly unattractive manhood.

Eve compared her own face in the mirror to the glossies on the walls. The look in her eyes was quietly appraising.

Then she noticed the crumpled note Tommy had been given by the young stagehand. She picked it up and opened it.

STAGE 12 PROPS, it read. *9:30.*

There was no signature.

Eve looked pensively at the note. Her beautiful eyes darkened as a series of calculations, cold as ice, went through her brain.

Then, like an impersonal surgeon deciding to amputate a diseased limb, she made her decision.

She left the dressing room and crossed the studio lot to the bungalow where she had her private telephone.

When she got there she made a call.

At nine-thirty that night Tommy Valentine kept his rendezvous on Stage 12.

He was crouched behind a large papier-mâché replica of a courtroom bench, lovingly sucking the penis of one of the studio's young male contract players.

His hands were cradling the young man's testicles. He sucked at the throbbing organ with deep, quick strokes, his tongue working with a passionate expertise born of years of experience. His own genitals were on fire as he felt his youthful lover began to strain in his mouth.

Suddenly a flash of light blinded them both. There was a loud click, and a sound of running feet.

The penis in Tommy's mouth went limp. He felt his lover tremble.

Tommy's blood ran cold. He had just heard the worst thing a young man in his position could ever hear.

It was the popping of a flashbulb.

The next morning an item appeared in a Hollywood gossip column authored by a venerable and influential columnist named Brewster Lannes.

"One of our top young male stars was caught with his pants down last night," the item read, *"in a most compromising position. Olympic Pictures had better be careful about letting its young stars engage in a kind of hanky-panky that should never see the light of day—particularly when those stars are being sold to the public as all-American boys to be admired and emulated by our nation's impressionable youth. Shame, shame, shame."*

A copy of the column, along with a shocking photograph, found its way to the Olympic Pictures brass that very afternoon. An hour later Tommy Valentine's contract was canceled by virtue of his violation of the morals clause.

Shooting on the latest "Jill and Johnny" film was stopped immediately, of course. There would be no more "Jill and Johnny" pictures.

Meanwhile, at Worldwide Pictures, Eve's own studio, a top-level meeting of the studio executives was held to decide the fate of Eve, who, despite her great acting talent and her immaculate reputation, had been unfairly tainted by her long collaboration with the disgraced Tommy Valentine.

It was decided that the best way to put distance between Eve and Tommy was to elevate her above her present status as a teen star and find her a lead role in an adult romantic comedy as soon as possible. The studio's writing staff was ordered to work up a project within two months, so that shooting could start within four.

An all-out publicity campaign was blueprinted, with an eye to selling Eve Sinclair as one of Worldwide Pictures' hottest new female leading ladies. The plan was discussed with Eve's agent, who promised the studio that his client would help in any way she could.

As for Tommy Valentine, he was barred from the studio the morning after his public humiliation, and never again appeared in films. His life took a rapid downhill course, and he died in a car accident in the Hollywood hills at age twenty-six, after a heavy evening of drinking at a homosexual bar in West Los Angeles.

Hollywood insiders knew that during Tommy's slide into disintegration, Eve Sinclair, his old friend and former co-star, helped him with money and sympathy on many occasions. This cemented Eve's reputation as a professional who never forgot her friends.

What no one knew was that Eve had personally and deliberately destroyed Tommy's career with a single phone call to columnist Brewster Lannes. It was thanks to that phone call that Lannes's photographer knew exactly where to hide at nine-thirty on that fateful night, in the prop room of Sound Stage 12 at Olympic Pictures. And it was thanks to the timely elimination of Tommy Valentine that, in the years immediately following the episode, Eve Sinclair's career took a giant leap toward superstardom in Hollywood romantic films.

As for Brewster Lannes himself, he received a private visit from young Eve Sinclair at his Malibu house a week after the dark deed he had accomplished at her bidding. She arrived in a sinuous silk dress that accentuated the sleek curves of her ripe young figure, and showed no trace of the candid adolescent she had played in her "Jill and Johnny" films.

After an intimate candlelit dinner to the sound of the Malibu waves breaking outside, Eve spent the night in Brewster Lannes's bed. Lannes was amazed at her prowess. She used her body like a master. She was as inventive in the sack as she was on the screen. Decidedly, she had the best tongue in Hollywood.

As she bent her pretty head over his penis Brewster Lannes had to smile at the irony of things. She was doing to him precisely what Tommy Valentine had been doing to that unfortunate young contract player on Stage 12. Only Eve was using her tongue to insure a great career for herself, while Tommy had used his to destroy his chances forever.

Well, Lannes mused, that was the difference in Hollywood—the difference between a survivor and a loser.

Eve was, if nothing else, a survivor. Woe betide anyone who got in her way.

LITTLE DID KATE REALIZE THAT THE NEXT NINE MONTHS OF her life were to be spent at the remote diner on Route 22, and that Ewell Stimson was to become closer to her than her own mother had ever been.

Mr. Stimson—"Call me Pop, if you like," he had said—was a grandfatherly character, so soft-spoken and retiring that Kate felt safe with him. He never asked her about her bruises the night she had arrived, or where she came from, or why she was running away. He did not try to find out who her parents were, and never asked her about her past.

The reasons for this were obvious. The old man was so desperately lonely, and so helpless in the face of the worsening condition of his diner, that he was even willing to accept a young runaway as his ward, in return for her services as "chief cook and bottle washer" in the diner.

For Kate surprised both Ewell Stimson and herself during the first weeks after her recovery by showing a remarkable talent for just the kind of hard work his enterprise needed.

She began by making friends with his part-time waitress/cook, a local girl named Pam, and giving the diner a thorough cleaning and redecoration. She designed a new menu, put little flowers on the tables, fixed the ripped and broken chairs, and repainted the entire place.

She also cleaned the old man's house, which bore the grime of years of neglect. She waxed the floors, beat the carpets, dusted thoroughly, and washed everything. She even mended his clothes. Ewell Stimson watched her in his helpless, dowdy way, reminding her constantly that seeing her do all this was almost like having his beloved Frances back in the house. He called Kate a "dynamo" and sang her praises to all those who paused long enough at the diner to chat with him.

In the diner Kate cooked as well as waited on tables. She quickly learned the intricate arts of short-order cooking—how to cook bacon and eggs for four on one griddle while making sandwiches six feet away, how to make a plate out of yesterday's meat loaf, warmed-over mashed potatoes and canned succotash, and make it taste good—and soon became an efficiency expert in the kitchen. She kept it clean and orderly, and the food she turned out was so far superior to what Ewell had managed on his own that soon there were more customers. Truckers and traveling salesmen heard that the place had taken a turn for the better, and now stopped not only for gas ("LAST GAS FOR 40 MILES"), but also to eat.

They came for more than the food. They enjoyed Kate's unusual good looks and her friendly personality. She opened up as time went on, and the same customers who had initially complained about her slowness in the kitchen became devoted regulars. They traded jokes with her about the hard times, and she became their confidante as they complained about the rigors of their traveling jobs and the henpecking of their wives back home.

Underneath their camaraderie they were of course ogling her fresh young body. She wore starched uniforms in a checked pattern which made her look brisk and efficient. But there was a secret behind those complicated eyes of hers, and it seemed to radiate through her sinuous limbs, the lush blond hair that fell to her shoulders when it wasn't pinned back for her work, and above all the feminine smoothness of her movements, so elegant that not even her tacky surroundings could tarnish its luster.

Most of them were half in love with her after first meeting

her, and came back for that reason alone. The only reason they didn't ask her out was her youth, combined with Ewell's made-up explanation that she was his "sister's only daughter," visiting from back East.

The restaurant and gas station did better and better. Ewell Stimson counted his new savings and had the booths in the diner reupholstered, bought some cheap but attractive landscapes for the walls, and put in a brand-new Wurlitzer jukebox. As a final gesture to the new era that had dawned for the diner, he took the plunge and leased the billboard on Route 22 that his wife had so often begged him to take on.

It was a good and busy life. After a hard day in the diner Ewell would sit with Kate in the parlor and listen to "Amos 'n' Andy" and "Eddie Cantor's Camel Caravan" on the old console radio in the living room. Kate would read a book or magazine as the radio shows played, and Ewell would sit in his easy chair, his tired eyes at half-mast, feigning good-humored wakefulness until the onset of sleep made his breathing heavier and finally forced the first snore from him. Then he would say his goodnight and slowly mount the stairs, leaving Kate to finish her reading and close things up before going to bed herself.

They talked a great deal during their time together. Ewell Stimson told Kate everything there was to know about his late wife, whom he had loved dearly and depended on perhaps more than was good for him, and about the daughter he still doted on despite her distance from him. Kate absorbed his stories with interest, fascinated by the complexities of human nature and refreshed by the old man's love for the women in his life. It helped her to forget her own mother, a selfish and cold creature, and her miserable years under the same roof with Ray.

Ewell Stimson's obvious admiration for Kate, combined with his respect for her privacy, allowed her to blossom under his kindly protection, and before long she felt, if not at home under his roof, then at least comfortable and safe there, more safe than she had felt in years. She did not perhaps know herself any better than before, and had no more idea than ever where her life was leading, but she felt relieved and secure in this unlikely stopping-off point.

Ewell Stimson had never been so happy. And Kate was growing more confident and beautiful every day. It was a new lease on life for both of them. They knew it could not go on forever, for Kate was a young woman with her own life to live. But they enjoyed each other and their hard work together, and did not think too much about the future. The hard times had made everyone appreciate little moments of security and contentment, and had purged people's normal instinct to expect any sort of permanence from the world. Today was all that mattered.

So their life continued as winter became spring, and Kate looked forward to the remainder of her first year with Ewell Stimson, and her seventeenth birthday.

Then things changed.

One day a young man appeared at the gas station, had Ewell fill his old coupé with ethyl, and had lunch at the counter. He had light brown hair and cautious gray eyes. He was very voluble and confident, despite his obvious poverty. He said he was en route to San Diego to take up a new job. He was slight of build, but wiry. Though not classically handsome, he had a youthful intensity that was appealing. There was something unusual about him that Kate could not make out. She had become rather expert at typing her customers after six months, but this young man was an odd case.

He chatted politely with her and listened to Ewell's stories about Frances and about the good fortune of having Kate come along to help him out.

"She's a wonder, that one is," Ewell said complacently. "Why, we've doubled our business since she got here. She keeps me on the straight and narrow, I can tell you."

At this the young man seemed more interested. He spoke privately with Ewell outside by the gas pumps.

"I don't suppose you could use some help around here," he said. "A hired man, so to speak. To tell you the honest truth, I'm a little short at the moment. I'll never make it all the way to San Diego without stopping to earn some money. I'm a good mechanic, I can pump gas, and I'm not afraid of hard work."

Ewell Stimson thought carefully. There was a lot of hard physical work around the place that needed doing—fixing the fence around the back, carpentry, loading and heavy cleaning that were beyond Kate's powers.

And there was some extra money to spare . . .

He looked into the young man's eyes. He saw sincerity there, and an air of youthful confidence that impressed him. Decidedly, it would be a blessing to have a strong young man around the place to help out, if only for a few weeks.

"I can pay you fifteen dollars a week," he said. "With meals included. There's a room in the back of the house, behind the kitchen. It's not beautiful, but it's livable."

"Thank you, sir. You won't regret it. I promise."

"Call me Ewell. Or Pop, if you like."

They shook hands and the young man parked his old coupé around the back, took out his suitcase and went into the back room to change his clothes.

That very afternoon a honeymoon couple came along in a car that was idling roughly and stalling at low speeds. The young man, who bore the unusual name Quentin Flowers, found the source of the trouble and cleaned the valves while Ewell Stimson smiled to himself.

He had found another gold mine.

Spring came, unseasonably warm, and then a hot and dusty summer. Quentin stayed longer than he had anticipated, explaining to Ewell that he wanted to put aside a little nest egg before heading for San Diego. He seemed to enjoy his work, and did it efficiently. Thanks to Quentin, business was better than ever in the station as well as the diner. He was a good mechanic, and charmed the station customers with his wit and volubility.

He told Kate all about himself, his family in Seattle, his married sisters, his widowed mother, and the disastrous effect of the hard times on their livelihood. He spoke of his misfortunes with some bitterness, but he had a boundless confidence in the future that outweighed his sadness about the past.

He was a young man who was going places, or so he claimed. The job he was to take in San Diego was in a large retailing business owned by an uncle. He considered it just a stepping-stone. He had big plans for his future. He would get a college degree in business at night school while he worked his way up in his uncle's business, and then start a career in management. He was convinced that hard times could not last forever. He would survive them, and when times got better he would be armed and ready for a new career.

"Of course, I'll have to be patient," he told Kate over coffee in the diner. "But that's one of my virtues. All things come to him who waits, my father used to say."

Quentin never tired of talking about himself and his plans. But somehow his conversation did not bore Kate. She was impressed by his unshakable sense of purpose. It was a quality she herself lacked, for she remained directionless despite her efficiency as a worker. And there was that inner intensity about Quentin, a sort of electric charge behind his gray eyes, that fascinated her.

As summer wore on she found herself noticing his physical attributes as well.

She saw the tattoo on his arm when he worked in his T-shirt at the pumps. He was slim, but his body was strong. His fingers, stained by motor oil and grease, were long and powerful.

Sometimes, when it was particularly hot, she would look out the window and see him out back working on his own coupé with his shirt off, or hammering at the fence posts, or carrying heavy automotive parts from one place to another, the sweat standing out on his forehead. He had a deep chest, a slim waist, and a look of tightly strung young muscles that caught her eye. He swung the ax with terrific power.

For the first time in her life Kate found herself looking at a young man's body with interest. Back home in Plainfield she had never even looked at the boys at school. And after her run-in with her stepfather she had not thought of male-female relations at all. Life with Ewell Stimson had helped her to forget all that.

But looking at Quentin in the back yard brought back the strange, almost painful ferment she had felt in her growing body, the sensitivity of her breasts, the slow heat between her legs.

She found it harder to take her eyes off him when he was working. He spent more time shirtless in the back, beneath her window, as the weather grew hotter in the valley. She asked herself once or twice whether he was showing himself off to her deliberately. After a moment's doubt she dismissed the thought.

Quentin treated her with unfailing respect, despite his comradely familiarity. He accepted Ewell's story about her being his niece and affected a comradely protectiveness toward her. Sometimes, when one of the customers in the diner showed too lively an interest in Kate's sensual good looks, Ewell felt relieved that Quentin was on the place to protect her.

But to Kate things were not so simple. Quentin was slowly getting under her skin. The feeling was at once dangerous and seductive. She began to hope that he would soon depart for his job in San Diego, and leave her to work out her life on her own.

Then one day the truth she had been hiding from for so long caught up with her.

It was a torrid Saturday in July.

Ewell had taken the pickup into town to buy supplies for the diner. Quentin had offered to go, but Ewell had asked him to watch the pumps while Kate handled the diner.

Kate and Pam worked a long day and closed up at six. They cleaned up the kitchen together, and after Pam had gone Kate went upstairs to take her shower.

Ewell had still not returned, but she was not worried about him. She knew he was a great talker and was probably bending the ears of some of his old friends in town with his stories. He often did not return from these trips until late.

Quentin was still downstairs, manning the pumps. Kate entered the bathroom, stripped off her uniform, took off her bra and panties, and got into the shower.

The shower head worked perfectly now, because Quentin had fixed it a month ago. The hot water coursed over Kate in long steady waves, making her skin tingle as the soap rinsed off the smells of restaurant food.

For an instant she looked up at the shower head and thought of Quentin's strong hands working on it in the shop downstairs. She saw his slim, hard body with the tight bands of muscle, and the tattoo on his arm. She recalled the mystery behind his eyes when he looked at her.

"Quentin," she heard herself say, and closed her mouth with a start. Her hand had been drawing the slippery bar of soap across her stomach and her breasts, and the name had escaped her lips without her realizing it.

She blushed. The female urges thrilling through her body these past weeks were undeniable now. She was a woman, with a woman's impulses and needs.

She slipped the soap between her legs, up and down the silken thighs and to the secret place which responded with a silent clamor to her touch. Her own thoughts shocked her. For so long she had been alone with herself. Now it seemed that her body was running away with her.

A bit cautiously she finished soaping herself and washed her hair. She emerged from the bathroom in the terry-cloth robe she had bought after coming here, and with a towel wrapped around her head.

She stopped dead in her tracks. Quentin was standing in the hallway, blocking her path to her bedroom. There was a knowing, oddly gentle look in his eyes.

"Feel better?" he asked.

She raised an eyebrow.

"What do you mean?" she asked.

"Nothing like a shower on a hot day to freshen you up," he said. "I could use one myself. After all that hot work outside."

He was wearing his T-shirt. His arms looked strong and somehow dangerous, with the tattoo on the wiry bicep. The smile in his eyes was decidedly strange, an expression she had never seen before.

"Well, I'm through," she said. "If you want the bathroom."

Her words rang false. Quentin never used the shower in the house. He always bathed in the shed outside. She had not been able to think of anything else to say. She wanted to get past him to her room.

"No," he said ambiguously, and stood there staring at her.

She took a step closer to him. He did not move.

"Can I get past?" she asked nervously. "I'd like to go to my room, please."

He said nothing. She saw his eyes travel down her freshly washed face, over the contours of her breasts and hips under the terry-cloth robe, and further down her legs.

She blushed.

"Quentin," she said irritably, "do you mind getting out of the way? I have to get dressed . . ."

"Why did you say my name?" he asked suddenly, moving a step forward to block her path the more securely. His face was close to hers. Surprisingly, he did not smell of station oil and gas at all. He smelled fresh and clean. He must have washed, she thought.

But his words had taken her aback.

"I—what?" she asked. "What are you talking about?"

"Just now," he smiled. "In the shower. You said, 'Quentin.' I heard you."

Kate's eyes opened wide. She stood facing him as though he were an accuser, in the silence of the hallway. Her blush deepened.

"What . . . ?" she said. "I don't understand."

"Come here," he said, touching her elbow. "I want to show you something."

He led her down the hall to Ewell Stimson's bedroom. She saw the old bed with its brass headboard, the pictures of Ewell's wife and daughter. The room smelled of old age. There was a mustiness about it that made her faintly ill.

To her surprise, Quentin opened the closet door and motioned her inside.

Reluctantly she followed. It was an old walk-in closet. There was a cracked mirror hanging on a hook. Quentin pushed it aside. Behind it was a hole in the wall.

"Take a look," he said, motioning her to the hole.

She looked through it. Her eyes widened. It offered a clear view to the inside of the bathtub. One could see the whole body of the person inside the shower, from the knees up.

Kate's breath came short. An odd, frightening sensation shot through her body. She could feel Quentin behind her.

"I got to noticing," he said, "that the old man always made it a point to be upstairs when you were taking your shower. He would come in from the diner, or up from downstairs if he was listening to the radio. One day when he was out and you were downstairs I did some investigating. It wasn't hard to figure it out."

There was a pause. The look in his eyes was penetrating, but not without a certain kindness.

"Now you see for yourself," he said.

Kate stood rooted to the spot. She could not find words to say. Everything she had taken for granted for nine months was revealed in a new light. And that light came straight from Quentin's glimmering eyes.

"I don't blame him," Quentin said. "He's an old guy, and he's been alone a long time. He doesn't mean any harm. What harm does it do to look?"

He had not moved, but Kate realized she was hemmed in by him here in the closet. She could not get around him. She looked away from him in her embarrassment.

"You're a very pretty girl," he said quietly. "And you have a beautiful body. I envy him."

Kate felt a tremor deep inside her as she reflected that, as she showered just now, Quentin had been looking at her, just as Ewell Stimson had looked. She had no secrets from him now.

And he had heard her say his name to herself in the privacy of the shower.

There was a silence. She wanted to tell Quentin to leave her alone, to mind his own business. But the look in his eyes, and his hard body hemming her in here in the closet, sapped her will.

"Why did you say my name?" he asked.

She trembled before him. She said nothing. But now her downcast eyes rose to meet his.

Very slowly he stepped forward and cupped her cheeks in his hands. His fingers moved to her temples, rubbing and soothing, and touched her wet hair under the towel.

Her eyes half closed in the shadows. The hole in the wall was behind her. The clothes on their hangers stirred slightly as the two bodies swayed in the cramped space.

Now the two hands slid downward along her neck, slipped under the shoulders of the robe, and eased it off her bare skin. The robe fell down to her waist, revealing the ripe girlish breasts. Quentin was silent, looking at her.

"You're so beautiful," he said.

Then he kissed her. It was a soft, featherlight kiss, pausing at each cheek before touching her lips. The painful longings she had been feeling these past months erupted inside her with a spasm. His tongue slipped into her mouth, sending flares of excitement through the quick of her.

The hands came to her breasts now and cupped them gently, the thumbs grazing her nipples, which hardened at their touch.

Kate knew what was about to happen. Her body had been waiting for this moment for a long time. She had tried to put it off, not to think about it, because of what had happened with her stepfather, and because of all the painful nights when, as a child, she had heard uncanny animal sounds coming from her mother's bedroom.

Now she was going to find out what it was all about.

She did not struggle or protest. She wanted to know.

Quentin slowly undid the knot at her waist, and the robe fell off entirely, landing with a sigh at her feet. She was completely naked. She watched his eyes as he admired her body. She could feel the mysterious male heat inside him as he looked at her breasts, her lush brown skin, her thighs and hips and the unclothed center of her.

"You said my name," he murmured.

She said nothing. The hands caressed her breasts and moved down to her hips. He kissed her again.

Then he picked her up in his arms and carried her to her bedroom. He seemed terribly strong. Though Kate was not a tiny young woman, and he was slight of build, he carried her as though she were a doll.

When he deposited her naked on her bed, the warm air of the room came to caress her skin with an almost sensual delicacy.

He bent to kiss her, first on the lips, then on each nipple, the smooth strokes of his tongue sending terrible waves of wanting through her.

He stood back and pulled off his shirt. The chest and arms she had admired from a distance were close to her now, and she could smell his fresh aroma.

He sat on the edge of the bed and leaned over her. His hand ran from her brow down her nose and chin to her breast, and down her stomach to her navel. Then his palm came to rest just above the fragrant triangle between her legs.

He kissed her again, softly, and stood up to undo his jeans.

Seeing the look in her eyes, he paused.

"Haven't you ever done it before?" he asked.

She shook her head, her expression candid as that of a schoolgirl.

He seemed to ponder for a moment. His fingers were still at his belt. He looked at her naked body.

At last he smiled.

"Then your first time will be the best," he said, undoing the belt and slipping the pants off. "I promise."

He stripped off his underpants and came to her. She caught a fascinated glimpse of the erect sex between his legs as he covered her with himself.

Her breath left her body as, for the first time, she felt the hard smoothness of male nudity fitting itself perfectly to her own soft skin. Her arms curled around his back.

Sensations came in waves, urgent and overpowering, making her blush and gasp and moan over and over again. Her body did not seem to belong to her. Desire thrilled through her limbs, making her pelvis undulate against him.

Gradually the center of all that heat revealed itself, between her legs, straining to beckon the hard man's sex inside. He knew the instant she was ready. His kisses became more urgent, the slow, stroking fingers smoothed her and heated her, and then, as her legs spread to receive him, he came inside her.

The flash of pain she felt at his coming was a strange coda to the hot excitement he had made her feel for weeks, and one with it somehow, so that it did not alarm her. He was slow and tender as he followed behind the pain, slipping in and out of her, comforting her with his kisses. Almost at once the hot length of him turned her pain to ecstatic pleasure.

She had never felt anything like this. She contemplated her own body, with its exulting sensations, as though from a great distance. She was awed to feel the power of his flesh over her, and the mystery of her own physical need. It seemed to throw a new light on everything she had ever experienced—her loneliness, her long nights of insomnia and worry, her distraction in class at school, her sense that an unnamed destiny beckoned to her.

What Quentin was doing to her now, and the huge excitement her body was taking from him, provided an answer she had been seeking a long time. Not the final answer, not the only one. But this answer was so deep and thrilling that it made her forget all her wonderings about who she really was and where she was going. Quentin banished it all with his body.

He seemed to sense that she was past the brink now, a woman initiated to pleasure and ready for the final fulfillment. He came deeper inside her, and deeper still, helping her with sure hands to move her thighs so he could penetrate further and further. Now the hardness inside her almost made her cry out with delight. She had been alone with her own body all her life; now she understood the why and wherefore of its softness, its destiny in welcoming this beautiful male thing.

She began to squirm, to gasp her pleasure in his arms. He held her closer, and closer still, burying himself deeper within her and holding steady so that the straining of her own pelvis would allow her to take her pleasure again and again. Her hands were in his hair, on his shoulders, then down at his hips to pull him deeper. And only those terrible slow strokes had meaning for her now, as the shadows of her girlhood gave way to the blinding light of this seduction.

When the spasm of his manhood came, sweet and liquid, she was ready to receive it. And the rasping groan in his throat as his body tensed told her she was good, told her that what she had given him was something precious that he valued.

They lay for a long time in silence, listening to the ebb of their gasping breaths. His hand made slow circles around her breasts and along her ribs, and he kissed her face again and again.

It was night now. The roadway was silent outside.

Suddenly she remembered the time.

"Ewell will come," she said.

He shook his head.

"His truck had a leak in the transmission line," he said. "He couldn't make it to town and back without the truck stopping."

He paused.

"I wanted to make sure," he said.

She nodded, too numbed by the pleasure still throbbing in her veins to protest.

But now, with the mention of his calculation, it occurred to her that she had done something wrong. Ewell had been kind to her. She did not like to think of him walking alone on the road with his old legs.

"You tricked me," she said.

Quentin smiled down at her, his eyes full of tenderness. His next words took her by surprise.

"I want you to go away with me," he said.

She looked at him, lying on her side, his hand on her hip.

"I can't," she said. "It wouldn't be right. Ewell needs me."

"He knew you would be leaving sooner or later," he said. "The time has come. I need you more than he does."

He paused, smiling. "You're not his niece," he said. "I know that, too, you see. I know everything. He has no claim on you."

Kate pondered his words. On one side was her image of

Ewell, his paternal ways, the friendship that had grown up between them these past months. On the other was the sensation thrilling through her still, a primordial passion whose existence she had never suspected until this day—and the penetrating eyes of the young man naked beside her.

"He'll be all right," he said. "I know a fellow in town who will take over the pump. I even asked him about it. And I found a girl who can help Pam in the kitchen. She's been a cook before. I left their names for Ewell downstairs. You see, babe, I thought of him all along. I want to do right by him, too. But I can't live without you."

Kate looked at him, confused.

"I shouldn't," she said. "He took me in. I can't just walk out."

"Why do you think I stayed here so long, when I had a good job waiting for me?" Quentin asked. "I couldn't leave without you, Kate. I knew that the first time I ever saw you."

His eyes, always mysterious, deepened even more.

"I love you, Kate," he said.

Kate could not believe what she was hearing. And yet the ecstasy he had just given her, so far beyond any experience she had ever had before, seemed to bear out his words. How could such physical joy come from anything but love?

"I can't go to San Diego without you," Quentin said. "I can't go anywhere without you. Don't you understand?"

There was a silence. She looked into his eyes, hypnotized.

"You're already halfway out the door," he said. "You were the day I met you. It's only one more step, Kate. Take it with me."

She could feel how right he was. All these months she had indeed been on the edge of something, her past life disappearing behind her like the wake of a speeding ship. But she had not wanted to face it.

Again she thought of Ewell, and her face clouded.

Quentin seemed to read her mind.

"He's an old man who stares at you through a hole in

the wall," he said. "You don't belong here. He'll be all right. I promise you, I've taken care of him."

He bent to kiss her breast again. Something in her collapsed at the touch of his lips.

"We'll get your things together, and we'll leave in my car," he said. "I've been fixing it up just for this moment, babe, because I knew all along that this moment was coming. Just as you did, deep down. Let's not put it off any longer."

She gazed up at him. Her will was broken. She belonged to him now.

"I love you," he repeated. "Don't say no. If you do, I'm finished."

She lay naked, her eyes shining amid the lush hair tumbled across the pillow.

"Kiss me again," she said.

Smiling, he bent to place his lips on hers.

• • •

At midnight that night, Kate became Mrs. Quentin Flowers at the home of a justice of the peace in a country town fifty miles from Ewell Stimson's gas station. She used her mother's maiden name on her marriage license, without quite knowing why. When Quentin asked her about it she told him that "Hamilton" was a false name she had used for convenience after she left home.

By the next morning, she was halfway to her honeymoon at Yosemite.

Kate never looked back.

She could not know that when Ewell Stimson returned to his station that night in the car of a friend who had passed on the highway, he found no note from Quentin about someone to take his place, or Kate's. Quentin had lied to Kate about the note.

Nor could she know that all the money had been removed from the till at the diner as well as the gas station, and that the savings Ewell kept in a locked box hidden in his bedroom were also gone.

Kate would never know these things.

9

JOSEPH KNIGHT'S FATHER WAS A WIFE-BEATER AND A PHI-
landerer. He stayed out until all hours carousing with loose
women, and returned drunk in the wee hours to quarrel
with his wife and inevitably to beat her.

During the boy's earliest youth he overheard these late
homecomings and quarrels, and they so scarred his mind
that he was unable to sleep through the night ever again
without waking at three or four in the morning, covered
with cold sweat, his heart filled with dread and nausea.

By the time he was ten he had become his mother's protector and confidant. He knew most of her secrets, and she
knew most of his. They lived only for each other. Yet the
father remained, a presence who was necessary only for
the paycheck he brought home, and who terrorized the
house as tribute for what he earned.

One day when the boy was thirteen years old he decided
this life had gone on long enough.

On a blustery March night the husband came home later
than usual, and drunker than usual. He staggered into the
tool shed behind the house, in search of a bottle of gin he
kept hidden there. He knocked over several boxes of tools.
Then he stumbled and fell.

The next morning he was found dead on the floor of the

tool shed, an awl from the work bench stuck deep in the back of his head.

The bizarre mishap looked like an accident. Nevertheless the police wanted to talk to the son, for they knew he had not been on good terms with his father. Before they could take him in for questioning, he disappeared. He was never seen in the town again. The police bulletin on him remained in effect.

The mother was left alone. She missed her son, but she knew how much he loved her, and what he had given up for her. Missing him was less painful for this.

She looked back on the circumstances of her cruel husband's sudden death and decided it was better not to think about it too much.

Soon thereafter she began to receive money orders from far-flung places, accompanied by laconic but tender notes from her son, notes that invariably said, "Am fine. Hope you are too. I love you." The notes were never signed.

She did not ask what the son did to make this money. Soon she was surprised by the amounts. There was enough for her to live well, much better than she had ever lived before with her husband. She paid off the mortgage on the house. She bought better clothes.

Then she began saving the money he sent her. She put it in a special account at her bank. She thought he might need this nest egg if his fortunes ever turned sour. She suspected it would never be necessary, but she reflected that in this way she could still be a mother to him, even from so far away.

The notes and money continued to arrive regularly, but the son never came home to visit her. She knew this was not merely because of the police's suspicions about his role in her husband's death. It was because of the unspoken knowledge shared by the mother and son about what had really happened, and why.

Her separation from her son filled her with sadness. But the reason for that separation was a secret bond between them, more intimate than his money orders and his brief notes.

Once he sent her a picture of himself. It showed a strong, handsome man, grown thick and balanced and muscular,

*much bigger and more powerful than she had ever imag-
ined he might grow.*

The mother was lonely.

But she was proud.

*One day, years later, the son received news that his
mother had died. He sent a legal representative to arrange
for her funeral and to bring him her personal effects. As
he was going through her affairs he found all his notes and
postcards, lovingly kept by her in a box. He also found her
bank account, and her will, which bequeathed to him all
her money, the money he himself had sent to her.*

*He was filled with sadness when he reflected that she
had saved the money for him and spent so little of it on
herself. His efforts had been vain, then, at least as far as
she was concerned.*

*Or had they? After all, the money he sent had assured
her of his success. And her own saving of that money for
his future had allowed her to feel she was still taking care
of him, still watching out for him. So that she could be a
mother, to the very end.*

*Ironically, there was perhaps no greater gift he could
have sent, no better way to make her feel secure in her
love for him.*

*As long as she was alive he had not been truly alone.
He understood this only now, as his solitude in the world
came home to him. Love had left his life, and he did not
expect to meet it again. He did not try to escape the void
within him, for this was his way of remembering his love
for her, a love that had nourished his boyhood and given
his later adventures a meaning.*

*Now the question of meaning, of justification, would
have to wait. He would see where his intellect and his
power could take him. If this was an empty game, he would
play it out to the end.*

*From now on he would live for the future. As for the
past, he would think of it no more.*

Joseph Knight stood looking at himself in the mirror.
The face he saw was a handsome one. The brow was

strong and dark, the jaw square. The dark eyes glowed with a strange energy that frightened men and attracted women. The nose was straight and strong. The cheekbones were a trifle high, the neck thick and powerful-looking. The rich dark hair mirrored in its own way the strength that shone in the tanned, weathered skin.

He looked older than his years. This suited him, for he did not want to look too young. It was important to him that people take him seriously from the first handshake.

He need not have worried.

He was a rich man now. Thanks to a hundred business deals, large and small, each carried out with scrupulous planning and research, and a sharp eye for the weaknesses and venality of those he dealt with, he had amassed holdings in businesses all over the East to go with his oil investments in Texas and Oklahoma. Among his operations were a percentage of a liquor distributorship in Maryland, a restaurant chain in Philadelphia, a precision-parts factory in New Hampshire, two hotels in Florida, and one of the most successful nightclubs in New York City.

He did not know how much he was worth, and he did not much care. Money no longer mattered to him. He lived for the day-to-day challenge of pushing the world in its weak spots and forcing it to make room for him. He lived for the exercise of his will.

For another moment he studied himself in the mirror. Then he got down on his knees, placed his hands on the floor, and did two hundred push-ups, slowly, mechanically. His lips pursed from the effort, but he did not gasp. After some experimentation a few years ago, he had found that 150 push-ups were the most his powerful arms and shoulders could handle without serious effort. So he had made it a habit to do 160 push-ups each morning until that amount, too, became easy. After a while he had increased the number to 170, then 180, and on to 200. The only reason he did not do more was that his time was too limited to accommodate them.

His theory was that one must never push oneself beyond one's natural endurance too fast. One must always stay within one's limit, do what comes easily—and then, step by step, increase that level of performance.

He regarded himself as a machine. He took good care of that machine. He knew what it was capable of. He would make it capable of more.

When he got up, breathing heavily, his face still red from the effort, he glanced at the small bookcase beside his bed. There were about a dozen books. Half of them were manuals on mining, applied physics and chemistry, finances, economics, and a fat volume about the Napoleonic Wars.

The other half were volumes of plays. These included works by Ibsen, O'Neill, Chekhov, and a very dog-eared Shakespeare.

His own interest in plays had surprised him when he discovered it several years ago. Until that time he had considered literature irrelevant to his life. But one day, browsing idly through a Shakespeare play in a bookstore, it had occurred to him that the dramatist's work mirrored remarkably the histories of warfare that had long fascinated him. The subject of each play was the strengths and weaknesses of the characters, and their strategic interplay. It was plotted as subtly as one of the great battles.

Joseph Knight became an avid reader of plays. Literature, he found, was a rich meditation upon the interactions of men, their calculations and venality and sexual obsessions. He read *Hamlet* and *Othello* and *King Lear* and *Macbeth* dozens of times, each time learning more about the subtleties of character and the awesome technical precision of the playwright.

Wherever he went, he took a volume of plays and at least one history of warfare. The stories of the great battles, the strategic insights and mistakes of the powerful generals, were an inspiration to him. Life resembled the great battles in which the judgment of one man must be sharp enough to gamble the lives of many men without losing them. A gamble that could change the history of a nation or even the world.

Joseph Knight's own battles for financial success were not on that level, of course. But he treated them as though they were. He was a perfectionist, careful and thorough in every move he made. He found his greatest pleasure in defeating other people by making their strengths work against them, and in circumventing his own weaknesses— lack of funds, lack of influence or friends.

He was an erudite man in some ways and an ignorant one in others. His knowledge had been gained by personal experience, and his reading was calculated to facilitate his path through life as an adventurer. Though a lively intellec- tual power, he did not read for pleasure. It never occurred to him that somewhere inside him was a true student, a mind that could have found satisfaction in a university doc- torate, a mind that might have enjoyed the pure acquisition of knowledge for its own sake, and even the expression of ideas that belonged to him by writing his own plays. He had no time for such thoughts. He was a man of action.

He looked at the face in the mirror again. The burning intensity of the black irises was familiar to him and without value, but he knew it had a powerful and sometimes irresist- ible effect on women.

He had had all the women he wanted almost from the time he left home. Something in them seemed to faint at the sight of him, and their bodies were his willing toys. He enjoyed himself with them when he felt the need, but was never touched deeply by them. They came too easily, and they never seemed to have any serious dreams or ambitions for themselves beyond the gaining of protection from a man through the use of their sexual wiles. Like members of a harem, they lived by a shallow self-interest that made him feel sorry for them, and more than a little contemptuous.

He had never known a woman who aspired to be an individual, who had her own heart and her own thoughts, irrespective of the little advantages she could gain in the world by flattering men. He had long since given up waiting to meet her.

Feeling as he did about women, he was impervious to their subtle manipulations, the way they used their bodies, their endearments, their tears, their complaints to try to chip away at the will of a man and make him do their bidding. All their blandishments had no effect on him. Nev- ertheless he treated them with deliberate consideration and, when he needed it, great charm. For more than once a woman's help had come in handy in his business endeavors.

He had no friends he trusted, no woman he cared deeply about. The mother he had loved and admired as a boy was now dead. But he did not allow himself the leisure or the weakness to consider himself lonely. He understood that the key to his existence was his lack of dependence on other people. So he trusted only himself. And because of this he found that he was always the stronger in his relations with others. He had no excess baggage to look after in his life, and he wanted it that way.

He never asked himself whether he was happy. He did not see the world in such terms. He followed the trail blazed by his own abilities, knowing that it led to greater power and greater achievements, and did not bother to wonder whether there were other thoughts a man might have about his life. If there was emptiness inside him, it was covered over by the relentless accumulation of his knowledge and his power.

Today Joseph Knight stood in his hotel suite in Chicago. He was on his way out to the office he kept in the Loop. He came here six or seven times a year to keep an eye on his midwestern interests. The office was rented in the name of a paper corporation called Midwest Associates, which he had created as a front for his many activities.

Today he was in something of a funk. His business seemed stale. The cold wind blowing off Lake Michigan looked bleak and inhospitable. He dreaded the boring day ahead. He needed a new challenge to stimulate him.

He did not know it yet, but the challenge was waiting in his office at this very moment.

His secretary greeted him by introducing him to a stranger who was dressed in a silk suit and carried a monogrammed briefcase.

"How do you do, Mr. Knight," the man said, rising to shake Joseph Knight's hand. "My name is Warren Dreyfus. I represent Carl Rizzo."

Knight looked into the stranger's eyes. He saw confidence there, and a polished air of quiet condescension.

This was understandable. Carl Rizzo was an important mob figure in Chicago and northern Illinois, a man with many connections and considerable power. Knight had heard of him often in the course of his business trips here, but never crossed his path.

Now, however, Rizzo had taken note of Knight's existence.

Joseph Knight smelled shakedown in the demeanor of Rizzo's envoy. But he ushered him courteously into his office and offered him coffee.

"Carl would like to meet you," Dreyfus said. "He's been hearing things about you, and he's favorably impressed. He likes to meet all the people who work in his territory. For the sake of friendship."

Joseph Knight smiled, measuring the force behind the stranger's invitation. Rumor had it that Carl Rizzo played very rough, and had had several men killed or run out of the state for not playing ball with him. Though not yet as high in the mafia hierarchy of the Midwest as he would like to be, he was a man of great ambition and power. His ruthlessness had made him friends as well as enemies. He was a man to be taken seriously.

"Of course," Joseph Knight said. "I'd be pleased to meet him any time."

"How about dinner tonight?" Dreyfus said. "At his estate in Glencoe. He'll send a car around at six. Will you be here?"

"Certainly," Joe said. "And please pass along my thanks and my respects."

The stranger left, a quiet smile on his face. Joseph Knight's show of respect had already convinced him that Knight would be no trouble to Rizzo.

As for Knight himself, he had already made his first move in the game. He resolved to keep his wits about him.

Carl Rizzo lived in a baronial setting in Glencoe, his mansion overlooking the cold, choppy waters of Lake Michigan. There were two Rolls-Royces, a Bentley, and a

Mercedes roadster in the driveway. The house looked like old money, from its tudor trim to the restrained furniture, all antique, that filled the rooms. There was not a trace of the nouveau riche. It was the house of an aggressive man on the make who goes to great lengths to present himself as a settled and staid one.

Knight had been picked up at his office by two men in a limousine, a silent driver and a second man, very stout and menacing-looking, who was obviously one of Rizzo's enforcers. Not a word had been said on the forty-five-minute journey northward.

Carl Rizzo greeted Knight personally. He was a man in his fifties, with iron-gray hair and careful eyes whose expression of languid hospitality concealed a cold watchfulness.

"Delighted that you could come, Mr. Knight," he said. "Let's have a drink."

The two men chatted over cocktails in the living room as the lake wind whistled outside. Their conversation ranged over innocent topics like the weather and the Chicago sports teams, wending its way ever closer to serious matters as they spoke of the hard times and their effect on business.

In the living room Joseph Knight observed several framed photographs of a beautiful young woman, obviously done by expert portrait photographers in a shadowed, glamorous style.

There was a full-length framed oil portrait of her above the mantel, showing her in a dress that made her look as though she had come from the cream of North Shore society. In the painting she wore a fabulous diamond necklace, with several bands of stones set in an exotic white gold arrangement about her slender swanlike neck. Her beauty was very pure and aristocratic.

She could only be Rizzo's wife—a wife he was proud of and wished to show off to his visitors. But she was not in evidence tonight. Rizzo had chosen to entertain his visitor alone.

Knight did not ask about her. He wanted to let Rizzo play his cards in his own way.

Over dinner Rizzo got down to business.

"I admire a young man like you," Rizzo said. "You have initiative, you have bright ideas. You're going to go far. I think it's important that we link up financially from the start. I'll help you out in every way I can. All I ask in return is a reasonable compensation, and the option to help you in your future interests."

"What sort of compensation?" Knight asked.

Rizzo glossed over the details with a wave of his manicured hand. But Joseph Knight got the message. Rizzo's deal amounted to nothing less than financial piracy. He required a tribute of 50 percent of all profits, off the top, plus contractual obligations making him a full partner in all of Knight's enterprises. The fine print was even worse. All the risk went to Knight. Most of the profit went to Rizzo.

In addition, there was a virtual option clause stating that Rizzo would be given 50 percent of any business that Knight might start or acquire in the next twenty years, as a full partner. It was the most onerous business deal imaginable.

Joseph Knight kept his thoughts to himself as he listened.

"That's asking a lot," he said at length, his voice expressing mingled respect and worry. "What do I get in return?"

Carl Rizzo smiled.

"Complete financial cooperation from me, with the benefit of all my resources," he said. "I haven't done bad in this town," he said, pointing to the beautiful house around him. "And I have lots of friends, in politics as well as in business. Believe me, Joe, you won't regret it."

A half hour later Joseph Knight thanked his host for the pleasant evening.

"Let me think over the details and get back to you," he said.

"Don't take too long," Rizzo said. "In this town a man needs all the friends he can get."

The threat was obvious. There was a cold gleam in Rizzo's eye as he bade his guest goodnight.

Knight was driven to his hotel by the two men who had picked him up earlier. This time the obese, evil-looking bodyguard sat in the back seat with him. He was clearly a dangerous fellow, his body built of sheer stone.

"I'm Salvatore," the man said, shaking Knight's hand with fingers like vises. "The boss said to make sure you got home safe."

"Thank you." Knight's voice seemed stifled, abashed.

"No problem. It's what I'm paid for."

Knight was careful to seem self-effacing to the point of pusillanimity. He could see the half smile of contempt on the big man's face.

When they reached their destination the fat man made a point of climbing across Joseph Knight to get out of the limousine. As he did so he managed, by apparent accident, to push a large knee between Knight's legs and squeeze the genitals, hard.

Knight winced and grunted, but did not say a word.

The fat man grinned. "Sorry, pal," he said, opening the door. "I didn't mean to hurt you. It won't happen again."

As the car pulled away Knight could see the fat man laughing with the driver. He had enjoyed his little joke, and clearly did not respect Knight enough to hide his amusement.

Joseph Knight went upstairs to his suite, lit his pipe, and stared out the windows at the skyline of the Loop. The wheels were turning quickly inside his brain.

What Carl Rizzo had proposed was nothing more nor less than financial rape. He intended to get a stranglehold on Knight's growing business empire and perhaps to kill it at its roots.

And what did he have to back his demand up? Intimidation. He had not had to mention what had been done to his earlier competitors, because it was common knowledge. He knew Knight must have heard about it.

Moreover, the disrespectful behavior of Rizzo's subordinates in the limousine had been an obvious sign of contempt and bravado, a message sent from their boss. He did not take Knight seriously. He expected prompt submission from him.

And this was a sign that, somewhere down the line,

Knight would be eliminated once he had been sucked dry. There could be no doubt about that.

The challenge to Joseph Knight was a serious one. He knew that Carl Rizzo had mob connections. In one form or another those connections went straight to the Vincent Monaco family, the key mafia organization of the city.

One might assume that the murders and other acts of violence committed by Rizzo's goons over the years had had the imprimatur of the mafia, and perhaps even involved its people.

But Joseph Knight did not make this assumption. His sharp eye had detected the weak spot in Rizzo's attack.

From his admittedly slight contacts with the crime families in other cities, Joseph Knight had not found that they asked for a cut anywhere near what Carl Rizzo was demanding. This suggested that Rizzo was acting on his own. True, Rizzo was using the public knowledge of his mob connections as part of the intimidation. But perhaps that public knowledge was an illusion. Perhaps Rizzo was a lone wolf.

The fat bodyguard, Salvatore, with his crude physical menace, supported this interpretation. An actual high-level mob approach would have been more subtle, more civilized. Rizzo was showing off too much. This suggested, strongly, that he was using intimidation to hide what was in fact a lack of real mob support.

Thus Joseph Knight found himself in a delicate situation.

He knew that in his future endeavors he would need friendly relations with the mob. No businessman of consequence can do without such friendly relations, even if he is legitimate. Once the mob decides a man is not its friend, it can hinder him, harry him limitlessly, in a thousand little ways, from unions to trucking to supplies, and even to banking and insurance.

So the long-range plan was clear: Joseph Knight must establish and maintain good relations with the mob.

The short-range problem was a conundrum: to get past Carl Rizzo with a minimum of loss to Knight's own interests, but without angering the mob or getting the reputation of a misfit.

But Rizzo was making this impossible. The deal he proposed was too onerous for Knight to accept and survive financially. More important, he could not accept it and hold his head up among other men as a man to be taken seriously. This was the key.

Therefore the course of action was clear. Carl Rizzo must be taken out of the picture.

But how?

Joseph Knight puffed at his pipe. He thought over his evening with Rizzo. He studied his memory of Rizzo's face, of his talk, and recalled the curious mixture of bravado and caution, of elegance and ill-concealed coarseness, in his demeanor. Rizzo was a man who was putting on an act. Such a man must have a weakness, an Achilles' heel.

Joseph Knight needed to find out what that weakness was.

And he already knew what his first step must be.

He had to find out more about the young woman in the portrait.

 10

HER NAME WAS ANNE.

Her maiden name was Pendleton. She had come from a small town in Maryland, where her father was a respected physician and her mother a well-known charity worker and organizer. As a girl Anne had attended the prestigious

Hotchkiss School for Girls in Baltimore, then the Hewitt Academy.

She had been a precocious child, full of energy and talent. Her IQ was high, and she had an equal facility with numbers and words. She could have grown up to become a mathematician, a writer, or anything else she liked.

But her extraordinary beauty had caused show business to beckon to her, and she had left college to become a dancer, over her parents' strenuous objections. She had gone to New York and then Hollywood in search of work. Her career had not gone well, for her abilities fell a bit short of her ambition. She ended up dancing at the Chez Paree in Chicago, a mere chorus girl. Her parents, hearing of this, disowned her.

Though not a success, Anne was beautiful. Her beauty was pure and blond and virginal. She was innocent and unspoiled, despite her profession, because she had refused the advances of dozens of club owners, fellow artists, and patrons. Her upbringing had been straitlaced, and she was delicate and feminine in her manner. She looked the part of the suburban princess that Carl Rizzo had cherished in his imagination throughout his own violent life in the Italian neighborhoods of the big city.

Rizzo was smitten the first time he picked her out from among the other chorus girls. He courted her with panache and elegance. He sent her flowers a dozen times before even asking her to dinner. When she accepted, he treated her like a queen. He took her to the Pump Room and the Ambassador and the Montmartre. He gave her lavish gifts, bought her dresses, and even used his influence to get her a starring dance role at the club. The role did not last, for she simply could not manage the elaborate steps required to be a headliner. But the romance took. Anne needed a protector, and she was seduced by Carl's attentions.

Carl showed her a brand-new mansion he was building in the city's most exclusive northern suburb, overlooking Lake Michigan. The place already looked venerable and stately, and Carl was having it furnished with priceless antiques.

"Marry me, Anne," he said, "and live here with me.

You don't have to dance any more unless you want to. You can stay right here and rule over your own domain." He smiled gently. "That includes me," he added.

Anne Pendleton hesitated. She knew what kind of man Carl Rizzo was. She had worked in clubs and casinos, and met the type before: the quiet, serious mob man with a dangerous look in his eyes, the man who knew his own power and feared no one.

Such men did not often take women seriously. She had known girls who became their concubines. The men were brutal, insensitive, indifferent. All her experience told her to keep a safe distance from his type.

But Carl's courtship was so respectful, and her own need so great—she was running out of money fast, and was too prideful to bear the idea of going back on her knees to her parents for support—that her loneliness carried the day over her common sense. She accepted him. They were married three months after their first meeting.

Carl's wedding gift to her was a priceless diamond necklace with a dozen flawless stones in a white gold setting. She knew it must be worth a hundred thousand dollars at the very least. It was this necklace that Anne wore when she sat for the portrait that was hung in the living room of their Glencoe house. It was made up of groups of stones, three, four, and five, separated by intricate little Italian gold beads in amazingly lovely patterns.

"I want you always to wear it," he said. "To remind you how much I love you, Anne."

Their honeymoon was brief, spent at Lake Tahoe. "Business" required Carl's quick return to Chicago. He was a man with responsibilities, a man on whom a lot of people depended. He expected his wife to understand this without explanation.

When they returned home Carl suddenly changed his tune about her dance career. He insisted that Anne give it up at once and live only as a housewife. "You have a name to live up to," he said. "No wife of Carl Rizzo dances in bars."

Anne agreed, with mingled relief at being freed from her difficult career and dread at the authoritarian manner in which her husband had mapped out her future. She was to stay at home, going out only for charity work in the community.

She began to realize that this quiet life might not be a bed of roses.

Carl Rizzo, it turned out, was a jealous husband.

Each day he was driven into the city by his chauffeur, accompanied by his bodyguard, a frightening-looking fellow named Salvatore, with a massive body and a cold look in his eye. Carl called Anne several times during the day from his office, his affectionate tone thinly masking his desire to check up on her.

Soon she realized that the servants, personally chosen by her husband, were spies for him. She could feel them watching her and making sure she was never alone for very long.

Carl kept his business activities a complete secret from his wife. She knew nothing about his financial interests, his associates, or his enemies. She had known before her marriage that he had connections with the Chicago mafia. Her considerable intelligence, combined with the little involuntary hints he gave, allowed her to deduce that he was not as high in the mob hierarchy as he would have liked. He was an ambitious man, and a ruthless one. He was powerful, and still on his way up. He had enemies, and he would no doubt make more of them.

It was best, Anne decided, that she not know more.

But as his wife it was necessary that she know what to do in the event of his death. With this in mind Carl told her that there was a safe in his private office, upstairs in the Glencoe mansion, where the most sensitive of his private papers were kept. He explained that in the event of illness or death on his part, she was to call his attorney, Max Begelman, immediately. Max would open the safe and take care of Carl's affairs.

She of course was not given the combination to the safe. Nor did Max have it. Carl was too secretive a man to trust even his attorney on that score. He told Anne that when the time came Max would know how to get into it. He,

Carl, had cleverly arranged a way to inform Max of the combination in the event of his death.

One evening when Carl took Anne out to dinner and an evening at the Chez Parée she saw an old professional associate, a dancer and comedian named Sonny Gallian. She had been in several shows with Sonny during her career. He was a good-looking, dark man with a ready wit and a flashing smile.

She invited him to join her at their table, introduced him to Carl, and got a few welcome laughs out of him. She realized that night that it had been more than a month since she had laughed. Life with Carl brought no laughter, but only a ponderous feeling of dread and watchfulness.

So Anne laughed, and kissed Sonny, and put her arms around him, and had a drink more than her usual quota. She had not had so much fun since her wedding.

"Goodbye, babe," Sonny said at the end of the evening, kissing Anne's cheek. And to Carl, "Take good care of this one. She needs someone steady like you."

Anne looked back on that isolated evening of levity with such fondness that two weeks later she was feeling lonely and called the club. She spoke to the owner, and asked him how she could get in touch with Sonny.

The owner sounded embarrassed.

"Haven't you heard, Anne? Sonny had an accident. He's in the hospital."

"What happened?" Anne asked warily.

"Somebody broke both his legs," the owner said. "It was bad. He'll be walking with a cane if he ever walks at all. Sonny's dancing days are over, believe me."

Anne hung up the phone. She was afraid to visit Sonny in the hospital, not only because of her suspicion of what had really happened, but because she feared that if she was seen visiting him, something even worse might happen to him.

So she contented herself with sending him an enormous bunch of flowers and a long sympathetic note. But she took the precaution of buying the flowers out of her own money, so there would be no trace of the purchase on Carl's household accounts.

Anne had learned her first hard lesson about the consequences of displeasing her husband.

After the Sonny Gallian episode Carl kept an even closer eye on his wife. Anne now realized that she was truly living like a prisoner.

What was worse, life inside her ivory tower was singularly unsatisfying.

Carl Rizzo was a terrible lover.

Anne had realized during their courtship that the act of love with Carl was brusque and not very sensual. But his other attentions at the time, so considerate and respectful, had combined with her own loneliness to cover over this fact.

Now, however, she could not hide the truth from herself any more. Carl made love like an animal, with no pretense of romance or kindness. He ordered her to take her clothes off, mounted her without so much as a kiss, and—usually painfully—entered her and took his pleasure without the slightest regard for her feelings.

Not only was he a crude lover, but he was an inadequate one. And on some level of his personality he seemed to realize this. His frustration only made him the more brutal. And it was this sense of owning her without satisfying her, of taking his pleasure while knowing he was giving her no pleasure of her own, that soon became part and parcel of his jealousy toward her. His morbid watchfulness increased in proportion as his sense of his own potency withered.

Of course, as far as the outside world could see, Carl put Anne on a pedestal. He dressed her in the costliest fashions, bought on Michigan Avenue. He gave her expensive jewelry, exotic perfumes. He let her decorate the house with whatever she liked, regardless of the cost. He showed her off to his friends. He had the portrait of her with her jeweled necklace done by the finest portrait painter in the city, and gave it the place of honor in his salon.

But inside her own house Anne was treated like a prisoner, and even like a slave. Carl never addressed her with tenderness or affection any more, but only with suspicion and a severity bereft of any respect at all.

She found herself wondering whether Carl had been brought up to treat a woman that way. Perhaps his father had treated his mother the same way, and the grandfather before him. Perhaps generations of hard Sicilian men had treated their women thus, without even thinking about it. Perhaps there was no genuine malice behind Carl's cruelty, but merely a blind acting-out of a traditional coarseness.

But this was not the way Anne had been brought up to live. And it was not the way she herself had dreamed of living during her days of loneliness and struggle as a dancer. She had dreamed of a loving, supportive husband, strong enough within himself to be truly gentle with her. A man whose love would pleasure her in bed while filling her heart with happiness and peace.

So Anne came to look on her husband with a mixture of fear and contempt. For she could see behind his power to his shallowness, his lack of real manhood.

Why did I marry him? she asked herself a hundred times. Why had she been such a fool? Why had she been so hasty? Why had she allowed Carl's blandishments to overcome her long-held suspicion concerning men of his type?

There was little use in asking these questions. It was too late now. She belonged to Carl Rizzo, and he was not the sort of man to let her go. They had been married in the Catholic Church.

Nothing short of his death or hers would ever get her out of this prison.

• • •

One day Anne was shopping on Michigan Avenue for a new dress when she met a stranger.

He walked up to her in the exclusive dress shop, a somewhat perplexed look on his face.

"I know you don't work here," he said, noting her beautiful clothes. "But I need the advice of someone objective, someone who's not trying to sell me anything. My wife is about your size. She has your coloring, too. I want to give her a dress for our anniversary, but I don't know how to begin. I've never bought her a dress before. I'd like it to be something really special."

Anne looked at him. He seemed sincere, and genuinely puzzled by his surroundings. At the same time she noticed how handsome he was. He was strongly built, with dark eyes, thick hair, and a sort of depth in his tanned face that made him look both intelligent and very masculine.

She decided to do as he had asked. She strolled about the shop with him, holding up various dresses in front of herself for him to judge. When they found one they both liked, she went into the dressing room and tried it on for him. His eyes lit up when she emerged.

Anne felt a curious sensation as he admired her in the dress.

"That's it," he said. "If it looks half as good on her as it does on you, she'll be thrilled. I can't thank you enough."

Anne could not help lingering in the store as he paid for the dress and had it boxed and gift-wrapped. He thanked her again, so thoughtfully and politely that she had to laugh at his courtliness.

When he left he shook her hand.

"You've been a great help," he said. "But I don't even know your name."

"It's Anne," she said. "Anne Rizzo."

"Joseph Knight," he said. "My friends call me Joe."

A subtle quiver went through her as the warm dry palm encircled her hand. His eyes met hers, and the dark irises caressed her with a softness that lulled her seductively.

Had he asked her to have a drink with him, or lunch, she would not have refused, even though she knew he was married. He was that attractive.

By the time she was in her car going home, Anne already knew she would not get him out of her mind. He would be one of those brief meetings every woman has in her life, like a glimpse through a door behind which a whole world awaited, a world of love she would never know because her life was committed elsewhere.

Had she been a happy woman, Anne would have looked back on the episode with a trace of wistful amusement at her own infatuation. But she was not a happy woman. She

felt desperately alone that night. She paced the house forlornly. Carl did not come home until late. He made love to
her in his clumsy, almost childish way, and went right to
sleep.

Anne did not sleep a wink. She was thinking of the
stranger. Over and over again she saw the complex light in
his eyes that harmonized so strangely with the hard, tanned
surface of his face. She had never encountered a man so
sure of his masculinity, a man who could afford to treat a
woman with such perfect respect and warmth because his
own personality was so secure.

Anne got out of bed the next morning with eyes smarting
from her insomnia and a hopeless feeling deep in her
senses. She bade her husband goodbye for the day and
retreated to the bedroom, where she sat in her nightgown
drinking coffee and staring out the window at the cold
angry lake. She had never felt so alone in her life.

Just before noon one of the servants brought a box from
the Michigan Avenue dress shop and placed it on Anne's
bed. The servant had assumed it was a delivery of something she had bought yesterday.

When Anne opened the box she saw the dress she had
tried on for the stranger.

Her breath caught in her throat. She read the note that
accompanied the dress.

*I decided not to give it to her. It would never have
looked as good as it did on you, so it seemed a crime.
Please wear it with the memory of my sincere thanks.*

The note was unsigned.

Anne gazed at the handwriting for a long moment. Then,
her senses tingling, she took off her nightgown and slowly
put on the dress. The fabric slipped over her naked limbs
like a caress. She adjusted it carefully and went to stand
before the mirror.

The look in her eyes in the glass shocked her. It was a
guilty look, full of delighted and covetous anticipation. It
almost seemed that the lovely silken fabric denuded her
instead of covering her, stripping away her disguises and

revealing her guiltiest thoughts. Its touch on her skin was like the touch of the stranger's lips on hers.

She was still standing there admiring herself in the dress and thinking of Joseph Knight when the phone rang.

"Did you get the dress?" came a deep smooth voice.

"I—yes," she said.

"I hope you aren't offended," the stranger said. "I am so grateful for your help, and I didn't know how else to thank you."

"How did you—find me?" she asked.

"The lady at the dress shop knew you," he said.

There was a silence.

"Does it look good?" he asked.

She got his point. He was guessing that she had put it on.

"Yes," she admitted daringly, gazing at herself in the mirror. "It looks wonderful."

"Please don't be offended if I ask you a favor," he asked. "Would you wear it for me sometime?"

Anne held her breath. Her eyes closed. She knew what he was asking. She knew the danger that lay behind his words. But she could not help herself. She looked at the bed in which her husband had mounted her so crudely last night. She was a woman. She had a heart. She could not go on living that way.

"When?" she asked, surrender in her voice.

They set a date for the following week. There was a banquet being given by Anne's charity group on behalf of one of the city's hospitals. Anne managed to convince one of her friends in the group to cover for her in the event that Carl called to ask for her during the evening. The friend, a married lady from Evanston, gave Anne a knowing look, but promised to do what she asked.

Thus Anne freed herself for one precious night.

She left home in Carl's Bentley, had her chauffeur let her off at the downtown hotel where the banquet was being given, and told him she would call him when she wanted him.

She waited until the Bentley was out of sight and then

took a cab to a small restaurant on Superior Street where Joseph Knight was waiting for her.

She was wearing the dress he had given her. The look in his eyes as he admired her in it told her what she had been dreaming of all this time: that he felt about her as she did about him.

You only live once, Anne told herself fatefully.

Their dinner was a quiet one. They said much more with their eyes than with their words. Joseph Knight told Anne a few insignificant facts about himself—he was a businessman, he said, with interests in Chicago—and asked her about her own life. She told him the bare essentials, not wanting to sully this occasion by having the name of Carl Rizzo pass her lips. Then they went dancing. He held her close as they danced, and so subtle was the touch of his hand that something in her surrendered at the nearness of him. He sensed this, and supported her with a delicate strength that sent unseen tremors through her body.

The evening passed as though in a dream. At eleven o'clock she found herself sitting with him in silence, looking into his dark eyes with an expression of helpless entreaty in her own.

He took her hand.

"Shall I take you home?" he asked.

She nodded. They both knew what he meant.

He took her to the penthouse suite at a small but elegant downtown hotel. She could see from the books on the shelves and the business papers on tabletops that this was where he lived.

But she saw the rooms for only a second, for no sooner had he taken her coat than Joseph Knight turned out the lights and took her in his arms.

His kiss penetrated her like a love potion. It left her limp with wanting. His strong hands were around her back, touching delicately at her shoulders, her ribcage, her waist as he pulled her closer to him.

She had never felt at once so protected and so defenseless. Her passion declared itself in a long, sweet sigh that made him smile in the darkness.

In one smooth movement he swept her off her feet and

carried her to the bedroom. For a moment he stood kissing her as he held her effortlessly in his powerful arms.

Then he placed her gently on the soft spread and began to take off her clothes. First he removed the dress itself, which he hung in the closet. He returned to look down at her in her slip. He pulled the straps down her shoulders and slid the garment off, watching her slender dancer's body emerge before him. Then he removed her stockings, unhooking them and peeling them down her legs with a sure touch.

He gazed at her for a long moment.

"You are beautiful," he said.

Anne could not speak. Desire had taken her breath away.

He knelt to take off her bra. The breasts were bared to him, nipples already taut with excitement. He cupped them for an instant with his dry hands, and then slipped off her panties. Her hair had come loose and was splayed across the pillows like a golden halo around her head.

He bent to kiss her. The male tongue was warm and exciting as it stroked her own. She grasped his arms and pulled him closer. The aroma of him, so seductive as they had danced, was more pungent now, and terribly masculine.

Softly he ran a finger across her brow and down her cheek, exploring her as though she were something precious seen for the first time, something to be touched worshipfully and thoroughly. He caressed her shoulders, her arms, her hips, his hands moving down her legs to her toes, making every nerve inside her sing with desire.

Then he stood up to take off his own clothes. The handsome jacket and slacks came off, and then the shirt, revealing a powerful muscled chest, a hard square waist, and strong legs. There was something massive about him, despite the lithe contours of youth, something rocklike and irresistible.

She watched in awe as the underpants came off. He stood erect before her, a male god carved in something beyond mere flesh, something more noble and thus infinitely more sexy.

She held out her arms to him, trembling.

The whole hard length of him came to caress her all at once, dry and warm and protective. But there was terrible power coiled behind that soft touch, and she thrilled to feel it come closer, hungry to possess her.

Her hands traveled lovingly over the strong shoulders she had admired, and then down his back, along bands of muscle hard as steel, and finally to the male loins pressed excitingly against her.

Her legs spread pliantly, her back arched to offer her breasts to him. He came closer; she felt a sweet slow probing at the tip of her, and, with a silent rush of power, he slid to his hilt inside her.

Never had she imagined that sex could be at once so tender and so overwhelming. He filled all of her, tight and hot and irresistible, and yet left room for her own identity, her own feelings. And as his slow strokes began to fire her passion to unspeakable heights, still the warm hands held her close, the terrible poised muscles held her as gently as a china teacup.

She shuddered as he brought her orgasm after orgasm, each more beautiful than the last. Her legs were wrapped tight about his waist, her hands slipping over his flesh, awed by the tense bands of muscle that were everywhere she touched.

Her head shook this way and that, her body shuddered with delight, her fingers scratched his tanned skin in their frenzy. And just when she thought she could stand the ecstasy no longer, that she would die of pleasure if it did not end, he pushed deeper, to a secret place she had not known she possessed, upraised her all at once, and gave her the white hot stream of his passion.

Her moans sounded in his ear for a long time after the greatest height had been reached, for her pleasure continued to burst in long spasmodic waves, making her tremble again and again in his arms.

For a long time she could not even find breath to whisper a word to him. She seemed to have taken leave of the earth and of herself. He had brought her something infinitely beyond her pathetic sexual encounters with her husband, beyond even her guiltiest girlish fantasies about what sex might one day be like. He had given her something transcendent, something from a dimension of delight she had never dreamed possible.

When at last she recovered some measure of control over herself, she snuggled gratefully in his embrace. How safe he made her feel! And how warm, how wanted . . .

She was so full of her delight in him that she was not surprised by the words he spoke.

"I lied about my wife, at the dress shop," he murmured. "I'm not married."

She simply nodded and kissed his lips.

"Good," she said. "Now I don't have to share you with anyone."

• • • •

Anne saw Joseph Knight as often as she could after that.

She had to move heaven and earth to free herself from her husband and his spies. She was forced to extremities of guile and cunning that surprised her.

She bribed salesgirls at expensive dress shops so that she could slip out the back for forty-five minutes. The same went for her hairdresser. She had to use her own money, which she had scrupulously saved from the allowance Carl Rizzo gave her.

She began to take dance classes "to keep in shape," she told Carl. She joined a class in sculpture. She began taking tennis lessons, assuring her social-climbing husband that she would teach him after she had learned, and they would play doubles with other North Shore couples. She took up horseback riding. She undertook a redecoration of several rooms of her house. This necessitated meetings with decorators, shopping trips, consultations with fabric designers and cabinetmakers.

All these activities became pretexts for brief escapes from her husband's dominion, escapes that led straight to Joseph Knight's arms.

She exhausted every trick in her book and managed to see Joseph Knight twice a week. During those magic trysts she forgot her lonely life and thought she was the luckiest woman on earth. Joseph Knight's caresses opened the door to a fantasy come true, a sunlit world in which she was respected, understood, and made safe and happy, even as her ecstasy burned hotter than ever.

When she was not with him she existed in a state of almost painful anticipation. Her body craved him with an urgency that would not be denied. At all hours of the day, when she was alone, she would think about him, about his warm lips and powerful hands, about his muscled nudity, and about the beautiful erect thing between his legs, a thing almost too fascinating for her to take her eyes off, were it not for her frantic haste to get it inside her and let it do its delightful work.

She was insatiable. She could not get enough of him. But her dependence on him was not only of the flesh. Something about his quiet seriousness, the personal strength that allowed him to be so kind and understanding, had stolen her heart. This man, Joseph Knight, was the man she was made for, the man she had dreamed of all through her girlhood. Carl Rizzo was a colossal mistake, a monstrous accident. Her heart sank when she thought of him, and her skin crawled when he touched her. But deep inside she cherished an infinite joy to think that at last fate had allowed her to meet Joe, the man of her dreams.

After the first month she knew she belonged to him forever. She would do anything, brave any danger, run any risk, to be with him. She did not care what the future brought. Her heart had found its home. Nothing could ever change that again.

Thus she was shocked, but quickly got over her shock, when, one day, Joseph Knight asked her an unexpected question.

"I need your help," he said. "It's something important."

"Anything," she said. "Darling, just ask."

"There is a safe in your husband's private office, at home," he said. "I need the combination."

ANNE RIZZO WAS THRILLED.

She was like the heroine of a romantic adventure. Her lover had given her a difficult quest, and she was going to prove herself equal to it, for his sake and for the sake of their love.

She was too intoxicated by her passion for Joseph Knight to be angry over the false pretenses under which he had approached her. It was too late for such scruples—her heart was lost.

Moreover, Knight had told her something of his professional relationship with her husband, and about her husband's business dealings. Not enough to involve her with guilty knowledge, but enough for her to realize what a rapacious and venal creature Carl Rizzo really was. He was a renegade, a man who broke all the rules of the mafia as well as of civilized society for the sake of his own gain.

This news did not entirely surprise Anne. She had suspected as much. She recalled Sonny Gallian, the innocent comedian who had been such a good friend to her, and what Carl had done to him. Now she truly realized the horror of her decision to marry Carl. He was a monster.

She would do anything Joseph Knight asked, and with no second thoughts. Not only was she head over heels in love with him, but she saw a chance to change the course of her life, a life she had so foolishly thrown away when she had married Carl. She dared to hope that when she had given Joseph Knight her ultimate commitment, shown him what she was made of, he would take her away from Carl. She did not doubt his ability to do so. One look in those burning dark eyes of his left no doubt that he feared no man on earth and was capable of even the most dangerous of exploits.

So she threw herself into her quest like the fearless heroine of a melodrama, bold and reckless and indifferent to the perils she faced.

Joseph Knight had explained that under normal circumstances he would not have dreamed of asking something so difficult and dangerous of her. But her husband's safe was a Minor, the finest safe money can buy. Even the best second-story man would have to blow such a safe rather than to attempt to crack it. There simply would not be enough time. Knight needed the combination. He needed an "inside man" to help him. And the inside man was Anne.

She began to pay closer attention to her husband's movements. She watched him when he went into his private office at night, and watched him when he came out.

She managed to get a look at his key ring when he was in the shower. She studied all the keys carefully. She found out which key matched the lock on the door to his private office. This was the one she needed.

But identifying it and getting it away from Carl were two different things. Carl guarded his keys jealously, and always kept the little office locked. It would not be easy to penetrate that inner sanctum.

Necessity, the mother of invention, gave Anne an inspiration.

One night she drugged her husband's cocktails with just enough of a powerful sedative to make him sleep like a rock. She made love to him to exhaust him the more; she demanded that he do it three times. The drug was already taking effect, so he became more tired each time, though flattered by her insatiability. He did not know that each time he touched her she was imagining it was Joseph Knight who held her in his arms.

When the husband was dead to the world Anne leapt out of bed, purloined the keys from his pocket, and went to an all-night locksmith who made her a copy of the office key. She was back by 3 A.M. It was enormously difficult to get out of and back into her own house without alarming the servants and the bodyguard Carl kept on duty. It was only because Anne knew the grounds and the house better than anyone else that she was able to slip out a corner of the lawn and get back in an hour and a half. Of course she could not use one of her own cars. There was a car waiting for her on a nearby street. It had been put there by Joseph Knight.

Luckily for Anne's purpose, her husband was often away from home at night. Carl Rizzo was a typical mob character who spent several evenings a week playing poker or drinking with his mafia friends. He expected his wife to be at his beck and call, but cared nothing for the lonely nights she spent while he was out carousing with his associates.

For this reason Anne had all the time she would need for what she had to do.

Two nights after she had had the key to his office copied, Carl went out for an evening downtown. As soon as the servants had retired to their own rooms Anne used her key to get into the office. She turned on the light and searched the small room for the safe. It was behind one of the oak panels of the walls. No serious attempt had been made to hide it. Carl obviously felt that the presence of his bodyguards and the high quality of the safe itself would suffice to protect his secrets.

Having seen the safe, Anne began to search through all the private papers she found in Carl's desk. She was looking for the combination.

She did not find it. Moreover, most of the papers she found were rather innocent. They included bank statements, investment records, and real estate certificates. Obviously the real evidence of the business life Carl led was hidden in the safe.

Anne looked for some sort of message left for attorney

Max Begelman in the event of Carl's death. A note, a sealed envelope—anything. She was unsuccessful. No such document was to be found in the office.

But she found a copy of Carl's will in his desk drawer. This he had of necessity placed where she and his attorney could find it in the event of his death.

Anne sat down at the expensive mahogany desk and read through the will. She reasoned that it must include some provision concerning the safe, and perhaps even the combination.

But she found nothing of the sort.

In passing she noticed Carl's instructions for the disposition of his assets. Most of them were to go directly to Anne. A small yearly stipend went to his mother in Italy, another to his sister in New Jersey.

So he loves me, after all, Anne mused contemptuously. She cared nothing any more for Carl Rizzo. Only Joseph Knight had a place in her heart now.

But the combination was not mentioned in the will. And she knew the safe must contain Carl's most important secrets. It occurred to Anne that whatever was in the safe was so sensitive, perhaps damningly illegal, that Carl would not want it opened by a probate court. It could not see the light of day.

Therefore he must have some other arrangement, more subtle, in mind.

She was about to close the will when something caught her eye. On the last page of the will a codicil had been added.

"I further direct," it read, *"that in the event of my death my wife's portrait shall on no account be disposed of in any fashion without the explicit consent and direction of my attorney, Max W. Begelman. In the event that Max W. Begelman is deceased or unavailable at that time, the portrait is to be handed over to a person or persons to be named by me in this testament."*

Anne Rizzo knew she had found what she was looking for.

There must be more to the little instruction than met the eye. Perhaps it was a sort of code between her husband

and Max Begelman, a clue that Max would know how to interpret.

She put away the will, left the office, and went downstairs to the living room. She turned on the recessed ceiling light that illuminated the portrait. On the surface there was nothing unusual about it. It was a beautiful picture, done by the most prestigious portrait artist in the Midwest, a man who had painted all the great ladies of the North Shore. It made Anne look sleek, sophisticated, and aristocratic. No doubt this was the way Carl saw her, or wanted to see her. She had grown so used to having it in the living room that she had barely glanced at it for many months.

Now she studied it carefully. She tried to look at it as Max Begelman, a clever man, would look at it after Carl's death. She wondered whether some sort of clue for Max was concealed under the paint, or in the frame, or in the canvas.

She got a magnifying glass from her writing desk and scoured the portrait for tiny marks or concealed figures. She studied the folds of her painted gown, the brush strokes of her hair, the background of drapery and light.

She found nothing. Her eyes were smarting from the effort, and her back hurt from craning her neck to stare through the glass at the painting.

Then something else in the portrait caught her eye.

It was the necklace she had worn for the sitting, the beautiful diamond necklace Carl had given her when he asked her to marry him.

In the portrait the necklace looked different somehow.

Anne studied it for a long moment, then padded silently to her bedroom to get the necklace itself from her jewelry box.

She returned and stood before the picture, looking from the necklace in her hand to the painted image, over and over again. She soon realized that the two were not the same.

The number of stones was different. So was their disposition between the gold settings. The difference was too small to be noticed by a casual observer, but too studied to be missed by someone on the lookout for just such a detail.

There were three groups of stones in the painting, as in the actual necklace. But the number of stones in each group had been altered by the artist, as had the number of Italian gold beads between the groups of stones.

The first group had five stones in reality, but six in the painting. The second group had been changed from eight to seven. The third group had been changed from eight to six. The number of Italian beads between each group had also been altered.

Anne was now sure she had found the clue she was looking for.

Her heart racing, she hurried to her writing desk, got a piece of paper, and wrote down the number of stones and beads in the painting. She turned off the light in the living room, went back to her bedroom, and studied the two series of numbers.

She began with the most simple strategy. She simply added the two numbers to make a two-digit figure. Where there were five stones in the necklace, but six in the painting, she got the number 56.

She tried adding the numbers, then subtracting. Then she began to try more complicated operations, studying the permutations and combinations offered by the numbers of beads and stones, factored in a variety of ways.

Anne's old talent as a student of mathematics came back to her as she worked at the numbers. A strange exhilaration thrilled through her senses and fired her intellect. She was taking action at last, seizing the reins of her fate. And she was doing it for Joseph Knight.

By three o'clock that morning, when Carl Rizzo came home, Anne had conceived eight basic ways to derive a combination to the office safe from the numbers implied by the portrait. When she heard the downstairs door open she hid her calculations in the bottom of her jewelry box—a nice irony, she thought—and hurriedly got under the covers. She made believe she was asleep when Carl entered the bedroom. To her relief he was too tired to think about sex and went immediately to bed.

Anne did not sleep that night at all. The excitement of her discovery kept her awake. She kept sifting the precious numbers this way and that in her mind, looking for new combinations.

The next day a new vigil began. Anne knew she could not get into the office while the house staff was awake. She must wait for Carl to go out at night again. But he stayed home that night, and the next, and again the next night. He forced her to listen to his monotonous conversation over dinner, and made love to her with clumsy delectation in the late evenings. Apparently her feigned passion of several nights ago had filled him with ideas about a new intimacy with her. He seemed to want to be close to her. He even treated her with more affection than usual. She thought she would burst under the weight of his embraces. The smell of his body, the taste of his tongue when he made love to her, made her want to retch. But she endured it, for Joseph Knight's sake.

At last, five nights after her initial session with the portrait, Carl went out again. Anne was ready. As soon as the house was quiet she padded along the hall in her bare feet and used her copied key to get into the office. She opened the wall panel and looked at the safe. In her trembling hand was the piece of paper on which she had written the series of possible combinations.

She tried the first. It failed. The safe remained securely locked.

Undaunted, she went on to the second series. Again her efforts met with failure.

She looked at the clock on the office desk. One o'clock. She had at least an hour before Carl returned. He never came home before two.

With fingers chilled by danger Anne kept trying the combinations. In her excitement she twirled the dial too quickly and had to start over again. Her breathing was shallow, her hand trembling.

After a half hour she heard a murmur of tumblers and a sudden tick as she turned the dial. The safe's handle stirred significantly. When she grasped it, the heavy door swung open. She had succeeded.

She had to suppress a cry of exultation. This was the

moment she had been waiting for. She had accomplished the mission Joseph Knight had given her.

Hurriedly she tried the combination again to make sure it worked, and memorized it. Then she began to close the safe door.

But curiosity stopped her hand. Cautiously she looked at the safe's contents. They shocked her. The safe was full of cash, negotiable securities, and records of an incredible variety of illegal transactions. Anne was no expert on illegal activity, but she saw clear evidence that her husband was involved in drug trafficking, prostitution, gambling, extortion, and worse. There was enough evidence in this safe to send him to federal prison for three lifetimes.

Shaking her head, she closed the safe, left the office, and returned to her bedroom. There she practiced the combination to make sure she had it completely memorized.

Then she got into bed and fell fast asleep.

Carl Rizzo got home at three that morning. He was in a mood to have sex with his wife, but when he saw how soundly she was sleeping, and how exhausted she looked, he did not have the heart to disturb her. He could not know that she had been awake into the wee hours, working to betray him, before she went to bed.

So he got into his pajamas and fell asleep by her side.

The next day, from a pay telephone at her tennis club, Anne Rizzo made a call to Joseph Knight's downtown office. In low tones she repeated the combination she had found and was thanked for her efforts.

Then she went home and sat down to wait.

A week and a half later Carl Rizzo's house was burglarized while he and his wife were out at the theater. It was a routine job, apparently done by amateurs, with some silverware and jewelry stolen. The only sign that there was anything unusual about the burglary was that the servants who were home at the time had all been knocked out with blackjacks.

When Carl Rizzo heard about the burglary he immediately checked the safe in his private office. What he saw inside it made his blood run cold.

His cash and negotiable securities had not been touched. Neither had the financial records that testified to the massive tax evasion he had been practicing for the past fifteen years.

But the private papers documenting the fact that he had been holding out on the Chicago crime syndicate through many lucrative years of loan-sharking, gambling, prostitution and drug sales, were missing from the safe. These papers proved that Carl Rizzo was a renegade, disloyal to the mafia to which he owed so much of his stature in the city.

Carl Rizzo knew that the absence of those damning documents represented his death warrant. He immediately tripled security in his house, hiring new bodyguards at high wages. He had himself driven to his downtown office, surrounded by heavily armed men, and made a pretense of conducting business as usual.

Then, without warning, he and Anne left the country.

Carl told his secretaries and associates that he and his wife needed a rest and were going to tour Europe. They would be gone at least three weeks.

What he did not tell anyone was that 90 percent of his assets went with him on the ship bound for Le Havre. These assets, in cash and negotiable securities, would be deposited in a Swiss bank account. Carl Rizzo intended never to return to the United States. He would start a new operation in Europe, where he was unknown. It would be a difficult transition, especially at his age. But he had no choice. This was a matter of survival. The mafia never forgot a grudge. Carl Rizzo would be a dead man if he ever set foot on American soil again.

On the ship Carl breathed a sigh of relief. If the country of his birth was behind him, so were the relentless hoods who would surely have killed him had he not fled.

He began to enjoy his first-class accommodations. He and his beautiful wife were invited to dine at the captain's table. He took Anne dancing in the ship's ballroom, and saw her admired by the first-class passengers in their formal dress. He stood with her on the promenade deck looking at the moonlight over the ocean and talking of their new life together. He was sick of Chicago, he said. It was a provincial city with horrible weather and unsophisticated inhabitants. Europe would be an exciting change for both of them.

Anne smiled and said nothing. She knew there were bodyguards watching her and Carl at this very moment. She had to seem thrilled with Carl's new plans. The last thing she wanted was to give him the slightest hint that she might have been involved in the misfortune that had forced him to flee his native city.

It was a romantic voyage for Carl Rizzo. He made love to Anne every night in his spacious stateroom. Each day he felt more secure as America receded behind the ship's churning wake, and the continent of Europe approached.

The voyage ended on a muggy morning at the port of Le Havre. The ship was escorted into the harbor by French tugboats. Harbor officials came on board to clear the vessel for arrival, and French Customs waited at the pier.

Carl Rizzo was standing at the rail beside his wife, smiling at the bustle of activity all around him. Porters were carrying luggage, ship's officers were hurrying this way and that, passengers were waving to relatives meeting them at the pier.

Suddenly Carl let out a low grunt and clutched his throat as though to gasp for breath. Anne turned to ask him what was the matter. He could not answer, but slumped slowly to the deck, his eyes glazing over as he stared up at her beautiful face.

The ship's doctor was called. He had Carl moved immediately to his examining room. Suspecting a stroke or a heart attack, he attempted emergency resuscitation, without success. Carl Rizzo was dead.

The doctor notified the local health officials, who had the body moved to a French hospital for examination. The French pathologist, unconvinced by the diagnosis of heart failure, soon found the cause of death. There was a tiny puncture mark at the back of Carl Rizzo's neck. The spinal cord had been neatly speared by a sharp object.

The pathologist, an experienced man who had seen more than his share of underworld killings, realized what had happened. Carl Rizzo had been murdered by an expert ice-pick man who had apparently concealed himself in the flow of porters and passengers on deck and stabbed his victim with a sure stroke before melting into the crowd.

Carl Rizzo returned to Chicago in a coffin. His widow accompanied him, carrying in her trunk not only the wardrobe she had intended for her extended European stay, but also the millions of dollars in cash and securities that constituted Carl Rizzo's nest egg.

Carl Rizzo's funeral was held at a downtown funeral home, far from his Glencoe house and close to his South Side roots.

The funeral was conspicuously boycotted by every one of Carl's erstwhile mob friends. Only Anne and the immediate Rizzo family were in attendance to hear the eulogy.

A week later Anne was present as Carl's will was read. Sure enough, nearly all of his assets went to her. She was now a millionairess several times over.

As for Joseph Knight, he pursued his business activities without further interference. His relations with the Chicago crime syndicate were cordial. Not long after Carl Rizzo's death Knight was invited to a reception for local businessmen given at the house of Vincent Monaco, the head of the syndicate. He spent a pleasant evening there, and was taken aside by Monaco to be assured of friendly relations and cooperation in the future.

Neither man alluded to Rizzo, to his recent death or to the burglary that had brought about his undoing. However, Monaco had been informed by his grapevine that Rizzo had tried to shake Knight down not long before the events leading to his misfortune. And the wily mob boss knew that nothing happens by accident.

Word went out that Joseph Knight was a man to be respected, a legitimate businessman who knew how to do a favor, but also how to return a wrong.

And there was another reason why Knight was held in considerable esteem.

On the very day that Carl Rizzo was murdered aboard his ship in the port of Le Havre, his stout bodyguard, Salvatore d'Amato, had been strangled in his home in Chicago.

Though the mob had been directly responsible for what had happened to Carl Rizzo, it had had nothing to do with the death of the burly bodyguard. That had been accomplished by an unknown outsider.

Salvatore's murderer had to have been a man of great force and courage. He had killed d'Amato with his bare hands, disdaining knife and gun.

It was known that Joseph Knight had been mistreated by Salvatore on the night of his first visit to Carl Rizzo. Vincent Monaco drew the obvious conclusion.

Decidedly, Joseph Knight was a man to be respected.

* * *

Three months after her husband's death, Anne Rizzo decided it was safe for her to contact Joseph Knight. There was no one to care about her fidelity to her husband's memory, after all. He had been a mobster, and hardly a pillar of the community.

She called Joseph Knight's office in Chicago. The secretary told her that Knight was out of town, seeing to his interests in the East. But he would return Anne's call when he came back to Chicago two weeks hence. She took Anne's name and thanked her for calling.

Joseph Knight did not return Anne's call.

Anne waited nervously, and then called Joseph Knight's office again.

This time the secretary politely told her that Joseph Knight was unavailable, that he was out of the country, and asked her what her business was. Anne refused to tell her.

A third call, a week and a half later, got the same response.

By now Anne Rizzo knew the secretary was lying.

Knight was at this moment in New York City. He had left explicit instructions to his secretary that under no circumstances was Anne Rizzo to be allowed to see him.

Such was the report of the detectives Anne had hired to track Knight's whereabouts and find out why he had not returned her calls.

She gave the detectives a bonus and ordered them to continue loose surveillance on Joseph Knight. She wanted to know where he was, who he was with, and what he was doing. At all times.

You don't know it yet, Joe, she mused. *But you're going to marry me.*

12

Eve Sinclair, Hollywood's youngest female leading lady—and perhaps the most talented of them all—has scored a triumph with her first film on her own, *The Youngest Heart*, in which she plays a delectable and warm-hearted young woman who marries for love despite the machinations of two willful families.

Not since Lillian Gish has an actress created such a furor of critical praise at so tender an age. No less a critic than Harrell Keaton of the *New York Times* has hailed Miss Sinclair as "an eighteen-year-old genius with the beauty of Carole Lombard and the depth of Bette Davis." We can't remember when an actress has launched a new stage of her career with more excitement than that created by Eve Sinclair in *The Youngest Heart*.

Rumor has it that Eve's stunning performance, combined with undisclosed prospects for future films, has netted her a renegotiated, record-breaking contract with Worldwide Pictures. Small wonder. The child star who made a name for herself at age eight and went on to become a nationwide celebrity through her excellent performances in the popular but ill-fated *Jill and Johnny* series with Tommy Valentine has shown every sign of major star potential for years. Some observers feared that her long-term association with the disgraced Valentine would taint her own career, but she has put all such talk to rest with her brilliant new film.

Will Eve Sinclair win an Oscar nomination for Best Actress this year? No doubt her tender age, and the relatively lightweight quality of *The Youngest Heart* as a film, will deny her that honor. But no one in the business will forget her superb performance—least of all Worldwide Pictures, which has just paid a reported seven figures for the privilege of launching Eve on the next phase of her great career.

Eve Sinclair sat in the office of her attorney, Craig M. Janus, of the prestigious Hollywood legal firm of Janus, Hubbard, and Eason.

She was seated comfortably in one of the large leather armchairs reserved for important visitors. She was dressed in a linen suit of classical beauty, and wore jewelry in white gold designed for her by Sybil Beneyton of Hollywood.

She was looking at Craig Janus, a venerable man in his sixties who had been a partner in his firm for twenty years. Eve herself had retained his services several months ago in anticipation of this day, and had used his firm to iron out the details of her new contract with Worldwide Pictures. Her association with Janus, Hubbard, and Eason was a key step in the new life she was making for herself as a major star.

Eve never once turned her eyes to the other visitors in the room.

One of them was her mother.

The other was her mother's lawyer.

Ethel Forrest—formerly Mrs. Roy Casale, and before that Mrs. Elliot Sonnenbaum—kept smiling at her daughter. She wanted to be on her best behavior today. She had spent a lifetime building Eve's career, and she wanted Eve to remember that.

But Eve never met her mother's eyes. She had arrived on her own and been here waiting when Mrs. Forrest and her attorney arrived. She had not looked away from Craig Janus's face since this meeting began.

"Well," Craig Janus said, "let's get down to cases. As you know, Mrs. Forrest, your daughter Eve has now reached her majority. She is eighteen years old. Under California law she is now entitled to control of all her earnings as an actress. Your stewardship of Eve's affairs as her legal guardian is no longer necessary. It falls to us now to make new arrangements."

There was a silence. Mrs. Forrest's attorney, a slippery and quite intelligent Hollywood lawyer named Lewis Isaacs, gave his client a sidelong look that reminded her to keep silent.

Craig Janus smiled.

"I'd like to thank you both for coming," he said urbanely, looking at his guests.

"Delighted to be here," said Lewis Isaacs. "Mrs. Forrest wants only the best for her daughter. She wishes to cooperate fully in any new arrangement."

Again Mrs. Forrest smiled at Eve. But Eve kept her eyes fixed on her attorney. Though Mrs. Forrest could see that this was a bad sign, she kept her own smile in place.

It was hard for the mother to contain her righteous anger. She cursed the recent changes in the California law that allowed youthful Hollywood performers to take over the reins of their finances at age eighteen. She felt that a child should have its interests protected by the family until at least age twenty-one, and possibly even beyond. A child of eighteen is hardly competent to administer hundreds of thousands of dollars. Only the concern and commitment of blood family can be trusted with such a responsibility.

Mrs. Forrest had handled Eve's money right from the beginning, when Eve signed her first studio contract as a helpless little girl of eight. Mrs. Forrest had stewarded her daughter into stardom, at great cost to herself in time, money, energy, and love. She saw no reason why she should not continue to do so. She and her attorney hoped at this meeting to convince Eve to give her legal authority to continue sharing in her earnings and administering them. Common sense and plain old ethics demanded that Eve not shut her mother out.

And there were additional reasons for the mother's concern.

Mrs. Forrest knew, as all of Hollywood knew, that Eve had just negotiated a contract through Craig Janus with Worldwide Pictures for a salary at least five times greater than any she had ever earned before.

That was a lot of money.

It was money Mrs. Forrest could use, money she needed.

Over the past ten years Eve had taken in over a million dollars as an actress. Her mother had been in charge of that money. Some of it she had spent on Eve's expenses, such as wardrobe, photography, and so on. The greater portion she had invested in the stock market, following the investment advice of her second husband, Roy Casale. What was left she had used to live high on the hog in the Brentwood mansion bought with Eve's earnings, and on travel to Europe, where she had also bought a villa in Sardinia.

Unfortunately, as the Depression deepened, Mrs. Forrest was virtually bankrupted by the loss of the hundreds of thousands of dollars she had put into the Market. It was this disaster, more than anything else, that brought about her divorce from Mr. Casale. Roy had been a lovable but irresponsible fellow, full of loud assurances about investments that were not often as sound as he claimed they were.

And Roy was an incorrigible philanderer. That had been the last straw.

Not that Mrs. Forrest could flatter herself that she was a perfect wife. She had had her own peccadilloes. One of them was a fling with a certain Don Forrest, a Los Angeles real estate man who knew how to make her laugh. It was Mr. Forrest that she married after her breakup with Roy Casale.

Soon after Ethel's marriage to Don, thanks to Eve's upward-climbing career and her series of hit films with Tommy Valentine, there was money to pay the bills with again, and considerable assets left over. These Ethel had invested in some exciting real estate ventures along the California coast on the advice of her third husband.

She had thought she was building a real nest egg for herself—and for Eve, of course. But it turned out that Don played fast and loose with the real estate market. In the last year he had taken a terrible beating with some of Ethel's investments, and she was virtually broke again.

Of course, Ethel herself was partly to blame for the way things had gone. She had spent a lot on herself—for Eve's sake, of course. She felt that, as Eve's mother and representative, she had to live well. There was the Brentwood mansion, which carried a sizable mortgage. There were her clothes, most of which came from the best Hollywood designers (she owed it to herself and Eve to look presentable when publicity stories were done on them both). There was her jewelry, and the two Rolls-Royces she owned, and the villa in Sardinia—none of it quite paid off, if truth be known.

And Ethel did like to gamble. It was a pleasure that excited her and soothed away the strain of her responsibilities as a star's mother. She had spent many an evening with Don at Cloudy's in the Hollywood hills, playing roulette and twenty-one.

To make a long story short, she had done everything a mother can do for her daughter, except put away a lot of savings. Frankly, she had counted on Eve's talent to see her through these hard times to better days. After the Tommy Valentine episode she had been worried. But Eve, true to form, had shown that she was a survivor, and had landed on her feet.

Even Ethel was amazed by Eve's performance in *The Youngest Heart,* the first film of her new career as a leading lady. She had not realized Eve possessed such maturity and depth as an actress. And she had been thrilled by the prospects the new film opened, for herself as well as for Eve. She intended to divorce Don Forrest this spring—he was really not much good for her after all—and perhaps get married again soon. She had met a charming man at the casino last winter, an automobile salesman from Pasadena . . .

But she had been surprised and a little shocked to hear that Eve herself had negotiated her new contract with Worldwide Pictures. Eve had made the deal through Janus, Hubbard, and Eason without telling either her mother or her agent about it. The new contract had been a fait accompli. Mrs. Forrest still did not know its precise terms, for she had not been shown it.

That was a sinister sign.

All the more reason for Mrs. Forrest to be on her best behavior today. If Eve wanted more control over her career now that she was growing up, her mother would not stand in her way. But a daughter must surely appreciate what a mother has done for her, and what she owes in return for a lifetime of loyalty.

So Ethel Forrest was on the edge of her seat as she waited for Craig Janus to speak. Everything depended on what happened today in this office.

Craig Janus cleared his throat.

"Eve is grateful to her mother," he said, "for taking care of her finances up to this point. As for the future, we want to assure Mrs. Forrest that she will always remain the object of her daughter's love and respect."

There was a silence. Mrs. Forrest felt a tremor in her heart. She looked at her lawyer. Lewis Isaacs was staring into space, as though absorbed by some private preoccupation that carried him far from this place.

She made a sound that brought Lewis back to earth. He smiled at Craig Janus and leaned forward in his chair.

"Do I understand," he asked delicately, "that Miss Sinclair wishes a financial association with her mother to be arranged through legal counsel?"

Craig Janus grew cold.

"On the contrary," he said. "There exists no financial association between Miss Sinclair and her mother as of this date. Nor is there any legal arrangement. From a financial point of view Miss Sinclair is free."

"But you can't do that!" Mrs. Forrest suddenly erupted

from her chair. She was a combative woman by nature, if not the most sharing or the most dependable of mothers. "You can't cut me off, Evie! I built you from nothing! Don't you remember how much I gave up for you? The sleepless nights, the struggles over contracts, the getting up at the crack of dawn to get you to the set on time . . . Why, I gave my life for you, Eve. Half of what you are you owe to me. You can't just turn your back on all that. Blood is thicker than water, after all."

No one said a word. Eve still did not look at her mother. Lewis Isaacs was perched on the edge of his chair like a marionette about to topple over. Craig Janus was looking down at his hands.

At last Lewis Isaacs spoke.

"Mr. Janus," he said, "as you know, Mrs. Forrest has invested substantial amounts of her own assets as well as her time and energy in furthering the career of her daughter. It's hard to put a price on devotion like that."

"Indeed," responded Craig Janus coldly.

"I don't know what a court would say about Miss Sinclair's obligation to her mother," Isaacs went on. "But I do know that Miss Sinclair, as an adult, must take responsibility for certain investments made on her behalf that have not paid off as handsomely as we might have expected. These investments were made in good faith, and Mrs. Forrest has suffered considerable distress . . ."

"Lewis," Craig Janus interrupted. "We know perfectly well what Mrs. Forrest has gained from her daughter's career, and what she has lost—on her own initiative. I might mention that the mortgages on the Brentwood house and the Italian villa are entirely Mrs. Forrest's responsibility, as are all debts incurred by her as her daughter's guardian. She has no legal right to claim any compensation from her daughter with regard to any properties or investments. If you feel that an injustice has been done to your client, I invite you here and now to bring suit against Miss Sinclair. We'll let the courts decide who owes whom."

Lewis Isaacs chewed at his lip nervously. He knew quite well that if Eve Sinclair chose to sue her mother for the money she had squandered over the years, Mrs. Forrest would be a big loser. The mother's only course, if she could not bend Eve through emotional appeals, was to get out while the getting was good. She had no one but herself to blame for her spendthrift ways and her rather unsavory adventures.

Craig Janus stood up abruptly.

"If there's nothing else," he said, "let me thank you again for coming, and bid you good day."

He held out a hand. Reluctantly Lewis Isaacs shook it. Then he turned to help his client out of the office.

Ethel Forrest was not so easily moved.

"Eve, you can't do this!" she cried. "I've given my whole life for you. My whole life . . . You owe me!"

Eve said nothing. Craig Janus interposed his body between his client and the visitors and herded them gently toward the office door.

"Thank you for coming," he repeated tactfully. "Thank you, thank you . . ."

Lewis Isaacs whispered in the mother's ear, "We'll talk about this outside, dear. Just calm down, and we'll get downstairs where we can talk . . ."

But Mrs. Forrest knew what was happening. Her whole life was being wrecked by an ungrateful daughter.

"You little bitch," she called over her shoulder. "I'll sue you till you're black and blue for this! You mark my words. You can't cut me off without a cent and get away with it. I'll take this to the highest courts . . ."

The office door closed on her plump body. Her bellowing voice could be heard from the outer office as she harangued her lawyer. It was an ugly sound that died away slowly as Eve sat staring out the window.

When it was gone at last, Eve turned to Craig Janus.

"That's it, then?" she asked. "Am I free?"

"Free as the birds, Miss Sinclair," the attorney smiled. "Your destiny is your own. May I congratulate you on how firmly you've taken over the reins in the past few months? You've shown yourself to be a thorough professional."

Eve did not acknowledge the compliment. She looked back out the window. The expression in her eyes was so cold that the attorney had to look away.

"What about Mother?" she asked.

"She has some rather serious debts," he said. "The house, the villa, the cars . . . And she has no assets anymore, since she's cut off from you. Personally, I think she'll have to sell everything quite soon in order to avoid bankruptcy. Unless she marries a wealthy man, that is, and right away . . ."

Eve looked into his eyes.

"What about the house?" she asked.

He opened a file folder on his desk and looked through the papers inside.

"The mortgage is enormous," he said, "and the interest hasn't been paid for several months. She has very little equity in the place. I should imagine it would be the first thing to go."

Eve stood up. She looked brisk and beautiful in her suit. Her sable coat was slung over her arm.

"Keep your eye on it," she said. "When she puts it on the market, make her an offer. As low as possible, of course. But enough to make her sell. I like that house."

I grew up there, she told herself with a bitter smile.

"All right," the attorney said, making a note on his pad. "I'll see to it. Is there anything else, Miss Sinclair?"

Eve was gazing out the window. The office had a magnificent view of Hollywood, with Wilshire Boulevard close by and the hills in the background.

Goodbye, Mother, she thought. For years she had looked forward to this moment, hoping that when her chance to strike came, her mother would be as financially overextended as possible. Now her dream had come true. Ethel Forrest would not share in her daughter's future fame and wealth. She would spend the rest of her life contemplating the fortune that had got away from her, thanks to Eve.

But already Eve's satisfaction over what she had done to her mother was fading, eclipsed by the dark resolve that always seized her heart when she saw Hollywood stretched out before her. It was a hostile and dangerous world, filled with clever and venal men and women. But it could be dominated by anyone whose will was as strong as her talent.

As of this moment, Eve Sinclair had all her weapons ready. She had survived the trials of her youth. She had used Tommy Valentine to the fullest before dropping him when he became an encumbrance. And now she had got rid of her mother. She was on the threshold of a great career, with the critics and the public at her feet. Her talent was a glittering sword, sharpened by patient years of hard work and experience. It could destroy anything and anyone who stood in her way. She had unfinished business in the world outside that window.

Try to stop me now, she said silently to the sunny hills and the busy city of dreams. *Just try to stop me.*

ON A BLUSTERY DECEMBER NIGHT SIX MONTHS AFTER THE death of Carl Rizzo, Joseph Knight was on his way home to his penthouse apartment on Manhattan's Upper West Side when a slender figure blocked his path.

"Hello, Joe."

At first he did not recognize Anne Rizzo. She did not look like herself. Something had changed her. There was a new intensity to her eyes, an odd wraithlike aspect to her body. Nevertheless he was struck once again by her great beauty, a beauty that only seemed to have increased since he knew her.

"Anne," he said. "It's nice to see you. What brings you here?"

Inside he was already preparing himself for trouble. The

look in her eyes spoke volumes. There was something ghostly, almost witchlike, in her demeanor.

"May I come in?" she asked.

Joseph Knight hesitated only for a second before replying.

"Of course."

He took her upstairs with him. She was silent in the elevator. She did not even look at him.

When they had entered the apartment she stood gazing out the windows at the spectacular view of the Park and midtown. He had bought the place for this view. It made Manhattan seem like a fairyland. One could not see the filth and danger of the streets, or the corruption behind the windows of all those offices and apartments. One saw only the architectural splendor of the metropolis, with its glittering lights and soaring angles. It was like a view of human aspiration purged of all the ugly venality that goes with it. The idol without the feet of clay . . .

"May I help you off with your coat?" he asked.

He touched her shoulders as he took the coat. Something communicated itself from her to him, sudden and imperious as an electric shock. He felt both attracted and repelled by it. This was not the way he remembered her.

His eyes opened wide as the coat came off. She was completely naked underneath it. Her magnificent dancer's body displayed its perfect curves before him. He saw the tender shoulders, the fresh young breasts, the flat stomach and lush hips, the long shapely legs. She had a body that could steal a man's heart.

She turned to look at him. She saw his reaction to her nudity.

"What's the matter?" she asked. "Had you forgotten what I look like with no clothes on? Is your memory so short, Joe?"

Despite the alarm sounding at the back of his mind, he took her in his arms and kissed her. Then he picked her up, a creamy naked doll in his arms, and carried her to his bedroom. He placed her on the bed and stood looking down at her. She was staring up at him through eyes glittering with passion.

He knew he should kick her out of here now, this minute. But the sight of her as she lay gazing up at him in her nakedness was irresistible. He took off his clothes and lay down beside her.

He kissed her. He felt her tongue slip into his mouth and caress him eagerly. His body stirred despite himself, and in an instant his sex had found its way to hers.

Then he was inside her, drawn by a terrible female force that seemed to grasp his sex and take possession of it. Her sexual hunger was amazing. She was very different from the young woman he had seduced in Chicago. That young woman had been innocent, even virginal, despite her marriage. Knight had used his caresses to arouse her to a need she had never known before. And she had responded with great excitement.

But that earlier response had been candid and girlish. The creature in his arms now was a woman through and through, aroused by an enormous passion, giving all of herself and expecting all of him in return.

Physically, Joe was seduced by the transformation. The urgency of her caresses inflamed him, and he found himself straining madly, excited more and more by the feel of her hands in his hair, the soft rubbing of her thighs against his hips, and the terrible hunger inside her that gripped his sex and would not let it go.

At last, when he could stand it no longer, he held her close and let himself come into her. His whole body shuddered. He felt drained. His breath scalded his throat. As she held him he heard her purr softly, deeply, with a great and ominous satisfaction.

They lay for a long time in silence before either spoke. Then she turned on her side and looked at him.

"Why did you leave me?" she asked.

Inwardly Joseph Knight sighed. *I should have known,* he thought to himself.

"I left because I had to leave," he said carefully.

"What does that mean?" she asked, her beautiful breasts stirring as she leaned her head on her hand.

Joe realized now that he had made a serious mistake in letting her into his home. It was obvious she had pursued him here. She had taken great pains to find out his New York address and to be here waiting for him.

With no clothes on under her raincoat.

"I had to move on," he said. "So did you. We both had our lives to live."

He saw her shake her head, an eloquent movement full of complete denial, as though he had said something absurd and childish.

"But I love you," she said.

There was a long pause. She stared into his eyes, looking for the effect of her words on him. At length his silence told her what she had probably feared the most.

Now her look grew cold.

"You think it's that easy?" she asked.

He looked into her eyes.

"Nothing is easy," he said. "It wasn't easy to deal with your husband. He was trying to ruin me. I had no choice but to defend myself. And it wasn't easy to leave you. But I had to do that, too. As I say, we both had our lives to live . . ."

"Joe, we killed him," she said suddenly. "You and I. We killed Carl."

"That's not true."

Again he saw that stubborn little shake of her head.

"Oh, we didn't wield the knife, perhaps," she said. "But we made it happen. I helped you, and you set him up. You set him up so that his own people would destroy him. Do you think you can walk away from that?"

"I have to walk away from it," Joe said, studying her. "Carl got what he deserved. That's the end of the story."

"Is it, Joe?" she asked, raising one of her delicate eyebrows. "Is it?"

"What do you mean?" he asked, sitting up. "What are you saying, Anne? What is it you want?"

"I want you to marry me." The words were spoken in a deceptively small voice, with an enormous conviction behind them. Lying there in the sheets, so beautifully naked, she really looked like a witch now, dangerous and cunning.

Joseph Knight thought carefully. He was accustomed to dealing with men. He knew their strengths and weaknesses like he knew his own. But Anne was a creature of another essence. He had never taken women seriously enough to wonder how their souls worked. Now here was one, aroused, driven by a mysterious force he himself had never felt inside him.

He weighed his words before answering her. He realized that defensive cajoling maneuvers would be pointless. She meant business. She would not take a polite no for an answer.

So Joseph Knight fell back on his old instincts and thought like a businessman. She had the initiative. She had gone to great trouble to get it, and she was going to use it. He had to get it back from her. This was his first rule as a businessman, and as a man. He would follow it now.

"I don't love you, Anne," he said. "I don't want to marry you."

He saw a brief spasm shake her body. Her eyes opened wide. She looked as though she had been stabbed. It was a pitiful sight to behold. His words had taken her by surprise.

But she recovered.

The expression of unspeakable loneliness and abandonment disappeared, eclipsed by the former look of stubborn certainty.

"You killed my husband," she said.

"Your husband got what was coming to him," he corrected. "You're a free woman now, Anne. That's the important thing."

Again she shook her head, impatiently, as though he was deliberately trying to confuse her with childish absurdities when she knew the real, adult truth.

"I gave you my heart," she said, "and you killed my husband. You must do the right thing, Joe. You must marry me. That's why I came here."

Joseph Knight hesitated. He searched for the right words. There were no right words.

"No," he said. "I won't, Anne."

Her look darkened. "I'll turn you in," she said.

He sighed. He did not want to hurt her. But he had to protect himself.

"Turn me in to who? And for what?" he asked. "Your husband was killed by members of a well-known crime syndicate.

I didn't pay them to do it, or ask them to do it. There is no evidence connecting me with them. You can't turn me in, Anne. And even if you could, you'd have to confess your own role in the business. You'd end up in prison."

"I already am in prison," she said.

Joseph Knight had no answer for that.

He stood up and looked down at her. She was so touching in her nudity, but so frightening in her resolve. Her lovely, vulnerable body made an uncanny contrast with the ice-blue eyes burning up at him.

"I never told you I loved you," he said. "I never asked you to marry me. I'm not going to do so now. You can't change that, Anne."

"Oh, yes, I can," she hissed, leaping up at him from the bed.

Before he could stop her she got a grasp of his neck and held him tight. He felt her legs curl violently around him. She scratched at his eyes and cheeks and neck, hitting and clawing. He heard a low groan of rage in her voice. The frail legs clung to him with an inhuman urgency as he struggled to get her off him.

He heard curses, remarkably crude, on her beautiful lips.

"Bastard . . . You dirty bastard . . ."

He felt the sting of her scratches. He grunted in pain. At last he got a grip on her wrists and pulled her off him. He threw her on the bed. She lay on her side, clutching his knees, her grip no longer violent, but despairing. Tears were streaming down her cheeks.

"I love you," she wept. "I gave up everything . . . I love you. You can't leave me now. Oh, my God . . ."

Her hopelessness wrung at Joe's heart. He had never seen or imagined such intense grief. And he was its cause.

But he could not give in to her. She had no place in his life. No woman ever had, and, he believed, no woman ever would. His freedom was at stake. He could not give it up.

He gently dislodged her arms from around his legs, and she lay back on the bed, sobbing uncontrollably. She looked so alone, so forsaken, that he had to avert his eyes.

He saw his clothes lying tumbled on the floor. He put on slacks and a shirt and went to the bathroom mirror to fix his hair, which had been mussed by her passion and her anger. He saw blood on his cheeks from her scratches, and cleaned it off. Then he came back to her.

"Where are you staying?" he asked. "I'll get you a cab."

She was quiet now. Still naked on the bed, she looked up at him. For a long moment she stared at him through eyes like a child's, eyes that could not believe he could abandon her this way. Innocent, tragic eyes.

Then that dark, burning glow he had never seen before tonight came back, and she was looking up at him with an extraordinary hatred.

"I don't need your cab," she said.

"You can't go home that way," he said, gesturing to her nudity.

"I came this way," she replied with an irony that sounded strange on her lips. "I guess I can go the same way."

For a fleeting instant he thought of an infant coming into the world naked and leaving it the same way after a long and complicated lifetime.

He watched her put on her coat.

"Anne, I'm sorry," he said.

"Don't apologize," she said angrily. "It doesn't suit you. Besides . . ." she began, and then caught herself.

She paused at the door, buttoning her raincoat. She looked at him. Now her eyes had found yet another expression. Gone were her pleading, her hurt, and even her anger. In their place was a cold determination.

"You haven't seen the last of me," she said.

Joe felt a tremor in his nerves as she shut the door behind her with a quiet click.

After that night Joseph Knight was on his guard. He took Anne Rizzo at her word. He believed he was not through with her yet.

Though he did not see her at close quarters again, his suspicions seemed well-founded.

During the week after her visit to his apartment, he received several anonymous telephone calls both at home and at the office. The caller hung up immediately, as though it were a wrong number, and yet Joe thought he knew who it was.

He also had the feeling he was being watched, perhaps from a great distance, as he walked from his apartment to the cab stand down the block, or as he walked into his office building in midtown. He wondered whether the feelings were a result of the phone calls or of Anne's terrible despair and hatred the night she had been at his apartment.

He lay in bed at night thinking about Anne. He recalled her nudity—she had been thinner, he recalled now, thinner because of her grief and obsession over him—and her despair. It was a despair that had made him want to enfold her in his arms, until the sight of her hatred had drained him of all tenderness and filled him with loathing.

He had spent long years training himself not to take women seriously, not to be touched by their possessiveness, their need to be protected. But now, despite his precautions, a woman he had used for his own ends wanted to be repaid for her sacrifice, for her love. He could not deny her right to that emotion. Nor could he give in to it.

He lay in bed, naked—he never wore pajamas—and remembered the way she had made love that night. It was as though she was at once trying to devour him and to give herself so completely that nothing would remain of her. Trying to consume both of them.

And something about her macabre combination of passion and gigantic female anger made him feel aroused even now. Making love to her had been like making love to a panther, a tigress.

He tried to put her out of his mind. But it was not easy.

Because of his desire to forget Anne, and the lingering sexual ferment left by the memory of her, Joseph Knight felt the need for a woman.

The next week he made a date with a woman he knew in Mamaroneck. She was the wife of a wealthy member of the Stock Exchange, an aged financier who had married her for her mind, of all things, and almost never touched her sexually.

Joseph Knight had met her at a meeting of investors several years ago and kept up an amicable physical relationship with her ever since. She genuinely liked her husband, enjoyed his money, and was a good companion to him. She got her physical pleasures where she could, tactfully, and her husband was intelligent enough to respect her needs and to leave her alone.

Her name was Yvonne.

She and Joseph Knight saw each other every two weeks or so when he was in New York. Yvonne would drive in to a small Manhattan hotel and register as Mrs. Joseph Knight, and he would meet her; or, as tonight, he would drive out to Mamaroneck, just to get out of the city, and join her at a small apartment she kept there for their trysts.

Joseph Knight spent a relaxed evening with her in the tastefully decorated flat, drinking champagne and having a light supper between lovemaking. To his surprise he found that his always-impressive physical prowess as a lover was even greater than usual. Yvonne complimented him on it.

"What's got into you, Joe? You're like a stallion tonight. I'm going to be sore in the morning."

"Just those eyes of yours," he joked. But behind her eyes he saw those of Anne Rizzo, passionate and dangerous.

At 1 A.M. he left the flat and began the long drive back to Manhattan.

Halfway to the city he noticed a car following him.

It came at high speed, its lights glaring in his rearview mirror. He wondered why he had not noticed it before.

The car came closer, tailgating him. He could hear the roar of its engine behind him.

Cursing under his breath, he stuck a hand out the window to wave the other driver on.

His gesture was ignored. The car came up close to his rear bumper, again and again. Its engine snarled angrily. He could not see the driver's face.

Then all at once the other car changed lanes and darted out beside him. Glancing to his left he saw who the driver was.

It was Anne Rizzo.

Before he could completely take in the mad expression in her eyes, she had swerved to the right and rammed him hard, her fender striking directly at the driver's door, inches from his ribs.

He slammed on the brakes. She did so as well, and fell behind. But she kept up her pursuit. Her engine roared again and again as she pumped the accelerator.

With a sinking feeling Joseph Knight realized that Anne must have followed him all the way out here to his tryst with Yvonne. He cursed himself for not having kept a better watch to make sure he wasn't followed. It was too late for that now.

He looked at the speedometer. He had inched up over sixty. She was right behind him, the howl of her engine seeming to echo the wild look in her eyes. He looked in his rearview mirror. Her face was not visible now, but her blond hair was like a halo of fire.

Once again her car came closer to his bumper, dangerously close.

Somehow the idea that she had followed him, that she was pursuing him so recklessly, made Joseph Knight see red. He had never had to deal with the fury of a woman scorned before, and he disliked the feeling. She had actually tried to kill him just now. And the tragic determination of her pursuit maddened him.

He had spent his whole adult life leaving women behind him. Here was one who refused to be left. She would gladly die if she could take him with her. That was obvious in the way she was driving.

Before he could follow this thought any further she overtook him again. He saw her face, truly insane this time, glaring at him through the windows of the two cars.

In that split second it occurred to him that it was jealousy that was flaming in her eyes. She knew he had been with a woman tonight, and she intended to punish him. Her plan to get him back was eclipsed by the rage possessing her. She wanted only to hurt him.

Infuriated, he pushed the accelerator, hard. He would increase his speed to defeat her. He never doubted for an instant that he could outmaneuver her behind the wheel. No woman was a match for him at handling a car. He would leave her in the dust.

At that instant something flashed across his field of vision, pulling his eyes from the rearview mirror back to the road.

It was a deer. It had wandered out onto the deserted highway in the silence of the night, and now stood stock still, terrified by the headlights approaching it.

Joseph Knight had only a split second in which to react. He jerked the wheel to the right and drove the car at seventy miles an hour onto the pebbled shoulder of the highway.

It was difficult to control the heavy sedan at this high speed on such a surface. The wheels began to skid. Joseph Knight had to fling the steering wheel this way and that to avoid hurtling off the shoulder into the deep ditch that ran alongside the highway.

"Damn . . ."

Clenching his teeth, he managed to get the car back onto the pavement, the wheels screeching.

He was beginning to sigh his relief when the sound of a crash behind him brought him up short.

He looked through the rearview mirror. Anne's car had gone off the road, hurtled into the ditch and turned over.

He braked hard and slowed his sedan to a crawl. He gazed through his rearview mirror at the overturned car a hundred yards behind him. His hands clenched the wheel in consternation.

As he watched, an enormous explosion erupted from the overturned car. The gas tank had ignited. Flames shot skyward in the empty night.

Now he realized what had happened. Anne must have followed him when he swerved to avoid the frightened deer. But she had lacked his driving skill, and was unable to handle her car when it skidded on the gravel shoulder. She had driven straight into the deep ditch and turned over at high speed.

Anne was dead. One glance at the flames feeding on the crumpled wreck left no doubt of that.

He continued to crawl forward at ten miles an hour, looking in the rearview mirror and pondering his situation. He noticed to his surprise that his hands were trembling on the wheel. He looked up and down the highway. There was not a car in sight. None but his own, and Anne's.

Joseph Knight felt something collapse deep within him. He had not wanted this to happen. Yet he felt responsible for it, in more ways than one.

He had caused Anne to follow him out here into the night-darkened suburbs. It was because he had made her love him that she had pursued him here to New York. It was only because she had given him her heart that she had helped him to destroy her husband.

He had underestimated her. He had tried to use her and forget her, and she had not allowed him to.

Had he slowed down just now, as she was pursuing him, and tried to talk to her, she would still be alive. But her vengeful pursuit had made him see red, and he had increased his speed, challenging her to keep up with him. At that instant the terrified deer had forced him into a maneuver that Anne could not execute.

And now Anne was dead.

A year ago, before she ever met him, she was safe, if unhappy, with Carl Rizzo. Now she was dead. Because of Joseph Knight.

He drove on slowly, staring back at the flaming wreck. In another few minutes, he knew, the police would be here.

They would find her ruined body and her death, and they would wonder why. Perhaps, familiar with this area, they would assume a deer crossing the road had caused the accident.

But they would never know the real reason.

And they would not find Joe Knight.

Slowly he began to pick up speed, twenty miles per hour, then thirty. He dared not turn around and go back to examine her car more closely. He could not afford to be seen, and he did not want to see what was inside that wreck.

So he drove away. Curiously, the flaming wreck did not seem to get smaller as he increased his distance, but to grow larger, and to loom in the rearview mirror like something waiting ahead of him, something coming closer, rather than a thing he could leave behind.

The flames were the passion of Anne Rizzo, a passion that refused to wither even in death. But she was dying alone with her love and her agony as he drove away from her.

Cursing, Joseph Knight pressed the accelerator.

He had never felt more like a coward in his life.

 **14**

LIFE WITH QUENTIN FLOWERS WAS NOT WHAT KATE HAD been led to expect.

Their honeymoon consisted of two days in a cheap motel in Yosemite. Then they spent an exhausting day driving through the overheated California valleys to San Diego.

The job in San Diego Quentin had talked about with such high hopes turned out to be a low-paying clerk's position at a barely solvent hardware and notions store owned by an uncle who himself hardly seemed a great success in life.

The man, whose name was Eden "Dink" Bellamy, treated Quentin with amused contempt, as though Quentin was a long-awaited bad penny that had finally turned up. Eden made good on his promise to give Quentin a job, but with a knowing shrug that clearly implied he did not expect Quentin to be around for long.

Moreover, Eden seemed very surprised that Quentin was married. "I didn't know you had it in you, boy," he joked with a little sidelong wink at Kate's beauty. He found it amusing and more than a little incredible that Quentin had convinced any girl at all to marry him, much less a girl who seemed quite clean and intelligent, like Kate.

But if Eden treated Quentin as though he obviously did not take him seriously, he took a genuine liking to Kate. He made her comfortable when she visited the store, invited her and Quentin to dinner—his wife Miriam hit it off well with Kate—and talked to her with genuine respect. He admired her, but was puzzled by the incredible fact that she could have hooked up with a boy like Quentin.

Perhaps it was because of this display on the part of Eden that Quentin soon forbade Kate to go anywhere near the store or to have anything to do with Eden or his wife. Work was work, Quentin told Kate. His home life with her was to be kept rigorously separate.

Home life turned out to be a cheap apartment near the waterfront, an area chiefly occupied by poor working people and a scattering of street hustlers and others who were down on their luck. Kate soon realized as she explored the city that Quentin had settled in a needlessly run-down neighborhood. He could have picked a much nicer place. But when she broached the subject he told her with surprising violence to shut up. He said he knew well enough where he and his wife ought to live.

Soon after their arrival Quentin went to a downtown clothing store and brought home two natty suits of clothes, one a handsome gray and the other a dark blue. Both were rather flashy in their cut. They reminded Kate uncomfortably of her stepfather, Ray, who used to put on his gaudy suits and wing-tip shoes, his loud ties and tie tacks, when he went out on "business."

Kate wondered what Quentin planned to do with those two suits. They did not seem appropriate to his modest job at the store. But she did not ask, for his demeanor made it obvious he did not wish to be cross-examined by her.

There was not much money left over after Quentin had bought the two suits. He and Kate had to live cheaply in their little efficiency apartment. Kate rattled around the place alone while Quentin was gone all day.

One day, dying of boredom, she decided to surprise him

at the store with a lunch she had made at home. When she got there Eden was alone in the store. He told her somewhat pityingly that Quentin was not there and that it was up to her if she wanted to ask her husband any questions about it. Kate could not fail to understand from this that Quentin had not been going to the store for some time.

That night she dared to ask Quentin about it.

"Why haven't you been working?" she asked.

Quentin grabbed Kate by her shoulders and shook her hard.

"Didn't I tell you never to go over there?" he said. "Listen, Kate, and listen good. What I do when I go out of this place is my business, not yours. I'm the one who brings home the bacon. Your job is to keep house for me—and not to ask questions. Have you got that?"

Kate accepted his chastisement. She was young, and inexperienced about men. She hopefully assumed that Quentin was sensitive about his lack of immediate financial prospects and was doing everything in his power to improve their lot. This, she hoped, was why he had taken time off from work at the store—to look for something better.

Quentin kept Kate off balance in more ways than one during those first months. His moods were unpredictable when he came home at night. He could be silent and preoccupied, or unexpectedly lively and full of fun, or smoldering with an incomprehensible anger. Sometimes he could be surprisingly tender, bringing her home a rose or a little gift. Once he took her out to dinner, presenting her with a new dress for the occasion. He could be quite romantic when he wanted to.

But no matter what his mood, when evening reached its end and it was time for bed he took Kate in his arms and made love to her. At these moments his passion was undeniable, and his touch, grown more expert in finding her pleasure points since their marriage, raised her to heights of excitement that left her limp and almost drugged when it was over.

When she wandered around the dingy little apartment alone during the day and felt herself giving in to reproach against her husband for the life she was leading, she could not help looking forward to the caresses that would bring a coda to her day and send her into pleasant sleep at night. She could forgive Quentin a lot, and hide her own growing despair from herself, because of the power of his love-making.

Curiously, though Quentin played her body like a violin and could drive her almost crazy with excitement when he wanted to, she often felt as though she were watching from outside herself as she responded in hot spasms to his touch. There seemed something impersonal about this clamor of the flesh, something from which she felt herself separated as though by an invisible barrier.

She wondered if Quentin noticed this. At times she thought he did not. At other times she felt an impalpable tension in his caresses, a sort of frustration. Sometimes he would withdraw from her with a sigh after lovemaking and curl up on himself on his side of the bed. She felt his distance, and suffered from it. She feared she was inadequate as a lover, and worried about her own femininity.

She did not dare to face the thought that perhaps she had been too hasty in getting married. As she sat around the little apartment with nothing to do, she sometimes suspected that she was no closer to her own self or to her destiny now than before, and that she felt every bit as exiled here in Quentin's world as she had been back home with her mother.

But she banished the thought. This was a life she had chosen for herself. Life with Mother and Ray had been something thrust on her, something she had had to escape. And if things were not ideal between her and Quentin, one could hardly expect perfect understanding at the beginning of a marriage. People need time to get used to each other. Perhaps the mysterious destiny she had so long sensed within herself, haunting her life like a private shadow, was merely an illusion of youth, a thing she would get over when she learned how to cope with real life.

Things went on this way for two months, then four, then six. Kate was growing increasingly restless. Her young mind required stimulation, just as her body required more activity than her pacing of the apartment could provide.

She wished she had some new clothes, and places to wear them. She wished her life had some purpose.

Quentin sensed her distress and tried to reassure her that things would not always be this way.

"Don't worry, babe," he said. "I'm working on something big. Very big. That's why it has to be a secret. When it comes off you'll be the best-dressed woman in California. Not even those Hollywood babes will have a thing on you."

But time went by, and the "something big" did not come. Despite her best efforts to be understanding of Quentin's predicament in these hard times, Kate felt her patience wearing thin. Being a prisoner, she discovered, did not suit her. She felt she was going to explode if something didn't change.

Then, from an unexpected direction, came her deliverance.

One day there was a knock at the door when she was sitting by the window distractedly reading a magazine.

She opened the door to find a fat, angry man staring at her, a master key in his hand.

"Is your husband here?" he asked.

Kate shook her head. "He's out . . . working," she said.

A smirk lit his face.

"Do you know who I am?" he asked.

"I—no," Kate said, stepping back a pace.

"I own this building," he said. "And I don't make a living by giving people free housing. You haven't paid your rent in three months. Your husband keeps telling me it's coming, but he doesn't pay. I'm sorry to bother you with something that's your husband's responsibility, miss. But if you don't pay up this month I'm going to have the sheriff evict you. That's it."

Kate was taken aback.

"I'm sorry," she said. "I didn't know."

"Well, you know now," the landlord said. "Believe me, miss, I mean business. This is your last warning. You tell that husband of yours he has three days to pay what he owes. After that, out you go."

"I'm awfully sorry," Kate said. "I think he just forgot. Here, I think I have some money for you."

She went to the dresser and found the little money she had managed to save from her days with Ewell Stimson. She had been saving it for just such a rainy day as this.

It was enough to pay a month and a half's rent. The landlord seemed mollified. She assured him she would see that the rent was paid and begged him not to approach her husband.

Then she sat down to think. Despite her embarrassment at the landlord's visit and her increasing suspicions of Quentin, an exciting idea was taking shape in her mind, banishing her worries.

She would get a job. That way she could contribute to the rent, and at the same time get out of the apartment and do something productive.

She did not tell Quentin of her plan, perhaps because she wanted to surprise him, or perhaps because she feared his disapproval—she was not sure which.

It was surprisingly easy. Kate presented herself at a local restaurant that was particularly busy. She told the manager she was an experienced waitress—which was in part true— and within two days he called her to fill in for one of the other girls. She did so well that at week's end he hired her permanently.

Kate was a skilled waitress, and the customers liked her. She genuinely enjoyed her work, and it showed. Needless to say, the sight of her beautiful body stirring under her crisp black-and-white uniform made its impression on the male clientele, who were mostly businessmen enjoying corporate lunches.

She also discovered a new talent in herself. This was a real restaurant, not a diner, and the customers expected to be treated with polished hospitality. Kate found she could sense what a customer wanted within the first two seconds of greeting him. And she adjusted her manner, her smiles, her humor accordingly. For each tableful of customers she put on a special little performance intended to charm them and make them feel at home. The results were immediate. She became a great favorite among the customers, and received consistently higher tips than even the most experienced of the waitresses.

Her boss appreciated her contribution to his business. He gave Kate a raise in salary after her first month.

She used her first paychecks to pay off the landlord, who now seemed satisfied and promised not to bother her husband about the rent. She felt proud and happy. She had a place to go every day, people to relate to, a job she was good at—and she was making money. She was contributing to her household, and making things easier for Quentin.

One day she would tell him about her job. She would find a way to inform him delicately, so that he would not feel offended by her independent initiative on his own behalf.

But before she could break the news to him, he found her out.

She came home from work one afternoon to find Quentin waiting for her. He was dressed in one of his fancy suits and looked as though he had interrupted something important to come home in the middle of the day. She smiled as she closed the door.

Without a word he hit her hard across the face with his open hand. She fell back on the bed. She lay gazing up at him, touching her burning cheek, amazed at what had happened.

"I went to see the landlord today," he said. "I wanted to pay him some money I owed him. He told me my *wife* had taken care of it already."

Too late she realized that this slight to his manhood was even worse than what she had tried to avoid.

"Where'd you get the money?" he asked.

"I—had it," she lied. "In my suitcase."

"Liar," he said, hitting her again. "I know what's in your suitcase, and I know what isn't there. You'd better come clean, pussy, and quick, or I'll beat you into the ground."

Kate stared at him, still pondering the fact that for the first time in their marriage he had struck her.

"I got a job," she said.

She told him about her job at the restaurant. She explained that the landlord had complained about the rent, and that she had tried to help out.

Quentin's face turned red, then pale, then red again as she spoke. He paced back and forth in front of her like an angry panther.

"Listen," he said when she had finished. "And listen good. Your job is to stay here and keep house for me, and to be here when I come home. The rent is my business, not yours. I don't know what put these crazy ideas into your head, but you'd better forget them, and fast, if you want to keep living."

He came to a stop before her and raised his hand again to hit her.

"Goddamned women," he shouted. "They look for any way they can find to cut your balls off. I thought you were different, Kate. I see I was wrong."

His hand was poised to hit her. But he looked down and saw the red welt on her cheek from his first blow. A kaleidoscope of expressions flashed through his gray eyes, including regret, anger, and a deep suspicion she had never seen there before.

Then, without warning, he suddenly softened.

"All right," he said. "Okay. You did what you thought you had to do. It was my fault, babe. Don't blame yourself." There was something curiously abstract in his words, as though he were articulating an argument to himself rather than speaking to her. He sounded deliberate and measured, almost calculating.

Then he smiled.

"Anyway," he said, sitting down and lighting a cigarette, "the hard times are all behind us now. I have a job for you. Something a lot more important than pushing plates in a chophouse. You're going to do something big, babe. And I got it for you."

Kate sat up on the bed. "What is it, Quentin?" she asked.

He puffed at his cigarette, studying her.

"Can you keep a secret?" he asked. "This is sensitive work. It has to be strictly on the QT. Understand? This is no job for a blabby amateur. It took me a long time to set it up, believe me."

"I can keep a secret, Quentin," Kate said eagerly, looking up at him. "Please, tell me what it is. What do you want me to do?"

She had felt her marriage growing weaker these past weeks as her guilt about her job and her worry about Quentin increased. Now she saw a chance to put it all back together.

"All right," Quentin said, putting out his cigarette. "There's a fellow I want you to meet . . ."

15

THE YOUNG MAN'S NAME WAS CHRISTOPHER HETTINGER. He came from one of the wealthiest families in the city. His father, Judd Hettinger, had built his small five-and-dime business into the most prestigious department store in the metropolitan area. Hettinger's was a San Diego institution, with an enormous ten-story main store downtown and two branches in nearby cities.

Christopher was his father's only son and heir. He was twenty-three years old and had graduated from Stanford. Now he was being groomed by his father to take over the business. He worked at the central store here in San Diego as assistant manager of one of the clothing departments.

That was all Quentin would tell Kate.

"Your job is to get friendly with this kid," he said. "He's lonely since he got back from college. He needs a friend. You're going to be that friend. I'll handle the rest. I may have more instructions for you later. For the moment, keep that waitress job of yours as a cover. It fits right in with my plans. It's best that you not know more."

Kate gave him a long look.

"Quentin, I don't like the sound of this," she said.

Before she could say anything more he seized her by both arms and shook her hard. "Your job isn't to like," he said dangerously. "I've been planning this thing for months. From now on you do exactly as you're told. Is that understood?"

She nodded obediently. He looked at her for another long moment, his eyes full of suspicion.

Then he released her.

"Besides," he laughed, "do you think I'd ask you to do something wrong? Never, babe. This is just a question of business. And don't think I want you to get *too* friendly with this guy. I'm the jealous type, remember. No: just be his friend. Make him like you, make him trust you. And let me handle the rest."

Kate looked into her husband's eyes. She could see that he was hiding something from her. She did not like what she was getting into.

But she had no choice. Her marriage to Quentin was all she had in the world, and it was at stake. She would not know where to start if she lost Quentin.

So she resolved to do what he asked, but to make sure he did nothing wrong. She would see to that part of it herself.

"All right," she said.

"That's my girl." Quentin was visibly pleased. He bent to kiss her. His arms encircled her and pulled her to him. She felt his soft kiss on her lips, quickly growing more intimate as he lay down beside her on the bed.

Soon the rhythm of her passion made her forget everything but him.

Kate followed her instructions.

On a warm evening in April she crossed paths with Christopher Hettinger. She had learned his route home from his work and had planned her approach with Quentin. She dropped her bag of groceries as the young man was walking by her outside a grocery store.

"Here, let me help you," he said, bending to scoop up the fallen apples and cans and a loaf of bread.

She had only seen him in photographs and from a distance with Quentin. Up close she saw how innocent he was. He was tall, but soft. He had sandy hair not unlike her own in color, and blue eyes. There was a sweet, boyish air about him that made it obvious he could not hurt a fly.

"I'm so clumsy," she said. "I don't know what's the matter with me. I've been dropping things all day."

"Can I carry this for you?" he asked, holding the bag. "I'd be happy to walk you home."

"No, thanks," Kate said. "You're very kind. Thank you very much."

Despite her refusal of his offer, she met his eyes with a smile in which she put all the welcome she could. She saw him respond. She knew, as she walked away down the block with her groceries, that he would not forget her.

A week later she arranged to cross his path again.

This time he was on his lunch hour. He usually spent it alone, away from his father's business. He was walking through a local park on his way to a café when she passed alongside him.

They both stopped in their tracks.

"Oh—it's you," Kate said.

"It's you," he repeated.

There was a moment's embarrassed silence, after which they both laughed.

"Well," he said, obviously mustering his courage to talk to her. "How have you been?"

"Oh, fine," she said. "I haven't dropped anything since the last time I saw you."

"That's good," he said. "Dropping things can get expensive."

"Yes."

Again there was a silence. She knew now that he had

been thinking about her this past week. It was written in his eyes.

"Listen," he said. "It must be fate that we crossed paths twice. Why don't you have lunch with me?"

"Well, I . . ." she said, looking away. "I don't know . . ."

His courage flagged as he saw her hesitate. Then he brightened.

"I know," he said. "You can't accept an invitation from a total stranger. Allow me to introduce myself. Chris Hettinger." He extended a hand.

Reluctantly Kate took his hand. It was warm and gentle.

"Kate," she said. "Kate Flowers." She used her real name, in accordance with Quentin's instructions. But she wore no wedding ring. Her orders were to make the young man think she was single.

"What a lovely name," he said. "Do people call you Katie?"

She shook her head.

"Oh, well," he said. "Anyway, now we know each other. You can accept a lunch invitation from a friend, can't you?"

"Well, I shouldn't . . ." Kate said. Then, seeing his stricken look, she smiled. "But I guess it's all right."

He took her to a small restaurant in the center of town, a place frequented by ladies on shopping outings. Kate had the feeling he was not known there. He looked embarrassed, but thrilled by the adventure of being alone with her.

He asked her about herself. She told him she had come from Stockton, was a high-school graduate, and was working as a waitress here in the city while she waited to find a better job. She told him a made-up story about her family, claiming she had a father and mother she loved very much and explaining that she had left her home town because of the hard times. By omission she made sure he believed she was not married.

It was hard to lie at first. But then Kate found herself thinking about her real father as she expressed affection for her family. Her feelings for him made her lie seem genuine, and Christopher Hettinger was clearly impressed by her sincerity.

This opened him up. He told her about himself, about his family, his education. He told her about the two older sisters he disliked, about the mother he felt close to, and his dictatorial, remote father. He described his four years at Stanford as a miserable experience, adding that he had gone there only because his father was a Stanford alumnus. He was eloquent in describing how much he hated being in his father's business, and chafed to get out from under Judd Hettinger's wing. He wanted a career of his own. But so far he had not been able to muster the courage to tell his father off.

And he told her about his girlfriend.

"Her name is Jane," he said. "Jane Garretson."

He pulled out his wallet and showed Kate a picture of a young woman with dark hair. She seemed neither attractive nor unattractive, though it was possible the picture did not do her justice. There was something faintly rigid about her expression, though she had pretty eyes. Chris looked at the photograph with reverence.

"She's a great girl," he said. "We've been going together, sort of secretly, for several years."

He confided to Kate that his parents did not approve of the girl because her own family was poor. But he was informally engaged to her and determined to marry her. He had kept up his relationship with her throughout his years at Stanford, writing her frequent letters and seeing her whenever he was home. His rebellion against his father seemed wrapped up in his commitment to this girl.

Somehow Kate got the impression that both the boy and the young woman were virgins and were saving themselves for each other. She could not be sure of this, but her intuition was very strong.

Chris spoke of his father with a combination of dread and contempt. To judge by the boy's report, the father was an insensitive, money-grubbing robber baron who cared for nothing but his business and his reputation in the community. He had apparently picked out a wealthy local girl for his son, and would not even hear him speak the name of his beloved Jane without flying into a rage. The boy could not bear his father's interference in his love life. But he did not yet dare to brave his father's wrath by going ahead and marrying Jane. He seemed to be gathering his courage for a confrontation that was yet to come.

For her part Jane Garretson was a very old-fashioned and upright girl. She was not ashamed of her impoverished family, and expected to be courted for love rather than money. She respected herself and did not like hiding behind corners. She wanted Chris to openly propose to her. She would not wait forever.

And she demanded fidelity. It was clear she wanted Chris and took their relationship as seriously as if it were a true engagement, even now. As a matter of fact the young man had spent a lot of money on a secret engagement ring he had given her. Engraved inside the band was a wedding date. He had sworn to adhere to it.

Kate was astonished to hear so much about Christopher Hettinger's conflict-ridden young life during one brief lunch. He had bared his soul to her with a candor that both touched her and put her ill at ease. She was not used to presenting herself to someone under false pretenses. The manipulative role she was playing made her uncomfortable, particularly since she was succeeding so quickly in getting into the boy's confidence.

Perhaps he saw her discomfort, for he laughed.

"But here I am telling a total stranger all my innermost secrets," he said. "Forgive me. I didn't mean to burden you."

"Not at all," Kate laughed. "You can tell me whatever you want. After all, we know each other now, don't we? We're friends."

The boy's face lit up.

"Friends, yes," he said.

At the end of their lunch he said, "Well, goodbye, Miss Flowers. I have to get back to work. They'll kill me if I'm late."

"You can call me Kate if you like," she said, uncomfortable with the falsity of being called "Miss."

He shook her hand, smiling.

"Kate," he said. As he took his leave he looked as though a great weight had been lifted from his shoulders.

Ironically, Kate felt as though an equal weight had suddenly been thrust upon her. And she was not sure she liked it.

Kate saw Chris Hettinger again. She met him for walks in the business district near his father's store, and they sat on a bench in Balboa Park and fed the pigeons together. She let him call her at the restaurant where she worked, telling him to "just ask for Kate." He invited her to lunch again. Their friendship quickly deepened.

Chris unburdened himself to Kate more and more. He told her he felt caught between his fiancée on one hand and his family on the other. He had no one to trust with his feelings except Kate herself. He could not talk to his mother, who was too much in awe of her husband to take any but a spectator's role in the family conflict. His sisters were spoiled, selfish creatures who had never been close to him and who were both married now and absorbed in their own families. He had no male friends left over from high school, and his only college friend, a trusted roommate, was far away now, in Massachusetts.

Kate was all he had.

She took advantage of this sudden closeness. She encouraged Chris about his fiancée, telling him to stick to his guns, telling him his life was his own and that he must stand up to his father come what may.

Of course, her role as confidante was only a subterfuge, blueprinted by Quentin. But she found more of herself engaged in her relationship with Chris than she had planned. It was with real sincerity that she urged him to find his own life and not to let others use him for their own selfish ends.

Saying this, it suddenly occurred to her that she might as well have been talking to herself. She identified with Chris's sense of entrapment and with his youthful yearning. She wanted to urge him with every fiber of her being to choose love over expediency and to find real happiness for himself, at whatever the cost.

This insight increased her discomfort at what she was doing, for all her advice was being given under false pretenses. Yet the sincerity she expressed from behind her mask made her feel closer than ever to Chris. And she liked the feeling.

Meanwhile she had begun to suspect, from what Chris had told her about Jane Garretson, that Jane was not as forthright as she seemed, and was using Chris for her own ends. Kate was becoming suspicious of the poor but demanding girl who seemed so rigid and possessive about Chris. Perhaps Jane might not make him a good wife after all.

Kate could not help feeling a secret pang of jealousy over the unseen girl to whom Chris had pledged his heart. And this unbidden emotion made her unsure of her own instincts. Were her suspicions about Jane merely a result of her own budding affection for Chris?

She did not know. She knew only that the closer she grew to this vulnerable young man, the more distressed she was by her own falseness toward him.

And perhaps her falseness toward herself, as well. Her advice to Chris that he follow his heart brought her a profound sense of unease. Deep inside her there stirred the suspicion that what joined her to Quentin was not really love, but was merely Quentin's self-interest combined with the sexual spell he had cast over her. She did not like to confront this suspicion, but every time she looked into Chris's candid, trusting eyes it came back to haunt her.

Perhaps in order to flee these feelings, she complained to Quentin about her task.

"I'm getting nervous about this," she said. "How much longer does this have to go on? I feel funny. I don't know where I stand. I wish I knew where it was all leading . . ."

"You're doing fine," Quentin said. "Just let things take their course. It's best that you not know more. Believe me, Kate, you're just a contingency plan, you're on the sidelines of the real action. But you're doing a bang-up job."

Perhaps to mollify Kate, he asked her to get a simple piece of information out of the boy about his father's company. She did so—a routine figure about the company's dividends that was, in fact, public knowledge—and was calmed for a while. She tried to believe what Quentin said, that she was not part of the real action.

But her heart told her differently.

Meanwhile she and Chris Hettinger became more intimate. The process moved quickly, as though on an unseen timetable of its own. Kate hardly had to help it along. Each lunch with Chris, each walk, each conversation, cemented their friendship. The boy depended on her more and more. And, despite herself, she was coming to depend on him, too, for something she had never had before in her young life—real friendship.

Chris's innocence seemed to reach out to a vulnerability deep inside Kate that had long been buried, first by her miserable life with her mother and Ray, and then by her strange and troubling existence with Quentin. The closer she became to Chris the more she doubted her own life.

She saw more clearly how important sex was to her marriage, and wondered if there was anything more substantial binding her to Quentin. She realized that Chris had a different sort of thing to offer a woman. He offered his heart, his trust, his sincerity. These were things that Quentin did not seem to possess. Talking about Chris's future with Jane made Kate feel more and more alone, because in opening this door for himself Chris seemed to be closing it for Kate.

Kate now found herself becoming consciously jealous of Jane, whom she had never seen. She began to find herself playing the devil's advocate in her own mind, arguing that Jane was not in fact good enough for Chris, and that Chris would see this in time.

She even began to have daydreams in which somehow she herself was free, and Chris married her. How different her life would be then!

She had seductive, tormenting fantasies about sex with him. She was more than ever convinced he was a virgin. His purity sang in his every gesture. She wondered what it would be like if the clock were turned back and she herself were still a virgin. If her first time was with Chris, instead of with Quentin. Perhaps in Chris's arms she would never have known the amazing sensual heat Quentin had stirred in her. But might she have experienced something more delicate, more precious?

These thoughts alarmed her more than ever. And once again she complained to Quentin.

"I don't like it," she said. "He trusts me too much. He's trying to get too close to me. I want it to end."

But Quentin seemed delighted.

"The closer the better," he said. "Believe me, you're really helping the kid. Go ahead and encourage him. That fits right into my plans. And don't worry. Nothing you do will cause any harm."

And he kissed her, hard. The warm feel of his embrace, and the taste of his lips on hers, eased the distress inside her while silencing her scruples, at least for the moment.

April had given way to May, and May to June.

Chris Hettinger invited Kate to have a special picnic with him one Saturday, in a secret place he had known since his boyhood.

"It's a meadow with some oak trees, out in the pastures," he told her. "Nobody knows about it except me. I'm sure you'll like it."

She packed a picnic lunch under the watchful eye of Quentin.

"Be good," Quentin told her. "I have to be out of town today and tonight. I won't see you until late. Have a good time."

She met Chris in town and he drove her out into the farm and orchard country. He parked on a dirt lane between two pastures and they walked to the place he had told her about.

It was truly magnificent. The meadow overlooked a tranquil valley, with pastures dotted by sleepy cows. There was a summery freshness in the air. The grass was soft under her bare feet. The breeze caressed her cheeks almost lovingly.

"It's beautiful," she said as Chris spread the blanket out on the grass. "I haven't seen a place like this in as long as I can remember. Do you bring Jane here?"

"I haven't yet," he said. "I used to come here to think, when I was little. I sort of kept it to myself." He smiled. "You're the first person I've shared it with," he added.

They sat for a long time in silence. Kate lay on her back and watched the tree limbs sway in the gentle breeze above her head. Chris lay down beside her.

"I used to think the clouds were speaking to me," he said. "I thought they were telling a story."

She smiled.

"I used to think the trees were talking to the wind when they swayed," she said. "I always thought the whisper of the leaves was a kind of language. The groan of the branches, too. Some trees were sadder than others . . ."

"What about this one?" he asked, pointing to the large oak.

She smiled. "This one is happy. It's happy because we're here to see it."

"Maybe it's happy because we're together," Chris said. He turned on his side and looked at her. She smiled.

He looked troubled.

"What's the matter?" Kate asked.

"Time is running out," he said. "Soon I'm going to take your advice and get officially engaged. When that happens, it won't really be right for me to have a friend like you. I don't know what I'm going to do without you."

There was an anxious look in his blue eyes that made Kate feel a strange sad longing. She wished she had met him a long time ago.

"We're together now, aren't we?" she said. "That's something, isn't it?"

He nodded.

"But I don't want that to end," he said. "I can't imagine life without you, Kate. It sounds crazy, since I haven't known you that long, but it's true. I'd rather cut off my right arm than live without you. You make me happy in a way I've never been before. I don't want to lose that."

"You don't have to lose it," she said. "We can be friends forever."

She could see by the look in his eyes that she had missed his point. But she herself did not want to hear what he was trying to say.

So instead, she reached out and touched his cheek.

He grasped her hand in his.

"When I look at you," he said, "it makes me feel as though an open door was right in front of me. A door I can't walk through. All my steps are taking me away from it. But my real self, the person I want to be, is behind that door. And if I don't go through it, I'm wasting everything."

She said nothing.

"It makes me dizzy," he said with a nervous little laugh.

She smiled. "Well, my friends always called me a dizzy dame," she said.

There was a brief, scalded sound in his throat. He pulled Kate to him and kissed her.

The touch of his lips on her own made Kate feel faint. Her eyes closed in pleasure. His kiss was full of a youthful candor that stirred strange embers inside her.

Then she realized how forbidden this response was on her part. With some difficulty she managed to pull back from his embrace.

They lay facing each other. She looked into his eyes. The sweet expression she saw there had an effect almost more intoxicating than his kiss.

"Oh, Kate," he said. "Kate, my dear . . ."

His hand was on her shoulder. He pulled her closer. He covered her face with kisses. And her own hands were on his chest now, undecided as to whether to push him away or to draw him closer. To her shock she was responding to him with something inside her body that had never been there before he touched it. She felt a loss of control that was as delicious as it was upsetting.

She tried to gain possession of herself, and failed. He went on kissing her. His hands stroked her shoulders, her cheeks. Soon he dared to touch her hip, then her breast.

Kate knew she was in trouble now. But the surrender coursing through her could not be stopped. The body in Chris's arms had long known the touch of Quentin's lips and fingers, but it came alive now in a different and irresistible way. It was an experienced woman who tried to keep herself from giving in to Chris, but it was an innocent girl, naive and passionate, who fell further into the magic of his touch at every instant.

"We shouldn't," she managed to say, trembling in his embrace.

He did not reply. Like every young man who has found the woman to whom he gives himself for the first time, his body was his answer.

He loosened the first button of her blouse, then the second. She did not stop him.

Now that she had taken the fatal step, the rest was slow and sweet—the gentle kisses, the murmurs, the soft sounds of clothes coming off, the caress of the warm air and sun on naked skin.

And soon, with a delicacy that belied his youth and inexperience, he had parted her thighs and found his way inside her. Passion made Kate arch her back and grasp him to pull him deeper inside, and moans she had never heard before stirred in her throat. The creamy flesh of young womanhood offered itself to him unhesitatingly, and his own groans sounded in her ears like anthems of innocence.

He was deep inside her now, his every stroke charged with an affection that broke down her last defenses. And what was coming out of her body to greet him, to welcome him and inflame him, was also something over which she had no control. It was so shy and yet so hungry, so innocent yet so overpowering, that she soon gave in to it with her whole heart, as he did.

Her legs were curled about his waist. He strained inside her. A long musical sigh escaped her lips. He heard it, and trembled in his ecstasy inside her. The core of her opened eagerly to receive him.

It was over. They lay gasping in each other's arms, stunned by pleasure.

For a long time they did not move. Both were surprised by what had happened. Then she felt his smile against her cheek. He had found what he sought. He had stepped over the threshold he perceived in her.

But Kate herself felt as though she had crossed over a more dangerous line. For in lying to this boy about who she was, she had lost her own grip on her identity. And in giving herself to him she had sacrificed far more than she had intended.

Kate closed her eyes and pulled Chris closer, as though the rampart of his young flesh might blind her to the truth burning painfully inside her.

She knew she had just taken the first step into a world she had not known before. Its perils might be infinitely greater than the joy she had just experienced.

But it was too late to turn back. The damage had been done.

16

KATE WAS IN LIMBO. THE CHANGE TAKING PLACE INSIDE HER was so powerful that it seemed she no longer knew herself.

In an odd, furtive way she felt as though she herself were a girl who has just lost her virginity to the one boy who really matters, the one boy who already owns her heart. She was full of innocent, girlish feelings about Chris, feelings of wonder and exultation and worry about what he thought of her now.

Yet these very feelings filled Kate with horror, for she knew she had done something terribly wrong, and false, in losing herself that way in Chris's arms. She could hardly flatter herself with comparisons to a virgin. The more appropriate comparison to her behavior was something she dared not name.

Quentin seemed to sense the change in her. He was rather distant toward her. He seemed preoccupied when they were together. And he did not make love to her. She wondered if, seeing the tip of the iceberg that loomed within her, he realized that she would not be able to respond to him in the old way. In any case, she was glad he did not touch her. Her body felt so different, so new, that she wanted to be alone with herself for a while.

And she wanted to see Chris again. She could not make bold to call him herself after such an event. He must call, he must let her know he really cared, let her know that his heart had really been involved in what had taken place. The fantasy of belonging to him was truly running away with Kate now.

A few days after the incident in the meadow, Chris did call.

The call came at the restaurant, which was the only number Kate had given him.

Chris sounded terribly excited. "Kate, I've been doing a lot of thinking," he said. "I love you. I want to marry you."

Kate was so taken aback that she could not even find words to answer him.

"I know this must be a shock, after all my talk about Jane," he explained. "But you've got to believe me, Kate. It's you I want. You're all I want in the world. I love you, Kate!"

She struggled to think of something to say to him. In a practical sense his proposal was a disaster. It proved she had carried her subterfuge too far, played her part too well. Yet, in her heart, it was like a dream come true, a guilty dream she never should have entertained.

"Chris, please don't," she pleaded. "You don't really know me. You're just being noble, because of what happened between us." She had to speak in a whisper so as not to be overheard by the other waitresses. "Believe me, you don't owe me anything."

"Owe you!" he exclaimed. "Kate, I love you! I'm not being noble. I'm in love with you. Can't you see? All my life I've been looking in the wrong direction for what I wanted. Oh, Kate, I've been so blind, so stupid . . . But now I see everything clearly. Please, don't say no. Say you'll think about it."

Kate had turned pale. The phone was shaking in her hand. She felt like a criminal caught red-handed.

"I . . ." she stammered.

"Just say you'll think about it," he insisted, the candid joy in his voice breaking her heart. "Or better yet, don't say anything. I'll meet you for lunch tomorrow. We'll talk then. All right?"

Relieved to be let off the hook at least for now, Kate agreed. She decided she would spend tonight thinking up an explanation that would let Chris down easy. It would be one of the most difficult nights of her life. But she would endure it, as she would endure the heart-wrenching agony of refusing him.

She hung up the phone.

The next day was Friday, June 13. It was a date that Kate would remember for the rest of her life.

She had spent a sleepless night, and was still rehearsing what she would say to Chris, when an item in the morning newspaper caught her eye.

LOCAL MAN DIES

A local man whose family has been a financial pillar of San Diego society for many years died suddenly last night in what police have called a suicide.

Christopher M. Hettinger, the 23-year-old son of businessman Judd Hettinger, founder and President of Hettinger's, Inc., was found dead in his La Jolla home by his parents early Friday morning upon their return from a party. He had died of a single gunshot wound to the head, apparently inflicted by a family-owned revolver which was found beside the body.

Christopher Hettinger worked as an assistant manager at Hettinger's. He was a graduate of Exeter Academy (1932) and Stanford University (1936). Besides his parents he leaves two sisters, Judith and Shielah.

Services will be held at the Todd Funeral Chapel Monday at 11 A.M.

Kate held the newspaper in her frozen hands, reading the item over and over again. It made no sense to her. But it filled her with a mortal, paralyzing dread as well as an almost unbearable grief.

She could think of no earthly reason why Chris should take his own life. Only yesterday he had been full of a boundless joy as he proposed to her. What could possibly have happened in those few hours to make him commit suicide?

Kate's entire body began to tremble. A secret suspicion, leaping in all her senses, was telling her that she was responsible for what had happened.

She closed her eyes and fought to gain control of her emotions. She was still sitting at the kitchen table, dressed in her waitress uniform, when Quentin suddenly came in the door. She looked up in surprise. He had left early this morning, and she had not expected to see him until tonight.

Quentin seemed bright and somehow chipper.

"I've got good news, babe," he said. "Our business came through with flying colors. Better than I could have hoped. We're going to celebrate tonight. I'll take you out to Carlucci's. I want you to go out today and shop for a new dress. And forget about that waitress front," he added, gesturing to her uniform. "You won't be needing that any more. We're in the money, babe."

She looked up at him, dazed. She still held the newspaper in her hands. Her eyes were brimming with tears.

"What?" she asked.

He looked at her. "I said everything worked out," he repeated. "You did your job, I did my job, and we made hay."

Kate was staring at him. She held out the newspaper.

"What happened?" she asked, pointing to the item announcing Chris's death.

"Oh, that," Quentin said. "That's nothing that need concern you, babe. A family problem. None of our business."

Kate was on her feet now, moving toward him.

"Quentin, I want the truth," she said. "I spoke to Chris only yesterday, and he was perfectly fine. And now he's—

he's dead! It's impossible. You've got to tell me what happened. I want the truth, Quentin. I have to know. I have to!''

She had moved close to him and placed her hands on his arms. She was gripping him hard, though she did not realize it.

Only now did she notice that the excited gleam in Quentin's eyes had something sinister about it. His smile was not really happy at all, but malicious and angry. He was measuring her own panic with increasing rage.

He disengaged her hands with a jerk and picked up the newspaper. He glanced at the item about Chris with a complacent smirk.

"What's to know?" he asked. "The kid got depressed. Maybe he had a fight with his girlfriend. Why is that your business?"

"Quentin!" Kate cried, white with anger. "Tell me the truth!"

He looked at her appraisingly. Then, with brutal suddenness, he hit her hard across the face with his open hand. She staggered backward. He pushed her down on the bed and stood looking at her, his lips curled in hatred.

Then he picked up the newspaper and threw it at her. The pages fell away from each other, raining down on her like ungainly paper rags.

"So baby wants to know the truth, does she?" he said, standing over her. "Since she did her part, she wants to know what it all meant? Is that it?"

Frightened, Kate nodded.

"All right, then," he said, releasing her abruptly. "I'll tell you the truth."

He went to the closet and pulled out a large manila envelope. He tore it open, produced a sheaf of eight-by-ten glossy photographs, and threw them at her. They fell over the bed, already littered by the tumbled newspaper.

She picked up one of them and looked at it. She turned pale as she saw an image of herself, naked, in the arms of Chris Hettinger on the blanket in the meadow. She could see the shadow of the oak tree's branches covering their bodies as they made love. The look on her face in the photo was passionate, enraptured.

Quentin was staring down at her, his eyes full of dark triumph.

"How come you never look like that when you're in bed with me, babe?" he asked savagely.

Kate looked from her husband to the photograph. Her hands were trembling.

"I—what does this mean?" she asked.

He smiled ominously. "Are you sure you want to know?" he asked. "You may not like what you hear, babe."

"Tell me, Quentin. I've got to know."

"All right." He lit a cigarette, pulled a chair toward him and sat down, straddling the seat, his arms over the back. "You want to know the awful truth? I'll tell you, then. Your lover boy is dead because of you."

Kate's eyes opened wider.

"What do you mean?" she asked.

"I'll spell it out for you," Quentin said. "A few months ago I managed to make contact with Mr. Hettinger Senior. He was concerned because his son was fooling around with some girl who came from the wrong side of the tracks, a penniless frill whom the boy had taken it into his head to marry. Well, the father couldn't live with this, because he wanted his boy to marry money. He didn't want to waste that Stanford education and a big career at Hettinger's on some nobody. But the son had made up his mind. He was as stubborn as his father."

Quentin smiled. "There was one wrinkle that had caused the father to look for a guy like me to help him. The little girl his son was nuts about was a stickler for fidelity. A virgin, in fact. She was saving herself for little Chris, and expected him to do the same. She wasn't going to pop her cherry until their wedding night. The old man found this out by stealing some letters the boy had received from the girl. He passed the information on to me, and we had a little discussion about it."

He looked at Kate.

"Naturally, I thought of you," he said. "You're a good-looking piece of tail, with a nice personality. And you're not above a little hanky-panky, as we both know," he added cruelly. "I told the old man not to worry, that I would see to it that his boy had a fling with someone, and that we would get proof that would make him look unfaithful to his little girl. That's when you entered the picture, babe. I had you get friendly with the boy. My intention was to get you in a compromising position, enough to show the boy was unfaithful to Miss Muffet. Then the old man could put the arm on the boy and get him to break his engagement."

Quentin's smile grew more evil.

"How could I know," he said, "that you would oblige me in such a dramatic way, babe? Far beyond my expectations. Far beyond what I had hoped. After all, I told you not to get too friendly with him. I told you I was the jealous type. I just assumed you'd never get past the hand-holding stage. But you really surprised me. You went all the way. A lucky thing I had somebody out in those hills to get it all on film. It was too beautiful a performance to go to waste."

"You—you had me followed?" Kate said.

He nodded.

"You're quite the little lover, aren't you?" he said, puffing at his cigarette. "Why, to look at those pictures, I'd swear you were actually in love with that boy. Yes, sirree: you look just like a young lady in love. You'd think you were popping your own cherry in that meadow."

Now his words came forth with a venom born of limitless rage.

"I confess that those pictures made me a little jealous," he said. "I looked at them and I said, *'That's my wife.'* That's what I said, babe. *'That's my wife in those pictures. That's my wife fucking that boy!'* Yes, indeed. Like I say, babe, I never saw that look on your face with me. No, sirree. Not that look."

Kate said nothing. Tears had welled in her eyes. She held the photo without looking at it. It represented her last view of Chris Hettinger, the last time she had seen him alive.

"Well," Quentin said, "when I showed the old man the

pictures, he was mighty pleased. This was just what he had wanted, and more. All he had to do was confront the son with this proof, and the son would have no choice but to call off his engagement to Little Miss Muffet and marry the girl of Daddy's choice. So I was paid handsomely for my trouble, and I shook hands with Daddy and took my leave."

Quentin stubbed out his cigarette and flexed his arms in a pleased manner. It was obvious he was enjoying his wife's agony, the more so since he knew it came from her grief over Chris as well as her shame.

"Of course, I couldn't stop there," he said. "Because, my sweet, you yourself didn't stop at making friends with the young fellow, did you? Not only did you fuck him, but you made him fall in love with you, didn't you? I'm not stupid, Katie girl. I know what was between you two. And a picture is worth a thousand words, isn't it? Any fool can see what is as plain as the nose on your face."

He smiled.

"So I paid a little visit to young Mr. Hettinger last night. I broke the news to him that you were my wife. I told him enough of what we were up to for him to understand what a cheap little impostor you are. He took it hard. I felt sorry for him, you know. After all, I myself know how it feels to find out that the woman you love is a cheap little whore, a liar, a phony, a two-timing little cunt who will do what suits her without caring who she hurts . . ."

Kate had curled up on the bed with her eyes averted, as though to defend herself against his slashing words. He saw her tears staining the pillow.

"The rest," he said, gesturing to the newspaper strewn around her body, "is history. Of course, I didn't intend to do little Chris any harm. Hell, babe, none of us intend harm when we play our little tricks, do we? You didn't intend harm when you played your little trick with Chris last week, did you? Hell, you were just having a good time. A very good time. Just a quiet little picnic for two. No, you didn't intend for anybody to die. Not you, babe . . ."

Kate could not move or speak. The full horror of what she had done, and of what Quentin had done, was exploding inside her like a bomb.

Quentin was still gazing down at her.

"Well?" he asked. "Don't you have anything to say for yourself?"

She could not find words to say. Not only was an innocent boy dead thanks to her. The life she had lived with Quentin was over. All the illusions that had sustained her so uncertainly since the day she left Ewell Stimson's house in Quentin's car were now destroyed. She was adrift among the fragments of that ruined life, just as the strewn newspaper and photographs on this bed were the proof that she deserved all that was happening to her.

Quentin seemed to sense the depth of the punishment he had inflicted on her and to glory in it. He was looking down appraisingly at her beautiful body, the body that had seduced poor Chris Hettinger just as it had seduced Quentin himself and pathetic old Ewell Stimson before him, Ewell Stimson the aged voyeur who had taken Kate under his wing.

"It looks like we have some pieces to pick up," Quentin said, savoring his metaphor as he looked at the papers and photographs on the bed. "I think we should let bygones be bygones, babe. What's done is done. Your boy is dead, and nothing can bring him back."

He knelt on the bed, and moved toward her.

"But," he said softly, "you still have me."

He pushed the debris out of the way and ran his hands over her uniform. She did not respond to his touch. She was too numb.

Slowly he found the hem of her skirt and pushed it up until he found her garter belt. He unhooked her stockings and pulled them off. Then he found the zipper and undid the uniform. She lay emptily as he slipped it off. He studied her in her bra and panties. Slowly he reached to touch her back with his finger and traced a letter there.

"The scarlet letter," he said. "A is for adultery, W is for whore."

He unhooked her bra. Then he pushed her down on her stomach and slipped the panties down her legs. He saw the perfectly shaped loins, the sweet young sex that had pleasured him so often since their marriage and that had now brought them to this moment at the cost of young Chris Hettinger's life.

"You still have me, babe," he murmured. "You still have daddy."

Slowly, cruelly, he poised himself over her and entered her from behind. He felt the tremor of her stunned body, and knew that his penetration was the final nail driven into her self-respect. He began to grind against her, enjoying his own cruelty.

"There you go," he murmured, excitement scalding his throat. "That's what baby wants, isn't it? You're all alike, you girls, aren't you? You like a little fun, and you don't care where you get it. Am I right? Am I right?"

And now he glanced down at the bed and saw one of the photographs of her in Chris Hettinger's arms. The rapt, exalted expression on Kate's face in the pictures inflamed him the more, and he worked himself deeper into her, more angry with each thrust, and more excited at his domination of her and her own despair.

"Nothing can bring him back," he hissed. "Never. Because you killed him, babe, as surely as if you pulled that trigger yourself. Never, never, never . . ."

At these words his seed exploded into her. Her quiet sobs joined his gasps in the silence of the room. She lay naked and pathetic under him, her tears wetting the pillow.

Without another word Quentin pulled out of her, as harshly as he could. Then he straightened his clothes, gave a quick look at his hair in the mirror, and walked out of the apartment.

Quentin was gone all night.

He spent the evening drinking with some of his friends downtown, and ended up sleeping with a girlfriend in her apartment. He wanted to make Kate jealous if possible, wanted to make her savor her loneliness and her guilt. Tomorrow he would perhaps lessen his severity toward her. But for tonight he wanted her to suffer.

He returned home at ten in the morning, almost twenty-four hours after their confrontation over Chris Hettinger's suicide.

Kate was gone.

There was no trace of her in the apartment. She had taken her clothes, her coats, her cosmetics, her few possessions. She had also taken the damning photos of herself with Chris, and the newspaper.

Quentin was amazed at the thoroughness of her departure. She had left nothing of herself behind.

He realized she had left him for good.

Quentin sat down and lit a cigarette. He looked at the apartment around him. He saw the rusty little stove on which Kate had cooked his meals, the tiny bathroom with its dripping faucet, the ugly walls, the chipped painted table and the sagging mattress.

This was where he lived. This was the home he had made for the wife who had now left him. It was a cheap and tacky place, fit for cheap and tacky people.

Kate, he realized dimly, had never fitted in that life. There was a mysterious nobility about her, despite her poverty and her youth and ignorance, that had impressed him even at Ewell Stimson's, and made him want her. That nobility had made him ill at ease after he had married her, for he knew it was a quality he himself did not possess, and a quality no woman he had ever known had possessed.

And he now saw that it was that quality that had caused her to be unfaithful to him. Her infidelity was not merely physical. In giving herself to the Hettinger boy she had expressed her aspiration for something Quentin could never give her.

Well, now the boy was dead, and Kate was gone.

Quentin thought for a moment of pursuing her. She could not have gotten very far.

Then he dismissed the idea.

Good riddance, he thought. She had been cramping his style long enough. He would be better off without her.

He puffed at his cigarette. For a moment he savored the idea of his new freedom. He could go where he wanted, get drunk when he wanted, lay all the girls he liked, without having to worry about Kate.

But then he looked at the battered old apartment door with its chain lock, the door through which Kate had walked out on him. Beyond it stretched a world of opportunities, of experiences that he, Quentin, would never enjoy, for his own limitations as a person immured him here in this shabby life as a permanent prison enforced by his own mediocrity.

His smile faded as this thought sank into his brain. He stared at the door. He wondered whether Kate, having gone through it, might some day enjoy those experiences, those fulfillments that he could never have offered her and would never taste himself because of what he was.

Again he thought of young Chris Hettinger, and of the impassioned look on Kate's face in the photographs. A sudden rage possessed him. He threw his cigarette at the closed door.

"Go on," he shouted aloud. "Have a nice life . . ."

Then a secret smile curled his sensual lips as he recalled something he knew, something Kate did not know.

"You'll be seeing me, pussy," Quentin said.

JOSEPH KNIGHT CONTINUED TO EXPAND HIS ENTERPRISES up and down the East Coast and in the Midwest. Taking advantage of the peculiar economic conditions produced by the Depression, he acquired controlling interests in struggling companies and used his financial cunning to make them turn a profit. With every passing month his wealth and influence increased.

He was known among his peers as a man with incisive

ideas, originality, and great personal force. A man who kept his promises but who was not to be crossed. Though his public profile was low, he was one of the most promising young entrepreneurs in the nation, a man on his way to a great future.

But his heart was not as light, or his spirit as calm, as before the death of Anne Rizzo. He was upset by the tragedy of her violent end, a death so untimely for a woman so young.

He recalled her touching innocence the first time he had met her, an innocence that had been reflected in the way she made love. It had seemed a shame to see so unspoiled a girl in the clutches of a man like Carl Rizzo. At the time Joseph Knight had thought he was doing a good thing by liberating her from Rizzo even as he got Rizzo out of his own way.

But it had all gone bad. Anne had come out of the episode obsessed with Joe and unable to face her own life without him. It was that obsession, growing from a part of her personality unsuspected by Joe himself, that had led to her death.

Why could she not simply have accepted the elimination of her cruel husband and taken the money she had inherited from Rizzo to start a new life? She was young and beautiful, she could easily have gone back to Maryland and married some nice young man. Her future was her own to choose.

But she had chosen Joseph Knight.

Joe would never forget her eloquent, fateful words when he had tried to tell her she was free of the prison of her marriage.

I am in prison, she had said.

Joseph Knight did not understand women. He could not comprehend a passion so consuming that a woman would sacrifice everything to pursue a man who did not want her. Or worse yet, a passion that could drive a woman to destroy both herself and the man she loves rather than to let him live away from her. Being a businessman who was accustomed to seeking realistic gains, to pushing the world where it would give and to backing off where it would not give, he could not understand a woman being willing to abandon life itself for something as unsubstantial as the love of a man.

Perhaps because Joe himself had never felt anything serious for a woman, he could not understand women's need to love totally and to be loved totally. Their passionate incompleteness, their profound desire to live as two instead of as one, puzzled him.

Yet this deep hunger, which Knight had not failed to observe in the heroines of the great playwrights and novelists, from Shakespeare to Ibsen, from Sophocles to Tolstoy, was of the essence of woman. A hunger so consuming that a woman would gladly brave death, and even destroy her lover, if she lost the chance of fulfilling herself through the spiritual nectar of his love.

Joseph Knight assumed that other males were as indifferent to women as himself. And thus he concluded that no man could possess anything worthy of the passion, the obsession, of an Anne Rizzo. Such women were chasing after phantoms, chimeras, pots of gold at the end of rainbows when they attached themselves to the empty hearts of men. It was a fool's paradise they pursued so frantically, and sometimes so nobly.

Joseph Knight could not understand this. He saw the passion of women from the outside. He could not put himself in their place. And because of this he had failed to understand Anne Rizzo before it was too late. His miscalculation had been disastrous for her.

It was this lingering sense of defeat, of sadness over needless tragedy, that kept Joseph Knight in a depressed state for many months. He threw himself into his work, but his spirits remained low. Not only did he feel sad—he felt curiously unfulfilled. It seemed as though the whole course of his life over the last ten active years no longer sufficed to sustain his interest. His many business activities did not seem to stimulate him.

He needed a new challenge, perhaps a change of scene.

Before he could make up his mind to do anything about his feelings of unrest, an opportunity suddenly presented itself, an opportunity whose fateful consequences were invisible to Joseph Knight at the time.

An old business acquaintance from Boston named Jerry Mercado came to Joe with an unusual idea.

"Joe, I want to do something exciting, and I want you to go in with me on it," Jerry said. "I want to produce a movie. Independently. I know some people on the Coast, and they're going to help me. Believe me, it will be fantastic. We can produce a good film on a shoestring and get it distributed through the big theater chains. We'll make a fortune."

At first Joseph Knight smiled. He had known Jerry for years. Jerry had been a movie nut for as long as he had known him. Jerry went to the movies nearly every day of his life, owned three theaters in the Boston area, and read the movie magazines religiously.

But Jerry was not as shrewd a businessman as Joe. He had a history of throwing himself into promising new ventures that turned out to be nothing. He often did not do his homework, did not thoroughly analyze a marketplace before investing his time and money in it.

Nevertheless Joseph Knight needed a change of scene. And nothing could be further from his present alleys than Hollywood. The very word brought images of refreshing foreignness to his mind. He had never expected to go anywhere near Hollywood in his business life.

This, then, was the new arena which his current restlessness demanded. It would help him forget Anne Rizzo and get him involved in the future again.

And his businessman's instinct put him on the alert when Jerry told him about the fabulous amounts of money to be made in the city by the Pacific Ocean. Naturally Jerry exaggerated his prospects and made the production of a film seem easy. But Joseph Knight had read enough about Hollywood to know how much the film companies made on a yearly basis. There was a great deal of money in the film industry—Depression or no Depression.

Joseph Knight decided to take a chance.

"Show me your property," he told Jerry Mercado. "If it looks good, I'm in."

Two weeks later Joseph Knight had delegated control over his major business interests to trusted lieutenants in Boston, Miami, Chicago, Philadelphia, and New York. He journeyed to Los Angeles with Jerry and settled into a suite at the Beverly Wilshire Hotel.

It was July. Joseph Knight was surprised by the California climate. Unlike the muggy East Coast and Midwest, it was dry, with fresh ocean breezes cooling the coastline, but with the inland valleys burning in desert heat and filled with citrus groves irrigated at high cost.

Los Angeles was a sprawling, ugly city, lacking New York's sculptured high-rise elegance, Boston's charm, Philadelphia's history or Chicago's magnificent architecture. But it had a certain antic energy to it. It looked like a place where deals were being made in innovative ways by people who were making up the rules as they went along.

As for Hollywood, it was quite simply the craziest place Joseph Knight had ever seen. Geographically it was nothing but a hillside community on the western edge of Los Angeles, separated from the ocean by a few miles of busy roads, and already contaminated by the smog and congestion of the city. The Hollywood "Flats," at the base of the mountains, were as shabby as the poorest parts of New Jersey. Yet only blocks away were the fabulous residences of the stars and movie executives, hidden behind high fences and lush landscaping in the hills and canyons overlooking the city.

Because of the enormous wealth generated by the high-risk movie business, Hollywood had in one generation turned itself from a sleepy country community into a showplace for the gaudy, the pretentious, the fantastic. New money was everywhere, in mansions flaunting masonry and fountains and furnishings imported from European castles. Inside these houses were shifty money men, most of them first-generation immigrants, men only a few years removed from their beginnings on the Lower East Side of New York but now tanned brown by the hot sun of the city they had conquered with their greed, their cunning, and their talent for the entertainment business.

Also inside these houses were actors who had begun as untrained contract players, naive youngsters from all corners of the country, and had been made into household names by the Hollywood image-makers, by the whims of the public, and sometimes by their own talent.

These were the stars, pampered slaves of the studios who worked backbreaking hours in a profession of the most ruthless competition, and lived in a splendor no less incongruous than that of the studio executives. For they were only half educated and no more accustomed to wealth and position than their bosses. They had to "pose" as confident and successful pillars of the community, just as in their acting roles they posed for the cameras. The unreality of their existence was matched by the terrible precariousness of their perch at the top of the Hollywood heap, a perch that could be dissolved at any moment by a single flop at the box office. No wonder so many of them had been destroyed by drugs, alcohol, and fast living. Illusion makes a poor ground under one's feet, even if that illusion brings in a colossal salary.

But if the anxiety of their position ate away at their insides, they could not show it outwardly. So they kept up a brave smile for their fans. And wherever they went, the publicity men were not far behind, snapping their pictures and recording their pre-digested patter for the eager public.

It was amazing to behold this ugly place filled with smog and traffic, where the movie studios sprawled over acres of land, with huge back lots full of sets, cavernous sound stages, and warehouses. Each one was a factory, where stars toiled alongside highly paid technicians and construction specialists to create the most profitable product in the smallest amount of time.

Yet this factory, so peculiarly American in its relentless mass production, was different from any factory Joseph Knight had seen in his business career. For this factory produced fantasy. A fantasy that was gobbled up greedily, day in and day out, by a public famished for escape from the hard times that were making real life almost unbearable in its hopelessness.

As a hardheaded businessman accustomed to realistic assessments of situations, Joseph Knight found Hollywood absurd. Nowhere in this landscape was a businessman's dream, the "sure thing," to be found. Here one found only stars whose ascension to the summits of popularity was as unpredictable as the most dangerous stocks on Wall Street. And the spectacle of the Hollywood money men, bankers turned esthetes, trying to gauge the public taste as they cranked out romantic potboilers and swashbuckling melodramas, was so incongruous as to baffle a real businessman who lived for bottom-line certainties.

Yet it was precisely this element of chance, of unlikelihood, that gave Hollywood its peculiar glamour. The whole town shared the gaudy imitation of high style, the shameless pursuit of overnight success, that gave the stars their fleeting luster. It was a place where the instincts of the gutter combined with the universal human need for dreams of glory. A hybrid world in which, insanely, business mingled with art.

Joseph Knight found himself attracted to this world, for it appealed to his sense of danger and challenge. And his intellect was stimulated by the product Hollywood turned out. The Hollywood movies were almost completely predictable stories, written according to formula and consumed like candy by the waiting public. Yet somewhere behind their stock characters and familiar dramas they had something in common with the great plays by Ibsen and Chekhov that Joseph Knight had learned to admire. What that something was, Joseph Knight did not yet know. But he saw that the Hollywood film was not a thing to be taken lightly. Not only did it appeal to universal human emotions, but it also made a great deal of money.

For this reason alone, Joseph Knight decided that he had made the right move in coming here.

But if Hollywood was a land where opportunity knocked, Jerry Mercado was hardly the man to open the door.

He had come out here with nothing in his pocket but an

informal arrangement with a small independent producer and a handshake agreement with a representative for one of the major theater chains.

The producer had engaged a fifth-rate writer to write a screenplay for a swashbuckling adventure called *High Seas*, with predictable romance elements and a ho-hum ending. Joseph Knight read the script and handed it back to Jerry with a polite nod, not wishing to throw cold water on the scheme until he knew more about it.

The producer had managed to line up some no-name talent for the starring roles, and non-union employees for the below-the-line work of sound, light, and so on. Facilities for shooting were to be rented from a minor studio in Culver City, at high cost.

Jerry Mercado was terribly excited about the venture. He was so thrilled at the prospect of seeing his own name on celluloid as the Associate Producer of *High Seas* that he paid no attention to the risks involved in the project.

After some thought Joseph Knight invested twenty thousand dollars in the venture. He stayed in the background as Jerry and his executive producer went through the complex process of casting and pre-production. He visited the set during shooting and absorbed all he could about the mechanics of filmmaking. He watched the dailies with Jerry and the others and privately noted the obvious inadequacies of the actors and the director.

And he learned.

Shooting took three weeks. When it was finished, post-production, from editing through publicity, took a mere two months. *High Seas* was hardly a major motion picture.

In the end the film was a colossal failure. As a finished product it looked like what it was: a stereotyped "B" picture, suitable only to run as a trailer for a first-run theatrical film, and a bit more forgettable than most.

As it turned out, the representative of the theater chain who had promised Jerry to distribute the film had to back off on his promise. The money men in New York who ran the theater chain had turned the film down, he said, because they were overbooked with blocks of films from their own Hollywood studio.

Jerry seemed surprised and disappointed by this unfortunate news. But Joseph Knight, who had been patiently doing his homework about the Hollywood studio system during the making of *High Seas,* was not surprised. He did not tell Jerry this. He kept his thoughts to himself.

High Seas was never shown in the United States. It was sold to a European theater chain, where it was seen briefly in a handful of locations before being dropped. All the money Joseph Knight and Jerry Mercado had invested in the project was lost.

Jerry was despondent for a while, and then shrugged his shoulders.

"Well, better luck next time, Joe," he smiled. "I guess it's a rougher game out here than I thought. I think I'll go back to Boston, where the pickings are better."

Joe nodded and bade his friend goodbye. As for himself, he stayed in Hollywood for a few more weeks, pondering the experience he had just had.

He had lost twenty thousand dollars on Jerry's ill-conceived venture. But he had got a valuable education out of his failure. And his initial impression of Hollywood as a place of absurdity and chaos had changed.

His business mind now told him that there were millions upon millions of dollars to be made out here. And those millions were being made by cautious, powerful men who had consolidated their hold on the studios over two tumultuous decades.

These men were monopolists. They force-fed the public with their own product through the system of block-booking, by which a theater owner had to show a studio's lesser efforts in order to show its top-of-the-line blockbusters. They insured their own success by keeping independent producers like Jerry Mercado off their turf.

Fabulous wealth, and a monopoly controlling the access to that wealth—such was Hollywood.

This dual equation appealed to Joseph Knight's sense of entrepreneurship. He was challenged by the idea of a closed market controlled by powerful and willful men. He relished the thought of penetrating that market and forcing it to make room for him. Such an ambition was far beyond the talents of an impulsive and undisciplined fellow like Jerry Mercado. But it was not necessarily beyond a Joseph Knight.

After several weeks of thought Knight made up his mind. He called his attorney and financial adviser, Elliot Fleischer, in New York.

"Elliot," he said, "I want you to keep an eye on things for me for a while. Call me at the Beverly Wilshire if there are problems. I'm staying here."

As Joseph Knight hung up the phone and prepared for a good night's sleep, neither he nor the busy city around him dreamed that his solitary decision was to change Hollywood history.

18

KATE HAMILTON WAS DEAD.

She had died in a bed in San Diego, surrounded by newspapers and glossy photos that chronicled a shame she could not bear to live with.

The body that belonged to her—the beautiful body of an eighteen-year-old girl, unspoiled and fresh, bearing no visible traces of the adventures that had already befallen it—continued to wander the earth. But the personality inside it had been burned to ashes by its own experiences. And, for a long time, no new personality came to replace it. Kate had a long journey to make before meeting herself again.

Time passed. Kate wandered. She held a dozen separate jobs in a dozen cities. Her travels took her from Arizona to the Florida keys, from St. Louis and Chicago to the northernmost tip of Maine. She saw a great deal of the United States without really noticing it. She met many people without paying them much attention. She had many experiences, some of them violent, without being marked by them. The self inside her was like a seedling protected from germination by its own hard casing. Nothing that happened to it until that new birth could have reality to her.

The people whose paths she crossed in those years would later recollect that she had never seemed "all there" in her dealings with them. There was a mystery about her, they would say, an abstraction, that made her intriguing and more than a little frightening.

The more so because, now, she was capable of the unexpected. And, when the situation demanded it, capable of violence.

In Santa Fe, one of her first stops after San Diego, she had found work as a waitress in a restaurant not so different from Ewell Stimson's truck-stop diner. There she fascinated the patrons with her catlike walk, her beautiful body, her sandy hair turned blond by the sun, her brown skin.

Once an unfortunate customer—a traveling salesman—took the unconscious sensuality of her manner for sexual invitation. He waited for her to get off work and approached her in the parking lot of the restaurant. Mistaking the empty expression in her eyes for acquiescence, he dared to put his hands on her.

She struck him in the face with a fist so sure in its trajectory and so perfectly balanced that he fell at her feet almost unconscious. She coolly overturned a garbage can full of restaurant scraps on him and walked away, forgetting the incident already.

In a town on the Gulf of Mexico, she worked in a real estate office for two months as a secretary/receptionist. One day her boss took her to a building site. There he opened his heart to her.

"Kate, I love you," he said. "I've held it in as long as I can. I can't bear to look at you in the office any more,

201

or to hear your voice. I can't sleep for thinking of you. Will you marry me?"

Kate's eyes widened in surprise. She had barely taken notice of his existence before this moment. She found it amazing that she could have had such an effect on him while he had had so little on her.

That night she left the town without bothering to quit her job. When she didn't come to work her boss made inquiries about her. She had given her landlady the apartment key, but left no forwarding address. No one had any idea where she had gone.

The boss never saw her again.

She did not hold jobs for long. She quickly lost interest in each place she settled in. From Duluth to Portland, from Rapid City to Baton Rouge, from El Paso to the Canadian Rockies, she traveled aimlessly, her direction determined by which train or bus was leaving soonest.

A true nomad, she could not stay in one place for long. And when she remained in a town more than a month or two, she changed her domicile. She would move into an apartment or furnished room, live in it for a few weeks without changing a thing or adding so much as a calendar. She never noticed the cockroaches crawling over her floors, or the cold draft coming in through the cracked window, or the noise from the neighbors' quarrels, or the children's shouts in the hallway.

Then, as though driven by an unseen natural force, she would abruptly move on, migrating to another apartment on the other side of town, where she would stay for a while before moving out again.

In one Pennsylvania town she lived in four apartments in as many months. She would lie on her bed staring at the ceiling, oblivious of her surroundings—and then one day awake to find the place intolerable, and move on, for a reason she herself did not know.

Those who saw the faraway look in her eyes assumed she was thinking about herself. They could not have been more wrong. Her physical peregrinations across the land corresponded to a mental wandering in which she never looked inside herself or back on the past. Her mother and stepfather,

Ewell Stimson, Quentin, and unfortunate Chris Hettinger were all absorbed by a sort of quicksand inside her mind.

Subtle transformations took place in her like seismic shifts of volcanic power that groaned beneath her silent surface, bringing about sudden, incomprehensible changes in her behavior.

One afternoon as she sat in her apartment on the south side of Baltimore, she heard strange music from down the hall. She got up, knocked at the neighbor's door, and saw that the radio was playing. She asked to be allowed to stay until the end. The neighbor, a young man, invited her to sit down.

When the music ended the announcer said that it was Beethoven's Seventh Symphony.

She went out to a music store and bought a record player. It was expensive, and cost her a lot of her savings. She bought a set of 78 RPM records of Beethoven's Seventh Symphony, played by the Berlin Philharmonic Orchestra under a man named Fürtwangler.

She took the player and the record home with her and played it through. Then she played it again and again.

After a couple of days the neighbor from down the hall came to knock at her door. He had heard the music playing on her gramophone and wanted to strike up an acquaintance with her. She closed the door in his face.

She listened to the records over and over again, oblivious to the scratches they collected as she handled them in her careless way. Her neighbors shook their heads as they heard the strange, pounding, exultant music again and again from behind her door. There was no sense in complaining to her about the noise, they knew. She would look you in the eye and nod, and then forget all about you.

She listened to the symphony for five weeks. Then, one rainy afternoon, as the orchestra was deep in the complexities of the second movement, she suddenly sat up, looked at the phonograph irritably, and pulled the needle off the record.

She never played the record again, or any other. It sat gathering dust on the turntable until the day she moved out. She gave the machine to a neighbor and thought no more about Beethoven, or about music, again.

*   *   *

She sometimes made friends, despite her distraction. Her mystery attracted them. Girls whose destiny was as predictable as their small-town speech, their ordinary clothes and their provincial dreams, saw something exotic and untamable in her. They confided everything to her, because she was an amazingly good listener, her inner emptiness allowing her to hear what they said without having to filter it through her own selfish concerns.

Often these girls became dependent on Kate, for they saw that in her silent way she possessed a kind of independence they would never have. Thus they were puzzled and hurt when, one day, she suddenly moved on without bothering to give them a forwarding address. They could not know that they had had no more reality for her than the dusty corners of her cheap apartment.

Men found her irresistible, and women could not take their envious eyes off her. There was something earthy and powerful about her that acted like a magnet upon other people. She had become more beautiful as she grew older. The enigma inside her added a strange luster to her long thighs, her firm rounded breasts, her brown skin, and the complex beauty of her face.

But no man succeeded in touching her. And no sexual longing came to trouble her inner emptiness. Her sexuality had fallen into a dreamless sleep from which, it seemed, it would never awaken. She never missed it.

The only people who seemed to understand her were children.

The daughter of her second landlady in Atlanta, a nine-year-old girl named Terry whose father had walked out years before and whose mother was an alcoholic civil-service worker, knocked on Kate's door one day.

"My mother won't be home until late," she said quietly. "Will you play Monopoly with me?"

Kate looked down at her visitor. The girl's mother had never said a word to Kate since she had moved in. The look in Kate's eyes had put her off. But the little girl did not seem scared of her.

"Come in," Kate said, opening the door.

The girl put the game on the coffee table in front of the fold-out bed and looked at Kate's bare walls.

"Why don't you put pictures on your walls?" she asked.

"So I can see what I want when I look at them," said Kate. "This is my room, not theirs."

The child thought she had never before heard an adult say anything so cogent or so attuned to her own way of thinking.

The Monopoly game remained unopened. The little girl conversed with Kate for the rest of the afternoon. She told Kate about her childish concerns and asked questions that Kate answered with blunt honesty. When it was time to go home, the little girl found it hard to tear herself away.

That night Terry told her mother that the lady in 2B was "nice."

She returned, and they spent hours together, playing checkers or drawing pictures or just talking. Often there were long silences between them, filled with a mute understanding that made conversation unnecessary. Terry adored Kate. She felt that Kate was the first grown-up person she had ever understood, or who had understood her.

Kate did not treat Terry like a child. Nor did she treat her like an adult—for Kate did not take adults seriously at all. Instead, she treated her as something above an adult. For adults, in Kate's eyes, were so petty and shallow in their self-interest as to be beneath contempt.

Terry was still unformed, full of empty spaces waiting to be filled. More yet, behind her child's mask of play and politeness, Terry was trying to outgrow her sordid past, to overcome her family and become a person. Kate related to this instantly, for it was exactly what she herself was trying to do.

When spring came they took the bus into the countryside. They walked together in the woods, sat down among tall grasses filled with cattails, and waded through streams. Terry was in heaven. She felt in Kate a flesh-and-blood extension of the world's mysteries, good mysteries, in which she could find a destiny for herself. Kate was the only person Terry had ever trusted.

Then Kate left town. She left no forwarding address, so

Terry could not get in touch with her. The little girl asked her mother what had become of the nice lady in 2B. Her mother said she did not know, and privately thanked her lucky stars that Kate was gone. She did not think such a creature, so wild and unpredictable, was good for her daughter.

The little girl took out the sketch pad on which she had drawn so many pictures with Kate, and did her best to draw an image of Kate herself as a keepsake. She found that it was impossible to capture Kate's essence, for it had never been visible in her physical features. But she kept the picture anyway, letting her imagination bring to it what her eyes could not.

As time went by she accepted her renewed solitude, and her memory of Kate's face and voice began to dim. Every once in a while, though, a postcard came from some far-away city with her name on it. Sometimes an unusual arti-fact would arrive in an envelope—a book, a magazine, a rabbit's foot, a sample of volcanic rock. And the little girl knew her friend had not forgotten her.

The complicated skein of Kate's wanderings took an un-expected turn when she found a job as a waitress in a small Nebraska restaurant and made a new friend.

Kate had drifted into town and applied for work at the first likely-looking restaurant. She was an old hand at this now. A streetwise and experienced young woman, she knew what she was doing.

The girl who waited on her wore a name tag that read "Melanie." She was extraordinarily pretty, with dark hair and green eyes and a rosy complexion. She was taller than Kate and had a model's figure.

"Can I get work here?" Kate asked after ordering her coffee.

"You need a job?" Melanie asked.

Kate nodded.

"Well," Melanie frowned, "the boss says he's not hiring. But I know two girls who are going to be leaving soon. One is getting married, and the other, well—she needs an operation, if you know what I mean. He wouldn't hire you if you asked, but I can put in a good word for you. What's your name?"

"Kate."

"Hi, Kate." Melanie did not need to ask if Kate had experience waitressing. One look at the way she sat in the booth made it clear she knew her way around restaurants.

"Leave it to me," Melanie said with a wink.

That night Kate had a job. And, since she did not have a hotel yet, she had a roommate as well, for Melanie insisted she stay with her.

Over the next few weeks the two young women drifted into a friendly relationship. Kate enjoyed Melanie's youthful optimism. Melanie, like many before her, fell under the spell of Kate's abilities as a listener. She did the talking for both of them.

Melanie was an innocent girl, somewhat scatterbrained but unspoiled. She adored the movies. She read all the film magazines and was an expert on every detail in the lives of the Hollywood stars—at least as reported by the tabloids. She had long cherished the dream of going to Hollywood to try her luck, but had stalled in this out-of-the-way place due to lack of money. She talked about the great actors and actresses, Gable and Harlow and Bette Davis and Carole Lombard, her eyes full of a yearning that touched Kate.

The only sour note in this friendship came from an unexpected direction.

The restaurant's chef/owner, a dictatorial man named Rolf, soon found himself attracted to Kate. He could not take his eyes off her when she worked. Something about her walk, her eyes, captivated him. There was a pride and a fierce sensuality in her that he had never seen in a woman before.

He did not fail to notice the hard armor around her personality, and for a long time was too intimidated to approach her. But at last his obsession grew too powerful to resist, and one night he tried to touch her.

She froze him with a look so dangerous that he had to beat a hasty retreat. There was murder in her eyes, he told himself. She was a woman capable of anything.

After that night he kept his distance. But he could not get Kate out of his mind. Sleep would not come. He could not concentrate on his work. He thought he would go crazy if he did not escape her spell. He wanted to fire her, but his desire would not allow him to let her go.

Finally, in desperation, he found himself turning his attention to Melanie. She was a beautiful girl herself. And she was Kate's roommate and only friend. Desiring her was almost as good as desiring Kate herself, and a lot less dangerous.

Rolf importuned Melanie with his attentions. He made subtle and not-so-subtle passes at her in the kitchen. He asked her out. He offered her money, gifts. When she refused he threatened her.

Melanie was not a terribly intelligent girl, but she did have her pride. Her sexual transgressions had been minor, and she flattered herself that she was keeping herself essentially intact for Mr. Right. She might stray from the path of righteousness if a male treated her with the proper tenderness and respect, but never for a greasy-smelling short-order cook named Rolf.

Things went from bad to worse. Rolf, on fire with a desire he could not assuage, besieged Melanie, who sensed the misdirection of his passion but did not know how to extricate herself from the situation.

One day, near closing time, the chef stumbled past the point of no return when he caught sight of Melanie changing out of her uniform in the back of the kitchen. His eyes feasting on her long, slim arms, firm little breasts and creamy thighs, he came at her like a bull in heat. Before she could defend herself he had locked her in his arms and was covering her with sloppy kisses as he ground her fragile body against his pelvis. The breath was squeezed out of her.

"Help!" she cried weakly. "Somebody help!"

At that instant a sharp gonglike sound was heard, so close to Melanie's head that her ears rang. Rolf crumpled in an inert lump at her feet. Behind him she saw Kate standing with an extra-large iron fry pan in her hand. She had hit Rolf full force over the top of his balding head with it.

Still breathless from her struggles, Melanie smiled gratefully at her savior.

"Thanks a lot," she said. "I don't know what I would have done if you hadn't come along." She stood half naked, the marks of her employer's hot hands still pink against her pale skin.

"Don't mention it," said Kate indifferently, dropping the pan calmly on her unconscious boss's chest.

"I'm afraid we're going to have to quit, though," Melanie said. "When he wakes up we'll both be fired, sure as anything."

Kate shrugged. "All right."

Melanie threw down her uniform and pulled her street dress out of the rusty little locker against the wall. Kate helped her with the zipper.

"Hey," Melanie said suddenly. "I've got an idea."

"What is it?" Kate asked.

"Let's go to Hollywood!" Melanie beamed.

Melanie's friendship with Kate, and the spectacle of Kate's violence toward Rolf, had somehow given her the courage to take the plunge, burn her bridges behind her, and set out after her dream at last.

But she could not make the journey without Kate.

Kate seemed unimpressed. "Hollywood?" she asked.

"Oh, please, Kate," Melanie cried. "It's where I've always wanted to go. But I never had the guts to take the first step until now. If you're with me, I believe I'll actually make it. Won't you come?"

Kate saw that there was truth in Melanie's words. Melanie was a dreamer, the sort of girl who would never have the courage to carry out her ambitions unless someone gave her needed support.

Kate flipped a mental coin. She did not much care where she went or who with. Why not do Melanie this small favor, then? The cost to herself was nothing.

She undid her apron and threw it on her boss's face.

"All right," she told Melanie. "Let's go."

That night they were on a bus bound for Los Angeles.

Little did Kate realize it, but it was not Melanie's destiny she was following on this nocturnal voyage.

It was her own.

ential, the marks of her employee's hot hands still pink
against her pale skin.

"Don't mention it," said Kate inadifferently, enjoying the
turn-caution on her unconscious boss's chest.

"If in afraid we're going to have to quit, Trunsh," Mellanie said. "Even the makeup we'll both be dead, sure as
anything."

Kate shrugged. "All right."

Mellanie threw down her unguard and rolled her fingers
out of the way until Kate looked against the wall. Kate
helped her with the zipper.

"Hey," Mellanie said casually, "if we got six glasses—"

"What is it?" Kate asked.

"Let's go to Hollywood!" Melanie beamed.

Melanie's friendship with Kate, and the spectacle of
Kate's violence toward Rolf, had somehow given her the
courage to take the plunge, bare her breast behind her,
and set out after her dream at last.

But who could put under the journey without Kate?

Kate seemed unimpressed. "Hollywood?" she asked.

"Oh, please, Kate. All the directors. I'll—here I've always wanted to go. But, I never had the guts to take the
first step until now. If you'll come with me; I could—I'll actually
make it. Won't you come?"

Kate saw that there was truth in Mellanie's words. Melanie was a dreamer, the sort of girl who would never have
the courage to carry out her ambitions unless someone have
her hand somehow.

Kate licked a meager crust. She all but shook with a new
sheer sun it. What with waiting just to Hollywood, she might
make? The reality beg—I was the boss?

She curled her arms and stretched on her boss's feet.

"All right," she told Mellanie.

That night they took on a bus bound for Los Angeles.

Lying in Kate's arms in their very say, Mellanie's destiny
she was following an idea certain to come

To see her own.

BOOK

TWO

JOSEPH KNIGHT STAYED IN HOLLYWOOD.

But he was no longer a mere tourist, or a filmmaking dilettante. Instead he was a man with a mission. Indifferent to the city around him, he immersed himself in the inner workings of the moviemaking industry, making himself an expert on the subject.

He studied the financial profile of every major studio. He quickly became familiar with the byzantine legal code that had sprung up in the last twenty-five years to accommodate the high-finance world of film. He studied the careers of Mayer, Thalberg, the Warners, and Sam Goldwyn, from their roots as sons of immigrant tradesmen through their rise to fame and power.

And he went to the movies.

Not only did he see every film being produced by the major studios—a nearly full-time job, for the studios were each producing from fifty to a hundred movies a year—but he went to the Hollywood Film Archives and immersed himself in the influential films of D.W. Griffith, Erich von Stroheim, King Vidor, and their peers.

He studied the tradition of the silent film, from the earliest one-reelers to the great Griffith melodramas like *Intoler-*

ance and *Birth of a Nation*. Then he studied the cataclysmic transition from silent to sound movies, and its effect not only on the stars but on the writers and directors who made films. He learned how the movies had coped with the financial pressures of the Depression as well as the emotional effects of devastating poverty on the public's taste.

The more he learned, the more convinced he was that Hollywood, despite its monopolistic superstructure, could be forced to make room for Joseph Knight.

His careful study of the film business had shown him that the studios were not the self-sufficient giants they claimed to be. In reality they were simply the production arms of huge corporations based in New York City, corporations whose source of income was their ownership of theater chains. From Paramount with its 1,200 theaters to Warners with 425 and Fox with 500, Continental with 650 and smaller Monarch with 400, these corporations made their money by keeping their theaters filled with customers. To this end they made films at their own studios to show in their theaters—main attractions with big stars, as well as modest "B" pictures with no-name talent, and newsreels and cartoons as filler.

The flamboyant studio heads in Hollywood—Mayer, Jack Warner, Harry Cohn—got a lot of attention because of their huge salaries and their high public profiles. But they were actually the puppets of the money men in New York—shadowy figures with little-known names like Katz, Mazur, Nagel, Speck—who paid their salaries in return for a steady supply of films to fill their theaters. It was these faceless money men who really ran the film business.

The power of the major film companies came less from the films they made than from the theaters they owned—theaters that dominated the market for film exhibition not only within the United States but throughout Britain and continental Europe as well. Theaters that were strictly closed to the work of that most hated of Hollywood interlopers, the independent producer.

This was the first and most important lesson Joseph Knight had learned about Hollywood. If he hoped to make money in the movie business, he would have to do it through one of the major studios.

The second lesson was that times were changing in Hollywood—whether the big studios liked it or not.

Escapism had dominated the film industry through the Depression-ridden mid-thirties, with Shirley Temple becoming the highest paid star in Hollywood, and lavish musical fantasies bringing in huge receipts at the nation's box offices. It was thanks to the musicals and their dramatic counterparts, the frilly historical costume dramas, that the major studios had been able to muddle through the worst of the hard times.

But now things had changed. Shirley Temple's popularity had plummeted as she grew into adolescence. The formula films that had been force-fed to the public throughout the Depression no longer seemed to be making quite as much money. The major stars of the decade were losing their luster. The public was fast tiring of the big studios' escapist melodramas with their cardboard characters and treacly endings.

But the studio moguls and their writing staffs had not yet decided how to react to the changes going on in the public's mind. Today's Hollywood films, with rare exceptions, remained stereotypes. They had no sense of human risk, human tragedy. They avoided believable characters and realistic endings like the plague. And yet, as had been shown by a handful of surprise hits like *All Quiet on the Western Front* and *Fury,* the public was not afraid of realistic stories, provided they had enough psychological truth to make them compelling to watch.

Joseph Knight pondered these facts at great length during his solitary walks around Hollywood and his evenings at home. He came to the conclusion that Hollywood was on the verge of a new era. Like it or not, the major studios needed new talent to survive the transition to a new decade. That meant new stars, new writers, new producers and directors. The movies would have to change with the times.

And this was where a man like Joseph Knight came in.

Joseph Knight had never been a movie fan before; he had been either too poor or, later, too busy to spend two or more hours of his valuable time watching shadows dance on a screen in a darkened movie theater. But now those shadows occupied the center of his attention, for he saw that they translated directly into dollars, and into great power for the men who knew how to manipulate them to please the public.

And as he watched and learned, something astonishing happened. He began to concoct stories in his mind.

The movies he had seen told him something about the consciousness of the moviegoing public, about its dreams, its fears, its fantasies. And now, as a sort of intellectual game that quickly became deadly serious, he tried to invent characters, situations, conflicts, and dramatic climaxes that would match those of the best films he had seen.

Just as he had often marshaled key facts about a marketplace in order to help create a successful product in the past, he now focused his considerable intelligence on molding characters that would appeal to today's public.

Or more precisely, the public of a year or two from now. For Joseph Knight was already thinking ahead.

Spending long hours alone in his hotel suite, Joseph Knight fleshed out his idea. Time passed without his noticing it. After six weeks of hard work he had the blueprint for a powerful Hollywood film in his mind. Though his lack of experience in the new business made him slow to trust his own instincts, he felt sure that the project, once completed, was capable of making millions of dollars at the box office.

The only thing that remained was to turn the blueprint into an actual screenplay.

Knight did some careful research about the available screenwriters working in Hollywood. He soon realized that all the truly gifted writers had long since been snapped up by the major studios. The only free-lance writers available were hacks whose mediocre talent might help to produce another instant flop like Jerry Mercado's *High Seas*, but never a serious contender for commercial success.

For a few days after this disappointing discovery, Joseph Knight was discouraged. He saw no way out for himself except to sell his idea to a major studio for a pittance and perhaps see it made into a major motion picture, with others taking all the credit and reaping the profits.

Then the instincts that had long since formed his own character, combined with a lifetime of experience in the marketplace, brought him to a surprising decision.

Well, then, I'll write it myself, he thought.

This momentous decision was made as coolly as any other business decision Joseph Knight had ever made. It involved enormous ambition and a level of risk from which any ordinary man would have prudently recoiled. But Knight was accustomed to great risk and believed in himself as no ordinary man does.

So he went to work on his project, translating his general ideas of character and plot into dramatic scenes, fleshed out with dialogue and visual structure. The work was much more difficult than he had imagined. The effects he had admired in so many successful plays and films—so sleek and effortless on the surface as they were performed by brilliant actors and captured by talented directors—were amazingly difficult to create from nothing.

But Joseph Knight persisted. He rewrote the scenes dozens of times, purging himself laboriously of his own inexperience, polishing and re-thinking until the scenes had the same power and impact as those of the finest films he had seen.

During those long days and nights of silent work, all Joseph Knight's personal capabilities and experience gradually came together in one potent weapon. His knowledge of popular movies and their structure equipped him to create fast, dramatic scenes that would play well on the screen. His knowledge of playwriting, gleaned from Shakespeare, Ibsen, and O'Neill, helped him to deepen the psychological level of the story he told and thus maintain audience interest. His newfound knowledge of Hollywood production methods helped him to visualize the actual filming of the project and to spot potential problems. His familiarity with the star system and the pool of working actors in Hollywood provided him with clever ideas about casting.

Even now, his hands dirty with the fruit of his own creative effort, Joseph Knight did not think of himself as an artist, or of what he was preparing as an esthetic project. He was simply a businessman, he felt, creating a product to be sold in the right marketplace and at the propitious moment.

Thus he never bothered to realize that, if he had not been a man of action by his own choice, he could easily have become a Pulitzer prize–winning playwright or the most successful scenarist in Hollywood. He was born to the task. The strength of personality that had carried him so far in the business world had always been accompanied by a quality of mind that he had never thought to call by its proper name—originality. Nor had he ever paused in his busy life to think that the realistic power of his intellect had from the beginning worked hand in hand with a remarkable power of imagination.

After two months of hard work Joseph Knight had completed a screenplay that had all the ingredients needed for commercial success. His doubts about his own talent were forgotten now. He knew in his heart that what he had created answered a need in the consciousness of the moviegoing public. The project was a hit just waiting to be made.

But now the weakness in his plan came clear to him.

Though he had created a property of infinitely greater quality and appeal than Jerry Mercado's lackluster *High Seas*, he still faced the same dilemma that had been Jerry's undoing. As an independent creator he remained outside the closed, oligarchic world of the Hollywood studios. And those studios had a monopoly on the stars, the directors, and the sophisticated production facilities without which his project could never become an important film.

The cruel alternatives remained the same: to sell his screenplay to a major studio for a pittance, or to see it condemned to obscurity. No matter what the creative and financial challenges facing Hollywood today, the studios would always close ranks against an outsider as their most basic instinct.

Unless, that is, a chink could be found in the armor that bound the studio heads together in their pursuit of monopoly and profit.

Faced with this dilemma, Joseph Knight made his most

important intellectual decision yet. It was a diabolically clever decision that even a man as subtle as Knight himself could not have conceived until this moment.

However, it would set him back by at least three months, and require a second siege of work as arduous as what he had just been through. He could not help wondering if his strength and initiative would hold out that long.

But if his plan worked, Knight would at last be in possession of the key that could open the doors of Hollywood to him—doors that had been firmly closed to every independent talent who had tried to break into the movie business in a generation.

So Joseph Knight went back to work.

Three months passed. Knight spent them in a concentration so intense that sometimes he forgot to eat or sleep for as long as thirty-six hours at a stretch. When the ordeal was over he felt older and more exhausted than he had ever felt in his life.

But he had accomplished what he set out to do.

Armed with the fruits of six months of effort, he now faced the greatest challenge of his business life. It was a challenge that played to Joseph Knight's talent: his keen eye for human weakness, and his ability to exploit that weakness to get what he wanted.

This time, though, it would not be the weakness of a man, but of a whole system, the system called Hollywood.

Joseph Knight was ready. He had planned this phase of his attack as meticulously as he had polished the tiniest details of the product he had to sell.

It was time to go into action.

On January 16, 1940, long after the failure of his independent film with Larry Mercado, Joseph Knight made the contact that was to be the most important of his career in Hollywood.

He used a business acquaintance from the East for whom he had done a very large favor a number of years ago to get himself an appointment with Owen Esser, one of the most important producers in Hollywood and perhaps the highest-paid producer at Continental Pictures, the most prestigious studio of them all.

He met Esser in his bungalow on the set of the picture he was currently producing. Esser was a flamboyant man who had won two Oscars for his films and been nominated for six more. Not only did he produce his own pictures, but he was a big wheel at Continental when it came to assignments of important projects to other producers under contract to the studio. He was very close to Bryant Hayes, the head of the studio, and was married to Hayes's niece.

"You have ten minutes, Mr. Knight," Esser said. He was a high-and-mighty sort of fellow, and conscious of his own importance. He was putting a golf ball across the carpet toward a makeshift hole, and made a point of not looking up at Knight.

"I appreciate your seeing me," Joseph Knight said. "I have a scenario that I think might interest your studio. I'd like to give you the broad lines of it, and let you be the judge."

Esser smiled patronizingly. He had listened to hundreds of script proposals from amateurs in his time. When, he wondered, would people begin to understand that it took a professional to know how to gauge the public taste, and to create a film that would make money?

Suppressing his yawn, he looked at his watch and said, "I'm listening."

Within thirty seconds his yawn had disappeared and he was listening intently indeed. He put down his putter and stood behind his desk, his eyes on his visitor.

The stranger was laying before him one of the most cannily conceived scenarios he had ever heard. It had every element that Continental Pictures' high-level idea men searched for in their meetings. It had romance, it had adventure, it had great roles for a leading man and leading lady. Like most of Continental's great successes, it was a costume story set against a sweeping historical background—in this case the Russian Revolution. The characters' psychological interplay was amazingly subtle, and contributed to the peculiar, riveting drama of the piece.

Esser had to hide his excitement. The story the stranger

had brought him was dynamite. It was as though the entire brain trust of the Continental scenario department had worked for a year to produce the quintessential Continental product. It was irresistible.

"The hero would be played by Guy Lavery," Joseph Knight said. "The heroine, of course, would be played by Moira Talbot."

Owen Esser nodded. The stranger's thinking was sound. Guy Lavery was an attractive and elegant leading man. Moira Talbot was Continental's top female star, a star whose box-office standing had been in the top five for the last six years. She was the perfect choice for a major costume property like this one. And there was an Oscar in it for her if she played her role well.

Joseph Knight had stopped speaking. Owen Esser raised an eyebrow. Something was missing, he realized.

"Well?" Esser said. "This sounds very interesting indeed. Tell me the rest. How does the story end?"

Joseph Knight smiled.

"You said I had ten minutes," he said, looking at his watch. "The ten minutes are up. I won't take up any more of your time."

"Never mind what I said," Esser retorted irritably. "Tell me the ending, for Christ's sake."

Knight shook his head.

"I don't want to insult you, Mr. Esser," he said. "And, believe me, I'm grateful to you for seeing me. But I'd prefer to discuss the ending with Mr. Hayes himself."

There was a long silence. Esser stared at Knight with a mixture of hatred and disbelief. He did not relish being treated as a subaltern who did not merit the hearing of the crucial ending. For insults like this he had hounded men to destruction in Hollywood.

On the other hand he had to admire the stranger's chutzpah. This Joseph Knight not only had a brilliant idea, but he knew what to do with it. Esser wondered why he had never heard of the fellow before. He had the skill and the cunning of the great Hollywood entrepreneurs written all over him.

But Owen Esser was not going to give in easily.

"Mr. Hayes never listens to ideas until they've been thoroughly worked over by his top staff," Esser said with a shrug. "I'm afraid what you ask is simply impossible."

Joseph Knight smiled.

"Thank you for your time," he said, standing up.

Esser spluttered. "Are you sure you won't . . . ?"

Knight extended a card. "I'm staying at the Beverly Wilshire Hotel," he said. "Leave me a message if you change your mind. It's been nice talking to you."

And without another word he left the office.

2

BRYANT HAYES, BORN SOLOMON WOLFSHEIM, WAS THE single most successful studio head in Hollywood.

He had started in silent films, in partnership with a financial speculator named Adolph Herman. They had formed Continental Pictures on a shoestring in 1922, and had produced silent comedies and adventure films.

The fledgling studio had struggled at first in its efforts to compete with Biograph, Famous Players-Lasky, and the other aggressive silent film producers. Then, in 1927, Hayes, who had always had a sharp eye for talent, discovered Christine Gant, a rather nondescript teenager from Iowa, in a bit part in one of his western adventure films. He saw the potential in her face, and put her in ingenue roles in two costume melodramas in which she was immediately noticed.

A year later Christine Gant was an international star. Bryant Hayes devoted the entire resources of Continental Studios to promoting her career and finding the right talent to play opposite her. She made a series of silent dramas so successful that Continental caught up financially with its competitors and outstripped most of them.

But the career of Christine Gant was ended by the unexpected advent of sound. Her voice, heard by the public for the first time in 1929, had an unpleasantly nasal quality with a midwestern twang that no voice coach could correct. Clearly she was unsuited to the new medium of sound film.

Bryant Hayes sadly bought out Christine Gant's contract and began to look around him for a star to replace her. But no sooner had he begun this process than the Stock Market Crash intervened, forcing Continental to sell off half its theaters and to begin a rigorous belt-tightening program.

It was during this interval that Bryant Hayes cannily bought out his partner, who was too shaken by the Crash to continue struggling for survival in the movie jungle. Hayes now had supreme authority over the creative end of the business. He stewarded it on a shoestring through the dark years of 1930, 1931, and 1932, making a series of modest adventure films and westerns, and managing to attract enough investors in New York to buy back some of the theaters he had lost.

Then his big break came.

In a brilliant move that required all his cunning and most of his money, Hayes lured Moira Talbot away from Paramount. Moira was a young, fresh-faced star with a peculiar aura of charm and elegance about her. Paramount was too busy with its other female stars to see her potential or to develop it, so she came to Continental.

Hayes immediately threw all his creative energy into building Moira's career. He showcased her in romantic comedies, costume dramas, and family films. Soon the public got used to her subtle beauty and fine technique, and she caught on. Her films became major box-office draws, and around her Hayes developed a new stable of talent. He used his increasing bankroll to attract the finest directors, producers, and writers to Continental, which soon became known as "the Cadillac of Hollywood studios."

By 1936 Continental Pictures had gained back everything it had lost during the hard times. Its assets matched those of its most powerful competitors, and its nationwide chain of 650 theaters was exceeded only by that of Paramount.

Bryant Hayes, through clever self-promotion, had managed to get himself recognized as the dean of American movie moguls. His salary was higher than that of any other studio head. His face was known to movie fans everywhere, as was his extravagant Bel Air mansion. He was a well-known philanthropist and a pillar of California society. No one remembered his past as a struggling young movie man, so few years ago, or his roots in the crowded streets of New York's Lower East Side.

Bryant Hayes had arrived.

Today Continental Pictures was famous for the consistent high quality of its films and for their box-office success. Though the studio was not known for the originality of its product—most of its movies were predictable potboilers and costume dramas—the box-office receipts did not lie. The public enjoyed Continental's colorful costumes, bigger-than-life settings, and reassuringly happy endings.

The studio's stars were household names. Topping the list were Moira Talbot and leading man Guy Lavery, who had made four hit films with Moira. The gossip columns had been buzzing for years about an offscreen romance between the two stars that might soon lead to matrimony. Moira and Guy were America's sweethearts. Continental's publicity department was in heaven.

Behind the scenes Bryant Hayes was as ruthless and ambitious today as he had been fifteen years ago. He went to extraordinary lengths to upstage his competitors and to sabotage their best-laid plans if possible. He ran the Hollywood end of Continental Pictures with an iron hand. The only threat to his power was the corporation's board chairman in New York, a dangerous financier named Arnold Speck. Speck had assumed a place on the board after he had acquired a large block of stock in the corporation, and through his talent as an investor he had quadrupled the firm's assets in the last five years. No matter how flamboyant a life Bryant Hayes led in Bel Air, he had to answer to Arnold Speck when it came to the bottom line. The two men had never liked each other. Hayes considered Speck a common Wall Street shark; Speck saw Hayes as a posturing Hollywood phony.

Hayes was convinced that Speck intended to destroy him one day. The canny money man was just waiting for something to tarnish Hayes's glamour before he struck.

But Hayes's string of successes at the box office made him invulnerable to Speck's inside maneuvering. Hayes was a household name. His position at Continental Pictures was assured.

Hayes was a recluse, insulated from the public and even from his own stars by a phalanx of assistants and executives. He had been called the hardest man to see in Hollywood. He did most of his work at his Bel Air home, not bothering to go to his Culver City office except for ceremonial occasions.

But today Bryant Hayes was seeing a visitor.

Joseph Knight arrived punctually at eleven and was shown into one of the mansion's formal salons, where he waited a half hour before being greeted by Hayes, who was dressed in a swimsuit and bathrobe.

"Why don't you come down to the pool?" Hayes asked. "Would you like to take a swim?"

"I'll watch, thanks," Joseph Knight said.

A small, rather shabby-looking butler had appeared from nowhere. He was a man in his sixties, and very worn-out. There was an almost comically melancholic expression in his eyes, a hangdog look.

"Karl," said Hayes curtly, "bring us a bottle of scotch and some soda at the pool, will you?"

The butler, whose soiled livery matched his sloppily shaven face and downcast demeanor, nodded without a word and melted away.

Hayes smiled at Joseph Knight. "I don't suppose you recognize my houseboy, do you?" he asked.

Knight shook his head.

"Well, you're too young to know Karl's era," Hayes said, squiring Knight through the house toward the recreation area. "His real name is Karlheinz Rächer. He was a fine director of silent films—one of the best, in fact. But the advent of sound destroyed him. He didn't know how to adjust to the new techniques. Then the Depression ruined him, because he had put all his money into the stock market. He was about to commit suicide when I talked him out of it. I got him some work at our studio—special effects, lighting design, and so forth—but by that time he had gone a bit soft in the head, and wasn't really dependable. Finally I brought him here as my houseboy and valet, just to keep him out of trouble. It's either me or the state hospital, I'm afraid. Don't be surprised at his appearance, or his demeanor. He's like a member of the family to me. I don't have the heart to discipline him."

Joseph Knight nodded. If this little story had a false ring to it, he did not show that he had noticed.

The two men strolled to the lavish swimming pool, which began inside the downstairs solarium and extended under an elaborate glass wall to the enormous back lawn of the mansion. Knight watched as Hayes took a languid swim and got out of the pool to accept a tall drink from the little butler. The studio head was a man in his sixties, accustomed to a sedentary career, and his body was not in good trim. But he swam well, with strong, even strokes. He enjoyed his dip, not hurrying to get out and speak to his visitor.

"Well," he said when he had emerged at last and was toweling himself off, "let's hear what all the fuss is about. Owen Esser tells me you have something really brilliant up your sleeve."

Joseph Knight described his scenario in detail, watching Hayes's gray eyes focus on his face as he spoke. The studio head showed neither disinterest nor interest. He sipped quietly at his drink.

When Knight had finished Hayes put down his drink.

"And now," he said, "may I hear the mysterious ending that all the flap is about?"

Joseph Knight told him the ending in a few well-chosen

words. It was a brilliant ending, almost too perfect to be believed. It grew with impeccable logic from the motivations of the characters and the conflicts of the story, but it was completely unexpected. Hayes listened, impressed. Not even his best idea men at the studio could have come up with such an ending. Its poetic justice would have escaped them.

It was a tragic ending. At the end of the film the hero died, and the heroine was left to carry on his work for him and live for his memory. Such an ending, for a costume drama about the Russian Revolution, was almost unthinkable. Yet it offered the heroine a chance to achieve a bigger-than-life romantic impact. For the actress who played the role it would be the chance of a lifetime.

Knight smiled. "I'm telling you this in confidence," he said, "because I respect you and know I can trust you. As you can see, a lot of work has gone into this idea. I don't want it to be wasted. That's why I went directly to the top. That is, to Continental Pictures, and to you."

Hayes weighed the stranger's flattery and his apparent candor. He had watched the handsome, tanned face of Joseph Knight as he listened to his speech. It was hard to make him out. His eyes were full of secrets. He was a young man, but he seemed older than his years. Clearly he was an individual of great force.

"Why haven't I heard of you?" Hayes asked, smiling. "This is a brilliant concept. I take my hat off to you. Where have you been all this time?"

"I've been in business," Joseph Knight said. "But I became intrigued by film, and thought I'd like to get into it, at least as a sideline."

Hayes nodded ruminatively. He looked at the copy of the screenplay that Knight had placed before him on the poolside table.

"Well, I'll tell you man to man," he said. "There's no way I could get a thing like this into production in the next six months. Maybe not in the next year. Our stars are booked. The right directors and producer are not available. That's the way life is at a successful studio, you know," he added with a trace of condescension to the outsider.

"But I'll give it some serious thought, and go over it with my people. If we all agree that it sounds promising, our rights people will make you an offer for the concept. I'm sure there will be a tidy sum involved for the film rights . . ."

Joseph Knight smiled, shaking his head.

"I'm not interested in selling the rights, Mr. Hayes," he said. "I want credit as writer and co-producer, and a percentage of the gross."

Hayes nodded, acknowledging his guest's intelligence. Knight would have to have been a complete fool to sell his concept outright. The studio would have paid peanuts for it, and taken all the profits from the finished film for its own.

"All right," Hayes said. "I'll lay your offer before my people, and we'll let you know as soon as we have a decision. How does that sound?"

Knight leaned forward. "It's not that I don't trust you," he said. "But I'd like to have some kind of guarantee . . ." He glanced down at the copy of the screenplay on the table.

Hayes smiled.

"Naturally," he said. "My legal people will be in touch with you by the end of the week. You'll be completely protected, I assure you."

Joseph Knight stood up. "I'm grateful to you for seeing me," he said. "You're an important man, and you took the time to listen to me personally. I won't forget that."

"Not at all," Hayes smiled. "That's what I'm here for. I'm always looking for good ideas. And we can't always find them from our own people. It's I who am grateful to you for coming to us."

It was time to shake hands and part. Joseph Knight knew he had had his chance. As a salesman he had done his best. The interview was over.

Suddenly they were interrupted.

An almost unbelievably beautiful young woman, no more than twenty-two or twenty-three years old, strode into the pool area dressed in a skimpy bathing suit and dived into the pool.

When she came up she noticed the two men.

"I didn't see you," she said, the water streaming down her hair onto her slim shoulders. "I'm sorry to have interrupted you."

"Not at all," Hayes smiled at her. "Daria Kane, I'd like you to meet Mr. Knight. We were just discussing some business together."

The girl glanced at Joseph Knight without extending a hand. There was a cool, narcissistic look about her. No wonder, he thought. She had an amazingly perfect body. Slender arms, lovely rounded breasts, a slim waist and ribcage, and nubile hips above the most beautiful pair of legs he had ever seen.

She looked at Joseph Knight as though she expected him to faint at the sight of her. When he did not, she turned to Hayes.

"Well, I won't bother you any more," she said. "I just wanted a quick dip before I went out."

She extended a hand behind her, and at that instant the tired little butler, as though on an invisible cue, appeared and placed a fluffy bath towel in her hand. She began to towel herself off, her body twisting this way and that with ill-disguised sensuality as the droplets of pool water slid down her satiny skin.

Then she paused, looking closely at the towel.

"Karl," she said, "this towel is dirty. Look at it."

With patrician contempt she held out the towel. The butler took it humbly.

"I am sorry, miss. I will get you another."

The butler looked so seedy that it somehow made sense that the towel he had brought was tainted by touching him. Joseph Knight noticed that the little man did not smell any too fresh.

"Where are you off to?" asked Hayes of Daria, who was standing virtually naked before them, the remaining water running down her shoulders and between her breasts. At this moment it occurred to Joseph Knight that she had played the little charade about the soiled towel in order to let him see more of her gorgeous body while the butler went to get her another towel. She was indeed an amazing sight in her swimsuit.

"I'm going to do some shopping," she replied to Hayes. "Sally is going with me."

There had been an undertone of jealousy in Hayes's inquiry, despite his effort to hide it. And in the girl's answering voice was the note of obedience common to girls who know that their men are jealous of them.

In that instant Joseph Knight recalled what he himself had learned about this girl in his research on Bryant Hayes.

Continental Pictures had put her under contract two years ago after Hayes himself had discovered her working for a small independent studio. Since then Continental had been grooming her for a major career. But the plan had been slowed down, rumor had it, by the fact that the girl had no talent and could not read lines.

In the interim Hayes had fallen completely under Daria Kane's sexual spell. She lived with him, saw to his physical needs, and had him wrapped around her little finger. He bought her fabulous clothes and took her everywhere with him. He was morbidly jealous, since he was an old man now and she still a young girl. The situation was in a state of uneasy equilibrium. It would be resolved either by the girl breaking through to some sort of starring career or by her becoming Hayes's wife. Either way she was sure to be a big winner, and she knew it. In the interim she had to put up with Hayes's jealousy and possessiveness. This was perhaps worth it to her, given what she was getting in return. A talentless starlet, she was the protégée of the most powerful man in Hollywood. It was not a bad spot for a girl of twenty-two with her whole life ahead of her.

Perhaps this was why she had glanced at Joseph Knight with that arrogant narcissism in her beautiful green eyes.

"I'll only be a couple of hours," she told Hayes, with the same note of submission in her voice. "I'll see you for dinner."

At this moment the little butler returned, humbly offering a second towel to the girl. She took it without looking at him and resumed toweling herself off. It was a faintly embarrassing moment, as Hayes and Knight both looked at her beautiful body, each man realizing that the other was looking at her and that she wanted them both to admire her.

"Really, Bryant," she said as she finished, throwing the towel on a nearby lounge chair. "Can't you at least get Karl to wash a little? He smells like the Paris subway. And he never shaves."

Hayes smiled.

"Karl's all right," he said, seemingly happy to be distracted from his jealousy. "I'll have a word with him. Have a good time shopping."

The girl stood in her tanned loveliness, almost too sensual to be real. Joseph Knight reflected that only in Hollywood could a beautiful girl have this peculiar halo of unreality.

Daria Kane looked from Hayes to his visitor, and back to Hayes again. At this small byplay Hayes's face darkened. Joseph Knight knew why. She was mentally comparing Hayes's flabby chest and flaccid muscles to Knight's own male magnetism.

Then she was gone.

"Well," Hayes said, "as I say, I'll follow this up. I'll let you know one way or another. If we can't do the picture, perhaps another studio can. But I won't forget your having come to me first. I owe you one, Mr. Knight."

"It's I who owe you, Mr. Hayes. Thank you again for your time."

They shook hands, and Knight left, accompanied to the front door by the melancholic little butler, who saw him out without a smile or a word.

Bryant Hayes looked down into the cool rippling waters of the swimming pool. He spent a long moment thinking about Joseph Knight.

There had been something calm and self-possessed about Knight that rubbed Hayes the wrong way. A sort of inner balance or force that spelled extreme aggressiveness. Joseph Knight was the embryo of a major Hollywood power, a Darryl Zanuck, a Mayer, a Thalberg in the making. All this man needed was a leg up, a little bit of help, and in two years he could be a power to be reckoned with. He had talent, and, what was infinitely more important, he had a killer instinct. It was visible in his eyes.

A major enemy.

Hayes put on his terry-cloth robe, retrieved the screenplay from the table, went inside to his office, and picked up the telephone.

"Get me Mr. Devlin in our legal department," he said. "I have some urgent work for him. And get me Esser. Tell him to be here in fifteen minutes. I want a full meeting of our top staff this afternoon at two."

He thought back on Joseph Knight, his dark, complex eyes, his thick strong body, and the way Daria had looked at him.

It was time to nip this evil in the bud.

WITHIN TWENTY-FOUR HOURS AFTER HIS ENCOUNTER WITH Joseph Knight, Bryant Hayes had initiated a collective effort on the part of Continental Pictures' brain trust to deal with Knight's suggested movie property.

In the first place Hayes ordered his legal department to institute a copyright search to find out if Joseph Knight had protected his film under current copyright laws.

In the second place, Hayes assigned research workers to find out everything they could about Joseph Knight's background.

In the third place, Hayes assembled his best team of writers and commanded them to get to work on the screenplay Knight had brought him. He wanted all the dialogue evaluated and supplemented if necessary within one month, so that Continental Pictures could use it to create a major blockbuster film for Moira Talbot and Guy Lavery within a year.

In short, Bryant Hayes was setting out to steal Joseph Knight's idea and to make the film on his own without having to pay Knight a penny.

Hayes did not go about this plan with a thrill of intrigue or with ill will in his heart toward Joseph Knight. On the contrary, he was simply following the instincts that had directed his business endeavors for twenty years and that had got him where he was today. Joseph Knight was a potential rival with a brilliant idea. Hayes's natural reaction was to steal the idea and neutralize the threat from Knight.

Within forty-eight hours Hayes's legal department had the answer he wanted. There was no copyright on Knight's concept. The film was completely unprotected.

Hayes now instructed his screenwriting team to fake memos on the scenario dating back eight months, memos in which the idea was hashed out piece by piece. Within days the job was done. Hayes was handed a massive dossier documenting work done at Continental Pictures on the concept, a dossier that would prove in a court of law that the concept had originated at Continental and that anyone who claimed the contrary was a liar.

A few days later the report from Hayes's investigators on Joseph Knight came through. Knight, according to the report, was a canny and aggressive businessman with interests in a dozen states. His assets, shrouded in various paper corporations and securities, far outweighed his rather modest lifestyle. He was a man to be taken seriously.

But Knight, if a ruthless and brilliant shark in business, was a novice where movies were concerned. His only experience in Hollywood had been a twenty-thousand-dollar investment in a flop "B" picture that had never even been exhibited in the United States.

Knight was a beginner. A dilettante.

At this news Bryant Hayes smiled. He knew he was completely protected. He could now make the film at his leisure, in the certain knowledge that Knight possessed no recourse against him. If Knight tried to sue Continental for stealing his idea, there was ample proof to defeat him in the courts.

Hayes was in the driver's seat. The handsome young man he had interviewed by his swimming pool was a wet-behind-the-ears entrepreneur full of naive ideas about storming Hollywood with his brilliant film. Hayes would clip the upstart's wings and make a great new picture in the process.

When Knight found out, a year down the line, that Continental Pictures' huge new feature starring Moira Talbot had been made from his idea, he would of course be angry. But his hands would be tied. The entire Hollywood system, financial and legal, would be against him. No individual could fight that system. Of this Hayes was certain.

That would be the end of Joseph Knight in Hollywood. He would perhaps take his entrepreneurial talents elsewhere, shrugging his shoulders over his failure to penetrate the closed world of Hollywood. And if he ever tried to come back, he would find himself facing the same brick wall: the major studios and their hammerlock on all the theaters in the nation.

It was precisely in this manner that Hollywood protected itself against outsiders and kept the enormous profits of the American film entertainment industry for a handful of film companies that monopolized the theater chains across the land. Hayes was not acting out of spite or anger; he was doing the only thing he could do as an agent of that monopoly against an outside force. He never questioned his own actions for a second.

Now the major priority was to make the film. It had all the earmarks of a classic Continental moneymaker.

With a few small changes to the basic idea, of course, to make it more palatable to the public taste.

After meeting with his writers on the question of those very changes, Bryant Hayes returned home to his Bel Air mansion.

He sat in the lounge overlooking his spacious acreage, with its priceless landscaping and its magnificent view of the hills. At length he picked up the house phone and dialed the number of his houseboy, Karl Rächer.

"Karl, bring me a whiskey and soda, will you? And Karl, bring a glass for yourself as well."

"Yes, sir."

A few moments later the little butler appeared with a tray, two glasses, and bottles of whiskey and soda.

"Thank you, Karl," said Hayes, watching Karl mix a highball as Hayes liked it, mild and spiced with a dash of bitters. "Make yourself one, as well."

He watched Karl pour whiskey into a glass for himself. There was a tense expression on the aged German's face as the whiskey swirled in the bottom of the glass.

"Come, come, man," said Hayes robustly. "Don't stint. Pour yourself a decent drink."

Tentatively the German filled the glass higher with whiskey, until there were three fingers in it. Hayes could see from his expression that he would have liked more. But Hayes let him understand by a little shrug of his shoulders that this was enough.

"Sit down, Karl, sit down," Hayes said.

The little man sat uncomfortably on the edge of the couch, the glass held in both his hands. He looked as melancholic and obedient as a house dog. It was obvious he was utterly dominated by Hayes.

"I have something I need your advice about, Karl," Hayes said. "With your experience in Hollywood, you may be able to help me."

"Yes, sir. Anything, sir." There was a pusillanimous note to the heavily accented German voice. Karl took a small sip from his glass, his hand shaking slightly.

"Karl, if you were making a film about the Russian Revolution," Hayes said, "how would you get a happy ending out of it? You're a European, after all. Suppose the main characters are White Russians. Suppose the Revolution comes between them, separates them."

The little man sat with a stupid look on his face.

Hayes smiled paternally.

"Come on, Karl," he said. "Surely you have a notion."

There was a pause. Hayes waited patiently. His staff of writers at Continental had been full of their usual half-baked ideas this afternoon. He wanted an independent opinion from someone he could trust.

"A costume drama, sir?" Karl asked.

"Yes," Hayes said. "A costume drama, Karl. With a happy ending."

In a few words Hayes told Karl the gist of Joseph Knight's scenario. He did not detail the tragic ending Knight had told him, but left the ending as a blank for Karl to fill in.

As he spoke, Karl held onto his drink, daring only to take a small sip or two, his hand trembling around the glass. It was obvious he wanted more to drink, a great deal more, and that a simple drink of whiskey, more than ample for anyone else, was a subtle torture for an alcoholic like Karl, whose craving was only whetted by such an amount.

Hayes could see this, and was enjoying it.

"Well?" he asked when he had finished his description of the property. "What's your opinion, Karl?"

He watched Karl's preoccupation with the drink vie with his concentration on the question he had been asked.

"Perhaps they would emigrate, sir," Karl said at length.

For a moment Hayes seemed lost in thought, pondering the notion. Then he smiled.

"Of course they would, Karl," he said. "Just so. They would emigrate together."

"Or meet in a foreign country after emigrating separately," Karl said. "The woman escaping first, the man left behind." A glimmer of inspiration shone in his bloodshot eyes. "Perhaps she believes the man is dead," he added. "His arrival in the foreign country comes as a surprise to her."

"Even better," Hayes smiled. "Thank you, Karl. Thank you very much. I value your advice. You know that."

Karl looked at his drink. He had barely touched it. There were still almost three fingers of golden liquid beckoning to him in the bottom of the costly crystal glass.

"That will be all, Karl," Hayes said with a sudden note of severity.

The servant realized that he was not to be allowed to drink the whiskey his employer had importuned him to pour into the glass in such quantity. He was being dismissed. His hand shaking slightly, he put the glass down on the tray and shambled out of the room.

Bryant Hayes sat alone, thinking about the brilliant new film he was going to make.

He had already forgotten the little game he had just played with Karl. It had been only a moment's amusement, and now he had more important things on his mind.

Hayes often used Karl as a sounding board for his own ideas, or made a show of asking Karl for advice. This was not, as it seemed, a way of being sympathetic to the little German. It was a subtle way of humiliating him.

A dozen years ago, Bryant Hayes and Continental Studios had paid a handsome sum to import Karlheinz Rächer from Berlin, where, after an early career as a photographer closely associated with the Expressionists, he had made silent films so influential that even today they were the subject of admiring critical studies.

As a photographer Rächer had had a stunning visual sense, accentuated by daring and very intricate darkroom techniques. He brought this visual power to his filmmaking, and was universally recognized as the most brilliant of the transplanted German directors, such as von Sternberg, Lubitsch, Erich von Stroheim, and the young Fritz Lang. Rächer had an inimitable style and a powerful inspiration that assured him a great career in America.

Then he had run afoul of Bryant Hayes.

The two men had met, of course, when Hayes first hired Rächer for Continental Pictures. Hayes had noticed a hint of Teutonic arrogance in the diminutive German's eyes during their first conversation. He could see that Rächer considered him a cheap American philistine who subordinated art to making money. He also sensed Rächer's great intelligence, and a hint that the German considered himself mentally above his American studio boss. This got under Hayes's skin because, though a businessman of extreme cunning, he lacked the esthetic taste of the highest talents he employed. He did not know a Picasso from a Matisse, could not tell Proust from Thomas Mann, and in every way incarnated the rather shallow Hollywood mogul whose brains are in his pocketbook.

Hayes decided to test Rächer.

After Rächer's first few efforts for Continental, effective psychological thrillers that made money, Hayes commanded the little director to make a silly costume drama filled with musical numbers. Rächer, not surprisingly, refused. He told Hayes, through one of the studio's most powerful producers—the same Owen Esser, as a matter of fact, whom Joseph Knight was later to encounter—that he had not been hired to make costume musicals, that there were other directors at Continental more suited to such work, and that his refusal was final. Hayes could take it or leave it, Rächer said.

At first it seemed that Hayes gave in. His request was withdrawn, and Karlheinz Rächer felt that he had won a battle and could hold his head high.

Then a deadly silence ensued. Karl Rächer's phone did not ring. No projects were brought to his office. The studio seemed to have forgotten his existence. There was no work for him.

Other foreign directors continued building their American careers while Karl sat on his hands. Enraged, he asked his agent to get him loan-out work with another studio. His agent informed him this was impossible. According to his contract, he could only be loaned out at the option of Continental Pictures. He could not work anywhere else without Bryant Hayes's express permission.

Infuriated now, Karl Rächer arranged meetings with the heads of the other major studios. He asked them if they would buy out his contract with Continental and give him a new start. But no one was buying. Though Rächer did not know it, Bryant Hayes had personally blackballed him. He could not work anywhere.

Rächer considered going back to Germany. But by now the German political situation was in chaos, the inflation had destroyed Germany's economy, and the Nazis were coming to power. Rächer, a Jew, did not dare return to his native land.

Karl Rächer was trapped under Bryant Hayes's thumb.

The studio head's silence continued. No scripts came Karl's way.

By this time Rächer's savings had been depleted by his lavish Hollywood lifestyle. He had to sell his Brentwood house and move into a bungalow not far from the studio. He raged to his agent, his friends and colleagues, about the injustice being done him. And they all sympathized. But no one could offer constructive advice, except the obvious: Karl Rächer must go to Bryant Hayes on his knees, declare his submission and his willingness to take on any project Hayes assigned him—and thus get back in the studio head's good graces.

This Karl Rächer could not do. His Teutonic pride would not let him. In his brief relationship with Bryant Hayes a fierce competition of wills had sprung up, abetted by an instinctive dislike and a need on the part of each man to feel mentally and creatively superior to the other.

So Karl Rächer withered on the vine, like his career. He began to drink. He spent his days in an alcoholic haze in his bungalow, cursing his fate. His bank account dwindled to nothing. His friends melted away, as friends in Hollywood always do when misfortune comes.

The battle of wills went on for two years. At the end of that time Karl Rächer was a shadow of his former proud self. He was dissipated, his skin was sallow, his eyes glazed. He was a broken man, surviving on the few dollars his remaining friends gave him as handouts. And most of those dollars he was drinking away.

At last Karl Rächer gave up.

One day he came, hat in hand, to ask Bryant Hayes to take him back. He would make any film Hayes asked, he said.

Their meeting took place in Hayes's office. Several high-level producers and studio executives were present, drinking cocktails with Hayes. There was also a beautiful young actress who at that time was one of the studio's budding stars.

Hayes made a point of not dismissing the others. He looked at Karl, a flicker of ill-disguised triumph in his eyes.

"You mean, Karl, that you would be willing to help this studio by directing, say, this script?" He held out the script for a college comedy, a silly "B" picture that Karl Rächer would not have looked at two years ago.

Karl nodded miserably. "Yes, sir," he said. "I will make any picture you like."

Hayes dangled the script, smiling. The others fell silent as they saw the cruel gleam in his eyes.

"What would you do for a chance to direct this script, Karl?" he asked.

"Anything, sir. Anything you like."

"Would you crawl?" Hayes asked, his eyebrow still raised in a sadistic look of interrogation.

The little German trembled slightly at these words, but did not flinch. He looked Hayes in the eye.

"Please, sir," he said.

"Would you?" Hayes asked. "Would you crawl?"

The silence in the room was charged with expectancy. The studio executives were looking curiously at Karl. The young starlet gazed at him with undisguised sadistic pleasure. She had seen Hayes humble people before, but this was a display of cruelty she found amazing and enjoyable— the more so since Hayes had taken her under his wing recently and she felt safe in the shadow of his enormous power.

"Let's see you do it," Hayes said. "Let me see you crawl, Karl."

A great tremor went through the little German, like a chemical change overwhelming his very being. Slowly he sank to the carpet and crawled on his hands and knees to Hayes while the others watched.

Karl Rächer crouched like a puppydog at Hayes's feet, his trembling face upraised.

Hayes let out a small laugh. Then he dropped the script on Karl Rächer's head.

"You start Monday, Karl," he said. "Now get out of here."

Karl Rächer picked up the script under the amused eyes

of the beautiful starlet and the powerful studio men, and left the office—on two feet.

But he never really walked on two feet after that day.

For Hayes's vengeance had only begun. After the college musical he assigned Karl Rächer only to "B" pictures of the worst kind, with no-name stars, mediocre writers, and second-rate below-the-line talent. He hounded Rächer's career pitilessly, forcing him into a long filmography of worthless pictures instead of the string of triumphs Rächer should have had to his credit.

In the end Karl Rächer fell apart completely, and drank so much that he could not effectively direct at all. Hayes exiled him to the Special Effects department, where Rächer fit in well because of his background in photography. Rächer was no longer a filmmaker but merely a photographic artisan, helping to graft images onto painted mattes and working with film stock.

When Rächer's seven-year contract with Continental Pictures ran out he applied for work at the other studios. But none would have him. His recommendation from Continental, for one thing, alluded to his drinking and the dissolution that had caused him to lose his directing assignments and be exiled to Special Effects. But beyond this, the personal handshake relationship of Bryant Hayes with the other studio heads effectively blackballed Karl Rächer for good.

To complete the humiliation, Bryant Hayes refused to renew Karl's contract at Continental. By this time the little German was a shabby bum. He had spent many a night in the Hollywood drunk tank and even, afflicted with delirium tremens, had to endure a stint in the state hospital.

Now Hayes administered the coup de grâce. He offered Rächer a job as his personal valet and houseboy. Rächer, an unemployable has-been, accepted. His spirit broken, his mind ruined by alcohol and humiliation, he behaved like the lapdog Hayes had made of him that awful day at the studio, in front of the studio executives and the sadistic young starlet. Metaphorically if not physically, he crawled. He dressed Bryant Hayes, cleaned his house, brought him drinks, and disintegrated further under Hayes's very eyes.

For Hayes made it possible for Karl to be in a constant

state of alcoholic intoxication, though never outright drunkenness. He let him drink, and had the other servants keep an eye on the liquor supply to facilitate Karl's tippling, within strict limits. He watched Karl deteriorate. He treated him with the careless indulgence of a master for a slave. Sometimes he made gentle fun of him. Sometimes he made the other servants clean him up. But generally he allowed Karl his seedy, hangdog look, and smiled when his guests noticed the broken little man and remarked on his dissipation.

"I take care of him," Hayes often said, just as he had said to Joseph Knight. "Without me, he'd be in the state hospital or the drunk tank. I'm all he's got."

And occasionally, as today, Hayes even asked the advice of Karl Rächer. The two men would have a drink together, and Hayes would pick Karl's brain, for he knew that a powerful intellect still remained behind the little German's dazed eyes. Sometimes the advice Karl gave was good. At other times, his mind too addled by dissipation to be lucid, he could only give rambling and worthless comments.

But Hayes kept him around and continued playing with him, like a cat with a dying mouse, just to remind himself and Karl that no man in Hollywood dared risk the wrath of Bryant Hayes for any reason—much less pretend, as Karl had done, to be intellectually and spiritually superior to Hayes. Sometimes, like today, he offered Karl a drink, and then made a point of dismissing him before he could actually touch more than a drop of it. This was his way of pouring a little more salt in Karl's wounds, just for the fun of it.

Eventually, Hayes assumed, Karl would either lose his mind completely or commit suicide. Hayes was waiting, with the patience of a jailer, to see which it would be. He enjoyed carrying out his decade-long revenge on Rächer, because he knew how brilliant Rächer had been. It was one thing to destroy a typical Hollywood yes-man. It was quite another to bring a proud and brilliant professional like Karl to his knees, and to destroy him in slow motion.

Karl Rächer had had his moment of rebellion—now ten years ago. And his punishment would continue until there was nothing human left inside him to punish. Hayes would keep him as a house pet, to be coddled with alcohol and stewarded to an early death, for his own amusement and the flattering of his own cruel pride.

Decidedly, Hayes had shown Karl Rächer who was the better man.

Today Hayes evaluated Rächer's advice. He decided that Karl was right. One could confect a happy ending out of the Russian Revolution if one tried. This would not be the ending Joseph Knight had built into the screenplay, but it would sell. The public craved happy endings in these hard times.

A year from now, if this film paid off, Moira Talbot would be right up there with Bette Davis and Katharine Hepburn at the top of the Hollywood heap. Continental Pictures, with this stunning success, would establish itself as the pre-eminent Hollywood studio, above MGM and Paramount.

And Bryant Hayes would have applied the finishing touches to his image as the greatest producer in Hollywood.

• • •

When Joseph Knight's phone did not ring during the week after his interview with Bryant Hayes, he was not surprised.

But he did not jump to conclusions about the meaning of Hayes's silence. It was precisely this that he had to discover.

He had never expected Hayes to accept his film on his terms. He understood the Hollywood system. A Hollywood studio would buy a property outright—for peanuts—but it would never allow an outsider to penetrate its ranks. Hayes had promised to call only as a means of getting rid of Knight. He never intended to see him again.

But this was not the key question. The key question was whether Hayes's refusal applied to the film itself, or only to Joseph Knight as the film's originator and proprietor.

One of two things had happened, Knight knew. Either

his film had stopped with Hayes himself and been forgotten the moment Knight walked out of Hayes's house, or, more significantly, the idea had hit home, and Hayes was planning to make the film while freezing Knight out of the production.

The latter result was the one Knight had hoped for from the outset. All his plans depended on it. He had intentionally left his property uncopyrighted and himself legally unprotected against the theft of his idea. He had offered the bait to Hayes like a carrot, in the hope that Hayes would be sufficiently impressed to put it into production.

Had Hayes taken the bait? That was the question.

But it was not until the end of his interview with Hayes that Joseph Knight had realized how he would find out his answer.

 4

A WEEK AFTER THE SWIMMING POOL MEETING BETWEEN Bryant Hayes and Joseph Knight, Daria Kane was on her way into a Wilshire Boulevard restaurant to meet Hayes for lunch when she passed a familiar face on the sidewalk.

It was the stranger who had been sitting by the pool at Bryant Hayes's mansion last week.

Joseph Knight looked at her with a moment's perplexity, followed by a light of recognition in his handsome eyes.

In that instant, to her surprise, Daria realized she had

not stopped thinking about him since her brief meeting with him. His image had been just beneath the surface of her thoughts throughout the past week.

This made her angry. The more so since she thought she saw a flicker of presumption in his dark eyes as he looked at her.

She cut the stranger dead, striding past him into the restaurant without greeting him or seeming to notice his existence. She behaved as though she was as distant as the remotest stars, and he a mere Hollywood tourist miles beneath her notice.

She thought no more about him that afternoon. She was buying a dress for a very important party. It was being given in honor of Bryant Hayes by the Academy of Motion Picture Arts and Sciences, and would be attended by all the major studio heads and dozens of stars. It was important that Daria look her best, not only to reflect well on Bryant Hayes but also to maximize her chances of a screen career.

She bought a magnificent gown in ice-blue satin, slit high up the thigh and with a low-cut bodice. She also bought a stunning sapphire necklace by Renée Girard for the occasion. She herself was amazed by her beauty when she tried the whole ensemble on at home. There was something at once sculptured and kittenishly sensual about her that made men gasp when they set eyes on her.

She showed the outfit to Hayes. He was pleased, and told her she had done well. Not surprisingly, the sight of her in the low-cut gown, with the outline of her magnificent hips and legs under the silken fabric, inflamed his aged libido, and he took her to bed.

As usual she felt nothing as he caressed her. When it came time for him to enter her she had her usual thought, *I'll be dry,* and tried to think of something to excite herself. To her surprise it was easy tonight. The image of the stranger, Joseph Knight, leapt into her mind with amazing urgency. She saw his eyes glowing mysteriously under the dark brows in the strange light of that burnished face, so masculine that a woman was thrown off her balance at the very sight of them. In his silent way, Joseph Knight was the sexiest man she had ever met.

Almost at once she was slippery and hot between her legs. And as Bryant Hayes took his pleasure from her, manifestly excited by her unaccustomed eagerness, she found herself gripped by the image of the stranger's dark eyes and hard, thick body.

She had the odd suspicion that, on Wilshire Boulevard today, Knight had known she had been thinking about him ever since last week, known it before she herself did. And underneath his polite smile of recognition was this intimate, mocking knowledge.

Once again the anger she had felt on the street came to her. But this time it came with a sensual rush that stunned her. Arching her pretty back, breasts shuddering under the fascinated gaze of Bryant Hayes, she suddenly had an almost painful orgasm. Her excitement was so contagious that Hayes himself came at once with a great burst within her.

Hayes kissed her and patted her cheek, smiling at his prowess. Then he rolled over and went to sleep.

But Daria was kept awake by anger, and by an involuntary excitement that lingered throughout her senses.

The stranger's smile hung before her eyes, penetrating, caressing. She wondered how he could have got so deep under her skin in two chance meetings.

She resolved to banish him from her thoughts, whatever the cost. She got up, went to the bathroom, and took a sleeping pill. She was damned if she was going to let that man make her lose sleep.

But Daria Kane did lose sleep over Joseph Knight. A lot of sleep.

In the first place, he crossed her path again.

It could only have been an accident. It could not have been premeditated. But there he was, getting out of a limousine in front of a downtown office building just as she was passing on her way to lunch with a friend.

This time he did not smile or indicate his recognition. He must have sensed from her chilly demeanor last time that she wanted no part of him. So he merely looked her in the eye with an expression of casual interest and perhaps the subtlest hint of shared memory. "You don't want to know me," his eyes said. "All right, then, I won't greet you." There was a quiet cooperativeness in this momentary glance.

And perhaps something more.

The hint of something more kept Daria awake that night and forced her to take a double dose of sleeping pills. Her nerves were on fire with involuntary excitement at the effect Knight had had on her, and with rage at this very excitement. She would not countenance such susceptibility in herself. She prided herself on her absolute self-control. It was that control that had snared Bryant Hayes as her lover and protector, and that control that was going to make her a power to be reckoned with in Hollywood.

It took until four o'clock that morning to get the stranger out of her mind. And even in sleep he took up residence in her dreams. Daria woke up exhausted and cranky.

But she was not finished with Joseph Knight yet.

At the end of that week she took Bryant Hayes to the airport. He was on his way to New York to meet with the board of directors of Continental Pictures. It was the most important meeting of the year, a financial meeting. The studio had been losing money during the last quarter. Hayes intended to let the board in on his brilliant new idea, the idea stolen from Joseph Knight. He expected this picture to be the biggest money-maker for the studio in the last five years.

Hayes had decided not to take Daria along with him. He needed all his wits about him on this trip, and did not want to be distracted, or too relaxed, by her lovemaking. He was to sell his new property to the board. And the board was run by Arnold Speck, a man who hated Bryant Hayes's guts and had been angling for years for a way to topple him from his Hollywood throne.

It was only thanks to Speck and his canny investments that the studio had survived the Depression as well as it had. Every member of the board knew how crucial Speck had become to the corporation. His power had never been greater.

But Speck, a man with an overweening ego, did not like to see Hayes, his old rival, getting all the credit in the press for the corporation's success. The more so since Hayes's filmmaking decisions had brought only modest financial success at the box office during that time. Speck was Continental's real money-maker.

And Speck had ambitions to take over the creative, Hollywood side of the operation himself one of these days. He did not advertise his ambition, but Hayes, a shrewd judge of human nature, was acutely aware of it.

Thus it was crucial that Hayes score a major box-office success soon, in order to establish himself once and for all as the creative head of Continental Pictures and to force Speck to stay in New York where he belonged.

The new Moira Talbot property suggested by Joseph Knight was the key to this strategy. It was an exciting, high-gloss product, sure to take in millions if it was properly produced and distributed. But it was also a big-budget film, requiring a heavy financial investment from the start. Hayes would need all his skills to sell it to the board, for it represented a major risk.

Speck had more power than Hayes where it counted: with the financial managers and stockholders of Continental. Hayes burned at the idea of having to pander to a man he hated. But on this trip he would have to flatter Speck, to soft-sell him, to wheedle him into approving the initial expenditures for the new film. It would be a loathsome experience, but Hayes would have to go through it. For this reason above all he did not want Daria along on the trip. He could not mix pleasure with this darkest side of his business.

He did not like leaving Daria behind on her own, for his jealousy was strong as always. She was a gorgeous young woman, nearly forty years younger than he, and he was often tormented by fantasies of her secret hungers and the furtive ways she might try to assuage them. This was why he had her closely watched whenever he was absent from home.

He bade her a tender goodbye at Los Angeles Airport. "I'll be back in three days," he said. "Keep an eye on things for me."

"I'll miss you," she said, her big eyes glistening. "Call me every night."

Touched at her loyalty, he kissed her. The feel of her tongue in his mouth excited him, and he wished wistfully that he could sleep with her tonight. But business was business.

At that instant, as she was kissing him, Daria glanced over his shoulder and saw something that made her start.

Waiting in a departure lounge a dozen yards away, dressed in a dark blue suit that set off his tanned skin strikingly, his briefcase beside him, his eyes calmly fixed to her face, was Joseph Knight. He smiled slightly and looked back down to his newspaper.

Daria closed her eyes in desperation. She had to force herself to finish her kiss with Bryant Hayes as though nothing had happened.

"Is anything wrong?" Hayes asked, studying her face carefully.

"No," she insisted. "I just wish you weren't going. Hurry back. And call me tonight."

"All right," he promised. "Take good care of yourself. And be a good girl."

She knew this was his way of saying he was keeping his eye on her. He often made oblique references to his jealousy, and to what would happen to her if she cheated on him.

The words had a particularly powerful ring today, because Joseph Knight was in all her senses as she hugged Hayes goodbye.

A moment later he was gone, having watched her blow him kisses from her post in the aisle.

She dared not turn around to see what had become of Joseph Knight until Hayes had gone through the gate to the plane. Her senses tingled as she waited. She could almost feel Knight's dark, penetrating eyes on her back as she stood waving goodbye to Hayes. She blew kiss after kiss, hoping the emotion in her face would be seen by Hayes as love for him.

At last he was gone.

Daria turned around. There was no sign of Joseph

Knight. The waiting area he had occupied was now full of passengers standing in line to get on their plane. She looked at the departure sign. The plane was going to Phoenix. Knight was nowhere in sight.

Shaken, Daria walked out of the airport, feeling hundreds of eyes turning to admire her beauty, and got into her limousine.

"Home," she told the driver.

She could hardly breathe. She needed to get back into her own bedroom, have a stiff drink, and try to forget the madness that was happening inside her.

But it was not so easy.

She had her drink, and a tranquilizer to boot, but nothing banished the image of Joseph Knight from her mind. She saw the look on his face at the airport. It was the same calm, appraising look he had worn every time she had seen him. But this time there had been a definite light of amusement at the back of his eyes. He knew somehow that he had got through her defenses, and he was enjoying her disarray.

The effect of the drink and the tranquilizer could not compete with the throbbing in Daria's senses. She spent the whole afternoon staring at the walls of her bedroom and fighting the wild ferment inside her. Though her mind hated Joseph Knight passionately for his quiet arrogance and his knowing looks, her body clamored to belong to him. Her skin was on fire. The tips of her breasts were absurdly alert and painfully sensitive as the silk fabric of her nightgown brushed against them. And between her legs there was an ache she had never felt before.

It was not so much the mere physical presence of Knight that inflamed her so. It was the look in his eyes, and his mysterious stillness. Unlike other men, he did not have to take a pace forward or say a word to tell her he desired her. His whole body proclaimed it in a way so masterful, so penetrating, that despite her fierce pride she found herself wanting to fall at his feet like a slave.

Over and over again she imagined him silently entering this room in the dead of night, sometime when Hayes was away and she was alone—such as now, for instance—and putting his warm, strong hands on her. She could feel his kiss, feel that hard powerful body pressed to hers, and her delicious surrender as he took her. She imagined it in a hundred ways, each more seductive than the last, but all having in common her furtive solitude in the bedroom and Knight's entry there, their guilty commingling and the sexual delights he alone would know how to bring her.

She tossed and turned in her bed all afternoon, unable to quell the fantasy or the waves of sensual longing coursing through her. Then she got up, took a cool shower, and prepared for dinner. She called a friend from the studio, one of Hayes's publicity men, a young man named Jon Diefenback whose company she could enjoy without fear because he was a homosexual. She also knew that Jon would tell Hayes of their dinner and Hayes would be reassured that Daria had been in safe company in his absence. Thus she would kill two birds with one stone.

The evening passed pleasantly enough. Jon regaled her with inside jokes about doings at the studio, and they both spoke about the new project that had Bryant Hayes so excited. Daria was hoping there would be a small role in it for her somewhere. Jon encouraged her.

At evening's end Jon took his leave with a smile, and Daria was alone. Exhausted, she said goodnight to the housekeeper and went to bed. She knew the servants had orders to keep an eye on her. That was one price she had to pay for being Hayes's mistress. But they would never make bold to enter her bedroom or even to knock after ten.

So she would be alone with her thoughts, and her fantasies.

Daria took off her dress and underwear and slipped on a sheer silk nightgown. The tickle of the fabric on her bare skin made her tremble. Her nipples were taut and straining. Her whole body was shaken by a thousand tiny tremors.

She read for half an hour. Then an enormous fatigue came over her. She gave up the fight to deny her emotions, and this seemed to bring her a semblance of peace. Guiltily she slipped off the nightgown. She would sleep nude tonight. Perhaps the only way to defeat her fantasies about Joseph Knight was to give in to them.

Even now, as she lay naked under the sheets, her pride made her hate Joseph Knight for having thrown her into this state. The more so since he probably had not wasted a moment's thought over her, to judge from his amused indifference when he looked at her.

She wished she could sneak out just for tonight, escape Bryant Hayes's expensive prison and find a man, any man, to give her a good deep fuck and make her feel like a woman. Then maybe she could forget Joseph Knight and get some decent rest.

But another man, any man, would be a poor substitute for the man she wanted. Try as she might, Daria could not deny this.

It was with this maddening thought that, her nerves deadened by the tranquilizer she had taken, she plummeted into uneasy sleep troubled by images of Joseph Knight.

She was awakened in the night's darkest hour by a featherlight touch of lips against her own.

At first she forgot where she was. The dream she had been having was so intense that her physical sensation seemed to grow naturally out of it. She felt Joseph Knight naked against her body, his mysterious, unreadable smile curling the soft lips that touched her own.

The kiss moved to her cheek, her brow, her eyelid, and back to her lips, spreading delight through her senses. She began to rise toward wakefulness, but the excitement of her dream pulled her back down into rapture. Her body strained to receive the caresses of her imaginary lover. A moan stirred in her throat.

The kiss was at her lips again, this time more intimate. A smooth male tongue penetrated her mouth and began to explore her. Still confused by her dream, she put her arms around the hard shoulders offered to her.

A voice in her mind told her that it was Bryant Hayes holding her in his arms. He was here in his bed, as usual. It was his kiss she was tasting.

But it did not feel like his kiss. This only served to increase the power of her dream. She began to forget Hayes. She did not need to think about him. She could give herself wholeheartedly to the thrill of her fantasy, feel her senses rise to the furtive wanting she had struggled against so long.

And as the kiss grew deeper, more knowing, a second inner voice began to warn that this was not a dream. This was really happening. And this kiss was not coming from aged Bryant Hayes. It was the kiss of a young, virile man. A man who was in her bedroom.

Even as part of Daria edged closer to wakefulness, the rest of her gave itself with abandon to the sensations hurrying through her. She held her lover, brought him closer, spread her legs to open herself to him. The smooth hard feel of his arms was a delight beyond words. Her nipples brushed against the hair on his chest. Her thighs slipped lovingly around his hips. Her dream was coming true at last, and more beautifully than even her guiltiest fantasies had presented it to her. It was Knight, Joseph Knight, here inside her mind, her body, all male and all for her.

The moan of her own excitement brought her awake.

She was not alone. There was a man in the room after all. In the bed, and on top of her.

Her eyes opened wide. In the shadows she could not see him. Fear made her want to cry out.

But the delicious kiss was still on her lips, and the large hands were holding her gently, and every sinew in her body had already opened itself to him in her sleep. She could not stem that tide of wanting so quickly. She had to get her bearings.

Gradually the room came into focus, looming over her in a moonlit glow, its details hidden by the dark figure of the man she already held in her arms. Her hands tensed on his ribcage, but did not let go, did not push him away.

She could not seem to find herself. Her own desire, and the intensity of her dream, had sapped her of the defenses she needed now. Surrender was already sighing in her senses, even as her mind fought for lucidity.

Mustering all her strength, she forced back the tide of delight in her limbs and pushed her dream lover back from her long enough to see his face.

A gasp caught in her throat. It was Joseph Knight.

A great tremor shook her as she pushed harder against his chest.

"You," she hissed. "What do you think you're doing?"

But even as her harsh whisper sounded, it shook and trembled on her lips. For desire was still more powerful than shock or anger.

She made a comic figure, nude in the bed, pushing against his chest with frail arms while her long legs were wrapped lovingly around his waist. Anger took possession of her hands, making them scratch and claw, even as desire still owned the lower part of her body, which had not yet been informed of her decision to fight him.

And even the soft hands that scratched at his flesh had not quite made up their minds, for there was a passion in their movements that did not come from refusal alone. And he seemed to sense that she was fighting against herself as well as him, that in her sleep he had conquered too much of her to lose his ground now.

"Ssshhh," he murmured, his hands cradling her trembling body with a delicacy that was the more strange because the hard length of his sex was already nestled between her thighs.

For a long agonized moment Daria teetered on the edge of an abyss. Her pride had joined her anger, and she wanted more than anything to throw this intruder out, to scream for the servants, to call Bryant Hayes in New York and have him unleash the full fury of his power against this arrogant upstart, this Joseph Knight.

But the feel of Knight's body, combined with the sensual aftereffects of her dream and the ferment she had been feeling in herself for a whole week, sapped her strength to resist. Her hands, rebelling against her will, began to caress his shoulders. The cry of anger in her throat sounded as a sensual sigh. Her skin was on fire.

In that instant he pressed his advantage. He pulled her face to his and kissed her hard. Powerful arms curled around her back and pulled her against the terrible male body hungry for her own. Her legs spread wider around him as her pliant woman's flesh was pressed to the hardness of him.

And in that fatal instant Daria lost the battle. Her body no longer belonged to her. Her hands fluttered over his back, her nipples rubbed delightedly against his chest. Her tongue came to join his own in a tense little dance of discovery. Forbidden female undulations made her loins stir against his, and already the sweet place between her legs was finding the tip of him and smoothing a path for him inside her.

"You bastard," she moaned. "Dirty bastard . . ."

But it was too late. His sex had felt her invitation, opened the waiting door, and with one long sighing movement he slid to the hilt inside her. She gasped. He was bigger than she had imagined, and more intimate in storming the quick of her.

From that moment her anger did not disappear, nor did her pride forget the insult being done to her. But these forces could only join hands with the delight in her flesh as she gave herself to him, fighting all the way, her struggles making her surrender sweeter and more perverse.

She ran her hands down his back to his loins. His body was thick with bands of muscle hard as steel. His hands were on her shoulders, pulling her down onto him, and her knees were upraised, helping him to come deeper. His thrusts were slow, knowing, unspeakably intimate. Daria had been with many men in her young life, but never with one who knew how to own a woman this way. His strokes found hot centers of ecstasy whose existence she had not suspected until this moment.

Her back arched, her hands clenching on the silk sheets, her breasts trembling against his chest, she gave him her first orgasm, and then, almost immediately, another. He felt her little spasms caressing his sex, but did not stop his stroking, for he seemed to know this was only the overture to her passion.

The powerful hands had slipped down her back to her loins, and he held the soft globes in his hands, positioning her like a doll in his grasp. His face remained dark, he was like a huge shadow that had fallen over her on this bewitched night. The silence of the room, the familiar walls, were like accomplices to the unspeakable act going on in the bed. Daria's head flung this way and that, her eyes unseeing in her ecstasy.

Deeper and deeper he came, while the large hands upraised her, fingers hard as iron poised on her tender flesh. Pleasure made her whimper and moan as the terrible male thing inside her stirred and moved and thrust with tiny shifts that kindled explosions throughout her senses.

"Bastard . . ." The word was no longer an accusation on her lips, but an anthem, the sensual song of her surrender.

And now even this word was silenced, for he was pulling her closer, tighter, and she felt the first tremor of his coming, more exciting than anything she had ever felt before, more dangerous and thrilling. Then, quickly, it was coming forward, storming like an express train, irresistible. And when at last it found her, upraising her to a height she could not bear, the explosion was greater than she had imagined possible.

It seemed to go on forever, the last coming of him, a possession so complete that she lost her soul and existed only as the slave of his body. He himself was motionless, buried in the quick of her, his sinews tensed like steel in that last embrace, while she shook with a thousand tremors of delight, her mind gone, her pride sacrificed on the altar of the ecstasy he had brought her.

When it was over, and she came to herself in slow stages like a dreamer finding her way tentatively back to reality, she knew already that her strong will had been burned out of her by what he had done to her. The rebellion she had felt only moments ago was gone now. All that remained was surrender, and the throbbing aftermath of a pleasure beyond her dreams, a pleasure on the edge of death itself.

He remained hard inside her, but now he cradled her with arms grown gentle and fatherly. He held her against his chest and kissed her brow with warm soft lips. And still the tremors shook her, for she had given so much that she could only return to her own flesh through a long series of stages, each one a little shock.

She tried to say something. At first she could not find

words. The English language seemed to have abandoned her.

"How did you . . ." she stammered, "get in here?"

He did not answer. He merely held her closer. She nestled lovingly against his chest, her legs still wrapped around him. Still the sex inside her did not ebb. Decidedly, he was not a mere man. He was something stronger than a man, more cunning, infinitely more powerful. She had suspected it when she saw him looking at her at the airport, but now she knew it with every fiber of her body.

"Never mind," she said, finding a remnant of humor somewhere in the heart of her surrender. "You're here now."

At that moment Daria Kane entered a new and perilous world.

 5

THREE WEEKS AFTER BRYANT HAYES'S BRIEF AND IMPORTANT visit to New York—a visit on which he successfully convinced his New York superiors of the enormous commercial potential of his new costume project—the head of a rival film studio, Monarch Pictures, received a visit from Joseph Knight.

It was the strangest visit he had ever received.

His name was Oscar Freund. His had been for fifteen years the leader among the smaller studios. He possessed a chain of four hundred theaters, none of which were the lavish downtown houses, but unpretentious neighborhood theaters patronized by working people and their families. He produced modest but money-making films, usually renting out stars from the bigger studios. He had managed to make a tidy profit, albeit far less than that of the major companies, by turning out strong "B" pictures, westerns, screwball comedies and shorts. And he had made headlines by producing a number of "serious," socially conscious dramas that won Oscars and gave his studio critical success.

Ironically, during the desperate years 1931 and 1932, when Universal and RKO were forced into receivership, and even the great Paramount went into bankruptcy, little Monarch Pictures had managed to turn its usual profit. This was thanks to Oscar Freund's canny sense of the marketplace and his unique ability to cut costs without sacrificing quality. Freund had a reputation for being open-minded about new things, trying offbeat ideas and odd combinations of stars. Sometimes his ideas flopped, but more often they made money.

Freund was a "survivor" in the finest sense of the word. He could make any picture for less than his competitors, and give it a high-gloss look, getting the best from his performers, cameramen, and technicians. A Freund picture always seemed to be more than the sum of its parts. Freund had made more than one major star through his clever productions—stars he could no longer afford after having made them, for they went to the more powerful studios to pursue their careers.

But he was a creative force in Hollywood. He had won more than his share of Oscars, often stealing the award from the major studios' more expensive films, and liked to boast that "Oscar" was a nickname celebrating his many awards rather than a mere given name. His studio had its own peculiar brand of prestige, and those in the know were always on hand to see each new Monarch picture.

And there was one more facet to Freund's personality, which interested Joseph Knight more than the others.

Oscar Freund hated Bryant Hayes.

His enmity dated back more than fifteen years, to the

time when he and Hayes were both ambitious young studio heads battling for supremacy during the silent era. A major deal had been struck between Freund and a large New York backer, a powerful financier who had more than three hundred East Coast theaters in his pocket. But Freund lacked the assets to go through with the project on his own, so he contacted Hayes and asked him if he would like to make it a partnership arrangement. Their combined assets could have made them co-owners of the biggest studio in Hollywood if the scheme paid off.

Hayes had delayed, saying he needed time to convince his then-partner, Adolph Herman, to accept the idea of a merger with Freund and Monarch Pictures. Freund had taken a brief vacation in Mexico while waiting for word from Hayes.

When Freund returned to Hollywood he was confronted with the news that Hayes had made a separate deal with the New York financier. Though the terms were never disclosed, it was obvious that Hayes had sweetened the deal in some secret and perhaps illegal ways in order to freeze Oscar Freund out.

Under Hayes's leadership, Continental Pictures went on to become one of the biggest studios in Hollywood. Oscar Freund never recovered from his missed opportunity. He watched Hayes become the dean of studio heads and a pillar of the community, while Freund himself had to pursue his career out of the limelight. By the end of the silent era Continental had cemented its reputation as the "Cadillac of studios" while Monarch remained a sort of disheveled bridesmaid, respected for its critical successes but never taken seriously as a financial power.

Oscar Freund's hatred of Bryant Hayes had grown more intense with the passage of the years.

Oscar Freund loved the movies. He loved every aspect of the work, and was not afraid to get his hands dirty in story conferences, on the set, and even in the editing room when he thought his directors needed a helping hand. He was often chaffed about his paternal interference in the business of others, but those under him at Monarch took his advice very seriously. His expertise at every aspect of filmmaking was unquestioned, and more than once his acute instincts had saved a Monarch film from mediocrity and brought results at the box office.

But neither Freund's great talent nor his hard work could bring Monarch up to the exalted level of Hayes's Continental Pictures. The tremendous financial might of Continental was too much for Freund. He could only hope to embarrass Bryant Hayes by upstaging him with a particularly brilliant film now and then, or outdoing him in a single financial quarter. This was the best that Freund could do against a competitor of such power and prestige.

But now his opportunity for revenge came.

It came in the form of a total stranger named Joseph Knight.

Knight found that Freund was much easier to see than Hayes and was a great contrast to the regal head of Continental Pictures. Freund greeted Knight in his office at Monarch Studios, an unpretentious room cluttered with scripts and bearing a musty aroma reminiscent of the Tin Pan Alley office where he had worked as a song plugger twenty-five years before. The atmosphere was one of harried hard work and the grime of high-tension competition. Freund was famous for his no-frills lifestyle, a lifestyle he encouraged for his employees, especially his stars.

"What can I do for you, Mr. Knight?" Freund asked. He looked impatient, and not without a knowledge of his own importance. "My time is limited, I'm afraid."

"I won't take up much of it," Joseph Knight said. "And I think I can promise I won't bore you."

He began to outline a story he had brought for Freund's consideration. It differed radically from the story he had given Bryant Hayes, though it was no less brilliant in its concept.

It was a harshly realistic story of the Depression and its effects on the lives of two people in love. The heroine was a young girl from a wealthy family who fell madly in love with a handsome young man from the other side of the tracks. When her family broke up the romance, the young man went off to seek his fortune. While he was turning himself into a millionaire, the girl's family was ruined by the Depression. By a cruel twist of fate, the young hero returned in triumph to ask for his first love's hand, only to find that during his absence she had married a poor suitor to whom her now-impoverished family could not object. Thus the hero had wasted his time in pursuing a golden idol as a means of winning the girl he loved.

Oscar Freund listened to Joseph Knight's recitation, smoking cigarette after cigarette, which he butted messily in the large ashtray on his desk. His quick brain was evaluating the scenario. It was a metaphor for the entire tragedy of the Depression. It also made a profound statement about America, the "land of opportunity" where, too often, money and its possession, or lack of it, stood between people. The theme of the story was that material success cannot bring people together. Only love can.

When Joseph Knight had finished, Oscar Freund nodded from behind his desk.

"All right, it's brilliant," he said. "I'm not afraid to call a spade a spade. I've been around this business long enough to know quality when I see it. It could do big business. It could make a lot of money for somebody."

He took a deep breath. "But not me," he added. "And not now."

There was a pause. The two men looked at each other, neither one flinching.

"Why not you?" asked Knight.

"Because I'm booked," Freund said. "I'm up to my ears in productions, each one more chancy than the last. If you knew how overextended I am . . . I just can't do it. I don't have the cash or the resources. Not now. Maybe next year, or the year after . . ."

Knight shook his head with a smile.

"It has to be now," he said. "But I'm not asking you to invest a dime in this. I'm only asking you to distribute it. I'll take all the financial risk. I'll do the hiring, I'll line up the investors. I'll be responsible for any loss. I'll put a million dollars in your bank as security tomorrow morning. All I need from you is your back lot for shooting, and those four hundred theaters of yours for distribution."

Freund seemed intrigued. "And what do you get out of this?" he asked.

"I produce," Knight said. "I control everything artistically. I choose all the below-the-line talent, and I do the casting. It's my picture."

Freund looked skeptical. "Do you have any experience at this sort of thing?" he asked.

"Enough," Knight said. If his own bravado astonished him, he did not show it.

A speculative look had come over Freund's face.

"What if the picture is a bomb?" he asked. "I can't afford to get egg on my face."

Knight smiled. "You've heard the story," he said. "Do you think it will be a bomb?"

Freund said nothing. He believed the picture had a chance to become a hit. The public was ready for a serious cinematic statement about the Depression that had been making the country's life miserable for a decade.

"Let me make it even easier for you," Knight said. "You don't have to associate your name with the picture, or put your studio's imprint on it, until you've seen the finished film and decided for yourself what it's worth. I will take all the risk."

Freund looked more closely at his visitor.

"And what is my cut if the picture makes money?" he asked.

"You name it," Knight smiled.

Freund named a percentage. Knight responded with half that percentage. Freund smiled. This was what he had expected to get for his studio's name, its facilities, and its distribution network.

Oscar Freund had now heard enough to know he was being offered a deal almost too good to be true. Yet, surprisingly, he seemed less interested than before. The expression in his eyes had become distant and ambiguous.

Joseph Knight knew what this look meant. Freund was preparing to refuse him. No matter how much a maverick Freund might be among Hollywood studio heads, he could not bring himself to break the unwritten code that bound that fraternity together. He could not allow an independent producer like Joseph Knight to penetrate his studio. Not at any price. He might buy Knight's property outright and make it himself at his leisure, but he would never empower Knight to use Monarch's facilities to become a major new Hollywood power on his own.

"I'm impressed by your offer," Freund said carefully. "But I don't think it's going to work out."

"Perhaps you'll change your mind," Joseph Knight rejoined, "when you hear the last piece of the puzzle."

Freund raised an eyebrow. "What else have you got up your sleeve?" he asked.

Joseph Knight leaned back in his chair.

"Bryant Hayes's next big production," he said. "It's his biggest-budget project in seven years. A costume epic about the Russian Revolution. It's scheduled for release next Christmas. It will star Moira Talbot and Guy Lavery. The publicity blitz will be bigger than anything he's done since before the Crash. I know every single word of the script."

"How is that?" Freund asked.

"Because I wrote it," Knight smiled.

Oscar Freund sat bolt upright.

"Maybe you'd like to tell me about that," he suggested.

In a few well-chosen words Joseph Knight told Oscar Freund about the project he had handed Bryant Hayes on a silver platter. He described the bigger-than-life costume drama, and also its unexpected, tragic ending. Without a hint of rancor he explained how Hayes had appropriated the property without compensating him.

And he said more. He told how the property had been submitted to Hayes's superiors in New York at a top-secret meeting and been approved for red-carpet treatment and blockbuster release next Christmas. He told about the casting decisions, the plans for location shooting, the assignment of producer and director. In short, he gave Oscar Freund the exclusive lowdown on a top-secret project, down to its tiniest details.

"How do you know all this?" Freund asked.

"Never mind how I know," Knight replied. "The important thing is that Hayes's picture will be your competition next Christmas. Our competition, I should say. And I just found out something that throws a new light on the whole problem.''

"What is that?" Oscar Freund asked.

"Three weeks ago," Knight said, "in consultation with his top script advisers, Hayes agreed to drop the tragic ending of the story and go with a Hollywood boy-gets-girl ending.''

Freund, on the edge of his seat, looked into Joseph Knight's eyes. "But the whole story depends on that ending," he said. "Without it the characters don't mean anything. What do those jerks think they're doing?"

"They're doing what their instincts tell them," Knight said. "They're backing off from taking a chance. They're going to give the public what they think it wants.''

Suddenly Freund's bright little eyes focused sharply on Knight. He wondered whether Knight had known from the outset that Hayes and his people would butcher the ending of his screenplay. Could he have seeded them with the idea, knowing all along what they would do with it? Could he be that clever?

Oscar Freund did not ask.

"So you're going to give the public something better than Continental," he said. "You're going to take the big gamble, and try to upstage Hayes.''

Knight smiled.

"They told me you were a smart man, Mr. Freund," he said. "I thought you'd get my meaning.''

Oscar Freund thought carefully. What he was being offered was the opportunity of a lifetime, and with no risk to himself. If he brought this picture out, and it upstaged Hayes's costume drama, it could be an enormous embarrassment to Hayes. And a bright feather in the cap of Monarch Pictures and Oscar Freund.

"You're a smart man yourself," he said to Knight. "You're a nobody. No one in this town has ever heard of you. And here you are telling me that the two biggest films to come out next Christmas will both be yours. One stolen by Hayes, and one distributed by me.''

Knight said nothing. His expression was as calm as though the two men were discussing the weather.

At that moment Oscar Freund's lifelong hatred of Bryant Hayes finally outweighed his loyalty to the Hollywood studio code against independent producers.

"All right," he said. "I'll help you. On the condition that you put up the money in front, and sign papers making you responsible for any loss to my studio. In return you get my facilities, my distribution, and any other help you need."

"There's one more condition," Knight said. "The entire project must be top secret. I want complete security. No one must know anything about this production. Not until we decide to let them know, that is. The element of surprise is the key."

Freund nodded. He saw the deviousness of his visitor's plan.

"All right," he said. "No one but you and I will know the details of production, or the schedule. If the word gets out, you'll know it was me who let the cat out of the bag."

Knight smiled. He was impressed by Freund's honesty. He had heard that Freund was a breath of fresh air in the fetid Hollywood atmosphere, and now he had the proof of it. The man was willing to take a chance, and to keep a secret.

They shook hands.

"I'd sure like to know where you get all your inside information about this Hayes picture," Oscar Freund repeated.

Knight smiled. "Why don't you let me worry about that?" he asked.

Freund shrugged. "As long as it's good information," he said. "It's your money."

Knight smiled again. The light in his eyes impressed Freund, who only now realized he was in the presence of someone who might one day become a great Hollywood power. This much talent combined with this much cunning was exactly what made a Zanuck, a Thalberg, a Mayer.

Under ordinary circumstances Oscar Freund, like any other studio head, would have done anything in his power to stand in the way of such an upstart. But Joseph Knight represented Freund's best chance—and perhaps his last—to get revenge on Bryant Hayes for the bad deed that had cast a shadow over his entire career. He was going to take this chance.

"Partners?" Knight asked, extending a hand.

"Partners," Oscar Freund agreed, shaking the hand warmly. He could feel the rocklike strength of Knight's personality in his handshake. It occurred to him in that instant that he had known both sharp entrepreneurs and brilliant artists in Hollywood. But the two qualities, cunning and inspiration, never seemed to be united in the same man. Until now, that is. Until Joseph Knight.

He walked the stranger to the studio gates and said goodbye. Then he hurried back in to his office to start making plans. He had not felt so excited in years.

As for Joseph Knight, he felt satisfaction mingling with a quiet exhilaration in his veins as he drove back to his hotel. He was about to embark on the biggest financial gamble of his career. At the same time he was about to assault the ramparts of the Hollywood fortress with a powerful property in his hands, and with a powerful ally at his side.

Two allies, that is.

The first was Oscar Freund, with his studio, his resources, and his hatred of Bryant Hayes.

The second was Daria Kane.

6

THE HOLLYWOOD THAT KATE HAMILTON FOUND ON HER arrival with Melanie was a far different place from the Hollywood seen by Joseph Knight from his room at the Beverly Wilshire Hotel, not to mention the baronial Hollywood of Bryant Hayes.

Rather than the Hollywood of high-rent offices and hotel suites with views of the hills, this was the Hollywood of cheap apartments and furnished rooms in the polluted Flats, an endless grid of dirty city streets whose buildings had seen better days and whose inhabitants were on a one-way trip to nowhere.

This was the Hollywood of starving extras and star-struck hopefuls whose dreams of glory were quickly devoured by the monster that was the film industry, a monster whose glittering facade concealed its murky core of venality. Young people driven by dreams of being "somebody" came here to escape their past, armed with their good looks and sometimes their talent in high-school productions or community theater. But the irony of Hollywood was that behind its glitter it was a faster and more vicious road to a dead end than any the hopefuls could have trod back home.

This was the Hollywood of low-level assistant directors, casting directors, and agents, driving second-hand Mercedes and Duesenbergs and Bugattis around Hollywood Boulevard to impress their girlfriends, the Hollywood of sleazy talent scouts and fly-by-night independent producers who exploited the star-struck "kids" (Hollywood's perennial name for the hopefuls) with dangled contracts and promises of one-line roles or nonspeaking walk-ons.

It was a land of cold, hard business, the business of making movies. It employed several thousand professionals in its huge studios, and it made a handful of performers very rich. But these few pampered stars, with their retinues of agents and publicity men, were in every way the exception to the rule where film acting and production were concerned.

The overriding majority of Hollywood actors were contract players to the big studios, with salaries barely large enough to support a lower-middle-class lifestyle, and with almost no job security. Most of these highly talented people were lucky to get billing in a "B" picture or two before their careers fizzled, sabotaged by an unfortunate profile, the changing whims of the casting directors, or the cruel passage of the years. And for every struggling contract player there were a thousand hopefuls who never found work at all.

Hollywood, the "land of opportunity," was in reality a place so surfeited by pretty faces, perfect figures, and raw acting talent that only one performer in a million stood a chance of making a career there.

But the hopefuls, the "kids," did not care about this reality. They came here driven by their dreams. And those dreams persisted even after harsh reality had made it obvious they had no chance of coming true. For that was perhaps the final irony of Hollywood, the "dream factory." Its vast store of hopefuls were themselves consumed by a dream, and so driven by it that a thousand humiliations could not tarnish it or diminish their indefatigable search for the success that receded before them a bit more each day.

This was the Hollywood whose corruption and venality were already the subject of dark legend: the seamy side of the illusion factory, the underbelly of the world of dreams.

It was a place that devoured youth and innocence, using as bait the promise of stardom in order to exploit the hopefuls who flocked here like flies to honey. That exploitation was moral, professional, and nearly always sexual.

The town was one gigantic trap, a quicksand disguised as nirvana. Though its fatal charms could attract only one type of victim—the "hopeful," the ambitious young person driven by a dream—such victims existed in inexhaustible quantity in a vast nation economically crippled by the Depression. So Hollywood thrived while its slaves languished in its musty corners.

Unlike those around her, Kate Hamilton was remarkably unfazed by the Hollywood she entered as a hard-boiled, beautiful young woman of twenty. She was indifferent to its perils because she was unattracted by its illusory pots of gold.

Kate entered this world provided with an invisible armor that made her absolutely impervious to its pervasive corruption. That armor had been built into her by her lonely childhood, the sudden loss of her home, and tempered further by her brief, disastrous marriage to Quentin and the shame she bore over what she had done to Chris Hettinger.

Kate was past being vulnerable to the promises held out like so many carrots by corrupt Hollywood, because Kate had no dreams left at all. She had long since lost her girlhood, and with it her capacity to fantasize about Prince Charming, or the glories of love, or that great universal substitute for love, Success.

Thus the sleazy underside of Hollywood, in the ugly Flats at the base of the storied hills, was no more depressing to Kate than any of the dozen other places she had lived since she began her wandering. And the glitter of Hollywood, shilled to tourists by tour buses whining their way through Bel Air and Brentwood, by Grauman's Chinese and the studio back lots and the HOLLYWOODLAND sign in the hills, was as indifferent to Kate as the Louvre or Notre-Dame is to Parisians who have walked by the old monuments a thousand times in their daily lives but never for a moment considered entering them to take pictures or buy postcards.

Hollywood to Kate was a place like any other. And she behaved here as she would have anyplace else. She quickly found a job as a waitress at a popular Wilshire Boulevard restaurant and was pleased to find that her income was excellent, for the Hollywood types who had lunch and dinner here—lunches and dinners filled with excited conversation about "properties" and "talent" and "concepts"—liked to impress their guests by leaving her large tips.

Kate's beauty was not even noticed by these customers. Beautiful girls were as plentiful as palm trees in Hollywood. But her personality, rendered confident and welcoming by years of waitressing, endeared her to her customers. And her long-perfected subtlety of manner, which made the customer like her and want her to like him back, only increased her appeal, and her tips.

But Kate was alone in her cool indifference to the snares of Hollywood. Her friend Melanie immediately threw herself into the hectic round of meat-market casting, the search for agents, the enrolling in acting classes and workshops, the reading of *Daily Variety* and *The Hollywood Reporter,* the endless hours of Hollywood gossip with her hopeful friends—and the quietly agonizing dilemma of selling each day a little more of her honor, a little more of her self-respect, in the inevitable grind of "being nice" to casting directors, assistant directors, and prospective agents.

Strangely enough, Kate, who alone remained aloof from the Hollywood grind, and who spent her working days here as calmly and routinely as she had in North Dakota or Illinois, became a sort of mother figure to Melanie and her friends. Most nights she returned from work to find one of them waiting to pour out her heart to her. They told her about their childhoods, their parents (most of whom had been abusive; Kate came to realize that the lure of Hollywood was particularly strong for young people who had been unwanted or abused as children), their dreams, and the crashing of those dreams against the daily disappointments and humiliations of Hollywood.

Kate was a good listener, and something about her inner stability made her sought after as a confidante. Perhaps it was her very invulnerability to Hollywood that made the hopefuls want to tell her their dreams. Perhaps she was a reflection of the independence of mind they wished they possessed.

Kate listened gently to their complaints about the assistant directors and agents and casting directors who made promises they did not keep, the men who bedded them and then did not call back. She listened, and she commiserated. But she quickly learned never to challenge the dream that kept these girls going back for more punishment. For if she made bold to suggest, even indirectly, that a particular casting director was never going to help a girl, that she should look elsewhere or even consider leaving Hollywood altogether, the girl looked at Kate with a combination of terrible anguish and utter incredulity. And Kate realized that her allusions to reality could cause these girls great mental suffering, but could never bring them one step closer to the truth. Their illusions were their life's blood. Nothing could penetrate them except, perhaps, time.

Kate learned a lot about illusion from Melanie and her friends. And she learned a lot about exploitation from their stories. But nothing she heard touched her personally. In Hollywood as elsewhere, she lived removed from her own circumstances. Hollywood's corrosive illusion made no more impression on Kate than the country customs of rural Iowa or the city slime of Chicago or Detroit. It was all the same thing: a world of cruel takers and willing victims, a world that did not concern her.

Her only concession to Hollywood took place one day when, on a bored whim, she allowed Melanie to convince her to have a photo portfolio done.

"Come on," Melanie pleaded. "You've got great looks, Kate. It's only the price of a few photographs. You can't leave this town without at least giving it a chance . . ."

Kate spent the money on the portfolio, and was amused to see the glossy photos of herself in a dozen glamorous poses, each one cast in a stereotyped mold so strict that she looked virtually indistinguishable from the major stars of the day.

The portfolio made Kate smile, but also disturbed her. It showed a creature as foreign to her as the man in the moon. Yet this was herself. And the face she saw in the mirror each day was almost as foreign to her as the face in the pictures, so great was her distance from her own life. She did not like to be reminded of the extent of her own alienation, so she put the pictures away and did not look at them again.

Not long after the portfolio was printed Melanie came home from a casting outing and excitedly told Kate she had found her a job.

"I took your portfolio with me," Melanie said. "I showed it to the assistant director. He said to have you come along. It's just a crowd scene, but it pays five dollars. Come on, Kate. Just for the hell of it."

Kate, who was not working that day, had no plans. She decided to accompany Melanie. The two young women showed up at Paramount Studios, where they were shown into a waiting area for extras. At length they were approached by a harried assistant director who greeted Melanie familiarly and looked at Kate.

"This is the girl I was telling you about," Melanie said. "I just know she'll be terrific if you give her the chance."

The young man shook Kate's hand and looked her over, noticing her tanned skin, her shapely limbs, and the peculiar lushness of her body, which stood out even in this town full of ripe young girls. Then he looked into her eyes. What he saw there seemed to impress him.

"All right," he said. "Stick with Melanie, Kate. She'll tell you what to do. You girls are lucky. It's not a crowd scene after all. You're going to be ten feet tall on that movie screen. It's a medium shot."

He gave Melanie a last smile that made it perfectly clear to Kate that he was sleeping with her.

The girls went to Wardrobe, where they were fitted with costumes. Each was given a business suit with a skirt and jacket.

Then they went to Makeup and had their faces done by friendly makeup artists for whom it was all in a day's work.

Finally they were taken to a sound stage where they waited over an hour and a half for their shot to be ready. It was a brief scene in a "B" picture. One of the secondary characters was to walk out of an elevator, pass by a handful of secretaries, and move off camera. The whole shot would take about three seconds. Melanie and Kate were to be two of the secretaries.

At last it was time to shoot the scene.

"All right," said the director. "Girls, find your marks. Ginger, I want you to turn and look at Tommy as he comes out of the elevator. The rest of you, just look right in front of your faces. Look busy. You're working girls. When I shout 'Action,' just walk two paces from where you are."

A moment later the actor had arrived. Kate recognized his face from a handful of second-rate movies she had seen over the years. He usually played dishonest cops or mobsters, or occasionally a hero's army buddy.

The actor got ready in the fake elevator, and the assistant director placed Kate and Melanie and the others on their marks.

"Quiet on the set!" shouted the assistant director. "Places, everybody."

The slate man came forward to the camera.

"Three's a Crowd," he said. "Scene one forty-three, take one." He snapped the slate.

"Roll camera . . . roll sound . . ." called the director. "And . . . action!"

The actor walked out of the elevator, glanced at the girls loitering in the hall, and walked off camera.

"Cut!" called the director. "Roy, get me some more light."

The light man moved one of the hot studio lights, and the scene was shot again.

"Cut!" called the director. "Honey . . . what's your name?"

"Melanie." Melanie had turned beet red.

"Honey, get your hair out of your eyes. Okay, everybody? Take three. Let's go, girls. Time is money."

In another three takes the shot was printed. The extras were dismissed.

On the bus homeward Melanie asked Kate what she had thought of her first acting experience.

"It was fun," Kate said noncommittally. "Thanks for asking me along."

"Now let's see if we end up in the movie," Melanie said. "About ninety percent of the work I've done has ended up on the cutting-room floor. Usually they decide to cut the scene, or change the background. However you slice it, I end up out of the picture. But we've been paid, thank God, and they can't take that back."

Melanie was prophetic, though she could not know why.

Three days after the shot Melanie and Kate had made, the brief piece of film was being viewed by an assistant director and an editor at Paramount's editing room. The editor, a seasoned professional who had worked on over five hundred pictures in his years on the lot, was viewing the piece of film on his Moviola and paused it.

"Hey," he said to the assistant director. "Look at this."

The assistant director came to his side and viewed the still frame, scratching his head.

"There's something wrong," he said.

"You're damned right there is," his colleague said. "Take a look at the blond extra behind the elevator boy. Jesus Christ, who let her in?"

The other man nodded. "She sticks out, doesn't she?" he said.

"You're not kidding. Like a sore thumb. She spoils the whole shot."

The assistant director sighed. "I'll have to tell Barry," he said. "We'll have to reshoot, or cut around it somehow."

The two of them sat for a moment lingering over the frame of film. All the girls who had been hired as extras blended perfectly into their roles. They looked like nondescript secretaries, on their way to work in the fictitious building where the actor was emerging from the elevator.

But Kate obviously did not belong. Why this was so,

neither man was sure. Something about her eyes, her body, her demeanor, seemed to distract the camera from its master shot and upstage every other visual element. There was something unpleasant and almost violent about the effect. Moreover, Kate did not look like a secretary. She failed to disappear into her function.

"She a friend of yours?" the editor asked with a raised eyebrow.

"Me? Hell, no," the assistant director said. "I never saw her before."

"Well, she messed up our shot pretty good," the editor said. "Somebody ought to tell her to go back to Kansas. I never saw a girl grab the camera that way. What an eyesore."

The editor, a man accustomed to responsibility, summarily threw the entire shot into the cutting-room trash bin. Shaking his head, he tried to forget about the waste of time and money the unknown blond extra had caused.

Thus Kate's brief appearance in a soon-to-be-forgotten "B" picture called *Three's a Crowd* went into the trash heap, never to be seen again. Only the studio's payroll records would record that Katherine Hamilton had worked as an extra on *Three's a Crowd*.

In future years film archivists and scholars would scour film vaults all over the world in search of that tiny piece of film which documented the very first appearance of Kate Hamilton before a camera.

But they would not find it. Like so many other seeds of future greatness, it had simply disappeared.

THE TITLE DECIDED ON BY BRYANT HAYES'S BRAIN TRUST FOR the film conceived by Joseph Knight was *Winter of Destiny*. The Continental executives thought the title suited the harsh Russian landscape and expressed the romantic sweep of the story.

It was to be a very big film, and thus it needed a grand title. Continental Pictures was pulling out all the stops on *Winter of Destiny*. Now that he had the go-ahead from Arnold Speck and the New York money men, Bryant Hayes put everything he had into making the new film a blockbuster.

First on the list, as always, came the publicity machine.

Word was leaked to the Hollywood press early in May that a major new film was in the works, starring Moira Talbot and Guy Lavery. Friendly Hollywood columnists, all beholden to Bryant Hayes for past favors, immediately began trumpeting the new film as the "culmination" of Moira Talbot's great career, a sure Oscar for the famed Continental actress.

In addition, the press began to buzz with heated rumors that the sweeping romantic story was bringing Moira Talbot together with Guy Lavery in scenes so torrid, so intimate, that the long-awaited marriage of the two great stars was sure to follow close upon the release of the film.

With the publicity machine humming, and *Winter of Destiny* being sold to the public as a history-making project involving a romance of the stars, Bryant Hayes threw himself and his best people into pre-production.

Hayes spared no expense. He freed top director Corbett Fischer from his current busy schedule and put him to work full time on *Winter of Destiny*. He put together a team of writers, the best Continental Pictures had, to polish the screenplay. He locked them in a bungalow on the studio lot from morning until night, telling them that only their best work would be acceptable for this once-in-a-lifetime project. They were promised huge bonuses in the event that *Winter of Destiny* was a box-office hit, and even greater rewards if the film won an Oscar for Best Screenplay or Best Picture. And they were warned that there would be dire consequences for all of them if the film failed.

Bryant Hayes himself would produce the film. He chose Owen Esser as executive producer. Together they spent weeks casting the supporting players for the film. They used all the best talent that Continental had to offer, and did not hesitate to cast the finest character actors on loanout from rival studios if they thought they could do a better job, and look better in the film, than the available Continental contract players.

From cinematographer to lighting director to sound man, all the "below-the-line" talent was the best in the business. No expense was to be spared to make *Winter of Destiny* a blockbuster. Bryant Hayes had a feeling about this film. He had had it ever since Joseph Knight first suggested it to him. It was a film of destiny, he felt—the quintessential Continental picture, high-gloss, romantic, dramatic, and coming at just the right time for Moira Talbot, for the studio, and for Hayes himself.

Nothing must stand in the way of this picture. It would be the key to Continental Pictures' finances and prestige for the next year. And if it succeeded, Bryant Hayes's standing as the top studio head in Hollywood would be assured—and his clout with the Continental board back in New York, and his power over Arnold Speck, would be solidified.

Pre-production ended on June 8, and an enormous gala was held at Ciro's to celebrate the beginning of production. Moira Talbot and Guy Lavery were presented to the press with such ceremony that one columnist compared the party to the launching of a battleship. "If *Winter of Destiny* were the *Titanic*," wrote the reporter for *Daily Variety*, "it couldn't have a better send-off."

The comparison was unintentionally ominous, but no one noticed that in all the excitement.

Shooting began on June 30. The set was closed, but daily reports on the progress of the great new film were given to the press, which waited eagerly in a special briefing room in the Continental executive office building. Each of these briefings became an occasion.

Soon everyone at Continental realized that the new film was going to cost more than anticipated.

The costumes alone cost hundreds of thousands of dollars. The finest designer in Hollywood had been hired to create Moira Talbot's gowns. Meanwhile the film's supporting players, not to mention its thousands of extras, required costumes too. And Bryant Hayes spared no expense in making sure these costumes were absolutely authentic. He hired a team of research consultants to guarantee their historical accuracy.

Location shooting was scheduled for Paris, London, and New York, not to mention the Italian Alps and the Mediterranean coast for sea and mountain scenery. Every place, in fact, except Russia itself, which was of course off limits because of political problems. Location shooting for this picture would cost more than any in Continental's history.

No expense was spared on sets, special camera effects, props, even genuine period furniture and draperies. Hayes pulled out all the stops to re-create the Russia of 1917. Specialists in Russian history, including a professor from UCLA, were hired to insure authenticity. Experts were hired to coach the principals on dialogue and accent. Russian wolfhounds were brought in, trained by an expert from Europe. Everything from sleighs to carriages to lanterns to samovars was absolutely authentic.

As the weeks passed, production ground on, an enormous endeavor that had to proceed slowly, for the sheer scope of the project tended to bog down shooting. Many scenes that would have been shot in an hour on another film took days on *Winter of Destiny*, so complex were the difficulties of lighting, special effects, and continuity, and so high were the ambitions of the filmmakers.

Inevitably, costs increased as the shooting schedule grew longer. Exhaustion became a factor among the actors and crew alike. Tempers began to flare as crucial scenes were shot twenty, thirty, fifty times in search of the right effect.

Moira Talbot, overworked by her difficult role, which required her to portray a fresh seventeen-year-old girl who grows into a woman in her late twenties during the film, fell prey to acute exhaustion and had to be excused from filming for ten days on the orders of her physicians. In her absence a careful study was made of the rushes of her early scenes. Bryant Hayes and director Corbett Fischer were worried. Moira was not as young as she once had been. Her scenes as the fresh-faced adolescent heroine did not look convincing. It was decided to reshoot the scenes after her recovery.

Guy Lavery, a dependable leading man, seemed to hold up better. But he was being asked to play a very masculine character, a role he was never very happy with because of a softness in his screen image that Continental's makeup artists and cameramen had had to work overtime to minimize for the past eight years. Guy, a homosexual, was best when he played gentle heroes, and he was weakest in the swashbuckling scenes. But his role in *Winter of Destiny* required him to be capable of great physical violence, to be hard and even brutal when necessary. These were qualities a little out of Guy's range, so he had to stretch himself to his limits.

But the actors were not the only problem bedeviling *Winter of Destiny*.

As time went on, and the Continental brain trust viewed the rushes, a few timid voices began to express reservations about the actual plot of the picture. It lacked punch, power, sweep, they said.

No one dared express an opinion as to why this was

so. One or two of Bryant Hayes's more intelligent writers suspected that the problem had originated with the change that had been made in the film's ending. Without the tragic finale that had originally been written for the script, the plot and characters lost their dark momentum. The film seemed to spin uncertainly toward its conclusion.

These writers dared not confide their theory to Bryant Hayes. Experienced yes-men as well as creative talents, they were paid to do what he told them to do, and not to contradict him. So they kept their mouths shut.

As for Bryant Hayes, he had made his decision. Happy endings were the heart and soul of Hollywood films, and of Continental films in particular—especially when those films were romantic costume epics. The public had had enough misery in its day-to-day life in the last decade. It did not go to the movies to see more unhappiness. It wanted hope, even if that hope had to be purchased with heavy doses of fantasy.

Hayes's best dialogue men had been working overtime for months to orchestrate the picture's happy ending, and he was not going to go back on it now. It was too late. So he ordered rewrites on the weakest scenes and commanded his writers to use the best of their imagination and talent to add punch to the scenario. Drama, he told them. Drama and more drama—or their heads would roll.

Rewrites went on around the clock. Scenes were added and dropped as Hayes and his director sought to restore the pace and intensity that seemed to have slipped out of their grasp. The actors became even more tired as they had to redo scenes they had already shot and reshot. The crew worked with their eyes at half-mast, drained by exhaustion.

As shooting ground into its third month Moira Talbot began to look simply too old for her part. As for Guy Lavery, he began to look puffy and sallow in the rushes. It was known that Guy had suffered from a drinking problem for many years. Rumor had it that the stress of shooting had forced him to start hitting the bottle again.

In a rage Bryant Hayes called his two stars in for a conference and told them in no uncertain terms that if they did not both shape up he would throw them off the picture and let their careers wither on the vine. He was giving them both a chance to win Oscars in the most important film of their careers. If they were not professional enough to take advantage of the opportunity, he would get someone else who was.

He hoped his threats had succeeded. But as shooting continued, he was not so sure.

Thus, bit by bit, as production lurched uncertainly forward, *Winter of Destiny* changed from the object of high hopes and great expectations to a beleaguered ritual of collective exhaustion and demoralization. No one seemed to be able to stem the tide of confusion dogging the project. Bryant Hayes finally had to fire director Corbett Fischer and replace him with another of Continental's top directors, a man who shared his own vision of the film and was willing to sacrifice all other considerations to it. New writers were brought in in handfuls to support or replace those who were already at work on the project. Work continued at a fevered pace, but nothing seemed to ease the general sense of frustration.

Winter of Destiny, still heralded by the obedient press as the greatest film of the decade, was fast becoming a white elephant. Yet Hayes and his people drove relentlessly onward, convinced despite their own nagging doubts that this picture would be the studio's best ever.

Little did Bryant Hayes suspect that his many difficulties with *Winter of Destiny,* scrupulously hidden from the public eye, were well known to Joseph Knight.

Nor did he suspect that a great many of the problems that were constantly arising to plague the picture were placed in his way by Joseph Knight, in the most diabolical manner possible.

Thanks to his backbreaking work schedule, Hayes was not able to keep as close an eye on pretty Daria Kane as usual. Sometimes he did not see her for thirty-six or even forty-eight hours at a stretch.

During these times Daria used her ingenuity to arrange trysts with Joseph Knight.

These private meetings, which took place at a variety

of safe and discreet locations, were the delight of Daria's existence.

They always began with lovemaking. Joseph Knight played Daria's beautiful body like a harp, orchestrating the waves of her excitement in a thousand inventive ways. When at last he entered her, the power of his sex almost unspeakable, he drove her to extremities of pleasure she had never imagined possible, and left her limp with satisfied desire.

Had Daria been a little more innocent, she would have fallen in love with him. The very thought of a lifetime of sex with such a man was like a dream come true. But Daria's Hollywood experiences had seared all the dreams out of her. She was smart enough to know that Joseph Knight did not love her and never would. He had seduced her for a reason. And she was willing to give him what he wanted in return for the pleasure he brought her.

So, in the quiet intervals after they made love, she talked to him about *Winter of Destiny*.

She knew all about the film's problems, because in her bedroom conversations with Bryant Hayes she had pumped Hayes to pour out his hopes and frustrations to her. Hayes, exasperated with the people he worked with on the set, was only too happy to use his lovely young mistress as a confidante. Thus Daria knew all about Hayes's troubles with Moira Talbot and Guy Lavery, with his directors, and with the endlessly rewritten screenplay of *Winter of Destiny*.

And everything Daria learned from Hayes she passed along to Joseph Knight.

Knight smiled as he thought of Hayes's consternation. For Knight had cannily built many traps into the screenplay for *Winter of Destiny*, traps he knew Hayes would fall into by natural inclination, by his ego, and by the constraints of his own studio.

The most important of these, of course, was the film's ending. Knight had used his own tragic ending to give the film psychological depth, and thus to make the property a bait that Bryant Hayes would not be able to resist. But in so doing, Knight had correctly predicted that Hayes, when it came to dollars and cents, would abandon the sad ending in favor of a stereotyped Continental Pictures boy-gets-girl denouement.

With this in mind Joseph Knight had purposely structured the entire story so that, without the tragic ending, the film would have no inner tension at all, no real life. Now his subtle sabotage was paying off. Bryant Hayes's high-priced screenwriters could not restore the bigger-than-life power of the original scenario, because its head had been chopped off when the ending had been changed.

But this was not the only trap Joseph Knight had laid for Bryant Hayes.

Knight had intentionally included crucial scenes involving the heroine as an adolescent, because he knew it would be a strain on aging Moira Talbot to carry off these scenes. And he had deliberately placed the hero in situations that would tax Guy Lavery's ability to carry them off in a masculine way.

As Hayes and his people fell into these traps, Knight was the first to learn about it, thanks to Daria.

And, also thanks to Daria, there was another and even more ruthless dimension to Joseph Knight's sabotage of *Winter of Destiny*.

Knight knew that Daria was Hayes's trusted confidante. So he began to seed Daria with ideas about how to correct some of the problems besetting the film. Daria in her turn suggested these ideas to Hayes as though they were her own, in the wake of her lovemaking with him.

Hayes was astonished by the incisiveness of his paramour's ideas. He had long given credit to Daria as a lover, but had never thought of her as a great brain. Now he had to change his mind.

Her advice was ingenious, on its face. She told him how to motivate Moira Talbot to look younger and more spontaneous. She made suggestions for how to make Guy Lavery look more masculine, more attractive. She read over the shooting script with Hayes and pointed out areas that seemed slack, lacking in punch.

Hayes listened to everything she said. More and more he acted on her suggestions. He even invited her to come to the set with him as his special adviser, but she cannily refused, saying she could be more lucid if she was removed from the hurly-burly of actual shooting. Her real reason, of course, was that she wanted to be free to spend time with Joe Knight while Hayes was busy on the set.

As time passed Hayes grew dependent on Daria's judgment. Since she was not directly involved with the film, and never visited the set, she seemed more objective and impartial than the people at Continental, who were too embroiled in the project's complexities to see the forest through the trees.

It never occurred to Bryant Hayes that Daria was playing a double game intended to increase his difficulties rather than to solve them.

In the short run Daria's suggestions seemed to help. But over time they resulted in more and more retakes, and more and more exhaustion for the stars and those behind the camera. Often she would cleverly find a flaw in a sequence that had been one of the costliest and most difficult to film. Hayes, unable to deny the logic of her criticism, would imperiously demand reshooting of the entire sequence. The result would be a week or more lost to the shooting schedule, and a hundred thousand dollars spent and spent again. The improvement to the scene would never be as great as the cost in exhaustion to the actors and crew.

Many of Daria's suggestions for script changes helped the pace of a particular scene while subtly weakening the whole picture in a way that would not be seen for weeks or even months afterward. For her suggestions dissipated the psychological and romantic tension that had been built into the original screenplay, and left the scenes brighter but also more shallow. This, also, Joseph Knight had intended.

Thus, like a complicated embroidery whose design is known only to its maker, the cumulative effect of Daria's clever suggestions was not really to improve *Winter of Destiny* but to lengthen its production and further demoralize its cast and crew.

And behind every word Daria said, every idea she expressed, and the resultant problems besetting *Winter of Destiny*, was Joseph Knight.

As time went on, every production delay, every conflict with the stars, every firing that took place on *Winter of Destiny*, became known to Joseph Knight, and he continued to play the chess game of seeding Hayes with ideas that seemed to help at first while hurting in the long run. Since *Winter of Destiny* had originated with Joseph Knight, he knew how to sabotage it better than anyone else alive.

And, with Daria's help, he did everything possible to add to Bryant Hayes's problems.

Meanwhile, at Monarch Pictures, the film conceived in secrecy by Joseph Knight and Oscar Freund made its way slowly through pre-production and into production. Everything about this project was the opposite of the monster that was being created with such hullabaloo at Continental.

The picture had no title. It had been relegated to the "B" pool of projects at Monarch and was looked upon by Monarch insiders as a "second feature" of no importance whatever, a film to be made on a shoestring and exhibited as a trailer for some larger Monarch feature, such as a detective film or one of the musical comedies for which the studio was famous.

Only Oscar Freund himself, and Joseph Knight, knew what was actually at stake.

Some of the finest talent in Hollywood had been cannily assembled by Joseph Knight for this top-secret project. They included scenarists, costume designers, a brilliant composer for the musical score, and one of the best production designers in Hollywood.

The director, hand-picked by Joseph Knight after a lengthy search, was Serge Lavitsky, a Polish immigrant who had started his career as a set designer and become one of the most distinctive directors in Hollywood before a series of run-ins with his superiors over artistic issues had caused his career to go downhill some five years ago. Lavitsky was a temperamental but brilliant director with a dazzling, unusual visual sense derived from his early years as an artist in Paris.

Joseph Knight, with his uncanny feel for personality, managed to tame Lavitsky and to get him excited about the visual and dramatic qualities of the film he had in mind. The story centered on the Depression and had many scenes set in New York City. There was ample opportunity for Lavitsky to turn the film into a symbolic visual statement about the agony the nation had been suffering for the past decade.

Lavitsky was excited by the project and threw himself into it with restored creative energy.

Within the first few weeks of pre-production Joseph Knight had made the major casting decisions for the new film. They came as a surprise to his collaborators.

For the heroine, whose tragic fate separates her from the man she loves, he chose Rebecca Sherwood, a beautiful but unsung contract player from Columbia who would be loaned out for this picture. She was a young actress with a remarkable face, at once innocent and sensual, and a flawless acting technique. The only reason she had not already become a major star was an unusual ambiguity of personality she had before the camera, a complexity of image that made her unsuitable for the major studios' stereotyped heroines and for the "bad girls" so dear to the hearts of 1930s producers.

Joseph Knight had chosen her for the indefinable undertone to her melodious voice, and a secret shadow of sadness he saw in her eyes. Other directors had not quite known what to do with her up to now. But Joseph Knight saw just how to mold her into the heroine he wanted.

But the great casting decision of the new picture, which was to be talked about in the future as the casting coup of the decade, was that of the male lead, and was made by Joseph Knight right under Oscar Freund's nose.

The actor's name was Samuel Raines. He had been in Hollywood for nearly twelve years, playing private detectives, crooks, policemen, airmen, soldiers, and all manner of roles requiring an actor with a masculine image. He was currently under contract to Oscar Freund and had worked on loan-out in an endless series of "B" pictures. His looks were dark but not classically handsome. His voice was somewhat gravelly, a quality that had contributed to his exile in so many unnoticed character parts. He was an unusual-looking man, somewhat disturbing in his masculinity, and the camera did not love him by instinct.

But Joseph Knight saw something special in Raines's powerful physique and smoldering dark eyes. And when he had the actor read for the part in the new picture, he found that a little careful coaching brought out a tenderness in his voice that had never been noticed before.

This time Oscar Freund balked at Joseph Knight's eccentric casting choice.

"The guy is nothing," he complained. "A second-rate character man, nothing more. If you make him your hero, you'll condemn your picture to the trash heap before you start."

"Let's test him with Rebecca," Joseph Knight rejoined, "and see if you're right."

The screen test was held a week later. Samuel Raines's performance opposite Rebecca Sherwood left no doubt that Joseph Knight had been right about him. Like the young Humphrey Bogart, Raines had been successful at playing evil and dangerous characters. But something truly magical happened when his frighteningly masculine looks were applied to a positive character. He projected a stunning integrity and power, combined with impressive sexiness.

The symbiosis between Samuel Raines and Rebecca Sherwood was extraordinary. Miss Sherwood instinctively played her own delicacy of manner off against Samuel's dark incisiveness. The strange glow of her lovely face seemed to gain in haunting effectiveness when she was on the screen with him. And Samuel Raines, an extremely intelligent actor despite the modest roles he had played in the past, managed to add a genuinely tragic quality to his sex appeal that made him almost unbearably attractive as Rebecca's great love.

Oscar Freund's skepticism about Samuel Raines remained, but he deferred to Joseph Knight's choice of the two lead performers. After all, the canny studio head told himself, it was Knight's picture. The egg would be on Knight's face if it flopped.

Besides, Oscar Freund had made a career out of taking

chances, and he was curious to see if Samuel Raines would really be able to bring off this most difficult assignment.

Director Serge Lavitsky warmed to the exciting challenge of making Samuel Raines and Rebecca Sherwood into a historic romantic combination. He shot them in striking ways, from odd angles and against unusual backgrounds. Their two faces became the visual center of the film, like a particular harmony at the center of a symphony.

Once the two principals had been cast, excitement about the film increased. The supporting cast was chosen from all over Hollywood. Each and every performer was chosen for a quality he or she had not previously exhibited in the stereotyped character roles he or she had played. All of them were given piquant new functions by Knight and Lavitsky. As a result the scenes played with a sparkling intensity that had not been seen on a Hollywood screen in many years.

Joseph Knight knew his film would have to compete with a lavish Continental extravaganza with fancy sets and thousands of extras. So he set out to counteract this superficial appeal with a deeper one of his own. He had meetings with Lavitsky and Oscar Freund in which they sketched out a visual plan for the film. They used the landscape of New York City in new, original ways. The Statue of Liberty, the Chrysler Building, and even the East River and the Brooklyn Bridge at dusk were given new, symbolic significance.

They used costumes, interior lighting, and sets to create a poetic, haunting contrast between the structural impersonality of the city and the intimate lives of the characters. They found visual themes and contrasts everywhere. Lighting director Fred Sokol worked long hours with Lavitsky and the set designers to create a visual image that would captivate the viewer without being intrusive or self-conscious.

Meanwhile Lavitsky's camera came to know the faces of the two stars with an unprecedented intimacy. Aided by Joseph Knight, he managed to milk more emotion out of one close-up of his hero and heroine than Hayes and his minions could get out of a panoramic shot with five hundred extras and the blaring of a symphony orchestra.

Joseph Knight had an uncanny knack for dialogue that

increased psychological tension. He could bring an audience to the edge of its seat in even the most routine scene, through the unseen conflicts he placed like traps under the simple dialogue. This knack had come from his many readings of the greatest playwrights and from his own untapped talent, a talent that had been waiting all his life for this chance to reveal itself.

And he had a peculiar, unique sense of romance. He managed to play off Rebecca Sherwood and Samuel Raines in a way that increased the sexiness of the scenes as well as their romantic tension. Every day the film grew in psychological intimacy, its dramatic story far exceeding in depth the ponderous, stereotyped scenes Hayes was creating for his two stars in *Winter of Destiny*.

The cast came to look upon Joseph Knight with a mixture of awe and affection. Though he was a daunting presence in his dark business suits as he controlled every aspect of filming, he took the time to consult at length with each player, no matter how small his or her role, and to let the actor himself contribute suggestions as to how best to give the role its greatest power.

The same went for the crew. Knight got to know all the grips and construction people, treating them with the same friendly camaraderie he enjoyed with the script supervisor, the assistant set designers, the continuity girl. He made everyone understand that if their best work went into this picture, the picture would be something they could be proud to see their names on.

Everyone responded. For teamwork is a Hollywood tradition, even if the absurdities of star and director egos, and the sudden changes of plan from studio heads and producers, often reduce Hollywood films to a hodgepodge. Teamwork united the Hollywood crews in their professionalism even under the worst of circumstances. And here was a producer who knew how to bring out the pride of his people by showing them how the finished product would benefit from their best efforts.

Meanwhile, in a thousand small ways, Oscar Freund contributed his own experience and savvy to help the picture. He showed Knight how to cut down on rehearsal time, how to manage the union people efficiently, how to "cut in the camera" to save time on editing, and gave him myriad little tips on how to smooth the filmmaking process and shorten the shooting schedule.

Thanks to the combination of Knight's brilliant intuition and Freund's sound practical advice, the film moved forward by leaps and bounds, inspiring everyone who came in contact with it. It would have been the hottest project of the decade were it not for the secrecy surrounding it. As things stood, though, it was the best-kept secret in the history of Monarch Pictures. The cloak-and-dagger aspect of production only increased the excitement of all concerned.

It was Rebecca Sherwood who suggested the title that Joseph Knight and Oscar Freund ultimately accepted for the film—*The Rainbow's End*. Rebecca's inspiration, born of her own deep commitment to the film, communicated its bittersweet commentary on the fantastic 1920s and the dream-ending Depression with perfect poetic justice.

Rebecca's suggestion was the finishing touch added to a project that was already the greatest single filmmaking quest in Oscar Freund's long memory. *The Rainbow's End* was the finest project he had ever worked on. And Joseph Knight—an amateur, a beginner!—was by far the most brilliant talent he had ever met in Hollywood.

Thus, through eleven difficult months, two of the most ambitious films in Hollywood history went through their birth agonies. Each in its own way was an enormous gamble. *Winter of Destiny* was an over-financed, over-produced costume epic starring two performers who were both reaching a bit beyond their talent. The film was made from a screenplay flawed by the decisions of its own producers, and had been beset with problems almost from the outset. Yet it was the product of the aggregate talent of the most successful studio in Hollywood.

As for *The Rainbow's End*, it was the brainchild of an unknown producer who had never made a film before. It starred untried talent and was directed by a temperamental has-been who had been fired from the major studios years before.

And, most dangerous of all, *The Rainbow's End* dared to depart from the tradition of the last ten years of Hollywood filmmaking and hit the public right in the face with a tragic ending. Disdaining the taste for fantasy that was so essential to Hollywood nowadays, *The Rainbow's End* plumbed the universal feelings of sadness, defeat, and grief spawned by the Depression, and used them to tear at the heart of its audience.

Whether the American filmgoing public would accept such a film was the biggest gamble of all.

Oscar Freund began to get cold feet toward the end. He feared that Bryant Hayes with his blockbuster *Winter of Destiny* would roll over *The Rainbow's End* and win a dozen Oscars.

When he confided his worries to Joseph Knight, Knight reassured him with a smile.

"Let me worry about that," Knight said. "The film is my responsibility. And look at it this way, Oscar: we've had a ball these past few months. Who can ask for more than that?"

Oscar Freund smiled. Joseph Knight was right. Win or lose, it had been worth the effort to collaborate on the kind of passionate filmmaking they had done on *The Rainbow's End*. Movies should be fun to make as well as to watch, Freund had always believed. And he had never enjoyed himself so thoroughly as on *The Rainbow's End*.

As for Bryant Hayes, he worked eighteen-hour days on his stolen property as if it were his own. While production on *Winter of Destiny* lurched painfully toward its end, he doubled and tripled his commitment to the film. All that he knew about moviemaking went into it. And if there were weaknesses, he felt he knew the public mind well enough to know that the appeal of his stars and his story would triumph over those weaknesses. He worked like a man possessed. And when his work made him exhausted or depressed, he sought refuge in the welcoming arms of beautiful Daria Kane.

Meanwhile Joseph Knight retained his calm professionalism as shooting on *The Rainbow's End* ended and post-production began. Though he drove himself and his associates mercilessly, he never showed a sign of fatigue or irritability. His own calm seemed to act as a soothing drug on those he worked with, giving them the courage to push themselves beyond the limits of their talent. If the enormous gamble of *The Rainbow's End* was eating away at his nerves, he never showed it.

The people at Monarch Pictures could not understand how Knight, a newcomer to the Hollywood madhouse, could handle so chancy a project with such equanimity.

Either he was a genius, they decided, or he knew something they didn't.

A few of them, including Oscar Freund, decided that both things were true.

EVE SINCLAIR WOKE UP ALONE IN HER MALIBU HOUSE.

The hushed thump of the surf outside was her only companion, though the smell of sex reminded her of the man who had spent the night with her.

He was a well-known Hollywood stud—a failed leading man—with a strong body, a very long penis, and a remarkable ability to keep himself hard for as long as he was asked. He was popular among many female stars and executives' wives, and made a better living off their money gifts than he did from his pint-sized studio contract.

He had given Eve a good time last night, but had disappeared early this morning in order to go somewhere he did not specify—perhaps to the arms of another woman, Eve surmised indifferently.

It was ten o'clock. Eve rarely got out of bed before this hour when she was not shooting. She almost always awoke alone, for her various lovers were early risers, and were off to their morning pursuits long before she slipped from the private world of her dreams back into the harsh light of Hollywood.

Stretching herself like a sleepy cat, she got up and padded to the kitchen, where she turned on the coffee. While it perked she got into a very hot shower, which she turned ice cold for two bracing minutes before she got out to towel herself off.

She returned to the kitchen wearing a silk robe, her hair wrapped in a towel, and poured coffee. She sat down to scan the newspapers. She always read the trade papers from New York as well as Hollywood, not to mention the *Wall Street Journal* to keep track of her many investments.

On page 3 of *The Hollywood Reporter* she noticed a mention of her name under a gossip columnist's byline.

"Svelte and elegant Eve Sinclair," read the column, *"was seen at the Trocadero Tuesday night on the arm of Columbia's heartthrob Dirk Chamberlain. Could romance be in the picture between these two supremely eligible stars? Our own crystal ball says yes. The look in lovely Eve's eyes left little doubt that what she has going with friend Dirk is HOT HOT HOT . . ."*

Eve smiled. There was no truth to the columnist's prattle. She had not even been with Chamberlain at the Trocadero. The item had been cooked up by Chamberlain's agent and her own, with some prodding from the publicity departments of their respective studios. Over the years Eve had been linked in the gossip press with dozens of matinee idols, but had never seriously dated one—unless, of course, one counted the purely sexual liaisons such as last night's guest. She hated actors. Their fragile egos, inflated by fame and ambition, made them impossible as friends, much less marital partners.

Not that she hadn't been married to one. Her first marriage had been to a male star whose career had been on the rise at the time. It was a studio marriage, arranged by the publicity men, and Eve had been grateful for the exposure at that delicate time in her career.

The marriage had ended abruptly when her husband's box-office position went down. She never missed her husband, for she had never really noticed him when he was married to her.

Her second marriage, to one of the more powerful producers at MGM, had lasted longer. But then one of the producer's spies had caught Eve *in flagrante* with one of her most handsome beaux, a congressman from New York who was just then running for the Senate.

There had been a scene. Eve had considered her options. The politician truly wanted her to marry him. But he insisted that she give up her film career to be a political wife. This notion Eve rejected out of hand. The result was that the producer gave her a generous divorce settlement, she dropped the politician, and had not married since. No man with credentials sufficient to advance her career had presented himself.

So Eve was completely alone in the world. She had no close or trusted friends—that was a luxury that the rigors of life in Hollywood had long since ruled out—and no immediate family.

The fate and whereabouts of her mother were unknown to her. She imagined that Mother was off somewhere hopping from marriage to marriage, in search of the wealthiest man she could snare. Eve would never see her again.

In the event of an illness or accident that might befall Eve, the people to be contacted would be her attorney, her financial adviser, and her agent—in that order. There was no one who loved her or cared enough for her to want to be informed. Of course, the studio brass would need to know, so they could make their plans accordingly . . .

Eve had no one. Strangely, she did not feel this as a lack. She felt it as a comforting inner emptiness, suited to the clarity of vision her profession required of her. Other people were unnecessary distractions. Her career was the only thing that really mattered to her.

Life as a child star and an adult Hollywood actress had long since purged Eve of a normal woman's need for love. Eve was a woman of action. She did not waste time thinking about her needs as a person. She lived for something beyond herself.

When she closed a major deal, or stole a scene from another actor, or beat out another star at the box office, or fooled a producer or director into doing what she wanted, she felt she was at the center of her being. If that center was empty, it nevertheless glowed with an electric excitement that kept her stimulated and made her feel real. No sexual experience she had ever had could compare to this hot core of intensity that was her ambition.

This beautiful house, which she had bought like everything else with her great earnings, was a pleasant haven, but it did not seem complete to her. She could not enjoy it the way a person basks in his hard-earned possessions. It was a stepping-stone, a mere rung on the way somewhere. Everything in Eve's life was this way. Everything was impermanent, incomplete, a mere step toward something bigger, toward the final accomplishment that would crown her efforts.

What that accomplishment was, Eve herself did not really know.

And if there was tragedy in this inner emptiness, this inability to feel that she was worth something in herself over and above what she could accomplish—if there was tragedy in this, Eve did not see it. She was pleased with the things she had accomplished, and she wanted more. Her infinite inner hunger sustained her. Fulfillment, love, happiness, were foreign concepts to her. Success had made them irrelevant.

Eve was sitting with her eyes closed, sipping at her coffee as she scanned the newspapers, when the phone rang again, startling her. She got up with a sigh and answered it.

"Hello."

"Eve, this is Freddy. I've got good news." It was her agent.

"What is it?" Eve's eyes were adjusting to the half-light.

"Your performance in *Capricorn* just won the London Critics' Award," Freddy said. "Congratulations, Evie."

Eve was silent.

"Well, that's good news," she said at length, thoughtfully.

"Better than good. You know what this means, don't you?"

She knew what it meant. She was certain to get an Oscar nomination for her performance, now that the London Critics had given it their seal of approval.

This result was not unexpected. Eve's work on *Capricorn*—a worthless romantic melodrama, but with a fine role for the female lead—had been at her highest level. In six weeks of shooting she had scarcely done a single take that was not worthy of final print. The script had been better than usual, and the director, a canny professional named Otto Rojek, had seen eye to eye with Eve about her character. The leading man, a handsome and fairly talented actor on loan-out from RKO, had done his work well. But it had been Eve's thorough professionalism and constantly inspired acting that had carried the production. Everyone knew that.

And the picture had done well at the box office, again thanks to Eve, who was one of the most bankable leading ladies in Hollywood. Not only did she rank consistently in the top ten women at the box office, but she managed, through varying degrees of blackmail, manipulation, and downright "screaming," to get only the best actors and production people for her pictures.

Eve had been nominated for two Oscars already. Few people in the business failed to realize that she was one of the finest actresses in Hollywood, perhaps the finest of them all after Garbo. Not only was she a quick study and thoroughly professional in her behavior on the sound stage, but she could tailor her looks and personality in uncanny ways to suit the most disparate of roles. And she used her considerable power as a star to make sure that her cameramen showed her only in the best light, that her scenarists saved the best lines for her, that her costume and makeup people did what suited her best, and, most important, that her directors understood that they were working on an Eve Sinclair picture and must devote all their talent to making her look good.

As far as people in the business were concerned, Eve was a thoroughbred, the best there was.

But to the public at large she was still one of the lesser lights in Hollywood, a fine actress who had never quite "made it" as an adult leading lady, despite her brilliant career as a child star and adolescent.

The reason for this was only too well known to Eve herself. Though she was beautiful and elegant, with an intelligence in her face that few performers could match, she lacked the smoldering sex appeal that allowed lesser actresses to catch the eye of producers and directors as well as the public.

More yet, she lacked that indefinable something that had come to be called "star quality" in Hollywood. She lacked the brassy sensuality of a Harlow, the bitchiness of a Bette Davis, the mannish elegance of Katharine Hepburn. She was simply not distinctive enough. This fact allowed her to play a great variety of roles with an almost incredible smoothness and believability. But it kept her out of the limelight, kept her from creating her own unique image. There was no "Eve Sinclair look" for other actresses to emulate, no "Eve Sinclair style" to match Hepburn's trousers or Bette Davis's eyes or Harlow's chesty sensuality.

This lack of a recognizable personal style had always been Eve's weakness as an actress. She had everything else: talent, technique, insight, skill of the highest possible order. But she lacked that impalpable appeal that made lesser actresses into household names while Eve remained on a lower rung of the Hollywood ladder.

The Hollywood money men had been waiting ten years now for Eve's great talent to translate at last into superstardom. So far they had waited in vain. Eve was a star, and a box-office draw. But she was not a great star. Not "Hollywood royalty." Not yet. And as long as she did not get that final push, seize the spotlight once and for all, every aspect of her career would suffer, from box office to salary to scripts and publicity. Eventually—a notion she did not like to linger over—the studio brass would give up on her and start looking for someone to take her place.

But this morning's news thrust these unpleasant thoughts out of Eve's mind.

An Oscar might be the final touch to her image that would at last make her into one of the great ladies of the screen. And this year she might actually win. The competition was not particularly strong, and her performance in *Capricorn* had been flawless.

Eve had grown accustomed to Oscar nominations. She had also grown accustomed to not winning the Oscar itself. She knew she would always be an also-ran as long as there were flashier actresses with higher public profiles and greater affection from the public to steal the honor from her.

But this year it might be different. This year she might win.

With this thought in mind Eve thanked her agent and hung up the phone. She turned back to the picture window behind which the waves rolled ceaselessly forward, and drummed a finger against her arm. Gone was her morning somnolence. Her nerves were alert now.

Opportunity was knocking at last. The opportunity she had worked a lifetime for, honing her art to a level of perfection rarely seen in Hollywood, and using her wits to extract favor from those who could help her while destroying anyone who stood in her way. She had played the toughest game in the world with matchless skills and a killer instinct. And she had come up just a little bit short—until now.

This was Eve's Oscar. It had to be!

Eve stood staring at the inscrutable ocean, an image of eternity whose significance was lost on her. There was nothing in her own imagination to match that spectacle of ceaseless, rhythmic repetition bordering on peace. Inside her mind she toiled onward and upward, relentlessly, toward a shadowy goal that receded a little more each day, just a bit out of reach.

But she would reach it. She would capture it at last.

And now it was almost in her hands.

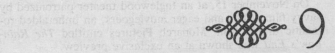 9

ON DECEMBER 1, IN TIME FOR THE CHRISTMAS SEASON, *Winter of Destiny* was to have its premiere at Grauman's Chinese Theater.

An unprecedented publicity blitz was poised to explode at the moment of the premiere. Full-page advertisements for the new film had been bought in newspapers everywhere. The cover of *Time* was reserved for Bryant Hayes, and a feature story written on this, his greatest production ever. Every film magazine in the land was prepared to ballyhoo the film. Unprecedented pressure was being put on the Academy of Motion Picture Arts and Sciences, behind the scenes, to insure as many Oscar nominations for this film as possible.

As for Moira Talbot and Guy Lavery, they were both freed from all other responsibilities so as to be completely available for publicity touring on behalf of the film. They would tour Europe as well as the United States. It was rumored they were even to travel to Russia to have their pictures taken with Russian officials in front of the actual locations where the film's story took place. This would be a goodwill joining of hands from America to Russia that might well reduce tensions between the two countries.

At least a thousand theaters nationwide had booked the picture. So great was the advance publicity that these theaters had been forced to accept an expensive block of Continental features and "B" pictures in order to have the privilege of exhibiting *Winter of Destiny*. Bryant Hayes was already counting his profits in the millions of dollars. Not since *Gone with the Wind* and the greatest de Mille epics had a single film generated so much excitement.

Then the unexpected happened.

On November 15, at an Inglewood theater patronized by savvy film critics and eager moviegoers, an unheralded romantic drama from Monarch Pictures entitled *The Rainbow's End* was shown at an exclusive preview.

In a surprise development that would later be part of a crucial chapter in American movie history, the preview created a sensation.

Rainbow was a hard-hitting, realistic drama that showed how the Depression destroyed people's lives and hopes. Its characters spoke directly to the American psyche—the hero through his ill-fated search for financial success as a guarantee of love, and the heroine through her tragic failure to marry the man of her choice when her wealthy family stood in her way. Male viewers related as profoundly to the hero as did women to the heroine. Though the story came to a tragic conclusion that separated the lovers forever, it nevertheless celebrated the mystical power of love even in conditions of hopeless adversity.

The film captured something essential, not only about the Depression, with its long years of cruel hardship, but about the era of prosperity that had preceded it, an era whose false optimism and childish belief in the indestructibility of human dreams seemed somehow to have brought on the great spiritual crash of 1929.

Thanks to its magnificent screenplay and brilliant direction, the film rose to a height of romantic intensity that left the preview audience stunned and started a wave of word of mouth that had swept through California in a single day and the entire nation within a week. *Rainbow* was clearly not a mere "B" picture. It was a film of the highest importance, a film that seemed to set a new style in moviemaking with one stroke.

On the heels of the explosive response to the preview,

Monarch Pictures started its own publicity campaign to spread the word about *Rainbow* from coast to coast.

The publicity, as it turned out, was not even necessary. It was almost as though there was a spell on the picture. People everywhere dropped whatever they were doing and lined up to pay any price to see it. Theaters were packed. Lines extended around the block. Overnight that rarest of Hollywood productions, the classic film, had revealed itself.

The excitement had spread to Europe within the first fortnight, and Monarch's dubbing studios were working on twenty-four-hour shifts to finish foreign versions of *Rainbow* in time to satisfy the demand. The Depression had hit Europe even harder than the United States, and the film's depiction of human tragedy and triumph in the face of economic disaster spoke to the hearts of Europeans as much as to Americans.

Samuel Raines, the film's hero, became an overnight superstar. His emergence as a bigger-than-life leading man left audiences breathless. Thanks to Joseph Knight's screenplay and the camera of Serge Lavitsky, a dimension of Raines's screen personality had emerged that had never been suspected in his previous roles. He was revealed as a heroic, sexy, and deeply romantic figure. Overnight he was the star of all the fan magazines. From now on he would rival Colman and Gable and Cary Grant as one of the elite leading men in Hollywood.

As for Rebecca Sherwood, her performance left audiences weeping. Her peculiarly delicate and tragic quality as an actress had been at the center of *Rainbow* and was quickly acclaimed by critics and public alike. Her nomination as Best Actress by the Academy was a certainty, and a great career stretched before her.

Everyone connected with the film became a celebrity. Articles on Oscar Freund and his courageous support of Joseph Knight's top-secret project filled magazines and newspapers. Serge Lavitsky saw his career resurrected with this brilliant effort, and was hailed as one of Hollywood's greatest directors. Oscar nominations were predicted for the film in at least a dozen categories, including

Best Actor, Best Actress, Best Original Screenplay, and, of course, Best Picture.

But no one benefited from this storm of public attention more than the "mystery man," the creative genius who had personally written and produced *The Rainbow's End*, Joseph Knight. His photo appeared in all the film journals and newspapers. His striking masculinity, combined with his youth, sparked curiosity about his private life and early career, and added to the luster of his triumph. It was a foregone conclusion that this daring young visionary would become the hottest producer in Hollywood, and that he could write his own ticket with any studio he chose.

By the end of November *The Rainbow's End* was making film history. Its box-office gross exceeded twenty million dollars, an amount never before attained by any film in so short a time. Such a performance by a film whose budget had been less than half a million dollars left all observers stunned.

And among those observers, none was more flabbergasted than Bryant Hayes.

Hayes was in a rage. His film, *Winter of Destiny*, had been upstaged with a vengeance by *The Rainbow's End*. The latter was obviously the hit of the holiday season.

In other circumstances Hayes would have withdrawn *Winter of Destiny* and saved it for release at a later date. But his hands were tied. He had booked the film into a thousand theaters nationwide and had no other film to replace it with. The publicity blitz he had orchestrated could not be stopped on a dime.

There was no choice but to go ahead with exhibition. And Hayes, a fighter by nature, decided to take the chance. He turned loose his publicity army and put his film into Grauman's Chinese as scheduled, on December 1.

The result was a disaster.

The public, in ecstasies over the intense, intimate emotional drama of *The Rainbow's End*, was in the worst possible frame of mind to welcome the predictable big-budget Hollywood costume drama that was Hayes's much-worked-over *Winter of Destiny*.

Movie fans were not fooled by the publicity stories about the film's two stars and their long-awaited marriage. No one cared any longer about the love lives of Moira Talbot and Guy Lavery. Everyone had seen them both in a dozen pictures, and familiarity had bred contempt. In fact, comically enough, it was the two stars' very attempt to achieve bigger-than-life status through their fancy costumes and artificial roles in *Winter of Destiny* that ended both their careers. Moira Talbot's advancing age and lack of real acting ability were shown to embarrassing proportions in her portrayal of the Russian heroine. And Guy Lavery's soft, almost simpering mannerisms showed through despite his attempts to be heroic.

Compared to the heartbreaking performance of Rebecca Sherwood as the tragic heroine of *The Rainbow's End* and the dramatic emergence of Samuel Raines as a major star opposite her, Moira Talbot and Guy Lavery looked like insipid contract players in *Winter of Destiny*. They alone sank the film, and their careers to boot. Neither of them would ever appear in a major production again.

But *Winter of Destiny*'s failure went much further. Audiences yawned at the lavish production sets and shrugged at the clumsily directed crowds of extras. The Russian story, so remote in time and so foreign, paled beside the crushingly immediate Depression tale of *The Rainbow's End,* a truly American story for a public that had been bottling up its painful emotions for nearly a decade.

"Joseph Knight's masterful *The Rainbow's End* has opened a wound in the American psyche," wrote an influential critic, "and helped us all to weep for our own lost hopes and to learn to admire ourselves for our stubborn courage in the face of adversity. This is more than a mere entertainment film: it is a national epiphany. And the rapt American public, standing in the rain and snow in lines three blocks long, is welcoming it as such. Oscar Freund and Monarch Pictures picked the perfect moment to show us two great characters and a drama of wrenching emotion. We have all suffered ten long years with this Depression, and for nearly as long we have swallowed huge doses of escapist screen pablum and fantasy from Hollywood, of which the ponderous Continental epic *Winter of Destiny* is a classic example. *This* winter the film of destiny is *The Rainbow's End,* and the man of the hour is Joseph Knight."

In comparison with *Rainbow*'s record-breaking triumph, Continental Pictures' *Winter of Destiny,* the film on which Bryant Hayes had gambled his reputation and millions of Continental dollars, was a monumental failure. It played to half-empty theaters for three weeks and then was withdrawn. Many of those same theaters, owned by Continental Pictures, had no choice but to book *The Rainbow's End* in order to recoup their losses on *Winter of Destiny.*

The trade papers were merciless.

COLD WINTER FOR CONTINENTAL, read one headline.

PIX NIX FOR HAYES FLOP, wrote *Daily Variety.*

WINTER OF MEDIOCRITY, proclaimed *The Hollywood Reporter.*

Thanks to the debacle of *Winter of Destiny,* Continental Pictures suffered its biggest quarterly financial loss since 1930. Bryant Hayes was left to explain to Arnold Speck and his money men in New York how this fiasco had happened. The failure of *Winter of Destiny* was the biggest single blow to his prestige and power since the incorporation of Continental Pictures. Even Hayes himself doubted he would recover from it any time soon.

The riot of excitement over *The Rainbow's End* went on and on. The film's financial success around the world was matched only by its unanimous critical reception.

On February 15 the expected happened, when the Academy Award nominations were announced. *The Rainbow's End* was nominated for an unprecedented fourteen Oscars. A sweep of the major awards at the April ceremony was predicted for this most unusual of films.

As for *Winter of Destiny,* it managed to garner nominations for three awards, including Best Special Effects, Best Cinematography, and—thanks to Bryant Hayes's personal influence—Best Picture.

But no one was fooled by these cosmetic nominations. *Winter of Destiny* was a colossal flop, and its ignominious performance at the box office had irrevocably tarnished the image of its producer. No longer would Bryant Hayes be the personification of the flamboyantly successful Hollywood mogul. That honor would now go to handsome, charismatic Joseph Knight. Knight incarnated the *working* Hollywood producer: young, idealistic, serious, sleeves rolled up, a genuine film artist with something to say to the world through his work. While Hayes, the cigar-smoking kingpin with his Bel Air mansion and his offices full of yesmen, was an anachronism, an image of the insensitive money man out to make a buck by trotting out timeworn formulas for bored audiences in search of escapism.

To Hayes this was the unkindest cut of all. Even more painful than the failure of his film was the humiliation of being upstaged by a nobody like Joseph Knight. Bryant Hayes was as concerned with his personal image as with his work. And that image had suffered a disastrous blow.

Of course, it never occurred to Hayes in his anger that the film on which he had worked so hard and gambled so much, *Winter of Destiny,* had been nothing more or less than stolen property. He himself had stolen the film's concept and original screenplay from none other than Joseph Knight.

Hayes hardly even remembered Knight's long-ago visit to his home and their discussion of the property Knight wanted Continental Pictures to produce. Hayes's theft of the property had been business as usual, so much so that he had barely given his own venality another thought.

Thus he failed to ponder the irony of what was happening to him now. Had he done so, he might have begun to suspect that Joseph Knight had had something to do with the way things turned out. And he might even have drawn the deeper conclusion as to Daria Kane's role in the disaster that had befallen *Winter of Destiny.*

But Bryant Hayes never looked in those directions. His rage blinded him to such devious subtleties. He only knew that Joseph Knight, in stealing the public's heart, had virtually cuckolded Bryant Hayes. Knight had made everyone think that he himself had single-handedly introduced a new level of talent and commitment to Hollywood filmmaking.

It was a new era, or so the movie publications claimed—an era of high aspirations and great new achievements, in which Knight would reign supreme.

From now on Bryant Hayes would have to look at the darkly handsome image of Joseph Knight in all the film magazines and hear the world trumpet Knight's glory while Hayes's own life's work, the result of twenty years of dedication, gathered dust in the public's short memory.

This was an insult that Bryant Hayes would not forget.

And when the day of reckoning came, he would avenge it.

But for now Hayes could only rage, and drink away his rage.

On the night the Oscar nominations were announced Hayes had his houseboy, Karl Rächer, bring him a bottle of aged single-malt scotch. So wrapped up was he in his own anger that he did not even take notice of Karl, who was his usual seedy self as he brought the bottle with the soda and ice on a tray.

Karl Rächer closed the door quietly on Bryant Hayes and smiled to himself as he returned to his own quarters.

No one knew Bryant Hayes's house like Karl Rächer.

Almost from the beginning Karl had known about Daria and Joseph Knight. He had used the combination of his great intelligence and his familiarity with Daria's habits to realize that Daria was involved with Knight. From his privileged position on the sidelines Karl had watched what was going on. And, himself a filmmaker, he had seen the subtle connection between Daria's intimacy with Knight and the innumerable accidents that had befallen *Winter of Destiny*.

Though not enough of a man himself ever to have repaid Bryant Hayes for what he had done to him, Karl Rächer could appreciate the cleverness and poetic justice of what Joseph Knight had done to Hayes and Continental Pictures. In the silence of his soul he applauded Knight and took sadistic pleasure in the discomfiture of Hayes.

And he resolved to keep Daria's secret. Neither Daria nor anyone else would ever know how much Karlheinz Rächer knew about the debacle of *Winter of Destiny* and its real cause.

10

April 10, 1941

KATE HAD GIVEN UP AUDITIONING.

She was sick of the cattle calls, the endless waiting, the scorn and unfriendliness of the casting directors and assistant directors, the walk-ons and extra roles that paid so little and never led anywhere.

But Melanie did not seem willing to let Kate give up on acting. She dragged her to the workshop she attended twice each week. Kate watched the proceedings with a bored look. Her pride was offended by the sight of a dozen desperate hopefuls cutting histrionic capers in front of a jaded coach who himself was a failed actor. The whole thing looked ridiculous and very sad.

The work Kate and Melanie did at the studios did not seem like real acting. Kate could not see that it had anything in common with what Bette Davis or Cary Grant or Spencer Tracy did on the movie screen. Those people were actors. Kate and Melanie were more like models, positioned before the indifferent camera for two seconds of film and then herded off the sound stage like cattle.

The only personal experience Kate had ever had that reminded her of real acting was, paradoxically, waitressing. In her restaurant work she had learned to use her voice and body to create an image designed to please a specific customer and get as big a tip as possible. Kate had made herself an expert at this. She could read many customers in the two seconds it took to approach their tables, and rearrange her personality in that tiny interval so as to arouse their sympathy or admiration.

But Kate never saw this as acting. To her it was just work. She was too hardheaded and practical to see the logical similarity between what she did for a living and the art of the great Hollywood stars.

Kate was weary of the whole routine. Her mind was slipping further and further away from her surroundings. Soon her body would follow, and she would pick up stakes and leave. The vastness of the American country beckoned to her. Hollywood was an absurd place, really, and more venal and disgusting than most. The frantic machinations of Melanie and the others to get roles seemed tragic and silly to Kate. These girls would never become real actresses, and they would never come a step closer to their own selves for all their efforts to get before a camera. They would be exploited, chewed up and spit out by Hollywood, and would end up as secretaries or shopgirls with used-up bodies and tainted souls.

Kate could feel her wanderlust stirring inside her. Soon it would be time to leave.

But before she could make up her mind, something happened that was to change her plans.

Oscar night was approaching. The awards ceremony would be held in the ballroom at the Ambassador Hotel. Melanie was burning to go and see the stars. She convinced an amused Kate to go with her.

On Oscar night the two dressed up in their best clothes and went to the hotel. There were searchlights lighting up the sky. The stars arrived in their limousines—Clark Gable, Ronald Colman, Bette Davis, James Cagney, Joan Crawford—dressed to the teeth in the latest Hollywood designer creations. Melanie and Kate, held behind the police cordon with hundreds of screaming fans, watched from a distance. Kate was astonished by Melanie's almost hysterical excitement.

When the stars had all arrived, the crowd did not disperse. The fans would wait all evening, listening to the ceremony inside through loudspeakers, and be here to applaud the winners when they emerged from the hotel.

The idea of standing out here all evening was too much for Kate.

"I'm not staying," she told Melanie. "You can if you want. I'll see you at home."

To her surprise Melanie agreed to leave also. The new shoes she had worn were hurting her feet, and she needed to sit down.

They stopped at a nearby coffee shop to rest and talk about what they had seen before going home.

They sat at the counter and ordered coffee. The coffee shop was almost empty. There were a couple of girls in a booth, and a man at the counter circling the names of horses on a racing form while a cigarette burned in an ashtray in front of him. Melanie was full of her usual mixture of excitement and frustration.

"Did you see Gable?" she asked. "Isn't he a dream? How can one man be that handsome? Those *teeth!* He's incredible. And Bette Davis's gown! If I could wear a dress like that just once in my life . . . And did you see the way Joan Crawford had done her hair?"

Kate listened disinterestedly. Though she found Melanie's enthusiasm touching, she herself had seen little to admire in the stars getting out of their limousines. With their fancy clothes and hairdos, their makeup and their smiles for the crowd, they looked to Kate more like circus performers than genuine celebrities. There was something freakish about the whole affair, something too unreal to arouse Kate's admiration.

Kate was not an intellectual by any means. But she had had her flings with the secret world of dreams as well as the seamiest side of reality. To her eye, the Hollywood stars with their posturing and their screaming fans were not glamorous. They were puppets, caught in the web of their fans' dreams. They were not really the masters of their own destiny, because their professional existence depended completely on pleasing other people. She imagined that their private lives were not at all pleasant. They probably had little time to themselves and even less peace of mind. Kate had fought too hard for her own independence to find such a prospect enticing.

But she smiled to hear Melanie exclaim about it all.

"John Garfield!" Melanie was saying. "To think that I saw John Garfield! And Eve Sinclair! Little old me, from Wichita, on the same sidewalk as Eve Sinclair. I've admired her since I was that high."

"I used to admire her, too," Kate said wistfully, recalling her girlhood worship of Eve Sinclair.

"What I wouldn't give to be in there right now seeing that ceremony!" Melanie was saying. "Just think, Kate. They're all listening to the speeches, and waiting for the great moment when the envelope is opened . . . If only we were in there, and not out here . . ."

"Well, it's not the end of the world," Kate said.

At that moment a deep voice interrupted them.

"I beg your pardon. I couldn't help overhearing you."

Kate looked up. It was the man who had been studying the racing form a few seats down from them at the counter. He had moved closer, and was smiling at them. He was in middle age, with a rather elegant William Powell look to him. He was dressed in a dark pin-striped suit with a vest and carried an old overcoat. He looked a trifle seedy and yet rather cultured. Just the sort of type one meets in Hollywood, Kate thought. Perhaps an old character actor down on his luck.

"I know how you can get into the Ambassador," he said. "It's really quite simple. If that's what you want, that is . . ."

Kate was looking at him suspiciously. Melanie was saying nothing.

The man hesitated, seeing their faces.

"Well, pardon the intrusion," he said. "I didn't mean to bother you . . ."

He turned away.

"Wait!" Melanie said suddenly.

He turned back, smiling.

"Do you really know a way in there?" Melanie asked.

He nodded. "You go down about half a block past the

side entrance," he said. "Then turn left into the alley, and you'll see an unmarked door in the side of the hotel. It won't be guarded. It never is. I used to sneak in that way when I didn't want to be seen in the lobby, for one reason or another. It's a delivery entrance. You simply take the freight elevator up to the lobby or the mezzanine, and you're in."

He had a rather wistful expression on his face. Kate noticed the lines under his eyes, and the thin, well-cared-for mustache that made him look even more like William Powell. He had a high hairline and dark hair, and a tanned face. There was something at once elegant and dissipated about him. Kate would have suspected that he was a drinker, but he seemed too self-possessed for that.

For an instant he looked at Kate, and she saw an odd expression in his tired eyes. There was something faraway about it, as though he saw that she was the type of girl that might have interested him a great deal, but a long time ago.

"Well," he said, "I won't trouble you any more. Good luck."

He turned away, placed a nickel on the counter beside his cup of coffee, and sauntered out of the coffee shop, his raincoat thrown over his arm. Kate saw that he had a peculiarly elegant gait, like a real gentleman, but with something faintly ironic about it, as though he wanted to show off his dissipation as well as his refinement.

Melanie was looking at her.

"Do you think he was on the level?" she asked. "Do you want to give it a try?"

Kate looked into Melanie's eyes. They were as excited as those of a child. Kate laughed.

"It can't hurt to try," she said. "The worst that can happen is that we'll get thrown out on our ear."

Five minutes later the two girls were moving carefully down the alley the stranger had described. They could still hear the crowd milling out front, and the voice of Bob Hope through the loudspeaker making jokes between the presentations of awards.

The door was there, just as the stranger had said. It was made of metal and covered with chipped brown paint. It looked like the door to a garbage room.

Cautiously Melanie opened it. Inside there was nothing but a few empty crates and pallets. Indeed, it was a delivery area.

Melanie and Kate stole through the room and found the freight elevator the stranger had mentioned. They pulled open the heavy door and got in. There were buttons for the lobby and mezzanine as well as all the floors. Melanie pushed the mezzanine button and the conveyance lurched upward.

A moment later the elevator stopped, and, peering out carefully, Melanie opened the door. The mezzanine area loomed before them. It was furnished in the classic style, with mahogany lowboys and ornate framed mirrors and Louis XVI armchairs.

Now it occurred to Kate that they had not bothered to ask the stranger where to go from here. Presumably the ballroom was on the lobby floor or mezzanine.

"Well, we might as well look for it," Kate said. "We've come this far."

They scouted the mezzanine cautiously, noticing themselves in one of the mirrors as they passed. They looked presentable enough to pass for two guests of the hotel, but hardly as two invitees to the presentation banquet.

They found a stairway down to the lobby floor, and at length heard from around the next corner the unmistakable sound of the crowd inside the ballroom. Kate peered around the corner and saw security guards flanking the doors.

"Let's try the back," she said to Melanie. "Maybe we can find a way into the wings somewhere."

They circled around to the back of the ballroom and looked for another door. The corridor was full of unmarked, inconspicuous-looking louvered doors leading to service rooms for the hotel. They chose one close to the ballroom and opened it.

Melanie slipped inside. Kate was about to follow her

when they both heard a voice from inside the ceremony room.

"And the winner of the award for Best Actress is . . ."

They both paused as they waited for the name to be announced.

"Miss Rebecca Sherwood, for *The Rainbow's End!*"

Applause rang out. Kate saw Melanie's eyes open wide at the announcement. Melanie had seen *The Rainbow's End* seven times, and identified strongly with Rebecca Sherwood as a young performer who came from obscurity to achieve great fame.

"Oh, Kate . . ." Melanie was exclaiming.

At that moment a male voice from the corridor interrupted them. Kate turned to see a hotel security guard approaching. "Miss," he was saying.

Quickly Kate closed the door on Melanie and turned to the guard. He was looking at her suspiciously.

"Can I help you, miss?" he asked.

Experienced at reading the looks in the eyes of men, Kate realized in that instant that he had not made up his mind that she did not belong here. He was trying to evaluate her from her clothing and demeanor.

Quickly she put on a confident, almost regal manner.

"Why, yes, you can," she said. "Is there a ladies' room?"

He looked at her carefully.

"Didn't you find the powder room inside, miss?" he asked.

She realized he must be talking about the powder room for the banquet guests inside the ballroom.

"It's full, I'm afraid," she said. "I don't want to wait half the night."

For one last instant doubt shone in his eyes. Kate gave him a bright, confident smile that dispelled his suspicion.

"Follow me, miss," he said.

He led her along a hall to an area adjacent to the ballroom. There was a ladies' room tucked away in a corner, barely marked.

"It's not used much," he said. "Comes in handy on nights like this."

"Why, thank you very much," Kate said. "You're very kind."

"Don't mention it, miss," the man said. "Things get pretty hectic around here this time of year."

On an impulse Kate reached into her purse and found a dollar, which she handed him as a tip.

"Why, thank you, miss, I'm sure." The guard walked away, entirely appeased, as Kate reflected ruefully that with that dollar gone she would have no lunch tomorrow or the next day.

She entered the ladies' room and looked at herself in the mirror. The expression of patrician condescension she had used for the security guard was still lingering on her face. For the thousandth time she reflected on the difference between her flesh, which lent itself so easily to illusion, and the inscrutable core of her real self, a self she still knew almost nothing about.

She heard the click of high-heeled shoes outside the powder room. On an impulse she ducked into one of the stalls, not wishing to enter into conversation with one of the hotel guests.

She sat down on the seat as someone entered the powder room. She would wait until the interloper had left, she decided, and then go to find Melanie.

But her thoughts were suddenly interrupted by a word hissed from the chair before the vanity mirror in the powder room.

"Rotten little bitch . . ."

The crude words were pronounced by a lovely, sibilant voice that was somehow familiar. They were followed by a barrage of barracks language in low but intense tones, an incredibly coarse display even for Kate's hardly tender ears.

Kate held her breath, intrigued by the voice. There was a note of desolation underneath its anger that struck a chord deep inside her.

What was more, the voice was becoming more familiar now.

Carefully Kate looked through the crack in the stall door. The woman had her back to her, but Kate could see her face in the vanity mirror. The woman was staring fixedly at her own reflection.

It was a young face, and a beautiful one. The eyes were blue, the complexion creamy and unlined. The hair was very dark, and styled in a smooth wave that fell gracefully to her slim shoulders. The chin, brow, cheeks, and nose were amazingly delicate and subtle. Her bone structure was as perfect as her skin.

But the expression on the face was twisted by hatred and frustration as the foul words sang perversely from her lips.

"Fucking, fucking bitch," she murmured. "Fucking no-talent bitch . . ."

Kate had to fight to conceal the abrupt intake of her breath. She was looking at Eve Sinclair.

Eve was studying herself with a mixture of fury and contempt. It was as though her anger were directed first at something outside herself and then, far more intimately, at herself above all.

Only now, in the presence of this embarrassingly intense emotion, did Kate recall what she and Melanie had just overheard: the awarding of the Oscar for Best Actress to Rebecca Sherwood. Kate recalled that Eve Sinclair had been up for that award, for her performance in a film which Kate had seen but whose title she could not remember. A mediocre movie in which Eve, as always, had been very brilliant.

And Rebecca Sherwood, the haunting, sensitive young star with her chiaroscuro performance in Joseph Knight's stunning film triumph, *The Rainbow's End*, had won the Oscar that Eve had no doubt wanted very badly.

These thoughts were going through Kate's mind as she eavesdropped on what must be one of the most painful moments in Eve Sinclair's life. For it was common knowledge in Hollywood that Eve Sinclair had done everything an actress can do to reach the top of her profession—except win the Oscar. Eve was a famous star in her own right, but despite her best efforts, she had always been consigned to the less glamorous, less stellar ranks of Hollywood actresses. And this in spite of the fact that her acting skill was hailed the world over.

"Rebecca . . ."

The word on Eve's lips, pronounced softly, meditatively, proved that Kate had read her thoughts. Kate felt almost embarrassed to be so close to this woman, seeing her without being seen, and knowing what was in her heart.

And now it occurred to Kate that she was looking at more than just an actress. She was looking at the grown-up image of her own childhood idol. She was looking at fresh, beautiful, elegant Eve Sinclair, the personification of perfection she had not only idealized throughout her youth but had cherished in her heart as the portal to a better and cleaner world, a world in which little girls were loved and cherished, a world of happy endings.

But she was seeing that cherubic face as it had been altered not only by time, and by the indescribable rigors of a Hollywood career that Kate could not even imagine—but also by a lifetime of frustration that had reached its peak this very evening.

In all her imaginings about Eve Sinclair, Kate had never once thought of her as a failure. But what she was witnessing now was failure at its most painful, the failure of a proud and brilliant professional who has given everything she has to her career and who has lost the honor she deserved to a newcomer, a young actress who could never have won the Oscar had it not been for the brilliant showcase given her by Joseph Knight in *The Rainbow's End*.

As Kate watched, a dizzying kaleidoscope of expressions crossed the face in the mirror. Most palpable of them, of course, was anger. But just beneath it, yawning like a black ocean, was loathing. Loathing for her failure? For the Academy's whim in bestowing its highest honor on youthful Rebecca Sherwood? Loathing for everything Hollywood represented? Or perhaps loathing for herself and for the life she had squandered in the vain pursuit of an acceptance that would never come?

Kate could not know, for Eve Sinclair, so familiar an image on the movie screen, was a stranger to her. But the power of Eve's hatred and disgust could encompass all these things and a thousand more. It was pitiful and frightening to behold.

As Kate watched, the beautiful face in the mirror was overtaken in slow waves by something new. It was a terrible sadness, a sort of bottomless, infinite regret.

Kate saw a single tear well up in Eve's eye and trickle forlornly down her cheek. At that moment Eve looked like a little girl, lonely and frightened and lost. The expression lingered only for a split second as the tear flowed down her cheek—and then was gone, eclipsed by the coarser emotions of an adult woman, just as a sand drawing is swept away by a salty wave.

Kate felt atrociously uncomfortable. She did not dare leave her stall, or even move. She could not bear to let Eve know she had been watched. She must remain here until Eve left.

At that moment there was a knock on the door.

"Eve?" came a male voice from outside. "Are you in there?"

The face in the mirror came to itself with a start, as though torn back cruelly from a private drama too intimate to see the light of day. The lovely features composed themselves with a quickness that amazed Kate. A hand dabbed at the tear on her cheek.

"Yes," Eve said loudly. "What is it?"

"Press, Evie," called the voice. "Sorry . . ."

There was a moment's hesitation. Eve's face registered an almost unbearable suffering. It was the loneliest face Kate had ever seen. Then, as though by a sudden shifting of inner forces unspeakable in their power, the face changed. All the emotions that had ravaged it were banished. An expression of calm, ladylike urbanity appeared, eclipsing all else.

Eve was preparing herself for the reporters.

This banishing of emotion was more impressive to Kate, in her hiding place, than all the performances she had ever seen Eve give on the screen. For the emotion inside Eve was clearly unbearable, an acid searing her very heart. And she was hiding it under an iron mask of self-control, to reassure the press and her fans of her eternal self-possession, her transcendent elegance, the indestructible nobility of the star.

Quickly Eve wiped away the last traces of the tear that had moistened her cheek, and dabbed at her makeup with a tissue. She pushed back her chair, stood up, and glanced at herself in the mirror for a last time.

And in that glance Kate saw—either because it was really there or because she herself could not forget it—the lonely and frightened little girl, peeking out through a tiny corner of Eve's carefully constructed image. Kate knew somehow that it would never again be invisible to her, that she would see it every time she looked at Eve Sinclair from now on. For it seemed to spread over the entire past, coloring not only the youthful image of Eve that Kate had so admired as a girl, but Kate's own girlhood, and her own loneliness.

Eve gave herself a last evaluative look in the mirror. Her eyes had the tired determination of a beaten soldier who vows to fight again another day. She spoke softly to her reflected image.

"One hundred and fifty percent," she said, her words mystifying Kate.

Then she turned and walked briskly from the room. A voice in the corridor greeted her, and she was gone.

A moment later Kate went to find Melanie. She did not tell Melanie what she had seen in the ladies' room, but stayed with her in her little closet to eavesdrop on the rest of the awards presentations.

Kate was less familiar with the winners than was Melanie, who seemed to know every set designer, composer, cinematographer and director in Hollywood. But she did notice the drift of the evening, which was in fact a historic occasion: the sweeping of nine Academy Awards by Joseph Knight's *The Rainbow's End*. Having seen and admired the film, Kate was not entirely surprised to see it garner so many honors. But she was astonished by the almost palpable electricity from the banquet room as Hollywood expressed its surprise and admiration for this most improbable of big winners.

Perhaps the most memorable moment of the evening was when Samuel Raines accepted the Best Actor award for his portrayal of the hero in *The Rainbow's End*. Raines, normally a taciturn and rather frightening screen presence, was very human and unpretentious as he accepted the award.

"I'd like to be able to say I earned this by myself," he told the audience. "But that would not be true. I've worked hard in this business for fifteen years. I've had my opportunities, and missed some of them, as all of us have. But what you see when you look at my performance in *The Rainbow's End* is not something I conceived. It is what a brilliant filmmaker made of me with his own vision. God knows I love Serge Lavitsky, and we all know he was behind the camera throughout the film, giving it his own brand of genius. But even Serge was transformed by *Rainbow,* as I'm sure he'll tell you. No—the man who made us all rise above ourselves for this film, the man who made us believe we could be better than we had before, and who lifted us to a level we hadn't aspired to—that man is Joe Knight. My thanks go to him first, and then to all of you, for making this the greatest night of my life."

Samuel Raines's acceptance speech was widely quoted and shown in a dozen newsreels, for it was the dramatic highlight of the evening. Its words were still sounding in Kate's ears as she and Melanie left their hiding place and went outside to join the crowd waiting to see the stars leave the hotel.

The mob scene outside was even more crazy than before the ceremony, perhaps because the fans were aware of the historic significance of *The Rainbow's End* and its huge success. Kate and Melanie were buffeted by hundreds of screaming, pushing fans held back by a line of scowling policemen, some of whom were on horseback. It was a wild scene, on the edge of insanity, and Kate could hardly wait for it to be over. She wished she were home in bed. She was only going through this final crazy episode for Melanie's sake.

The stars came out, couple by couple, their faces changed now that they knew who had won the coveted awards. Kate saw Bette Davis, Clark Gable, Joan Crawford, Ronald Colman, Walter Huston, Myrna Loy, and many others. Somehow they all looked rather melancholy and tired in the glare of the lights. Kate imagined them wishing to get home and out of their fancy clothes so they could have a nightcap and go to bed.

But when she saw Eve Sinclair emerge, something stirred inside Kate. Having had that face before her mind's eye all her life, Kate now knew it in its private anguish. For this reason she was glad, really glad that she had come to this ceremony tonight. She knew Eve better than she had ever known her before, and, in an obscure way, she knew herself better too.

She was still musing over this fact when a group of fans suddenly broke through the cordon and rushed toward the emerging stars. The police line erupted in chaos. Kate and Melanie were thrust forward by the force of the mob. It was a frightening moment. One of the horses reared, its eyes terrified, as its rider tried to rein it in. The hooves kicked violently upward into the night sky.

In that instant the crowd mingled with the celebrities who were leaving the hotel, and the police could not bring order. It was a wild, prohibited mingling of two groups that were supposed to be separated by logic as well as space—the exalted stars and the unwashed multitude that admired them from afar.

Before Kate knew what was happening she was separated from Melanie and borne by the heaving wave of humanity toward the steps of the hotel. Police were everywhere, waving billy clubs and shouting at the crowd, their faces distorted by anger.

Suddenly Kate found herself pushed roughly into the arms of one of the policemen. Apparently exasperated by his long evening's struggle against the crowd, he took out his anger on her, roughly flinging her aside so that she tumbled to the pavement at his feet.

"Get back," she heard him grumble, to her and anyone else within earshot. "Get back."

At that instant a pair of strong hands gripped Kate by both arms and helped her to her feet. Their touch was firm but gentle. She wondered if it was another policeman, more patient than the first.

But when she turned to thank her benefactor she saw a

handsome man in a tuxedo who was obviously one of the celebrities from the hotel. He was looking at her through dark eyes filled with concern.

"Are you all right?" he asked.

Before she could say anything she saw him dart an angry glance at the policeman who had thrown her down to the ground.

"Be more careful, Officer," he said in a low tone which stopped the officer in his tracks. "These are people, too."

The officer turned away, chastened. Kate looked again at the man who had helped her up. He seemed familiar, but she could not place him. Now she saw how physically powerful he was, and how masculine. He was still looking at her, his eyes full of lingering anger at the police officer and concern for her safety.

"I'm—I'm all right," Kate said. "Thank you. Sorry . . ."

Her words did not come easily, for the hands holding her were alive with a steely male power that almost took her breath away.

"Good." He released her. He began to turn away and then looked back at her, a sudden intensity stirring in his eyes, as though he wanted to fix her image in his mind before letting her go. She wondered whether he thought he knew her or whether this was a characteristic of him, this hard and quick fixing of people with his eyes.

She could not know, for in another instant he was gone, and she was being pushed back into the crowd, searching vainly for Melanie while still feeling the stranger's hands on her arms, an odd warm thrill unlike any feeling she had ever experienced before.

After a long search she found Melanie, and they began to extricate themselves from the crowd. Melanie seemed to have escaped the melee that had submerged Kate and was still full of childish excitement over all the stars she had seen.

"Nine Academy Awards!" she was exclaiming. "What a man! And look, Kate—there he is!"

Kate turned to follow the direction of Melanie's out-stretched hand and saw the stranger who had helped her, getting into a limousine while a phalanx of policemen kept the crowd back.

"Is that . . . ?" Kate said, her eyes lingering on the limousine as Melanie held her arm.

"That's him!" Melanie cried. "That's Joseph Knight! Isn't he a dream?"

Kate said nothing. A moment later the two girls were on their way home. When they got there Melanie wanted to talk all night about what she had seen at the Ambassador, but Kate had to work tomorrow, and yawningly sent her friend to bed.

For as long as she could remember Kate had not needed more than thirty seconds to get to sleep at night. But tonight she lay awake for what seemed a long time, thinking about the strange and unforgettable scene she had witnessed from her hiding place in the powder room at the hotel. Eve Sinclair, her girlhood idol, had sat within a few feet of her and unknowingly poured out her very heart through the reflected image of her tormented face. The moment seemed to have marked Kate in a way she could not understand.

But as somnolence stole forward at last to blur Kate's thoughts, she forgot about Eve Sinclair. The face of Joseph Knight, the handsome stranger who had helped her when the policeman threw her to the ground, banished all else from her mind. Dream images flowered before her vision, guiding her at last toward slumber. And they all seemed to take root in Joseph Knight's searching black eyes. When sleep took her in its arms at last, they were the arms of Joseph Knight, holding her firm to steady her on her own legs while somehow sweeping the earth out from beneath her, so that she fell quickly out of herself, and toward him.

To Kate this was just another night's sleep, albeit more pleasant than most. It would take her a long time to realize that on this fateful night she had crossed over the invisible line between the past she took for granted and the destiny that had been waiting for her all her life.

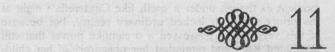

11

A WEEK AFTER THE OSCAR CEREMONY AT THE AMBASSADOR Hotel, Kate went out to find herself a theatrical agent.

She told no one about what she was doing, least of all Melanie. She felt oddly furtive and guilty about it. And she felt doubly uncomfortable because she was not sure why she was doing it. Kate was not in the habit of taking actions without knowing why.

Something about her experience on Oscar night had changed Kate. Before that night she had been indifferent about acting and frankly contemptuous of Hollywood. But now an irritating little impulse had been started in her, like the grain of sand around which a pearl grows. It was an impulse to give acting one serious try before she gave up the idea entirely.

Why she had changed she did not know. She was not introspective enough to ask herself whether it had something to do with her eavesdropping on Eve Sinclair's private grief, or with something about the Oscar ceremony itself. She only knew she felt different.

Of course, she would never be able to erase from her mind the tragic image of Eve's face in the ladies' room mirror, the beautiful features torn by painful emotions as Eve reflected on the Oscar she had lost to Rebecca Sherwood, the star of Joseph Knight's brilliant film, *The Rainbow's End*.

Nor would she forget Eve's astounding strength as she composed her face for the press before that same mirror, burying her private anguish by an act of will.

Kate looked back on Oscar night as a special moment somehow removed from the natural course of her life, a moment as though under a spell, like Cinderella's night at the prince's ball. It lacked ordinary reality, but because of this very fact it possessed a dreamlike power that still fascinated Kate and reminded her obscurely of her childhood fantasies about Eve Sinclair and the magical world she inhabited.

But these thoughts did not lead Kate toward an answer to the riddle of her behavior. She asked no questions. Instead, she moved forward boldly, just as she would have done in one of her quick, efficient searches for a waitressing job. She sent out copies of her portfolio, made phone calls, and soon got the answer she wanted.

Her first appointment was with an agent named Barnett Livingstone. She had heard Melanie mention the name many times as an agent who gave young performers a chance, provided they had talent. And something about the name struck Kate as distinguished. She felt a childish impulse to be represented by a man with so elegant a name.

She was surprised and a little dismayed when she arrived at his office.

It was a small, cluttered office with a frosted glass door in a run-down office building in downtown Hollywood. There was a secretary's desk, but no secretary. A balding man in shirtsleeves with a fat stomach and a cigar greeted her.

"Barney Livingstone," he said, ignoring the shocked look on her face. "And you are . . . ?"

"Katherine Hamilton," Kate said, managing a smile.

"Have a seat," he said. "I'm on the phone. I'll be right with you."

He left her and went into his inner office without closing the door. He picked up the phone and continued his conversation, the smoke from his cigar floating in plumes on the stale air.

"Okay, sure," he said to his unseen interlocutor. "I know she can do it. But *will* she do it? That's my whole point, Frankie. You can't count on her today the way you could a year or two ago. She's just not the actress she was. Everybody knows it. See, that's why I'm saying, just give this other girl a chance. Just let her test for the part. Nobody needs to know about it. It'll only take ten minutes, for Christ's sake. Just take this little chance for me, Frankie. Big stars have been discovered this way. You know that."

There was a long silence. The agent's back was to Kate. She could see him nodding as he listened to the person on the other end of the phone. He was leaning back in his swivel chair, his feet on the desk.

At length he leaned forward, smiling.

"Okay," he said. "Sounds good. You're a pal, Frankie."

He hung up the phone and stood up. He moved to the door.

"Come on in, honey," he said to Kate. "I've got your portfolio right here."

She went into the office. He remained in the outer office for a moment, looking at something on his secretary's desk, then came in, closing the door.

"Sorry to have kept you waiting," he said. "That was one of our favorite producers. I managed to get him to try out a client of ours. It was like pulling teeth, believe me."

He sat down and stubbed out his cigar. He looked from Kate to the portfolio on his desk. His eyes narrowed as he studied her.

"You're very attractive," he said. "Very distinctive-looking. I mean it. Haven't I seen you in something?"

Kate shook her head. "I've only done extras and a couple of walk-ons," she said. "My guess is they were all cut."

He nodded, appraising her.

"Very distinctive," he said. "Those looks of yours probably upset the editors. They like all girls to look the same.

I hope you're not discouraged, though. You've got something unusual."

He glanced down at the portfolio, shook his head, and closed it.

"Your photographer was trying to hide the quality I'm talking about," he said. "We can't blame him for that, that's what he thinks he's paid for. His job is to make you and everybody else look like Marlene Dietrich. But there's something special about you . . ."

He looked her over again. "Do you mind standing up?" he asked.

Kate stood up, leaving her purse on the floor beside her chair.

"Good," he said. "Just walk across the room and back. That's right. Fine. Now put your hands on your hips. Smile. Smile! Good . . . Okay, sit down."

Kate sat down and looked at him.

"Well, you've got something," he said with a sigh. "I'm not sure what it is, but it's something different. Tell me, can you read lines? Have you had any acting lessons?"

Kate shook her head. "Only a few workshop sessions," she said. "To tell the truth, I didn't take it seriously until— well, until recently. I think I can learn, though."

He seemed impressed by her candor.

"Here," he said, handing her a piece of typing paper. "Read me the first line."

Kate looked at the paper. It was very dirty, and had obviously been touched by many hands. It bore a list of lines of dialogue, typed in a column down the page without any connection to each other.

She read the first line.

"It's past ten, ma'am. Your mother is here."

The agent smiled.

"Honey, this isn't a morgue," he said. "Give it some oomph. Make it real."

Kate read the line again. He looked at her without expression.

"Now try number eighteen," he said.

She looked down the page and found the line.

"I don't have to take that from you," she read.

"Now: anger," he said. "Put some real anger into it. Think of the person you hated more in your life than anybody else. See that person's face, and say the line to him or her. Go on."

Kate thought of Ray, her stepfather.

"I don't have to take that from you," she said.

The agent stared at her for a long moment. Then he smiled.

"Okay," he said. "Maybe we can get you some acting lessons. For the moment, that face of yours may be good enough to get you some work. But you'll have to be prepared to work hard. Are you?"

Kate nodded, thinking ruefully of her waitress job and whether she would have to give it up.

"All right," he said, standing up. "I'll give you a shot. Hang on a minute."

He went into the other room and returned with a stapled sheaf of papers inside a blue cover.

"Sign three times on page ten and once on page eleven," he said, handing Kate a pen. "It's a standard contract. Five years, fifteen percent."

Kate looked at him, her eyes lighting up. He was accepting her!

"You're really . . . ?" she asked.

"I'm not making any promises, you understand," he said. "You seem like an intelligent girl. You know how tough this business is. But I'll try my best for you. That I do promise."

Kate skimmed over the contract's pages briefly. The fine print meant nothing to her. She signed where he had told her to and put the contract on his desk.

"Good girl," he said. "Now stand up."

She stood up.

"Drop 'em," he said.

Kate was taken aback by his words.

"I—what?" she said.

"I said drop 'em," he said. "Drop your pants. Come on, honey. I haven't got all day. I got a business to run here."

Kate frowned. "I don't know what you mean," she said.

He stood up, moved around the desk, and brushed her

327

breast with a tobacco-stained finger. She could smell the cigar on his breath, and a tang of cheap alcohol.

The look in his eyes was at once lascivious and cajoling.

"You could go far," he said. "You're really a looker, in your way."

His hand moved down her breast to her hips. He began to pull her toward him.

"You be nice to me . . ." he began.

Before he could finish Kate pushed him away with both her hands.

He looked surprised and angry.

"Honey, what's the matter with you?" he asked. "What planet are you from, anyway? This is Hollywood, U.S.A. Get it? Wake up."

Kate said nothing. She was looking at him through eyes more dangerous than she realized. But he did not see her expression, for he was too busy staring at the swelling breasts under her blouse.

He was truly excited now. He could see that she was, indeed, something special.

"Don't be stupid, honey," he said. "I haven't got all day. You want to work, or don't you? Drop those pants and spread 'em, or you get nothing."

He grasped her by her shoulders and tried to kiss her.

All at once Kate's knee came from nowhere to strike him hard between his legs. His eye opened wide. He gasped.

Before he could shout his distress Kate's fist smashed into his nose. Blood started from the injured organ instantly. The agent staggered backward from the force of the blow.

"You crazy bitch," he cursed. "You fucking cunt . . ."

Suddenly the pain between his legs made him double over. He fell to the floor with a gasp.

With a coolness that amazed herself, Kate placed one of her high heels firmly on his chest and held him down as she reached across his body to the desk top.

"Fucking bitch . . ." he coughed through his own blood.

Kate found the contract on the desk. Taking her foot off the agent's chest, she stood back and carefully tore the contract up. She put the pieces in her purse and stood looking down at Barney Livingstone. The blood was running down his lips and chin. He was looking at her with an expression of hatred and amazement. He could not believe what she had done.

Kate turned on her heel and left the office without hurry. An odd calm was inside her, along with a mental image of Ray, darting in and out of her consciousness along with the face of the agent.

By the time she reached the street she felt nothing at all, except a sudden hunger.

She walked a couple of blocks in the morning sun. The air felt fresher than usual. The sidewalk under her high heels seemed to glimmer pleasantly in the sunshine. The strange absence of emotion buoyed Kate and made her feel young and strong.

At length she found herself before a coffee shop that seemed familiar. She looked along the street to get her bearings, and saw the Ambassador Hotel a block away.

She turned to the coffee shop. This was the same place she had gone to the night of the Oscars with Melanie.

Kate went in and sat down at a booth. When the waitress came she ordered a sandwich and a cup of coffee. She was famished and exhilarated. A private smile played over her lips.

A deep, smooth voice suddenly sounded at her ear, making her start.

"Fancy meeting you here."

Kate turned to see a face that rapidly came back to her memory. It was the dapper-looking middle-aged man who had been here the night she came with Melanie, the man who had told them how to get into the Ambassador through the side entrance.

"Hello," she said with a smile. "It's a small world, isn't it?"

"You said it, my dear. In Hollywood, the one thing you can't do is avoid the people you've met already. That can be a curse as well as a blessing, believe me."

He was standing with his raincoat thrown over his arm, looking every bit as elegant and as shabby as the night she had met him. The smile on his face was infectious. His teeth were bright and sparkling, his mustache perfectly trimmed, and there was an air of benevolent humor about him that charmed her.

"I just left someone who won't be friendly if I meet him again," she said, surprising herself with her own openness.

He raised an ironic eyebrow.

"Don't tell me," he said. "Assistant director? Casting director?"

"Agent," she said.

"Ah-hah," he smiled knowingly. "Those are the worst. Did you give him something to remember you by, I hope?"

Kate nodded, grinning like a little girl.

"That's the stuff," he said. "Not every young actress has that gift. These fellows think they can pretty much write their own ticket."

Kate opened her purse and retrieved the torn-up contract. She held it up to him like a trophy.

"I had signed it," she said, "before he got fresh."

"Did you tear it up, or did he?" the stranger asked.

She pointed to herself.

Gently he clapped his gloved hands together. They made a quiet caressing sound.

"Bravo," he said. There was a paternal gleam in his eye. "Hollywood could use a lot more like you. Tell me, did you get into the Ambassador the other night?"

Kate nodded. "Thanks to you, yes."

"And was it interesting?" he asked.

Again she nodded. She could not begin to tell him how important that night had been for her. At the same time she realized that her sudden decision to make a serious try at acting had landed her here in this coffee shop with nothing but a torn-up contract to show for her efforts. In a crazy way she had come full circle. This amused her. She laughed out loud.

"I must say I admire the way you're taking this," the stranger said. "I suspect you're someone rather special. May I introduce myself? Norman Webb. Sometime screenwriter, and currently—well, currently between destinies."

Kate put the torn-up contract back in her purse, and then held out a hand.

"Kate Hamilton," she said. "Waitress."

The smile on his face widened.

"I like you better all the time," he said.

"Would you care to join me?" she asked.

He made a pretense of indecision, touching at his frayed silk tie.

"Well, I have an appointment at the racetrack," he said. "But I think the ponies will wait for me. Thank you very much."

He sat down in the booth, his gentlemanly demeanor unruffled as he folded his raincoat beside him. He took out a gold cigarette case and opened it, offering her a cigarette. She shook her head.

"Do you mind if I . . . ?" he asked.

"Not at all."

He took out a cigarette, tapped it against the case, and lit it with a scratched gold lighter that, like the cigarette case, seemed to have seen better days. Kate smiled. Every facet of him seemed to unite elegance with wear and tear, urbanity with decay. He seemed almost proud of it.

"Well," he said. "Now that the ice is broken, why don't you tell me all about yourself? What destiny brought you to our little Mecca?"

Kate told him an abbreviated version of her life story while she waited for her sandwich to arrive. She covered the major details of her childhood without stressing her unhappiness or revealing the reason why she had left home. She also left out her marriage to Quentin and its ugly aftermath. She had long ago consigned Quentin to ancient history in her mind, and had never even told Melanie about him.

She covered her wanderings about the country in one sentence, and told him how she had accompanied Melanie to Hollywood as a lark. She had just finished describing Oscar night and her sudden decision to give acting a try, when her sandwich came.

"You're a woman of few words," Norman Webb said. "As a writer—a sort of writer, I mean—I ought to be able to match you in brevity."

Watching her eat, he told her about himself. He had grown up abroad and returned to the United States to finish his education at Yale like his father and grandfather before him. He became a writer while at college and aspired to join the "lost generation" of writers that included Hemingway, Faulkner, and Scott Fitzgerald.

But before long he had realized that his talent was not on the same level as that of his heroes, so he had come to Hollywood to work as part of the growing stable of "idea men" who cranked out scenarios for silent movies, including comedy shorts, Keystone Kops one-reelers, and then the longer silent features.

These writers were treated like animals by the early studio heads, who saw nothing in common between their brand of gimmick-writing and the work of a serious writer. But with the advent of sound it became necessary for writers to produce dialogue, and here Norman had a real facility. Though his work lacked depth, he could write snappy, exciting dialogue, and he found himself a lucrative career writing screenplays for stylish early thirties comedies as well as cops-and-robbers thrillers and mysteries. He made a good living, although, like all Hollywood writers (most of whom were forced to work in committee form on their screenplays, with the assignment of screen credit being based on the whim of the producer), he was not treated with much respect.

Then, somewhere along the line, the incessant compromise and superficiality demanded by Hollywood, the contempt of the studio bosses and the overweening falseness of the film capital, got under Norman's skin. He began to weigh the absurdity of what he was doing against the luster of his boyhood dreams. The comparison was more than he could stand.

He divorced his first wife, married a much younger woman, and divorced her, too. Alimony payments began to vie with his increasing gambling debts for what was left of his studio salary. He began to turn up late for work, preferring the racetrack to the studio. He quarreled with producers, directors, and other writers about insignificant plot and dialogue problems. Discouragement ate into his soul.

His studio fired him. A second studio gave him one chance, which he threw away through his undependable behavior. Then he was blackballed. No one would hire him, because he now had a reputation as a loser.

At present he was making a shabby living writing adventure stories for pulp magazines. He lived alone in a tacky bungalow in the Flats, drank cheap whiskey, and went to the track nearly every day of the year, buying two-dollar tickets and juggling horses instead of women.

Like so many denizens of Hollywood, Norman Webb was washed up, a has-been who was also a never-was, a man whose potential had been eaten up by the Hollywood dream factory along with his self-respect and his hope for his own salvation as a man.

All these things Norman related with a cheerful cynicism that impressed Kate. He seemed amused by his failed life, almost as though it had happened to someone else. He hid nothing, glossing eloquently over the details of his disintegration as though it did not even touch him. Kate sensed great pain and disappointment inside Norman Webb. But she also felt a warm, paternal gentleness coming from him that was the first quality she had valued in a person in a long time. She was glad she had asked him to sit down. She felt much less lonely now.

"Well," she said, "we're two of a kind, I guess. But at least you've seen your day. Mine is never going to come. Not after what happened today. But that's okay. I enjoy being a waitress."

"It's an honorable profession," he said. "And it does, in fact, require a subtle kind of acting, among other qualities. Tell me, Kate—may I call you Kate?—what made you decide to try the agent route? To be an actress professionally, I mean?"

Kate frowned thoughtfully.

"I don't really know," she said. She thought of Eve Sinclair's face in the mirror, but decided there was no point in telling Norman Webb about that. She honestly did not know why acting had suddenly appealed to her.

He was smiling. "Well, no one really knows the why of things," he said. "That's a topic that quickly becomes boring, anyway. How do you feel now that the first skirmish has come out the way it has?"

Again Kate seemed thoughtful.

"Well," she said, "in his office—the agent's—I felt like I was going to kill him. It was strange . . . It was as though there was a power in me. I didn't care about the consequences. I just wasn't going to let him get the best of me. Afterward, on the street, I felt wonderful. Free as the birds. Then I felt terribly hungry, so I came here."

She shrugged and smiled. "Doesn't make much sense, does it?" she said.

"On the contrary," he replied, "it makes the best kind of sense. You see, young lady, Hollywood was getting set to plant its first hook in you. And there would have been a lot more where that came from. Each of those hooks drains a little blood and injects a little bit of poison. Like the bite of a leech. Let enough of them penetrate your soul, and there's nothing left inside. That's the secret of this town. But you were smarter than you perhaps realized. You stopped it before it could get started."

Kate said nothing. She was not sure what Norman Webb was getting at. But she could feel genuine affection and friendship in his words.

Suddenly he seemed to turn inward. A very serious look came over his face.

"I knew a writer once," he said. "A very talented man. Very bright, and ambitious. He let Hollywood get its hooks into him. He forgot who he was, why he was a writer. All he could see was the money, the mediocrity, the greed. He became demoralized, and his work started to suffer as well as his personal life. The leeches had finally got through to his talent, you see, and were patiently eating away at it. He was on the verge of being kicked out of his studio. Then one day the studio head called him into his office."

Norman paused to puff at his cigarette.

"Well, the studio head made jocular conversation for a few minutes, and then held out the story for a huge picture, a big-budget property. Several big stars were already committed. This single film could save the writer's career. Everybody knew what dire straits he was in, financially as well as creatively.

"The studio head eventually stopped beating around the bush and revealed the catch. In return for the big new picture he wanted the writer to betray one of his best friends. I won't bore you with the details, except to say that the best friend was also a writer, a much more talented one, in fact, to whom the studio head had taken a dislike. The best friend had a past, of course—don't we all?—and the needy writer was close enough to him to know about it. The producer wanted him to use his knowledge to set up his friend to be black-balled. The studio head was very paternal about it, very nice, like a doctor with a fine bedside manner. 'Just help me out on this, and your troubles are over.'

"Well, the writer knew what he was being asked. He thought it over for a long time—a long time, believe me, my dear—and then, having weighed his friendship against his career, he gave in. He did what he was asked. He was given the big film, he made a lot of money on a bonus from it. And his friend was drummed out of Hollywood and never seen again."

Norman flipped a bit of ash off the end of his cigarette with his little finger. He sighed.

"My friend found, to his surprise, that his new success had a bad taste to it. He couldn't seem to enjoy the money he had earned. The face of his banished friend haunted him. He bought a new house in Brentwood, got a new wife—everybody in Hollywood gets a new wife when it's time to celebrate some success or other—and had a child. He got better scripts to write and made a small fortune. But nothing helped. Eventually—just at the time when the fellow he had betrayed was making a name for himself back in New York as a novelist—my friend hanged himself in the rec room of that Brentwood house."

He looked at Kate.

"That's what Hollywood is, Kate," he said. "That smiling face that asks you to betray your best friend and dangles a contract as bait. 'Remember,' the smiling face says. 'It's your career.' Always those same three words. *It's your career*. Those are the three most fateful words in Hollywood. If you let them get a grip on your soul, you're finished."

He smiled at Kate. "My dear," he said, "today you took your first giant step toward preventing that from ever happening to you. Remember: it's not the career that counts. It's the soul. When they ask you to trade the one for the other, you know it's no dice. Say no, or you're finished."

Kate was serious, disturbed by the ugly story she had heard.

"Well," she said, "it looks as though there's no danger of me reaching high places. No one in this town will even bother to tempt me."

"Not so fast," Norman Webb said, leaning forward. "You sell yourself short, my dear. One agent does not make or break a career."

Kate could not know it, but the gray eyes of her guest were scrutinizing her from the vantage point of nearly fifteen years in the movie business. Norman Webb was fascinated by her. She had all the freshness of youth, and a lush sensuality to go with it. Yet there was something ageless about her, something feminine in a deep, earthy, and almost dangerous way.

He smiled to think of what she had done to poor Barney Livingstone—whom he knew vaguely from his years in Hollywood. She must have attacked like a jungle cat. She was proud and honest. There was nothing of the starlet in her. But, potentially, like depths under the moonlit surface of a dark lake, there was something of the real actress in her. His long years of Hollywood experience told him so.

"You've only just started," he said. "Barney Livingstone is merely a backwater of the great Hollywood stream. And, if you can accept the opinion of a man who's been around this town, Barney was right about one thing. You do have something special. A quality. I noticed it the other night, when you were here with your friend. And I notice it now."

Kate shrugged. Her skepticism was obvious.

"I'll wager," he said, "that I'm not the first person to tell you that."

"What?" she asked.

"That you're special. That you have a quality."

Kate laughed. "That's right. You're not the first. But most of the people who have said it were showing me the door. Whatever the quality is, they don't like it."

"We'll see about that," Norman Webb said. "Today's No is tomorrow's Yes, as someone who knows Hollywood once said. And Hollywood's experts are only good at remembering what sold last year. They don't have eyes to see next year's success."

Kate looked at him ambiguously. She seemed to be humoring him.

"I'll tell you what," he said with sudden firmness. "I'm going to leave you now, because, for reasons which you now know, I can't miss my appointment with the ladies and gentlemen of the track. But I'd very much like you to have dinner with me next week. And I'd like to ask you a favor: don't see any more agents until you've talked to me. I can give you a few pointers that may help you avoid hitting the submerged rocks in our murky little stream. Is it a deal?"

Kate smiled. She saw no reason to refuse, though she hardly expected his proposal to lead anywhere.

One thing she was sure of: Norman Webb was not another Barney Livingstone. He had no ulterior motives in asking her to dine with him. She could see the sincerity behind his blasé manner. Something about him inspired confidence, as well as a daughterly instinct to let him protect her.

Here, perhaps, was the friend she had lacked all these years. She did not much care whether he actually helped her to start a career in Hollywood. But she did want to see him again. In the last half hour she had felt, for the first time in five years, that she was in real contact with another human being. Was it Norman Webb's sadness that touched her? His loneliness? His checkered past? She did not know.

"All right," she said. "It's a deal."

Norman Webb smiled. Kate wrote down her phone number, handed it to him, and smiled back.

"It's a pay phone at the bottom of the stairs," she said. "I hope you don't mind."

He laughed, tapping the piece of paper against his fingers.

"Well, you know that part of Hollywood, anyway," he

said. "Your phone will ring before the week is out. Whatever the results at the track. Count on it, young lady."

He stood up, threw his folded raincoat over his arm, and twirled his hat in his hands.

"It's been a pleasure," he said.

"Me, too," Kate smiled.

And with the same genteel gait Kate had noticed the night of the Oscar ceremony, he sauntered out of the café.

Kate sighed and signaled to the waitress to bring her check. It was time to go home and put on her own waitress uniform.

But she would not return to her apartment as the same young woman who had left it. She had been changed this morning. By Barney Livingstone, to be sure. But perhaps more profoundly by Norman Webb.

Come what may, Kate thought, this had been a special day.

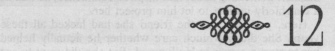

NORMAN WEBB WAS AS GOOD AS HIS WORD.

He called Kate's pay phone at the bottom of the stairs and took her out to dinner at an inexpensive but respectable Hollywood restaurant the next week. During their dinner he talked about Hollywood. His familiarity with every aspect of the movie business, from the nuts and bolts of acting and shooting to the machinations of powerful producers and studio executives, was a revelation to Kate. In talking to him she realized what a fantasy world her friends like Melanie had been living in all this time. These aspiring actresses saw Hollywood as a sort of Open Sesame that would lead them to fame and fortune if they simply pushed the right button. Norman made her see that the movies were a hard, competitive business in which staying power, grace under pressure, and a thousand tricks of the trade were required, even of those who had already opened the door.

At dinner's end Norman asked Kate to meet him the next morning at the corner of La Brea and Santa Monica. "It's time to begin your real education," he said.

Kate was there bright and early, sitting on a bench on the sidewalk. She smiled as she saw Norman turning the corner, his fedora on his head, his walking stick in his hand, and a fresh flower in his lapel.

"The early bird gets the worm, I see," he said, looking at her. "Sleeves rolled up? Ready to work?"

Kate stood up.

"Come on," he said, taking her arm. "I want to show you something."

He took her to the gates of Worldwide Pictures, spoke a few low words with the guard, and walked her right onto the lot.

"How did you . . . ?" Kate asked.

Norman laughed, swinging his cane as he walked.

"Norman Webb, the man who opens all doors," he said. "Didn't I get you and your friend into the Ambassador? Bear but a touch of my hand, young woman, and you shall be upheld in more than this."

He looked around the studio lot.

"I used to work here," he said. "Used to come in every morning and work in one of those bungalows you see by the south fence. Half soused most of the time . . . But I came in, by God, and I got the job done. For a while there, they couldn't do without me."

Kate was amazed by the studio lot. There were buildings and backdrops of all kinds. Western streets, old Boston mansions, French village squares, Italian palazzos, Renaissance facades. All of them had in common the fact that they were somewhat miniature in size—perhaps three quarters what they would be in real life—and that they looked completely and utterly fake.

When she mentioned this to Norman Webb he laughed.

"You're learning something about Hollywood, my dear," he said. "You see, the camera can't see detail or perspective the way the human eye can. Therefore the camera is just blind enough to mistake these fakes for the real thing. As for the size, you simply shoot the actors in the foreground, and the deep focus of the lens takes care of the rest. It all looks real. That's Hollywood, Kate. Illusion triumphant. Nobody sees the underside, so everyone thinks it's real."

"Where are we going?" Kate asked.

"Well, you and I need to do some work," he said. "I didn't want to take you to my house, because the neighbors might talk, you know—" He winked at her with his fine irony. "So I thought we'd use one of the old offices here. I no longer work here, and they wouldn't touch a screenplay of mine with a ten-foot pole, but I have a few old friends, like the fellow at the gate. So we're going to use Worldwide's facilities for our little tutorial."

"Tutorial?" Kate asked.

"You'll see," he said mysteriously.

He took her into one of the office buildings and showed her up to a small, poorly lit but presentable office. It contained a sofa, a small chair, and a large desk. Two of the walls were covered with large mirrors.

"It's never used," he said. "We'll have the privacy we need here."

Kate hung her coat on the coat rack and looked at him.

"There's a man I want you to meet," Norman said. "Not this week, or next, but soon. His name is Alfred Dozier. He is an actors' agent, and a most respected one. He handles few beginners. Most of his clients are established character actors or musical-comedy performers. They work constantly, and they keep him in business. He would not so much as look at a newcomer without a personal recommendation from someone he trusts."

"Then he won't look at me," Kate said.

Norman shook his head. Pointing to himself, "I am the trusted person," he said. "In the old days, when I was still somebody in this town, I did Alfred a few favors. Important favors. He knows I'm finished now, but he remembers a good turn. He will see you. He will listen to you read."

Kate looked at him neutrally.

"Now, that's all I can do for you," Norman said. "I can get you in the door. The rest you will have to do for yourself. You must remember that Alfred hates beginners. He can't stand taking a chance. He only bets on sure things. Therefore, Kate, we have to make you a sure thing before you enter his office."

Kate smiled. "That's a tall order."

Norman had sat down behind the desk. He rummaged through the drawers until he found a piece of paper, produced a large black fountain pen, and wrote down a single line.

"Here," he said. "Read this."

Kate looked at the piece of paper. Norman's handwriting was crabbed and eccentric, but readable. It was a line of dialogue.

"Mrs. Pembroke, there's someone at the door," Kate read.

Norman smiled. "You hang on to that," he said, "and watch me."

He stood up and came around the desk. Kate sat in the hard chair by the door and watched.

He stood up to his full height and held his arms to his sides.

"Mrs. Pembroke," he said gravely, "there's someone at the door."

Kate smiled. He was the very image of the English butler, though he had not bothered to put the slightest trace of an accent into his voice.

Now he unbuttoned his suit jacket, put one hand in his pocket, leaned back against the desk, and winked. "Mrs. Pembroke," he said significantly, "there's someone at the door . . ."

Kate almost laughed her astonishment. Norman had so

transformed himself as to be unrecognizable. This time he was not a butler. Far from it. He was a guest, perhaps a lover, in any case someone who knew Mrs. Pembroke very well, indeed too well. There was just enough knowing irony in the way he said "Mrs. Pembroke" to suggest that he knew some guilty secrets about the fictional lady and would not shrink from treachery to get what he wanted from her. The appearance of "someone at the door" had obviously interrupted a private and guilty dialogue between himself and Mrs. Pembroke.

"How did you do that?" Kate asked.

"Watch this," he said.

He joined his hands in front of him, leaned slightly forward, assumed a tragic expression full of dread, and said quietly, "Mrs. Pembroke, there's someone . . . there's someone at the door."

This time Kate had the overriding impression that the person at the door was bringing bad news, terrible news. And Norman himself was undeniably playing the role of a trusted maid or housekeeper or confidante—a woman, in any case. From a single change in his demeanor and delivery he had created a situation of dread, urgency, and downright tragedy.

Kate's eyes were opened wide. "That's amazing," she said. "Norman, were you an actor?"

Norman shook his head. "No, dear, but I know all their tricks. After all, I wrote for them for fifteen years. Especially in the silents, where body language is everything, and you have to get the message across with your face instead of your dialogue. I had to know the tools of their trade as well as my own. Now let me show you a few more things."

He read the line of dialogue six or seven more times. Each time, through a trick of his face, voice, or demeanor, he managed not only to alter the meaning of the line completely, but even to create a scenic atmosphere that gave the line context. The imaginary Mrs. Pembroke changed to suit his delivery, and the scene was given a new dramatic thrust every time he read the line.

It was a tour de force of acting know-how, and when it was finished Kate quietly applauded.

"That's incredible," she said.

Norman shook his head. "It's not incredible. It's just basic scene-stealing. It's the weapon every professional actor—every good one, at least—takes into an audition, Kate. And it's a double-edged sword. Half of it gets you the part. The other half makes you look good on the screen—or on the stage, depending on the role. You don't have to be a genius to learn it. But without it, you'll never get to first base in this town."

Kate frowned. "I don't think I can do it," she said.

Norman smiled. "You've been a successful waitress all these years, haven't you?"

She nodded. "But that's different . . ."

"Different, yes," Norman allowed. "But it's a variation on the same theme. Your problem, my dear, is to break through to the talent you already have, and make it work for you in a new arena. And I am here to help facilitate the transition."

Kate looked at him skeptically.

"Well . . ." she said.

"Well, nothing," Norman scoffed, putting a cigarette in his holder. "Roll up your sleeves, young lady. Let's get to work."

The next four weeks were quietly backbreaking for Kate. She met Norman Webb at Worldwide Studios, closeted herself with him in the same cramped office, and forced herself to learn the most basic skill in an actor's arsenal: how to identify herself totally with a fictional character who did not really exist.

Using the mirrors on the office wall to gauge the effect of her exercises, Kate read line after line, practicing hundreds of inflections and dramatic modulations. Forced by Norman to forget herself completely, she learned how to make her face, voice, and body into instruments of illusion. Alone before the mirror, she created situations, characters, hopes and sorrows, triumphs and disasters. None of them were real, but it was her job to make them convincing. The harder she worked at them, the less real she herself felt.

It was the most difficult thing Kate had ever done, for it

did not come naturally to her. All her life she had fought against the traps and seductions of the world by retreating into herself, by clinging to her independence and keeping the world at arm's length. Norman Webb was asking her to give up that precious security of her own identity and to throw herself headlong into imaginary people and situations.

Time and again Kate wanted to give up the whole project. She was convinced she lacked the basic instinct that makes an actress. But Norman was every bit as convinced of the contrary. He would not listen to her complaints, but worked her like a slave driver until she was ready to drop from exhaustion.

Just when Kate seemed at her lowest, bereft of courage and dying to give up the struggle, Norman suddenly surprised her by announcing, "That will do. You're ready."

Kate stared at him in stupefaction.

"You're not serious," she said.

"I've never been more serious in my life," Norman replied, an unaccustomed look of gravity on his lined face. "I've made you an appointment with Alfred Dozier for tomorrow morning. Ten o'clock."

Kate looked at him pleadingly. "I'm not ready," she said. "I've never felt less ready."

Norman smiled.

"I'll be the judge of that," he said. "You just dress up in something attractive, and be at eighty-five hundred Sunset Boulevard at ten tomorrow."

Sighing inwardly, Kate nodded her obedience. For Norman's sake, she would go through with this.

But she did not like to think about the look on his face when she failed.

The premises of the Alfred Dozier talent agency were as different as night from day from those of Barney Livingstone. Alfred Dozier seemed obsessed with appearance. His outer office was hung with proper British landscapes showing hunting dogs and horses and stately oaks. His furniture was in fine leather, his carpet an elegant Aubusson weave. His secretary, a middle-aged woman with bifocals, sat behind a polished walnut desk. There were several clients waiting to see Mr. Dozier. But, as Norman had promised, Kate did not have to wait. Her name was called promptly at ten. Alfred Dozier believed in punctuality.

Mr. Dozier greeted Kate and took her into his office. He was a little round-faced man with wire-rimmed glasses and a three-piece suit. He looked more like a loan officer at a bank than a Hollywood agent. He was polite, but not warm. Despite his roly-poly exterior, there was a great reserve about him. He held the visitors' chair decorously for her, and retreated behind his large desk, whose spacious leather-covered top bore only a fountain pen in a holder and a single file folder. There were no ashtrays in the office. Mr. Dozier did not approve of smoking.

"Well, Miss Hamilton," the little man said. "I understand you wish to be an actress."

Kate smiled. "I already am an actress, sir," she said. "I would like to be an actress represented by Alfred Dozier."

He smiled to acknowledge the distinction.

"You are aware, I am sure, of the unemployment statistics in your profession?" he said.

"Yes, sir," Kate answered simply.

"Well, then," he said, "let's see how you perform."

He produced a sheet of paper not unlike the one Barney Livingstone had handed her. It bore a series of lines of dialogue.

"Why don't you stand up," he suggested, "and read me the third line from the bottom?"

Kate stood up and moved to the center of the room where he could see her. She had chosen a clinging dress that showed off the lush contours of her body, and had her hair done for the occasion. She knew she looked attractive. But from the expression on Alfred Dozier's face he might as well have been looking at a clam. She suspected he was only trying to get her out of here as fast as possible. This reading was merely a formality.

She looked at the third line from the bottom.

Not until after your bedtime, it read.

Kate smiled at the agent.

"Is there a cue?" she asked.

He shook his head. "It's up to you," he said.

Kate nodded. She looked at the line for a moment.

Then she bent her body forward and looked down. A gentle smile came over her face, and she sketched a movement with her hand that looked like a caress.

"Not until after your bedtime," she said. It was more than obvious from the soft sound of her voice that she was a mother kissing her child goodnight. There was something maternal and sweet about Kate. She managed to draw attention to the imaginary child she was addressing, but also to herself as the mother.

"Very good," Alfred Dozier said, raising an eyebrow. "Can you give it to me another way?"

"Certainly," Kate said.

Now she stood back. She gave the agent an up-from-under look. She curled one foot behind the other and moved her knee slowly back and forth. She held her shoulders so as to show off her shapely breasts. Her tongue darted out to touch her upper lip.

"Not until after *your* bedtime," she said, sensuality breathing from every pore as the words crept out of her mouth.

This time she had changed the context completely. She was obviously a girl who had met a man at her place of work. The man must have asked her what time she got off work. And she was responding provocatively, mockingly, "Not until after *your* bedtime." Something about her delivery had the husky pungency of a mating call. Her entire body sketched a subtle pantomime of femininity conscious of its own attractiveness.

The agent was impressed. He was looking at Kate intently.

"That's very good," he said. "Very good, indeed. Tell me, Miss Hamilton. Haven't I seen you in anything? You seem familiar."

"Just a few walk-ons," Kate said. "No speaking parts yet. I've had some trouble getting to first base with the casting people."

There was a long silence. Alfred Dozier stared at her.

His eyes were as cold as little round ice cubes. His small delicate hands were joined on the desk top.

Then he smiled.

"Well, I think we can do something about that," he said. "Sit down, please, Miss Hamilton. I'd like to show you one of our standard contracts. You might want to have your attorney look at it . . ."

Kate shook her head. "That won't be necessary, Mr. Dozier. I know I can trust you."

He smiled. "Well, trust is a good beginning," he said.

He pushed the intercom button on his desk top and spoke to his secretary. A moment later Kate was signing her second contract with a Hollywood agency. When she had finished she shook hands with Alfred Dozier, who showed her out of the office with the same cold courtliness he had greeted her with only a few minutes before.

Kate breathed a deep sigh as she stood in the smoggy sunshine on Sunset Boulevard. She felt as though she had taken leave of reality. Her feet were off the ground, and she didn't know how to get back down again. Everything that had happened since she met Norman Webb and began her acting studies with him smacked of unreality. There was not a single link between this world and the life she had felt so sure of before.

Perhaps, she mused, this was what acting was all about— a willingness to take leave of the real world and breathe the strange air of illusion. Perhaps she had arrived in Hollywood at last.

A week after her interview with Alfred Dozier Kate auditioned for a speaking role in a western being made by Paramount Pictures. Armed with her portfolio, her new status as an Alfred Dozier client, and the skills taught her by Norman Webb—not to mention the iron determination of her own personality—she got the part.

Kate had one line to read. The shooting of her scene took twenty minutes. She was paid eighteen dollars, the standard salary for a bit player, which came to $14.52 after the deduction of Alfred Dozier's percentage and additional deductions for taxes.

Two weeks after that she got a part as a waitress in a speakeasy for an RKO musical. This time she had two lines, and earned twenty-two dollars.

A week after that Alfred Dozier called with an audition for a costume drama in which Kate played a lady's maid. Kate smiled when she saw that one of her three lines was *"Mr. Abernathy, your nephew is downstairs."*

Kate smiled, recalling her lessons with Norman. *Mrs. Pembroke, there's someone at the door,* she said to herself.

After receiving her salary for this job and the three that followed it, Kate added up her accounts. She had made more from acting than from waitressing in the last month.

Kate looked at herself in the mirror. Now, and only now, was she willing to admit that Norman Webb had been right.

She was an actress.

 13

THOUGH EVE SINCLAIR DID NOT KNOW IT, SHE HAD NOT FIN-
ished with Joseph Knight.

The first time she had crossed his path in Hollywood, he had stolen her Oscar and used it to make a star out of brilliant young Rebecca Sherwood, his leading lady in *The Rainbow's End.* This was one of the greatest blows Eve had ever suffered, personally and professionally. She had vowed that if her chance ever came to pay Joseph Knight back for what he had done to her, she would do so with pleasure.

But now her attitude was to change.

On June 23 her agent called to tell her some surprising news.

"Listen, Evie," he said. "You'll never guess who wants you to star in his new film."

"I don't play guessing games," Eve said coldly.

Her agent cleared his throat nervously. Eve was hard to deal with at the best of times. Thank God, he thought, he had good news for her.

"Joe Knight," he said, using the familiar first name despite the fact that he had never met Joseph Knight.

There was a silence at Eve's end of the line. She was thinking. Obviously the news had impressed her.

"What's the film?" she asked guardedly.

"It doesn't have a title yet," Freddy said. "But I got the script by messenger today. Knight wrote it himself. Believe me, it's dynamite. It's everything that *The Rainbow's End* was, and more."

Eve said nothing. She knew that Freddy, like all Hollywood agents, was incurably given to exaggeration. She never believed any of his claims about a property until she had read it herself.

But she knew without seeing the script that if Joseph Knight had written it, it was something to be taken seriously. Even in her hatred of Knight for indirectly stealing her Best Actress Oscar for young Rebecca Sherwood, she had realized that *The Rainbow's End* was no fluke. It was the work of a cinematic prodigy, a man whose lack of experience in making Hollywood films had not limited him at all, but on the contrary had given him the advantage of enormous spontaneity and originality.

Ever since the Oscars she had hated Joseph Knight. Yet, in her heart of hearts, she had known all along that she would give just about anything to work with him. Not only was he the most visible and exciting young producer in Hollywood, he was also without a doubt the most gifted.

So now Eve replied politely to her agent.

"When do I get to read it?" she asked.

"I'm having it sent over by messenger right now," Freddy said. "Knight has invited us to lunch at Chasen's for Wednesday. That will give you time to read the script and make up your mind. How does that sound, Evie?"

"Fine," Eve said. "I'll wait for the messenger."

She hung up the phone.

She was already thinking about what dress she would wear to her lunch with Joseph Knight. She hurried into her bedroom and opened her closet. Then she noticed her face in the mirror and began wondering how to make herself up for her lunch, how to do her hair.

Suddenly she shrugged and frowned at herself in the mirror.

"Get control of yourself, for Christ's sake," she hissed. "He's just a goddamned producer. You're acting like it's your first date."

She went back to the kitchen to make herself a cup of tea while she waited for the messenger to arrive. Her nerves were tingling. She could not deny that she felt excited. A starring role in a Joseph Knight picture could be the ticket to the superstardom she had sought so vainly throughout her career.

Knight had done it for Rebecca Sherwood. Perhaps now he would do it for Eve.

With this thought in her mind, Eve prepared to be at her best when she met Joseph Knight.

On Wednesday Eve and her agent arrived punctually at Chasen's. Eve looked elegant and self-assured in a pale pink suit designed by Howard Greer, a fashion that managed somehow to be businesslike, glamorous, sexy, and informal all at once. Despite herself Eve had tried a dozen other outfits, complete with accessories, before settling on this one. She had had her hair done this morning. She looked sensational, and she knew it.

André, the famed maître d'hôtel at Chasen's, met Eve at the door and squired her and Freddy to a secluded table where three men were seated. Joseph Knight got up to shake her hand. He was taller than she had expected, over six feet, but the muscled power of his body made him seem

shorter. He was built like a man, not a boy. He looked
older than his years. His face was tanned and very
handsome.

Eve was not the only Hollywood star never to have met
Joseph Knight. He avoided the Hollywood party scene,
preferring his solitude in the suite he kept at the Beverly
Wilshire Hotel. He apparently made all the business contacts he needed through his own methods, without needing
to socialize.

Knight introduced her to his colleagues. She recognized
Samuel Raines, the star of *The Rainbow's End* and now
one of the most sought-after leading men in Hollywood.
The other man was Lawrence Walsh, who would be executive producer of the new film.

Eve had had time to read the script and was more than
excited about it. It was a complex story of mystery and
intrigue, perfect for masculine Samuel Raines, and with a
unique role for the female lead.

Samuel Raines would play a detective who, in the course
of a dangerous investigation, gets involved with a "mystery
woman" who fascinates him and leads him deeper and
deeper into a web of deceit and danger. As he gets closer
and closer to her the detective falls in love with her. Despite her ambiguous warnings about the menace of those
around her, she falls for him as well. Her best efforts to
protect him and to extricate herself from the men she is
involved with fail, and in the final scene the detective dies
in her arms, a victim of her love and the dark forces surrounding it.

It was a classic *film noir*, with interesting psychological
subtleties and serious underlying themes. And it offered
infinite possibilities for Eve in the lead role. Her character
was passionate, mysterious, and fatal to herself as well as
others. The role had Oscar written all over it, provided Eve
gave it her best.

Eve accepted the vodka Gibson Knight had ordered for
her and asked the logical question.

"What made you think of me for this role, Mr. Knight?"

"Call me Joe, please." Knight had fixed his dark eyes
on her, a serious look on his face. "As you can see from

the script, we need an actress with a strong screen presence, but a lot of flexibility as well. The change in emotional tone from scene to scene is pretty severe. I need a great actress, Miss Sinclair. You were the first performer I thought of.''

Call me Eve—please.

Eve did not say these words. She was keeping her distance intentionally. She did not want this young producer to think she would kiss his feet for offering her this role. The fact that she considered it the plum of a lifetime did not affect her decision. She had her reputation and her pride to think of.

Meanwhile, at the back of Eve's mind was the canny perception that she was not in fact ideal for the role. The heroine Knight had conceived on paper had to be bigger-than-life, mysterious, sexually disturbing, and tragic. Eve lacked a powerfully sensual image, despite her beauty.

Knight, she mused, must have surveyed the female stars available and decided that Eve, though not a sex symbol, would nevertheless be able to carry off the role because of her great acting ability. She was thus a compromise between his ideal image of his heroine and what was available to him among Hollywood stars.

Of course Eve kept these thoughts to herself. She wanted to appear confident of her ability to handle the role, but not overeager. She wanted Knight to court her at this meeting—not the reverse.

It was a strange lunch. The atmosphere was thoroughly professional, almost too professional for Hollywood. There were none of the Hollywood hugs and kisses that usually punctuated such a meeting. Nor was there the usual cloying Hollywood flattery, or the excessive displays of excitement for the property and the stars that were *de rigueur* at a Hollywood lunch. Joseph Knight and his executive producer were polite, explanatory, and perfectly serious about their project. As the lunch wore on it became evident that Knight brought a quiet, intense concentration to his work that quickly infected those around him.

Knight had decided to direct the film as well as produce

it. Since he had written the screenplay, he would have complete artistic control over the project.

Eve was impressed. She already knew the screenplay was brilliant. She had little doubt that Knight would be an effective director. He knew his own talent and how best to use it in the nuts-and-bolts world of Hollywood finance and production. He was a man to be taken seriously at all times. That was obvious.

Eve's instincts told her to be on her best behavior. It was important that she impress Knight at this first meeting. He was doing her a favor, and he probably knew it, for he was smart about Hollywood and about the forces at work in the careers of the major stars. She wanted to get on his good side, to start off on the right foot.

Nevertheless, as lunch wore on she found herself irritated by him. Something about him got under her skin.

She was irked by Knight's seamless display of cool professionalism. It seemed to increase the magnetic masculinity that emanated from his strong body. Again and again her glance was drawn to his swarthy skin, his strong jaw, and those penetrating black eyes. Eyes that were too subtle to appraise her directly, or to try to joust with her in silent messages. Eyes that kept their distance even when he looked at her directly. Eyes that displayed respect for her as a professional while intentionally refusing to notice her as a woman.

This behavior both impressed Eve and annoyed her. She was accustomed to a certain amount of kowtowing, no matter what the occasion. After all, she was a star. She never went anywhere in Hollywood without having people fall all over themselves to flatter her—even her enemies. Most of all, perhaps, her enemies.

Meanwhile she reflected that Joseph Knight needed her in his film for more than just her talent. He needed her box-office appeal as well. The name Eve Sinclair on a marquee brought people into the theater. Knight must be taking this into his calculations. He needed a visible, glamorous, respected female lead for his picture. That was why he had come to Eve.

Yet he was not treating her like a star. Nor was he, in

the final analysis, treating her like a woman. To judge from his behavior, she might be an attorney he was hiring to write his will, or a banker he was asking to handle his mortgage. He was that distant.

For a few minutes Eve accepted this behavior on his part, measuring him carefully as she listened to him describe the new film. Then, on an impulse, she decided to take up the challenge and see if she could get through his armor. She was accustomed to having her way with the men she dealt with in Hollywood. Why should Joseph Knight be an exception? Could he be so full of himself that he thought he could treat a great star in this offhand manner?

She began to meet his eyes deliberately. She put the subtlest hints of female inquiry into her glances. She used her body in masterful, almost subliminal ways to attract his interest. She placed tiny hints in the things she said to him, hints that told him she knew where his male instincts were located, and knew just what to do with them whenever she wanted.

Eve put on a performance at that lunch as subtle and brilliant as anything she had ever done before a camera. Without for a moment departing from her cool, professional exterior, she sent out signals to handsome Joseph Knight that were as inviting as a mating call in a steaming jungle.

Her performance was a work of genius. But it failed completely.

Knight did not show the slightest sign of having noticed it. He remained as respectful, as impersonal, and as damnably handsome throughout lunch as he had been the first moment Eve saw him. And when he shook her hand in the smoggy sunshine outside Chasen's, he was as much a stranger as he had been at the outset.

They had agreed to work together, and all indications were that they were about to enter into a professional relationship that would be enormously beneficial to both. But Joseph Knight had shared absolutely nothing of himself with Eve. He had resisted her sly advances and withheld himself in a way she found, to her own consternation, unbearably seductive.

By the time she arrived home Eve was so rattled that she had to have a stiff drink and take a hot bath. She lay naked under the bubbles in her tub, feeling her body tingle with excitement. Again and again she saw the face of Joseph Knight before her mind's eye, and her proud personality bristled in hatred of him.

She asked herself why he had had this effect on her, why she had allowed him to upset her so. There was danger in her own susceptibility. She had made a career out of knowing exactly what she was doing where men were concerned. Hollywood was a jungle ruled by the male, so a successful actress had to be a consummate seductress in order to survive. Eve had spent a lifetime sharpening her female wiles and her bedroom skills so as to manipulate the males she came into contact with.

But she had obviously not manipulated Joseph Knight. What was worse, she had the atrocious suspicion that Knight had known precisely what he was about at Chasen's, from the moment he met her until he took his leave of her.

Of course, she could not prove this. More yet, her nerves were so jangled that she suspected her own impressions of being false and subjective. But the damning fact remained: Joseph Knight had penetrated her own defenses, and done so with a vengeance.

She resolved not to let him get away with it. No man had ever treated her so indifferently. She would get through to his male instincts somehow, and show him who was boss.

Satisfied with her resolve, Eve closed her eyes and lay back to enjoy her bath.

She never dreamed that she had just made the most dangerous decision of her life.

14

THERE WERE REHEARSALS, STORY CONFERENCES, CAST AND production staff meetings.

This was an important film, and it bore what was later to be known as the "Joseph Knight stamp" of careful drawing-board planning and preparation. Joseph Knight was a perfectionist about every aspect of his films. He expected no surprises on the set and prepared accordingly. He took a personal interest in everything from the stars' makeup and wardrobe to the health problems of the least important grips and stagehands.

And his perfectionism extended to the relationships between the people working for him. He spoke personally to everyone, made sure everyone knew exactly what was expected of him or her, and took great pains to develop a spirit of camaraderie and mutual respect among his people. He considered the film a group effort and did not believe it stood a chance of being good unless everyone involved felt important, felt needed, and gave his or her absolute best.

And Knight inspired the cast and crew by his own example. He worked long hours on every aspect of pre-production. He held meetings daily with various key people—his executive producer, the script supervisor, the set designer, the supporting players, and of course the stars—

to make absolutely sure they knew how things were developing and where they fit in. A Hollywood film is a sprawling enterprise, often involving so many people that each one feels like a tiny cog in an enormous wheel that he or she doesn't understand. Joseph Knight set out to counteract this feeling, and to involve and commit everyone as deeply as possible.

Knight prided himself on anticipating problems and solving them before they had time to become serious and threaten his film.

But this time his precautions were no match for what was to become the worst problem he would ever face as a filmmaker.

During pre-production Eve Sinclair was polite and distant to Knight. Her behavior was thoroughly professional as always. But she was not friendly.

Joseph Knight could not know that under her coldness was a simmering cauldron of feelings she could barely keep under control.

Since the day of her lunch with him at Chasen's, Eve had noticed that Joseph Knight had not changed in his demeanor toward her. He was polite, deferential, but always well within himself, sharing nothing of his private personality with her. As the days passed his mystery seemed to deepen. And as he grew more inscrutable, less comprehensible to her as a man, his body seemed to grow more attractive.

Though he always came to the meetings dressed in dark suits, he often took off his jacket and loosened his tie. Eve was struck by the broad muscled shoulders under his shirts, his strong neck and square jaw. When he rolled back the cuffs of his sleeves she saw thick, powerful wrists. His hands looked strong enough to tear telephone books in half.

Or to pick up a woman without effort and bear her away in his arms . . .

There was a balance, a control, in everything Knight did. There were no sudden movements, no displays of anger or emotion. He always sat impressively still, particularly when he was listening to someone else's advice or opinion. The economy of his movements accentuated the inner power of the man.

Hollywood was a place where people showed off their success, shouted their demands, exaggerated their compliments and their threats. Part of its subculture was this flamboyance of ego, this gaudy melodrama of gesture. In this arena Joseph Knight was like a visitor from another planet. He was tightly controlled, unfailingly polite—and yet his restraint communicated an enormous, almost frightening confidence, and commanded respect from all who came in contact with him.

In a word, Joseph Knight possessed integrity. It was the rarest quality to be found in Hollywood, and it applied to his character as a man no less than to his professional behavior.

Eve found this quality unbearably attractive, and downright maddening, because it prevented Joseph Knight from taking her femininity into account or making any effort to flatter her. Knight did not treat Eve with any special or personal consideration at all. She was no different from the supporting players, the extras, or even the stagehands.

Eve's proud personality could not bear this kind of treatment. And so, just before the start of production, she reached a point at which she could stand it no more.

It was the night before shooting was to begin.

Eve had come to join Joseph Knight and some key cast and crew members on Sound Stage 7 at Monarch Pictures to take a look at the sets to be used during the first few days of shooting. The lights were not turned on and the cameras were idle, but the actors got an idea of their marks and movements, and everyone was shown the shooting schedule. It was to be a tight one. Oscar Freund always worked on a tight schedule to save money, and Joseph Knight agreed with him.

Larry Walsh, the executive producer, showed Eve the trailer that had been brought to the set as her dressing room. When the meeting broke up at nine-thirty she told Walsh she would like to speak to Joseph Knight privately in her trailer.

After the others had gone a quiet knock came at her door.

"Come in," she said.

The door opened a crack, and Joseph Knight's handsome face appeared in it. He did not enter the trailer.

"Did you want to see me, Eve?" he asked.

"Yes," she said. "If you're not too busy. Come on in."

He came in and sat down in the canvas chair by the door. His powerful body dwarfed the tiny room. His tanned face looked dark and dangerous under the vanity mirror lights.

She had turned toward him. Her breasts were outlined by her silken blouse, her hair flowing over her shoulders. There was the ghost of a smile on her lips. He was amazingly handsome as he sat looking at her curiously.

"What's the problem?" he asked. The look in his eyes expressed polite interest and nothing more.

"It's about my character, the mystery woman," she said. "I've been meaning to discuss it with you for some time, but there always seems to be someone else around . . ."

He smiled, urging her to go on.

"Well, I've been thinking about her," Eve said. "And it occurs to me that in a strange way she isn't really aware of her own sexuality. That's what makes her so complex. She's rather repressed, even though she uses men to get what she wants."

Joseph Knight nodded.

"I think you could say that," he agreed in a neutral tone.

"Well," she said, a tiny lilt in her voice now, "it seems to me, from the technical standpoint, that I should actually overplay her sensuality a little. From the inside out, I mean. Not so that it becomes an attitude, but between the lines, as it were."

He nodded. "I wouldn't be surprised if it works out that way," he said. "We'll find out for sure on the set. But I think you're certainly on the right track."

He was sitting quietly, his hands folded, looking into her eyes. She saw the complex depth of his irises, that coiled explosive quality he had. It seemed to be inviting her to take a chance.

She stood up and moved a pace toward him, making sure he could see the outline of her slim thighs under her slacks. She was wearing one of her most sensual perfumes.

"What I mean is," she said in a husky voice, "some women don't really have any idea of their own sexuality. They live as though it weren't even there. Whereas there is another kind of woman—the kind who knows what she wants, physically, and goes out and gets it. I don't mean a tramp—I just mean a woman who has strong needs, and who is in touch with those needs. Do you see what I mean?"

Knight was still sitting before her, his hands folded. His look had become more ambiguous now. But she decided to press her advantage. She knew every signal of a man's desire; she had needed that radar in her years in the business, and it had seen her through many a difficult spot.

"She knows when a man desires her," she said, moving a step closer to him. "And she knows when to keep him waiting, and when to give him what he wants."

She was standing directly in front of Knight, her pelvis at a level with his eyes. He said nothing.

"After all," she murmured, "what is the point of beating around the bush? We all know what we need. The least we can do is to be generous with each other . . . I, for one, always know exactly what I want . . ."

Now her sex was within an inch of his face.

Suddenly she sank to her knees and brought her lips to his. She kissed him, slowly and intimately. She put her arms around him and pressed her breasts to his chest. He did not move, but the scent of him nearly drove her mad with desire. She had not been wrong in all her guilty imaginings about him. There was an enormous sensuality under that quiet, businesslike exterior. It smoldered inside him like the hot core of a volcano.

She began to sigh, to whimper.

"Come on," she breathed through her kiss. "Don't tease me. You know we were attracted to each other from the beginning. Don't play hard to get now. I'm not in the habit of having to beg for it . . ."

Hot shudders were running up and down her legs, making

her tremble. She drank in the taste and smell of him like a sensual elixir. She felt him take both her wrists. She was sure he was going to push her down on the floor and take her right here. That was how urgent the sheer maleness of him was. She could hardly wait to feel him inside her.

What happened next came as the surprise of Eve's life.

Holding both her wrists, Joseph Knight pushed her away from him. Then he stood up, still holding her wrists in an iron grip, and pulled her to her feet.

"That's nice of you," he said, his tone as polite and distant as ever. "But I couldn't impose. I have to be going now. See you on the set."

She was still close to him. He released her hands. She did not know whether to slap his face or grab him around his handsome waist with all her strength. The wanting inside her was burning out of control. She was breathless with desire.

She took one more chance.

"Oh, come on, Joe," she said. "Don't let my billing scare you. Underneath all that star quality, I'm just a girl who wants to be loved, like any other girl."

Her hands came to rest on his waist. As she spoke her palms began to slide down his hips, the fingers working their way across his thighs, inward, closer and closer to the secret place between his legs.

She had almost found the sex when he stopped her again. Now the look in his eyes was darker.

"I said, no thanks," he said with finality. "I'll see you tomorrow."

Had there been a note of contempt mixed with the firmness in his voice? Eve was not sure.

But the mere suspicion was enough to outrage her. No man had ever dared to treat her this way.

She slapped him suddenly, very hard, across his face. Two of her fingernails left little pink trails across his tanned cheek.

"People don't say no to Eve Sinclair in this town," she said.

The look in his eyes had not changed. It was like an armor ten feet thick, absolutely impervious to her boldest weapons. She could not fail to feel the insult in his very indifference.

"I'm sorry if I've offended you," he said, not moving. "Do you see any problem in our working together?"

She gave him a look that burned with hatred.

Then, very slowly, she said, "No, Mr. Knight. I don't see any problem. No problem at all."

"Good." His smile was perfunctory, even impersonal. "See you on the set, then."

He left, closing the door behind him. Eve stood alone, trembling from the insult he had subjected her to, and from the throbbing ache of her desire.

Then she turned back to the vanity.

In the mirror she saw a face she had never seen before.

It was the face of a woman scorned.

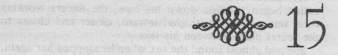

15

On a hot day in August Kate Hamilton reported to Sound Stage 7 of Monarch Pictures to audition for a role in a film whose title and subject matter remained a mystery to her.

The audition had been procured for her by Alfred Dozier. He had given Kate a brief scrap of dialogue from the working script, sent by the casting director with the cryptic description of character: *"girl who helps hero."*

That was all the explanation Kate had to work from. As was so often the case in Hollywood, the actor knows no more about the production than the fact that he or she is to show up at a particular casting location on a particular day. That was all Kate knew today.

Except for one thing. The new film was a Joseph Knight production. Therefore it would be a huge plum for Kate if she got the role. No film would be more eagerly awaited than this one. Despite herself Kate was excited.

The casting director, Tom Gianos, was a friendly and professional man whom Kate, in her inexperience, had never met before. He sat her down in his office and told her a bit about her role.

"This is a detective story," he said. "You play a pretty girl the detective passes on the street. There's a brief scene in which he smiles at you, and you smile back. You have a line of dialogue. Then, later in the picture, the hero is on the run, pursued both by crooks and police. He knocks on a strange door, and surprise, you're the one who opens it. You take him in, hide him from his enemies, and then he leaves. You have about four or five more lines during this scene. It's a small role, but you'll sure as hell be noticed in it. You have to be very sexy, but also rather endearing. Think you can handle it?"

"Sure," Kate said, remembering Norman's coaching about how to handle casting directors. "No problem."

Kate was asked to wait while a screen test was set up for her on the set. She studied her lines carefully. They were well-written, subtle lines of dialogue. There was a tongue-in-cheek humor about them, a sly sophistication, that was not lost on her. She was to be an attractive, sexy girl who took a maternal interest in the hero but was eclipsed by the larger plot of the picture, in which the hero pursues a mystery woman who turns out to be his undoing.

It was a foggy, complex thriller in which Kate was to provide a bit of light and humor. She crossed her fingers. This would be the biggest role she had got so far if she was cast. She intended to do her best.

Tom Gianos returned after a half hour and took her to Makeup. She was made up to look sensual and mysterious, and her hair was combed out to fall over the shoulders of her raincoat.

After another half hour's wait, Kate was called for by an assistant director and taken to the sound stage, where lights were set up before a backdrop of a doorway.

"All right," the young man said. "I'm going to read with you. But remember: Samuel Raines will be playing the hero. Just imagine you're with him. Look very interested, very attracted, but also a bit mysterious in your own right. Okay?"

"Okay," Kate said.

The assistant director posed her in half profile and consulted with the cameraman for a moment. Then the hot sound stage lights went on, the makeup girl touched up Kate's face, and they ran through the scene.

Kate put everything she had learned from Norman Webb into her reading, and more. She knew that the camera was concentrating on her face, really watching her with interest—something that had not happened in the bit roles she had played in other films. She had to make a strong impression, but without overplaying her part.

Kate gave the moment all she had. She was miked closely, so she did not have to speak loudly. She made her words a sibilant murmur of invitation. She allowed her natural sexuality to spring forward in her manner. But she left just enough complexity in her reading to make the character interesting.

She was asked to repeat the lines as the camera shot her from several angles. Then she was taken to another set with a street scene background, the set where she would cross the hero's path in the first half of the film. She was shot walking, several times.

Then the assistant director thanked her and told her she could go.

Though Kate could not know it from his friendly face, he had already made up his mind not to give her the role.

As a matter of fact, of the eight actresses who were tested for the part, Kate was the first to be rejected.

In passing along the bad news to Alfred Dozier the casting director explained that Kate's screen presence was too "hot" for the role. She stuck out too much. True, the character required an actress with a certain power, but Kate was simply too much.

Tom Gianos did not say what was really in his mind. He felt that Kate's sexuality was a bit too strong even for this role, which was to be deliberately sexy. He was afraid she would detract from the star, Eve Sinclair, who was not an impressively sensual actress. The best course was to opt for someone simpler, cuter, for the small role.

Alfred Dozier called Kate with the bad news.

"I'm sorry, dear," he said paternally. "You simply weren't what they were looking for. But Tom Gianos assured me you were excellent before the camera. Try to hang on to that."

Kate thanked him for getting her the opportunity, and shrugged off her disappointment. She knew that her career did not stand or fall with one small role. She had the long pull to think about.

She had already half forgotten the whole episode when her phone rang at ten o'clock the same night.

"Miss Hamilton? This is Joseph Knight. I'm sorry to bother you at home. Have I caught you at a bad time?"

"I—no," Kate stammered. "What can I do for you?"

"Well, I've been looking at the rushes from our screen tests over here at Monarch Studios, and I saw your test for the new film. You were very impressive. Really excellent."

"Oh. Well, I'm glad you liked them," Kate said. She could not think what else to say. She already knew she had been turned down for the role.

Suddenly she remembered what Melanie and so many other girls had been put through by Hollywood producers, directors, and casting people. Perhaps Joseph Knight had taken a liking to Kate's looks based on her screen test, and wanted a date with her. Perhaps he intended to dangle promises of future tests, bit parts, or talk of a bigger role, to seduce her. Perhaps, indeed, he thought his exalted reputation alone would suffice to sweep her off her feet.

So Kate waited suspiciously for his next words.

"There was a mix-up among us at the studio," Knight said. "I apologize for the inconvenience. We've cast you definitely for the role. I'm having the contract sent by messenger to Alfred Dozier tomorrow morning. I hope you're still available?"

"I—so far as I know, yes, I am," Kate said.

"I hope this comes as good news," he said. "If your performance is anything like your test, I think you'll be brilliant."

"Well, thank you," Kate said. "I'll certainly do my best."

"Tell me," Joseph Knight said. "Your face looked awfully familiar in the test. Have I seen your work somewhere?"

Kate smiled. It seemed she heard this question every time anyone in Hollywood spoke to her.

"Well, I've been in a few things," she said. "Mostly bit parts and walk-ons. You might have seen me without really noticing me."

"I see. Well, this is a part in which you'll get noticed. I think I can promise you that. I'll have my production people get in touch with Mr. Dozier about a shooting schedule. Congratulations, and thanks again for being available. I'm sorry about the mix-up."

"No problem, Mr. Knight. I'll be looking forward to working with you. Goodbye, then."

"Goodbye, Miss Hamilton. And thanks again."

With a raised eyebrow Kate hung up the phone. This was a pleasant surprise, to be sure. She had already given up on the role, and now, just like that, she had it.

But even as her thick-skinned auditioner's personality was adjusting to the unexpected good news, a sudden shiver ran down her spine, for she realized that this was not the first time she had spoken to Joseph Knight. The voice on the phone just now belonged to the same man who had helped her to her feet in the confusion of Oscar night at the Ambassador Hotel, a man whose handsome face and protective manner had never been entirely absent from her dreams since she first saw him.

Kate could not suppress the feeling that there was something fateful about Joseph Knight crossing her path for a second time. She needed all the hard-boiled realism she could muster to shrug off her emotion and go to bed as though nothing had happened.

The next morning the contract arrived at Alfred Dozier's office, just as Joseph Knight had promised.

A week later Kate reported to Monarch Studios for preliminary costume tests and rehearsals with the first assistant director.

She was in the middle of the test for her first scene, dressed in the raincoat she was to wear on camera, when she met Joseph Knight.

Knight came onto the set and introduced himself.

"Joe Knight," he said. "We spoke on the phone. I'm very glad you're working with us. Your test was great."

He extended his hand. She was surprised by his looks. Her memory of him from Oscar night at the Ambassador had been eclipsed by a hundred photos of him in the press. Now it seemed that the stranger before her brought a third face, more complex, to her mental image of Joseph Knight. She was astonished at how handsome he was. She had never seen so attractive a man. There was a force about him that combined oddly with his mild-mannered exterior. At first glance he seemed too young for his great fame and power. Yet there was something calm and mature in him that outreached his youth and gave him a remarkable balance and smoothness.

Then something unexpected happened.

As Kate shook Knight's hand she felt a tightness in her throat. Her hand felt cold inside his warm palm. A strange, almost painful tremor coursed through her body. Her knees felt weak.

Embarrassed, she met his gaze. To her surprise, he himself seemed affected by touching her. Something had coiled suddenly in the depths of his eyes. She saw him hide it behind his friendly smile, but its intensity lingered in his handshake, which seemed to hold her closer.

Let me go, she thought suddenly. A nameless fear had come over her, deeper than any fear she had allowed herself to feel in many years. She thought she was losing herself.

Whether because Knight saw her alarmed look or felt her hand go tense inside his own, he released her.

"It's funny," he said, looking at her speculatively. "I could swear we've met before. I'm usually very good at faces. But I can't recall, somehow . . ."

"I'm sure I would have remembered . . ." Even as she said these words Kate wondered why she was lying. For some reason she did not want him to recall their first meeting. It seemed so long ago, and so far removed from this moment. At the same time she felt trapped, suffocated, as she watched him search for her in his memory. It was as though he was feeling for her in a darkness that joined them. She did not want him to find her.

Knight broke the spell.

"Well," he said, "perhaps I did see you in one of those movie roles of yours. Anyway, let's get to work, shall we?"

He sat Kate down with the assistant director and went over her character with her. He was precise and rather distant as he discussed the role.

Then he turned to the lighting director, who was standing by.

"Tony," he said, "be sure to give her a dark background in your close-up. I want to see those eyes. And change her scarf to a darker color. See me before you do her other scene."

He turned to Kate. "I'll be in and out," he said. "I have a number of scenes to keep track of. Good luck. I'm glad you're with us."

Kate felt him begin to extend his hand and then hold it back. She was glad not to shake it again. She did not like the effect he had on her. Reassuring though he was, he made her feel naked and somehow guilty. It was as though she had committed some sort of crime, perhaps long ago, and it was coming back to haunt her.

She watched him leave the set. She was glad to see him go, and yet she looked forward to the future moment when he would come back. It was a strange and confusing emotion.

Gratefully Kate turned her mind back to her work.

* * *

On his way back to his office Joseph Knight thought about Kate Hamilton.

He had overruled his subordinates last week after reviewing her screen test. He had needed only a moment to make up his mind. One look at the natural intensity in her eyes and at the earthy sensuality of her body had made him sit up and take notice. The sound of her voice, sibilant and husky, had done the rest. She was a performer with a future.

Knight understood why his casting people had turned her down. They were afraid of her sexuality, afraid she would upstage his star, Eve Sinclair. But Joseph Knight was not worried about that. He could tone Kate down in the direction. He would get the most out of her without hurting the film.

Joseph Knight had learned during the shooting of *The Rainbow's End* that it never pays to be overly conservative. In casting, as in every other aspect of production, one must dare to gamble, to take chances on people with talent. He would not let an actress like Kate Hamilton slip away just to protect his star. He would instead get the most out of both of them.

When he called the Hamilton girl to tell her she had the role, her voice had seemed completely unfamiliar. But today on the set he again had the odd feeling that he had seen her before. Yet he could not seem to place her.

He moved quickly toward the far end of the sound stage. He had a lot of work to do this morning. Actors and stagehands were greeting him as he passed.

But the image of Kate Hamilton lingered stubbornly before his mind's eye. There was something disturbing about the feeling it engendered. It was a nagging familiarity without recognition. And a sort of longing, or perhaps loneliness. He could still feel her small hand in his, pliant and cool, yet full of a strange energy.

What was it about her, he wondered, that threw him off balance? The fine earthy figure, the smooth brown skin, the gentle voice? The womanly bearing, so full of an odd depth beyond her years? Or was it the sadness in those soft golden eyes, so palpable that one almost felt a lump in one's throat just to look at her?

He did not know. But he had a movie to make. He had no time to linger over his own susceptibilities.

With that last firm thought he put Kate Hamilton out of his mind.

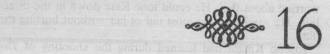

16

EVE SINCLAIR WAS OUT OF CONTROL.

For the first time in her long Hollywood memory, emotion had outstripped the iron grip of her will.

The shooting of Joseph Knight's new film—now tentatively entitled *The Velvet Web*—was an ordeal that grew worse each day.

Every morning Eve arrived on the set with red eyes and a tortured heart. As the makeup people worked on her eyes, she fought blindly with her emotions.

She had spent the night tossing and turning in her bed, thinking about Joseph Knight.

Something about the impersonal look in his handsome eyes, and the cold, final way in which he had refused her attempted seduction, drove her crazy with hatred and frustrated desire.

Each night she went home to study her lines for the next day's shooting. But instead of preparing the lines she had to speak in the film, she found herself rehearsing the things she would like to say to Joseph Knight.

They were withering, contemptuous words. She wanted to insult Knight, to demean him, to let him know in no uncertain terms that he was a flash in the pan, a wet-behind-the-ears beginner in Hollywood, an ambitious boy in a man's world. He had only got where he was today by blind luck and a little bit of talent. While she, Eve Sinclair, was a professional who had paid her dues long since, survived in the worst jungle on the face of the earth, and honed her art to a level he could neither aspire to nor really appreciate.

In her fantasies she insulted Knight a thousand times over. She reduced him to ashes. She destroyed him utterly.

Yet, at the end of all those fantasies, more powerful than her own hatred, more compelling than her humiliation and her thirst for revenge, was the haunting image of Knight's handsome face coming closer to hers, the strange black eyes caressing her, the warm lips touching hers as he enfolded her in his arms.

Eve cursed her own schoolgirl emotions. She was shocked at herself. She could not understand why this man, this Joseph Knight, was having such an effect on her. She had known dozens of handsome, powerful men in Hollywood. Most of them she had got around without a false step. Others, too dangerous to seduce, she had avoided by instinct, or sometimes manipulated from afar through one subtle means or another.

But never had any of them penetrated the thick rampart of her ambition and got through to her heart.

Until now.

Eve rebelled with all the force of her strong character against what was happening inside her. She resolved to give the performance of her life in this film, just to show Joseph Knight what she was made of. She would carry the film herself, as she had so many films in the past. She would win Knight an Oscar through her own efforts. Then she would throw it in his face and turn her back on him forever.

But it did not work out that way.

The Velvet Web was a troubled film during the first weeks of shooting, thanks to Eve.

Eve was petulant and temperamental on the set. She quarreled with everybody. She reproached the cinematographer for lighting her badly. She sneered at the costume and makeup artists for making her look drab and inelegant in her key scenes. She reproached her co-stars, including the puzzled Samuel Raines, for feeding her lines with poor pace, for failing to understand their own characters, for stealing scenes from her.

She criticized the script. She challenged the lines she had to read, claiming they were weak, lacking in drama, psychologically false. Time and again she stopped in the middle of a take—an unforgivable sin for a professional Hollywood actress—and announced with a sigh that she could not read these clumsy lines, that they must be changed.

Those around Eve looked away nervously. They knew the script had been written by Joseph Knight himself. In attacking it, Eve was hitting Knight with the lowest blow she could, for this was his screenplay, and the entire film his own conception.

The common denominator of all Eve's tantrums seemed to be that, in her view, *The Velvet Web* was being made by amateurs, beginners who did not have enough experience to understand the subtleties of filmmaking. Eve herself, a seasoned professional, made a great show of her exasperation at the amateurishness of the production.

No one else shared this view or supported Eve in it. But this did not stop her from expressing it over and over again with varying degrees of bluntness.

By the second week of shooting Eve had made herself a monumental nuisance. She had insulted virtually everybody on the picture, and ruined at least a hundred takes through her displays of pique. The cast and crew of *The Velvet Web* were dumbfounded. Many of them had worked with Eve before. She had always been easy to work with and unfailingly polite, the very definition of a professional. Now she seemed completely changed, unrecognizable.

The only person she did not fight with openly on the set was Joseph Knight. Her resistance to him was on another, more devious level. She listened in silence to his murmured instructions for each take, nodding apparent compliance, and then ignored them, reading her lines as she saw fit—when she read them at all, that is.

Joseph Knight refused to take the bait she was so blatantly offering him. He ordered re-take after re-take, gently, politely, always suggesting to Eve that she "try it his way," and never exploding or disciplining her in front of the others when she ignored his orders. Clearly Knight was pondering the situation and looking for a course of action that would save his film. Studio time was expensive. Two hundred people were working on this picture. Eve was its star. He could not allow confrontation with her to ruin the film.

But, try though he might to be diplomatic with Eve, Joseph Knight could not help being close to her on the set, and this physical proximity was the real flame behind her impossible behavior.

There he was, behind the camera for each and every shot, or coming to her side between takes to discuss her lines. Her hands ached to reach out to his handsome body, to hurt, to caress. And after each consultation, he walked away, just as he had walked away that fateful night in her trailer, retreating into his bland professionalism while she was left to try to hide her frayed emotions from the watching camera.

And Eve could not hide her disarray, for she was caught in pitiless close-up, and her image in the finished film would be fifteen feet high on theater screens all over the world. Thus the technical medium of Eve's stardom came back to haunt her, now that her skill at manipulating her own image was destroyed by the power of the emotions she was feeling.

The daily rushes told an eloquent story. Eve was missing her character almost completely. She was supposed to be playing a sensual, mysterious woman who bears a dark and fatal curse, as dangerous to herself as it is to the man who loves her. The role was on the borderline between romance and tragedy. It required the most sensitive modulations on the part of the actress.

Eve was not playing this role at all. In her scenes she looked like a furious woman out for revenge. She looked like a petulant schoolgirl. She looked like an angry woman scorned. She looked like anything but her character.

And yet—as Joseph Knight might have noticed as he studied the rushes, shaking his head—there was one thing in common, ironically, between Eve's absurd behavior before the camera and the character she played: they were both women in love.

Everyone could see the state Eve was in, but she alone knew the reason for it. How could she admit that her performance was suffering because the director would not fuck her? It was impossible, demeaning, unbearable.

After the first ten days of shooting Joseph Knight took Eve aside, in company with the executive producer, to tell her there was a problem with her performance. He wanted her to tell him if there was something bothering her, to clear the air.

Eve curled her lip as she looked at the two men. She saw that Knight did not want to be alone with her. He had his associate with him as a shield. She blandly assured them both that there was no problem. She would do whatever they asked, if they would simply be clear about it. It was their film, after all, not hers, she added with a note of contempt.

And she looked daggers at Joseph Knight as he saw her out of his office.

After that meeting, the atmosphere on the set was worse instead of better. Tempers were beginning to flare all over the sound stage. Eve was sowing discord through her angry and childish behavior. Everyone could feel the film beginning to sink. Their collective inspiration was flagging under the weight of Eve's resistance.

But Eve would not admit that anything was wrong. To those who gently tried to reason with her she was offhanded and indifferent. What was everybody so worried about? she demanded. Why did they not let her alone so she could do her job?

Inside her trailer she felt an angry surge of self-satisfaction. She had Knight where she wanted him now. She knew he could not get another star. The cost would be prohibitive, for one thing. For another, Eve's great box-office ap-

peal was an obvious key to the picture's future. That was
why Knight had cast her in the first place. He could not
do without her now. It was too late. Thus for practical as
well as commercial reasons she had him by the balls.

And she intended to squeeze him until he treated her
right.

● ● ● ●

Somewhere in the midst of the chaos of those weeks,
Kate Hamilton's brief sidewalk scene with Samuel Raines
was shot, as was the longer scene in which she greeted him
at the door of her apartment and hid him from his pursuers.

Joseph Knight himself directed both scenes. Kate found
him a gentle and helpful director. He was a perfectionist,
and not afraid to shoot a scene many times in order to get
the desired effect. But he treated his actors with respect
and consideration for their fatigue as well as their talent.

"Now, look out at him enigmatically," he told her as
they shot the doorway scene, tilting her head at just the
right angle by touching her chin. "Remember, you're a
woman of mystery yourself. Your past is a checkered one,
though we never get to hear about it. You're a girl who's
been around. You're attracted by him, but you also like
him. You can see he is in trouble, and you want to help."

Kate did the scene as she was told, and patiently went
through several re-takes in which she was asked to change
certain details of her performance. Knight came close to
her, and their eyes met as he explained what he wanted.
Kate felt the same strange discomfort at his nearness that
she had felt the first time they shook hands. She managed
to hide it behind her performance, and he seemed pleased.

"Good work," he said when the last take was done. "I
think it will be a strong scene. Thank you, Miss Hamilton."

"Call me Kate. And thank you."

The morning after Kate's scene was shot Joseph Knight
looked at the rushes of her performance. He was surprised
by what he saw. That strange, haunting look of sadness
was visible in her eyes, the look he remembered from the
first time he had met her on the set. It communicated itself

to the camera with an enormous coiled power. Knight was so struck by it that he asked his associates in the screening room whether they saw it too.

Their responses were noncommittal.

"She's hot, but she's playing the part," said Larry Walsh.

"The camera likes her a lot," said the first assistant director. "Maybe too much. She sticks out. But maybe you want that . . ."

"It's up to you, Joe," said the cinematographer.

Knight looked again at the screen. He seemed thoughtful.

"Larry," he said suddenly. "I want you to get this girl into the last scene of the picture. The death scene. When Sam gets shot, I want her there. A head-to-toe in her raincoat, and a close-up. I think she's just what that scene needs. Let's call her agent tomorrow and line her up."

"Will do," said Larry Walsh.

They went on to another scene. Joseph Knight felt the face of Kate Hamilton lingering in his memory. He wondered whether he had decided to use her in the finale because of her performance on film or because of the odd effect she had on him personally. On one hand she seemed to be just the touch the film needed. Or was she, on the contrary, a walking flaw that he was making worse by adding her to another scene, for reasons he himself did not understand?

He did not know.

Puzzled, he again put Kate Hamilton out of his mind.

This time it was harder.

On September 21 the volcano that had been building under *The Velvet Web* at last erupted.

The assembled cast was shooting the most important ensemble scene of the film, the scene in which the hero, having been shot by a misguided police detective on a crowded street, speaks to the mystery woman for the last time. It was the dramatic highlight of the film, an image on which Joseph Knight had worked for many months.

Eve's character, hitherto mysterious and alluring, was now to become maternal and kind as she took her leave of the hero whose undoing she had unwillingly brought about. She had to communicate a womanly sympathy, as well as a tragic guilt over the havoc she had caused.

Samuel Raines, playing the dying hero, looked very masculine and yet vulnerable as he lay in the heroine's arms. Eve had to hold him tenderly while the camera focused on their faces in a tight close-up before receding to take in the crowd looking on, a crowd that included several key characters from earlier scenes of the film. Then, without a cut, the camera was to pull back on its crane to reveal the entire street, and the indifferent city beyond. The words THE END would be superimposed over this final image.

It was an expensive shot, involving many well-paid actors and extras, not to mention stagehands, a crane operator, and lighting specialists. It had to be done perfectly.

It was on this shot that Eve chose to push her intolerable behavior a step too far.

She did the scene completely wrong. She ignored the emotion her character was supposed to communicate, and behaved in a crude and rather childish manner that ruined the take and wasted Samuel Raines's fine effort.

The scene was shot again and again. With each re-take the destructive effect of Eve's performance became more obvious. At this moment, when the greatest subtlety of characterization was required, she was deliberately sabotaging not only her own character but the entire scene as well.

Joseph Knight watched in consternation from behind the camera. He wished he could stop and shoot the whole scene again another day. But the shooting schedule was tight, the budget limited. The shot had to be done now.

Yet Eve's behavior before the camera was absolutely hopeless. Because of her, not a single foot of the film shot so far could be printed.

Joseph Knight came to her side between takes and patiently explained what he needed, talking to her as though she were a child. Forcing back the angry words he wanted to say to her, he managed to be polite and logical.

Eve listened with a bored, stubborn look, and in the next take played the scene precisely as she had done before.

She even seemed to repeat her absurd performance in its finest details, just to rub it in.

At last Joseph Knight stopped the action and told the crew to take five. He took Eve aside for a serious conference. He explained how much was riding on this shot. He told her how important her cooperation was for the success of the film. He told her how much he counted on her professionalism. He knew she would not let him down, he said.

She listened in silence. After their conference Knight called everyone back and shot the scene again. Once again Eve's performance was completely unacceptable. The triumph in her eyes at the end of the scene was obvious. She was enjoying the consternation she was causing.

"Cut," Joseph Knight called. "Stay where you are, everybody."

There was a pause on the set, pregnant with violence. It was obvious to anyone with eyes to see that Eve Sinclair was intentionally trying to ruin Joseph Knight's film. For three weeks everyone had been wondering how much longer Knight would stand for her behavior.

Now the answer came.

Joseph Knight walked slowly from behind the camera onto the set. Eve was still in her position, holding Samuel Raines in her arms.

"Sam, step off the set a minute, will you?" he said to his male star.

Samuel Raines, pale with the embarrassment of the moment, got up and left the set. Joseph Knight stood looking down at Eve. She stared up at him defiantly.

The look in Joseph Knight's eyes was not angry. Yet it contained something so dangerous that everyone on the sound stage held their breath.

"You're fired," he said to Eve. "Get off my set."

He had made no effort to lower his voice. The deep tones echoed among the actors, extras, and grips crowding the sound stage.

Eve looked up at him through wide eyes. She was genuinely shocked.

"What . . . what did you say?" she asked.

His expression was calm, almost intimate.

"I said you're fired," he repeated. "You're off the picture."

Eve let out a brief, nervous laugh.

"I don't believe this," she said. "*You* are firing *me?*"

Joseph Knight said nothing.

Eve's features became distorted by hatred as she realized the gravity of her situation.

"Why, you good-for-nothing animal," she said. "You think you can fire Eve Sinclair? Who in hell do you think you are? I can buy and sell you any time I like. You goddamned ambitious little prick. I can buy and sell you! You don't fire Eve Sinclair, you . . . you . . ."

Rage kept her from finding her words. She was still sitting on the floor, gazing up at him in loathing.

He moved forward suddenly and jerked her to her feet. He held her by both wrists and spoke to his first assistant director.

"Call security," he said. "I want her kept away from this set until she's packed her things. Have her out of the building in half an hour."

Eve had begun kicking at him. He held her at a distance until a security man arrived, and then handed her over. She was escorted to her trailer, shouting curses which echoed across the silent sound stage. When the trailer door closed she could be heard inside, still cursing, her voice somewhere between a shout and a moan.

Joseph Knight stood in the middle of the set. He seemed lost in thought. The stunned cast and crew watched him, terrified by the coiled power in his posture. "You could hear a pin drop," witnesses would say years later about this extraordinary moment. No one dared move.

Knight surveyed the assembled actors and crew. He touched his chin meditatively. Those present could almost feel him measuring the damage that had been done to his film by Eve Sinclair and wondering whether the project could be saved at all. He was a professional, as smart as they came. He had stolen nine Oscars from Bryant Hayes. His quick mind must be even now looking for a way out of this crisis.

He walked silently about the set. He looked at the actors.

They did not meet his eyes. He looked at the anxious crew. He saw the camera operator in his crane, waiting for instructions.

Suddenly Knight's eyes came to rest on Kate Hamilton. She was standing on her mark, dressed in her raincoat, as he had instructed his assistants to have her do for this final shot. Her blond hair fell to her shoulders. Her eyes were fixed on him. Alone among the actors present, she did not look away. He saw the same expression that had fascinated him in their previous encounters, a sad and very feminine look that had never been entirely absent from his thoughts since he first saw her screen test.

He seemed to decide something all at once. He went to her side. He looked closely at her.

"Come with me," he said. "I need you."

She pointed to herself inquiringly. "Me?" she formed the word with her lips.

He took her hand and brought her to the center of the set.

"Do you know what this scene is about?" he asked in a low voice.

She nodded. "I've been watching it for the last forty-five minutes," she said.

"I want you to play it for me," he said.

Her eyes opened wide. She could not believe what she was hearing.

"Now, remember," he said. "She has caused his death. She didn't want to, but she suspected all along that she was going to. She loves him, but she's never been able to tell him that. She has to tell him now, with her eyes. Your eyes. Do you understand?"

Kate was still staring at him in a sort of shock. But the force of his will seemed to possess her.

"You've killed him," he repeated. "You've killed him because you loved him. It's too late for you both. Say it with your eyes."

She looked at him dubiously.

"Will you help me?" he asked.

Slowly Kate nodded. She felt he was asking something far beyond her powers, something almost insane. But she knew she would crawl through jungles for him, or climb mountains.

He gestured to Samuel Raines, who came forward and resumed his position. Kate sank to her knees and held his head in her arms. At a gesture from Knight, the camera came forward.

The slate man came over, more than a bit confused.

"*The Velvet Web*," he said to the camera. "Scene four sixty-three, take sixteen."

He snapped the slate and disappeared.

Samuel Raines, ever the professional, looked into Kate's eyes. He was completely in character. One could never tell from his expression that he had just changed leading ladies.

"I guess we meet again," he said, reading his line.

Kate said nothing. But inside herself she thought of Joseph Knight, and of the feelings she had been having ever since she met him in this building four weeks ago. A light came into her eyes, touched by melancholy and tenderness.

"I'll be seeing you," Samuel Raines said, a dying smile on his lips. "They say everything comes around again. Do you believe that?"

Kate responded without words. Her face was full of despair, and of love. The camera inched closer.

"Kiss me once," Samuel Raines said.

As she bent to touch her lips to his forehead, his eyes closed. The camera receded slowly, the crane lifting it higher and higher. Kate did not move. She knew, as did everyone else, that the film would end with this image.

A sigh of collective relief was heard on the sound stage. Everyone was in a state of shock, not only from the scene between Knight and Eve Sinclair but from the performance they had just witnessed.

Joseph Knight stood behind the camera, gazing into the face of Kate Hamilton. His look was contemplative, appraising.

"Cut," he said.

He came to Samuel Raines's side.

"Good work, Sam," he said, helping him up.

Now he stood looking down at Kate. He extended his hand. She took it.

She stood up. He did not relinquish her hand. His eyes swept over the cast and crew, who all seemed emotionally exhausted.

"You can all go home," he said. "I'll see you tomorrow morning."

The set slowly emptied. The silence was as heavy as before. No one knew what was going to happen.

Only Joseph Knight could provide the answers now.

As for Kate, she knew nothing, and felt nothing, except the warm hand still holding her own. It was a gentle grip, and yet a firm one, as though he never intended to let her go.

"I'll need you to help me tonight," he said. "Can you spare the time?"

Kate nodded.

"Of course, Mr. Knight."

Kate was up most of the night with Joseph Knight, Larry Walsh, and the cameraman, going through the key scenes of *The Velvet Web* on the deserted sound stage. She was dismissed at four A.M. and sent home in a studio limousine to get some sleep.

At six A.M. Joseph Knight called a meeting of the production staff. Present were Oscar Freund, several of Monarch Pictures' top executives, and the head of the studio's legal department.

"Gentlemen," Knight said, "Kate Hamilton will be our new leading lady."

He listened impassively to the collective intake of breath around the conference table.

"Dan," he said to the studio attorney, "I want Eve Sinclair's contract torn up today. Draw up a contract for Kate Hamilton and get it to Alfred Dozier as soon as possible."

He turned to Larry Walsh.

"Larry," he said, "I want Miss Hamilton taken to Wardrobe this morning. We'll need to fit her for Eve's costumes right away. Tell Makeup I want a conference this afternoon. I want to start re-shooting Sam's scenes with Miss Hamilton by next week at the latest. Let's move, everybody. We're short on time."

He closed the meeting and returned to the set to shoot whatever scenes he could until Kate was ready to step in as the leading lady.

Behind him he left a film studio in a state of shock.

The next morning the story of Eve Sinclair's firing was the headline on every trade publication in show business.

KNIGHT FIRES EVE SINCLAIR ON SET, announced *Daily Variety*.

STORM ON SET OF KNIGHT FILM, trumpeted *The Hollywood Reporter*.

SINCLAIR GETS BOOT FROM KNIGHT, said the *Los Angeles Times*.

It was the biggest story in a decade. Joseph Knight, already the hottest filmmaker in Hollywood since his stunning humiliation of Bryant Hayes and his nine Oscars for *The Rainbow's End,* had once again shocked the film world. Eve Sinclair, long considered one of the most bankable female stars in Hollywood, had been fired off a picture in front of the assembled cast and crew. In her place an unknown had been cast on the spot by Joseph Knight, and would now be his star.

This was a story to end all stories. The press buzzed like a beehive.

But the firing of Eve Sinclair was only the beginning of an episode that was to shake Hollywood to its foundations.

Ten days after firing Eve Sinclair, Joseph Knight married Kate Hamilton.

17

The Hollywood Reporter, October 10, 1941

KNIGHT MARRIES HIS NEW STAR

Joseph Knight, Hollywood's hottest new producer/director, has stunned the film world by marrying unknown actress Katherine Hamilton after giving her the starring role in his new film, *The Velvet Web.*

Knight had rocked Hollywood only a few days before by abruptly firing star Eve Sinclair in the midst of shooting of one of the film's key scenes. "Creative differences" were cited by a spokesman for the film as the reason for Sinclair's firing, but loud rumors have it that Sinclair had been virtually uncontrollable on the set because of an unspecified antipathy toward Knight.

It was against the background of this explosive situation that Knight suddenly fired Sinclair and actually reshot the film's climactic scene with Hamilton, a minor player in the film and a Hollywood unknown whose only screen credits include a handful of walk-ons and bit parts. Twenty-four hours after these events Knight announced that Hamilton would be his new leading lady.

Ten days later, completing the almost unbelievable turn of events, Knight and Hamilton were married by a justice of the peace in downtown Los Angeles, only a few miles from Monarch Studios, where *The Velvet Web* is being shot.

Knight and his new bride—the first marriage for both—were denied the luxury of a honeymoon by the tight shooting schedule of *The Velvet Web,* already reportedly hundreds of thousands of dollars over budget because of the necessity of re-shooting all the Eve Sinclair scenes. The newlyweds will be getting to know each other with Knight's camera as intermediary.

Hollywood observers remained baffled by Knight's actions. Knight had no comment either on the change of stars or on his marriage. He would say only that the word on *The Velvet Web* is "full steam ahead."

Bryant Hayes let out a brief laugh as he put down the newspaper.

So Joe Knight is human, too, he thought. Knight, the ice man, the relentless professional, the celebrated fount of talent and determination, had his Achilles' heel, just like everyone else in Hollywood.

And that weakness was located right between Knight's legs.

Knight had fired Eve Sinclair, one of the most reliable leading ladies in Hollywood, and replaced her with a nobody. Coming from any other producer, such a blunder would have been embarrassing enough. But coming from Knight, with his prestige, his reputation for integrity and clearheadedness, it boggled the mind.

Nevertheless, Bryant Hayes mused, it must have been precisely Knight's overnight success, that enormous adulation surrounding him, that had blinded him to reality. Knight must have felt so invincible, so superhuman in his talent and his instincts, that he had dared to try this silly stunt and think he could get away with it.

Throwing away Eve Sinclair, with her name, her box-office power, and her great ability, for a no-talent starlet! An actress no one had ever heard of, a beginner.

Bryant Hayes rubbed his hands together. Now was the time for some hard thinking. He had made all his plans over the past several months based on the notion that Knight's new film would be a huge hit. With Eve Sinclair in the title role opposite Samuel Raines, the new film seemed surefire. Hayes had re-scheduled distribution of two of Continental Pictures' biggest new properties just to make sure they didn't hit the theaters in competition with *The Velvet Web*. Since the disaster of *Winter of Destiny* he was taking no chances. He was going to yield the spotlight to Knight and build slowly to recoup his losses.

But now everything was different. Now Hayes would go ahead with guns blazing, and hit the public with his best new pictures, taking on *The Velvet Web* head-to-head if necessary.

Provided, that is, that Knight ever finished his new opus. There was a strong possibility that with Eve Sinclair gone, the no-talent newcomer Knight had just married would soon show herself unequal to the challenge of a starring role. The money men at Oscar Freund's Monarch Pictures, already exasperated by the film's enormous production delays, might decide to bail out on the entire project. *The Velvet Web* would thus sink under the weight of its producer-director's inflated ego.

That would be even better for Continental Pictures. And better for Bryant Hayes. It would leave the field open for him to make a bundle in the theaters and take a giant step toward restoring Continental to its pre-eminent position among Hollywood studios.

And Hayes's success would be a powerful blow to Arnold Speck back in New York. Speck's maneuvering with the board would lose much of its effect if Hayes could produce a couple of big hits this year.

Yes, indeed, Bryant Hayes mused happily. Joseph Knight had stumbled at last. The public's adored new idol had feet of clay.

18

FOR KATE HAMILTON THE FIRST DAYS AFTER HER SURPRISE casting by Joseph Knight in *The Velvet Web* were a revolution that cut her off from her past and plunged her into a world whose rules were new to her.

For years Kate had been in total control of her life. She had kept her feet firmly on the ground and fought off anyone who tried to manipulate, confuse, or abuse her. At the price of an inner darkness that left her somehow separate from herself, she controlled her own destiny. If she did not know who she was, at least she knew who she wasn't. She made all her own decisions.

But now she was completely at sea. The profession of acting, which had been at most an experiment in her mind, had suddenly thrust her into the starring role in a major motion picture, conceived and directed by the most brilliant producer/director in Hollywood. Kate could not even begin to frame the challenge in her mind, much less live up to it. She was in a daze.

Her immediate response to this dilemma was simply to do what she was told. Ever since the first time she had met Joseph Knight she had felt an instinctive loyalty to him, a willingness to do whatever he asked of her. She gave herself to that emotion now.

Joseph Knight had budgeted a week of intense rehearsal

before re-shooting the film with Kate in the lead role. As he explained the scenario to Kate and helped her to read scenes with Samuel Raines, there was a remarkable look in his dark eyes. On the surface it expressed confidence and friendliness, but underneath it bespoke an almost frightening resolve. Knight had already seen Eve Sinclair do her best to ruin his film. Having fired Eve at one violent stroke, he was going through with the project. Nothing would stop him.

Once Kate had seen that look of smoldering purpose, she dared not think of letting Joseph Knight down. She would do what he asked of her, or die trying.

She had to force herself not to notice the production people around her, for she could feel their lack of confidence in her. They seemed to be waiting for Joseph Knight to come to his senses, fire the nobody he had impulsively hired, and find a genuine professional actress, a star, to play his heroine.

So Kate put blinders on and did not look anywhere but into the eyes of Joseph Knight. She tried to make herself putty in his hands so that, by being completely obedient, she would not make any mistakes.

But she soon found out that this was not what Joseph Knight wanted of her.

"No," he smiled during one of their first rehearsals for a major scene. "You're giving me what you think I want. Don't go about it that way, Miss Hamilton. It has to come from you. From inside. All right?"

Embarrassed to feel him read her mind so efficiently, Kate nodded and tried the scene again. She felt completely out of her element. The acting techniques she had learned from Norman Webb were like a mental game, an exercise in pure strategy without the participation of the heart. But Joseph Knight was asking her to bare her soul for the camera in a way she had never dreamed of attempting. In a sense he was invading her privacy, a privacy she had spent many years protecting with all the force of her strong will.

There were many false starts. Over and over again she tried to do what he wanted, but found herself faced with an invisible brick wall inside her. Joseph Knight shook his head, smiled encouragingly, and told her to try it again. She did, and failed once more. How could she tell him that the door he was asking her to open for him was a door she had never even opened for herself?

He kept up the pressure, his attitude becoming more and more serious with each passing day. She was convinced she could not give him what he wanted. She had never expected to make such a sacrifice, and did not think she had it in her.

Then one morning a change occurred. Kate was reading one of her most important lines under Joseph Knight's watchful eye. They had already been over it six times. She felt utterly hemmed in, and exhausted to the point of panic. Her concentration flagged for an instant. She felt faint. Then a sudden inner spasm, somewhere between rebellion and surrender, shot through her senses. The line emerged from her lips with an electric freshness, as though a chemical change had taken place inside her. She herself was taken aback and wondered whether she had crossed the line into emotional collapse.

Joseph Knight was smiling at her.

"There," he said. "That's what I wanted. I knew you'd get it."

Kate smiled weakly. "I'm glad *you* knew," she said.

"Now let's do it again," Joseph Knight said.

From that point their work together really began.

As the excruciating days went by, with Kate teetering between her fear of her own inadequacy and her fascination with the challenge Joseph Knight had given her, she began to see her situation in a new and unsettling light. In giving herself to the role of the mystery woman, she mused, she was also giving herself to Joseph Knight. It was his demand she was obeying, his personality she was surrendering to. The deepest part of her emotional life, not really felt by herself for years, was coming out of hiding and showing itself at last, for him and for the character he had created.

What was more, she thought she saw a response to this sacrifice of hers in Joseph Knight. She was not sure, for Knight himself was obviously the most private of men; but she sensed a flicker of acknowledgment, a reaching out, a mental taking of her hand to join her in her challenge.

Kate was torn by this intuition, for something about Knight's daunting masculinity had made her want to escape him, to hide from him, ever since their first meeting. On the other hand, she clung to her growing closeness with him as a desperately needed weapon against her own self-doubt.

Soon she began to suspect that her need was more dangerous than she realized. The veneer of bland professionalism that she showed to Knight in their daily work was cracking around the edges. Deep inside, beyond the reach of her self-control, the vulnerable female heart she had left behind so long ago was awakening to the attraction of Joseph Knight as a man.

A hardheaded woman, Kate fought back the emotion with all her powers, trying to concentrate on the role and to forget what was going on inside her. She knew Joseph Knight was not for her. He was a celebrity, a great man. They lived in separate worlds.

But even in warning herself this way Kate was acknowledging the seductive yearning that made her heart melt each time Knight was near. With every passing hour she became less sure of herself, more obsessed with him. She lay awake at night thinking about him when she should have been resting for the day ahead.

She began to feel an atrocious discomfort in rehearsals when Knight was near her, giving advice and encouragement, demanding more and more of her. Now she knew how Eve Sinclair must have felt when, playing the same role Kate was now playing, she had fallen under Joseph Knight's spell and lost her bearings as an actress and a woman. It had been one thing to observe Eve's antics from afar and to wonder about the antipathy between her and Knight. But now, close to Knight's handsome face and powerful body as well as his brilliant, probing mind, Kate realized that Eve had been in love with him. Her own tortured feelings left no doubt of it.

Kate's obsession grew worse and worse, and she feared that her inner struggle was contaminating every scene she played. What was more, she thought Joseph Knight sensed her upset. He no longer seemed at ease in his proximity to her. She was sure he was having second thoughts about her ability to bring off the role but was hesitating before confronting her with his decision. The look in his eyes was pained, as though he was struggling with himself. No doubt he was giving his Kate Hamilton experiment a few more days before calling it off and looking for a better actress.

Kate's position was unbearable. All she could do was to keep trying, to keep throwing herself into every scene with everything she had, and to wait for the blow to fall. She felt completely inadequate and emotionally out of control. She just wanted the whole ordeal to end.

Seven days after it began, it ended.

On the Friday before shooting was to resume, Joseph Knight knocked at the door of Kate's trailer.

"Miss Hamilton? May I speak to you for a moment?"

Kate glanced at herself in the vanity mirror. She looked awful. The day's rehearsal had left her pale and exhausted. She was wearing slacks and a sweatshirt. She wore no makeup, and her hair fell in tangled waves to her shoulders.

"Come on in," she smiled, mustering a brittle mask of goodfellowship as she watched him enter the trailer. He seemed to dwarf the tiny space. He was in shirtsleeves, and his muscled strength shone through the garments he wore. He looked fresh, crisp, and terribly handsome, as always.

He sat down and looked at her for a long moment. He seemed embarrassed.

"What's the matter, Mr. Knight?" she asked. "Is everything all right?"

He looked surprised. "Is that what you've been calling me?" he asked. "Haven't I ever told you to call me Joe?"

Kate smiled. "Yes, you did," she said. "But I didn't have the courage."

He did not seem to hear her. He looked around the trailer slowly, his eyes scanning all its details without seeing them. She had never seen him look so preoccupied.

Then he looked into her eyes. For the first time since

she had met him, his usual self-possession had vanished. He seemed to search clumsily for something to say.

"Kate," he said. "May I call you Kate?"

She smiled. "Of course."

He clasped his hands tightly together and took a deep breath.

"Kate, will you marry me?" he asked.

She looked shocked. She said nothing.

For a long moment they stared at each other as though unable to believe what had just passed between them.

His hands were clenched more tightly, the knuckles white.

"Kate," he said softly, "I love you."

Still she was silent. She looked away for an instant and saw his image in the mirror, a large man poised on the edge of his chair, his hands clenched as he gazed in supplication at a woman who was Kate herself.

All at once she shuddered. When she looked back at him her eyes were full of tears.

"You . . . ?" She fought for words, but nothing would come. She felt she had misunderstood everything. For nearly a week she had been on the edge of madness. If that were true, she might be dreaming this entire scene.

But her hands were held out to him, and he got up from his chair and came to kneel beside her. He touched her tangled hair, then her cheek. He gazed at her with an intensity she had never seen in a human face.

"I love you," he repeated. "Please, don't say no."

Her hands came to rest on his cheeks. She drew him to her breast. She could feel him breathing against her heart. There was not a thought in her mind.

She tried to come to her senses. The incongruity of holding him that way, protectively as a mother, while his terrible strength knelt down to her and placed itself on her breast, filled her with awe.

But already her lips were forming words as new and unexpected as any she had spoken for him before.

"I love you," she said. "I love you, Joe."

He raised his eyes to hers. He looked relieved and at the

same time incredibly excited. A boyish expression she had never seen on his face now lit it up.

"I haven't even kissed you," he said.

She said nothing. The look in her eyes said what she had to say.

He took her in his arms. As his handsome face came closer, all her fantasies and worries about him flew from her like gossamer. The warm lips touched her own. For a tiny instant she hovered painfully between herself and him, her heart recalling the Kate Hamilton she had clung to and sheltered throughout her life. Then she gave up the past and held him to her with gentle hands.

"You're kissing me now," she said.

An hour later they were in his bed, their naked bodies joined in the act of love.

Kate's breasts, on fire from his kisses, were pressed to his chest. Her hair was splayed out on the pillow in a golden halo. Her hands held his cheeks softly as he came deeper inside her. His strokes were slow and passionate. Her back arched against the sheets, and the long supple thighs he had noticed under her skirts were now grazing his hips with subtle tremors of delight.

She felt her femininity arouse him, and felt the huge power of his sex come closer to its pleasure. But the revolution in her heart went far deeper than the excitement of her body. She knew from every kiss, every stroke, that she belonged to him. The old Kate Hamilton had ceased to exist and was as forgotten as a previous incarnation. She was being born on this day to be Joseph Knight's woman.

She slid her hands down his back with soft urgency, to pull him deeper. His lips came to hers, and she kissed him again as her legs gripped him tighter. She felt his mystery, his own darkness, come forward to join hers. A thrill of danger surged inside her at the change he had wrought in her, but she did not shrink from it. She thanked her lucky stars for the opportunity of losing herself to a fate so great.

It seemed to Kate that her whole life had been leading to this moment, and that all the loneliness she had endured was the price she had had to pay in order to deserve Joseph

Knight. Her steps had been taking her toward him since before she was a woman, perhaps since her girlhood adoration of famous Eve Sinclair, or even before.

But thought was melting into passion in her mind, and there was no more time to wonder at the magic transforming her. The final wave came with a terrible rush. As her body cried out its ecstasy, she tried to look inside herself for a last time, to find out who she was. But in the darkness of her soul she saw only the eyes of Joseph Knight, gazing out at her with their look of fascination and secret knowledge.

19

IT WAS THE CRAZIEST HONEYMOON ANYONE EVER SPENT. And, in a strange way, the most intimate.

It took place during a six-week shooting schedule that was already far over budget, thanks to the Eve Sinclair debacle. Joseph Knight spent his short nights at home holding his new wife in his arms, but it was during their eighteen-hour days on the set together that they really got to know each other.

Years later, when Kate Hamilton's films were studied by expert scholars, the critical consensus would be that her amazing power as an actress had undergone its birth pangs during those crucial six weeks, as Joseph Knight and his camera plumbed her mystery more and more deeply and at the same time fell more and more in love with her.

Each morning, fueled in her spirit by the passion her husband had inspired in her the night before, Kate went before the cameras. And the intimacy that was quickly deepening between her and Joe gave her the courage to try new and adventurous things in her performance. She hid nothing from Joe's camera—neither the qualities she knew she possessed nor the secrets she had never suspected in herself until this moment.

Because of this abandon, Kate's performance became an underground sensation among Hollywood insiders long before *The Velvet Web* was released. The strange inner light that would one day be called "the Kate Hamilton mystique" was born under the eye of Joseph Knight's camera. It was an uncanny presence, almost supernatural in its attractiveness. It seemed to express the essence of femininity, not only in its sensuality but also in its tragic seriousness. In years to come, dozens of actresses would try to imitate it, but none would succeed.

For Kate was herself a mystery woman, filled with complexities as invisible to herself as they were captivating to others. It was as though she knew things without realizing it, had dared things without knowing it, had explored forbidden places without deciding to. There was a world of secrets behind her sensual eyes, a world full of intimate hurts and pleasures, perhaps even transgressions, that captivated her audience.

The morning rushes were so exciting that dozens of top studio executives joined those directly involved in the film in coming to admire them. Everyone saw the same thing: a great star was being born before their eyes.

So overwhelming was Kate's screen presence that few observers thought to recall Eve Sinclair's participation in *The Velvet Web*. Eve, with her polished talent, her tantrums, and her malevolent hatred of Joseph Knight, was barely a memory now. At her best she could never have brought to *The Velvet Web* a depth such as Kate Hamilton was giving to the lead role now.

It was like the passing of a torch from one generation of

actresses to another, an ineluctable dividing line between past and future.

And Kate Hamilton was the future.

As for Joseph Knight, he could hardly contain the exultation that fueled him as he drove Kate to the sound stage each morning and put her before the cameras. Nor could he control the excitement he felt as he took her home at night to hold her in his arms and make love to her.

Kate was growing into her leading role so quickly that it was obvious her innate acting talent was of enormous dimensions. She matched newly found technique to unsuspected depths, both in the character and in herself, with a dizzying power. Something volcanic and dangerous inside her communicated itself to the camera. There was no doubt in Joseph Knight's mind that she was a great actress in the making.

And the source of her attractiveness as a woman was as mysterious as the source of her power as an actress. True, she had a magnificent, lush body and a beautiful face with the most haunting golden eyes he had ever seen. But the principle of her sensuality, and of her amazing depth, came from something secret, something unseen that Joe could not capture with his mind, though he touched it with his love a bit more each day.

He realized that Kate had lived her life with a fierce pride and an intensity of experience that other people, male or female, never dream of. Underneath her blond beauty there was an independence of will to match her beautiful, natural vulnerability.

She was completely free of the ready-made beliefs and prejudices, the petty concerns, the shallow desires that had characterized the people Joe had known all his life. Despite her modest manner, she lived entirely by her own rules, scorning the conventions and expectations of others. She possessed an inner courage that bordered on recklessness, even on transgression.

There was a nobility about Kate that filled him with admiration. When he held her in his arms it was her separate existence, her freedom that he held, like a wild thing tamed only by her love for him. And in this embrace he gave up something of his own soul, rather than merely possessing her as he had possessed so many women before.

This was a new experience for him, the experience of losing himself to a woman. For the first time in his life he felt freed from the monotonous preoccupation with his own future, his own success, that had been his lot since he ran away from home as a boy. In loving Kate infinitely, he stopped caring for himself. This was a great liberation, greater than anything he had ever dreamed for himself in all his years of hard work and achievement. He was as thrilled as a child, and his delight shone in his dark eyes every time he looked at her.

When they made love Joe felt as though he was in the Garden of Eden, discovering woman for the very first time. And it seemed to him that his own manhood, having wasted itself in chimerical adventures throughout his life, was being born only now.

He could not know that Kate felt exactly the same thing. She was being created at this moment, in Joseph Knight's love, after languishing all her life in an existence that had no meaning and no reality. She had been a ghost when she had walked the earth before meeting Joe; now, as his wife, she was a human being at last.

During shooting Kate lived with Joe in his suite at the Beverly Wilshire. The two talked about buying a house in the Hollywood hills after shooting ended, but they could think only about the film for now.

Their hours alone together were so stunned by passion that they barely found time to tell each other about the past they had lived through before they met. Kate spoke of her dead father, her indifferent mother and stepfather, her wanderings. She left out Quentin. Not only did her first marriage seem irrelevant, almost nonexistent compared to what she now had with Joe, but it seemed a sacrilege to sully her love for Joe by mentioning Quentin's name. Quentin had existed before her rebirth. He had no reality now.

She listened to Joe's equally laconic story of his lost mother, his solitary travels, the business pursuits that had finally led him to Hollywood. He did not hide the fact that his many achievements had left him feeling empty and un-used as a man. Kate could see that he had had many adven-tures, but she did not press him for details, for she felt, as he did, that nothing of the past mattered except the marvel-ous, improbable fact that they had met. The past was wiped out, and only the future mattered now.

On one stolen weekend Joe was able to take Kate away from Hollywood for eighteen precious hours. He drove her into the Sierras to show her the cabin he had bought there a year before. It was a very private retreat, beside an extraordi-narily deep mountain lake—two hundred feet at its deepest—created by a glacial anomaly millions of years ago. Joe joked about how cold the water was and demonstrated how easy it was to get used to by diving in before Kate's eyes.

The cabin was a lovely, rustic place, built from heavy oak beams, with overstuffed furniture, thick rugs, and walls studded with paintings and tapestries. Joe explained that there were no other cabins on the lake, because he wanted no neighbors. He had bought all the land and taken mea-sures to keep trespassers out. He knew how important soli-tude was going to be for him now that the Hollywood publicity hounds had chosen him for their hero. The situa-tion could only get worse as Kate's fame increased—a fact he took for granted.

"When we're not shooting," he said, "we'll be able to come up here every weekend. There are trout in this lake. Shall I teach you how to fish, Kate?"

You can teach me anything you want. Kate's face beamed with pleasure as she thought of a lifetime to be spent with Joseph Knight. It all seemed too good to be true.

But thoughts of the future had to wait, for shooting was grinding inexorably toward its conclusion. The work seemed harder than ever, and more intense, with all the actors and production people pushing themselves more and more as they sensed that the near-debacle caused by Eve Sinclair's troublemaking on the set was being transformed by Joseph Knight into a film that had a chance for real greatness.

The collective effort went on in a frenzy of fatigue and excitement until, one day in mid-November, it ended. *The*

Velvet Web was completely shot. Only the laborious process of editing and post-production stood between the film and its public.

Joseph Knight and his new wife were drained by the drawn-out challenge of shooting but excited about what they had achieved. They were eager to see what the film would look like in its final edited form, and fascinated to find out what the public would think of it.

After a brief house-hunting search Joe and Kate bought a modest little home in Benedict Canyon, and Kate spent her days furnishing it while Joe worked on post-production with Larry Walsh and Oscar Freund at the studio. Each day she was waiting for him when he came home, and they made love lingeringly in the silence of their bedroom before thinking about dinner or the evening to come.

They had never felt closer or more fulfilled by each other. And yet it was at this moment of apparent calm that Joe and Kate began to feel a new and unsuspected hunger in themselves. Though they were deeper in love than ever, and more carried away by each other, a strange lack of fulfillment began to hang over their life together.

It fell to Joe to put their shared longing into words.

One night in early December he took Kate in his arms.

"Let's make a baby," he said.

Kate's face lit up.

"Do you really mean it, Joe?" she asked.

The look in his eyes was the only answer she needed. It was a look of passionate desire. He had already given her his heart. He wanted to take the final step that would make their love complete.

They made love into the wee hours, as though to seal their promise with the heat of their bodies. Their desire knew myriad forms, innumerable varieties of passion. Kate felt that her past was wiped out completely now that the final promise had been made, the last step toward eternity taken by her and her new husband.

It might take a while—such things usually did—but she would get pregnant. She and Joe had all the time in the world now.

But the next morning that time ran out.

20

December 7, 1941

KATE AWOKE FIRST. AS SHE MADE COFFEE IN THE KITCHEN she turned on the radio to see if there was any important news. The international situation had been getting worse and worse in recent months. And like all Americans, Kate was worried about what might come next.

Today her fears came true.

"Early this morning, Pacific time," said the announcer, *"the Japanese air force attacked the American military base at Pearl Harbor."*

Kate's breath caught in her throat. She dropped what she was doing and stared at the radio, her hands trembling.

". . . According to early reports," the broadcaster continued, *"the attacking force comprised three hundred or more Japanese war planes. American military spokesmen estimate that at least eight U.S. battleships, including the Arizona, as well as fourteen smaller ships, were sunk or seriously damaged. As many as two hundred American aircraft were destroyed, and two to three thousand military and civilian personnel on the ground killed or wounded. U.S. government spokesmen agree that this is the worst single attack on U.S. soil in the history of our nation. It is expected that America will declare war on Japan within hours."*

400

Kate looked up. Joe was standing in the doorway, gazing at her.

"You know what this means," he said.

Kate shook her head. She did not want to hear.

"I'll have to go," he said. "I'll enlist as soon as I can."

Kate's heart missed a beat inside her breast. Her handsome husband had never looked so young, so strong, and yet so vulnerable as at this moment, when he was preparing to fight for his country. She had never felt so proud of him, or so terrified for his safety.

She felt a pang of secret guilt. It was as though his coming into her life had been magical, unreal, like Cinderella's Prince Charming. She had done nothing great or noble to deserve him. Perhaps he was too good to be true. Perhaps their love was too good to be true. Perhaps her own lack of worthiness had pricked the fates to take him away from her. She had never felt so frightened in her life.

"Do you have to go?" she asked weakly. "We've only just . . ."

"I have to go," he said. And, quickly, Kate nodded.

The light burning in his black eyes grew hotter as he looked at her. It was as though he felt the world coming between them for the first time, and saw its power to separate them. She did her best to smile, so he would know that whatever happened, he owned all of her, and always would.

"Nothing can come between us now," he said. "You know that, don't you?"

For an answer she rushed to his side and hugged him with all her might.

As they stood in silence, the voice came on the radio again, to tell of the end of the world that had been and the beginning of a new one.

Kate looked up; Joe was standing in the doorway, gazing at her.

"You know what this means," he said.

Kate shook her head. She did not want to hear.

"I'll have to go," he said. "I'll enlist as soon as I can."

Kate's heart missed a beat inside her breast. Her hand sought her husband; had never looked so young, so strong, and yet so vulnerable as at this moment, when he was preparing to fight for his country. She had never felt so proud of him, or so terrified for his safety.

She felt a pang of secret guilt. It was as though the crisis had been magical, unreal, like Cinderella's Prince Charming. She had done nothing great or noble to deserve him. Perhaps he was too good to be true. Perhaps their love was too good to be true. Perhaps her own lack of worthiness had pricked the fates to take him away from her. She had never felt so frightened in her life.

"Do you have to go?" she asked weakly. "We've only just—"

"I have to go," he said. And, quickly, Kate nodded.

The light burning in his black eyes grew hotter as he looked at her. It was as though he felt the world coming between them for the first time, and saw its power to separate them. She did her best to smile, so he would know that whatever happened, he owned all of her, and always would.

"Nothing can come between us now," he said. "You know that, don't you?"

For an answer she rushed to his side and hugged him with all her might.

As they stood in silence, the voice came on the radio again, to tell of the end of the world that had been and the beginning of a new era.

BOOK

THREE

BOOK

THREE

1

Two and One-half Years Later
The Allied Air Campaign over Europe

Monarch Pictures Newsreel, May 18, 1944

Pilots of the Eighth and Ninth Air Forces, flying battle-tested B-17 Flying Fortresses accompanied by P-47 fighters, have done serious damage to enemy manufacturing and munitions plants throughout Germany, Austria, and Axis-controlled Eastern Europe in the past three weeks.

Flying high-altitude daylight raids, the forts and their daring ten-man crews have dropped countless tons of 500- and 1,000-pound bombs on the Axis targets. The battle against German anti-aircraft and fighters has been a tough one, but Axis losses in matériel are said to be enormous.

Back on the home front, American women are working overtime in munitions factories to keep the bombs rolling for our courageous pilots . . .

Kate Knight had watched the newsreel with her heart in her mouth. She knew the Air Force always put the best face on things. And the letters she received from Joe, who was a pilot with the 125th Group of the Eighth Air Force's First Division, were of little help. Joe offered no hard information, and if he had they would have censored it anyway. His letters were full of the brisk cheerfulness that all servicemen affected when they were in situations of great danger. "The worst thing about this war is missing you," he wrote. "The second worst thing is the food." He never mentioned danger, for he did not want her to worry.

The newsreel had been shown in a special screening at Monarch Studios. Oscar Freund had invited Kate to see it, for he knew it contained news of Joe's bomber group. Kate had driven to the studio to see it and then gone home to bed. Even now, she realized as she slipped between the sheets, it was dawn over Europe. The pilots were taking off for their missions. Joe could be heading into danger at this very moment.

Her worry was particularly intense for two reasons. Joe had been home for a ten-day furlough a month ago, and she had felt so close to him, and yet so far, that her mind seemed almost to go crazy from love for him and from longing.

They had made love constantly, starved for each other by their long separation. It almost seemed as though they were trying to melt into each other, blotting out the world so it could never come between them again.

And yet, at the heart of this physical closeness, there was separation. Joe could not or would not talk about the war, so Kate was shut off from a whole spectrum of his emotions, emotions that were visible to her in Joe's handsome face even as he refused to share them with her. She could feel the terrible stress the war was subjecting him to, but he would not allow her to endure it with him.

The war was changing him, as it was changing so many brave American men. But Kate's distress was more acute than that of other women, for she had hardly had time to get to know Joe in the first place before the war took him away from her. Now he was being scarred in ways she could not see, could not share.

There was nothing to do but take what she could of him. And he offered his love generously, totally. They spent hours in silent communion, reaching out to each other across the emotional chasm the war had placed between them and trying desperately to make up for lost time by deepening their intimacy as best they could during this brief interval. They both knew they would have to go on loving in this strange and painful way until the war ended.

When Joe left, Kate was so drained that it took her a week simply to get her nerves back and resume the vigil of waiting and gritting her teeth. As bad as it was to hold him in her arms while the war owned so much of his soul, it was infinitely worse to know that now he was back in the arena of greatest danger, flying his bomber in the face of the terrible German war machine.

Then a surprise had come.

Kate missed her period two weeks after Joe's furlough. She knew instantly that she was pregnant, for she had not missed a period since her puberty. A visit to her gynecologist had confirmed things yesterday afternoon.

She had written Joe this morning but not yet sent the letter. Oscar's call about the newsreel had set her nerves on edge. She wanted to hear the news of the 125th and wait until tomorrow to send Joe a letter through military channels.

Excited by her own news, but haunted by fear of the war, Kate settled into uneasy somnolence. She saw Joe's face before her mind's eye, and concentrated lovingly on each of the features. The straight nose, the tanned, smooth skin; the strong cheekbones and square jaw, the lined forehead that made him look older than he was. The crisp dark hair and the black, black eyes, so penetrating that they seemed to see into one's soul. The strength of Joe's gaze was so terrible that many people could not bear to meet his eyes. But when Kate looked into them she saw only love reaching out to caress her and protect her.

She saw them now, and tried to send him her love over the thousands of miles separating them. With her hands clasped over her stomach, she fell into troubled sleep. It seemed she had not slept well a single night since he left. But she was not alone in this. All American women with men in the armed forces slept with one eye open, a sort of antenna in their hearts tuned to potential disaster.

• •

At the instant when Kate finally fell asleep, Joseph Knight's hands were frozen on the wheel of his B-17, an aged "E" model nicknamed Broken Arrow. The German countryside, dotted by rivers glistening in the morning sun, looked deceptively placid 28,000 feet below. The mission, announced to the crews at four-thirty this morning, was to the German ball-bearing plants at Schweinfurt, about seventy miles from Frankfurt. It was one of the most heavily defended and dangerous targets in Europe. The mission involved hours of flying over Germany, and a struggle against German air defenses beefed up by fighters brought back from the Russian front to stave off the recent increase in American bomber attacks.

Joe was flying low group today. It was the most dangerous position in the attack group, because it caught more flak and fighter attacks than the higher positions. As wing pilot he had to maneuver expertly, so as not to throw off the other planes.

It was crucial to stay in formation, because in a head-to-head battle a B-17 could not defend itself against an attacking ME 109 or FW 190. Since the B-17s' turret gunners could not shoot absolutely level because of the turret design, the savvy German fighters loved to come in for the attack at twelve o'clock. The only chance of beating them was to stay in formation, where the other bombers' gunners could help fight them off.

This was where the men were separated from the boys. An inexperienced pilot would "throttle-jockey" to hold his position in the formation, a maneuver that immediately drew the attention of the enemy. The experienced German pilots licked their chops at the sight of green Americans, particularly during daylight raids. They could spot a green pilot in a hurry and come straight at him in their 109s or 190s, the dreaded "bogies" that might appear by the hundreds as a bomber group approached an important target.

These daylight raids, despite the optimistic news reports, were costing the Americans a lot of B-17s. The British, who had preferred night raids since the start of the war, thought the Americans' day raids were ill-advised and irresponsible. And lately it seemed they were right. In one mission alone last month the Americans lost sixty bombers. That was a lot of aircraft, and a lot of dead ten-man crews. Churchill and Roosevelt were still at loggerheads over the correct strategy, and it seemed that only a few more missions and the comparison of dead pilots to destroyed munitions plants would decide the issue.

As Joe held the wheel with his frozen hands, he reflected bitterly that the newsreels and Air Force press releases never bothered to report the single most significant thing about flying a B-17: the intense and relentless cold. At 28,000 feet the temperature inside the plane could drop to fifty degrees below zero.

The effect of that freezing cold on the nerves over a five-hour stretch was murder. Not to mention the hands and feet. Any part of the body that touched the cold steel of the fuselage felt frozen stiff after a few minutes. Frostbite was one of the prime sources of injury to the men. The Air Force had invented electric gloves and shoes in an effort to alleviate the situation, but, typically, their solution was half-baked. The electric wires were located in the palms of the hands, leaving the fingers to freeze anyway. And the electric shoes were sadly inefficient. The crew rubbed a greasy salve over the parts of their faces not covered by their oxygen masks in an effort to cut down on frostbite.

For today's raid Joe's group, the 125th, had joined the 98th, the 217th, and the 432nd. Each group would have comprised eighteen planes under ideal circumstances. But the 125th had lost seven planes in the last two weeks in brutal flak-ridden raids over Austria and France. The 98th was short five planes, the 217th was down by three, and the 432nd flying at half-strength. Roosevelt's campaign to convince the British of the viability of daylight raids had been costly.

Joe had lost a lot of friends in the last three months. The Germans were ready for the Americans with vicious flak barrages and hundreds of German fighters lobbing 20-mm cannon shells, 30-mm machine-gun bullets, and rockets into the formations.

The worst thing about these missions was that the P-47 fighter escorts could not carry enough fuel to escort the bombers all the way to the target. They would have to turn back at some point, leaving the bombers to go on to the target alone. That was where the German fighters waited. The trick to reaching the target and getting back alive was to stay in formation and fight off the bogies, pray you got through the flak, drop your bombs, and reach a position where a new group of fighters, American or British, could escort you home.

Today's mission was Joe's thirty-seventh. If he survived it he would have only thirteen more to go. Like the other pilots, he had long since stopped counting, because he had seen so many of his buddies killed that it was emotionally unbearable to count, or to hope. One simply survived a day at a time. The pilots displayed a sort of childish levity, cracking jokes and telling stories about their exploits and close calls, as though the daily proximity of death were nothing to worry about. Their emotions were buried too deep for their fear to come near the surface.

Joe's visit home to Kate a month ago was eclipsed now by the accumulated dread of his missions. He kept the memory in a secret place, where he could contact it in his private moments. It was difficult to think of Kate, because every time he saw her beautiful face in his mind's eye, and thought about the last time they had kissed, he imagined himself being blown into a million pieces by a German rocket tomorrow morning. And the thought of his own extinction was less excruciating than the vision of Kate's beautiful face contorted by grief over his loss.

So he kept her inside him, but thought about her only when the anguish of war gave him a brief respite.

Today he was his usual confident self, ready to take on the German air force with everything he had.

His only worry was that today was the fiftieth mission for his co-pilot, Henry Upchurch, a soft-spoken young man of twenty-five from Arkansas. Henry did not disguise his delight at the prospect of no more missions, but he did not speak of it openly, because all the crews shared a terror of the last mission. So many men seemed to get killed on their last mission that it had come to be considered a jinx. Everyone was uncomfortable when one of the crew was on his fiftieth.

Henry had married his childhood sweetheart before enlisting, and she was now the proud mother of their eighteen-month-old baby. Perhaps because of his own failure to give Kate a child before leaving Hollywood, Joe felt a paternal responsibility to reunite Henry with his little family by bringing him through this last mission safe and sound.

Joe had tried to put Henry at his ease this morning over their breakfast of powdered eggs and Spam, telling him the mission would be an easy one.

"Flak shouldn't be too bad according to Group," Joe had said. "And I'll get you past the bogies, Henry. You have my word on that."

Henry had made a show of being reassured, though he knew perfectly well that Schweinfurt meant grave danger. He was glad to be flying with Joe, who was known as one of the savviest pilots in the entire Wing, a conservative and cautious pilot who had saved more than one ship by holding the right position, fighting off the Germans with sure maneuvers, and flying just above or just below the flak. His crews were always relieved to know he was at the controls, because they thought he was their best chance of getting home alive.

Because of cloud cover, the groups had to descend to 17,500 feet as the IP—the Initial Point of the bomb run—approached. The P-47s had already had to turn back, and the bombers were on their own, flying in tight formation. They had come in west of Koblenz, and when they passed Frankfurt the Germans realized that they were coming for Schweinfurt. Everyone knew a terrible battle lay ahead.

Joe was holding position, checking every few seconds with the navigator about altitude and distance to the target, when the flak started. The crew heard the sickening CRUMP! of 88- and 105-mm anti-aircraft shells exploding all over the sky.

"Damn it," Joe muttered under his breath. The flak was accurate. Schweinfurt was an important target, the weather was good, and the Germans were ready and waiting.

He was still wondering how to pick his way through the flak field when voices started calling on the intercom.

"Ball to crew." It was the ball gunner, the most exposed man on the plane. "Fighters at ten o'clock low."

"Right Waist to crew. Fighters at three o'clock high!"

"Turret to pilot. Two forts hit ahead of us. One of 'em's burning, the other's already going down."

"Ball to co-pilot. More bogies nine o'clock level. Looks like a bunch of 'em. We're in for it."

Joe spoke into the intercom. "Pilot to navigator. How far to the target?"

"About five minutes," the navigator said.

Joe gritted his teeth. The key to survival at this point was to get rid of the weight of the bombs and increase altitude to get above the flak. But he had to try to hold out until the target was reached. These were the most critical minutes in every crew's life.

He looked at Henry. Henry's eyes looked frightened inside his helmet.

Joe shot him a reassuring glance and pushed the throttle. "Let's get this over with," he said.

Joe continued to hold position in the formation as the flak barrage got worse and worse. German fighters were everywhere, lobbing cannon fire and rockets at the bombers. Thankfully, none of them had come straight in yet.

Joe's hands were frozen on the wheel when the navigator's voice came over the intercom.

"Bombs away in one minute," he said.

The bombardier was opening the doors already. The squadron was poised to drop. Joe began to breathe a sigh of relief.

Suddenly a thunderous explosion was heard. The plane lurched wildly, and Joe had to fight the wheel for control. He scanned the gauges quickly. But before he even saw them, his nose told him the fuel line had been hit. The stench of 100-octane gasoline filled the air.

"Co-pilot to pilot," Henry was saying. "Engine one is out. Number four is on fire."

"Christ," Joe cursed, trying to take in everything that was happening. "Feather those engines. Pilot to bombardier. Are you ready to drop?"

There was no answer from the bombardier.

"Pilot to co-pilot," Joe said into the intercom. "Henry, leave the engines to me. Crawl into the bomb bay and make sure those bombs drop. We're losing hydraulic pressure fast."

"Roger." Henry unbuckled himself and left the cockpit. He was a slight young fellow, weighing no more than 145 pounds despite his height. This was a good thing, for the catwalk in the bomb bay was so narrow that a man of ordinary size could barely squeeze through it.

While fighting the controls, Joe called out to the crew on the intercom. Neither waist gunner answered. The tail gunner said he was fine, but the radio operator did not answer.

"Pilot to turret," Joe called to the turret gunner, a bright twenty-three-year-old recruit from California named Roy Hodges. "See if you can find out what's happened to the waist gunners. Report on damage."

Apparently the bomber had taken a powerful flak or rocket burst amidships and a simultaneous hit on the wing. One look at the fuel gauge and the hydraulic gauge left no doubt. They would not make it home today.

Ahead of them other forts were hit. The German fighters were having a field day, and the flak was deadly accurate. Bombers were dropping their loads, or even salvoing their bombs short of the target so as to avoid crashing after being hit. The formation was in shambles. It was going to be a costly mission.

"Turret to pilot. Right waist is dead. He took a piece of flak in the belly. Left waist is out cold. I think his oxygen failed."

"Pilot to turret. Try connecting Mike to the right oxygen system. Everybody get your chutes on."

"Co-pilot to pilot. The bombardier is hit. I think he's dead." Henry's voice sounded small and frightened. "There's a lot of gas in the air back here," he added.

Joe thought of Henry and the fifty-mission jinx. The bombs had not dropped yet, for he had not felt the sudden upward lurch that always shook a B-17 when the five-hundred- and one-thousand-pounders tumbled from the bomb bay.

"Pilot to co-pilot," he said into the intercom. "Henry, drop those bombs and get out of there. Everybody else prepare for bail-out. Check your chutes and make sure you have your bail-out kits."

The bail-out kit included a compass, a rubber map of the area being flown over, a water container and water purification tablets, as well as concentrated chocolates and Benzedrine tablets for shock.

"Pilot to co-pilot," Joe said. "Henry, what's going on? Are those bombs hung up?"

There was no answer.

"Pilot to co-pilot. Henry, are you there?"

Still no answer. The powerful fuel fumes in the air made Joe suspect that two things had happened simultaneously. The oxygen supply lines had been severed by the hit amidships, and the ruptured fuel line was filling the air with deadly fumes. The crew could not breathe.

He looked at the altimeter. Since the hit the plane had already lost five thousand feet. There was no question of trying to reach friendly territory, much less get home. They would have to go down right here, and take their chances as prisoners of war in the heart of Germany. The priority was to bail out and stay alive.

The fuselage began to shake. The plane was losing stability. At any moment one of those wings might snap.

"Pilot to crew," Joe said into the intercom. "Bail out. Repeat, bail out."

The tattered formation was turning for home. Burning forts were circling out of control. The German fighters were everywhere, their cannons and rockets bursting wildly in the blue sky. It was a terrifying sight to behold.

Even as Joe was thinking this thought, a burst of German 20-mm cannon fire crashed into the cockpit, and a feeling somewhat like the blow of a giant fist struck him somewhere in his pelvis. He was hit, and hit hard.

He tried to speak into the intercom, but could not seem to find breath. He did not know whether this was because of the gas fumes in the air or because of the hit he had taken.

"Pilot to crew," he managed to whisper into the intercom. "Do you read me? Who's still on board?"

There was no answer. Those crew members who had not bailed out were either dead, wounded, or overcome by the poisonous fumes filling the plane.

Joe looked at the controls. The plane was down to six thousand feet and losing altitude fast. Engine One was on fire, and the wing was vibrating badly. There was no time to feather, no time to fight for control. No time to do anything but get out.

Joe thought of Henry. Why had he not answered in all this time?

Despite the wave of pain building in his hip and pelvis, Joe unbuckled his seat belt, pulled on his chute, and headed back to look for Henry. He might still be alive in the bomb bay. If he was, they could bail out together.

Joe grabbed his walkaround oxygen bottle—good for about four minutes at the most—and a bail-out kit, and left the cockpit, setting the wheel and throttle. The pain in his hip made him grunt. He noticed that his uniform was drenched in blood, and looked away.

Gritting his teeth, he dragged himself into the bomb bay. The air was filled with droplets of gasoline. The bombardier was dead. Henry was unconscious, his arm still curled over the bomb shackle release.

Wincing at the pain in his hip and pelvis, Joe grabbed Henry and yanked him upright. Then he released all the bombs. The ship lurched upward. The decrease in weight might allow them a few more seconds of altitude, enough to bail out safely.

There was no more time to worry about the rest of the crew. The plane was beginning the low, swooping circular dive characteristic of B-17s that are out of control. There was no chance of saving it. Joe could only hope that those crew members who were still alive had consciousness enough to pull their D-rings and save their lives.

Joe looked at Henry. Henry's face inside his helmet had the innocence of a slumbering baby. But his color was not good. His skin was turning dark from lack of oxygen. Joe grasped him, checking his chute, and took hold of his D-ring. Few maneuvers were more dangerous than helping an unconscious man out of an aircraft. When the slipstream hit both men, their bodies could kill each other, so great was the force of the wind. And when the D-ring was pulled, they could get caught in each other's chutes, with certain death resulting.

"Okay, Henry," Joe murmured. "Don't worry about a thing. We're getting out of here."

He grabbed Henry tight, stood on the catwalk above the bomb-bay doors, and looked down. The plane had lost so much altitude that he could see the crops in the farm fields below.

Grasping Henry hard, he dropped forward through the bomb bay.

•   •   •

Kate was in the grip of a terrible nightmare.

She saw Joe in his plane, hurtling toward the ground. The plane had been hit, or had exploded. It was turning around and around, almost like a toy. She could see through Joe's eyes. The mountains were flinging around and around, the sun shining brightly.

There was violence everywhere. It seemed that in that instant the world was coming to an end. But Joe seemed indifferent to all this. His eyes were glazed and he was glancing over his shoulder, calm as death, watching it all happen without making a move to save himself. There was someone close beside him, a faceless person who did not make a sound.

Kate thrashed in the bed, little muted cries of anguish escaping her lips. It seemed that death had taken Joe into its arms like a mother, paralyzing his will so that he could not fight back. His expression was dazed, indifferent, like a man who has just been awakened from a pleasant sleep and is wondering what time it is.

This indifference was the most horrible thing about the dream. Kate called out madly, trying to wake Joe up, to tell him he was going to die unless he fought back. But it was useless. He plummeted toward the earth, turning around and around, the smell of burning gasoline all around him.

Kate woke up screaming. She realized there was more to her distress than the horror of the nightmare. She felt an intense pain in her pelvis. As she got up from the bed she felt blood flowing down her legs and a terrible grinding of cramps deep inside her.

By the time she got to the bathroom she knew she was having a miscarriage.

• • •

Joe held Henry with all his strength as the uprush caught them both. Then he pulled Henry's D-ring and let go quickly as the chute jerked Henry high into the sky above him.

Joe looked down as he fell. He could not be more than seven or eight hundred feet above the ground. He pulled his D-ring and heard the lines sliding as the canopy caught the air.

The jerk of the chute sent a wave of pain through his hip. He could feel blood coursing down the uniform between his legs. Then, for a long interval, he floated, lazy as a drifting gull, watching the land inch up toward him as planes fought with each other in the sky. The gasoline, the flames, the handful of parachutes, the diving fighters and falling bombers, all had an absurd and childish look. It was hard to believe that the best thing men could think to do with this beautiful azure sky was to fill it with flames and screaming soldiers.

Damn, he thought, recalling Henry's sweet young face in unconsciousness.

He cursed the war, the Germans, the planes, the indifferent sky.

"Damn, damn, damn."

He went on cursing until the ground rose up to meet him.

There was a sharp smack of impact in his legs, then through the ruined middle of his body and up his back as he crumpled to the ground.

The chute came down around him, but he was too weak to gather it in. He must have lost a lot of blood, he realized. He lay on his back, staring up at the sky filled with planes and parachutes, all of which now had a strange, faraway look.

He was on the verge of losing consciousness when the Germans arrived. They were in a jeep. He heard their voices.

They came close. He saw the familiar helmets, the faces preoccupied by the air battle going on overhead.

Their machine guns were aimed at him. They quickly saw that he was no danger to them. One of them said something that made the others smile.

Joe was gazing at them calmly, almost as though they were friends. Loss of blood was sapping what was left of his lucidity. Nothing seemed quite real.

The German who had spoken was a sergeant, at least ten years older than the others. He looked down at Joe.

"Du hast dich verletzt," he said as he saw the blood-soaked section of Joe's uniform at the right side of his hip. A slow smile curled his lips.

The German raised his combat boot and stepped on the shattered hip with all his weight. Joe cried out, an animal bellow of agony that roared from his lungs with a force he had not imagined himself capable of.

Before the pain drove him into unconsciousness he saw the Germans dragging Henry Upchurch's dead body toward him.

BOOK

FOUR

BOOK

FOUR

1

Two Years Later

Daily Variety, April 18, 1946

MR. AND MRS. KNIGHT TO RIDE AGAIN

The day is here.

Joseph Knight and his wife, Katherine Hamilton, who made box-office history four years ago with *The Velvet Web,* are working on a new film.

This is big news in Hollywood, because Kate Hamilton has not worked since she became an overnight legend through her amazingly powerful performance in *Web.* The actress's only public activity has been speaking tours for war bonds and several USO appearances in Europe and the Pacific, where her pinup figure is a popular item among the troops.

As for Joseph Knight, who received the Purple Heart and the Distinguished Service Cross for his bravery as a pilot over Europe, he has been slowly recuperating from serious wounds to the back, hip, and pelvis, and from the aftereffects of eleven months in a German POW camp. Knight is reported to be progressing steadily toward renewed health, though the combined effects of his shattered hip and pelvic wounds have left him in constant pain.

Knight held a press conference at Oscar Freund's Monarch Pictures to describe his new property, which he himself has scripted during his convalescence and will direct as well as produce.

"I wanted to write a picture about the war," he said. "And I wanted Kate to be the star. But both things posed challenges. I wasn't sure I could be objective about the war so soon after coming home. And I wasn't sure I could be objective, as a filmmaker, about Kate. I've worked very hard on this scenario, and I'm excited about it."

The script is reportedly about the effect of the war on the love life of a typical American girl. When the man she loves goes off to war, she assumes that if he returns safe they will be able to take up their life where they left off. But Knight's canny scenario shows what many Americans are now learning—that life after the war often cannot be what it was before.

As for Kate Hamilton, she expressed joy and anticipation at the prospect of working with husband Joe again. "I've seen him spend twelve hours a day on this script for nearly a year," she said. "When he finally showed it to me, I was thrilled. It's going to be a privilege to work with him again. I love him as a man, and I respect him equally as a filmmaker."

The film reportedly has a juicy role for the hero—expected to be played by Samuel Raines—and a very special supporting role for another actress. We predict that every female in Hollywood will be after that role with a vengeance. Good hunting, ladies.

Bryant Hayes closed the copy of *Variety* and sat back to stare at the sloping lawn of his Bel Air mansion.

Hayes was not a happy man. And the return of Joseph Knight to filmmaking, at this particular time and with this particular property, was not good news for Hayes or for Continental Pictures.

Hayes had been hurt badly by *The Velvet Web* four years

ago. Gambling that Joseph Knight had blundered by replacing the polished Eve Sinclair with an amateur, Hayes had run his best film of the year—a lavish costume drama in the classic Continental style—against *Web*. He had taken a bath at the box office, because Joseph Knight, like a magician pulling a rabbit from a hat, somehow turned *Web* into a classic and in the process launched Kate Hamilton as a great star. It was a wildly improbable turn of events, but it had happened, and *Web* had won eight Oscars, once again making Bryant Hayes and Continental Pictures look foolish.

At the time Hayes had cursed Knight, recalling the debacle of Continental's *Winter of Destiny* against Knight's first hit, *The Rainbow's End*. Now Knight had done it to him again. Hayes had almost prayed aloud that Knight would not return from the war alive. He did not want to have to compete with him again. Knight was like a jinx to Hayes.

The war years had not been kind to Continental Pictures. The studio had tried to muddle through them by making a series of inexpensive war movies to go along with some family films and musicals. None of the films had won awards, and few had made money. Continental's prestige, never restored since the *Winter of Destiny* debacle, was at a low ebb.

This year Hayes and his top writers had concocted a big new film, a romantic adventure entitled *Tides of Fortune*. Hayes had decided to pull out all the stops, overloading *Tides of Fortune* with big-name stars, a high-profile director, and expensive action sequences. With this film Continental hoped to start the postwar era with a bang and recapture its past glory.

But now Joseph Knight was back in the fray. And every time Knight made a film, it seemed to hurt Continental Pictures and Bryant Hayes.

As Hayes was thinking this, the phone rang. It was New York.

"Bryant, how are you? This is Arnold."

It was Arnold Speck, the last voice in the world Hayes wanted to hear just now.

"Hello, Arnold."

"Have you seen the papers?"

"Yes, I have, Arnold. In reference to what?"

"To Joe Knight."

There was a pause. Hayes already knew why Speck was calling. Speck never called unless it was to torment Hayes with pressure over money.

"I'm just thinking about our balance of payments for this year," Speck said. "We're pretty much overextended on *Tides of Fortune*. I'd hate to see us lose money on that one."

Hayes sighed. If *Tides of Fortune* was upstaged by Knight's new opus and lost money, it could be the last nail in the coffin for Bryant Hayes as president of Continental Pictures.

"I don't think there's any cause for alarm, Arnold," Hayes said. *"Tides of Fortune* is going to be a big winner. I can feel it in my bones. This Knight project is nothing to worry about. He can't possibly get it finished in time for Christmas distribution. And even if he does, we'll knock him out of the water. I feel sure of it."

"But can you *make* sure?" That was Speck's classic ultimatum.

Hayes sighed.

"Nothing is for sure, Arnold," he said. "You know that. All we can do is our best. We have a great film. It should make us a lot of money."

There was a silence, pregnant with menace. This was another of Speck's favorite tricks, the ominous silence.

"Well, as you say, Bryant," he said at last, "nothing is sure. Not in this business."

You mean my job. That was what Hayes heard in Speck's oily voice. This call was an ultimatum. Either make sure that Joseph Knight's new picture did not have a negative impact on Continental's yearly gross—or this could be the end for Bryant Hayes as head of the studio.

For five long years, ever since the disaster of *Winter of Destiny*, Bryant Hayes had been teetering on this tightrope, constantly prodded and tormented by Speck, whose influence with the board in New York had increased in proportion as Hayes's power in Hollywood had waned. Now

Speck was turning the screws tighter. Hayes was beginning his final battle. His weapon was *Tides of Fortune*. His adversaries were Joe Knight, with his creative powers and his commercial genius, and Kate Hamilton, with her huge box-office appeal.

There was no tomorrow.

"Don't worry, Arnold," Hayes said weakly. "We'll beat them. I'll find a way."

"I'm glad to hear you say that, Bryant," said Speck. "But actions speak louder than words."

"I really think . . ." Before Hayes could say another word he realized that Speck had hung up.

Furious, Bryant Hayes slammed down the phone.

The moment of truth had come. He *had* to find a way to get around Knight—and this year.

But how?

He had done everything humanly possible to bring the studio back in the four years since *The Velvet Web* made Kate Hamilton a star.

And he had anticipated this moment and tried to find weapons to use against Knight and his wife when the time came.

So far he had failed.

Since Knight went off to the war Hayes had had detectives watch Kate Knight's every move. Their reports had been depressing. During Joseph Knight's four-year absence his wife had lived like a nun, staying in her Benedict Canyon house when she was not doing war work and seeing only a small group of friends that included Oscar Freund and a few others from Monarch Studios. She also had a lot of lunches and walks in the hills with an unlikely friend, a washed-up Hollywood writer named Norman Webb.

Since Knight's return from the war Kate had devoted herself tirelessly to his convalescence, staying by his side religiously. Neither now nor during his absence had there been the slightest hint of infidelity on her part. She was a model wife—an almost extinct creature in Hollywood.

Today the Knights' lives were exemplary. They lived like a quiet married couple in a very ordinary house in the hills. Neither of them went to parties, played around, or used drugs or alcohol. They completely contradicted the Hollywood style.

But now the stakes were higher. Hayes had to find something, some way to hurt Knight, to throw a monkey wrench into his plans for another big movie. He had ordered the detectives to redouble their efforts, and to investigate every person connected with the Knights, no matter how remotely, in search of a weak link that could be used against them.

Hayes could only hope for the best. There had been no mistaking the finality in Speck's voice on the phone just now, or the menace in the way Speck had hung up on him. Speck smelled blood. Indeed, Speck was probably hoping that Continental's *Tides of Fortune* would bomb out against Knight's new picture, so that he could finish Hayes once and for all.

Bryant Hayes's whole career was on the line. Hollywood was not big enough for him and Joseph Knight together. Arnold Speck had made that clear. Hayes must either defeat Knight this time around, or lose his livelihood.

There was no middle ground.

* * *

As for Kate Knight, she now knew a new kind of happiness, far different from the hectic joy she had experienced during her whirlwind romance with Joe Knight but, in its own way, no less beautiful.

The first thing she had noticed about Joe upon his return was how thin he was. He did not look like the same man she had married. He seemed very tall, emaciated, and somehow inward. The Joe Knight she had known had been built like a professional athlete, his height belied by the massive force of his thickly muscled body, his eyes sharply focused on the outer world. Now his vision seemed directed within, where a mysterious pain occupied him.

In fact, Joe was badly wounded. His hip had been shattered by shrapnel, and he had received only the most cursory treatment at the POW camp in Germany. In the first month after his return he had a massive and complicated hip operation. Four months later another surgery followed.

Since the operations he remained in intense pain. He had to take large gray pills three times a day, and despite their obvious chemical power his eyes still bore the expression of a man in physical distress.

But he would not admit to Kate that he was in pain. "A little stiffness," he said, "on rainy days. Like any other veteran," he added with a smile.

Nor would he talk about his eleven months in the POW camp under Nazi supervision. "It was mostly boredom," he said. "The only thing about it that really got me down was being away from you."

He was infuriated by the surgery, because it prevented him from making love to Kate. Like any red-blooded man, he wanted to make up for lost time with his beautiful young wife.

But there was something deeper. It was as though, having looked death in the face in Germany, Joe now realized he was not immortal, that there were dark forces in the world more powerful than his own strength. He must use the time he had with Kate wisely, for it was not perhaps unlimited, as he had taken for granted when he first met and married her.

When at last he was able to make love to Kate, she could feel that he needed her more. It was obvious that missing her had been a wound as serious as any other he had suffered.

There was a new intimacy in his caresses, not less exciting than before he left for the war, but different. Where once he had swept Kate off her feet and taken her to sensual extremities that had left her numbed with pleasure, now he seemed to be probing for something more spiritual within her, and giving something more of himself than before. It was as though there were more mortality in his lovemaking now than before. As though death, once a remote thing banished by his love, had now come forward as a part of life he could not ignore, and added its strange dark luster to his love.

This did not alarm Kate, for she soon realized that all Joe had suffered had not in any way diminished his love for her. And in salving his pain with her body as well as her love, Kate felt more truly married to him now. She had been his wife for only two short months when he first left her. Now she could feel something eternal, an almost cosmic connection, binding him to her.

During his convalescence he seemed to doubt himself in ways he would not avow to her. The draining weight of his pain, combined with his inability to make love to her, cast a shadow over his personality. The Hollywood gossip mill made things worse, for it was full of rumors to the effect that Joe's wounds had sapped his creative energy and effectively ended his career as a major filmmaker.

Perhaps for this reason, Joe threw himself into his new screenplay with an almost obsessive concentration. Day after day, week in and week out, he divided his time between long hours at the typewriter and silent intervals spent alone in the back yard of his house, staring at the hills as he struggled mentally with the problems posed by his new project.

Kate respected his privacy during this delicate time, for she knew he was struggling with himself as much as with the new film. When he got up from his typewriter one sunny morning to tell her the screenplay was finished, she could see in his eyes that it was a success.

She was the first to read it, and realized instantly that his confidence was more than justified. It was a magnificent screenplay. In describing the separation of two young lovers by the war, and the unforeseeable future that follows—a future with tragic effects—Joe's story said something essential about war, and about the peculiar intimacy of love and violence.

When Joe told Kate that he had written the female lead for her, she was alarmed. She had not been before a camera in more than four years. And prior to *The Velvet Web* she had been a mere beginner. It seemed as though her one experience as an actress had been as fleeting as her first weeks of marriage to Joe, before the war had separated them.

But she knew she could not say no to Joe. Writing the screenplay had brought him more than halfway back to life. The rest was up to the film itself—and to her. If he thought she possessed the skill and depth as an actress to bring off the new role, she would give it her best for his sake.

In no time her own excitement over the project had eclipsed her worries, and she was anxious for the challenge of going before the cameras. Just as Joe was coming back to life as a professional, so must Kate herself.

Joe's war was over, as was Kate's. They were together at last. It was time to live again.

• • •

In a small café, unnoticed by the other customers, a man sat reading the item in *Daily Variety* about Joseph Knight's new film. The item was accompanied by a photo of Knight with Kate Hamilton.

Traffic streaked by soundlessly behind the window of the café. A cup of coffee sat before him, along with a half-eaten doughnut. His forgotten cigarette smoldered in the bent metal ashtray on the counter.

He nodded as he read the part about Knight's war wounds. He knew what that was like, for he had wounds himself, a souvenir of Guadalcanal. He was a veteran, too.

Now he looked at what Kate had told the reporters.

"I love him as a man, and I respect him equally as a filmmaker . . ."

The man smiled, curling his lip ironically.

So you've got it all, don't you, babe? he thought. *Your man is back and your career is ready to take off again. Good for you . . .*

He had watched Kate's rise to stardom with interest four years ago. He had seen her in *The Velvet Web* a dozen times, shaking his head in appreciation of her talent and that of her new husband.

But he had not made a move. He had waited to see where her career would go next. He did not want to act until she was an established star, a great celebrity.

Then the war had come and forced him to delay his plans. He had served four years in the Marines, hard, frightening years. He had come back from the war tempered by violence and ready for anything.

Ready for Kate . . .

He took a last look at her beautiful face in the tabloid's

photograph. How glamorous she looked! How bigger-than-life . . . But Hollywood did that to people. She was still just Kate.

Still his wife.

It's time, Katie girl. Here I come.

Throwing a dime on the counter for the waitress, Quentin Flowers got up and left his cigarette burning in the ashtray. He walked to the door of the café, pushed it open, and strolled out into the sun on Santa Monica Boulevard, Hollywood, California.

EVE SINCLAIR AWOKE ALONE.

The room around her was in shadow. She did not know whether it was night or day. Her mind was a blank, emptied of all memory by the alcohol she had consumed last night and more so by the life she had led for the last four years. A life whose ugly colors were painted by liquor, by drugs, by faceless, anonymous men, and by the nightmare thoughts that had driven her a million miles from her once-proud self.

She was lying on the couch in the living room of her Malibu house. She could hear the waves booming outside, ceaseless and sinister. Her eyes opened with a pained flutter. For a moment she stared before her like a dumb animal at the dawn of time, looking at the darkness as at a thing completely obscure, completely senseless.

Then she came to herself enough to know who she was.

Her confusion gave way to loathing. The world unveiled its familiar face, hideous and hopeless. The crushing headache brought by her hangover came to eclipse the cottony dullness in her senses.

She got up and staggered to the bathroom, bumping into chairs, couches, and tables littered with half-empty liquor glasses on her way. She opened the medicine cabinet without turning on the bathroom light and took four aspirin. The fresh tap water tasted like the bottom of a muddy pool, so jaded were her taste buds.

Still without looking in the mirror—her face was a sight that had become less and less bearable to behold in the past few years—she stood waiting to see if she would be able to keep the aspirin down.

To her pleasant surprise, her stomach accepted them. She pondered only for a moment before adding a Benzedrine to the chemical mix inside her. Then she swallowed some antacid and shuffled to the kitchen.

The place was a mess. She had kept the maid away for most of the last week, preferring to do her drinking in peace. Her fingers trembled uncooperatively as she spooned coffee grounds into the percolator, poured in the water, and turned it on. She managed to throw away a few of the beer and liquor bottles and scraps of food littering the counters. Then, her strength depleted, she returned to the living room to smoke a cigarette and wait for the coffee to perk and the Benzedrine to take effect.

She looked around the place with an eye practiced by her own dissipation. She honestly could not recall whether a man had been here with her last night or not. There were signs that more than one drinker had been present. There were cigarette butts of more than one brand. Pillows were tumbled here and there on the sofas. Had she perhaps shared her flesh with a stranger on the big couch before the fireplace? Or even on the floor?

She did not know. If there had been someone, he was gone. Whoever he was.

A shudder of loneliness went through Eve at this thought. For an instant she felt small and scared. She was like a little girl inside a woman's body, crying out soundlessly for a comfort she could not have, as she watched the smoke drift upward from the cigarette in the adult fingers that did not belong to her.

The fingers were shaking now, so violently that Eve reached for the nearest bottle, poured a shot of what turned out to be scotch, and drank it at a gulp. She closed her eyes and felt the liquor scorch her insides. Her physical pain was intense. But it was nothing compared to the mental pain her many drugs were intended to keep at bay.

She sat on her couch, listening to the relentless thump of the surf and waiting for the shakes to subside. She entered into her regular morning discipline: the effort not to think, not to remember.

In the last four years Eve Sinclair had lost the stardom she had won at so high a price, and plummeted to complete oblivion. The Hollywood nightmare that had consumed so many of her friends and enemies over the years had overtaken her at last. She was washed up.

Thanks to Joseph Knight, and thanks to *The Velvet Web*.

Knight's film had won eight Academy Awards, including Best Picture. He himself had won an Oscar as Best Director.

Kate Hamilton, the ingenue who had taken over the starring role from Eve—and married Joseph Knight—had won the Oscar for Best Actress.

In the chorus of adulation for that film, and for Knight and Kate—who was hailed as one of the great film actresses in the world after only one performance—Eve Sinclair was forgotten. Her tantrums on the set of the film, and her firing by Joseph Knight, were ancient history, eclipsed by the glory of Knight and his new wife, his new star.

No one in Hollywood thought to remember Eve Sinclair after Kate took her place. So no one besides Eve's agent or Eve herself noticed that all her roles dried up almost from the day Joseph Knight fired her off *The Velvet Web*.

Her own studio decided that she no longer existed. There were no scripts for her to read. Each day her studio mailbox was empty. None of the studio brass would answer her calls. She stopped being invited to even the most unimportant parties.

The silence of the phone was deafening. As those first hellish weeks passed, Eve realized the enormity of her predicament. Not only had her childish and destructive behavior on Joseph Knight's set hurt her reputation, but something more fundamental had occurred. Kate Hamilton, in her powerful performance in the finished film, had inaugurated a new image for leading ladies, a new style. It was an earthy, sensual image, tragic and profound, and it captured the public imagination instantly. In doing so it completely eclipsed Eve Sinclair's sleek, somewhat shallow image and made her an instant relic.

Almost overnight, Eve Sinclair was finished. The public, notorious for its fickleness and its short memory, quickly forgot her. The studios did not need her. They had plenty of other actresses, younger actresses, supple young stars whom they could try to mold into a look that would steal some of Kate Hamilton's glory.

It was as though Eve Sinclair had never existed.

On the basis of herculean efforts at fence-mending by her agent, her studio eventually offered her four "B" pictures in a row. Potboilers, cops-and-robbers melodramas, westerns, even a cheap musical. Eve refused them all. She knew that her appearance in a "B" picture would be the end of her career as a major star. She had to wait out the storm, and try to come out a winner somehow.

After the four "B" offers, there were no more. Eve was out in the cold, unbankable, finished.

She had fallen from the Top Ten Box-Office list within weeks of her firing by Joseph Knight. She knew she would never get back on it.

And all because of Joseph Knight—and Kate Hamilton.

During the first months after the disaster Eve had spent long hours in this room plotting ways to recoup her losses. She had thought of every studio executive or star who owed her a favor. She had thought of every angle, every dubious, dishonest, even scurrilous thing she could do to regain even a small part of what she had lost.

But it was no use. All her finely honed weapons were useless to her now. There were no producers to seduce, no aspiring directors to entice into her corner, no brilliant writers to offer favors to in return for tailoring a new script to her talents. Hollywood had turned its collective back on her.

And all because of the improbable and somehow crazy fact that Joseph Knight had come along to put his poison into her heart, to weaken her iron control over her own career for one disastrous and irremediable moment.

As the truth sank in at last, Eve began to drink. She realized that alcohol was a precious antidote for the unbearable pain assailing her at every moment, the despair boiling up inside her veins.

Soon she had begun mixing other drugs with the liquor, and finding to her pleasure that the shroud between herself and reality grew thicker. She stopped thinking about her career. She began thinking of how to kill each day until nightfall.

She found new companions. Perverse, lowlife companions to drink with, to sleep with. She barely remembered their faces afterward. At least she did not have to worry about running into them at a party some day. She wasn't invited to parties any more.

They weren't really here at all, those companions, with their boozy breath, their insincere voices, their hands and cocks and tongues. Eve was alone.

That was the essence of her torture—she was completely alone on earth. It had been a condition she accepted pridefully in the old days, when she was a success. But now that she was a failure, a has-been, solitude was an agony. There was no one in the world to care about her. No one to notice her pain, her despair, and to try to comfort her out of simple human kindness . . .

For once Eve missed her mother. Or rather, the idea of a mother. Not the grasping, selfish creature who had helped her launch her career so many years ago, but a real mother, to take care of her, enfold her in her arms and dry her tears.

But no. There was no one.

So the bottle became her only companion. And this ambiguous darkness, neither day nor night, this shroud that separated her from the waves, the shore, the people of the earth—this was her only element.

An element that made it possible not to look at her face in the mirror, not to think of the past that was lost, or the future that would never be.

She was still rocking on the edge of her seat, waiting for the headache to abate, when the phone rang.

She staggered across the room and picked it up. It was her agent.

"How are you, Evie?" he asked. She smiled bitterly to hear the discomfort in his voice. He knew how low she was. He avoided calling her as much as possible, because he did not want to be a witness to her hopelessness.

The handful of radio shows and publicity appearances he had managed to get her in the past two years—dates he had to scrounge himself, since her studio's publicity department would no longer acknowledge her existence, much less do something for her on its own—had come to nothing. At first she had refused them. Then, when she accepted a few, her disintegration was so obvious that everyone concerned knew she would have been better off not to have attempted them.

In the last six months, there had been nothing at all.

But today he had some news for her.

"Listen, Evie," he said. "I've got something that could be very, very big for you. Very big. But you're going to have to have an open mind about it. This is no time for egos. You've got to think of the future. This could be the start of something big, a whole new career, if you play your cards right."

"What is it?" Eve asked hoarsely.

"I have a script here," he said. "I've just finished reading it. It has a part in it that's perfect for you. More than perfect, in fact. I don't think there's anybody alive who could play this role as you could—if you put your mind to it."

Eve stood swaying in the darkened living room, holding her head and listening to the throbbing inside her brain.

"What kind of part?" she asked, trying to hide the tremor in her voice.

"You'll see. I'll send it right over," Freddy said. "You won't believe your eyes."

"Who offered it?" she asked.

"Well, it's a little more complicated than that," Freddy replied uncomfortably. "It's not exactly an offer. They haven't cast it yet, you see. But I have it on good authority that they would be very, very interested in seeing you test for it."

"Test for it?" Eve cried, hurting her headache with her own vehemence. "You want me to test for it? Who do you think I am, Freddy? Eve Sinclair doesn't do screen tests."

There was a pause. Freddy's silence was eloquent. He was waiting for Eve to face facts. Her days as a star were over. It was time to look for work wherever it presented itself.

"I'm sorry, kid," Freddy said. "That's the best I can do. As a matter of fact, they're afraid to offer it to you outright, because they think you'll refuse out of hand."

He was lying—no one had even thought of Eve for the part—but he hoped his lie would shake her from her lethargy.

"Who . . . who are you talking about?" Eve asked.

"Well . . . It's the new film by Joe Knight," he said.

Eve turned pale. Her hands began to shake.

A new film by Knight! And he was interested in her for the lead! Could it be? Could Knight have some crazy idea of resurrecting her career, the career he had personally destroyed?

"You've got to be kidding," she said. She managed a smile. "Wouldn't that be a plum for the gossip press? *Eve Sinclair to star in Joseph Knight's new film . . .*" Despite her irony she was getting very excited. Her fingers were cold as she held the receiver.

There was an uncomfortable silence on the line.

"Well, honey," Freddy said, "it's not exactly the lead."

Eve's face fell. She went from excitement to depression

in one instant. What sort of humiliation were they planning to subject her to? Was there no end to her torment at the hands of Knight?

On the other end of the phone Freddy was biting his lip in consternation. He had hoped Eve would have heard already that Kate Hamilton was to play the lead in the new Knight film. But now he realized that Eve had not heard, no doubt because she had stopped reading the trade papers, and because no one close to her would have dared mention the news about Kate Hamilton's new triumph.

"Who's starring?" Eve asked.

"Well, Kate Hamilton will be starring," Freddy said. "But, honey, you've got to believe me. This supporting role is even better than the female lead. It's a great, great role. Believe me."

"And they're not offering me the role?" she asked. "They're offering me a test?"

"Well . . ." Freddy said. "They're not exactly offering it. But I can get it. I'm positive I can get it. Once they see it as I see it . . . I mean, no one could do it the way you could . . ."

Eve felt the room wheel around her. She thought she was going to faint. How, she wondered, could her proud existence have been reduced to this degradation? They weren't even offering her a test. Freddy had simply got his hands on the script and thought she might do well in a test, if he went to Knight and his minions on his knees to get it for her.

What a joke! Just a few years ago Eve Sinclair had been at the pinnacle of Hollywood. And today she was reduced to going on her knees to the very man who had toppled her from that pinnacle, to beg him to test her for a supporting role in the picture that starred the girl who had replaced Eve four years ago and helped ruin her career!

Eve was reaching for the scotch bottle. There was no glass handy. She would have to drink right out of the bottle.

But she hesitated.

The wheels turned inside her mind, rusty but still efficient. She had been in bad spots before in her career and had used the cunning of a criminal as well as the talent of a star to save herself.

She had never been this low before. Until this instant she had been sure she was finished.

But here was a chance. And Eve Sinclair had spent twenty years learning never to let a chance pass her by. She was no longer the woman or the star she had once been. But she was still Eve Sinclair. She was a fighter, and a talented actress.

She put down the bottle.

"You have the script in hand?" she said into the phone.

"Right here, honey. Wait till you . . ."

"Send it over now," she said. "By messenger. I want it here in twenty minutes."

She did not hear Freddy's bubbling response. Slowly she hung up the phone.

She saw how crucial this opportunity was. But more importantly, she saw its poetic justice. The fine ironic hand of destiny was making her path cross that of Joseph Knight one more time. Knight was the man who had ruined her. Now she had a chance to work with him again, and perhaps to save herself through him. For good or ill, this chance was no accident. Fate was taking a hand.

Opportunity was knocking, perhaps for the last time. Eve would open the door.

JOSEPH KNIGHT WAS WAITING, ALONG WITH KATE AND EXEC-
utive producer Larry Walsh, when Eve arrived punctually
at eight o'clock in the morning for her screen test.

A lot of the people present had expected fireworks this
morning. Few could believe that Joseph Knight had asked
Eve Sinclair to test for a role in his new picture. He had
fired her from his last one after she had put on one of the
worst displays of on-set behavior in the history of Hollywood. That firing had led to the annihilation of Eve's career
and a tailspin in her personal life, while leading to an almost
legendary stardom for Kate Hamilton.

And Kate was to star in this picture, while Eve, if her
test was successful, would play the first supporting role of
her adult acting career.

During her starring years Eve would never have consented even to read a script for a supporting role. And even
now it almost defied reason to think that she would consider playing a supporting role in a picture that starred her
nemesis, Kate Hamilton.

So everything was in place for the explosion of the year.
The casting director, stagehands, and light and sound men
were on tenterhooks, as was the handful of observers from
the production team. Even Joseph Knight, Larry Walsh,
and Kate herself were unsure what to expect.

As it turned out, their worry was unnecessary.

Eve slipped onto the sound stage quietly and humbly, almost like an extra or a bit player waiting to be told what to do. She was dressed in a raincoat and scarf. When she took off her dark glasses it was obvious what the alcohol and drugs she had been using these past years had done to her face. The fresh glow of youth that had long been her trademark was gone. She looked used, almost battered.

But there was something determined and honest about her expression that impressed everyone on the set. She seemed to realize that the supporting role Joseph Knight had created was, in its way, a plum for her, and a challenge. It would not resurrect her career as a leading lady, of course. That was gone forever. But it offered her a last chance to show that she was a professional and still had a future ahead of her. On the heels of her long career in Hollywood, starting when she was just a child, here was a last symbolic battle to fight, a last hill to climb.

She walked straight up to Joseph Knight and held out her hand.

"You don't owe me this," she said. "I know how big a favor you're doing me. Thank you."

Joe shook her hand.

"It's not a favor," he said. "You've read the script. I need someone special in this role. I think you may be it."

"Call it what you like," Eve smiled. "I want you to know I'm grateful for the chance. I acted like a spoiled child on *The Velvet Web,* and I almost ruined your film. No actress has a right to behave that way. If you decide to use me this time, I'll be a big girl. I can promise you that."

She turned to Kate, and shook her hand as well.

"We've never really met," Eve said, "but I'm a great admirer of your work."

"The feeling is mutual," Kate said. She was about to add that she had adored Eve Sinclair throughout her childhood, but stopped herself in time. She did not want to remind Eve of the passage of the years, or of her past stardom. "You're a great actress, Miss Sinclair."

"Call me Eve." Eve smiled sadly. "I hope you don't

feel bad or embarrassed that you got your start by taking over from me in *The Velvet Web*. Believe me, you gave a lot more to that role than I ever could have—even at my best. You have a special quality that us mere mortals will never have. It shows up on the screen. I know you have a great career ahead of you. I'd like this chance to be a small part of it."

She laughed. "Isn't it ironic? Four years ago you were a small part of my film. Now I'm trying to be a small part of yours. The shoe is on the other foot. But I'll tell you something: that's where it belongs. Things are in their proper place now."

Kate did not know what to say. Such humility on the part of so great a star left her speechless. She watched Eve go to Makeup and pondered the odd fact that her childhood idol was crossing her path, not for the first time, or even the second, but for the third time—since Kate was counting the strange, almost enchanted night of the Oscars when she had seen Eve in the ladies' room mirror.

As Eve had herself made up she listened to Joseph Knight go over the role. If Joe had any reservations about being at close quarters with Eve, they were unnecessary. Eve listened intently and respectfully to his words.

"This role is very important," he said, "as you know from reading the script."

Eve nodded. The film was about the effect of the war on a young woman who falls in love with an impoverished young man of whom her family does not approve. Just when she has made her decision to give up her family for her love, the war intervenes, and her lover enlists in the army. She discovers after his departure that she is pregnant. She has his baby and holds out the hope that he will return to her. But when he does, a fatal intervention on the part of her best friend convinces the hero that the baby is someone else's, and he leaves without seeing his love. They never meet again. In retrospect, their goodbye at the train station as he left for the war was the last time they would ever see each other.

The role Eve was to play was that of the heroine's best friend, a friend who appears to abet the heroine's forbidden love while secretly falling in love with the young man herself, and who eventually separates them forever by preventing the hero from finding out that the heroine has his child and has been waiting faithfully for him since his departure.

"You're the heroine's best friend," Joseph Knight said. "But more than that, you're her virtual sister. You grew up with her. You've told each other everything—or almost everything—from the time when you were little girls. That includes boys and romance, of course. But now things change. When the hero enters the picture he puts a strain on this long-standing relationship. You begin to think about yourself, and you find that your own romantic needs conflict with those of the heroine. You have to hide this fact for all you're worth. This subterfuge is the essence of your character, and of your performance. A change has taken place inside you, and you have to hide that change, and make the heroine—and the audience—believe that you're just the same as always. The conflict is eating you up, but you have to hide that, too—until we're ready to let the audience in on it."

Eve listened carefully. She had read the script, and knew how pivotal her role as the best friend was. When the hero swept the heroine off her feet, no one realized that the best friend, Eve's role—named Susan in the script—had fallen for him as well.

The role of Susan was a classic one. Susan was a genuinely loyal and true friend to the heroine, until love came along to transform her heart and eclipse friendship. Her one lie to the hero changed the destinies of all the major characters and prevented the happy ending that was so close at hand when the hero returned from the war. Yet she could not do otherwise, because her love was too strong for her to resist.

Eve could feel Joseph Knight's excitement about the role as he described it to her.

"Throughout the film," he said, "you continually hide what's really motivating you. Even from yourself, because you can't face your own temptation to betray the heroine. But you're going to be dropping some very subtle clues as to your private conflict, so that when it is revealed, the viewer will see the poetic justice of it."

Eve nodded respectfully. She had read many a script in her time. She could recognize a great screenplay when she saw it. She knew that Joseph Knight had outdone himself in creating the role of Susan as a foil for his heroine. It was a stroke of genius.

But it was not a starring role.

Joseph Knight felt an impulse to smile as he compared Eve's obedience today with that of four years ago, when she had put on a sarcastic imitation of attentive obedience only to disobey his instructions as soon as the cameras started to roll.

But today something told him it would be different.

And it was.

What happened that morning on Sound Stage 7 at Monarch Pictures would never be forgotten in Hollywood.

Eve Sinclair emerged from her makeshift dressing room costumed and made up to look like an attractive but ordinary small-town girl. Everything about her expressed wholesomeness, simplicity, and a self-effacing good humor.

The makeup artistry that had been marshaled for ten years to make Eve look more sensual, more glamorous than she really was, now was used to the opposite effect, to make her look simple, friendly, and companionable.

A tremendous display of acting skill went into her performance before the cameras. She was sensational in every scene. With her friend the heroine—read by Kate—she was funny, endearing, natural. She expressed an intimacy born of long years of friendship, an intimacy that showed itself in a hundred little signs of affection and familiarity. With the hero, whose part was read by Joseph Knight, she was amiable and happy-go-lucky. Yet one could see from sidelong hints of almost unbelievable subtlety that she was not as indifferent to the hero as her overt behavior suggested. There was a sort of shadow behind all her gestures, a secret that peeked out like a musical grace note from her every smile and laugh.

It was an acting *tour de force* that left everyone on the

sound stage breathless. Not only was Eve's acting technique a phenomenon to behold, but so was the tragic halo she brought to her characterization of the best friend, a young woman who feels her own steadfast loyalty to the heroine slipping away under the irresistible force of her prohibited love for the hero.

A powerful chemistry soon made itself felt between Eve and Kate as they read their scenes together. Kate felt challenged as she had never been challenged before. Eve's performance brought out the best in her, and deepened her own understanding of her character.

By the end of the test, which took nearly two hours, Kate had made up her own mind. She took Joe aside and told him her opinion.

"I can't tell you what to do," she said. "But I think you've got to cast her. You've just got to. She will make your film great. And she'll make me a lot better than I ever would be without her. She's a genius. If only a little bit of that rubs off, I'll be the luckiest actress in the world."

Joe looked pleased. "I'll think over what you've said," he murmured.

When he had left Kate he went to join his director of photography, Wayne Prater.

"Joe," Wayne said, "Eve looks terrible. She's so dissolute. Her face looks like it's been through a dry cleaner."

Joe nodded. "I don't think that's a problem," he said. "She's a trouper. What she doesn't fix herself, Makeup can take care of. Besides, I like this somewhat weathered look. It fits her character. We don't want the girl to be a raving beauty. She's an ordinary girl."

Wayne went away shaking his head. He could see that Joe had made up his mind.

Larry Walsh, the executive producer, was even more negative about Eve.

"She'll be trouble in production," he warned. "She's never played a supporting role before. She's had the spotlight for twenty years. She'll crack up, Joe, I'm warning you. I know women like her. Once they come apart, you can't put them back together again. Eve Sinclair has been finished for four years. She's burnt out. You know she's been drinking. If you cast her you'll be asking for trouble."

Joseph Knight said nothing.

The casting director, Tom Gianos, was the last to speak to Joe.

"I have several other actresses lined up for today," he said hopefully. "Good ones. I think you should give them a chance, Joe."

Joseph Knight shook his head.

"Go through with the tests, for insurance," he said. "But I'm going to call Eve's agent right now and get a contract signed. She's our girl."

Joseph Knight had made up his mind. Kate's insistent support of Eve for the role of Susan had eliminated the last of his reservations. If Kate was so sure that Eve would be good for her own performance and for the film as a whole, then he would take a chance on her.

He had never been afraid of a gamble.

Eve was given the good news by Joseph Knight before she left the studio.

"We'll make it official later today or tomorrow," Joe said. "But as far as Kate and I are concerned, you're our Susan."

Eve's face lit up.

"Thank you," she said. "Thank you so much. You won't regret it, I promise you."

"I don't intend to," Joe smiled. "You were great today. I know you'll be great all the way down the line."

Kate shook Eve's hand warmly and congratulated her.

"I can hardly wait to start rehearsing," she said.

"Me, too," Eve agreed.

A few minutes later Eve was in a studio limousine, being driven home. The smog made her eyes smart, but she had never felt more clear-headed.

She had a lot of challenges ahead of her. But the biggest challenge was already behind.

She had got the job.

Today Eve Sinclair had put on the performance of her life.

May 16, 1946

NORMAN WEBB SAT IN THE BATTERED ARMCHAIR IN HIS Hollywood Flats bungalow, watching the smoke from his cigarette drift upward into the dusty air.

Behind the plume of smoke, as behind a screen, sat a man, a visitor. He was seated on the couch, his knees spread apart, twirling his fedora with dry, calm hands.

The visitor presented an oddly composite appearance. Though his clothes were flashy and lacking in taste, he carried himself with an impressive dignity. There was something balanced and even venerable about him.

But the look in his slate-gray eyes was not friendly.

"You asked for a week," he said, "and we gave you a week. Now, Mr. Webb, your week is up."

Norman puffed at his cigarette. There was a strange intimacy between the two men, as between old acquaintances. Though the visitor presented an obvious threat, Norman seemed familiar with it, so familiar that he was beyond normal fear. Fear was replaced by a sort of dissipation. Norman was almost comfortable with his enemy, as he was with his own weakness.

"One more week," Norman said. "I have some royalties coming in. I swear it. I can call my publisher."

The stranger shook his head with a smile.

"When will you guys learn?" he asked. "We are not in

the business of charity. We are in the business of lending money. People who welsh on us give the whole business a bad name. It can't be allowed, Mr. Webb. There comes a point at which push comes to shove. I don't want to see you get badly hurt. Now, you've had your fun at the track. You've got to pay the piper."

Norman looked more worried now.

"Three days," he said. "I'll call my publisher right now. While you're here. I know I can get the money."

The stranger stared at Norman. Though the look in his eyes was still dangerous, he seemed somewhat mollified by this latest proposal.

"So call," he said.

Stubbing out his cigarette, Norman reached for the phone. It rang before his hand touched it. He almost jumped at the strident noise. He was more nervous than he had realized.

He picked up the receiver.

"Hello?" he said.

There was a pause.

"Katie!" he exclaimed, the happiness in his voice accompanied by a sidelong glance at his companion. "What's new? Long time, no hear, sweetie."

Again a pause, Norman's eyes asking his visitor for patience while he listened to Kate.

"My goodness," he said, frowning. "Eve Sinclair? What in the world has got into Joe? She's washed up. Besides, she hates his guts. Or so I thought. Has Joe taken leave of his senses?"

He listened as Kate explained the situation. He began to nod as he heard her describe Eve's brilliant test for the new film. He could hear Kate's own excitement at the prospect of working with Eve.

"Well," he said, "it's the damnedest thing I ever heard. But if you think she'll work out, I'm happy for you. For Joe, too. Tell him I'll be cheering from the sidelines. How's he feeling, by the way?"

He listened, nodding. His eyes darted to his visitor as Kate asked how Norman himself was doing.

"Oh, fine, fine," he lied. "Just the usual routine. *Métro, boulot, dodo,* as they say in French. Between the track and my writing hobby, I keep rather busy." He glanced ironically at his visitor.

There was another pause.

"No, I can't make it, honey," Norman said. "I'd love to, but I have a couple of unsavory old acquaintances I have to entertain. I'll take a rain check, though. See you sometime later in the week. Keep in touch, all right?"

He hung up the phone.

The visitor was smiling at Norman.

"Why don't you ask her?" he said. "She's doing well for herself. She'll float a loan for an old friend like you, Mr. Webb."

Norman smiled sadly.

"It's obvious, my friend," he said, "that you have not read Proust. The two ways must never meet. That's basic material, pal."

Like all truly serious gamblers, Norman never allowed the tendrils of his secret life to touch his respectable friendships. He would no more have asked Kate or Joe to lend him money for a gambling debt than he would have asked them, had he been a homosexual or a pedophile, to make dates for him or help him seduce a child. His shame had to be kept private.

"You'll get your money, though," he said to the man on the couch. "You can count on that. I've always made out before. I will this time, too."

The man seemed skeptical.

"For your sake," he said, "I hope you do."

The look in his eyes sent an involuntary chill up Norman's spine. He had put these people off for a long time, wasting on them the ingenuity he should have been using all these years on writing. Now his bag of tricks was almost empty.

Unless he gave them what they wanted soon, he would have to pay for his sins with his own blood.

5

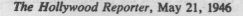

The Hollywood Reporter, May 21, 1946

EVE AND KATE MAKE MAGIC ON SET

Many observers expected prompt disaster from the improbable collaboration of Eve Sinclair and Kate Hamilton on Joseph Knight's new film, tentatively entitled *Farewell to Love*. After all, it was only four and a half years ago that Hamilton took over Sinclair's starring role in the now-legendary Knight film *The Velvet Web*, making herself into a great star on the ruins of Sinclair's career as a leading lady. Few could imagine these two actresses working together at all, much less joining forces on a film by Joseph Knight with Sinclair in her first supporting role ever.

But Hollywood is full of surprises. Though the set is closed, Monarch Pictures insiders tell us the Hamilton/Sinclair collaboration is not only running smoothly, but bringing brilliant results. *Farewell to Love,* an intense love story set against the background of the world war, shows all the signs of becoming another Joseph Knight classic.

If Knight knows a way to make two such different

stars work together so well under what can only be difficult circumstances, there are a hundred Hollywood directors who would like to know his secret.

In the meantime, we join the millions of movie fans who are waiting on the edge of their seats to see the finished film that Hamilton and Sinclair are making with their tempestuous common link, supermovieman Joseph Knight.

On the set of *Farewell to Love* at Monarch Pictures, Oscar Freund watched Kate Hamilton and Eve Sinclair as they shot one of their important early scenes in the new film.

The two women were dressed as small-town best friends easy in their companionship, and they acted the part perfectly. They were walking together in the scene, and gesturing languidly as they joked about the townspeople around them.

Even this relatively straightforward scene was remarkable, Oscar Freund noticed, for the subtlety of the dialogue and of the two young women's demeanor. The camera was close to them, tracking slowly as it followed their walk. Joseph Knight was crouched behind it with Wayne Prater, the cinematographer.

Oscar would be excited to see the rushes of this scene tomorrow. He was sitting too far away to get a good look at the actresses' faces. But he could feel the power of their performances, and the intense watchfulness of Joseph Knight's camera as it captured all the nuances of their eyes and voices.

Oscar Freund was impressed by what he was watching. He knew the public would stand in line to see this picture. Not only because it was the first Joseph Knight film since his return from the war, and Kate Hamilton's first film since *The Velvet Web*. It was also Eve Sinclair's first performance in a supporting role, opposite the very woman who had toppled her from her hard-won stardom four years ago. And it was—as the studio's publicity department unhesitatingly leaked to the trade press—a major statement about the war just won, and its effects on the lives of all Americans.

As a studio head Oscar Freund was full of excitement and anticipation. As a filmmaker he was in awe of Joseph Knight's talent, as Knight once again used his camera to bring out amazing depths in his actors. And he was thrilled by the performances of these two actresses—Kate, because of her extraordinary expressive power at so young an age, and Eve, because of her courage and flexibility in taking on a role so foreign to her previous career and playing it with such brilliance and conviction.

But as a man who had spent a lifetime in Hollywood and knew Hollywood people, Oscar Freund was deeply worried.

Something on that sound stage was not right. He could feel it in his bones.

Kate and Eve were working together *too* well, too smoothly. The film was progressing almost too easily. Each scene was falling into place automatically, as though the whole thing were a jigsaw puzzle that had tumbled from its box and fallen somehow into its finished form, all the pieces meshing together by a weird alchemy.

It was as though the fates wanted this film to be made for their own sinister purposes, and were facilitating every aspect of it, annihilating all the false starts, headaches, and aggravations that afflict every normal film.

Yes, it was all too good to be true.

And it seemed to Oscar that Eve Sinclair was at the center of this uncanny jelling of forces.

Eve was playing her character with an insight that defied description. In her finest starring performances she had never been this deep, this intuitive. And, in a thousand little ways, almost unnoticeable to others, she was feeding her own insights to Kate, helping Kate to outdo herself in the starring role of the girl who loses her great love to the war.

At the same time, Oscar had never seen an actress perform as self-effacingly as Eve. She seemed to want to pull her character in, to hide her deepest motivation from the camera, so that it was always Kate who stood out, Kate who took center stage with her innocence, her love, her sensuality and freshness.

Oscar Freund knew Hollywood actresses. They were all ego. Stealing scenes was their *raison d'être*. They did not willingly defer to other actresses as Eve was doing now.

Something about all this did not ring true.

Oscar knew that Eve Sinclair had no earthly reason to love Kate Hamilton, or to wish her well. He also knew she had more than one reason to want to hurt Joseph Knight and his new film. Having been on the scene for Eve's debacle in *The Velvet Web*, Oscar knew there had been more than mere pique in her disastrous first encounter with Knight. She had been in love with Knight. She had tried hard to hide it, but Oscar Freund had seen through her act. Her behavior had been that of a woman scorned, not a mere Hollywood prima donna.

And Kate Hamilton was the woman Joe Knight had chosen for his wife as well as his star after he threw Eve off his picture and ruined her career in one blow.

And now, remarkably, the very story Kate and Eve were filming made a striking mirror image to their own lives. Was it not the story of two women in love with the same man? Was it not the story of a woman who, failing to attain the love of that man, arranges events so as to destroy his relationship with the woman he does love? Was it not the story of a man so wrapped up in his worldly mission, and so confident of his love, that he fails to see the danger until it is too late?

These reflections made Oscar Freund extremely nervous.

Oscar had spent his own professional life spinning stories for an eager public. He saw two stories on that sound stage, not one. He could not help wondering whether, in a perverse and fateful way, life might not decide to imitate art in *Farewell to Love*. He would have thought his own fears absurd—after all, Joe and Kate were safely married, and happy together as no couple he had ever known—were it not for that strange, haunting chemistry he saw between the two women on the set and in the rushes each day.

It was as though *Farewell to Love* was under some sort of spell, a spell that kept the production team on the edge of its seat and filled everyone at Monarch Pictures with thrilled anticipation—but that might be leading to no good end.

As a studio head, Oscar Freund had never been so excited.

Or so afraid.

On the set, the scene was finished.

Joseph Knight came around the camera and shook hands with Eve.

"It's another winner," he said. "You were magnificent, Eve. Susan is getting better every day. You're giving her just the quality she needs."

Now it was Kate's turn to shake Eve's hand.

"You gave me just what I needed, too," she said. "I'm grateful."

She knew Eve would understand what she meant. Though the scene they had just played looked simple enough on film, it had not been easy to perform. Both actresses had to communicate a tension just beneath the surface of their characters, while hiding that tension behind their smiles and their easygoing chatter. The task called for great acting technique, and Kate had felt she was reaching beyond herself to make it work.

But, with a subtlety invisible to outsiders, Eve had helped Kate through the scene. Using tricks of timing and gesture that only a master could know, Eve fed Kate her lines so as to smooth the way for her responses, and acted as a psychological anchor for Kate to play off.

It was not only an acting performance. It was a display of support and generosity for which Kate could only feel gratitude as well as admiration. Eve was using her great talent and experience to help Kate look better on the screen and play her character with the greatest possible depth and balance. Indeed, Eve's contribution went beyond professional courtesy. It was more like genuine friendship.

"Thanks again," Kate said, squeezing Eve's hand. "I appreciate it."

"Not at all," Eve smiled. "I'm the one who should be doing the thanking. I don't think you realize just how good you are up there, Kate. Now I know why you won that

Oscar. I'm hoping a little bit of that magic of yours will rub off.''

There was truth to what Eve said. Kate's star quality, her mystique, was indeed captivating to all those present. But if Kate was a natural genius, she was also still inexperienced. Eve, a lesser screen presence but a more seasoned performer, was helping her to perfect her art all the quicker.

Now Kate hugged Joseph Knight. They did not speak, but Joe's hug communicated his love as well as his pride in his wife's talent. There was something so intimate about their embrace that Eve averted her eyes.

"Well," Joe said to Eve, still holding Kate in his arms, "I think you ladies have done more than enough for one day. Let's call it a day and start fresh tomorrow with scene two-seventeen.''

His smile was full of his usual friendly camaraderie toward all his actors. Joe was a slavedriver, but so nice about it, and so hardworking himself, that no one could deny him anything.

As he turned Kate toward her trailer, Eve suspected that there was one more facet to his smile, and to his embrace. He wanted to get his young wife home so he could make love to her.

In the old days, when Eve first encountered Joseph Knight, she had been impressed and finally maddened by the secretiveness of his eyes. They had concealed his thoughts utterly. But since the war he was different. Surviving so perilous an adventure—at the cost of serious wounds from which he still had not completely recovered—seemed to have softened him and made him more open.

The proximity of his beloved wife accentuated the transformation in him. He did not bother to hide the male instincts behind his admiration for her, or his desire to be close to her physically after working so hard with her on the set all day. His feelings were more natural, easier to understand.

"See you in the morning," Eve smiled, leaving them to each other.

She walked to her own trailer, script in hand, and opened the door. Before going in she turned for an instant to see

Joe and Kate swaying together in the shadows of the sound stage. How much like lovers they looked!

And Eve, like the character she played in the film, was going home to her lonely life while their love deepened before her eyes.

Inside her trailer Eve found the copy of *The Hollywood Reporter* with today's story about *Farewell to Love*. There were blown-up pictures of Kate and herself on the cover, with a smaller one of Joe on the sound stage in his shirtsleeves.

Eve sat down and began taking off her makeup. She looked at the face in the mirror. How much it had changed over the past few years! She barely recognized herself. Her famous look of statuesque elegance was gone, wiped out by time and despair. It was all the makeup people could do to make her look girlish and unspoiled for this role.

Then she looked at the photo of Kate on the cover of the tabloid. Kate had not changed at all. She was the same sensual, mysterious creature she had been four years ago, when Joe picked her out of the crowd of actors on the set of *The Velvet Web* and told her to take over Eve's role.

A sensual, enigmatic woman, and yet so young, so fresh . . . No wonder Joe could not resist her. Even from playing opposite her, and reading lines with her, Eve could hardly keep from falling under her spell. There was something about Kate that was bigger than life, something almost fateful about her beauty.

With this thought Eve had picked up the small pair of scissors from her makeup kit, intending to clip away a rough spot on one of her fingernails. But she hesitated, the scissors in her hand, as she glanced from the image of Kate to her own face in the vanity mirror. For a long moment she seemed lost in a daydream.

A darkness came over her vision, eclipsing both the face on the printed page and the one in the mirror. She saw a fleeting image of Joseph Knight and his wife removing each other's clothes, and then she was overcome by dizziness. The room seemed to whirl around her. A wave of nausea made her moan aloud.

Then she looked down at the newspaper. Kate's photo was

stained by a drop of Eve's own blood. In surprise, Eve looked down at her own hand. There was a deep puncture wound in the center of her palm. Blood was coursing smoothly out of it, forming a small dark pool on the newspaper.

Eve was amazed. The wound was very deep, and yet she had felt no puncture and no pain. It was as though the wound had come from nowhere.

She looked at the newspaper. The pool of blood was spreading over the face of Kate Knight, obliterating it.

Eve did not make a move to find a tissue or to stop the bleeding. She stared in fascination as her own blood drowned the beautiful face before her, each drop being absorbed thickly into the newsprint as another drop came to supplement it, the surface of the little pool shining red as death before her eyes.

Eve took a deep breath. Her eyes half closed. The emotion she felt was strange to her. There was no pain. Not in her finger, not even in her heart.

She felt only relief.

TWO DAYS LATER KATE WAS SHOPPING ON WILSHIRE Boulevard.

She had been granted the morning off by Joe, who was filming one of Eve's scenes with Samuel Raines at the climax of the film. Kate would have two hard scenes to work on this afternoon, one with Eve and one with the character actress who played the heroine's mother in the film.

For the moment Kate was free. She had slept in, waking up refreshed at ten, and decided to see her favorite designer about a dress for the premiere of the film. While she was on Wilshire Boulevard she would window-shop in search of outfits for other upcoming studio events.

She was walking briskly along the street, dressed in slacks, a sweater, and sunglasses. It was surprisingly easy to disguise herself this way. In her dark glasses she looked like a thousand other blondes to be found on the streets of Hollywood. Her famous face was immediately recognizable only when her golden eyes were showing.

She stopped in front of a shop, looking at a display of shoes. She realized that she needed shoes badly. The ones she had been wearing to the studio were worn and ragged.

She was on the verge of going in when she saw the reflection of a man behind her in the window.

"Hey, there, honey pie," came a familiar voice. "Long time, no see."

Kate went rigid. She did not turn around. The face was blurred in the sunlit window, but the voice was as clear to her as the sinking feeling in her stomach.

It was Quentin.

She studied his reflection. He was dressed in a cheap-looking suit, with a rather loud tie and a hat with a colorful band. His lips were opened wide, and she could see his flashing teeth as he smiled.

"How did you recognize me?" she asked without turning around.

He laughed. "That's easy," he said. "Who doesn't know the famous face of Kate Hamilton, Hollywood's greatest star? No one else looks quite like you, Katie."

She bristled at his use of the nickname, but said nothing.

He looked at her body, so effectively camouflaged by her simple attire, and at her dark glasses.

"Not a bad disguise you're wearing," he said. "But a man recognizes his own wife all right, doesn't he?"

A cold chill crept quickly through Kate's bones. She realized that for a long time a voice inside her had been warning her that this moment would come one day. She should have listened. Now it was too late.

Still she said nothing.

"Actually, you've been wearing quite a few disguises lately, haven't you?" Quentin said, his smile glowing in the window. "You're all things to all people, aren't you, babe?"

There was a pause. Kate felt its significance.

"But to me, you're still a wife," he concluded. "That's all that counts, isn't it?"

Kate began to tremble despite herself. Fear waged a vicious battle with a wave of anger that rose up inside her. A whole lifetime had passed since she last saw Quentin. She was not going to let him turn back the clock.

"You're not scaring me," she said.

And she realized that, on some deep level, she was right. The years had made her fierce and proud. Her love for Joseph Knight had made her even stronger. Quentin was a cheap crook, a stick figure out of her past. Nothing he might threaten her with could change what she was.

He raised an eyebrow.

"Oh, really?" he asked. "You're not scared? Well, that makes you a brave lady. I thought bigamy would scare just about anybody."

He paused to let his words sink in. Kate said nothing.

"Does your husband know about me?" he asked. "Does he know what sort of fellow you were still married to when you tied the knot with him?"

Kate was taken aback. It had been years since she had given Quentin so much as a thought. Her marriage to him had been an event so small, so tainted, so completely eclipsed by the long tumultuous years of her life, that it had no reality to her. Quentin had no more right to rise up in front of her this way than did Ray, or her mother, or any of the boys who had taunted her about her budding figure or her low social standing at school a lifetime ago.

Quentin was an insect. He barely existed. His sordid little life could not concern her now.

Yet he was her husband. This she could not deny.

She turned to look at him. She saw his liquid blue eyes

shining with their combination of sensuality, greed, and cunning. He was studying her closely.

"You still don't scare me," she said.

He raised an eyebrow in acknowledgment of her courage.

"You're a gutsy little bitch, I'll say that for you," he said. "But I guess success does that for a woman. You've fooled a lot of people, Katie. Big Hollywood star, and all that. Doesn't anybody suspect who you really are? Isn't anybody curious about where you really came from?"

Kate looked at him without flinching.

"I don't care who's curious," she said. "And I don't care what anybody knows. If you've got an ax to grind, Quentin, call my lawyer. He'll take care of you. Now get out of my sight."

She was surprised at her own bravado. She hoped she could keep up this act until he went away.

He was looking at her appraisingly. She could feel him measuring her resolve.

She worked up a bit more courage.

"You're out of my life," she said. "And you're going to stay out."

Her beautiful lips curled in a dangerous smile.

"Shall I call a cop?" she asked.

Quentin looked at her once more. In that instant she saw the secret behind his eyes. He had something more, a weapon of some sort. She had failed to intimidate him.

What happened next wiped the smile off Kate's face.

In a smooth, leisurely movement Quentin opened one side of his sport jacket. Pinned to the lining Kate saw an enlarged glossy photograph.

Her breath caught in her throat when she recognized it.

It was a photograph of herself, nude, in the embrace of Chris Hettinger.

Chris, who had committed suicide eight years ago, because of her, and because of Quentin.

Her eyes were open wide, glued to the picture. Unhurriedly Quentin closed his jacket.

"Still want to call a cop?" he asked.

His face bore the almost boyish, mischievous look she

had once known so well. But now he meant business. There was a hateful curl to his lip.

Kate could barely catch her breath. The brief vision inside his jacket had torn at the foundations of her world. She still could not believe it.

"You . . . I thought . . ." she stammered.

"You thought you had them all," he finished for her. "Uh-uh, babe. You thought wrong. I had the negatives copied as a precaution. I was always careful, remember? I always took care of business. I think you underestimated me in those days, Katie girl. Don't underestimate me now."

Kate looked from his leering face to the sport jacket behind which she could almost feel the image of the nude, entangled bodies. She fought for control of her nerves. Lucidity came and went in little bursts, like an electrical signal snapping in and out.

She looked for words to say, and could find none. This was too much to take in all at once.

"I think we should talk, you and I," Quentin said. He was buttoning his jacket primly.

Now he spread his legs to stand more firmly before her. She saw his body stir beneath his clothes, slim and wiry. The years had not thickened him as they did other men— probably because, in his narcissism, he worked out often. The very familiarity of his flesh filled her with loathing. All at once she remembered how he tasted, how he smelled when he made love. The thought made her feel sick to her stomach.

He could feel his advantage over her. The picture had sapped her courage.

"When and where?" he asked.

She thought desperately of her shooting schedule.

"We're in the middle of shooting a picture," she said. "It's almost impossible to get away."

Again he raised his mocking eyebrow, to acknowledge her success and her busy life.

"Oh, I think you can figure out a way," he said. "You're a resourceful girl."

Kate sighed and ran a hand through her hair.

"Where can I reach you?" she asked.

He produced a pen. Then, to her shock, he pulled the eight-by-ten photograph from inside his jacket and wrote on the back of it. He handed it to her, mockingly unconcerned by the passersby who might see the image of the naked bodies.

"Brookmont Hotel," he said. "I wrote down the room number, and the phone. Call me before eleven tonight. Otherwise I call you."

She had hurriedly folded the damning picture. She thrust it into her purse. For a long instant she stood looking up at him. He could feel her fear through her dark glasses.

A sardonic grin curled his lips.

"Queen of the silver screen," he said, obvious malice in his voice. "You've fooled a lot of people, haven't you, Katie girl?"

Kate managed to suppress the tremor in her voice.

"Get out of my sight," she said coldly.

Quentin's grin widened. Touching the brim of his hat in an ironic gesture of respect, he turned on his heel and walked off along the sidewalk. His stride was jaunty and unhurried.

He looked like what he was, and always had been—a cheap crook. He had not changed in all these years.

While Kate had come a thousand miles from who and what she was when she knew him.

But now he held her future in his hands. And he knew it.

QUENTIN WAS WAITING IN HIS ROOM AT THE BROOKMONT
Hotel when the call came.

"All right, I've called you," Kate said coldly. "What do
you want?"

"I want a meeting," Quentin said, puffing at his cigarette
as he lay back in his bed. "You and I have things to talk
about."

There was a silence.

"I'll meet you once," Kate said. "And whatever it is
you want, I'll give it to you once. After that I never want
to see you again. Is that clear?"

Quentin smiled. So she had had time to think things over,
he mused.

"All right, babe," he said. "If that's the way you want
it. All I want is a fair deal, and I'm out of your life. Where
do you want to meet?"

"I don't want to meet you anywhere in Hollywood," she
said. "It has to be someplace out of town."

Quentin thought for a moment.

"How about Santa Monica?" he said. "Down by the
ocean. Or maybe up the coast a little. Any place will do."

"I'm worried about being recognized," Kate said.

"So wear a wig," Quentin yawned. "You didn't look

very recognizable today. You worry too much, babe. You're getting a case of nerves."

"Wait a minute," Kate said. "Joe and—my husband and I have a cabin in the mountains. It's by a lake. It's very isolated. There are no other cabins. It's a perfect place. I can tell you how to get there without having to pass any other houses. No one will ever know we've been there."

"How far is it?" Quentin asked.

"About two hours," she said. "It's in the Sierras."

Quentin sighed. "All right," he said with a trace of irritation. "Tell me how to get there."

But the wheels were turning quickly in his mind. He was on the alert.

Kate gave him precise directions to the tiny town and told him how to get to the cabin without being seen.

"I'll meet you there tomorrow night," she said. "Eleven o'clock. It won't be easy for me to get away. We're right in the middle of shooting. But I'll make it somehow."

"That's the ticket, babe," Quentin smiled, stubbing out his cigarette in the twisted metal ashtray. "Bring fifty thousand dollars. That will do it."

There was a silence.

"I don't have that kind of money," Kate said. "You must be crazy."

Quentin grinned, his lips close to the dirty receiver of the hotel phone.

"That's too bad," he said. "Then the whole world will have to know you're a bigamist, Katie. And a whore, and a blackmailer. I guess we have nothing more to talk about."

"Wait!" He could feel her thinking on the other end of the line.

He lit another cigarette. He was in no hurry.

"I can get hold of twenty or thirty thousand tomorrow," she said. "I'll have to send you the rest later. That's the best I can do. I don't have the kind of money you think I do."

"Don't make yourself look stupid by trying to hold out on me," Quentin said. "I know what you're worth—you and that husband of yours. I've done my research, babe."

"Then you know I can't lay my hands on that kind of money in one day," Kate insisted. "Money doesn't just sit in the bank. It's tied up in investments. It takes time to get at it. You ought to know that."

Again there was a silence.

"Well?" Kate asked, trying unsuccessfully to hide the fear in her voice.

"All right," Quentin said at last. "Bring what you have, and I'll give you an address where you can send the rest."

"And make sure you have everything with you," she insisted. "All the pictures, all the negatives. Is that clear?"

"Well," Quentin hedged, "if I have to wait for the rest of my money, then you'll have to wait for the last negative. Fair is fair, babe."

He listened, smiling, as Kate considered his bargain.

"All right," she said. "I guess that's the way it will have to be. But I don't want to see you after tomorrow night. This is the only meeting. Do you understand?"

"Sure, hon. Sure. We understand each other."

"Goodbye." The coldness in her voice was eloquent.

Quentin hung up the phone.

He lay for a moment on the cheap hotel bed, hands behind his head, staring at the ceiling. Then he got up and took a suitcase from under the bed. He snapped it open and took out two manila envelopes. He opened one and looked inside it. It contained a dozen or so pictures of Kate, a girl of seventeen who looked rather older, in the arms of Chris Hettinger, back in San Diego. Naked, Kate had a look of pleasure on her face so intense that it bordered on beatitude. She held the boy tenderly, her hands pressed into the small of his back.

Quentin's jaw clenched as he looked at the pictures. With a muted curse he stuffed them back into the envelope. Inside it were the negatives. He threw the envelope on the dresser. He would take it with him tomorrow.

Now he stooped to open the bottom drawer of the dresser. It was empty. He pulled it all the way out and carried it to the bed. He turned it upside down. Then he took the second manila envelope and placed it on the over-turned drawer. He found the roll of adhesive tape he had bought yesterday and taped the envelope to the bottom of the drawer. He put the drawer back in the dresser. Then he threw the tape into the waste basket.

He smiled. In the envelope was a duplicate set of negatives and prints. Tomorrow night would not be the last time Kate saw him. Not by a long chalk.

He put on his suit, fixed his tie with care, and studied himself with pleasure in the mirror. He looked good, he thought. Confident, strong, smart.

No woman was a match for him. Kate should have known that long ago.

He would teach her a lesson tomorrow.

With that thought he decided to go out for a drink to celebrate. He needed a woman, anyway. His interview with Kate had had an irritating effect on his senses.

On his way out of the hotel room he noticed the adhesive-tape dispenser in the bottom of the waste basket. After a moment's thought he picked it up and took it with him. He would throw it into a garbage can out on the street somewhere.

There was no sense in taking unnecessary chances. Quentin took pride in his attention to details.

The next evening he set out for the mountains. He gave himself a lot of extra time for the drive, not only because the terrain was unfamiliar to him, but because he had no intention of arriving at the appointed hour. Expecting a trap, he would get there at least an hour early.

And he would be ready for anything. That was why he had a snub-nosed .38 revolver in his pocket.

The drive was long and pleasant. Once the city was behind him he traveled rustic mountain roads that hummed by quietly under the heavy wheels of his Packard. He passed through several towns, which grew smaller as he went higher into the mountains.

When he reached the little town mentioned by Kate he paused at the sign.

Clifton Springs
Pop. 275

He pulled off the main road, according to Kate's directions, and found the side road that bypassed the village, with its general store and handful of houses, and led directly to the lake.

He followed the road to a turn-off into a dirt track with a thick tuft of grass down the middle. There was a large sign that read PRIVATE PROPERTY. NO TRESPASSING. Kate had told him to expect it.

He turned into the private road. A mile and a half along it, he saw the cabin. It was just as Kate had described it, nestled in a stand of pines and cedars. The lake was invisible, on the other side of the trees.

Quentin found the place where Kate had told him to park the car. It was behind a clump of brush, well out of sight of anyone who might improbably come down the private road at this hour.

But Quentin did not park there. After studying the terrain he found another place, a hundred yards distant, that was equally invisible, not only from passersby but, more significantly, from someone approaching the cabin by the route he himself had just taken.

He hid the car there and walked the rest of the way to the cabin.

He circled the little place, making sure his shoes did not brush against twigs or piles of pine needles. He looked at his watch. It was nine-thirty. He was an hour and a half early.

The cabin was dark. Quentin tiptoed silently across the porch and tried the door. It was locked. After a moment's hesitation he knocked loudly. There was no answer.

He went around to a side window and, using a burglar's tool, opened it. He did not make a sound. He slipped inside, closed the window behind him, and produced a penlight.

He searched the cabin, looking in all the cupboards and closets. There was nothing remarkable about the place. It was a simple, rustic mountain cabin with kitchen equipment, boating and fishing supplies, and some simple camp clothes. It was surprisingly unpretentious for the vacation hideaway of a big Hollywood star and her producer husband.

In one of the bedroom drawers he found several women's bathing suits. He picked one up and brought it to his face. He found the crotch and kissed it, an ironic smile on his lips.

He looked at the bed. It was a double bed with a quilted cover. This was where Kate slept with her husband. This was where she fucked Joseph Knight.

This was the nest she had feathered for her happiness. Quentin felt a momentary upsurge of hatred as he thought of her wealth, her fabulous marriage, and his own continuing poverty. She had had all the breaks, and he had had none.

Well, tonight that would change.

After another tour around the cabin he sat down to wait. He felt the urge for a cigarette, but decided to refrain out of caution.

After what seemed a long time the distant purr of an engine made him sit up. He moved to the living room window, where he watched through the curtains as the car approached.

It seemed to take a long time, the tires murmuring on the dirt track. The car parked out of sight. Quentin waited, his breathing shallow, his ears pricked up. He looked at his watch. It was ten forty-five. So she had not tried to arrive early and set a trap for him after all.

He ducked behind the large living room couch, like a burglar, and waited.

At length he heard a soft step on the porch, a key in the lock. The door opened quietly, and then closed.

Quentin stayed where he was as a light was turned on. Peeking out from his hiding place, he saw Kate taking off her coat. She hung it in the coat closet and moved toward the kitchen. He saw her put water in a teapot to boil.

Then she went into the bathroom. He heard water running. When she came out she had taken off her shoes. She was dressed in a simple skirt and sweater. She touched a thermostat on the wall, and the thump of gas heat was heard. Only now did Quentin realize how cold the cabin was. This mountain air was chilly.

Kate returned to the kitchen, where the teapot was beginning to groan as the water heated up.

She looked different now. Without her sunglasses he could see her eyes and measure the difference the years had made in her face.

She seemed tense and nervous, but she was remarkably beautiful. Much more beautiful than when Quentin had known her. In those days she had been a girl, unformed, without real character. A good body, a good lay, but just a girl. Now she was a woman. Years of living had shaped her, given her depth and a special kind of beauty.

And a sensuality he had never known in her. It shone in her every movement as she paced about the kitchen, believing herself unobserved. It was not the same sensuality she had shown on the screen in *The Velvet Web*—a film Quentin had seen at least a dozen times—but it was linked to it somehow. The movie camera created a false image, idealized, and yet connected to the real woman by mysterious threads. Kate was not the character she had played in the film, but no other actress could have played that character with as much sexual intensity.

Quentin felt a tickle in his loins at the sight of her, his wife. Many was the time he had seen *The Velvet Web* and gone straight from the theater to find a woman, thinking only of Kate, of his desire and his hatred, as he fucked the stranger in his arms. Somehow the glorification of Kate's sex by the camera had increased her mystique in his own heart.

And now, seeing the natural, all-too-human woman in the kitchen in her stockinged feet, her skirt and sweater, Quentin felt a surge of wanting that almost took away his composure.

But he forced it back, knowing he had to be lucid tonight. It was the most important night of his life.

Kate was standing in the kitchen, staring bleakly into space as the kettle began to boil. Quentin realized there was no point in hiding himself any longer.

As she reached to pour her tea, he spoke.

"Nice place you have here."

A strangled cry escaped her lips at the sound of his voice. She dropped the kettle on the stove. Boiling water hissed over the stove top, and she jumped backward. She turned off the gas and looked at him.

"How did you . . . ?" she asked.

Quentin smiled and moved toward her.

"Didn't see my car, eh?" he said. "Well, I took a precaution or two. You know me, babe. Always careful. I like to know what I'm getting into before I get into it."

She was looking at him, fear in her eyes. It gave him a pleasurable feeling of power. And the sight of her body, trembling slightly at his nearness, excited him. This was the body that millions of men dreamed of every night of their lives, the body of the woman of mystery, the sensual goddess who had haunted the imagination of the world since *The Velvet Web*.

His wife . . .

She put the kettle back on the burner, forgetting her tea, and faced him.

"Let's get it over with," she said. "Where are the pictures?"

Quentin smiled. "Show me the color of your money first."

She padded across the room to her purse and opened it. He watched her body move, from the slim shoulders down her back to the beautiful ass, the supple thighs stirring under her skirt. Fear made her more beautiful.

She produced a manila envelope full of bills and handed it to him.

"That's twenty-eight thousand dollars," she said. "It was the best I could do. I'll have to send you the rest after I get paid for the new film. That will be at least two months. I can't do any better, so you'll have to take it or leave it."

Quentin nodded appraisingly as he looked at her.

"Well?" she asked. "Where are the pictures?"

"The pictures are here," he said. "As I told you, I like to take precautions. You'll get them before I leave."

He fell silent, looking at her.

"Well?" she asked, irritated and frightened. "What are we waiting for? I haven't got all night."

Slowly Quentin shook his head.

"You know," he said, "you're still my wife."

She recoiled from him with a look of disgust on her face.

He watched her fight for control of her emotions. She was trying to erect a wall against him, a wall of class and status as well as anger.

"I was never your wife," she said. "You have no place in my life. I've given you your money. Now give me the pictures and get out of here. And don't flatter yourself that there's anything between you and me, Quentin. You can blackmail me, but you can't touch me."

A flare of anger erupted in Quentin's gut, almost too powerful to control.

"That's a pretty speech," he said. "But the law is on my side, babe. I've got the marriage license to prove it. You may think I belong to your past, but you're still Mrs. Quentin Flowers."

Kate was looking at him hard.

"What do we do about that?" she said.

"Nothing," he replied. "It's nobody's business but ours. After tonight the marriage certificate will just be a souvenir. You won't see me any more. Our little business arrangement cancels everything. But," he added, "don't try to make believe we never meant anything to each other. That insults me, babe. And it isn't true."

He watched for her reaction to his words. She seemed wary. His eyes slid down her body, whose sensual contours had made millions of men shudder with desire.

"All right," she said. "Give me the pictures, and an address where I can send you the money. Then get out."

"You'll get your pictures," he smiled. "And your address. But first you have to show your good faith."

"What is that supposed to mean?" she asked.

He put the envelope full of money on the counter.

"Katie," he said, "you're riding pretty high these days. But I'm just a regular Joe. I work for a living, I live in a cheap hotel room. I eat crummy food. I'm part of the great unwashed who try to make ends meet, and who pay their good money to see you on the screen in their local theater."

Kate frowned, puzzled. "What are you getting at?"

"I've seen you in the movies," he said, "strutting your stuff, showing yourself off for millions of men. And I've sat there in the theater, looking at that body of yours up on that screen while other guys just like myself sat all around me. GIs, when I was in the service, and now ordinary slobs who work for a living. And I've gone home to my lonely bed, just like millions of men, and thought about you, and wished you were beside me."

Kate said nothing. Her eyes had narrowed, and she was watching him cautiously.

"But there's one difference between me and those millions of schmucks," Quentin said with a bitter smile. "You're my wife."

There was a silence. Now she knew what he was talking about.

"Any time I wanted to," he said, "I could have sat up in that movie theater and said to anyone who would listen, *'That's my wife up there!'* And, even if they thought I was crazy, I would have been telling God's own truth. Now, what do you think of that, Katie girl?"

Kate stared at him, incredulity mingling with the contempt in her eyes.

"I don't think anything of it," she said. "And you shouldn't either, Quentin."

"Oh, but I do," he corrected. "It gives me rights under the law. And I'm going to be big enough to waive all those rights. After tonight."

His words sent a tremor through her body. She felt her hands turn cold.

"Get out," she said. "We made our arrangement. You're not going to touch me."

He shook his head. "Not so fast," he said. "One for the road, babe. Just a little farewell kiss, between you and me. Then we part company for good."

Kate had stepped back a pace. He could see the revulsion in her eyes. Somehow it excited him all the more.

"Otherwise," he said, "I blow the whistle. What do you

think the world would think of you if it knew you had helped me blackmail an innocent boy to his death? If it knew how you had used that sexy body of yours to kill that boy? And what about that big-shot husband of yours? I'd like to meet him. We could compare notes about you—if you know what I mean . . ."

"If you ever go near him, I'll kill you," Kate said.

Quentin said nothing. The knowing look in his eyes did his talking for him. He knew Kate would do anything in the world to keep her two lives separate.

"Who says I'm going near him?" he asked. "We're finishing things tonight, babe. Our deal cancels everything. A promise is a promise. Am I right?"

Kate stared at him. He could see the wheels turning inside her mind as she weighed contingencies and cast about for an escape from what must happen now. There was no way out for her. He had seen to that.

Something seemed to collapse inside her.

"All right," she said. "You win."

She walked past him to the lamp and turned it off. Then she preceded him to the bedroom. She started to take off her clothes, briskly.

"Not so fast," he said.

He turned on the bedside lamp.

"I want to see you," he said. "I've waited for this moment, Katie, and I'm going to enjoy it."

He came to her side and kissed her on the lips. She did not respond. Slowly he took off her sweater, keeping his face close to hers. Smelling his cheap cologne, she averted her eyes.

He looked at her bra, and at the smooth brown skin of her shoulders. Then he took the bra off. Her breasts stood out, firm and supple. He cupped them in his hands, enjoying the tremor he felt in her body. So these were the breasts that had swelled under her costumes, blown up to a hundred times their real size by Joseph Knight's camera, blown up to fascinate and tempt a whole generation of men.

Then he knelt to undo her skirt, and watched it fall to the floor. She had nothing on under it but her panties. He slipped them down her legs and looked at the golden tuft between her legs.

The sight of her sex fascinated him. Years ago he had known it very well, so well that sometimes it even bored him when she did not seem responsive enough. He had cheated on her often in those days.

But now that same sex had a mystique, provided by her fame and her film image, an image that had made her bigger than life. Many was the time that Quentin had seen *The Velvet Web* and felt his senses quicken at the sight of Kate's clothed body on the movie screen. And he had thought of the warm little pussy hidden by those clothes and that bigger-than-life image, and longed to touch it and kiss it, as though somehow it must be made of a magic sexual substance, higher and more magnificent than the mere cunt of a woman. Even though he had once known it so well and taken it for granted.

And now, somehow, he was not disappointed. There was indeed something bigger than life about Kate. He had seen it when she was in the kitchen, thinking herself unobserved. He had seen it in her fear and her antipathy as she spoke to him. And he saw it now in her nakedness as she stood before him.

She was indeed a special woman, a woman different from other women. The magic she projected on the screen was not mere illusion. There was something real about it. Something that emanated from her.

No wonder, he thought, that Joseph Knight had found her irresistible and had married her almost as soon as he had cast her for *The Velvet Web*, making the Hollywood gossip mill buzz.

No wonder.

But tonight she did not belong to Joseph Knight. Tonight she was all for Quentin.

He picked her up in his arms. He smelled her perfume, and the sweet natural scent of her body, which he remembered from the old days..

But she was cold and distant. He felt her horror at his touch. He knew now how completely she loved Knight. Quentin himself was a worm to her, a low and vile thing.

This thought made him smile. He enjoyed the perversity of being able to shock and disgust her even as he took his pleasure from her. This was a more complete victory over her than he had planned.

He threw her on the bed, roughly. He saw the full length of her on the spread, naked and defenseless. He took off his clothes, slowly, removing the gun from his belt and putting it on the dresser. Kate never looked at his body. Her eyes remained fixed to his, an expression of utter emptiness in her golden irises.

He turned out the light and came to crouch atop her in the shadows. To his delight a shaft of moonlight came in the window, casting a blue glow over her body. She looked like a delicious ghost.

He spread her thighs and felt them tremble at his touch. His sex was hard and straining between his legs. He could hardly contain the excitement inside him.

He reached to touch her, and felt her tense.

"Warm up, babe," he said. "Relax. I always knew how to push your buttons. You know that."

He kissed her breasts, savoring her nipples with his tongue. Then he kissed his way down her stomach to her navel, feeling her body shudder. At last he touched his lips to her sex. The fine feminine taste of her overcame him like a potion. The fire of wanting inside him burned out of control. She was magnificent. And she was his.

But the tension inside her had not subsided. She was unresponsive, strung tight as a wire.

Irritated by her coldness, he sat upright on his haunches and poised his sex against hers. He was slippery enough for both of them, and worked his way inside her easily. A great surge of triumph went through him as he realized he was fucking the one and only Kate Hamilton, the great star, the wife of Joseph Knight, the sex symbol of the ages.

"There, now," he crooned. "That's not so bad, is it? Come on, babe. Love me a little. The way you used to do."

There was no response. She was like a dead body in his embrace. He humped her harder, pulling her down onto himself. Her passivity enraged him.

"God damn it," he hissed. "Let me see you fuck, Katie. You'd better warm up."

She did not move. She was like a woman submitting passively to a rape.

He struck her hard across her face with his open hand.

"Come on!" he said. "You'd better get used to it, Katie girl. You're going to be my baby . . ."

He caught himself in mid-sentence. He realized he had said too much. He had not intended to reveal that until later. But now it was too late. And as he felt her lithe body respond to this worst of all threats, he began to lose control. He jerked harder, thrusting into her with all his might.

"You might as well get used to it . . ." he repeated, beside himself now. "You belong to me. You'll always be mine. No Joseph Knight can change that . . ." He laughed, dizzy with rage and exultation.

"All mine . . ."

The words caught in his throat as Kate's hands came from nowhere to strike his face. Her thumbs, guided by an unnameable instinct, plunged straight into his eye sockets. He gave a sharp cry and jerked backward.

Then he fell sideways on the bed, curled on himself, cursing and holding his hands to his eyes. Kate leapt to her feet and stood looking down at him.

Rage made him indifferent to the pain she had caused him.

"You're finished," he snarled. "You belong to me. I'm going to fix you for good, bitch. Wait till that husband of yours hears about me . . ."

As his words sank in Kate saw the gun on the dresser where he had left it.

"I'll tell him everything," Quentin was saying, feeling for her on the bed beside him. "Wait till he hears about you . . ."

Kate grasped the gun and pointed it at Quentin's head. Her hand shook. She moved closer to him so that the gun was only an inch from his temple. Her whole body trembled, but her finger found the trigger.

"You thought you'd gotten rid of me," Quentin was saying. "You'll never get rid of me, babe. Not as long as you . . ."

The gun went off before he could finish. His head was

flung backward. His body jerked suddenly, and was still. Naked, he lay almost like a child before Kate's eyes. A stain of blood began to spread under his face.

Kate knew he was dead. The empty glare of his eyes and the position of his slumped body left no doubt of it.

She recoiled from him, still pointing the gun meaninglessly, as though to keep him at a distance. Her finger was frozen on the trigger, which she had not released.

The emotions she had been burying inside herself since the moment she had seen Quentin on Wilshire Boulevard were boiling up with a rush. But she forced them back down. Her work was not finished yet. She had a life to protect, her life with Joe Knight. She was going to finish the job.

If only she could silence the roaring inside her brain, and make her woman's flesh move according to her will . . .

She stood there like an automaton for several minutes, too overcome by what had happened to get control of herself. Then she noticed the blood spreading over the bed from the gaping wound in Quentin's skull. She hurriedly placed a pillow under his head and stood back staring at him. She barely breathed. A knot had formed in the middle of her chest, making her feel faint.

At last cool reason began to stir inside her. She put the gun down and grasped the bedspread with both hands. Laboriously she pulled Quentin's body to the floor and wrapped it in the spread.

Murmuring instructions to herself, she went to hunt for a cord of some sort. She found a length of rope in the tool closet and used it to bind the spread around Quentin.

Only now did she think of her nakedness. She got an old pair of jeans from the dresser and pulled them on hurriedly. She put on a T-shirt and found a pair of deck shoes in the closet.

Still whispering to herself nervously, she dragged Quentin's body through the living room and out the front door. Scouting the yard to make sure no one was around, she pulled the body down the path to the dock and loaded it into the rowboat.

Then she stood looking up and down the shore, biting a fingernail as she pondered what to do next.

In the moonlight she caught sight of several large stones at the water's edge. She hurried to them, one after the other, soaking her jeans in the frigid water as she carried them to the boat.

Retrieving the rope from the house, she tied two of the largest stones to Quentin's body, one at the chest and the other behind the knees. She got into the boat and rowed it to the deepest part of the lake. With trembling hands she pushed Quentin over the gunwale. His body disappeared into the dark water, dragged down two hundred feet by the weight of the heavy stones. There were a few bubbles, then nothing.

Now Kate thought of the gun.

She rowed back to shore, darted back into the house, returned with the .38 and rowed to a spot about a hundred yards from where she had dumped Quentin. She threw the gun into the lake.

For a moment she sat staring at the moonlit water around her. Only she and the lake knew her secret. Quentin could never hurt her now.

Then she returned to the cabin. She had work to do.

She was shaking continuously now, a sort of seismic tremor that hummed under her skin while allowing her to do what she had to do. She removed the bedclothes and remade the bed. Then she searched Quentin's clothes. She found his wallet, some change, a penlight, and a key ring on which there were car keys and what looked like a key to a safety deposit box. There was also a room key from the Brookmont Hotel with the number 412 on it.

Kate wrapped the bedding and Quentin's clothes in two pillowcases. She took them outside and placed them by the door.

Then she looked for Quentin's car. She knew the area around the cabin well, and her search only took a few minutes. She opened the car door with the key she had taken from Quentin's trousers. In the trunk she found the manila envelope containing the pictures and envelopes. For a moment she mused over them, wondering when he had intended to hand them over to her.

She put the envelope into the pillowcase containing Quentin's clothes. She threw both pillowcases into the trunk of the car. Then she returned to the cabin, found a gallon can of gasoline, and put it into the trunk as well.

She cleaned the cabin thoroughly, erasing all traces of Quentin and herself. Thankfully there was no blood to be found in the bedroom. It had not soaked through the bedspread. She wiped the place for fingerprints, trying to find all the places Quentin might have touched.

Then she took a shower to get the blood off herself. When she emerged she took a long last look around, making sure that the cabin looked just as it always had. She put on the clothes she had worn on her drive from Hollywood and put her jeans and T-shirt into the trunk of Quentin's car with the other clothes.

It was time to leave.

After locking the cabin Kate walked out to the dock and looked at the black surface of the lake. For an instant her breath caught in her throat as she thought she saw something break the surface. Quentin's body, her crime rising to the surface to betray her . . . Then she saw that she had been mistaken. It was just a trick of the moonlight on the water. She turned on her heel and walked back into the woods.

She drove Quentin's car several miles along empty country roads until she found a deserted dump site. There she soaked the clothes and pillowcases in gasoline and set them afire in a metal drum. She watched patiently as the clothes burned, prodding at the smoking mass with a stick. She saw the pictures of herself, naked in Chris Hettinger's arms, burning before her eyes. She tended the fire carefully until there was nothing left but unrecognizable ash.

She looked at her watch. It was twelve-fifteen.

She got into Quentin's car and drove it back to Hollywood.

She knew she could not leave the car anywhere near the cabin, or even anywhere along the route to the cabin. This was the most important step of all. She had to return it to the vicinity of Quentin's hotel in Hollywood.

The two-hour drive seemed to pass in an instant. Kate thought of nothing the whole time, except her life with Joseph Knight and what she was doing to save it. The smooth silent shaking of her limbs did not stop, but remained with her all the way.

The long approach down the mountains to L.A. was easy, for there was little traffic at this hour. Kate stopped at a phone booth and found the address of the Brookmont Hotel in the white pages. She drove to the address, cruised the neighborhood briefly, and left the car on the street two blocks from the hotel. After wiping her fingerprints from the steering wheel, gearshift, and keys, she left the car key in the ignition. The other keys she kept.

She looked at her wristwatch. It was only two-thirty. The whole night was ahead of her.

She would need it.

There was still the question of her own car. It was parked beside the cabin at the lake. She had to retrieve it.

She had foreseen this moment during her drive down the mountain. It was the most dangerous one of all, the one that required the risk of trusting another person.

She went to a pay phone and dialed a number.

A deep male voice answered, wide awake. She smiled. She had suspected he would be awake at this hour.

"Hello, Norman," she said. "This is me."

"Katie!" Norman cried. "Why aren't you in bed? For God's sake, girl, you have shooting tomorrow. You're not in any trouble, are you?"

"Norman, I need your help. Right away. Can you meet me at the corner of La Brea and Sunset?"

"I . . . well, sure. But . . ."

"Bring your car," Kate said. "We're going to be taking a drive."

"Will do, honey. You just stay put. Norman's your man."

Kate hung up the phone. In a few minutes, she knew, Norman would be with her, prepared to do anything in the world to help her, and to keep his mouth shut about it. He was her only friend.

She looked back on the last twenty-four hours. She had faced the greatest challenge of her young life, but she had been equal to it.

Once she had removed her car from the vicinity of the cabin, no trace of her journey would exist outside Norman's memory of having driven her up there. Everything inside the cabin was normal, except for a changed bed sheet and a couple of missing pillowcases that no one but she knew about. The place had been wiped clean of all traces of Quentin. His car was back in Los Angeles. The evidence he had brought with him to the cabin was destroyed.

And Quentin himself was at the bottom of the lake, where he would never be found.

Everything was covered. Kate's crime had left no traces. Joseph Knight would never know the truth about her.

AT ELEVEN O'CLOCK THE NEXT MORNING NORMAN WEBB entered the Brookmont Hotel on Melrose Avenue. In his pocket was the key to Room 412, given to him by Kate last night.

Norman had slept no more than two hours after driving Kate up to the mountains and driving back down alone. But he looked fresh and jaunty. A perennial insomniac who had once done his best creative work in the wee hours, he was accustomed to functioning on little sleep.

He strolled into the lobby and saw a lazy desk clerk chewing gum behind his counter. Perhaps half of the cubbyholes had keys in them. This was obviously a transient hotel, used by drifters who needed as cheap a place as possible to stay for a few weeks at the most.

The clerk looked up at him with the familiar mixture of

boredom and suspicion requisite of a man in his position. His beady little eyes sized up Norman's haircut and the probable cost of his clothes. Luckily for Norman, he looked the part of a man down on his luck. His collar was a bit frayed, and his suit and shoes were very old.

"Morning," Norman said. "Got a room?"

Without speaking the man turned and took a key from a cubbyhole.

"For how long?" he asked.

"Just tonight," Norman said. "If I like the room I'll maybe stay a week. And make it high up, would you? I can't stand those restaurant smells."

With a little shrug of irritation the clerk turned, put the first key away, and took out a second one.

"Nine seventy-three," he said. "That high enough for you?"

"Thanks," Norman said.

"No luggage?" the clerk asked with a trace of bored suspicion.

"I'll bring it over later," Norman said. "If I like the room, that is," he added with a little air of superiority intended to annoy the clerk more.

"You'll like it," the clerk retorted, looking again at Norman's clothes. "Need a bellhop?"

"No, thanks." Norman smiled. Since he had no luggage, the only reason he might need a bellboy was to get him a girl for the night. He did not intend to be in this building more than twenty minutes.

He signed the register, took the key, and rode the small elevator to the ninth floor. He emerged on a landing with an old cracked mirror, a threadbare carpet, and walls that had a lumpy look under their fifty coats of whitewash.

Norman went down the hall until he saw the staircase. Without entering his own room, he took the stairs to the fourth floor. The staircase was filthy and littered. When he emerged on the fourth floor he walked carefully along the corridor. There was no sign of a maid.

He found 412 without difficulty and tried the key Kate had given him in the door. He slipped inside and closed the door noiselessly behind him.

He turned to see a typical transient room. The bed was made. The rest of the room had the sloppily domestic look of a furnished room rather than a hotel room.

A cockroach moved languidly along one of the floor-boards. There was a chipped table by the window, with a newspaper, an ashtray cleaned of butts by the maid, and a pint of cheap rye whiskey.

A suitcase was sitting against the wall by the armoire. Inside the armoire were three shirts, all cheap, and two pairs of trousers. There were two sport jackets, both a little loud, and an extra pair of shoes. The tenant was perhaps a bit of a clothes horse, though he obviously traveled light.

In the bathroom was a toothbrush in a glass with a tube of toothpaste. There was a shaving brush and shaving cream, and a straight razor. A small bottle of cheap men's cologne stood on the shelf. There was no hairbrush. The towels were fresh. Evidently the maid had returned since the client was last in the room.

Beside the bed was a small chest of drawers. Norman opened the top drawer. It held several articles of dirty laundry and a girlie magazine.

The other two drawers were empty.

Norman stood thinking. He could feel there was something missing here. So far there was not a single sign as to the identity of the tenant. He must have overlooked something—or else the tenant had taken steps to hide his identity.

Then Norman looked at the chipped table beside the window.

He went over and picked up the newspaper that was on the table. It was folded to the racing form, and the names of several horses running yesterday at Santa Anita were circled.

Norman smiled approvingly. Those were the same horses he himself had picked yesterday.

As he put the newspaper aside he noticed a piece of paper on the tabletop. There was writing on it.

Take Santa Monica to Route 14. Take 14 north to 395. Turn left at Clifton Springs. Follow county road to gas station, left one mile, right on dirt road to cabin.

Norman nodded as he read. These were directions to the Knights' cabin in the mountains. He had driven that very route with Kate in his car last night and left her near the cabin at four-thirty in the morning.

He assumed she had driven back in her own car. At her own request he had not asked further questions. But he could not help making assumptions.

Kate had left her own car at the cabin, and had him take her up there so she could drive it home.

Why?

Carefully Norman folded the note and put it in his pocket. Then he turned to examine the room again.

Kate had asked him to come here, get into Room 412, and search it thoroughly. In her obvious distress she left no doubt that she expected something dangerous, something compromising, to be in this room. Norman's job was to find it.

He tried to think like a detective. He knew there must be something here. He looked under the mattress, then under the bed. Nothing. He looked through the armoire. He checked all the corners of the room.

Then he pulled all the drawers out of the chest of drawers.

Under the bottom drawer he found what he was looking for. It was a large manila envelope, taped to the underside of the drawer.

He removed it, replaced the drawers, sat on the bed, and produced a penknife from his pocket. He slit open the envelope.

His eyes opened wide as he shook the contents loose across the bedspread.

There were newspaper clippings. Something about the suicide of a young man. There were two or three letters. He recognized Kate's handwriting, though it looked somehow different.

And there were photographs.

Seven of them, he counted. They showed Kate, naked, in the arms of a young man. The couple was lying on a blanket in some sort of grassy area. The film was grainy, as though a telephoto lens had been used. But the photographs were eloquent. The couple was locked in the embrace of youthful passion. The young man held Kate tenderly in his arms, and she had her arm curled around his neck. In some of the pictures her legs were wrapped about his waist. In others he kissed her breast, the swell of pearly skin looking ripe and delicious against his lips.

In three of the photos they were obviously having intercourse. The boy was atop her, his youthful body hard and straining. Kate's face was full of rapt girlish ecstasy and a tenderness that made her extraordinarily beautiful.

She was much younger in the pictures. They had to be at least seven or eight years old. She could not have been more than a teenager. Her face was unformed, adolescent, a long way from the mature face whose complex beauty dominated *The Velvet Web* and now *Farewell to Love*. But her body already showed that strange earthy femininity that today made it irresistible to millions of moviegoers. And here, revealed for the first time, at least to Norman, was the nudity that was hidden by Kate's clothes, on the Hollywood screen and when she was with him.

Something about the sight of her nipples, her breasts, and the dark place between her legs made her seem at once irresistibly sensual and sweetly innocent. The look in her eyes as she cradled the boy on her breast was haunting. It displayed the gentleness of youth superimposed over something ageless and knowing. Innocence and experience, as it were, overlapping one another poetically in one human visage, a most beautiful face.

Norman looked at the pictures for a long time. Then he looked in the envelope. Sure enough, there were negatives. He counted them. There were more negatives than prints.

Now he looked at the newspaper articles. There was a picture of the suicide victim. He compared it to the boy in the pictures. It was clear enough that this was the same boy.

Norman used his writer's instincts to put two and two together. Of course, it was obvious these pictures were being used to blackmail Kate. This room belonged to the blackmailer.

But it seemed as though the pictures had also been used,

years ago, to blackmail the boy himself, or perhaps his family. They were pictures of the boy engaged in guilty sex with a girl who was forbidden to him in some way. The girl was Kate.

And that was why the boy had committed suicide. Or so it seemed.

Therefore the blackmailer was getting double duty out of his photographs.

Who was the blackmailer?

Idly Norman looked around the room again. There was not a clue to the identity of the tenant, except the hand-writing on the note.

Norman paused in front of the pictures, still arranged across the bed. For a reason he could not fathom, his eyes misted as he looked at Kate's naked body and her innocent passion. She was so beautiful! And such a mystery . . .

Then he put the pictures back in the envelope with the newspaper clippings and the negatives. He picked up the handwritten note and put it in his pocket.

He sat down in the chair by the window and thought for a long moment, his eyes scanning the room. Then he opened the suitcase on the bed and began putting every-thing he had found in the room into it. The razor, the tooth-brush, the clothes, even the newspaper.

When he had finished he studied the room. He took out his handkerchief and wiped the few places where his own fingerprints might have been left.

He closed the suitcase, surveyed the room, made sure he still had the key, and left.

He walked down the hall to the stairs and took them up to the ninth floor, where he entered his own room. He tore off the bedspread and made the bed look as though some-one had slept in it. He went into the bathroom, used the water glass, opened the bar of soap on the sink, and ran some water in the shower.

He thought of smoking a cigarette and leaving the butt in the ashtray, but decided that was too risky a detail to leave behind him.

When he was satisfied that the room looked lived in, he

put the key on the table and left, closing the door quietly behind him.

Then he took the stairs back down to the rear entrance of the hotel. It gave on an alleyway adjacent to the street. Carrying the suitcase, Norman left with an easy gait, trying not to attract attention to himself.

Ten minutes later he had arrived at his car. He started the engine and drove away. He had one stop to make on the way to Monarch Studios.

In his car he had the evidence of Kate's past, safely hidden from prying eyes. He was satisfied with his bit of cloak-and-dagger work.

It never occurred to him to make sure he was not being followed.

Kate was on the set on Sound Stage 12 at Monarch Studios, doing the fifth take of one of her most important scenes.

It was obvious to everyone on the set that Kate was not herself. She seemed tired, and she was taking her cues with little false starts that were not characteristic of her. Her co-star, Samuel Raines, was doing his best to help her through the scene, but she could not seem to get a grip on herself.

"Cut," called Joseph Knight, aborting the take. He came around the camera and took Kate aside.

"Kate," he said, "are you all right? Maybe we should forget this scene for now. You look like you need a rest."

Kate looked uncomfortably into his eyes. "No," she insisted. "I'll get it right. I'm sure of it. I'm sorry I'm causing so much bother. Just give me one more chance."

"Are you sure?" he asked. "Frankly, you look as though you had seen a ghost."

He looked at her. He was obviously concerned. Last night she had told him she had had an urgent call from her old friend Melanie. A sudden crisis had come up in Melanie's life—man trouble, Kate had explained—and Melanie needed the comfort of a friend. Kate had left the studio early, telling Joe she would spend the night at Melanie's and be back for work in the morning.

Her excuse had worked, except for the fact that after her harrowing night she was emotionally exhausted and in no shape to perform before the cameras. She was pushing herself beyond her own limits to give a creditable imitation of acting this morning, but it did not seem to be working.

Each time Samuel Raines kissed her, held her in his arms, she could feel Quentin's arms around her last night, taste the foulness of Quentin's kiss. And the terrible urgent readiness of her body as she prepared to attack Quentin, the awful spring of her limbs as she struck at his eyes with her hands, came back stubbornly to her now, an undeniable presence under what was supposed to be a tender love scene with Samuel Raines. Joseph Knight, behind the camera, sensed her tension immediately, and called for re-take after re-take. Now he was giving up on her, and trying to offer her an easy way out by canceling the scene for today.

"Are you sure?" he asked. "To be frank, you look all in. I don't think we're going to get something printable."

"Just let me try it one more time . . ." Kate was repeating. Suddenly she stopped. At the back of the sound stage she saw Norman Webb giving her the high sign.

"Joe," she said, "could I take five? If I could just have a few minutes to get myself together . . ."

Her husband still looked concerned. Kate seemed far away, and not at all herself.

"All right, everybody," he called to those on the set. "Take five. We'll come back with the same scene."

Kate excused herself and hurried toward her trailer. Norman intercepted her halfway there.

The look in her eyes left no doubt as to how worried she was.

"Did you . . . ?" she asked.

Norman leaned forward and spoke in a conspiratorial murmur.

"Mission accomplished, chief," he said. "Not only did I police the place, but I took everything out of it and left the room key behind on the table. Just as though the party simply packed up and left. I have everything in a suitcase in a locker at the bus station."

He reached into his pocket and handed her a locker key.

"There it is," he said. "So far as I know, that's the only trace of the missing party. And it's all yours."

Kate held the key nervously in her hand. She had gone white.

Norman looked at her.

"Sweetie," he said, "are you all right? It can't be as bad as all that. Believe me, I got it all."

She looked at him pleadingly.

"Norman," she said, "what did you find in that room?"

"Personal effects," he said. "A couple of cheap sport coats, some shoes, a newspaper with the ponies circled on the racing page—that endeared me to the tenant, whoever he was—and a toothbrush. Nothing of any note. It's all in the suitcase now. Except this."

He handed Kate a folded piece of paper. She looked at it. It contained directions to Joe's cabin, in Quentin's handwriting.

"That was the only thing in the room that gave a clue as to the tenant's identity," Norman said. "Except fingerprints, I suppose. And a place like that must have the fingerprints of a thousand people in it."

Kate stared at the note for a moment, thinking of the scene at the cabin last night. Then she folded it and put it in her pocket.

She was still holding the locker key in her hand. She grasped it as though it held her fate, or her undoing.

"Didn't you . . ." she stammered. "Didn't you find anything else? Something hidden? You see, I think there was something hidden . . ."

Norman shook his head.

"Honey, I went through that room like Philo Vance and Sherlock Holmes rolled into one. There was nothing."

She breathed a sigh of relief. She thought of the safety deposit box key she had found on Quentin. If there were duplicates of the photos and negatives—and, knowing Quentin, she could only believe there must be duplicates—they must be in the safety deposit box, wherever it was. And without Quentin to open the box, it would never be opened, and its contents never discovered.

In taking Quentin out of the picture, she had saved herself.

"Thank you," she said. "Thank you, Norman. You've done me a great favor."

Norman Webb smiled.

"Any time, sweetie," he said, patting her hand. "Any time."

She looked gratefully into his eyes. She saw nothing in the tawny irises but friendship.

KATE WAS ALONE IN THE BENEDICT CANYON HOUSE.

She had been given the afternoon off from the studio by Joe, who rightly felt she simply could not do her best work in her present frazzled condition. Without pressing her for explanations of her distress, he had insisted she go home to rest. She had cunningly accepted his offer, knowing she had important things to do before she could go home.

Now she was walking the floor restlessly, like a jungle cat trapped in a cage in a zoo, pacing its imprisonment and its silent rage and panic while curious observers watched, indifferent to its private anguish.

She felt as though something was closing in on her from the past, from the dark world outside her love for Joe. Something much too sinister for her to fight, despite all her desperate actions and her extreme precautions.

In a garbage dumpster a mile away she had put Quentin's suitcase. It was empty. She had taken out his personal possessions and dispersed them in garbage cans all over the Hollywood Flats.

Every trace of Quentin's tenure in that hotel room was now destroyed, including, most important, the note in Quentin's handwriting with directions to Joe's cabin in the Sierras. Kate had burned the note this morning in her trailer at Monarch Pictures.

It had made Kate physically ill to touch Quentin's trousers, his shirts, his underpants as she searched through the suitcase. She could actually smell his body on the dirty clothes. It smelled like the past, and it smelled like death.

At this moment Quentin's body was rotting under the black water of the lake in the mountains. Kate could almost see it rocked by the lake's quiet currents, already decomposing, perhaps being nibbled by lake fish. Thinking of this, she had to hurry to the bathroom to throw up.

She could not help recalling that this cruel, shallow man, whom she had killed, had been the man who deflowered her when she was only a girl. Her first lover . . . It made her feel not only nauseated but sick at heart, morally sick, to think that the innocence of her sex had first been given to someone so evil. The fact seemed to taint her whole life.

She did not regret killing Quentin. She had had no choice. Her payment of money to him would never have stopped him. He had actually said as much as he made love to her, seconds before his death, when sexual excitement overcame his own instinct for caution. She knew Quentin. There was no way to stop him from coming back and back and back, with his memories, his knowledge about her, his marriage certificate, and his blackmail. There was no limit to his evil.

She was not sorry Quentin was dead. That was a good deed, sure to help the dozens of people who were already under his shadow, and the others who would have been harmed by crossing his path in the future.

What was horrible was this ineradicable taint of having been touched by him, soiled by him in her very essence. In her nervous state it seemed to Kate that that was why

Quentin had found his way unerringly back to her. Because he could smell his own scent on her, follow that scent, see his own mark on her, and thus follow her to the ends of the earth.

Well, now Quentin himself was gone. But the foul taint remained. It filled her with loathing for herself and her ugly past.

And even now that taint was on her body, the body that belonged to Joseph Knight. How could she keep it from revealing itself to Joe somehow? How could she keep his clear eyes from seeing it, his heart from feeling it?

A little water clears us of this deed.

She recalled the words of Lady Macbeth. She had read the play at Norman's recommendation a year ago. Norman loved tragedies, and enjoyed educating Kate as to the psychological subtleties that lead characters into acts that inexorably bring about their destruction.

Even at the time, because of her checkered past, Kate had empathized with Lady Macbeth's unbearable guilt. But only now, now that murder was on her own conscience, did she understand the full weight of Shakespeare's tragedy.

She tried to comfort herself by thinking of how carefully she had erased all the traces of Quentin. She had even taken all the papers out of his wallet, burned them, and thrown the wallet away. The locker key was back in the locker, and Quentin's hotel room key back in the hotel. His car key was still in the ignition of his car, which would eventually be towed to a police garage, never to be claimed. No trace of Quentin would ever be found.

The only thing she had kept was the safety deposit box key. She knew this was an unwise act. She had hidden the key away, not yet daring to throw it away entirely. It was like a talisman that represented her small degree of control over what had happened and what might happen. Also, perversely, it represented her link with Quentin. She had the odd feeling that it was only by not trying to deny this link, by accepting it and taking responsibility for it, that she could hope to control Quentin's influence after his death, to keep him buried where he belonged.

The key seemed to represent both her prison and her escape, both the poison of Quentin and the antidote to stop that poison. It was only by holding it in her own possession that she could keep Quentin away for good. She must be the rampart, the shield, that protected Joe and her love from the past.

All these thoughts were on the borderline between cool calculation and plain irrationality. For Kate was desperately trying to save a situation that went straight to her very heart. The three men involved—Chris Hettinger included—were the only men on earth who had ever touched her in any important way. It was impossible to be entirely sane where something so terribly intimate was concerned.

So Kate paced, and thought, and prayed she had done enough, prayed the past would haunt her no more.

She was still pacing quietly, absorbed in her own silent panic, when she heard the door open in the kitchen.

She nearly jumped out of her skin.

She looked into the kitchen. It was Joe. He was dressed in his dark suit and tie, as every night when he returned from the studio. Though his work day had been a long one, he seemed somehow fresher and more handsome than she had ever seen him before.

He was looking at her, concern mingling with affection in his dark eyes.

Before he could say anything she rushed into his arms.

She held him tight and kissed him. Pressing herself against him, she tried to melt into him, as though to banish all space, all difference between them.

He laughed to see her so amorous.

"What's got into you?" he asked.

For a long time she could say nothing. When she did find her voice it sounded tremulous and weak.

"Just missed you, that's all," she said. "I felt so lonely . . ."

He held her cheeks in his palms and looked at her. The familiar light of tenderness shone in his eyes. She smelled his clean male scent, and saw the lush black hair above his tanned face. There was inquiry in his eyes, but also love, the same unconditional, passionate love she always saw there.

"I've missed you," he said simply. "One night without you is much too much."

They were both so accustomed to being together nearly every minute of the day, like halves of a whole person who could not bear to be apart, that to Joe it seemed unnatural and even criminal to have been separated from her by a whole night and most of today.

"How is Melanie?" he asked.

Kate's eyes clouded. She had almost forgotten her absurd subterfuge about Melanie, and it sounded false on his lips.

"She's fine," she said evasively. "I left her with another friend. I won't—won't have to see her again. I won't have to leave you again."

The words were like a prayer. She hoped Joe heard them as a simple assurance. He knew her so well that it was almost impossible to imagine he did not see through her lie of last night, did not know everything, simply by reading her heart.

The look in his eyes had changed. Its intensity was different now, touched by desire. She returned his gaze. All at once the old flame leapt suddenly between them. She placed her hands on his cheeks. Her body trembled in his embrace.

He kissed her, long and slow. Then, without a word, he picked her up in his arms and carried her to the bedroom. He placed her on the bed and sat down beside her, his fingers in her hair.

"I missed you," he said. "You seemed so far away . . ."

"I felt far away," she nodded. "Oh, Joe, let's never be apart again. Not even for a moment."

For an answer he kissed her again. The tension inside her body flamed suddenly to hot desire, infecting him instantly. He began to strip her clothes off, his breath coming short in his throat. The soft, beloved shoulders, tanned by the California sun, emerged from her blouse, and then the firm breasts with their tawny nipples, as her bra came off. She had never seemed more full of wanting.

She arched her back to help him as he slipped off her skirt. Her long, supple thighs came into view, almost unbearably sensual as they fell under his touch. He bent to kiss her breasts, her stomach, to drink in her magnificent female aroma as the panties came off, revealing the golden triangle between her legs.

A terrible need overcame him, born of his worry about her over these past twenty-four hours. He stood up, pulled off his jacket and shirt with one quick motion, and stepped out of his slacks. She saw the erect power of his sex as the underpants quickly slid down his thighs. She was awed by the beauty of his body, and breathless to get him inside her. But more urgent than her wanting was her joy at having him back. The events of last night had separated her from him by a spiritual chasm so enormous that she had feared, in some crazy way, that she would never seen him again.

Yet here he was, bending over her to kiss her tenderly, his tongue slipping inside her mouth, his hands buried in her hair. And once again the hard male limbs she loved so much were covering her, caressing her own nudity with the sure touch of long familiarity.

With a little groan she spread her thighs to invite him to her. His hands still around her face, his kisses on her lips, he probed softly at the center of her with himself, caressed her to moistness with the tip of him, slipped into her a sweet delicate inch, then an inch more, and finally slid to his hilt inside her.

From that instant it was quick, deliciously quick and hot, as their combined wanting consumed them. She gripped him closer than ever before, her legs wrapped around him, hands pressed to the small of his back, female sinews undulating and shuddering so seductively that in a few hot moments the great wave of their rapture was breaking over them. Kate held nothing back, pulling her husband into the deepest part of her, so that he could own her everywhere and banish the traces of Quentin that even now clung to her most private recesses. She wanted Joe to know that he alone owned her, that she lived only for him.

The spasm of their ecstasy was almost painful, for it sang of their separation as well as their reunion, and of a frantic attempt to beat back time and reality and circumstance in favor of their love. Kate did not know whether Joe was feeling this as intensely as she was, but she knew her body was proclaiming it with every sigh, every moan.

Did he guess at her secret? She hoped not. She prayed that the bestowal of her love would blind him to any worries he might have felt these last twenty-four hours.

But even now she knew that no matter how totally Joe filled her, he could never obliterate her secret entirely. The leering face of Quentin hung before her as she held her husband in her arms. The smooth, once-familiar feel of Quentin's arms, the taste of his kiss, lingered mockingly as Joe's body covered her.

She pulled Joe closer, held him tighter, as though to protect him against the ghost haunting her. Loving him entirely, she kept a private flame of hate alive inside her, so she could murder the tiny part of her that still bore the trace of Quentin.

When the wave of their passion had ebbed she held Joe like a mother, stroking his hard shoulder with her fingers, touching his hair, kissing his brow.

And at last, for this lovely moment, it seemed that nothing had happened, nothing had come to threaten them. The clock had been turned back, and their love was intact. She was still her old proud self, and he was the man to whom she belonged with all her heart.

He turned to look into her eyes.

"Kate," he said. "What's the matter? You're not yourself."

Despite herself she tensed. She feared that the essence of her guilt had somehow made itself known to him. She felt naked, transparent.

"Only that I missed you," she said. "It—it made me nervous. Being away from you."

His expression was penetrating, as though he could read

495

into her soul. Yet it was not frightening. Affection canceled all menace in it.

He touched her shoulder with a gentle finger.

"Kate," he said. "If something were ever wrong—I mean really wrong—you'd tell me, wouldn't you? If you were in trouble, I mean."

Kate managed a tense smile.

"Of course I would," she laughed. "But nothing is wrong, Joe. Nothing at all."

"I've worried about you since yesterday," he said. "It occurred to me that I love you so much that I've never really talked to you about certain things. You know, Kate, any trouble that was ever yours is also mine. There's nothing I wouldn't do to help you."

She said nothing. She was frightened to feel him probe so close to her secrets.

"The very idea that you might have trouble, serious trouble," he said, "and have to face it alone, without me, is awful. That would be a kind of—of sin against our love. Do you see what I mean?"

She nodded. Desperately she tried to be as much of an actress at this moment as she had ever been before the cameras.

"I understand," she said. "But all the troubles in my life went away when you came along. Do you believe me?"

For an answer he pulled her to him.

"Just hold me close," she said against his chest. "And never let me go. Will you promise that?"

"It's a promise," he said.

Perversely Kate felt she was using the protection of his own strength, of his love, to arm her to hide the truth from him. And she could not help feeling that this little lie at the heart of their love could only bring misfortune.

But at this moment, for the hundredth time since she first saw the terrible reflection of Quentin in the shop window before her, she steeled herself to fight off this evil alone. She would never let it touch Joe. He must never know the crimes she had committed, the evil that had touched her so long ago and that even now left its traces within her. She would hide it from him with the last breath in her body.

The two separate threads of her life—one good, the other evil—must never meet. She would die to keep them apart.

And now, in her husband's embrace, she felt encouraged. Quentin was under the earth where he belonged. His weapons were useless now. All traces of his entry into her life were erased.

She had done it alone, to save her life with Joe.

But not quite alone.

She had had a friend. The first real friend of her life, and just when she needed a friend most.

Thank God for Norman, Kate thought as she held Joe closer.

•   •   •

Nine miles away, Bryant Hayes sat behind his executive desk. On the desk top before him was a manila envelope. Across from him was a visitor.

Hayes took a puff of his cigar, studying his visitor's face. He drummed a finger ruminatively on the envelope. A slight smile gleamed in his eyes, and then was replaced by a look of paternal protectiveness.

"I don't want you to feel badly about this," Hayes said. "You've done the right thing. In fact, the only thing, for you as well as me. For everyone."

He looked the visitor in the eye.

"You got in over your head," Hayes said. "You needed money. Your career was going nowhere. You were in trouble. You couldn't go on that way."

He smiled complacently. "As of this morning, your troubles are over. You'll be right back on top again. You'll have scripts. You'll have respect. No more loan sharks and mafia tough guys for you. You'll be somebody again."

He glanced at the envelope. "Of course," he said, "you'll want to make yourself scarce for a while. I understand that. It will take a while for all this to blow over. But you've done the right thing for Hollywood as well as for yourself. This kind of thing," he gestured to the envelope with a frown, "is bad. It can ruin all of us. Our collective reputation has to be spotless. It may seem cruel now—

she is a fine woman, I understand, a good woman—but in the end you'll see it was for the best."

There was a long pause. Hayes studied his visitor. If there was a gleam of sadism in his eyes, it was veiled by his look of sympathy. But he could see that the visitor was suffering terrible moral scruples. This did not bother Hayes. He wanted it that way. He liked to see people suffer when they gave in to him. It proved that their capitulation was genuine and complete.

"Well, I think that concludes our business," he said, watching the visitor pick up the stack of bills that Hayes had placed on the desk moments before. "Take a vacation. Rest awhile. But stay away from Las Vegas. No gambling for you. I can't bail you out twice. Just have a nice rest. And when you return, there will be a whole new career waiting for you."

He paused. Then with a languid movement, he upended the envelope. Photographs, negatives, and scraps of newspaper clippings tumbled out across the desk top. The photographs were of Kate with Chris Hettinger.

For a moment Hayes looked at the photographs, fascinated. Then his brow furrowed in impatience.

"That will be all, Norman," he said. "You can go now."

His shoulders stooped by defeat, his face an agony of shame, Norman Webb stood up, put the money in his pocket, and left the office.

Hayes sat behind his desk, smiling.

It's an old rule, he thought to himself. But it's still as true as it ever was. *Every man has his price.*

10

The Hollywood Insider, June 3, 1946

Poor Kate Hamilton. It seems her ugly past has caught up with her. And just when she is on the verge of finishing her second prestigious film with Joseph Knight, the much-ballyhooed *Farewell to Love.*

Insider reporters have learned that not nine years ago, when dear Kate was a not-so-innocent teenager, she was involved in a sordid blackmail scheme that resulted in the death of a San Diego department-store scion named Christopher Hettinger. It seems that Hettinger, a white-as-snow Stanford graduate with a great future, was seduced by youthful Kate as part of a plan to prevent young Hettinger from marrying a local girl disapproved of by his family. The idea was to present all concerned with photographic evidence of the youth's hanky-panky with a local waitress named— Kate Hamilton.

All went weill. The romance was consummated, as the photographs on our cover and pages 6 and 7 document. But the innocent Hettinger boy, ashamed of his fling with Kate and despondent over its consequences for his family, committed suicide.

Kate went on to become a drifter, moving from town to town across America—and getting involved in who knows how many dubious affairs along the way—until, miraculously, she managed to get her hooks into none other than Joseph Knight five years ago. Knight was sufficiently besotted to fire the star of his second film, *The Velvet Web*, the respected actress Eve Sinclair, and to cast in her place Miss Hamilton—whom he married ten days later.

Knight has since become a war hero, returned from his flying exploits in Europe with scars and medals to show for his war experience, and begun a new film with—who else?—his loving Kate.

But it seems the past is not so easily buried. The chickens, as they say, have come home to roost. We wonder how Kate will explain away the all-too-eloquent pictures of herself with an innocent doomed boy named Chris Hettinger—to hubby Joseph Knight, to her colleagues on the new Knight film, to Hollywood, and to the American people.

Bryant Hayes sat at the enormous walnut desk in his private office at home. The *Insider* front page, with its headline and its photograph of Kate in the arms of Chris Hettinger, was spread before him.

Inside the tabloid, on the editorial page, was a long and eloquent editorial by the newspaper's publisher, Calder Sutherland—a very old and trusted friend of Bryant Hayes, and one for whom Continental Pictures' publicity department had done many favors over the years—demanding in the name of all that was holy that Kate Hamilton quit the movies altogether and that the Legion of Decency prevent the release of the new film in which Kate was starring. Her appearance before the public would be an affront to morality, the editorial said. She must be hounded from Hollywood, and the sooner the better.

The photographs on pages 6 and 7 were even more damning than the blow-up on the cover. While cropped to hide the sexual parts of Kate's lovely young body, they left no doubt as to what she was doing with Christopher Hettinger. The *Insider* had pulled out all the stops.

Hayes was smiling at the paper. In his hand he held a phone.

"Yes," he was saying. "Yes, Harvey. You can give the board my absolute assurance. And make sure Speck hears about this immediately. I give the board my personal word that *Farewell to Love* will never be completed, much less exhibited. This Kate Hamilton business ends things."

Bryant Hayes sat back comfortably. The triumph he had just scored was beyond his wildest dreams. *Farewell to Love,* a sure box-office smash thanks to the triple threat of Joseph Knight, Kate Hamilton and Eve Sinclair, would never see the light of day.

Thanks to Bryant Hayes.

That left the door open for Continental Pictures to rush to distribution with *Tides of Fortune,* the big-budget epic whose fate in the theaters seemed to have been sealed by the imminent release of *Farewell to Love.*

The course of action was obvious. *Tides of Fortune* would be premiered next spring, two months ahead of schedule. All the publicity stops would be pulled out. From Joseph Knight's debacle, Bryant Hayes and Continental Pictures would make a fortune. If *Tides of Fortune* did as well at the box office as expected, Continental Pictures would be the top-grossing studio in Hollywood this year.

And Hayes's personal power on the board in New York would double.

Hayes smiled as he spoke into the receiver.

"You just tell them they have my personal word on it," he said. "And make sure they understand who made this happen."

Hayes hung up the phone. For the first time since *The Velvet Web* had made Kate Hamilton a star, he felt that his destiny was in his own hands. He had spent five long years waiting for his chance to wreak vengeance upon Joseph Knight and his beautiful wife while putting a stop forever to Arnold Speck's maneuverings with the board back in New York.

And now his chance had come.

It had come in the unlikely form of a washed-up Hollywood writer named Norman Webb.

Since Hayes's detectives had been unable to find anything scandalous in the behavior of either Joseph Knight or his young wife, Hayes had become curious about Kate Hamilton's unlikely friendship with Norman Webb. There was the outside chance that Norman was in a position to know some dirt about Kate or Joe—or to find it out.

Norman Webb was not only a washed-up writer, Hayes soon learned. He was also an inveterate gambler, whose betting at the track had got him into some rather serious trouble with the local loan sharks. He was a man in the midst of an accelerating personal disintegration.

Hayes had ordered his detectives to keep an eye on Webb himself, just for the sake of thoroughness.

And now Norman had paid off, just when Hayes had needed a break most.

Last week Kate had met a stranger on Wilshire Boulevard, a man Hayes's detectives had never seen her with before. They followed the man to the Brookmont Hotel, a fleabag on Melrose Avenue, and kept loose surveillance on him.

Then they lost him Tuesday evening, as he maneuvered his old Packard through traffic. That was a disappointment, but it indicated they were on the right track. The stranger was important enough to go to some trouble to lose a tail.

As luck would have it, that same night, at two-thirty in the morning, the operative watching Norman Webb's bungalow saw Webb go out in his car and meet none other than Kate Hamilton on a corner in downtown Hollywood. Norman drove Kate all the way up into the Sierras, to a lake where it was known Kate and her husband had a cabin. The two returned in two cars, Kate's and Norman's.

Now the detectives knew they were onto something.

They were still watching the mysterious stranger's hotel the next morning when, lo and behold, Norman Webb was seen entering the place and emerging a half hour later with a suitcase he had not had when he went in. He took the suitcase to a bus-station locker and then hurried to Monarch Pictures, where he saw Kate and was observed in serious conversation with her.

What was in that suitcase? What sort of intrigue were Kate and Norman involved in? What had become of the mysterious stranger?

This was Bryant Hayes's moment of inspiration. He summoned Norman Webb to his office here at home. He told enough of what his operatives had seen to make it look as though he knew Webb had been an accessory to a serious crime. He played rough, making Webb fear for his freedom. Then he offered to cover up what he knew, to pay off Webb's gambling debts and guarantee him a lucrative screenwriting future, if Webb turned over what he had found in that hotel room.

After some obvious moral struggles, Norman had caved in. He gave Hayes what he wanted. An envelope full of pictures.

At this moment Norman was holed up in Tahoe or Reno or Las Vegas, counting his ill-gotten gain and waiting for the crucifixion of Kate Knight to be over before he slunk back to Hollywood.

Norman had behaved like the typical Hollywood creature. He actually liked Kate, and he revered Joe Knight. But friendship is no match for a Hollywood contract—particularly when the alternative to surrender is a term in jail.

And now the damning evidence of Kate's past was on the front page of Calder Sutherland's *Hollywood Insider*—to the delight of Sutherland, the eternal chagrin of Kate Knight, and the decided corporate advantage of Bryant Hayes.

Kate would be destroyed by those pictures within hours. And Joseph Knight, the real target of everything, would have to abandon his film and his heroine at one stroke. He would no doubt divorce Kate within weeks.

In this serpentine manner, after five long years of trying, Bryant Hayes would have his revenge on Joseph Knight.

And, if Continental had the kind of financial year Hayes expected, with *Farewell to Love* out of the picture, this might at last be the coup de grâce that allowed Hayes to sweep away the pernicious influence of Arnold Speck on the board, and assume sole power over the destiny of Continental Pictures.

Bryant Hayes was pleased with himself. He had followed the golden rule of Hollywood. He had waited. He had swal-

lowed his humiliations with good grace, knowing that today's humiliation is tomorrow's revenge. He had probed
for the weaknesses of all those who opposed him, and,
when his chance came to strike back, he was ready.

Everyone has his Achilles' heel. In the case of Joseph
Knight, the weakness was Kate Hamilton. And in the case
of Kate, it was her past—and her best friend, Norman
Webb.

The battle was over. All that remained was for Joseph
Knight to surrender, as Norman had surrendered.

As Hayes was thinking this the phone on his desk rang.
It was one of his vice-presidents.

"I thought you'd want to know, sir," the man said, "that
the Legion of Decency has scheduled a hearing on the Katherine Hamilton matter. They're considering barring the new
Knight film from distribution if Hamilton is in the lead
role."

"When is the hearing?" Hayes asked.

"Monday," the vice-president said. "They want you to
be there, since it was you who provided the photos to the
Insider."

Hayes smiled. The Legion was offering him a front-row
seat for the sacrifice of Kate Hamilton.

"Fine," he said. "I wouldn't miss it for the world."

Hayes got up to go to his pool for a swim.

He left the negatives in his desk drawer.

He did not bother to lock them away in his safe.

After all, this was his own house.

*   *   *

In the canyon house Kate sat numb as a statue, looking
at the cover of the Hollywood Insider.

Across the table from her sat Joseph Knight.

The tabloid had been published today, and Oscar
Freund's lawyers, in a panic, had called to ask whether
they were genuine. Joe had kept them from Kate until the
shooting day was finished, and had brought her straight
home to discuss them before deciding whether to suspend
shooting or to go on.

Now Joseph Knight was gazing intently into his wife's eyes.

Kate had just told him everything. About her running away from home, her brief unhappy marriage to Quentin, her affair with Chris Hettinger, and the boy's terrible death.

Everything but her murder of Quentin, that is.

In Joseph Knight's face there was no jealousy, no reproach. But there was sadness.

"I thought I knew you so well," he said. "I thought I was here to help you, to support you. It hurts to think that you had to suffer with these memories alone, with no help from me . . ."

Kate looked at him.

"They were part of my past," she said. "The memory of that boy, and of what Quentin did to him, and of my part in it—that made me what I was, Joe. An empty shell. When I met you it was like being reborn. I felt I had never existed before you. The last thing I wanted to do was to reopen that door."

He touched her hand. She could see that he understood.

Joseph Knight did not say what was in his mind. He had his secrets, too. Things he had not told her about, either because he wanted to be the only one to remember them, or because he did not want to remember them at all. The image of a woman's impassioned face, and of a burning automobile, flashed before his mind's eye for an instant, and then, mercifully, was gone.

"And how did this happen?" he asked, glancing at the tabloid on the table between them.

"Quentin came back," she said. "Ten days ago. He threatened to use the pictures. He wanted money. A lot of money. I—"

Words failed her. How could she admit to her husband that she was a murderess?

But she had already hidden so much, for so long . . . What good had lying done her?

"I tried to stop him," she said at last. "I guess I failed."

There was a silence as husband and wife pondered the gulf that had existed between them despite their love. A great sadness seemed to join them now.

"You should have told me," Joe said. "I would have taken care of it for you."

Kate nodded ruefully. She should have thought of that, she supposed. Quentin Flowers, a cheap crook, would have been no match for Joseph Knight.

But the whole point of her actions had been to keep Joe separate from her past. The idea of Joe and Quentin meeting, talking, had been more than she could bear. She had done the only thing she could do.

"What—what do we do now?" she asked despairingly.

Joe took both her hands in his.

"We face what comes," he said. "Together."

"Together . . ." Kate murmured, holding onto the precious word as to a lifeline. Despite herself she looked away from her husband.

"The last obstacle separating us is gone now," he said, his voice serious as it had never been before, even in their most intimate moments. "Let the world do its worst. It will never come between us again. Shall we promise each other that?"

She looked into his eyes. The love she saw there was undiminished, and perhaps even deeper than ever before. Deepened by disaster, she mused.

For no matter how absolute the love she saw in those handsome eyes, a shadow hung over them like a shroud. It was the shadow of the misfortune she had brought upon them both through her own sins, a misfortune that not even Joseph Knight could wipe away now.

It was too late.

"Is it a promise?" Joe repeated.

For an answer Kate buried her face against his chest and wept. He had never seemed so real, so solid, and yet she feared he was about to disappear and leave her in the empty solitude that had been her only world before she knew him.

Long ago she had asked herself whether their love was too good to be true, a paradise she had not deserved. At this moment, with her sins gathered around them both, it seemed that no promise could save her from the fate bearing down upon her.

She hugged him closer, her embrace full of love, but not of hope.

506

11

A WEEK AFTER THE DAMNING PHOTO STORY ON KATE HAD appeared in the *Hollywood Insider,* a meeting was held in a conference room at the Los Angeles County Courthouse. Present were members of the Legion of Decency and their attorney. Also present was Calder Sutherland, publisher of the *Hollywood Insider,* along with two of his newspaper's attorneys. Bryant Hayes, as promised, had a ringside seat.

Also present were Oscar Freund, Joseph Knight, and Kate, along with three lawyers from Monarch Pictures and an attorney for Kate herself.

The assembled legal brain trust made quite a crowd. There was an atmosphere of quiet melodrama in the room. Everyone knew that two great film careers were at stake—Kate's and Joe's—as well as the future of an embattled film, *Farewell to Love,* which had been spoken of as a sure Oscar winner until the present scandal erupted.

It fell to the Legion of Decency's attorney, Ellis Lippincott, to gavel the meeting to order.

"Gentlemen, and lady," he said, nodding to Kate, "we all know why we are here. A story has been published about Mrs. Knight in the *Hollywood Insider* which makes serious claims about her past associations and behavior. Mrs. Knight's attorneys, in conjunction with the legal department of Monarch Pictures, have instituted a twenty-million-dollar lawsuit against the *Insider* for slander."

Glances were exchanged around the table. The dollar amount of the lawsuit was enormous for these times. To an outsider it would have indicated a serious intention to fight on the part of Oscar Freund and Kate Knight.

But Oscar and Joseph Knight were painfully aware that the lawsuit was merely a holding action. Since there was no way to deny that the girl in the damning photographs was indeed Kate, and that poor Chris Hettinger had committed suicide in the immediate wake of his relationship with Kate, there was no real hope of saving Kate from a scandal of career-ending proportions. Kate's lawyers, under Joseph Knight's orders, had decided to delay things as long as possible, and, when cornered, to try to show that Kate had been an innocent dupe in the Hettinger affair and not personally responsible for the boy's death.

It was already too late, of course, for such a claim to do much good. But Kate's attorneys were as accustomed to defending guilty defendants as innocent ones, and would use every trick in their book to minimize the damage to Kate's reputation.

Ellis Lippincott cleared his throat. "Now, the Legion has called this meeting because it feels it cannot wait for the result of this lawsuit, which may take many months. The Legion must make its recommendation as to the suitability of a film starring Mrs. Knight for public viewing. The courts will decide the suit; but the Legion will hear evidence on both sides today with a view to making its recommendation to the appropriate authorities. Gentlemen, any introductory remarks?"

He nodded to Kate Knight's attorney, Burris Cody, of the prestigious Los Angeles firm of Cody, Smight, Griffin, Brent, and Sherman.

"Gentlemen," Cody said, "in the spirit of cooperation Mr. and Mrs. Knight have consented to be here today. But we feel this hearing is unnecessary. The story in the *Insider* is slanderous and irresponsible. Mrs. Knight is innocent of all the charges against her. There is no legal or moral reason why filming of Mr. Knight's film, *Farewell to Love,* should not proceed with all speed, followed by distribution on schedule to theaters in the United States and abroad."

He paused, not without a touch of drama.

"We would also like to see a full retraction and public apology in the *Hollywood Insider* for the false and slanderous charges made against Mrs. Knight. Such a retraction might make the civil suit unnecessary, and would avoid a great deal of trouble and legal expense for all concerned."

Burris Cody sat down, his air of lawyerly sternness masking his knowledge of how flimsy his bluff really was.

Bryant Hayes glanced at Calder Sutherland, a slight smile on his face. Calder Sutherland looked confident. He was sure of his information, sure of Kate's guilt. He had it all on the best authority. He had the photos to prove it.

His own counsel spoke up.

"The *Insider* stands by its story," he said simply. There was arrogance in his voice. "If counsel for Mr. and Mrs. Knight wishes to present evidence to the contrary, we'll be happy to listen. Under no circumstances will the *Insider* retract its story or apologize to anybody."

There was a silence.

"Very well," said Ellis Lippincott. "We all know where we stand. Does anyone else have anything to say before we proceed to the evidence?"

The lawyers shook their heads.

Then the unexpected happened.

"I have my own witness to bring forward, if you gentlemen don't mind," said Ellis Lippincott. "This witness has been retained by the Legion itself, and in these informal circumstances I see no reason why we shouldn't hear what he has to say."

Eyebrows were raised around the table. The lawyers, girded to have at each other with every weapon in their legal arsenal, had not expected the Legion to produce its own witness.

Ellis Lippincott motioned to the clerk at the door. A man was ushered in, dressed in a brown pinstriped suit. He wore glasses and carried a large portfolio.

"Gentlemen," Ellis Lippincott said, "may I present Mr. Thomas Avila. Mr. Avila is a photographic expert for the

U.S. Armed Forces, specializing in aerial surveillance and microphotography. We have asked Mr. Avila to examine the negatives of the photographs published in the *Insider* with a view to verifying their authenticity."

The bespectacled man sat quietly with his portfolio as Ellis Lippincott went through the list of his qualifications as an expert witness. The list was so long that by the time Lippincott finished, most of the lawyers present were yawning.

"Mr. Avila, may we have your testimony, please?" asked Ellis Lippincott.

"Yes, sir."

Avila opened his portfolio and produced an enlarged photograph, which he placed on an easel brought by one of the legal assistants.

It was a blown-up photograph of Kate Knight's head from one of the photos published by the *Insider*. The enlargement was so big that Kate's face was grainy and almost indistinct. But the photo was clearly recognizable.

"Gentlemen," Avila said. "I was asked to examine the negative from which this print, and the prints used in the *Insider*, were made. What you see here is a four-hundred-times enlargement of that portion of the negative showing Mrs. Knight's head."

He took a small pointer from his portfolio and pointed at the picture.

"As you will notice," he said, encircling the head with the pointer, "there is a hairline cut mark around the head. The detail of light and shadow has been very carefully airbrushed around this cut in order to make a match between the image of Mrs. Knight's head and the area surrounding it."

Seeing the expressions of disbelief around the table, he removed the large photograph and passed it around the table. As Sutherland and his lawyers saw the picture, their faces turned red.

"You'll notice, gentlemen," Avila said, "that some airbrushing has been done on the face and hair of Mrs. Knight as well. This was done, I believe, in order to cover up evidence of light and shadow which would have shown that she was photographed in another time and place. It is an expert job, invisible to the naked eye. Only under the microscope can one see that the images have been doctored.''

There was a pause as those present weighed the implications of what they had heard.

''I find that all seven negatives from which the prints were made contain the same evidence of manipulation,'' Avila said. ''The work is very subtle, very expert. But the pictures are not genuine. In a court of law they could not be used as evidence that Mrs. Knight was in the place where these images were photographed. That concludes my demonstration, gentlemen.''

There was a pause. Calder Sutherland, having turned pale during the expert's speech, leaned over to whisper in the ear of his chief counsel.

''What do you think?'' he asked.

''It doesn't look good,'' the attorney whispered back. ''Why didn't you check the authenticity of the photographs independently?''

Sutherland shook his head with a sigh. ''I thought I had the photos from the best authority,'' he said with a glance at Bryant Hayes. ''There was no reason to think they were fakes. I guess I should have checked. Where do we stand?''

The lawyer smiled.

''We're in up to our necks,'' he whispered.

Across the table the attorneys for Kate and Monarch Pictures were engaged in a whispered consultation no less intense than that of their adversaries. Hiding their own shock as best they could, they consulted with each other and with Oscar Freund and Joseph Knight about what to do next.

It was Kate's attorney, Burris Cody, who spoke for them all.

''In view of the expert testimony we have just heard,'' he said, ''Mrs. Knight, Mr. Freund, and their attorneys would like to suggest the following as a solution to our problems. If the *Insider* prints a complete retraction and apology for its slanderous allegations, and contributes the sum of two million dollars to the Actors' Relief Fund, we will drop our civil suit and consider the entire matter closed. Gentlemen, we would like to hear your reply to this.''

Calder Sutherland again leaned close to his chief attorney.

"What do you think?" he asked. "Two million is tantamount to admitting guilt."

The lawyer spoke in a whisper. "They're offering you a way out. Just pay the money. It will look like a generous gesture on your part. Print that apology. Be contrite. Be complimentary to Kate. And thank your lucky stars you're getting out this easy. Twenty million dollars in a lawsuit is a lot of money. They've got you by the balls now, and they know it. Kate Knight is close to being a screen legend. If you sling mud at her and lose, your circulation could go out the window."

Calder Sutherland thought for a moment. He was an intelligent man. He had needed to be cunning to steward his tabloid through fifteen years of legal troubles and still make enormous profits. He realized he had no hope of winning this battle in the courts, much less in the forum of public opinion.

"Okay," he said. "Pay the ticket. Let's get out from under."

"Gentlemen," said his attorney, standing up, "the *Insider* has a reputation for fairness and integrity to protect. This story, and the accompanying photographs, were printed in good faith. To the best of our knowledge at the time, they were genuine. We deeply regret the error and any distress it may have caused Mrs. Knight. We will print a full retraction as requested, and Mr. Sutherland will be happy to make the suggested donation to the Actors' Relief Fund."

There was a collective sigh of relief around the table. Joseph Knight kissed his wife's cheek and then stood up to thank his attorneys, who hid their amazement at the unexpected turn of events behind happy smiles and handshakes.

The representative of the Legion of Decency seemed pleased. He was a personal fan of Katherine Hamilton and had looked with great regret upon the prospect of an untimely end to her career.

Calder Sutherland, surrounded by his attorneys, left the room. As he did so he darted a look into the eyes of Bryant Hayes. It was not the look of a friend.

A few minutes later the conference room was empty. Joseph Knight and Kate were on their way back to Monarch Pictures to resume shooting. Oscar Freund rode in the limousine with them. The various lawyers involved were on their way to lunch together at Louise's, a favorite downtown restaurant patronized by attorneys and judges.

As for Bryant Hayes, he was on his way back to Continental Pictures to decide what his next move must be. He still could not believe what had happened. He had had Joseph Knight and his wife cornered at last, and they had escaped.

Hayes's curses rang out steadily in the back of his limousine. But they could not silence the inner voice warning him that because of today's events he was no longer the hunter, but the prey.

The Hollywood Insider, June 17, 1946

In an unprecedented move, the publisher of the *Insider* has personally retracted a photo essay on actress Kate Hamilton, published two weeks ago in this newspaper (see Editorial Page). The publisher, Calder Sutherland, acknowledges that the photos involved were fakes, apologizes to Mr. and Mrs. Joseph Knight for any distress caused by the article, and agrees to pay two million dollars to the Actors' Relief Fund by way of reparation for the embarrassment caused Mrs. Knight by this erroneous report.

Says the editorial, "The *Insider,* its publisher, its editors and staff deeply regret this grave insult to the integrity of one of Hollywood's greatest stars, and a woman whose personal integrity and honesty are beyond question."

Insider reporters have learned a startling secret about this report and its provenance. It seems that the photographs of Kate Hamilton, purporting to show her in the act of sexual intercourse with a young San Diego man who subsequently committed suicide, were provided to the editors of the *Insider* by none other than representatives of Bryant Hayes, head of Continental Pictures and a bitter enemy of Joseph Knight and his wife for several years.

Hayes, apparently angered by Knight's dramatic upstaging of his big-budget film *Winter of Destiny* in 1940 with his own epoch-making film *The Rainbow's End,* and further angered by the huge success of Kate Hamilton in Knight's later film *The Velvet Web,* personally had the faked photographs sent to the *Insider* as part of a vendetta against Knight.

Bryant Hayes's plan seems to have blown up in his face, as the apology in today's Editorial Column makes clear. We can only wonder what this blow to Hayes's prestige will mean to financially troubled Continental Pictures, which has been struggling for five years to recover its prestige in the wake of the disaster of *Winter of Destiny.* Some observers have suggested that Hayes's nine lives as head of Continental have finally run out, and that it is time for him to step down in favor of new leadership for the troubled studio.

Bryant Hayes stood on the carpet before the desk of Arnold Speck in the office high above Sixth Avenue in New York City.

Though he held himself with his accustomed dignity,

Hayes's hat was metaphorically in his hand, and he knew it. He had been undone legally by the Legion of Decency's surprise photographic witness. The photos in which he had invested so much had been revealed as fakes, and Joseph Knight had frustrated him once again.

Far worse, however, was the action of Calder Sutherland in naming Hayes on the front page of his newspaper as the source of the false accusations against Kate Knight. Thanks to that revelation Hayes would henceforth be viewed throughout Hollywood and the nation as a spiteful tyrant who, for the sake of his studio's financial gain, had stooped to slander in order to harm a great filmmaker and his legendary wife.

The blow to Bryant Hayes's reputation as the venerable head of a major film studio was devastating.

Thus, after all these years of struggle, of feint and parry and attack, Arnold Speck at last had the ammunition he needed to destroy Bryant Hayes.

Speck was sitting behind his desk, a self-satisfied look on his face.

"I did what I could with the board, Bryant," Speck said with ill-disguised triumph. "But to no avail. It has been decided that, under the circumstances, the only thing that will help is your resignation. Effective immediately."

He sat back and puffed at his cigar.

Though the words were not unexpected, they struck Bryant Hayes a hammer blow. His legs felt weak under him. He wanted to slump into the leather chair at his side, but even at this terrible moment he could not give Speck the satisfaction of appearing weak before him.

"I suppose you're not interested in hearing my side of this," he said.

Speck smiled.

"Of course I'm interested, Bryant," he said. "I feel for you. I'm on your side. You've got to know that, after all these years. But I'm afraid the board's decision is final. You'll have to fly back to Hollywood right away and start clearing your things out. We'll have a replacement there by the beginning of the week."

Hayes narrowed his eyes.

"And who will that be?" he asked.

Speck flicked ash from the end of his cigar.

"I'm going in temporarily," he said. "After all, I know the financial issues. And I have a nodding acquaintance with the creative problems, having had the benefit of quite a few years of advice from you. I'll do my best to pick up the slack."

Hayes smiled bitterly. He knew that this new arrangement would not be temporary. For many years Arnold Speck had been angling to take over the Hollywood end of Continental as well as the financial reins. It had taken all Hayes's ingenuity and cunning to hold off Speck this long. But, despite all his great triumphs, Hayes had made his mistakes and had his misfortunes.

The worst misfortune of all had been the day Joseph Knight crossed his path. From that day on, Knight had been his nemesis, upstaging him, outguessing him, tormenting him with stiff competition, forcing him into ill-considered decisions, disastrous errors in judgment.

And this latest one, the attempt to destroy Kate Hamilton and get at Knight through her, had been Hayes's final blunder.

If only Calder Sutherland had not named Hayes in his retraction! He owed Hayes innumerable favors. For fifteen years Hayes had provided the *Insider* with half its dirt, half its scoops, no matter who was hurt or helped by the stories. Together they had practically ruled Hollywood.

But Sutherland had had little choice when faced with the photography expert's damning testimony. He had opted to save himself and his newspaper, at Bryant Hayes's expense. Not even friendship or loyalty could have prevented him from choosing his own survival. Least of all Hollywood friendship or Hollywood loyalty.

What was done was done. Because of Calder Sutherland and Joseph Knight, Hayes was unbankable. His long and illustrious career was over.

Mustering what was left of his dignity, Hayes stepped forward and extended a hand.

"Arnold," he said, "it's been nice working with you. Best of luck."

"You, too, Bryant," Speck said. "You've been a hell of a studio head. We'll miss you."

Speck's words dripped with insincerity. Triumph glistened sadistically in his eyes. He held Hayes's hand a moment too long, to let the insult sink in.

Bryant Hayes endured the moment as long as he could, then extricated his hand. He turned on his heel and left.

It was over.

After Hayes had left the office, Arnold Speck sat lost in thought, a smile curling his lips as the smoke from his cigar plumed toward the ceiling above his head.

Then he leaned forward and buzzed his secretary.

"Get me Bryant Hayes's home phone in California," he said.

There was a pause.

"But didn't Mr. Hayes just leave your office?" the secretary queried in a puzzled voice.

Despite his irritation, Arnold Speck had to smile.

"Carol," he said, "when are you going to learn to do what I tell you?"

"Right away, sir." The secretary sounded chastened.

Arnold Speck sat back to wait for the long-distance connection to come through. As he blew smoke from his cigar toward the ceiling, a sound not unlike the purring of a cat escaped his lips.

13

As Bryant Hayes was leaving Arnold Speck's office in New York, his little German houseboy, Karlheinz Rächer, was sitting alone beside the swimming pool in Hayes's Bel Air mansion, drinking a bottle of the finest champagne in Hayes's vast wine cellar.

Karl did not hurry his enjoyment of the champagne. He drank in dainty sips, savoring the taste of the fine wine as his eyes traveled over the palatial domain of his employer and oldest enemy.

Karl Rächer was happy today, happier than he had ever been in his chaotic, mismanaged life.

For today he had defeated Bryant Hayes.

Karl knew perfectly well why Hayes had been summoned to New York by the board. He knew because he had seen the retraction printed by the *Hollywood Insider,* and the tabloid's pointing of its own finger at Bryant Hayes in the heart of its apology to Kate Hamilton and Joseph Knight.

At this moment, Karl mused, Bryant Hayes must be wondering how in the world his sure-fire photographic indictment of Kate Knight had blown up in his face, and cursing Calder Sutherland with all the fury in his own black heart for throwing him to the wolves. But Hayes would never know the real truth about his own downfall.

The man who had orchestrated Bryant Hayes's comeuppance was little Karl Rächer.

Hayes had been very clever in extorting the damning photographs of Kate Knight from poor Norman Webb. His Hollywood instincts had served him well, and the gutless Webb had been no match for him. In using his old cohort Calder Sutherland to publish the pictures in the *Hollywood Insider,* Hayes was behaving as a true Hollywood shark, scenting blood in the water and going for the quick kill.

But Hayes had conducted all this sensitive business in his own house, disdaining his studio office. This was his habit, because under his own roof he felt more in control of things. He had even left the negatives of Kate Hamilton and the Hettinger boy right in his desk drawer.

Hayes in his arrogance never dreamed that his home was ruled by Karl Rächer, who knew every cranny of it and eavesdropped on every conversation that took place within its walls.

So it was that Karl Rächer learned of the Kate Hamilton photos almost before anyone else, and found the negatives where Hayes had so imprudently left them.

Having overheard Hayes on the phone to New York, Karl realized that Hayes was staking everything on those photographs and on the destruction of Kate Hamilton. Continental Studios would budget its whole coming year on the proposition that *Farewell to Love* would never be completed, much less released.

And all this depended on the negatives that Hayes had brought home and left in his desk.

This was the opportunity of a lifetime.

An expert on everything having to do with film from his many years as a photographer as well as a special effects expert, Karl needed only an hour's thought before deciding what to do. He purloined the negatives when he knew Hayes would not be looking. He rented a darkroom in a busy section of Olympic Boulevard. With the patience of a master, he snipped the head of Kate Hamilton out of each of the negatives and then, after a few subtle manipulations of the exposure and a little airbrushing, put it right back where it had been—only now demonstrably doctored.

A couple of discreet phone calls had done the rest.

As he sipped his employer's champagne Karl Rächer could not help smiling at the final irony of his life in Hollywood. In his rented darkroom he had taken the real and made it look unreal. He had made the genuine seem fake. And thus, in a court of law, the fatal negatives could not be accepted for what they in fact were: evidence of Kate Hamilton's youthful peccadillo.

That was Hollywood, Karl mused: a power of illusion greater than reality itself. A power that could destroy lives, careers, honesty, truth. It had destroyed Norman Webb, and Rächer himself, and countless others. But for once, in this case, illusion had been marshaled to save a good young woman's career, and perhaps her whole future.

At the expense of the erstwhile master of illusion, and of the evil that illusion does: Bryant Hayes.

What Karl Rächer had started in the darkroom, Calder Sutherland had finished on the front page of his tabloid, the *Hollywood Insider*. And today the coup de grâce was being administered to Bryant Hayes by his superiors in New York.

With this thought Karl Rächer raised his glass.

The phone rang before he could bring the glass to his lips.

He picked it up.

"Mr. Hayes's residence," he said in his thick German accent.

"Karl, is that you?" said a voice he quickly recognized.

"Yes, sir," Karl said, looking at the champagne bubbling in his glass. "It is me."

"Everything went off as expected," said Arnold Speck, his voice firm and robust despite the crackle of the long-distance connection. "You did a beautiful job. Congratulations."

"Thank you, sir," Karl said, twirling the glass. "It was a pleasure."

"Your contract will be in the mail this afternoon," Speck said. "Seven years at five thousand a week, with bonuses for every picture you direct, and special incentives for all those Oscars we expect you to win for Continental. You're going to be right back up on top again, Karl—where you belong."

"Thank you, sir," Karl smiled. "You are most kind."

"I'll be on the coast by Monday," Speck said. "We'll have lunch."

"I'll look forward to it, sir," Karl said. "And thank you."

"Thank *you*, Karl. I never forget a favor. And the one you've done me is a beauty. I expect us to have a long and happy relationship."

They hung up. Karl raised his champagne glass with a smile, glancing around the domain of Bryant Hayes.

To he who laughs last, he mused, a smile on his lips. *Prosit*.

ON AUGUST 12, 1946, *FAREWELL TO LOVE* WAS FINISHED.

In the hectic weeks after the brief crisis over the photos of Kate in the *Hollywood Insider*—a crisis that had cost Bryant Hayes his Hollywood career and increased public interest in *Farewell to Love* a hundredfold—Joseph Knight had thrown every ounce of his creative energy into completing the film.

He had worked Kate and Eve and Samuel Raines into near-prostration, doing re-take after re-take on their key scenes, searching for that tiny inflection, that infinitesimal trick of light and shadow and expression, that would give the film an inner psychological sweep to match the enormity of the war in its effect on Americans' lives.

The most important scene of all was the last to be shot. It was Kate's goodbye scene with the hero at the train station when he left for the war. The scene was first seen only halfway through the film, when Kate's character was still a fresh and callow young girl head over heels in love, saying goodbye to her lover and fearing for his physical safety in battle.

But the same scene would also end the entire film—this time as a memory in the heroine's mind, now that she knows she has lost the hero forever, not because of the war itself but because of the complexity of circumstances during her long separation from him. She is now the mother of his child, a grown-up woman tempered by experience, and she looks back with tragic nostalgia on her earlier, more innocent self, realizing that her tearful farewell to the hero at the train station years before was the last time she would ever see him.

Because of this dual function of the farewell scene Joseph Knight directed Kate to deepen her character at that crucial moment, so that she saw beyond her own youthful naïveté to something dark and irrevocable about her farewell. He also added Eve to the scene after the hero's departure, in the role of the heroine's best friend who appears at the station to offer moral support as the heroine watches the train pull out.

The heroine, distracted by her grief over leaving her lover, does not pause to wonder what her best friend is thinking at that moment. Thus she never thinks about the possibility that the friend has been jealously watching her farewell with the hero, and feeling her own private grief as the man she herself loves leaves for war, even though his goodbye is for another woman.

It was the fine irony of this romantic triangle, expressed visually by the closeness of the two girls on the platform, that Joe wanted to capture. The camera would show the two women holding hands, joined forever by their love for the same man and the tragedy this love was to bring about.

Joe wanted the physical contact of the hands to be an integral part of the scene.

"Are we ready?" Joe said.

Kate and Eve nodded.

"Roll 'em," Joe said.

The slate man came forward.

"*Farewell to Love,*" he said, snapping the slate. "Scene four ninety-two, take one."

"Action," Joe said.

The camera came in close on Kate and Eve. So alike was the look in their eyes that in that instant they looked like sisters. Love for the same man made them almost resemble each other.

Kate clutched Eve's hands.

"I'm never going to see him again," she said. "I can feel it."

Eve, in character, held Kate close.

"It's not true," she said. "He'll come back. I know he will."

And, after a small pause, she added, with a pained wistfulness, "Love never dies. Nothing can kill it, not even time."

At this crucial point in the film, only the sharpest of spectators would guess from the look in Eve's eyes that it was for herself that she held out this hope, that she was not thinking of her friend at all. Love had blinded her to right and wrong, and made her forget her friendship entirely.

It fell to Kate to say the last line, as the camera came closer, cutting off the face of Eve and making Kate's close-up the last image of the film.

"Goodbye," she said. "Goodbye, my love."

The camera came closer and closer, until Kate's eyes filled the screen. The image of the receding train was reflected in her eyes, thanks to the brilliant work of the cinematographer. She had to hold her pose for two full minutes, enough time for the final credits to go up the screen. This would be one of the most important close-ups that Joseph Knight had ever filmed.

Kate did not flinch. The intensity of emotion in her eyes

was almost unbearable. Her eyes communicated a depth of love and a presentiment of dark fate so powerful that the few observers on the sound stage were in tears at the sight of her.

At last it was over.

"Cut," said Joseph Knight. He came around the camera and kissed both women, first Eve and then Kate. He took the hand of each and squeezed, letting his own flesh join them. Words were unnecessary now. The look in his eyes said everything.

Both women's performances were so perfect that Joe did not even try a re-take. He was sure he could never capture the same intensity again. And there was something mystical about the symbiosis between Eve and Kate that had made this strange, haunting shot possible. For Joe as a filmmaker it was the opportunity of a lifetime, never to be repeated.

Kate and Eve left the studio early, while Joe stayed on to finish some work with the production staff before the sets were struck.

Though it was only four-thirty in the afternoon, both actresses were emotionally exhausted. Kate realized she might not be seeing Eve Sinclair for a long time after today. Their work together had been so intense that it was hard to imagine life without Eve.

"Will you come home with me?" Kate asked impulsively.

Eve hesitated.

"Just for a drink," Kate said. "I've always wanted you to see our place. It seems—it seems bad to say goodbye here."

Eve smiled. "I'd love to."

Kate drove into the hills with Eve following in her little MG. When they reached the Benedict Canyon house Eve seemed surprised.

"So this is where you live," she said, looking at the little house with its attractive hedges and garden. "Why, I've been down this road a thousand times. I can't believe I've never noticed it."

Kate had to admit that the house was easy to bypass. It

was small and unpretentious, more or less like any attractive suburban house with two or three bedrooms. It had a cozy look that differed greatly from the houses of the great stars and big producers.

The two women entered the house. They left their scripts—no longer needed now, like the schoolbooks of young girls on the first day of summer vacation—on the foyer table and moved into the living room.

"It's lovely," Eve said. "Not your typical Hollywood spread. It's homey. I like it."

Kate smiled. "Joe can't stand big places," she said. "He says they make him feel at sea. I can't have much of an opinion, because I've lived in furnished rooms most of my adult life. To me this is a palace. What can I get you to drink, Eve?"

"Anything soft," Eve said. "Club soda, ginger ale—or iced tea, if you have it."

Eve had sworn off hard liquor and pills for the duration of shooting. She needed to be her best and look her best for this role. As things stood, it had been difficult for the makeup department to hide the traces of her dissipation. But in the rushes she looked good. Her acting talent, combined with the skill of Joseph Knight's cameraman, was hiding her true face and making her look young and innocent.

Today, even though shooting was over, Eve did not want a serious drink. For an unnamed reason she still felt she had to be on her toes.

"Iced tea," Kate smiled. "I'll have some with you. It will only take a minute. Make yourself at home."

She disappeared into the kitchen, and Eve heard water running. Then, almost immediately, Kate stuck her head out of the kitchen.

"Hey," she called. "How about a swim?"

Eve hesitated for an instant. It had been a long time since she had been in a bathing suit. Her fear of the combined effects of age and dissipation on her body made her uncomfortable about showing herself in public.

"I don't have a suit," she called.

"Oh, I'm sure I have one of mine that will fit you," Kate called. "No problem."

"All right, then," Eve called back after an instant. "Sounds good."

She could feel the grime of the day's shooting all over her. A dip in the pool would pick her up. Besides, she did not want to leave Kate yet. Their swim would allow her to stay longer.

She heard Kate go upstairs. She got up from her seat and walked idly around the living room. The place was nicely appointed, but really very simple, almost spartan. It had cane furniture, decorative tropical-looking landscapes on the walls, and a beautiful braided rug of exotic weave and design that seemed to give the whole place an air of freshness and intimacy.

There was a picture of Kate on the piano, a still from her role in *The Velvet Web*. It was a remarkable picture, capturing Kate's peculiar combination of innocence, worldly wisdom, and sadness, along with, of course, her haunting sensuality.

It was obvious why Joseph Knight liked to have that picture near him. This was Kate as he had first known her, and as his own camera had first captured her for *The Velvet Web*.

Eve got up and peeked into the study that was off the living room. The large desk was cluttered with Joseph Knight's piled-up scripts and other business papers. There was a typewriter with a page still in it. She tiptoed forward and looked at it. It was the scene from *Farewell to Love* that they had shot today. Eve recognized a small change in dialogue that Joe had informed her of this morning on the set. He must have been mulling over the script only last night, looking for changes that might add to the impact of that crucial scene.

Eve looked around the office. There was another picture of Kate on the desk, this one a snapshot taken with a lake in the background. Kate was dressed in a gorgeous bathing suit, her wet hair looking dark and stringy as it fell over her shoulders. The look in her eyes was ambiguous, on the edge of levity and fatigue, with something else added. Eve was impressed by the picture, but did not linger over it long enough to see that it was the picture of a young woman who wanted to make love and was trying to tell her husband so with her eyes.

Eve did not recognize the lake, but assumed it was the place in the mountains where Joe and Kate had their cabin. Perhaps the picture had been taken during their honeymoon, just after Kate had taken over Eve's role in *The Velvet Web*.

There were no other photographs or personal touches in the office. Eve went back to the living room and glanced into the kitchen. Kate was still upstairs.

Now Eve realized what was strange about this place. Though it had a very cozy and familial look, neither Kate nor Joe had any pictures of relatives. No pictures of parents, brothers and sisters, weddings, family gatherings.

It was as though the past did not exist for them. As though time began here in this house, with their love. As though there were no world beyond themselves.

Eve sat back down in the living room. She began to feel the strange, compelling intimacy of the house. This was a place where two people loved each other intensely, obsessively. They hardly noticed their surroundings, so wrapped up were they in each other and in their love.

A little uncomfortably Eve got up and moved to the sliding doors that led to the back lawn. There was a garden there, with tulips, birds of paradise, zinnias, tiger lilies. And a small swimming pool. Very small, by Hollywood standards. The water chuckled as a hose refilled the pool. Beyond the small back lawn was a lovely view of the hills, not as spectacular as the one Eve used to have before she sold her Brentwood house, but very beautiful.

There were several chaise longues and small tables around the pool. It was a pretty scene, the more attractive for its unpretentiousness.

Eve turned from the lawn and went back into the living room. She looked at the simple furniture again.

And in that instant she realized what had been prodding at her intellect since she entered this place.

There was something else missing from this house, beyond the expected pictures of family.

A child.

Eve could almost feel the absence. This was the house of a couple who were deeply in love. The only thing it lacked was the baby they both wanted so much. That was why it looked not only intimate, but somehow incomplete. How Eve was so sure of this she did not know. But it struck her with the force of the self-evident. Joe and Kate were eager for their first child, and probably trying hard.

With this thought, Eve sat down. She could still hear the muffled sound of Kate's bare feet padding about upstairs. Pensively she awaited the return of her hostess.

Upstairs Kate was rummaging through her drawers in search of a bathing suit that would fit Eve.

Half the time Kate did not know where her clothes were. She kept them in haphazard order. She was as indifferent about her clothes today as she had been five years ago. Marriage and love had not changed her on that score. She wore the first thing that presented itself, fluffed out her hair, and often did not bother to look at her makeup in the mirror. She hated shopping for clothes, and did so only when it was absolutely necessary for a studio occasion.

Joe did not mind her casual appearance. In fact, he encouraged it. He had never before met a woman who dared to be so natural about her appearance, a woman with no narcissism. It added to Kate's freshness, even to her innocence, he thought. And it added to her sensuality in a way that invariably excited him. Kate with no makeup, hair hastily thrown back or tied with a rubber band, dressed in jeans and a T-shirt, was more beautiful to him than Garbo in an Adrian creation. Kate was as natural as a young girl. Joe loved her for this.

A smile played about Kate's lips as she searched through the drawers. She was glad to have Eve here. She felt almost like a teenager who is bringing a new friend home for the first time and is eager to show off her room, her possessions, to share her thoughts and dreams. She and Eve had become strangely intimate during these past months, though they had never had a real conversation from woman to woman. Their acting had been the sole link between their personalities. But it had been a deep link, and one that would always leave its mark on Kate.

At length Kate found a dark one-piece suit that looked as though it would fit Eve perfectly. She took it downstairs with her and handed it to Eve.

"I'm sure it will fit," she said. "You can use our bathroom. I'll meet you by the pool."

Eve went into the bathroom and took off her clothes. She noticed Kate's few toilet articles. Predictably, Kate kept the bare minimum of makeup supplies on hand. As Eve's naked body came into view, she imagined for a split second that she was Kate, looking into this mirror. This, after all, was the mirror that saw Kate every day of her life.

What would the mirror see?

Eve already knew. It would see a young woman so confident in herself and in her marriage that she never for an instant doubted herself, suspected a taint or an unworthiness in herself. A woman who glowed right back at the mirror from the depths of a heart filled with happiness.

A woman in love . . .

This mirror must also see Kate and Joe together, for they obviously used the same bathroom, just like a modest young couple who could not afford two bathrooms. Perhaps sometimes they stood here together, after making love, or just before. Eve could almost see Joseph Knight's black eyes glowing with desire and love as his hands encircled Kate's slim shoulders, her hips, her breasts.

Eve pulled on the suit. Indeed, it fit perfectly. She was amazed that she and Kate were more or less the same size. For everything about Eve was slimness, trimness, svelte elegance—that is, during her better days—while everything about Kate was earthy lushness, curves, excitement, deep and disturbing female sensuality.

As Eve pondered these thoughts something stirred deep inside her, and a faint tremor shook her limbs. She was pulling the suit tighter, up her waist and between her legs. For a brief instant she thought of the sex Kate bore so easily in her own loins, the sex Joseph Knight adored and had possessed so many times. This suit had been close to that sex, touching it . . .

Eve put the thought out of her mind and padded out to the patio, where Kate was pouring iced tea from a pitcher into two tall glasses. Everything about Kate's demeanor had the same charming unpretentiousness as the house itself, almost as though she were a young housewife in her back yard in Ohio instead of a famous star in her Hollywood hills home. She looked absolutely gorgeous in her suit, a bright yellow design that hugged the lush fruitlike contours of her beautiful body.

A body that sang its readiness for childbirth . . .

Eve looked at Kate's face. As usual, it bore no makeup. Her hair, tousled by the mountain breeze, fell about her shoulders. For the hundredth time Eve tried to fathom the strange beauty of that face, a beauty that shone even more brightly without makeup than on the screen.

All at once she realized what Kate's secret was. At twenty-seven Kate was a beautiful woman. But if one looked closely at her face one realized that at thirty-five and forty and even fifty, Kate would be just as beautiful. And she would probably still be spurning makeup, and still letting her hair tumble where it liked.

Where did she get this quality? This inner glow, this pure desirability that other women would kill for? Did it come from a purity of heart that Eve could not herself imagine? Or perhaps from something darker and more complicated . . .

In any case, it was no wonder she had captured Joe Knight's heart so easily, and so quickly.

"You look great," Kate said, admiring Eve in her bathing suit. "I had a feeling that one would fit you perfectly."

Before Eve could answer Kate had dived into the pool and come up with water streaming through her hair and down her cheeks.

"Come on in," she called. "The water's fine."

Eve tested the water with her toe and found it warm and inviting. She sat down on the edge of the pool and, more cautious than Kate, let herself descend slowly into the water. It was heavenly, a slippery balm that washed away all her exhaustion and nerves.

"That's wonderful," she said, treading water. "I don't know why I don't do this every day. I haven't been in my own pool in months."

"Joe and I take a swim like this every night," Kate said. "Even if we get home late. It takes the sting out of the work days. I think it also helps Joe to sleep better."

Eve recalled the serious wounds Joe had brought back from the war. Neither he nor Kate spoke of them, or of the pain he must be in much of the time. On the set he was always handsome and full of his accustomed energy, though he remained thinner than he had been before the war.

Eve could imagine Joe and Kate swimming together in this intimate setting after a long day's work. Swimming before they made love, perhaps, or afterward . . . Backyard swimming pools were made for young couples in love.

And for children, of course.

After their swim Eve and Kate sat and chatted idly for a few minutes. They talked about shooting, and complained jokingly about what Joseph Knight had done to them with his rigorous shooting schedule. But now that it was over they felt joined by a quiet happiness, and by pride in their joint achievement. They were excited about the film. They knew it was something special, and they could hardly wait until it was edited and ready to be seen by the public.

Then, fatigue weighing them down, they were silent for a moment, staring at the hills. Eve felt a strange languor in all her limbs. She had not felt this relaxed or this at home in as long as she could remember.

"I wish I could sit here forever," she said. "Just forget Hollywood, forget everything but this little yard and that waning sun."

There was a pause.

"You know," Kate said at length, "I've never told you this, but you were my heroine when I was growing up. Those pictures you made as a little girl . . ."

Eve laughed. "How strange," she said. "What did you like about them?"

Kate smiled. "You were always so happy. Your character, I mean. You were surrounded by people who loved you. Like a little princess. And when they were in trouble, you saved them. There was so much love . . . At least that was what it looked like to me. I needed love then . . ."

Eve shook her head. A look of bitterness vied with something wistful in her expression. "Hollywood," she said.

"What do you mean?" Kate asked.

Eve suddenly looked serious. Then her face changed as she saw how touched Kate was by her own memory of her youth.

"Never mind," she said. "If it helped you in any way, it was worth it."

Again there was a silence. Each woman understood how unhappy the other had been as a child. The knowledge seemed to bring them closer.

"Tell me," Eve asked, "what was your life like before—before Joe?"

Kate looked wistfully at the hills.

"There was no life," she said. "There was no me. I just sort of woke up one day—and there he was. That's when I started living. Everything that went before was like a sad dream. Easy to forget, not pleasant to remember."

"There was never a man before?" Eve asked.

Kate seemed to come back to herself with a shock.

"Oh, yes," she smiled. "I was married once, for a short time. It was such a disaster, such a waste, that I often go for months at a time without even remembering that it ever happened."

"Were you very young?" Eve asked.

"Let me see . . . Seventeen," Kate said. "Yes, very young. Not even alive, really."

Eve saw the pain in Kate's face as she pondered the memory.

"Sorry I brought it up," she said. "Ancient history."

"Oh, never mind," Kate said. Then, looking at Eve, "How about you, Eve? Any important men?"

Eve blushed despite herself. The only man she had ever loved had been Joseph Knight. It suddenly occurred to her how false were the pretenses of this amiable conversation, and indeed of her being here today.

"No," she said. "My marriages were publicity stunts. I lived for career. I never let a man interfere with that. That was my biggest mistake, Kate. You're lucky. You know who you are."

"I wouldn't say that, exactly," Kate smiled.

There was a silence as Eve pondered these words. They were true. Part of Kate's mystery, both on screen and off, came from the fact that she did not really know herself any more than her fascinated fans or admirers did. She floated atop her own opaque essence like a reflection dancing on the surface of a dark pool.

But she had found Joseph Knight. And so, even if she was not sure who she was inside, she did know where she belonged. She knew she was loved. And that obviously was all she needed. This thought sent a pang of longing through Eve.

"Anyway," Eve said, "you've evaded Hollywood's most fatal trap. You're loved, Kate. And you know the difference between what's important and what's not important. Love is the only thing that matters. If the rest of us had known that, we never would have let Hollywood eat us up the way it did."

Kate's strange beautiful eyes, at once so candid and so mysterious, were fixed on her guest. She said nothing.

Eve looked away. She noticed the setting sun reflected in the pool water.

"Hey," Kate asked. "Why don't you stay for dinner? I can call Joe and see when he's coming home . . ."

"No, thanks," Eve said. "As a matter of fact, I've got a date. Have to get home and get ready."

Kate's lips curled in a little conspiratorial smile. "Someone special?" she asked.

"That remains to be seen," Eve said, stretching as she stood up. "In this town, you never know. I think I ought to give it a chance."

She wondered if Kate could see through her lie. She would be alone tonight, of course.

But Kate gave no sign. "You go ahead and change," she

said. "I'm going to clear up out here and call Joe and see how he's doing."

Eve went into the bathroom and took off Kate's suit. As she looked at the garment, a mere handful of fabric once she had taken it off, her heart went out to Kate. Kate was so honest, so unspoiled. And, most important, Kate had paid a price for that innocence. There was a fierce pride in her that had seen her through life without the moral compromises that had corrupted Eve herself and so many others.

And Kate had been lucky. Fate had allowed her to fight her way through the world while remaining good. That was a rare gift, vouchsafed to few human beings anywhere, much less to women in Hollywood.

And because of it Kate had come out of nowhere to steal Joseph Knight's heart and to become a great star with a single performance, in *The Velvet Web*.

How could Eve Sinclair, as an actress or a woman, ever hope to compete with a creature of so rare an essence?

Eve had put on her clothes and was standing in the bedroom, looking at the double bed in which Kate and her husband slept each night.

Suddenly she saw their bodies, joined by slumber in those soft sheets, saw Joseph Knight's powerful body in Kate's embrace. The bed was small, not a king-size, as most Hollywood couples used. Obviously they wanted to be close, as close as possible. Perhaps, since his war wounds, Kate cradled him to her breast like a mother, sensitive to his pain and to what he had been through.

But not for long. Soon the heat of his caresses would make her forget everything but her wanting, and the sheer power of him . . .

The damp suit was still in Eve's hand. She was looking at the bed, and yet not looking at it somehow. Her whole life yawned behind her like quicksand eager to devour its victim. And the future of Joseph Knight and Kate, the children they would have, their happiness, lay before her in that bed, a vision she could no more look in the face than she could stare into the emptiness of her own soul.

The room had gone black, and she was standing there as

still as a statue, when the soft touch of a hand on her shoulder startled her out of her reverie.

"What?" she said, her eyes blank as those of a person suddenly awakened from a deep sleep.

It was Kate.

"Didn't you hear me?" she said softly. "I saw you standing here and asked you if something was the matter. You didn't answer. Are you okay, Eve?"

Eve turned away from the bed in embarrassment. She looked into Kate's eyes, the golden irises luminous in the waning glow of sunset. Eve wanted to put her arms around Kate, to hold on to her for dear life. At the same instant she wanted to banish her from the world, to make it so that she had never existed. In this way, at least, she could breathe . . .

"I—oh, I'm fine," she said. "Just out of gas, I guess. Shooting does that to me."

"I know how you feel," Kate said, taking the suit from her. "Can you drive home all right?"

"Sure. I'll be fine," Eve smiled. "I'd better get moving. Mr. Wonderful will be calling around eight."

Impulsively she kissed Kate on the cheek as she left. Kate watched as Eve got into her sports car and turned on the engine. Kate waved, her gesture brisk and candid as that of a girl, as Eve backed down the driveway.

Then Eve threw the car into gear and headed down the mountain. Kate's smiling image was eclipsed from her vision, and only the canyon road filled the windshield.

Eve Sinclair took a deep breath. When she let it out, it came as a sob. The anguish in her heart twisted like the cruelest of knives.

Another ten minutes in that house, she mused, and she would have exploded. She had got out in the nick of time.

15

Three Months Later

THE GALA PREMIERE OF *FAREWELL TO LOVE* WOULD TAKE
place tomorrow night at Grauman's Chinese Theater in
Hollywood.

The film had opened to an eager preview audience two
weeks ago in Pasadena. Kate's recent brush with scandal
in the pages of the *Hollywood Insider* had combined with
public curiosity about Eve's first supporting role and Joseph Knight's return to filmmaking after a five-year hiatus
to insure the interest of the film.

But not even those closest to the production had anticipated the emotional response of the preview audience or
the enormous success of the first three weeks in selected
theaters across the country. *Farewell to Love* struck a
nerve in the psyche of the nation. Millions of American
women had seen the men they loved leave for the war in
Europe or the Pacific, and hoped against hope that those
men would return so they could pick up their lives where
they had left off. But in so many cases, that parting closed
a door forever on the life that had gone before. Separation
and the outer and inner wounds of war changed life for
good. Love, too often, was not as strong as fate.

It was that deeper and more tragic significance of parting
that the film depicted. And American women felt their
hearts break at the sight of Kate and what happened to her.

Her story was that of a love that could not be denied, but that also could not be ultimately fulfilled. A love that could lead only to separation even as it led to a cosmic union.

Rare was the woman who had not cherished at some point in her life a man to whom she had given her heart, but to whom she could not belong in this world. And the war was a symbol of this gigantic sundering, this core of pain inserted like a void at the center of human lives that seemed quiet and uneventful on their surface.

Farewell to Love was an immediate success, filling theaters all over the world. But Joseph Knight's film was more than a movie hit, more even than a movie classic. It was a mirror held up to a tumultuous time in world history and to the secret scars in the hearts of millions of people who had survived that time. The film would stand forever as a monument to its era, and a document of human courage in the face of irremediable loss.

No one doubted today, after three weeks of exhibition, that the film would win many Oscars. For Joe as producer, it would almost certainly bring an unprecedented third straight Best Picture Academy Award, along with probable awards for his sensitive, probing direction and his magnificent screenplay. Joe would go down in movie history as one of the greatest prodigies ever to make films.

For Eve Sinclair, *Farewell to Love* was a resurrection. The reviews of her performance were so excited, so thrilled, that their praise extended back over her whole career, wiping out the dark spots and painting her in the colors of a great actress.

"After twenty years as a trouper in the trenches of the toughest business in the world," wrote the influential critic for the *Los Angeles Times*, "Eve Sinclair has finally emerged as a great star. The fine irony is that she has done so in the first supporting role of her adult career. Yet it is in this role, so full of darkness and light, so colored by sin and goodness, by saintliness and temptation, that she has found herself at last. It is safe to say that a new career is now opening for her, perhaps not as the slick and commercial leading lady she once was, but as something infinitely more important—one of Hollywood's *great* ladies of the screen."

The other reviews were equally enthusiastic. Eve was considered a sure bet for Best Supporting Actress. She had taken the apparently thankless part of a girl who tries to steal her best friend's lover, and turned it into a classic role—the role of a young woman who is not lucky enough to be good, but who finds nobility of a sort even in her own tragic weakness, a weakness born of love.

Women everywhere identified with Eve. For what woman has been lucky enough to live out her life with the man of her dreams? Most women have to fight, and even to sin, in order to gain the man they want. Love knows no right and wrong, but obeys a law of its own. Eve had shown that cruel truth with a superb combination of dignity and pathos.

Yet even in her great glory, Eve was upstaged by Kate Knight.

The critics were calling Kate's performance "a role for the ages." The unique combination of earthy sensuality and feminine depth that Kate had shown so precociously in *The Velvet Web* attained an even higher level in *Farewell to Love*.

Audiences were on the edge of their seats from the moment Kate first appeared on the screen. The power of Joseph Knight's direction, and the subtleties of theme and dialogue provided by his screenplay, joined with the haunting look in Kate's eyes to warn the audience right from the start that tragedy was in store for her in her great love.

By the time her character said goodbye to the hero at the train station, audiences were in tears. And when, to conclude the film, the camera returned to Kate's face on the railway platform, and moved slowly closer and closer, her face became a living symbol of love and of loss.

"One of the classic camera shots in film history," wrote an influential European film critic. "Joseph Knight uses his camera the way Rembrandt used his brush. This is not a mere camera studying the face of an actress. It is an instrument of love, looking past the flesh into the spirit and essence of womanhood. The statement Knight makes is about Kate Knight's genius as an actress, about a tragic character, and about the nature of film—and, perhaps as much as anything, about himself.''

Of course, Kate's career as an actress was assured by her performance in *Farewell to Love*. But this performance went beyond the box office. Many observers felt that Kate would never have to appear again before the cameras to have made her final, unforgettable statement as an actress.

Kate alone knew that Joseph Knight had done this for her. It was his camera, and his personality, that had allowed her to play her role with a power she had never dreamed herself capable of. She also owed a lot to Eve's incomparable support. But was it not Joseph Knight who had cast Eve, Joseph Knight who had foreseen everything, creating this film from the depths of his own inspiration?

Yes, behind everything was Joe, with his creative talent, his love, and his incomparable strength. *Farewell to Love* was his picture.

•   •   •   •   •

Joe, Kate and Eve were at the cabin in the Sierras the day before the premiere. It was a quiet time for all three. Eve had driven up in her little MG to keep them company as they prepared for the ceremony at Grauman's Chinese, which would be covered by journalists from all over the world.

The three felt a bit strange together. For the last several months, since the last of their editing and dubbing obligations ended, they had not been together.

Something had come between them. Though Kate repeatedly invited Eve to lunch or dinner at the Benedict Canyon house, Eve always found an excuse not to come. In an unspoken way Eve seemed to be saying that she did not want to disturb Kate's privacy with her husband. She realized that ever since the inception of *Farewell to Love* Joe and Kate had not really had an interval of peaceful intimacy. The stress of shooting, combined with the crisis of the tabloid attack on Kate, and finally Joe's backbreaking work on editing and post-production at the studio, had kept them from their marriage to each other. It was time for them to rest and relax.

Finally Kate had decided to respect her friend's wishes, and no longer invited her. But she called her every few days, simply to talk about the film or to pass the time of day. And the telephone became a sort of lifeline between them, keeping them in touch while maintaining the distance that Eve seemed to require.

Kate did not ask Eve whether she had another acting job in the works. Nor did Eve ask Kate whether she had future acting plans. The two women kept silent on that score. Partially because it was a sore subject, particularly with Eve, whose career had been at a low ebb since *The Velvet Web*—and partly because neither of them had energy enough to talk about the future yet. They were still in the thrall of *Farewell to Love*. Their personal and professional lives were inextricably knitted to it.

But this weekend was different. Eve had driven up to the cabin to help Joe and Kate celebrate. The three had spent a quiet evening drinking champagne and listening to the sounds of the woods and the distant ripple of the lake.

Joe had been the first to go to bed. His work at the studio had made him more tired than he realized, and he wanted to give the two women some time together, since they had not seen each other in several weeks.

It was also clear from the somewhat drawn look on his face that he was in physical pain from the wounds he had suffered in the war. From casual remarks Kate had made over the months, Eve knew that Joe refused to take painkillers during his work days, but required powerful medication to sleep through the night.

So Eve and Kate were left alone.

They sat together on the couch.

"I'm so glad you're here," Kate said. "I don't know what it would be like if you weren't. I've missed you, Eve."

"Me, too," Eve said, a trifle less forthcomingly. "It's been a long time. How have you been, Kate?"

Kate's glowing smile was her answer. She obviously was

the happiest of women, a woman completely fulfilled by her man.

"I have a secret to tell you," she said.

Eve's eyes lit up. "Goodie," she said. "I love secrets."

"Well," Kate beamed as she spoke, "I'm going to have a baby."

An odd light flickered in Eve's irises, like a tiny strangled explosion, and was gone. Then her lips curled in a smile that quickly opened to embrace her friend. She hugged Kate.

"I'm so happy for you," she said. "Have you told Joe yet?"

"After the premiere," Kate said. "I don't want to break his concentration on the film yet. Besides, it will be fun to have two things to celebrate."

Eve's smile was touched by sympathy now. "I guess you two have waited a long time for this, haven't you?" she said.

Kate nodded. She had never been close enough to Eve to confide in her about the problems she had had in getting pregnant.

"We've been trying ever since we got married," she said. "But somehow it wouldn't happen. We've been to doctors . . . After the war Joe worried about the shrapnel he took in his pelvis, and I—well, I was worried about everything. Believe me, I'm relieved."

"Joe is going to be so thrilled," Eve said. "I know how he feels about the film, but nothing could mean so much to him as this. Are you sure you want to wait?"

Kate nodded. "I think it's best," she said. "We're both so wrapped up in the film, I think it would be just too much to tell him now."

Eve smiled and squeezed Kate's hand. "Well, I'll keep your secret," she said. "And congratulations, Kate. I always—I always wanted this for you."

There was a pause. Then Eve yawned.

"I'm sorry," she said. "I must be more tired than I thought. The drive up here did me in, I guess."

"We all need some rest," Kate said. "Come on."

She showed Eve to the guest room and then went to join

Joe. His breathing was quiet, regular, subdued by the drug he had taken. She lay close to him, as always. She heard the distant sound of Eve taking a shower. Then she drifted off to happy sleep beside the man she loved.

Their sleep was not untroubled, as it turned out.

Kate found herself awakening again and again, too excited about the premiere to give herself over to her dreams. When she woke up she found Joe tossing and turning by her side. Apparently his medication was not strong enough to keep him asleep on so important a night.

Neither of them realized it, but in her own room, Eve Sinclair did not sleep a wink. She remained motionless the whole night through, her eyes staring at the ceiling.

At three forty-five in the morning they all crossed paths on the way to the bathroom. They laughed at their collective insomnia and sat down in the living room to have a drink together. Kate made hot milk with whiskey. They sat in sleepy-eyed goodfellowship, wondering whether to abandon the idea of going back to bed and just get up now. Then, not wanting to be exhausted for the premiere, they decided to give sleep one more try. They returned to their separate rooms. Kate fell into a sweet, dreamless sleep in her husband's embrace.

The next morning they all had coffee and a quick breakfast before getting ready to drive to Hollywood. They wanted to make an early start, for both Kate and Eve would need all day to get themselves ready for the gala premiere, with designer dresses, makeup, and coiffures for the occasion. As for Joe, he needed to get to a noon meeting at the studio with Oscar Freund and to have several more meetings in the course of the afternoon about the film's exhibition schedule and foreign rights.

At nine o'clock Joe found that his car would not start. He examined the engine and electrical system and quickly found the problem.

"The distributor is shot," he told Kate. "We'll have to call Bob at the station in the village and see if he's got something that will get us going."

They were not lucky. The little village station did not

have the necessary part. But Bob, a resourceful friend who was aware of how important today was to Kate and Joe, had an idea.

"There's a station about forty minutes from here that has more parts than we do," he said. "Let me call them. If they've got it I'll drive down there and bring the part back to you."

"That's a lot of trouble for you," Joe said.

"No trouble at all," the gregarious station owner said. "Hell, I'd drive you down to Hollywood myself if I had to. But I'll bet you they'll have what you need."

A few minutes later he called to say the other station had the part. He could drive there and back in an hour and a half.

Joe looked at his watch. That would get him to Hollywood by one in the afternoon, an hour late.

Eve was looking at him.

"Take my car," she said. "You and Kate go on ahead. I'll wait here for Bob. When he brings the part, I'll lock up the cabin for you and follow you down the mountain. I'm not in that much of a hurry."

Joe shook his head. "No, that's too much trouble for you," he said. "I know you women need to see your hairdressers. You two take Eve's car, and I'll wait."

"Nonsense," Eve said. "You're the one who's in the real hurry. For heaven's sake, just go on. Take my car."

There was a moment of rather absurd wrangling about which two should take Eve's car, and which one should remain behind. It was finally decided that Eve and Joe should go ahead, with Kate to follow in her own car when it was repaired. Kate's old indifference to hairdressers and makeup decided the issue.

"If I make it, I make it," she said. "If I don't, I don't. I don't really care. I'll call you when I'm home. Have a good trip."

After some casual goodbyes punctuated by laughter about the car trouble and somewhat nervous jokes about the premiere, Joe and Eve got into the little MG. Eve was behind the wheel. Though Joe had offered to drive, she said she knew the little car's quirks, and joked that she didn't trust him on these mountain roads.

Secretly Joe was delighted. He had slept badly, and saw a chance to nap in the car on the way down the mountains.

Kate watched them leave, waving as they wended their way down the dirt track along the bank of pines. When they were out of sight she went into the cabin and tidied up before packing her bag. She did not do a very thorough job, for she knew she and Joe would be back here within a couple of days, or next weekend at the latest.

When she had finished she felt a wave of delicious fatigue come over her. The excitement of the past few weeks had left her more tired than she realized. She went into the bedroom to lie down and rest until Bob arrived to fix the car.

No sooner had her head touched the pillow than she was fast asleep.

Almost instantly, it seemed, she was dreaming. Faces were floating past her mind's eye in dizzying succession. She saw her own past, her indifferent mother, and Ray, pathetic ugly Ray, sitting in his armchair in the old living room. She saw Quentin. She saw Chris Hettinger, and Norman Webb, and Barney Livingstone, and Melanie, and so many other people who had crossed her path after she left home, touching her life as insubstantially as images on a movie screen.

And somehow, in her somnolence, she saw the tragedy of these people, some selfish, others not, some with evil intentions, others merely scared or confused, people who had shared the earth with her and yet not shared her heart. It all seemed dark and hopeless.

But now all the images in Kate's dreams were eclipsed by that of Joe. She saw Joe's face, smiling, handsome, with its curious mixture of hard, almost brutal strength and loving tenderness. It was the most wonderful face Kate had ever seen or imagined, the face that contained her own fate, and was her heart's only home.

But a shadow fell over it at this moment, and over Kate's slumber. It was no longer Joe's normal face, full of strength and initiative, that she saw. It was his face from the nightmare she had had more than once during the war, the night-mare in which his plane plummeted to the earth while he showed no emotion at all.

Kate moaned softly in her sleep. She saw the plane turn-ing over and over, trailing flames behind it across the harsh blue sky. And Joe sat in the cockpit like a somnambulist, indifferent to his own impending doom, a languid and some-how preoccupied look in his eyes.

In her sleep Kate cried out to him, emptying her lungs in a desperate effort to warn him of the disaster engulfing him. But he could not hear her, and the horror of the dream grew greater as the plane bore him toward the hard pitiless earth while he did nothing to save himself.

Kate felt an unearthly tension building within her, so enormous that it seemed impossible she could still be asleep. Her cries mingled with the ugly and mortal drone of the falling plane. Despair had locked her in a grip that would suffocate her unless she escaped it.

And when she opened her eyes to look around her and assure herself that this nightmare was only a dream, she realized to her amazement that she was already on her feet, rushing out of the cabin into the morning sunlight.

Somehow it did not look like sunlight. The glare of the day burst into her eyes like a blinding darkness. And the mountains rearing before her looked like sinister giants poised to crush her.

As she rushed forward Kate felt she was fleeing a thing more awful than a mere dream. She knew something terri-ble was about to happen. It had been approaching from her past all this time, ready to destroy her heart, and had only used the war, Joe's plane crash, and her miscarriage to fool her into thinking the danger was past. The war had been only the prelude. Her crime was to be punished now, on this day. Or so it seemed to Kate in her panic.

The cabin and the silent lake receded behind her as she ran. Before her were the cruel mountains, thrusting their ugly humps skyward while the ravines between them swal-lowed everything that dared to flutter above their depths. The earth itself seemed a giant executioner, weighted like a fist to punish all human hope.

And in Joe's dazed eyes was nothing but indifference to the fate that had been creeping up on him all this time, the fate that had waited until today to sunder him from Kate forever.

"No!" Kate screamed. "No!"

Like a madwoman she plunged down the drive, frantic to reach Joe and save him. But even now, as her love flung her forward into space, she sensed that it was destiny pulling her down the mountain, and that it was already too late, for herself as well as the man she loved. Rage and longing scalded her throat. She would not come to her senses until much later.

Inside the cabin the phone was ringing, but Kate did not hear it.

16

WHILE HOLLYWOOD WAITED AT THE BOTTOM OF THE SIERRAS for their triumphant return to its places of celebration, like the descent of gods from Olympus to the surface of the earth, Eve and Joe drove along the twisting mountain roads.

Eve handled the car easily. She had often driven all around the Hollywood hills and surrounding mountains in solitude, as a way of clearing her mind. She had had the little MG fitted to her specifications with a high-torque engine to handle the steep mountain grades. She loved to drive fast—and to drive alone.

But today she was not alone. Joe Knight was by her side.

She savored the odd situation, glancing at him as she handled the wheel. He was looking through the windshield, an unreadable expression on his face. He seemed thoughtful and yet good-humored. Perhaps he was remembering their sleepless night with Kate. Perhaps he was looking forward to the premiere.

He seemed very tired. No wonder, Eve thought. For nearly two years *Farewell to Love,* from casting to postproduction, had rested entirely on his own shoulders. Eve and Kate and the others had given their best, but the film was Joe's responsibility. Each day they had all looked to him for guidance, encouragement, and a clarity of vision about the whole project which he alone seemed to possess.

Glancing at him again, Eve could also see that he was obviously in physical pain. He had slept badly, despite his medication. Who could tell what morning agonies he suffered from the deep wounds of war after a restless night? Since he never spoke of his pain, it remained a mystery, like so many other things about him.

Perhaps only Kate had often seen him this tired before, as she awoke with him each morning to face the day of shooting.

Eve's heart moved to think of Kate's solicitude, and her intimacy with this most remarkable of men. What a joyous burden it would be to take care of him, to know his fatigue as well as his strength, to be able to comfort him in his hours of need, even of self-doubt. Perhaps last night, when they all finally went to bed after their toddy, Kate had enfolded him in her arms, gathered him to her breast, and helped him to sleep.

Kate, who was going to have his child . . .

Eve pondered the beauty of the love between Joe and Kate. They were perfectly matched. No man in the world was so masculine, so strong as Joe. And none was as sure in his treatment of other people. Oddly, Joe's very equanimity toward others, which contrasted so sharply with the shouting and tantrums of other producers and directors, came from the fact that he knew other people's weaknesses and forgave them. He showed others respect and consideration, treated them kindly, and got the best out of them. He could do this because of his complete confidence in his own strength, a strength that seemed to rub off on those who worked with him.

With this in mind Eve ruefully recalled her clumsy attempt to seduce him when they first worked together, and her inexcusably childish behavior on the set. Joe had been as composed and calm in refusing her seduction as he was later when, left with no choice, he fired her. He never lost his dignity, even when she was using every trick she knew to throw him off balance, to make him angry, to hurt his feelings.

Had she known him well in those days, she would have realized that the petulant behavior of ordinary women, and even their most vicious barbs, could have no more effect on him than their physical charms. Joe was looking for something deeper in a woman, a sort of dignity, of nobility perhaps, that ordinary women do not have.

How delighted, how fulfilled he must have felt when he first met Kate, who alone among women had that precious quality of trusting herself and respecting herself, a faculty that kept her heart safe from the rot and decay of the world, and of its worst outpost of corruption, Hollywood. Joe must have thought he was the luckiest man on earth the day he first set eyes on her and saw in her that special inner light of spiritual strength he had sought in vain for so long.

And when he saw that the camera could capture that light, that cosmic femininity, he must have felt blessed by the gods.

No wonder, then, that he had married Kate and made her a star all in the same moment, almost immediately after meeting her for the first time. There could not have been a second's doubt that this was the woman he had been waiting for all his life.

And all the others, the pathetic ladies-in-waiting, including Eve herself, must have flown from his consciousness like paper dolls when he at last looked into the beautiful face of Kate and gave her his heart with a marvelous sense of relief.

Ever since then, the two of them, and their marriage, had been the stuff of legend. They could not make a move without the whole film world reacting, turning to gaze at them in admiration and wonder.

And why not? They were truly bigger than life. Not simply because of their achievements, but because of that quality of character that placed them above other human beings, above the petty concerns of the earth, in a place where they had eyes only for each other.

And perhaps it was only because each of them had this rarest of qualities that they had found each other at all. Perhaps this was how the gods smiled on such creatures and lifted them from the rotting surface of the planet to a place where they could love in peace and happiness.

And now Kate was going to have his child.

Eve looked at Joe. She was going to say something, but she saw that he was asleep. Lulled by the movement of the car, he had nodded off, probably knocked out by his restless night and the relentless throbbing of his pain. He looked very peaceful and vulnerable, slumped in the seat of the little car.

They were approaching Coulter Bend, the steepest and most visually exciting part of the drive down the mountains. The road crept out on the edge of an enormous canyon, a drop of over a thousand feet nearly straight down. Across the chasm several craggy peaks rose angrily toward the sky, as though thrust upward by some spasmodic inner force that filled them with agony and longing.

The guardrail was small here, a mere strand of wire attached to steel posts two or three feet high. There were warning signs: TRUCKS USE LOW GEAR NEXT 10 MILES. Drivers held their steering wheels tighter through this stretch, and women passengers caught their breath and closed their eyes.

Eve looked at Joe again. He was dead to the world. His pain was visible in his face, a shadow of tightness, of effort in sleep. And yet there was something inexpressibly peaceful about him. He was probably dreaming of Kate.

Eve looked back to the road, and then to the emptiness beyond the drop-off. Her smile faded. For at that moment the pitiless bath of sunlight had sent a golden beam of lucidity into the deepest part of her mind.

She wondered why she had not thought of it before. It seemed to have been staring her in the face for as long as she could remember. But she could not have fathomed it before. She needed to be above the earth this way, alone with Joe, in order to understand.

You have his child, she thought, seeing Kate's face before her mind's eye. His gift of eternity, of immortality, had already been bestowed on Kate, along with the light of his love. The future was for Kate. But this was not all of Joseph Knight. The other half, the darkness, was for Eve. Was it not this darkness she had walked through all her life, trying vainly to escape it? Was this not the void that had been catching up with her all this time, closing off her future as surely as Joseph Knight's heart closed off her love?

There is justice in the world. This was the truth Eve saw only now, and seized with all her strength. All these years she had been half a woman, half a heart, limping through time like a cripple. But now, in this precious moment, her chance to make herself whole was presenting itself. Joseph Knight had made Kate whole. Now he would do the same for Eve.

She looked over the precipice into the chasm before her. It beckoned deliciously. She smiled, feeling the same beautiful combination of rage and peace that she had felt the day her blood spilled over the newspaper image of Kate in the silence of her trailer on the set of *Farewell to Love*. She seemed to understand what everything meant, and why things had to turn out the way they did. She had always been falling, and all her unhappiness had come from struggling against the fall that was her nature and her fate. Now she would give up the struggle, and let things take their natural course.

You have his child. Love was immortal, Eve knew. Neither time nor separation nor even destruction could alter it, diminish it in the least. Therefore, in taking what was hers at last, she would not really be stealing anything from

Kate. She would only be hastening the inevitable, confirming the eternal.

Her eyes on Joe, she jerked the wheel hard to the right. The car, traveling at sixty miles per hour, lurched into the flimsy guardrail and leapt over it. There was a shudder as the machine lost its grip on land and took to the air.

At that instant Joe woke up. He saw Eve looking at him. He seemed dazed, like a man awakened from deep sleep by some unwelcome interruption. Then he saw the expression in Eve's eyes, and his face changed. He was realizing that he had been incautious, that he should have seen this moment coming, that he had let it happen through his own lack of vigilance. There was a hint of pity for Eve in this glance.

He turned to look back up the mountain. She knew what this meant. He was looking backward toward Kate, toward the only thing that mattered to him. In this instant before death, he felt no fear of his own obliteration, but only his longing for the woman he loved.

And, sure enough, his lips opened, and he said, "Kate . . ."

Now the car was turning over, its flight skewed by the guardrail into an ungainly and yet somehow graceful twisting dive. Eve savored this plunge out of the world, this whirling deliverance.

For an instant she thought of Tommy Valentine. Her own past sins came up at her hard, like the steep walls of the canyon, angry to strike her, quick to punish. But she no longer cared. What did sin matter now? She was above the earth, lifted there by Joseph Knight, if only for a second that lasted an eternity.

The car struck an outhanging boulder and lurched end over end, already in flames. It tore down the mountainside, leaving a scar of hate and pain behind it.

They were both dead before it reached the bottom.

EPILOGUE

EPILOGUE

Los Angeles Times, April 22, 1947

The Academy of Motion Picture Arts and Sciences yesterday inaugurated the Joseph Knight Award, to be given each year for the most outstanding feature film by a first-time director. The award is intended to encourage original work by young filmmakers, and will be presented at each year's Academy Awards ceremony.

The inauguration of the award was announced at last night's Oscar ceremony at the Ambassador Hotel. At that ceremony Joseph Knight's last film, *Farewell to Love,* was awarded the Oscar for Best Picture. Katherine Hamilton, Knight's widow, received the Oscar for Best Actress. Knight himself was posthumously awarded Oscars for his direction and original screenplay, and the late Eve Sinclair, who was killed with Knight in an automobile accident last November, posthumously received the Oscar for Best Supporting Actress.

Farewell to Love received a total of nine Academy Awards. In his brief Hollywood career Joseph Knight made three films, which were nominated for a total of thirty-eight Academy Awards and won a total of twenty-six Oscars. No filmmaker in the history of Hollywood has achieved so great an accolade from his professional peers. The three films, *Farewell to Love, The Velvet Web,* and *The Rainbow's End,* are all considered screen classics. According to Jean Hersholt, the president of the Academy, "the Joseph Knight Award is intended not only to reward young talent and initiative, but to stand as a memorial to one of the finest filmmakers in screen history, and a man who personified courage, integrity, and respect for himself and others, both in his films and in his personal life."

Katherine Hamilton accepted her late husband's awards. Miss Hamilton, who is expecting Joseph Knight's child in July, was brief and gracious in thanking the Academy on her husband's behalf.

Though Miss Hamilton declined to participate in post-ceremony interviews, she had told friends and former associates that she will never again perform in a film.

The theater was not full.

It was a lazy Tuesday afternoon, in the middle of a busy work week. The only people here were young wives or mothers taking a break from their children, working girls on their days off, or neighborhood people with time on their hands. The Depression was a thing of the past now, and theaters were no longer full of unemployed people with nowhere to go.

On the screen was the face of a young woman. She was in the arms of a man. Behind her was the vague bustle of a train station.

Her eyes seemed to grow larger as she clung to her lover. "Somehow," she said, "I feel that my heart is losing you. That I've committed a sin without realizing it, and that's why you're leaving me."

"You've committed no sin," the man said. "Unless love is a crime."

Tears glistened in her eyes. The camera, already poised

close to her face, came closer still, and her emotion seemed to flow beyond herself, filling the silent theater.

"When love comes," she said, more to herself than to him, "you plunge without thinking. You see that your life was an empty shell before love came, so you turn your back on the past without a second thought. And then, when the world comes back to claim its own, there's no way to fight it, because you have no heart to endure loneliness any more. You've thrown it away, like a child throwing away a paper toy."

She looked into his eyes.

"That's the crime, you see," she said. "That's what has to be paid for."

Now the man was taking his leave, receding from her. She was alone.

"The whole of life gone by," she murmured, "and nothing left but goodbye . . ."

Sobs were heard in the audience. Many spectators turned their eyes away from the screen. Though the theater was not full, it seemed to overflow with grief.

Now the train was disappearing down the track, and the young heroine was left with her girlfriend, holding hands. The friend whispered words of comfort—"Love never dies. Nothing can kill it, not even time."—but the heroine seemed alone, lost in herself.

Her final words came as a voice-over, resounding through the theater as the camera moved closer and closer to her stricken face.

"Was that the word I heard that first day?" asked her eyes. "When the past was obliterated by your face, and suddenly the future stretched before me like heaven? Was that what I heard? *Goodbye* . . ."

By now the camera's intimacy with her face was unspeakably tragic. The audience was rooted to the spot, and yet seemed to want to escape, so painful was the spectacle it was watching. The credits began to roll up the screen. Not one person arose to leave.

In the last row, unnoticed by the other spectators, Kate looked up at her own face.

This was the first time she had ever seen *Farewell to Love*. As the film made its triumphant run, breaking box-office records everywhere and leaving a trail of praise throughout the critical establishment, an instant classic blazing like a comet through the film world, she had hidden herself away from it, afraid to look.

And only now, on this lazy weekday afternoon, had she finally found the courage to come and see it. In her seat at the back of the theater, she looked like a pregnant young wife, no different from countless others like her in this postwar America. No one would recognize her.

But for the first time, on that screen, she recognized herself.

It seemed to her that only now was she seeing herself as she really was, and seeing her life as she should have seen it all along—through the eyes of Joseph Knight, the only human being on earth who ever really knew her.

She pondered the irony of that final image. The film's heroine had lost her lover forever, but possessed his child, the child of their great love. Just as Kate now possessed Joe's child, in her womb, a child that would be born a few months hence, never to know its father.

Just as hundreds of thousands of American children would be born to wives whose husbands had not returned from the war. Joseph Knight seemed to have foreseen everything in his film, and understood everything, including his own disappearance.

And in that final image on the screen Kate was holding hands with Eve. Eve, who had given her so much, meant so much to her, and then departed the earth with Joe, a fate Kate had always expected for herself.

How strange, Kate mused, that Eve, who had been part of her life even when she was a little girl, filling her mind with fantasies of love and happiness from the magic mirror of the movie screen, should be with her now, at the end. Yet even now Eve was projected on a movie screen, still wearing the colors of illusion, still a bit removed from the flesh-and-blood reality in which Kate had tried to join her.

Such was the power of illusion to bring people together, and yet to linger between them like a shining barrier which, despite its frailty, could never be penetrated by human effort.

"Life imitates art." Kate heard the old expression inside her mind, a blithe pleasantry hiding a sinister and fateful truth. The strange crucible that was *Farewell to Love* seemed to contain the destinies of Joseph Knight, Eve, and Kate herself, almost as though Joe had been looking into a crystal ball when he conceived the screenplay.

And now it was over for all of them. Joe and Eve were dead. For Eve, *Farewell to Love* would stand as the culmination of her long, frustrating career and her great talent. For Joe, it would always stand as the monument to a rich creative future that was cut off too soon, unfairly soon.

And to his love . . .

To Kate, it was her last chance to look at herself and see what Joe saw. This was the only Kate she cared about. And seeing herself fade as the screen went dark was like seeing her own heart go dark, never to awaken again to love.

Kate felt she was seeing a terrible and beautiful truth on that screen. She and Joe had loved each other too much, too completely, and in showing that love for all the world to see, Joe had somehow given away a secret that should have been kept from the watchful fates. Perhaps there was a sin in loving that way, so totally, so daringly, without caring for the consequences . . .

She heard the heroine's words inside her, their truth illuminating every corner of her soul. *I've committed a sin without realizing it. That's why you're leaving me.*

The screen had gone dark. Kate crossed her arms over her stomach and hugged the unborn life waiting within her. And now she reflected that she had one more gift to give Joseph Knight. In three months his child would be born, never to know him, never perhaps to know the love that had brought it into this world, but still to carry on for him in some mysterious way, just as Kate would carry on for him until her dying day.

She did not cry, for she had no tears left to shed. She realized that the fates in their capricious wisdom had given her more than she deserved in freeing her from her life alone and bringing Joseph Knight to cross her path and make her heart his own.

On the condition that she lose him . . .

If the words in the screenplay were true, if love was a sin that must be punished by eternal separation and a longing that cannot be cured, then only at the price of sin can eternity be touched by the human hand. Perhaps goodness alone is not a strong enough charm to see the human being through life. Perhaps only the sin of love, which cares nothing for right or wrong, but only for itself, can bring eternity into the heart. Perhaps that was the real meaning of that mysterious word, *forever.*

Kate's eyes were closed, her lips moving softly as the fateful lines came back to her.

Was that the word I heard that first day? When the past was obliterated by your face, and suddenly the future stretched before me like heaven? Was that what I heard? Goodbye . . .

Kate clasped her hands around the life within her, her heart wedded to the life she had lost.

Goodbye, my love . . .

She did not hear her own words. No one around her saw her face, or heard her whisper, as they left the theater, their eyes already poised to blink at the bright sunshine outside.

Kate remained alone. The face of Joseph Knight was all she saw, and the past she had given up for him so joyfully, and the door opening inside her to a future that belonged only to him.

For a long time she sat there, savoring the void around her. Then, bidden by a voice that echoed from somewhere behind her pain, she got up to leave the screen and the darkness behind her.

Slowly, but moving on steady legs that had already carried her a long way through life, Kate walked back into the light.